'THE SIXTH BOOK IN THE RED GAMBIT SERIES'

INITIAT♟VE

COLIN GEE

Initiative

WRITTEN BY COLIN GEE

The Sixth book in the 'Red Gambit' series.

25th April 1946 to 19th August 1946.

ISBN-10: 1517169259

ISBN-13: 978-1517169251

If I might take the opportunity to explain copyright in the simplest terms. It means that those of you who decide to violate my rights by posting this and others of my books on websites that permit downloading of copyrighted materials, are not only breaking the law, but also depriving me of money.

You may not see that as an issue, but I spend a lot of my limited funds to travel and research, just to make sure I get things as right as I can.

I ask you sincerely, please do not break the copyright, and permit me to profit properly from the labours I have undertaken.

Thank you.

Series Dedication

The Red Gambit series of books is dedicated to my grandfather, the boss-fellah, Jack 'Chalky' White, Chief Petty Officer [Engine Room] RN, my de facto father until his untimely death from cancer in 1983, and a man who, along with many millions of others, participated in the epic of history that we know as World War Two.

Their efforts and sacrifices made it possible for us to read of it, in freedom, today.

Thank you, for everything.

Overview by author Colin Gee

If you have already read the first five books in this series, then what follows will serve as a small reminder of what went before.

If this is your first toe dipped in the waters of 'Red Gambit', then I can only advise you to read the previous books when you can.

In the interim, this is mainly for you.

After the end of the German War, the leaders of the Soviet Union found sufficient cause to distrust their former Allies, to the point of launching an assault on Western Europe. Those causes and the decision-making behind the full scale attack lie within 'Opening Moves', as do the battles of the first week, commencing on 6th August 1945.

After that initial week, the Soviets continued to grind away at the Western Allies, trading lives and materiel for ground, whilst reducing the combat efficiency of Allied units from the Baltic to the Alps.

In 'Breakthrough', the Red Army inflicts defeat after defeat upon their enemy, but at growing cost to themselves.

The attrition is awful.

Matters come to a head in 'Stalemate' as circumstances force Marshall Zhukov to focus attacks on specific zones. The resulting battles bring death and horror on an unprecedented scale, neither Army coming away unscathed or unscarred.

In the Pacific, the Soviet Union has courted the Empire of Japan, and has provided unusual support in its struggle against the Chinese. That support has faded and, despite small scale Soviet intervention, the writing is on the wall.

'Impasse' brought a swing, perhaps imperceptible at first, with the initiative lost by the Red Army, but difficult to pick up for the Allies.

The Red Air Force is almost spent, and Allied air power starts to make its superiority felt across the spectrum of operations.

The war takes on a bestial nature, as both sides visit excesses on each other.

Allied planning deals a deadly blow to the Soviet Baltic forces, in the air, on the sea, and on the ground. However, their own ground assaults are met with stiff resistance, and peter out as General Winter spreads his frosty fingers across the continent, bringing with him the coldest weather in living memory.

'Sacrifice' sees the Allied nations embark on their recovery, assaults pushing back the weakening red Army, for whom supply has become the pivotal issue.

Its soldiers are undernourished, its tanks lack enough fuel, and its guns are often without shells.

Soviet air power is a matter of memory, and the Allies have mastery of the skies.

In the five previous books, the reader has journeyed from June 1945, all the way to April 1946. The combat and intrigue has focussed in Europe, but men have also died in the Pacific, over and under the cold waters of the Atlantic, and on the shores of small islands in Greenland.

Battles have occurred from the Baltic to the Adriatic, some large, some small, some insignificant, and some of huge import.

In Initiative, the fighting develops again, and the book deals with that, as well as the other matters of war, that will take the reader from the Kalahari Desert to an airfield on Tinian, from China to the Black Sea coast, and from a Swedish castle to a hotel in Bretton Woods, New Hampshire.

As I did the research for this alternate history series, I often wondered why it was that we, west and east, did not come to blows once more.

We must all give thanks it did not all go badly wrong in that hot summer of 1945, and that the events described in the Red Gambit series did not come to pass.

My profound thanks to all those who have contributed in whatever way to this project, as every little piece of help brought me closer to my goal.

[For additional information, progress reports, orders of battle, discussion, freebies, and interaction with the author please find time to visit and register at one of the following-

www.redgambitseries.com, www.redgambitseries.co.uk, www.redgambitseries.eu,

Also, feel free to join Facebook Group 'Red Gambit'.]

Thank you.

I have received a great deal of assistance in researching, translating, advice, and support during the years that this project has so far run.

In no particular order, I would like to record my thanks to all of the following for their contributions. Gary Wild, Jan Wild, Jason Litchfield, Peter Kellie, Jim Crail, Craig Dressman, Mario Wildenauer, Loren Weaver, Pat Walsh, Keith Lange, Philippe Vanhauwermeiren, Elena Schuster, Stilla Fendt, Luitpold Krieger, Mark Lambert, Simon Haines, Carl Jones, Greg Winton, Greg Percival, Robert Prideaux, Tyler Weaver, Giselle Janiszewski, James Hanebury, Renata Loveridge, Jeffrey Durnford, Brian Proctor, Steve Bailey, Paul Dryden, Steve Riordan, Bruce Towers, Gary Banner, Victoria Coling, Alexandra Coling, Heather Coling, Isabel Pierce Ward, Hany Hamouda, Ahmed Al-Obeidi, Sharon Shmueli, and finally BW-UK Gaming Clan.

It is with sadness that I must record the passing of Luitpold Krieger, who succumbed to cancer after a hard fight.

One name is missing on the request of the party involved, who perversely has given me more help and guidance in this project than most, but whose desire to remain in the background on all things means I have to observe his wish not to name him.

None the less, to you, my oldest friend, thank you.

Wikipedia is a wonderful thing and I have used it as my first port of call for much of the research for the series. Use it and support it.

My thanks to the US Army Center of Military History and Franklin D Roosevelt Presidential Library websites for providing the out of copyright images.

All map work is original, save for the Château outline, which derives from a public domain handout.

6

Particular thanks go to Steen Ammentorp, who is responsible for the wonderful www.generals.dk site, which is a superb place to visit in search of details on generals of all nations. The site has proven invaluable in compiling many of the biographies dealing with the senior officers found in these books.

If I have missed anyone or any agency I apologise and promise to rectify the omission at the earliest opportunity.

At one stage in the writing of 'Initiative', I found myself at a real crunch point, where I wondered about one part of my overall story, and fortunately had the sense to put it to a group of American members of the Facebook group. I am extremely grateful that I did so, as it was quickly established that a crucial piece of my 'US' story simply wouldn't stand up to close examination by an American audience.

I am very indebted to the following members of the Facebook group for coming to my aid.

Thanks go to Giselle Janezewski, James Hanebury, Gary Banner, Keith Lange, Bruce Towers, Jim Crail, and Robert Clarke.

Author's note.

The correlation between the Allied and Soviet forces is difficult to assess for a number of reasons.

Neither side could claim that their units were all at full strength, and information on the relevant strengths over the period this book is set in is limited as far as the Allies are concerned and relatively non-existent for the Soviet forces.

I have had to use some licence regarding force strengths and I hope that the critics will not be too harsh with me if I get things wrong in that regard. A Soviet Rifle Division could vary in strength from the size of two thousand men to be as high as nine thousand men, and in some special cases could be even more.

Indeed, the very names used do not help the reader to understand unless they are already knowledgeable.

A prime example is the Corps. For the British and US forces, a Corps was a collection of Divisions and Brigades directly subservient to an Army. A Soviet Corps, such as the 2nd Guards Tank Corps, bore no relation to a unit such as British XXX Corps. The 2nd G.T.C. was a Tank Division by another name and this difference in 'naming' continues to the Soviet Army, which was more akin to the Allied Corps.

The Army Group was mirrored by the Soviet Front.

Going down from the Corps, the differences continue, where a Russian rifle division should probably be more looked at as the equivalent of a US Infantry regiment or British Infantry Brigade, although this was not always the case. The decision to leave the correct nomenclature in place was made early on. In that, I felt that those who already possess knowledge would not become disillusioned, and that those who were new to the concept could acquire knowledge that would stand them in good stead when reading factual accounts of WW2.

There are also some difficulties encountered with ranks. Some readers may feel that a certain battle would have been left in the command of a more senior rank, and the reverse case where seniors seem to have few forces under their authority. Casualties will have played their part but, particularly in the Soviet Army, seniority and rank was a complicated affair, sometimes with Colonels in charge of Divisions larger than those commanded by a General. It is easier for me to attach a chart to give the reader a rough guide of how the ranks equate.

Also, please remember, that by now attrition has downsized units in all armies.

Fig # 1 – Table of comparative ranks.

SOVIET UNION	WAFFEN-SS	WEHRMACHT	UNITED STATES	UK/COMMONWEALTH	FRANCE
KA - SOLDIER	SCHUTZE	SCHUTZE	PRIVATE	PRIVATE	SOLDAT DEUXIEME CLASSE
YEFREYTOR	STURMMANN	GEFREITER	PRIVATE 1ST CLASS	LANCE-CORPORAL	CAPORAL
MLADSHIY SERZHANT	ROTTENFUHRER	OBERGEFREITER	CORPORAL	CORPORAL	CAPORAL-CHEF
SERZHANT	UNTERSCHARFUHRER	UNTEROFFIZIER	SERGEANT	SERGEANT	SERGENT-CHEF
STARSHIY SERZHANT	OBERSCHARFUHRER	FELDWEBEL	SERGEANT 1ST CLASS	C.S.M.	ADJUDANT-CHEF
STARSHINA	STURMSCHARFUHRER	STABSFELDWEBEL	SERGEANT-MAJOR [WO/CWO]	R.S.M.	MAJOR
MLADSHIY LEYTENANT	UNTERSTURMFUHRER	LEUTNANT	2ND LIEUTENANT	2ND LIEUTENANT	SOUS-LIEUTENANT
LEYTENANT	OBERSTURMFUHRER	OBERLEUTNANT	1ST LIEUTENANT	LIEUTENANT	LIEUTENANT
STARSHIY LEYTENANT					
KAPITAN	HAUPTSTURMFUHRER	HAUPTMANN	CAPTAIN	CAPTAIN	CAPITAINE
MAYOR	STURMBANNFUHRER	MAJOR	MAJOR	MAJOR	COMMANDANT 1
PODPOLKOVNIK	OBERSTURMBANNFUHRER	OBERSTLEUTNANT	LIEUTENANT-COLONEL	LIEUTENANT-COLONEL	LIEUTENANT-COLONEL 2
POLKOVNIK	STANDARTENFUHRER	OBERST	COLONEL	COLONEL	COLONEL 3
GENERAL-MAYOR	BRIGADEFUHRER	GENERALMAJOR	BRIGADIER GENERAL	BRIGADIER	GENERAL DE BRIGADE
GENERAL-LEYTENANT	GRUPPENFUHRER	GENERALLEUTNANT	MAJOR GENERAL	MAJOR GENERAL	GENERAL DE DIVISION
GENERAL-POLKOVNIK	OBERGRUPPENFUHRER	GENERAL DER INFANTERIE*	LIEUTENANT GENERAL	LIEUTENANT GENERAL	GENERAL DE CORPS D'ARMEE
GENERAL-ARMII	OBERSTGRUPPENFUHRER	GENERALOBERST	GENERAL	GENERAL	GENERAL DE ARMEE
MARSHALL		GENERALFELDMARSCHALL	GENERAL OF THE ARMY	FIELD-MARSHALL	MARECHAL DE FRANCE

* OR ARTILLERY, PANZERTRUPPEN ETC

1 CAPITAINE de CORVETTE 2 CAPITAINE de FREGATE 3 CAPITAINE de VAISSEAU

ROUGH GUIDE TO THE RANKS OF COMBATANT NATIONS.

Book Dedication

History is a strange beast.

It contains lessons from which we never seem to truly learn.

And yet, the recorded matters of our past are constantly scrutinised and replayed by academicians and amateurs alike, criticising and second-guessing those who did what they thought was right at the time, and did so without either the benefit and safety of armchair comforts or time to make an extended and reasoned judgement.

World War Two has been replayed in minds since the final shots echoed into history and, in some cases, whilst the firing was still going on.

The armchair warriors and professors often decide that things were not done right, opportunities were missed, or that moral lines were overstepped.

On that last point, I almost always find myself in total disagreement with those who would seek to undermine and criticise those who undertook the missions and tasks that fall under scrutiny post-era.

RAF's Bomber Command was vilified for many years, a stance first adopted by Churchill, who offered up an opinion about the attack on Dresden that was interpreted as critical, and as distancing himself from the efforts made in the bombing offensive.

We British, as a nation, should be disgusted that we only chose to honour their efforts recently, when most of the survivors had passed away.

The truth is quite simple.

We were at war, total war, and the bombing of civilians and towns was undertaken by all sides.

Not an excuse but an undeniable fact.

History simply teaches that the RAF, USAAF, and Allied units were far better at it than our then enemy, and had far better equipment with which to wage total war.

The dropping of the bombs on Hiroshima and Nagasaki has been criticised from the moment they were detonated.

Even now, the arguments continue to evolve, and criticism is laid at the door of the pilots and men who flew the Silverbirds, and those who commanded them to do the deeds over Japan.

Regardless of how you see the Lancaster over Dresden or the B-29 over Nagasaki, the boys inside were doing a job for their country, under orders, and doing it to the best of their ability, and far too often, at the cost of their lives.

No matter what the arguments, we cannot disparage those who fought for us and carried the battle to the enemy and who did their duty, and what they thought was right, and certainly not because they were more proficient or had technology in excess of the enemy.

They honoured us with their efforts, so how can we dishonour them with criticism of their motivation and their morality?

So, to all those who did their duty and were pilloried by act or omission, I dedicate 'Initiative' to you.

May I remind the reader that his book is written primarily in English, not American English. Therefore, please expect the unashamed use of 'U', such as in honour and armoured, unless I am using the American version to remain true to a character or situation.

By example, I will write the 11th Armoured Division and the 11th US Armored Division, as each is correct in national context.

Where using dialogue, the character uses the correct rank, such as Mayor, instead of Major for the Soviet dialogue, or Maior for the German dialogue.

Otherwise, in non-dialogue circumstances, all ranks and units will be in English.

Although I never served in the Armed forces, I wore a uniform with pride, and carry my own long-term injuries from my service. My admiration for our young service men and women serving in all our names in dangerous areas throughout the world is limitless. As a result, 'the Star and Garter Homes' is a charity that is extremely close to my heart. My fictitious characters carry no real-life heartache with them, whereas every news bulletin from the military stations abroad brings a terrible reality with its own impact, angst, and personal challenges for those left behind when one of our military pays the ultimate price. Therefore, I make donations to 'the Star and Garter Homes', and would encourage you to do so too.

Book #1 - Opening Moves [Chapters 1-54]
Book #2 - Breakthrough [Chapters 55-77]
Book #3 - Stalemate [Chapters 78-102]
Book #4 – Impasse [Chapters 103 – 125]
Book #5 - Sacrifice [Chapters 126 - 148]
Book #6 – Initiative [Chapters 149 - 171]
Book #7 - Endgame [Chapters 172 - ?]

List of chapters and sections.

14

17

21

Fig # 179 – Europe, May 1946.

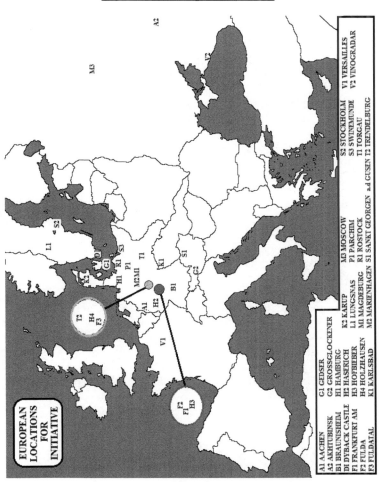

Now I am become death, destroyer of worlds.

Robert Oppenheimer, quoting Krishna, avatar of Vishnu, from the Hindu text, the Bhagavad Gita.

Chapter 149 - THE POWER

1000 hrs, Tuesday 30th April, Frankenberg an der Eder, Germany.

It was the eighty-third anniversary, and the French Foreign Legion's most important and significant day of the year.

Camerone Day celebrated the lost battle of Camerone, named for a hacienda in Mexico, where sixty-five legionnaires resisted a force of nearly three thousand Mexican soldiers.

It, above all other Legion battles, had created the mystique that surrounded the unit from that day forward.

The commander on the day, a Captain Jean Danjou, was killed early on in the battle, but his false wooden hand was subsequently found, and became the subject of veneration each Camerone Day, when the icon, the symbol of the Legion's fighting spirit against all odds, was paraded in front of ranks of legionnaires.

The honour of holding the icon and marching with it in front of assembled legion units was a singular one, an honour that had once been afforded to the long dead Vernais, tortured to death in front of Brumath.

Normally, the most precious item in the Legion's inventory remained safely within the confines of its headquarters but, as most of the Legion was in the field in Germany, the Camerone Day parade was being held in a large open green space on the north bank of the Eder River.

Every Legion unit in the French First Army had a representative section present, the main guard being mounted by men of the 1st Régiment Étrangere D'Infanterie.

The Legion Corps D'Assaut group was led by a proud Lavalle, the mix of ex-SS and long-service Legionnaires blending seamlessly into one group, and into the parade in general.

It had been too much to expect one of the new German contingent to be included in the direct parading of Danjou's hand, but it was a source of celebration and immense pride that Haefali had been honoured with command of the parade, and the singular honour of carrying the sacred relic had been granted to a Marseille-born Legion

24

Caporal-chef from the Alma, and command of the honour guard given to Oscar Durand, Lieutenant in the 1st Régiment de Marche.

There was even a small honorary squad comprising members of the 16th US Armored Division, until recently a solid member of the Legion Corps, their tank being one of two on parade that day.

The other vehicle was the only noticeable singularly German contribution to proceedings.

The 16th's Sherman M4A3E8 led the way, followed closely by the noisier and larger Tiger Ie.

Only a day beforehand, a Legion tank crew had been assembled at the repair facility and presented with their vehicle, lovingly restored by cannibalism from wrecks found across the battlefields, or by manufacturing those pieces that escaped detection.

Each of the five men wept as Walter Fiedler, the workshops officer, presented them with the repaired heavy tank...

...Lohengrin.

[http://en.wikipedia.org/wiki/Battle_of_Camarón]
[http://en.wikipedia.org/wiki/Jean_Danjou]

1100 hrs, Wednesday, 1st May, 1946, Red Square, Moscow, USSR, and the Oval Office, Washington DC, USA.

Stalin stood upright and proud amongst the political and military leadership of the Soviet Union, as large bodies of troops and vehicles swept past, the traditional 'urrahs' launched from thousands of enthusiastic throats.

It was an impressive display, that fact more appreciated by the hierarchy than the multitude of citizens gathered for the traditional International Workers' Day parade, who saw nothing unexpected about the standard huge display of Soviet military might.

For the citizenry it was as impressive as ever but, in reality, it was an illusion.

The participants had been stripped from internal commands, soldiers on leave, those recuperating from wounds; anything that could drive, stand, or march was on parade.

The Soviet war machine was nowhere near the powerful all-conquering monster it had been the previous year.

Of course, all received rapturous receptions. T-34m46's, with thicker armour and adapted to take the 100mm, T-44's similarly armed, followed by a phalanx of one hundred and twenty IS-III battle tanks, decked out as a Guards formation, the assembled citizenry appreciated all as clear indicators of continued Soviet military superiority. Had they known the real truth, and not consumed their spoon-fed daily bulletins comprising specifically edited reports of fighting in the frontline, they may have felt differently.

The fly past of Red Air Force regiments was extremely impressive.

The political decision to retain the majority of new and replacement aircraft, depriving the front line units solely to ensure sufficient numbers were on display on May Day, had been heavily contested by the military contingent, but to no avail.

More importantly to the hierarchy, the large numbers of aircraft were also there to protect them from any Allied attempt to disrupt the Soviet showpiece.

None the less, the new jets were impressive, although those with experience would have noticed the gaps in formation left by the three that had failed to take off, one drastically so, smashing back into the runway and spreading its experienced regimental commander across the airfield.

The captured V2s, now in their new Soviet green, red, and white livery, were also impressive, although virtually useless for anything but fooling civilians.

Almost unnoticed, four large football-like shapes, huge bombs carried on Red Air Force vehicles, passed by, their arrival and departure overshadowed by more jets and the very latest in Soviet technological advances; the IS-IV heavy battle tank and ISU-152-45, once known as Obiekt 704, brought to fruition for the heavy tank and tank destroyer brigades in Europe.

Almost unnoticed, the four mock-up representations of the pumpkin bomb found on the crashed B-29, left the square, and were immediately surrounded by a heavily armed contingent of NKVD troops.

Almost unnoticed, but not quite...

As the Marshal climbed the steps to the top of Lenin's Mausoleum, his heart protested, reaching and exceeding its point of toleration before he reached the top.

Zhukov, panting and eyes screwed up with pain, collapsed heavily.

"So that's that then. We've batted this around for months in anticipation of this moment, and we're still doing it now."

Truman wasn't scolding, just trying to draw a line under matters so they could progress.

The conversations still went on around him.

"Gentlemen, gentlemen... please."

The four other men settled down in silence, looking at the chief executive in anticipation.

"One final word... a sentence or two, no more. George?"

The outsider, George C. Marshall, Chief of Staff of the US Army, spoke in considered fashion.

"The scientists assure us of no consequences globally. It **will** save thousands of American boy's lives. No brainer for me, Sir."

"Thank you. Jimmy?"

Acting Secretary of State James S. Byrnes was slightly more animated.

"Sir, I support delay. Offer them the Mikado, lessen the terms, and they will fold. Blockade and conventional bombing will stop them. Soviet support is of little consequence to them now."

"Thank you, Jimmy. James?"

"I agree with Jimmy. We can still come back to this solution, but offer up the Mikado, and I see them collapsing. As stated, Soviet support counts for nothing now... in fact, I've been thinking that it might work in our favour."

"How so?"

It was Marshall that posed the question and, surprisingly, it was Truman that answered it.

"They've been raised up, and now they're back down lower than a rattler's belly."

Marshall nodded his understanding.

"Thank you, James."

Forrestal, Secretary of the Navy, settled back into the comfortable couch.

"Henry? This is your baby."

"I'd have it in the air right now, Sir. Yes, the Nips might fold, but then, they might not. They'll fold once the weapon is deployed. Also, as I've said before, the use may be enough to guarantee this world's future."

"Thank you, Henry."

Henry L. Stimson, Secretary of War, even though he had trotted out his position before, wanted to say so much more.

He wanted to say that this weapon could make war obsolete, solely by its use, so awful as its use would be, therefore demonstrating that future wars could hold no advantages for aggressors.

Actually, no advantages for anyone.

He wanted to say that its use would end the Japanese war now; not in a year's time, but now.

He wanted to say that the forces freed up by this act would help defeat the Soviets all the quicker.

He wanted, God, how he wanted to resign and walk away from the pressures of government, his body announcing its displeasure at his continued exposure on almost a daily basis.

Most of all he wanted the whole goddamn war to be over, and that meant using more bombs; lots more.

Thus far, the notion of deploying them on the Soviet Homeland had been avoided, sidestepped, even ignored.

Military minds saw advantages in spades, and almost no problems, but the political considerations were many, from whose air space the bombers would fly over, where the bombers would be based, guarantees from scientists that there would be no repercussions to basic objections on moral grounds.

But Stimson understood that to defeat the Soviets, they would have to demonstrate to them the idiocy of further aggression, and that was best done, at least initially, by exterminating an area of the Japanese home islands.

"Thank you, gentlemen. Give me a moment."

Truman rose and moved to the window, taking in the view across the well-kept grass, noting the gardeners hard at work.

'Not a care in the world.'

He laughed perceptibly, but unintentionally.

He stared hard at an old man deadheading a flower stand, and sent his silent message through his eyes.

'Care to swap?'

The work continued, his offer unheard.

'Very wise, sir… very wise.'

"Gentlemen...I've made my decision. The mission is a go."

In the Soviet army it takes more courage to retreat than advance.

Joseph Stalin.

Chapter 150 – THE DISBELIEF

1007hrs, Thursday, 2nd May 1946, the Kremlin, Moscow, USSR.

Vasilevsky took a moment to sip the water as the men around him took in the information he had laid before them.

Normally, it would have been Stalin that led off, but today Bulganin spoke first.

"So that's that? We've stopped the Fascist bastards?"

All eyes turned to the commander of the Red Banner Forces of Soviet Europe.

"I can only repeat, Comrade. They have stopped advancing across the whole front. All their advances. There is nothing moving forward now. Our soldiers have performed magnificently... truly astounding... glorious... and yet..."

"And yet, we look at a situation where we've ceded much ground that was won at the cost of many, many Soviet lives."

The attention swivelled immediately to Stalin as he interrupted Vasilevsky.

"Yes, Comrade General Secretary."

Stalin resisted the urge for nicotine and pressed ahead, his voice raised in anger and frustration.

"And yet you seem to portray this as some sort of victory? Some sort of magnificent undertaking by the Army? Something we can tell our Comrades is an achievement on a parallel with Kursk? Leningrad? What...even Stalingrad?"

The sarcasm stung and the wound was deep.

Vasilevsky stood his ground.

"Comrade General Secretary... Comrades... I say to you that the Red Army and Air Force are performing miracles in the defence of our Motherland. The enemy is strong and well supported, with no shortages in any department. Our forces, whilst high on morale and fervour, are constantly short of the goods of war because of the logistical situation and the bombing."

His hand ran down the map he had used to break to them the loss of much of the German territorial gains.

"Yes, we have lost much of what we gained, but we still have an Army... intact and capable. Our supply lines are shorter, which can only be an improvement."

Stalin raised his hand imperiously.

"Tell me you're not intending to retreat to the Urals to make the supply line easier, Comrade Vasilevsky?"

A number of men laughed before Stalin's icy stare cut them short and chilled their hearts.

He had intended no humour.

"No, Comrade General Secretary."

"No."

A silence descended on the room, one that was oppressive and dangerous.

The Soviet leader succumbed to his craving and lit up a cigarette.

"So, Comrade Marshal. Paint this rosy picture for us. Tell us how well things are really going, eh?"

There was danger in Stalin's sarcasm, but the increasingly resilient Vasilevsky did not step back.

"We have lost a tremendous number of men and a great deal of war materiel. Historically, our nation and army have shown themselves capable of sustaining such losses and still being able to function effectively."

Molotov went to say something, but Stalin's unspoken warning stopped him on the in-breath.

"The Allies are softer... not as soft as we once thought, Comrades, but definitely less resilient when it comes to hardship and national spirit."

Vasilevsky took another moment to moisten his mouth.

"They have sustained huge losses too, spread across the range of nations arraigned against us."

He sought a document and nodded in thanks to the person who had provided it.

"General Nazarbayeva's department has already advised me that the Brazilians are seeking to withdraw to a support role, following public criticism of casualties at home."

A number of minds wondered why the woman hadn't informed members of the GKO first and were decidedly unhappy, even though Vasilevsky's briefing had taken priority over hers.

"Similarly, I would expect public support in the main Allied countries to be wilting with every son or husband we put in the ground... or send home broken by war."

Stalin coughed uncontrollably.

Vasilevsky pushed his water across the table, which Stalin waved away as he coughed more, and his displaced cigarette end burnt a penny-sized hole in a priceless Chinese rug.

He recovered, wiping his face with a handkerchief that had been proffered up by he knew not who.

"Comrade Marshal. Are you trying to tell us that, despite the loss of much of the Fascist lands, and a considerable portion of our army and air force, we have, in some way, gained an advantage?"

"No, Comrade General Secretary. Militarily, we have been beaten back, but with resilience of heart and Communist will, we have stopped a well-supplied enemy ahead of his planned timetable. In essence, Comrades, whilst we have lost ground, the present result is a draw."

"A fucking draw? We do not draw... not with the Fascists... not with the Amerikanski... not with that drunken fuck Churchill.... we do not draw!"

The echoes of Stalin's words continued long after he had closed his mouth and his eyes burned more penny-sized holes through his commander in chief.

"We did not draw against the fucking Nazis! We destroyed them!"

"Comrade General Secretary, the situation now is different. This is not a small group of countries arraigned against us, controlled by a single madman, with limited resources and manpower at their disposal."

He turned his back on the ensemble to address the map.

"We have lost ground... lost men... lost tanks and aircraft... the Baltic is lost... our Japanese allies stand on the brink of defeat... and yet..."

He turned back.

"...I believe that we have done great damage to their cause."

He held up Nazarbayeva's report.

"This shows a chink in their armour, a weakness, brought about by the casualties this nation received."

He nodded at Beria.

"Who knows what information Comrade Marshal Beria might develop... or even... what mischief he and his men could cause in the home countries of our enemies. Agitate, cause political instability. These democracies are weak, and if the proletariat and workers rise up in protest... well, Comrades, you are the politicians here and will understand how best to exploit the damage our valiant soldiers and airmen have inflicted on the Allied armies."

31

It was as if a light was switched on and the room was bathed in its warm glow, as Stalin understood the situation with greater clarity than ever.

"Yes… you may be right, in some respects… our comrades on the GRU and NKVD will find out as quickly as possible."

Stalin's words translated into definite orders in the minds of both Beria and Nazarbayeva.

"But that is for later. For now, tell us what you intend to do about that."

Vasilevsky inwardly relaxed, knowing that he had passed an important point and would not be relieved, or worse, this day.

"Comrades, whether I am right or wrong, I intend to go with my gut feeling and attack our enemy… mainly one enemy… attack hard and without mercy, where I cannot attack, I will defend fanatically, using every resource at my disposal," his voice almost slipped into a soft fairy tale tone as he slipped his eyes over the map, eyeing the points where he would implement his plan, "…With the intention of bringing him to his knees politically… to inflict awful loss upon him… savage him… kill him in huge numbers…"

Vasilevsky suddenly remembered where he was and turned back to the GKO.

"We will knock him out of the war by using his own political system against him. Kill their sons and husbands in such numbers that the will to fight will go and the political pressure to withdraw will be irresistible."

Stalin and his cronies were amazed at Vasilevsky's presentation, seeing it appear to lapse into more of a political diatribe than a military presentation.

"Which of the lackeys will we turn, Comrade Marshal?"

Vasilevsky smiled at Molotov's question.

"Oh no, Comrade Molotov, you don't understand. Not a lackey, but the leader. We will drive the Amerikanski out of the war."

By the end of all the presentations, the malaise had lifted from the GKO and a new spirit of optimism positively oozed from every pore.

Beria and Nazarbayeva had definite orders to support Vasilevsky's military plan, and Vasilevsky had confidently put his intentions over, intentions that were approved there and then.

The ever-present supply and fuel issues were addressed, and positive sounds made, although there the military men present retained doubts that the promises would be met, given that none made in the last eight months had even been close to actual figures arriving at the front. Plus, the last vestiges of production from the Caucasian, Caspian oil fields, and from Ploesti, had come to an end, courtesy of the intense Allied bombing campaign.

Never the less, the fuel was promised, and no one dared to question the figures in the face of such positive feelings.

To back up the promise, an impeccably dressed professor was hustled into the meeting, just to deliver a small presentation on how to obtain fuel from other sources.

Stalin and most of the GKO pretended to take in the science of the hydrogenation of coal, with the possibilities for future fuel uses.

The presentation also covered octane levels and the need for high-octane fuels, especially for aircraft, which was received with a modicum of understanding.

They nearly grasped the process of extracting synthetic fuel from coal, although the Fischer-Tropsch process was well over everyone's head, except for the scientist summoned to try and explain it.

They understood far better that the oilfields discovered in Tatarstan and Orsk now secretly pumped their products to the new refinery at Yamansarovo, a facility constructed in record time and, importantly, one as yet undetected by the Allies.

Even though they were still months away from anything like decent production from Yamansarovo, it was a much happier group that went their separate ways as Thursday slipped quietly into Friday.

1106 hrs, Friday 10th May 1946, one kilometre south of Gedser, Denmark.

The Gedser-Warnemünde ferry had pulled out exactly on schedule, carrying a leavening of civilian traffic alongside the German military unit to be transported to the mainland that day.

At 1106 precisely, the bow of the ferry briefly encountered one of the mines released during the destruction of L3 'Frunzenets', the Soviet mine-laying submarine lost during the Spectrum operations months beforehand.

All over the ship, men, women, and children were knocked off their feet by the shock that hammered through the structure. The harmful waves of energy sought out weakness and opened up leaks from plates to shaft stuffing boxes.

The whole front of the ferry opened like a whale's mouth, scooping up the sea as the engines drove the vessel forward and under the water.

Boats hastily put out from Gedser, but found little to rescue, and spent more time recovering the dead.

Pionier-Bataillon 230 of the 169th Infanterie Division lost all but two dozen men, and only three of the party of children from the Nykøbing Katedralskole survived to return to their loved ones.

The long dead crew of 'Frunzenets' had added over six hundred lives to their haul of victims.

1956 hrs, Monday 13th May 1946, Mount Washington Hotel, Bretton Woods, New Hampshire, USA.

Gently moving backwards and forwards in the comfortable rattan rocking chair, Olivia Francesca von Sandow checked out the other occupants of the hemicycle, a leavening of the rich and famous in American society, all enjoying the lavish surroundings and the strange pseudo anonymity offered by the presence of those of similar status.

A recent arrival in Washington society, von Sandow was the deputy cultural attaché at the reopened German Embassy, and already one of the first names on the list of the 'A' party circuit.

The reasons for that were not only her exquisite looks and fabulous figure, but also for her intellect and wit, a quadruple combination that made her irresistible to men of power.

Which was why she was waiting patiently in the hemicycle, her hastily arranged leave from work in place, allowing her to meet 'clandestinely' with her latest lover.

He arrived on cue, flourishing roses and chocolates.

"Darling Olivia… you look wonderful, honey."

He kissed her firmly on the offered cheek and she accepted the offerings as if they were nectar from the Gods.

"Humphrey, darling, so punctual… and thank you… they're wonderful."

He smiled the usual dazzling smile, the one that his reputation as a ladies man was founded upon.

"Only the best for you, honey."

34

He looked at his watch and made his move.

"Now, do you need to freshen up after your journey, or shall we have dinner first?"

Olivia von Sandow half closed her eyes, pursing her lips in an innocent but completely not in the slightest bit innocent fashion.

"Actually, Humphrey, I wondered if we might eat in the room? I'm really very tired and would much prefer something more intimate... if that's ok with you, darling?"

Seven minutes later, Humphrey exploded noisily inside her mouth, her expert ministrations relieving his pent-up sexual frustration.

"Fucking hell, Olivia. And on a first date too!"

She gave a little shrug.

"Is any purpose served by beating about the bush, Humphrey? You're here to fuck me... I'm here because I want to be fucked by you."

Her direct approach was like an aphrodisiac to his ears.

"Anyway, you really did need that, didn't you, darling Humphrey?"

Looking down with the biggest of grins, he ran his fingers through her long dark hair and cupped her chin with great tenderness.

"I will always need you, sweetheart."

She kissed the head of his softening member.

"And now that you've emptied yourself, we can relax and have a nice meal, eh?"

Von Sandow giggled and stood up, kissing him lightly on the cheek as she straightened out her clothes.

"Now I feel hungry. Shall we go down, darling?"

On their way to the elegant main dining room, Olivia nodded to someone she knew, informing Humphrey that he worked at the embassy, but not to worry, as he was also there for the same reasons as them.

She coughed and wiped her mouth with a small handkerchief, sharing a knowing and decidedly sexual look with her escort, before disappearing into the restaurant, where the maître di immediately swept the couple off to a private corner, as Humphrey Forbes had previously requested.

The man, for whom the nod was a simple signal, waited whilst the couple disappeared, and gave them time to settle before acting.

That he worked at the German Embassy was correct, but his reason for being at the hotel was other than von Sandow suggested.

He walked quickly up to the front desk with an envelope he produced from his pocket, marked with the name that Olivia was using in her 'secret' liaison.

The clerk was immediately attentive.

"Good evening, Sir. How may I assist?"

"Hi there. I've an envelope for Miss Jacqueline Dawson. I wonder if you could retain it and pass it to her as soon as is possible please?"

He offered up the envelope, which the clerk took with great care, examining the details.

"Most certainly, Sir. I will attend to it personally. Miss Dawson is dining at the moment, and I will pass it to her the moment she leaves the restaurant, if that's acceptable to you?"

"Yes, thanks. That'll be just fine."

The clerk turned and slotted the envelope into a numbered hole in the rack.

'104.'

"Thank you."

The German Intelligence officer moved away from the desk and waited until the clerk was heavily engaged with another guest before swiftly mounting the stairs, two at a time, and finding himself in front of the door to suite 104.

The hotel door lock could not defeat a trained spy for long, and a few twists of his picklocks were enough for him to gain entry.

He found the small briefcase easily, and his camera started to record its contents.

Another pair of eyes had registered Olivia's movement through the lobby and into the dining room.

Michael Green, having a well-earned break away from his clothing business, watched von Sandow through the periphery of his vision, all the time engaging his NKVD contact and lover in conversation.

Seemingly, no signal was passed, none that could have been detected for what it was in any case, but Green, also known as Iskhak Abdulovich Akhmerov, and presently the NKVD rezident in America, understood the cough and handkerchief to be a definite confirmation that his agent had snared her target, and that it was likely

36

that the information would soon start to flow from the senator from Illinois, namely Humphrey Randall Forbes.

With professional care, he idly cased the room again, and made eye contact with the huge breasted woman sat three sofas away, drawing a coquettish smile that promised everything he wished for.

He intended to enjoy the sexual delights that Dilara Bölükbaşı would offer when she would clandestinely slip into his room later.

For now, he accepted her smile with the natural nod of a man interested but too shy to approach, and resumed reading the sports pages of his paper.

The FBI pair assigned to watch Dilara Bölükbaşı, suspected as being a member of Turkish Intelligence, and also suspected of being a double agent for the NKVD, saw the exchange, but neither felt it was anything but a man-woman thing, based around the wares the Turkish woman had prominently on display. There had been a number of other such non-events in the hour that they had observed her.

Of greater concern to them now was the presence of the Senator, member of the recently established Armed Services Committee. One agent slipped away to make an urgent call, summoning reinforcements.

The third angel sounded, and a great star fell from Heaven, burning like a torch, and it fell upon a third of the rivers, and on the springs of waters. The name of the Star is called Wormwood, and a third of the waters became Wormwood, and many men died of the waters, because they were made bitter.

Revelations 8:11

Chapter 151 – THE HORROR

0601 hrs, Monday, 27th May 1946, Briefing room, North Field, Tinian, Mariana Island Group.

They had practised the mission hard, as much as the short time span would permit, which had meant, including the day the order had arrived, twenty-five days of take-offs, precise navigation, dropping inactive bombs, three actual bombing missions, and all things that had generally welded them into a first-class team.

The day beforehand, their B-29 had dropped a pumpkin bomb on Miyazaki, as part of a group of B-29s sent on a milk run job over an ailing enemy nation.

It had been a singularly rude awakening when two of the Superfortresses were chopped from the sky by Japanese fighters of a type never seen before.

One rear gunner, Staff Sergeant Arthur Hanebury, took out one of the impressive fighters, sending it spinning away into the sea, important pieces detaching themselves with every rotation.

The surviving two fighters damaged two more B-29s before drawing off, ahead of the arrival of a wave of protective US fighters.

It was Hanebury's fourth kill, and second as a Superfort gunner, and the previous evening's celebrations, although muted by the loss of two crews, were still heavy enough to have left a mark.

Not so much of a mark that he and the men of 'Dimples 98' were not ready and raring to go.

"Ten-hut!"

The assembled crews sprang to their feet as the door at the end of the Quonset hut flew open, and the progress of their unit commander and S-2 were announced by the sharp sound of feet marching in unison.

The two officers reached the end of the briefing hut and came to a position of parade rest.

38

"Be seated."

The crews dropped into their chairs in eager anticipation, recognising their own excitement mirrored in the CO's face.

"Special mission 17 is go. We go the day aft..."

The whistles and yells drowned out the rest of Tibbets' words, so he stopped and let his boys have their moment.

The noise subsided gradually, as senior aircrew called the rest to order.

"We go on Wednesday 29th. You all know the mission profile... this is what we've been training for... and soon it all comes good."

He nodded at his Intelligence officer to start.

Lieutenant Colonel Hazen Payette, the 509th Composite's intelligence officer, pulled back the red cover, revealing the map, with its taped routes and targets clear in the eye of every man present.

As he spoke, occasionally pointing at the map, notes were taken, even by those who were not tasked for Mission 17, just in case a failure or a loss promoted them to participating in the greatest bombing raid in history.

Hazen drew their attention to the new fighter aircraft that had wounded and killed men from other units in the 313th Bombardment Wing the day beforehand.

"Intelligence suggests that they're Nakajima 87's, a specialised high-altitude interceptor. Seems like 679th Bombardment Squadron also had a run-in a couple of days beforehand."

No one stated the obvious about the lack of intelligence communications on the matter.

"Anyway, they don't seem to have many of them, but they're bad news for sure. The powers-that-be've upgraded our fighter support, and three squadrons of long-range Mustangs, not one, will be staging out of our foothold on Taiwan to escort you all the way in and out."

Nods gave the seal of approval to the upgrade in fighter protection.

Hazen finished up and ceded the floor to Colonel Tibbets.

"Final mission allocation, gentlemen."

He pulled aside the black cloth, revealing the aircraft assigned to which task.

There were whoops and groans, depending on the job allocated, the deeper groans from those whose call sign was not on display and therefore had no role in Special mission 17.

Major JP Crail spoke to his boys through the hubbub of joy and disappointment.

39

"At least we get to fly, boys. And who knows, eh?"

There were three possible targets for the mission, a situation brought about by the unpredictable nature of Japanese weather. The alternates were listed, should there be obscuration issues over target number one.

Hiroshima.

The B-29 could bomb by radar, but the mission parameters required a visual drop.

Hiroshima and the two alternates, Kokura and Nagasaki, each had a weather assessment aircraft assigned, the three B-29 crews happy to be involved, but restrained because they had no active role to play.

Dimples 85, 71, and 83 were assigned to Hiroshima, Nagasaki, and Kokura, each aircraft recorded by their nose name, as 'Straight Flush', 'Jabit III', and 'Full House' respectively.

Dimples 89, 'The Great Artiste', was slated for the bombing group, its blast measuring gear there to record what happened when the mission hit the target.

'Necessary Evil', call sign Dimples 91, was also in the bomb group, included as official observation and photography unit.

Tibbets would take 'Enola Gay', Dimples 82, and carry the Atomic bomb, serial number L-11, as primary strike aircraft on the mission.

Which left Crail and his crew, in Dimples 98, who would be armed with L-9, a fully operational device that they would take into the air and bring back home, unless Tibbets and Enola Gay fell by the wayside.

Crail smiled across at Eddie Costello of 'Laggin Dragon', who was not rostered to play any part.

The hurt in his friend's eyes gave him a moment's pause.

In the background, he heard the 'dismiss', which was underlined by the scrape of chairs as men rose up.

He nodded sympathetically to Costello and brought his attention back to his disappointed crew.

"Could be worse, guys," he inclined his head towards the silent crew of the 'Dragon'.

"Now, let's grab some chow."

Crail's crew were a quality team, brought together by their excellence at their individual crafts, and welded into a tight and efficient group by training, and training, and yet more training.

They were mainly good friends, although there were frictions, as there always will be.

They were officers and NCOs, college boys and farmer's sons, whose only common ground was servicing the Silverbird B-29 and the country whose uniform they wore.

Fig # 180 – The Japanese Home Islands.

0301 hrs, Wednesday, 29th May 1946, North Field, Tinian, Marianas Island Group.

'Miss Merlene' rose into the dark sky with as much grace as its overweight frame would permit, throttles pressed hard against the stops to extract maximum power.

41

In the blackness below, the sight of headlights and torches flitting around the shape of a B-29 stood out, the more so because of the importance of what had happened precisely six minutes beforehand.

Special mission 17, now known as Centerboard One, had not started well.

'Enola Gay' was fourth off, and had been taxiing to the runway when her outside port engine did what the Wright R-3350s did now and again.

Normally such failures were based around an issue with the valves, the ground crew called it 'eating them', where the valves were somehow drawn into the engine.

The alloy crankcase meant that any combustion was abetted by the magnesium, making such failures frequently fatal to the engine and mission, and if airborne, highly dangerous for the crews.

The fire had been brought under control speedily, as the strip had twice the normal allocation of emergency response considered standard for a 'Very Heavy' bomb group.

But Tibbets and his aircraft were spent, which meant that the burden of the attack now fell upon 'Miss Merlene' and her crew instead.

The training cut in, so Crail moved up to the take-off position and waited whilst the Weaponeer and his assistant were speedily transferred from the lame duck to his craft.

No sooner were the two Navy men aboard than permission to take-off was in hand, and 'Miss Merlene' rolled down the North runway to a date with history.

The sun rose over Japan at 0428 hrs precisely, bathing cockpits and crew positions in a penetrating light that seemed to almost single out each man in a beam of focussed attention, as a spotlight plays upon an actor on a stage.

Most of the crew saw the patterns of the 'Rising Sun' flag within the beams of light that radiated outwards from the fiery ball, and each felt the sight was an omen... one way, or the other.

And then, when the beauty and awe of the sight fell away, each man felt uncomfortable at the attention the sun gave him, as if the rays singled him out, and him alone, making him a target, vulnerable and exposed to what was to come.

'The Great Artiste', 'Necessary Evil', and 'Miss Merlene' came together over Iwo Jima and set course for the primary target, Hiroshima.

Ahead of them, the three meteorological birds plied their craft, and fed back mission-changing data.

Crail listened as Jones, the radio operator, passed on the information from 'Straight Flush' over Hiroshima.

'Solid cloud... Ten-tenths... No chance of bombing visually.'

"Damn."

The mission protocol was quite clear, but the decision was not his to make.

That responsibility lay with William Parsons, mission commander and weaponeer, a US Navy Captain presently working in the bomb bay, finishing up arming the 'Little Boy' bomb.

Three minutes later, Parsons arrived in the cockpit and announced the successful arming of L-9.

Crail briefed him in a minimum number of words.

"Shit. We could consider radar delivery?"

"No, Sir. The orders are quite specific on that. Visual delivery only."

"Shit."

Army Air Force and Navy agreed on the situation, and Hiroshima gained a reprieve.

"Alternate one?"

"Patchy cloud cover, but probably will be fine by our time over target."

"Alternate two?"

"Perfect so far, predicted best conditions for time on target."

"Mission implications, Major?"

"Eight minutes difference in flight time. Alternate mission profile allows for increased enemy defensive measures, but nothing that would skip past our escort guys."

"Your recommendation?"

"Get another check... we don't need to commit for another...err... six minutes. A lot could change in that time, Sir."

Parsons nodded.

"Make that call, Major. I need a drink."

The Naval officer disappeared to seek out one of the thermos flasks whilst Crail confirmed the latest from the Met planes.

Five minutes passed in the blink of an eye, and Parsons, accompanied by Naval 2nd Lieutenant Jeppson, appeared back in the cockpit.

Crail got in first.

"No change on primary. Alternate One has increasing cloud cover. Alternate Two is clear, Sir."

Parsons exchanged looks with Jeppson, who simply nodded.

"Alternate Two is the target. Send it, Major."

The radio operator, Staff Sergeant P.S. Jones the Third, fired out the one word transmission three times.

'Burnside... Burnside... Burnside...'

In Hiroshima, the primary target, and Nagasaki, Alternate One, no one felt relieved, no one celebrated, and no one thanked their God for sending a modicum of cloud to spare them from the horrors of Atomic warfare.

Both cities, plus a number of others, had been spared from heavy attack until this day, a conscious cold-blooded decision made so that the bomb could be used on a relatively intact target, to permit proper understanding of its destructive force.

The people in Kokura thanked their ancestors, or their God, for the continued sparing of lives, although they had no understanding of why the Yankees did not darken the skies above them, as they did most other places in the Empire.

In Kokura, life went on as normal.

The workers in the Arsenal, one of the last major production facilities available to the Empire of Japan, went about their business, blissfully unaware that a decision, made high up in the sky many miles away, was bringing death on a biblical scale to their front doors that very day.

Centerboard One was coming.

0708 hrs, Wednesday, 29th May 1946, airborne, one hour from Alternate 2, Kyūshū Island, Japan.

Jeppson was in the bomb bay, removing the final safeties from L-9, turning an inanimate object into an all-powerful weapon of war.

The rest of the crew were quiet, the normal banter that broke up mission boredom absent, probably as the enormity of their task started to gnaw away at them.

Hanebury surveyed the sky, seeking signs of enemy aircraft approaching, and saw nothing but the lightening sky.

44

Once, he had caught sight of some of the escort, at distance, behind and slightly above them, intent on shepherding the trio of B-29s to the target and back to Okinawa intact.

He unscrewed his thermos flask and took a belt of the sweet black coffee.

As he tipped his head back he caught the minutest flash of light, a microsecond that revealed the presence of something sharing the sky with them.

His reputation for having the eyes of a hawk was well deserved.

"Tail gunner, unidentified aircraft above and behind, distant, probably six thousand."

The message galvanised the entire crew, with the exception of Jeppson, who remained working in the bomb bay, blissfully unaware that there was a possible threat close at hand.

The three B-29s were flying in a relaxed V, but, with the imminent threat, drew in tighter.

The radio waves burst into life, imploring the escort to deal with whatever it was that was closing fast.

0709 hrs, Wednesday, 29th May 1946, airborne, just over an hour from Alternate 2, Kyūshū Island, Japan.

Hanebury had got it wrong.

There were two of them, flying tight together, making the spotting error extremely easy.

To give them their proper designations, the pair of killers were Nakajima Ki-87 fighter-interceptors, designed specifically to counter the B-29 threat.

The creaking Japanese manufacturing base had managed to produce five before Nakajima's Mushashino facility received a visit from the very aircraft they were designed to shoot down, and production was ended permanently.

Such important beasts were entrusted only to experienced pilots, and the two Japanese fliers were as experienced as they came.

The three B-29s were led by 'Miss Merlene', the nose position being considered the least vulnerable.

"Zuiho-Two, take the right. On my order… attack!"

The two Ki-87s moved apart, each pilot focussing on one of the rear bombers.

Interception group commander, Lieutenant Commander Kurisu Ashara, bore down on 'The Great Artiste', ready to let fly with the array of 20mm and 30mm cannons.

45

His wingman, Chief Petty Officer Kenzo Nobunaga, shouted a warning and made his own rapid manoeuvre, as tracers swept past the left side of his aircraft, passing through the space he had only just vacated.

Both pilots moved their Mitsubishi engines into emergency power, the turbochargers adding even more impetus as they dived away, pursued by Mustangs from the escort.

Ashara had the reflexes of a cat, but still a few bullets struck his machine as he flicked left and rolled away underneath the bomber formation, turning to starboard after his Number Two..

No fire came from the three B-29s, for fear of hitting one of their saviours, although many eyes followed the two killers as they were hounded by friendlies.

Pushing the boundaries of their upper 430mph limit, the two Nakajimas of Zuiho flight continued on a starboard turn, trying to come back round and up behind the B-29s, intent on making a successful run against the lumbering heavies.

The escorting USAAF fighters knew their business, and the curving attack approach suddenly became very dangerous, forcing both Nakajimas to flick away to port.

Six escorts suddenly became twelve, as the rest of the Mustang squadron entered the arena in pursuit of three Nakajimas Ki-84 Hayates.

Unlike the aircraft of Zuiho flight, the three Hayates were not in their prime, were equipped with worn out engines, and using sub-standard fuel.

Hanebury was able to call out the destruction of two in as many seconds, before the last survivor, and the gaggle of pursuers, disappeared from his view.

By the time he looked back at the two Ki-87s, he winced as a smoking Mustang rolled over and the pilot pushed himself out into the morning air.

The tail plane hammered into the man's form hard enough for those who watched to be able to imagine the sound reaching their ears above the drone of aero-engines. The body, for he must surely have died on impact, dropped away towards the sea below, and there was no sign of a deploying parachute to offer the hope of a heart still beating.

His killer, Ashara, exploited the pause and flicked onto an attack path, again selecting 'The Great Artiste' for attention.

The Ho-105 cannon had an effective range of under 1000 metres, just about half that of the defensive armament on the B-29, so Ashara was already taking fire from the tail gunner's .50cal.

However, the 30mm Ho-105 packed a lot more punch when it arrived on target, and so it proved, as first the rear gun position and then the tail plane suffered appalling damage.

Ashara manoeuvred slightly left and introduced the 20mm Ho-5s into the attack.

'The Great Artiste' staggered under the brief attack, the port outboard engine coming apart, the combination of its own energy and the damaging impact of explosive shells proving too much.

The entire engine dropped away, leaving a hollow mounting that trailed flame until the fuel was cut and there was nothing left to feed the fire.

Ashara pulled up and to port, pursued by a pair of vengeful Mustangs.

Nobunaga failed yet again, his attempted attack run interrupted by the melee of escort fighters.

Two bullets clipped the tip of his wing but otherwise, he was unscathed.

Conscious of his lowered fuel state, he knew he could make one last effort before breaking off the attack.

He seized a moment, created by the Mustang's anticipating that he would turn again for a rear shot, and rolled into a sharp port turn.

The Ki-87 slipped through the air, responding to his commands like a thoroughbred, prescribing a tightening arc around the nose of the lead aircraft before, lining up a swift burst on the port front quarter, Nobunaga pumped some 30mm shells into the lead bomber, before dragging the nose to starboard and sending a few more 30mm into the already damaged 'The Great Artiste'.

A shudder and sudden lack of response signalled some damage, as the tail gunner of the lead aircraft, 'Miss Merlene', put a few .50cal on target.

Nobunaga dove hard, believing that he could out dive the Mustangs.

"Zuiho-Two breaking off, diving to sea level, over."

"Zuiho-One breaking off, will join you, course 003, out."

The two sleek Japanese fighters dropped away unpursued, the USAAF escort commander calling off his eager pilots, keen to conserve fuel for the full operation and content with driving off the enemy at the cost of three of their dwindling fighter assets.

As Ashara and Nobunaga made their escape, the drama continued above them.

Parsons was in deep discussion with Crail.

"I'd say they can't go on, but that ain't my call, Captain."

The two men had taken turns to view the smoking B-29 on their port rear quarter.

'The Great Artiste's' pilot made the call, and reluctantly informed the mission commander that the B-29 had to return.

After the normal acknowledgements and best wishes, the damaged B-29 turned gently and headed for Okinawa, escorted by a pair of Mustangs.

"Mission abort?"

It was not a question, more the opening of a short discussion.

Parsons, as mission commander, had that call, whereas Crail, as aircraft commander, made decisions on his B-29 and its capabilities.

"Captain, she was the numbers bird. We can't do the measuring the high-ups want but, unless I'm missing something, her loss doesn't take us below mission success parameters."

"And us? What damage have we got and are you waving the mission off?"

Crail shook his head dramatically.

"No way, no how, Captain. My numbers all look good, and the aircraft feels good, so unless my boys find something," the crew had been detailed to do a damage inspection, "We are good to go."

The shells had struck in the bomb bay and central area, slightly injuring both Jeppson and Burnett, the flight engineer.

Jeppson was already inspecting L-9 for any sign of damage, and the rest of Crail's boys were looking for anything that might inhibit the huge airplane in her mission.

Parsons looked at his watch, mentally allocating a decision point.

Before it was reached, Crail was able to confirm that 'Miss Merlene' was fit for purpose.

Jeppson's report was less encouraging, and Parsons virtually leapt from the cockpit to go and see the damage to the atomic bomb's tail assembly himself.

Crail busied himself with re-checking every part of his aircraft's performance and, once satisfied, checked it all over again.

A voice in his ear, one that sounded heavy with the stress of command, requested the bomb-aimer to come to the bomb bay.

The B-29 was a pressurised vessel, with the crew spaces airtight and regulated.

The bomb bay was open to outside air and unpressurised, something that had meant modification to enable the bombs to be armed and de-safetied in the air.

This modification did not permit three men to work on the bombs at the same time, neither did it enable a single man to work on the damaged tail assembly.

It only just permitted a modicum of sight on the tail, but there had been enough for Jeppson to see damaged metal present.

Richard Loveless, the bomb-aimer, squinted through the observation port and took in as much as he could.

His eyes assessed the damage and he gave a running commentary as he thought through the issue.

"The good news is it's only the internal structure, not the external faces."

The tail assembly of the L-9 was a square box stabiliser, mounted on four angled fins. It was clear that one of these fins had been damaged, and the metal twisted.

"Definitely gonna affect the trajectory and move it off line some. What are you asking me, Captain?"

"Is it safe to drop from your point of view? I need to know that it's not going to go a-wanderin'. I want to know that you're confident you can still put the thing on target enough to do the job."

Loveless moved back into the same compartment as the two naval officers.

"Captain, it'll move off course some, bound to, but if I can't put the goddamned thing on top of a city... well... then you can throw me out after it."

Parsons smiled, nodded, and thumbed his mike.

"Mission commander speaking. We are go, repeat, we are go."

Centerboard One moved closer to the Empire of Japan.

Another psychological hurdle had come and gone, with the thought that the mission might be scrubbed because of the loss of 'Artiste' or the damaged fin, followed by the confirmation that it was still on, and the bomb would be dropped, come hell or high water.

Jones, radioed back a sitrep along with Parson's decision to carry on.

Pretty much everyone on the crew expected some sort of guidance or interference from base, but there was none; just a curt acknowledgement.

Whilst the automatic routines of flying combat missions were performed without thought, the concept of the attack, the nature

49

of their weapon, and the likely human and moral cost, became the focus of their active minds.

Only Loveless, on his own in the nose, and Hanebury, happy with his own company in the tail, could not discuss the matter with one of their friends.

At the control, Crail sat pondering the enormity of what he was about to do.

All of them had received psyche evaluations and training, preparing them for the mission, the expected results, and the impact on their moral soul, as one of the padres had put it.

They had taken it in their stride, as young men do, but now, in the reality of the minutes before visiting hell upon thousands of people, it was different.

Very different.

So different as to make all their previous thoughts and preparation meaningless.

'Damn.'

"Major?"

Crail had given voice to his thought.

"Sorry?"

"You said something, JP."

"I did?"

"Yep. Worrying isn't it?"

Crail flicked his eyes across the gauges, giving himself time to reply.

"They haven't prepared us for it, not right, I mean."

His co-pilot hummed in agreement.

"All that mumbo-jumbo, all that bullshit about righteous act, saving lives, ending the war, blah blah blah… it doesn't mean shit when you're up here about to do the deed… leastways that's how I feel. What about you, George?"

"I agree, JP. I thought I was ok with it… but I'm not so sure now… I mean… we all gotta live with it after the thing is done."

The two dropped into the sort of heavy silence generated by minds deep in thought.

Crail started, his mind suddenly overcoming a hurdle. He thumbed his mike.

"Dick, come up to the deck will you."

Loveless appeared a moment later, his face inquisitive.

Junior Pershing Crail got straight to the point.

"You got any problems with dropping the bomb, Dick?"

The reply was instant.

"Not a one, JP."

50

Nelleson barked back immediately

"None at all?"

"None, George, none whatsoever."

Dick Loveless looked at the two Doubting Thomases in front of him, and at the silent spectators, Burnett sat at the flight engineer's panel, and Blockridge, the assistant flight engineer, stood beside him.

As he took in their concerns, Parsons and Jeppson came back into view, their checking of the bomb complete.

Parsons couldn't help himself.

"Trouble, Major?"

His hand automatically checked the presence of his firearm.

"No, Captain, we're just talking here."

Loveless looked at Crail, silently seeking advice on whether to continue, or just disappear back into his greenhouse.

Crail bit the bullet.

"Carry on, Dick."

"Okay, Major. I have absolutely no problem with this whatsoever, and I'll tell you why."

Loveless pushed the cap back, adjusting the headphones so he could hear his own words properly.

"For a start, the Nips started it. We didn't... so they have whatever coming."

The silence drew him on.

"Yes, we're bringing something new and awful, but they'd use it on us for sure..." he waved his finger to emphasise his point, "You **know** they'd use it on us, so I have no problem with that."

Parsons piped up.

"Well, they tried that plague stuff out at the start of this war, and on the Chinese in the last war, so we know they have no moral stops on killing hundreds at a time with anything they can get their hands on."

George Nelleson jumped on that comment immediately.

"We're not talking hundreds, we're talking thousands, and not just military personnel either. We're going to kill a fucking city here!"

Crail went to speak, but Loveless was faster.

"Yes, George, we are. We are going to kill thousands of people in one moment of light."

He cleared his throat and continued.

"Is that any worse than killing millions slowly by starvation, eh? The Nips are starving, dying in their droves every day,

51

because we blockade them and they can't work the land. Any worse than shooting them down in their tens of thousands when we try and invade... when our soldiers too will be shot down in their thousands on the beaches and in the goddamned paddy fields, all because the war goes on and on and on, eh?"

"No but..."

"No, but nothing, George."

He slapped his friend's knee, trying to defuse the sudden adversarial tension.

"I don't believe half of the bullshit that we were spoon-fed, no more than any of us do, I 'spect."

Loveless suddenly realised that everyman who could see was fixed on him, eyes staring directly at him.

"Err, don't forget we've an aircraft to fly here, folks!"

The moment broken, the pilots and flight engineers looked over their instruments, the two naval officers relaxed their tensed muscles and leant against the bulkheads.

"Look fellahs, I really believe that this'll shorten the war and save lives. I actually believe it'll save Japanese lives too, in the long run. It has to, surely?"

He left that hanging for a moment.

The point had been debated and turned over many times before, but not in this situation... not on the flight deck of a B-29 less than an hour out from deploying the first atomic bomb ever dropped on an enemy state.

Such imminence of action crystallised thinking much more than debate in some warm and safe Quonset hut back on Saipan.

Burnett spoke up from the flight engineer's position.

"Yeah, but look at Hamburg and Dresden. Conventional bombing was supposed to shorten the war, and look at what those RAF boys went through afterwards from the press and politicians. And that was normal bombs and stuff, not atomics. Just imagine what lies in wait for us poor doggies, eh?"

1st Lieutenant Fletcher, the navigator, joined in.

"Fair point, Ralph. Even Prime Minister Churchill had his piece of that action."

"Yeah, exactly... plus Hamburg, Cologne, Dresden, and all the others put up a defence. These poor bastards ain't got a chance."

Crail couldn't help himself.

"So it would all be fine if they could shoot us down, yeah? Well, in case you boys ain't noticed, we're already sporting a little extra ventilation, and that's before we do the deed."

His voice carried the humour he intended and again the situation relaxed perceptibly.

Crail's mind had debated, listened to the words of others, and made a firm decision.

"And, for the record, I'm doing what I think is right, regardless of what the press might judge now or in twenty years' time."

"Amen to that, Major. Boys, I see we've a chance to stop this war here and now... I mean the nip part obviously. I also believe the shrinks and generals when they say it'll affect the Commies too...has to."

Loveless moved upwards, to make sure he could get his point over with his eyes and face as well as his mouth.

"We put the nips to bed with this bomb and that has to send a message to the Commies... don't fuck with us, Uncle Joe, we've got something that's badass as hell and we're not afraid to use it."

A number of nods showed his message was hitting home. Again, a message that had been heard before, but not under these circumstances, in this time frame, on this aircraft, nearing the coast of Japan.

"Think of the lives we'll save then. Our boys have bled dry over in Europe, and have done well. Just think... we now, the few of us, could save them in their thousands, save European civilians in their millions."

He sensed a new resolve amongst his comrades and chucked in a moment of humour to end his 'presentation'.

"Anyways... what you bastards worried about? I'm the poor bastard who has to drop it."

Not a laughing matter, but tension releases itself in strange ways sometimes, and they all laughed.

"Navigator, time to point Alpha."

"Skipper, point Alpha, twenty-six minutes on this course."

"Roger that."

He took a deep breath.

"OK Guys, let's get this done by the numbers."

Crail checked his watch automatically.

It was 0729.

'Miss Merlene' flew on to her date with destiny.

Centerboard One was almost there.

0755 hrs, Wednesday, 29th May 1946, Point Alpha, over Kyūshū Island, Japan.

"Course 018, prepare to execute, on my mark… three…two…one…mark."

Crail dropped the right wing and adjusted the B-29s course as the mission moved over point Alpha and turned for the bomb run to Kokura.

In the nose, Loveless checked and re-checked the aerial photographs of the Kokura Arsenal, specifically the configuration of the northeast corner, his precise target for dropping L-9.

The rest of the crew applied themselves, making sure that their particular area of responsibility was right up to the mark, ensuring that they did their bit to the absolute best of their ability.

The last weather report had talked of a slight worsening of conditions, but nothing that would cause an abort.

Loveless was calling the shots now.

His calm voice delivered the adjustments required, and the pilots acted, bringing the B-29 into the correct approach.

The navigator supplied his information in a steady matter of fact tone, suggesting nothing of the inner tension he felt… they all felt…

The intercom came to life.

"Navigator, Pilot…two minutes to release point."

Crail acknowledged and gave Nelleson the nod.

The bomb bay doors were opened, illuminating the Little Boy with natural light.

Jeppson took the opportunity to re-examine L-9 before he made the required report, and saw nothing untoward, other than the wounded tail plane.

"Pilot, Bomb Bay, doors fully open… weapon is ready."

"Roger, Bomb bay."

Crail looked Parsons, his eyes seeking a required response.

"Major, the mission is a go, Release is authorised."

He nodded at the naval officer, the final hurdle overcome in a few words.

"Pilot, Bomb-aimer, release authorised."

The process was left until the last moments to ensure that every opportunity for a safe and accurate launch was available.

Crail had rehearsed this moment.

"Pilot, crew, stand by for release… we are about to drop our bomb, and show the world that war has no place in our future. Good luck to us all. Pilot out."

54

The thought settled in the collective minds as the final seconds ticked away, and then individual brains made their own minds up concerning what was about to pass.

Crail... *just hold steady, Marlene baby, nice and steady...*

Hanebury... *get it done, Lovey, and get it done right...*

Parsons... *Please God, let this be righteous...*

Burnett... *They have it coming...*

Nelleson... *Sweet lord, what am I part of here...*

Fletcher... *Don't fuck with America!...*

Jones... *Kill to stop the killing... are we right... really right?...*

Loveless.................................. *that's it!*

"Bomb away!"

Everyone on 'Miss Merlene' understood that as the B-29, suddenly nine thousand seven hundred pounds lighter, rose instantly.

The procedure now called for a hi-speed turn, placing the rear towards the epicentre of the burst.

Hanebury, the man who would now have a direct view of L-9's act of immolation, already had the goggles on, an item that he had strict orders to wear to protect his eyes.

A timer, initiated the instant L-9 fell away, came to life fifteen seconds later.

The timer did its job, and the altimeters were made ready to activate the device, once the barometer had told them it was at its designated height.

The barometer was simple but considered insufficiently accurate to initiate the device by itself.

At six thousand, seven hundred and seventy-two feet, the barometer membrane curved sufficiently to complete the circuit, fully arming the altimeters.

They registered the rapidly decreasing height.

At one thousand, nine hundred and two feet, they permitted an electrical impulse to ignite the three Mk15M1 Naval gun primers.

Fifty-eight seconds from the moment the bomb left 'Miss Merlene', those primers ignited the cordite charges, which in turn propelled a modest sized uranium projectile into another, smaller piece of uranium.

A total of one hundred and forty-one pounds of enriched uranium collided at nearly one thousand feet per second.

Catastrophically so.

The reaction took place in a micro-second.

Its effects would be felt for a thousand years.

At first, there was light.

A pure light, all-powerful, and a clear pre-cursor to something truly horrible.

Then there was fire.

A huge ball rolling upwards and outwards.

The pressure wave was tangible, and those on the observation bird watched in awe as it rammed through the air, seemingly carrying all before it.

Thousands of people died in an instant, blast and fire claiming lives without effort.

The wave bumped 'Miss Merlene', and Crail and Nelleson gripped their controls with firmer hands until it passed.

"Pilot, tail. Check in."

There was silence.

"Pilot, tail, check in, you okay, Art?"

The voice that came back quite clearly belonged to Art Hanebury, and it equally clearly carried the true horror he had just witnessed.

His procedures had required him to report successful ignition and, although the sound and shockwave had done the job for him, Crail was a stickler.

Normally Hanebury would have been on the ball, but this was not normal, and his eyes had been assailed by a vision of hell that had never been seen before.

"Tail, Pilot, ignition confirmed... sorry JP... I mean, Major... I mean... my God..."

Crail thumbed his mike.

"Yeah I know, Art, we all know... horrible thing... worse than we could have imagined... but it had to be done."

Hanebury pursed his lips unobserved and lashed out at the metal surrounding him, splitting his hand in a bloody thwack.

He bit back the pain.

"Roger that, JP. I know... but that's...," again unseen, he nodded towards the huge mushroom cloud that rose above the destroyed city of Kokura, "... that's just so awful."

Loveless seized on the slight pause.

"Then we must all pray that it's the last time atomics are dropped on any one."

More than one brain continued the thought.

'... and maybe they are right... if it's that horrible then we might just've ended war as we know it!'

The thought sat comfortably and eased many minds.

Crail consulted with Parsons, who issued the order.

"Pilot, radio operator. Send Dante, repeat, send Dante. Confirm."

"Radio, pilot, send Dante. Over."

"Roger. Out."

As Staff Sergeant Jones sent the mission success code word, 'Miss Merlene' flew on, leaving behind death on a biblical scale.

0827 hrs, Wednesday, 29th May 1946, Kanoya Airfield, Kyūshū, Japan.

Reactions differed.

Some men screamed.

Some men wept silently.

Some took oaths of vengeance.

A single Aichi aircraft had been airborne nearby, and the two shocked crewmen had born witness to the moment when L-9 had destroyed Kokura.

News would have been patchy and slowly distributed, had the aircrew not witnessed the attack, and reported it within minutes.

The Japanese communications were badly damaged and not every station received word or orders, but Kanoya was an important base, and efforts to restore her links were constant.

And so it was that word of the attack reached the pilots of the Kogekitai, the Tokkôtai Special Attack Squadrons, and the men of the 301st Fighter Squadron, part of the 343rd Naval Air Group, all based at Kanoya, Kyūshū.

With clarity of thought, Chief Petty Officer Kenzo Nobunaga worked out that he and Ashara had failed to stop the aircraft responsible, the Yankee silver machines that had evaded their attacks had to be the ones who had destroyed Kokura.

He was sure of it.

Ashara was in the hospital, such as it was after many air attacks, being fussed over as befitted a naval air ace of his standing.

He had sustained a minor wound in the air battle, but his attempts to pass it off had fallen on stony ground, and unequivocal orders were given.

Nobunaga's aircraft was receiving attention, the defensive fire having damaged his ailerons.

He suddenly filled with a resolve to act, one he concealed with an outward calm as he surveyed the Intelligence Officer's maps, whilst the IO himself wailed inconsolably in the next room, believing his family slain in the awful attack.

Nobunaga studied the return routes of Yankee aircraft, seeking some pattern that would allow him to act.

He found none.

The tracks were drawn, reflecting previous missions and interceptions on the bomber's return.

He closed his eyes and beseeched his ancestors to intercede, to give him sign, some clue, a way of understanding the plethora of lines that confused the map in front of him.

"Mount Tara, Kenzo."

He opened his eyes and stiffened immediately.

Captain Sunyo stood before him.

"Sir?"

"There's a report they were seen from the observation post on Mount Tara, likely heading to Okinawa."

Nobunaga looked again and, in his mind, most of the lines fell away, leaving only two, one that ran over Mount Tara and another to the east, both of which headed towards Okinawa.

He nodded, acknowledging the precious gifts his ancestors had granted him.

"With your permission, Captain."

The Air Group commander nodded sorrowfully.

"You will not return, Nobunaga."

"Hai."

He bent his waist into a deep formal bow, acknowledging his superior's unspoken permission, agreeing with his summation, and in deep respect for the veteran pilot.

Chief Petty Officer Nobunaga strode from the IO's office and headed towards Ashara's silent Ki-87.

Four minutes later, the Nakajima rose into the morning, heading towards the Uji Islands.

0902 hrs, Wednesday, 28th May 1946, above the Hayatonoseto Strait, Uji Island Group, Japan.

They had all long since settled down, with no open expressions of their feelings and fears, the standard intercom banter flowing, albeit not as barbed and punchy as normal.

The return flight pattern took them through the Hayatonoseto Straits, between Uji and Ujimukae Islands.

A handful of ancient Japanese craft rose up in challenge, and none of them got close as the escort fell upon them and sent every single one into the sea below, the majority of the aircraft prescribing fiery trails, as unprotected aviation spirit tanks discharged their contents, fuelling the smallest blaze and ensuring an awful end to both aircraft and pilot.

Jubilant Mustang pilots filled the airwaves with their celebrations.

Relaxed bomber crews exchanged jibes and banter.

Nobunaga dived.

Hanebury yawned, oblivious to the approaching killer.

Nobunaga made a slight adjustment to starboard.

It was enough.

Hanebury yelled, "Fighter attacking! Turn to port, turn to port!", and thumbed his firing triggers.

Nobunaga yelled "Banzai! Banzai! Banzai!", and lined up on the centre point of the B-29.

Bullets from the other Superfortress rattled his tail section, knocking pieces off, but none prevented his inexorable rendezvous.

Hanebury shifted his aim as 'Miss Merlene' swung rapidly in line with his warning.

The Ki-87 drove in hard, even as Mustangs desperately tried to get a deflection shot in before the bombers made shooting impossible.

Hanebury's bullets struck the cowling, the wing root, the tail plane, and the cockpit, missing anything of importance.

Inside the Nakajima, fuel vapours started to make Nobunaga's eyes sting, and the narcotic effect of the leaking spirit started to numb his mind.

'No matter, Tennouheika Banzai!'

Hanebury fired a last burst as the heavy Nakajima fighter closed, two rounds of which smashed into the engine, two in Nobunaga's left leg and knee, and one that merely clipped a gauge on the way through the instrument panel and into the Japanese CPO's chest.

There was an instant fiery ignition, but Nobunaga's pain was momentary.

Ki-87 Number 343-A-05 struck 'Miss Merlene' amidships, although Hanebury's burst had altered the suicide aircraft's path sufficiently that the heavy engine clipped the underneath of the Superfortress, its propeller chewing up the aluminium skin and into the airframe beneath, before its momentum carried it out and below the fuselage and on a descent to the Hayatonoseto Strait below.

The port wing momentarily slapped the underside before fluttering away like a shiny Sycamore seed.

The Ki-87's fuselage and right wing explored the damaged skin and penetrated inside, tossing a modest amount of burning fuel forward and into the crew compartment.

The weight of the aircraft hammered into the airframe and, although much lessened by the absence of the engine, was sufficient to create havoc with 'Miss Merlene's' integrity and ability to stay airborne.

Apart from Hanebury's earlier shout, there had been no warning, and so Crail and Nelleson were taken unawares as the controls first lightened with the impact and then went very tight, all in the briefest of moments.

Something was wrong, big time.

"Crew, call in. What's happened?"

As he sought information, Crail was already taking 'Miss Merlene' lower, suspecting that the pressurised rear position might have been compromised.

Hanebury was first, and his voice betrayed the urgency of the situation as much as the heavy controls.

"He crashed into us, just rammed us."

Crail inwardly had two opposed thoughts.

Firstly, if Hanebury's intercom still worked then it can't be too bad.

Secondly, if an aircraft had crashed into them, then it had to be bad.

"Pilot, radar, report."

Nothing.

"Pilot, radar…Pick… Al… come in?"

There was no reply and Crail acted swiftly.

"Art, I need a sitrep. Get up there and have a look."

"Roger."

Arthur Hanebury quickly grabbed at a portable oxygen cylinder and made his way towards the pressurised compartment door.

As he moved forward from his tail gunner's post, Crail and Nelleson struggled to level the ailing B-29 out, the starboard side inexplicably and constantly fighting to rise.

Smoke and fumes greeted Arthur Hanebury as he opened up his pressurised door. He grabbed one of the fire extinguishers by his hatch and moved towards the radar operator's position.

The bomb bay emergency exit door, that should have protected their compartment, was open and bent by the force of impact.

60

The first thing he really noted was the hole, wide enough for him to spread his arms and still fall out, a tall enough for him to stand in, almost perpendicular to the damaged floor.

The remains of a man lay amongst the carnage, destroyed by the passage of metal through the crew space, and then swiftly flash burnt as the brief fire swelled and virtually died.

There was no sign of the second man, the one whose position lay at the point of impact.

Using the extinguisher to knock down the last few flames, he became aware of the noise created by the wind rushing through the compartment. The passing air stream created a Venturi effect and was sucking loose matter out of the hole.

Papers momentarily hung in the air and then rushed out into the atmosphere.

Hanebury plugged his intercom in and drew a deep breath before speaking.

"Tail, pilot."

Crail responded, anxiously awaiting the news.

"JP, all depressurised here. I don't think the Nip hit us square, just a glancing blow. We've a big hole in the starboard size, six foot across easy, and just as high, with damage to the air frame extending beyond and above that... can't see below impact point yet, over."

"Roger, Any more? How are the boys, over?"

"Both gone, JP. They'd no chance. No fire present... knocked out the little bit that remained... checking for further damage, over."

"Roger, Art. Help's on its way, out."

Nelleson and Blockridge were already in the tube, moving back to the rear compartment, Loveless having assumed the second pilot's seat, purely to have another set of hands on the controls.

As Nelleson emerged into the rear crew space, Hanebury's voice summoned Crail's attention away from his instruments.

"Pilot, tail. I've found trouble. Some damaged cables here, stand by."

Suddenly, colour became all-important.

It was Nelleson's voice that announced the bad news.

"Pilot, co-pilot. Yellow and black are slightly damaged, but should be fine. We can do something with them. Green are partially cut through. Repeat, green are partially cut through, over."

Crail digested the information.

It didn't explain the inability to level the airplane, but it might explain why certain movements seemed to catch and hang up.

Green was the right rudder cable.

'*Shit!*'

He swallowed before thumbing the mike.

"Can you rig it, over?"

Nelleson answered hesitantly.

"We can try, JP, we can try."

'*Shit!*'

Crail elected for a calmer spoken response.

"Do what you can. I'll keep her level and steady, and no rudder commands without warning. Out."

Crail exchanged looks with Loveless.

"Pilot, navigator, plot the shortest course to the nearest strip that can handle us, over."

1st Lieutenant Chris Fletcher was not considered a wizard navigator for nothing, and his response was instant.

"Okinawa, Pilot. Kadena airfield, with seven thousand, five hundred feet of runway, is closest…range five hundred and eight miles. Futenma field is nine thousand feet of metalled if you want more distance, but is five miles more, over."

Crail made a quick decision.

"Futenma. We'll go for the extra feet, over."

"Roger, Pilot. Course 187, over."

"Roger."

The work party in the radar compartment received the manoeuvre warning and warily observed the damaged cable as the B-29 adjusted the few degrees to starboard to assume the right course for Futenma Airbase, Okinawa.

[Author's note – It is without a doubt that Chief Petty Officer Kenzo Nobunaga took off in Ashara's aircraft, in the full knowledge that it had virtually no ammunition on board, such was the effect of US bombing missions on Japan's munitions and distribution network. I have therefore written of his death and ramming of 'Miss Merlene' as a deliberate suicidal act.

His body was recovered two days later and, despite the attention of ravenous sea dwellers, revealed the three wounds I have written of.]

In the wrecked radar section, Nelleson and Hanebury moved some pieces of twisted metal aside, metal that extended into the space better occupied by control cables.

The co-pilot thought out loud.

"This is a major problem. It's catching on this piece of frame."

He turned to Blockridge, who had remained within the communications tube.

"Go and grab the tool kit, Austin."

Blockridge disappeared and Nelleson made his report.

"Co-pilot, pilot, over."

"Talk to me, Nellie."

"Surface lock cable isn't in the run. Must have been severed. We need to work on the area round the damaged cable, and try and reinforce it. Austin's on his way back for tools. Recommend no heavy manoeuvres at any time, over."

"Roger, Nellie, tools on the way back to you right now, out."

"Art, open the cable panel down by your station. Find the red/black coupling... undo it... it's fucked anyway... recover the wire so we can rig something here. OK?"

Hanebury nodded and set off towards the tail as the tube hatch opened and Blockridge returned with the small toolbox.

The two men set to work with a small prise bar and a screwdriver, working the damaged metal away from the cable run.

"Oh fuck, Nellie, look at that!"

Nelleson looked at where Blockridge's eyes were fixed.

"Oh God."

The area above the hole and across the top of the radar station had a small but very discernible defect in the metal skin.

Staff Sergeant Austin Blockridge looked around him, checking things out, one side, then the other, then back up above his head.

"Compression. The frame's bending upwards!"

Nelleson repeated the assessment exercise and saw angles where there should be straight lines.

"Shit! You're right."

Blockridge grabbed the measure and took a few moments to compare the frame distances on either side of the fuselage.

"Three inches out on starboard side."

Now that the numbers were available, the eye could make out the lean on two of the frames.

"Rig something quick. Stop them shifting."

The NCO grabbed the body and dragged it to one side, laying the unidentifiable corpse on one of the crew berths, just to give himself some room in which to work.

The small table had taken a hit, but the metal and wood top surface looked a hell of a lot like it was of a size for part of the job.

Blockridge grabbed it and worked in between the most forward problem frame and the rigid part.

Grabbing the hammer from the kit, a few hefty taps jammed it in place.

Hanebury returned, carefully avoiding the grisly lump of meat now laid on a crew bed, a looped piece of cable held tightly in his hand.

He passed the cable across to Nelleson as Blockridge grabbed his shoulder.

"We need to fill in between these two frames here. The fuselage is bending," his hand pointed out the compression fold in the upper fuselage, which Hanebury studied in horror, whilst the assistant flight engineer noted the obvious deterioration.

"Grab the hacksaw, Art."

Blockridge measured up and pulled out a grease pen.

"Strip the mattress off that bunk."

The light mattress went flying in an instant and Nelleson marked out the cuts he wanted made.

"Get these cut out and we can wedge these in as struts. Quick as you can, Art."

There was no reply, just the urgent sound of a hacksaw biting into metal, as Hanebury set about creating the metalwork to stop the frames moving.

Nelleson increased Crail's stress, and for the matter, the stress levels of everyone who heard his report.

"Roger, out."

Crail didn't know whether to grip the stick more firmly or relax his hands.

The starboard inner made his mind up for him.

"That's hot," the flight engineer declared to no one in particular, reading the gauge that relayed the oil temperature.

"Say again, Ralph?"

"JP, the starboard inner oil is running red hot. Shot up very suddenly."

"Pressure's dropping too…"

Eyes craned for a view, and Loveless announced a new problem in synch with the assistant flight engineer.

"Black smoke, she's just belched black smoke."

64

"JP, starboard inner oil pressure's gone!"

Eighty-five US gallons of lubricating oil were deposited within the engine mount in a matter of seconds.

Crail reacted quickly, closing the starboard inner down and feathering the prop, the assistant flight engineer also doing his part.

He adjusted the aircraft, tinkered with the throttle settings and trims, and found no new handling problems.

He informed the crew, adding to their collective mental anguish.

"Pilot, co-pilot. Talk to me, Nellie."

Nelleson replied, his words punctuated by the sound of background hammering, as Blockridge and Hanebury did their best to increase the integrity of the airframe, despite the pain of their recently acquired scalds.

"Co-pilot, pilot, we just got a wash of hot engine oil. Send down the aid kit, over."

"Pilot, co-pilot, starboard inner just let go. Everyone OK, over?"

"We're still working, JP, but it hurts like hell, over."

Nelleson had taken the lion's share of the scalding hot oil, the left side of his face sticky and already swollen.

"Nellie, aid kit is on its way. How's the aircraft, over?"

"Co-pilot, pilot, we're reinforcing the framework with metal struts. Seems to be holding, but we're doubling up to make sure, over"

He looked at the destroyed bed frames, all victims of Hanebury's hacksaw.

"Once they're through, we'll get on doing summat about reinforcing the rudder cable, over."

"Roger."

Jeppson had done all he could with the first aid kit. When the bandages ran out, a nearby damaged parachute was shredded and provided much needed protection for blistered and oily skin.

The metalwork looked like something from a Laurel and Hardy film, a jury rig seemingly lacking rhyme or reason, but Blockridge was satisfied that it would hold and see them home.

'Probably.'

Wire and tape did its best to hold things in place in case of a reverse in the stresses.

Nelleson had worked with pliers, screwdrivers, and hacksaw, creating a tensioned support that took up the strain on either side of the damaged section on the green control wire.

At his behest, Crail started slow rudder movements, designed to see the parameters of movement in the 'repair'.

"Pilot, co-pilot. Came close to stop on right rudder. Left rudder all fine, over."

"Roger. Will repeat rudder. Shout out when at stop, over."

"Roger."

'Miss Merlene' moved gently in response as three pair of eyes watched the rudder cable close on the stop.

"Mark!"

In the glasshouse, Crail made a grease pen mark on the boss of his stick, giving him a rough reminder of where he could to, or, more importantly, not go beyond.

'Should be enough… I hope…'

The three men in the radar compartment decided on more work, and teased and cut a little more, to give some more right rudder if it was needed.

Crail re-marked the boss.

Nelleson returned to resume his co-pilot role, leaving Blockridge and Hanebury to ride it out in the damaged compartment.

The two spent their time equally between monitoring the cable and strut work, the compression fold in the fuselage, and creating more struts, just in case.

It was Art Hanebury who realised that the lower fuselage had its own major problems.

There was daylight where daylight should not be.

The skin had split in three places, an obvious but previously undetected opposite reaction to the compression issues.

"Anything you can do, Art, over?"

"Nothing except pray, JP, over."

"Roger, out."

'Prayer will have to do.'

1113 hrs, Wednesday, 29th May, 1946, on approach to Futenma Airfield, Okinawa.

The Mustangs had long since left their charges to their own devices, and the air now contained only a CAP of three Shooting Star jet fighters, and the two B-29s.

'Necessary Evil' would normally have landed first but this was not a normal time.

Given the lack of manoeuvrability and damage to 'Miss Merlene', as well as the proximity of Kadena, the damaged bird was first to land

On the airstrip's perimeter, crowds of Marines, Army personnel, and Sailors gathered to watch the show, the genuinely curious mixing with those of more ghoulish nature, all having been drawn by tannoyed announcements and the frantic deployments of meat wagons and fire trucks.

"Necessary Evil' did a low pass, gathering vital information to pass on to the wounded 'Miss Merlene'.

"Dimples-nine-one, received. Dimples-nine-eight, over and out."

Jones had opened the radio to the intercom so that Crail could get the information direct from 'Necessary Evil'.

What he heard was encouraging and he continued his descent with increased confidence.

The other B-29 circled lazily above as 'Miss Merlene' deployed her undercarriage.

An F4U Corsair, scrambled from Futenma to act as an observation plane, slipped in closer to inspect the landing gear.

"Dimples-nine-eight, Roughrider-five-one. Gear is down, starboard inner tyre appears deflated, over."

Burnett's board and Crail's display both showed that the gear was locked.

Crail spoke briefly on the intercom and Jones relayed his words.

"Roughrider-five-one, Dimples-nine-eight, confirm only one deflation on starboard gear, over."

The Corsair came in closer, level with the gash in 'Miss Merlene's' starboard side, and close enough to get a really good look at the two starboard wheels.

As he did so, Blockridge already had his head out, making his own assessment.

"Dimples-nine-eight, Roughrider-five-one, confirm, inner tyre definitely damaged and appears deflated. Outer tyre appears undamaged and to pressure, over."

"Roger, Roughrider-five-one, out."

Crail thumbed his mike.

"Remember, we're a cut-down Silverbird with weight already shed, boys. I'm going for a standard landing. I'll just protect the starboard gear some. Standby for landing. Merlene'll get us home, Boys. Good luck."

The weary B-29 steadily ate up the remaining yards, Crail and Nelleson gently nursing the wounded 'Miss Merlene', throttles set, flaps set, descending as if on a formal landing exercise with the Squadron commander stood behind them, assessing their technical abilities.

Blockridge's report was in agreement with that of the fighter jock, and the two pilots had already agreed a way to mollycoddle the starboard gear.

Both men were sweating.

In fact, everyone was sweating, and not because of the temperature in the aircraft.

The B-29 slid over the top of the base security fence, the control tower operative's voice a constant on their ears.

"Here we go, George."

The left gear touched and then decided to part company with Mother Earth once more.

No words were spoken.

The assembly caught the runway a second time, and Nelleson eased back on the throttles.

Crail held the right wing up as the airspeed started to disappear.

He gently dropped the damaged wheel set down, and the single inflated tyre kissed the ground beneath.

The 'feel' of the aircraft was good, but a lot of the nine thousand feet had already been consumed in the extended manoeuvre.

'Now then, sweet Merlene, look after us all, baby.'

Crail let the assembly take the full weight.

Not one breath was taken from glasshouse to radar position.

'You beautiful girl!'

"OK, let's stop the airplane!"

Power was put on full to the three remaining engines, and reverse pitch applied to the propellers.

Both men put pressure on the brakes, increasing it slowly as they grew more confident in the starboard undercarriage.

Behind them, a posse of emergency vehicles jockeyed for position, their engines screaming as they fell behind the fast-moving aircraft.

The audience, which had swollen to over two thousand, shouted, clapped, whistled, prayed, or combinations of all of those, as the stricken bird rolled down the runway towards the rapidly approaching point where runway became unstable and uneven ground.

The rear section, propped by the efforts of her crew, suddenly had a different set of forces act upon her tortured frames.

Firstly, many of the hand-manufactured struts fell out, no longer held in place by pressure, as physics decided to reverse its forces, with compression now primary on the underside, swapping itself with tension, now applied to the upper surfaces, tension which was sufficient to catastrophically open up the fault line that had developed in flight.

In turn, the stressed underside, started to detach, as frame supports and skin gave up the unequal struggle.

The tailskid had been deployed, and it was this modest metal support that held the tail in place whilst the fuselage decided whether it would stay intact, or come apart.

In the end, the skid failed and the tail section partially fell away.

In the cockpit, whilst the speed was no longer a problem, the additional drag of the tail assisting in decelerating the aircraft, 'Miss Merlene' was being dragged off course, as the starboard side of the rear end acted on the runway, creating an anchor effect.

Part of the metalled runway matting snagged and increased the forces dragging the B-29 off course.

The interlocking Marsden Matting started to pull up off the ground in one large bending piece.

The forward momentum was beaten by the grip of the runway metal, and the tail section tore off in stages, as each frame yielded up its hold.

No one up front heard the screams behind them.

'Miss Merlene' was suddenly free.

Too late to prevent the starboard gear running off the runway and into the softer ground.

Too late to prevent the ground taking the damaged gear in its embrace.

Too late to prevent the undercarriage straining in its mount and becoming detached.

The right wing cut into the soft ground, slewing the B-29 even more to the right.

The port undercarriage met with the yielding ground and struggled to remain intact, the wheels clogging as the earth invaded and clung.

Despite the futility of it all, Crail and Nelleson continued to try to steer, gripping their control columns, and feeling every hump and bump as the aircraft moved inexorably on towards…

… towards men who suddenly realised their predicament, and for whom an exercise in curiosity suddenly became a race for life.

The observers ran for their lives as 'Miss Merlene' came closer, her port undercarriage trying hard to stay intact under the colossal strain.

The right wing started to disintegrate as the starboard outer engine caught the ground and was ripped off, turning the B-29 more to the right.

By a miracle, the left wingtip swept over the top of a number of huts which, although unoccupied at the time, would have added to the risks for 'Miss Merlene's' crew.

Through the glasshouse, Loveless observed the approaching fuel bowser and fuelling station, the pair sat inevitably in the area through which the Superfortress would pass.

He gritted his teeth, and a slow moan escaped his mouth as the aircraft took the shortest possible route towards…

… towards…

With a lurch, Dimples-nine-eight came to a halt less than four feet from the bowser, the nose stove in but not breached, the soft earth surrounding it like a rolled comfort blanket.

"Crew out! Crew out!"

Pilots and flight engineers switched off everything and undid their harnesses, as the others rightly broke world records in their haste to get outside of the death trap, the smell of aviation spirit heavy in the air already.

Crail stood back as Fletcher dragged the unconscious Jones to the hatch and passed him out to the waiting Nelleson and Loveless.

Jeppson, bleeding heavily from a head wound, stumbled past, disorientated by the crash-landing and the blood in his eyes. Crail grabbed him and guided him to safety, the heavy fuel fumes already causing his brain to ache.

He dropped to the ground, ignoring the momentary pain, and urged the men to move away from 'Miss Merlene'.

Faithful to the last, the aircraft did not catch fire, and soon the crew were overwhelmed with rescuers of all shapes and sizes.

Ambulances opened their doors and Crail counted the boys in one by one, sharing hugs and handshakes with each and every man.

When all but he and Nelleson were loaded up, Crail saw what had happened to his aircraft, appreciating for the first time how lucky they had all been.

But there was something else that suddenly exercised him, and he ran as best as his sprained ankle allowed, closely followed by his co-pilot, moving towards the gaping hole that used to have a tail attached.

"Oh my lord!"

Nelleson shared the sentiment, the absence of either man quite apparent.

Both of them turned to look back down the runway, barely acknowledging the low run of 'Necessary Evil', a gentle wing waggle showing their relief at the incredible landing.

The tail section lay virtually upright, no more than a degree or two out of the vertical.

Three vehicles were in position, and both men could see rescuers moving slowly, unhurried, and lacking in urgency.

A USMC jeep screeched to a halt.

"You two's wanna see the rest of your plane?"

No second invitation was needed, and the pilots hopped aboard as the jeep sped off towards the other bit of 'Miss Merlene'.

The reason for the lack of urgency was soon apparent.

Blockridge was sat smoking a huge cigar, courtesy of a US infantry officer who, despite still being out of breath from his 'olympic' run to assist, had found time to produce a Cuban to celebrate the incredible survival of the two airmen.

A navy corpsman was working on Blockridge's broken left arm, fussing around and gently scolding whenever the Staff Sergeant moved even slightly.

Hanebury, a non-smoker, was coughing his way through his first Lucky Strike, still mentally examining his body for missing pieces and surprisingly coming up with negative results.

Both men were surrounded by rescuers who wanted nothing more than to shake their hand, touch their uniforms, or do anything to acquire a modicum of the luck that had preserved them.

The USMC jeep came to a halt, discharging Crail and Nelleson, who immediately set about burrowing through the crowd.

The two NCOs stood and gave formal salutes, which were returned by the two pilots. All observed by a mixture of Army, Navy, and Marine personnel who now had absolute confirmation that all airmen were completely gaga.

An Army Air Force Colonel arrived and ordered the four survivors into an ambulance, which immediately sped off to the sick bay, where the crew of 'Miss Merlene' were reunited.

USAAF senior officers had planned to present Tibbets with a DSC the moment he landed. That went out the window the second that Enola Gay fell out of line.

So there was no immediate presentation made to the crew of the first Atomic Bomb mission, but that issue was addressed when General MacArthur himself flew in to the repaired Futenma Air strip two days later.

On his orders, 'Miss Merlene' had not been bulldozed into the scrap heap, but Seabees and Air Force personnel had recovered her carefully, preserving most of her remaining structure and integrity.

Assessments were still being made as to what would be done with the historic machine.

Her crew stood in a rough line within the medical facility as Macarthur waxed lyrical about their success and how the end of the Japanese war had come closer with their efforts.

For JP Crail, Richard Loveless, George Nelleson, Ralph Burnett and Art Hanebury, there were well deserved DSCs. For everyone else, including the dead Mario Piccolo and the missing Al Cannington, there were Silver Stars.

Centerboard One had lost two aircraft, with twelve personnel killed or missing.

In Japan, the devastated Kokura had suffered over sixty thousand dead.

1444 hrs, Wednesday, 29th May 1946, Office of the General Secretary, the Kremlin, Moscow, USSR.

The first information had arrived with Molotov, through diplomatic channels.

Subsequently, information arrived on the desks of Marshall Beria and Colonel General Kuznetsov, as NKVD and GRU sources became aware of the historic events in Japan.

The GKO had been informed, and all but the ill Bulganin were present to hear Molotov recite the message he had received from the Soviet Embassy in Tokyo.

Beria held four messages. One in support of Molotov's, and two from another continent, their content almost taunting him.

And one other.

He read out the communication from the NKVD rezident in Japan, which did little more than confirm everything that Molotov had said.

Stalin waited for the three other messages, already apprised of most of their content during a brief telephone conversation an hour previously.

Beria continued.

"These two messages, Comrades, are from agents placed within the Amerikanski atomic programme. They warn of a likely immediate use, but are unable to speculate on the target. They also speak of a higher capability than previous suspected."

"Meaning what exactly, Comrade Marshal?"

"Meaning, Comrade Molotov, that they have more devices than we expected, and are ready to use them."

Beria had decided to keep part of the message from Agents Alkonost and Gamayun secret for now, for fear of making himself look inept.

The communication from the Imperial High Command was for him and Stalin alone.

For once, Stalin was calm and collected in his response, offering direction to the assembly.

"Comrades, we must consider this attack and new information carefully, and not make hasty judgements."

Stalin looked at the old clock and made a swift calculation.

"We will reconvene at seven. Use the time wisely, Comrades. Polkovnik General Kuznetsov, ensure that our Japanese allies are made aware of everything we now know."

The GRU commander nodded his understanding.

"We will deal with our intelligence failures another time."

The flatly delivered statement more than successfully carried the intended threat.

"Until seven then, Comrades."

The meeting broke up.

"Comrade Beria, a moment please."

The door closed before Stalin spoke again.

"Now, Lavrentiy, what else do you have to tell me?"

There was no way out for Beria, and he knew it.

"Comrade General Secretary, I did not consider it prudent to reveal everything from the messages I received from our agents, not before informing you first."

Stalin didn't bother asking why he hadn't been told over the phone; he understood Beria's game perfectly.

Beria passed across the Alkonost and Gamayun messages, adding the Japanese one as an afterthought.

The silence was deafening, although the effect upon Stalin was marked, his face flushed and his eyes narrowed.

He read the first message again, this time slowly and aloud, punctuating his recital with the occasional look at his man.

> *[priority code] QQQ*
> *[agent] Alkonost*
> *[date code] 250546d*
> *[personal code as an authenticator] FB21162285*
> *[distribution1] route x-eyes only*
> *[distribution1] AalphaA [Comrade Marshal Beria]*
> *[message]* Higher production of uranium weapons *confirmed A+. Minimum double suspected B-. Use is imminent A+ Groves. Possibly deliberately misleading project staff. Own view B+. Successful test on plutonium bomb A+ self-observed. Increased security threat to self. Interaction impossible. Hotel-Eagle.*
> *[message ends]*

> *Message authenticates. Codes for non-compromisation valid.*

> *RECEIVED 12:58 29/05/46 B.V. LEMSKY*

Beria readied himself, and was right to do so.

Stalin skim read the next two messages, his anger slowly overcoming him.

And then he cracked.

"What the fuck are we doing finding out now, eh?"

The messages were thrown at Beria with vigour, although their lack of aerodynamic form meant they missed their intended target.

"You've failed... failed me... failed the party... failed the Motherland!"

Beria shrank back as Stalin rose and advanced on him.

Gesticulating wildly, Stalin put the whole thing in a nutshell.

"We have Raduga underway, intent on hitting them before they have themselves organised, both politically and technically, and now I find we are so fucking far behind that I might as well toss fucking acorns at them!"

74

Beria wisely remained silent as Stalin's finger waggled, both in accusation and in indignation.

"What do we do now, eh? Let the bastards bomb the Motherland from Vladivostok to Archangelsk, cover the land with their atomic bombs? Raduga is smart… Raduga is an excellent idea… but it's not a war winner by any means, not like these… these terror bombs are."

He turned away, seeking solace in a cigarette and a sip of his tea.

He returned to staring at Beria, his eyes burning into the NKVD leader's very soul. Deliberately seating himself, Stalin seethed and plotted, reasoned and schemed.

His eyes betrayed processes in his brain, processes Beria chose not to interrupt, although his own mind was already working on responses to the changed world situation.

Suddenly the NKVD head realised that he had been caught up in a maelstrom of ideas, and had missed something extremely vital.

Stalin was looking directly at him, and with chilling intent.

"Comrade General Secretary?"

"This changes nothing, except makes our plans more urgent, Lavrentiy."

Stalin rose dramatically, invigorated by a renewed sense of purpose and belief.

"This is an opportunity for us… we must exploit it politically. These bombs… they bring issues, do they not?"

The GKO had been briefed on the likely effects of an atomic explosion, and it had made sufficient impact for Stalin to remember it now.

"We must use everything we have to foment unrest. Agitate in every political arena we can. Make the continued use of these weapons unimaginable to the capitalist's workers… make the politicians scared for their own positions… agitate… undermine… confuse…"

Stalin stopped and moved towards the window, recalling Vasilevsky's briefing, and the ideas that resulted.

"Yes, yes, yes…we have an opportunity here. Frighten the European allies with the after-effects of this bomb… play it up as much as possible… target the Amerikanski as Vasilevsky plans… break them inside and out… and when they are about to collapse…"

Stalin turned quickly, making Beria start.

The look demanded an answer from the NKVD chairman.

"And when they are about to collapse, we initiate Raduga, Comrade General Secretary?"

"We initiate the preliminary phase of Raduga immediately, Comrade Marshal."

Stalin paused for a moment, drank the last of his tea, and with studied care, replaced the cup in its saucer.

"Make sure the fucking Turks can do their part in this. Without them... just make sure the useless bastards get their part ready."

Beria could only nod, the Turkish part in the whole operation had always been a sticking point, but an unavoidable one.

Stalin continued, suddenly enthused.

"But we create a new Raduga, one we can adapt with every new development. If our Japanese allies can still provide their part of the operation, then let us revisit the plan, and make it more than it was."

After a few minutes of quieter, clandestine discussion, the General Secretary and head of the NKVD went their separate ways, reinvigorated by new plans and objectives, having been handed part of their needs by the Allies themselves.

Raduga had grown.

There was no huge response from the Empire of the Rising Sun to the Centerboard strike, save that of outrage and condemnation, of accusations and national resilience; certainly nothing to make anyone think that the Japanese had been struck a heavy enough blow as to change their national view, or undermine their commitment.

On Monday 3rd June, Tibbets finally got to drop L-11, turning the city of Hiroshima into a sea of fire.

The following Friday, 7th June, Little Boy L-10 fell from 'Big Stink', piloted by Lieutenant Colonel Thomas J Classen.

Beneath the B-29, the naval installation, port, and town of Yokosuka was obliterated, the attack being the final straw for the Battleship Nagato, which sank in shallow water for the loss of all but two of her crew.

The fourth Centerboard mission was scheduled for Tuesday 11th June 1946, destined for the city of Hakodate.

It was never flown.

When you realise the value of all life, you dwell less on what has passed, and concentrate more on the preservation of the future.

Dian Fossey.

Chapter 152 – THE MIKADO

0958 hrs, Monday, 10th June 1946, the Oval Office, Washington DC, USA.

The atmosphere was taut.

Water and coffee eased dry throats, as nerves gnawed away at the men waiting by the radio, the US Naval signaller checking he had the correct settings for the hundredth time.

The clock inexorably moved its hands to the ten o'clock position and, to the second, the silence was broken by the soft orchestral strains of 'Kimigayo', anthem of the Empire of Japan.

Just over a minute passed before the music faded out and was replaced by an announcer, declaring the identity of the main speaker.

Shōwa-Tennō, or as he was known outside the Empire of Japan, the Mikado… Emperor Hirohito.

The tension inside the Oval Office was incalculable.

A soft voice started to speak, the words translated immediately by a white house linguist.

"To our good and loyal subjects. After pondering deeply the general trends of the world and the actual conditions obtaining in our empire today, we have decided to effect a settlement of the present situation by resorting to an extraordinary measure.

We have ordered our Government to communicate to the Governments of the United States, Great Britain, and China that our empire accepts the provisions of their joint declaration.

To strive for the common prosperity and happiness of all nations, as well as the security and well-being of our subjects, is the solemn obligation which has been handed down by our imperial ancestors, and which we lay close to the heart.

Indeed, we declared war on America and Britain out of our sincere desire to insure Japan's self-preservation and the stabilization of East Asia, it being far from our thought either to infringe upon the sovereignty of other nations or to embark upon territorial aggrandizement.

But now the war has lasted for over five years. Despite the best that has been done by everyone--the gallant fighting of our military and naval forces, the diligence and assiduity of out servants of the State and the devoted service of our 100,000,000 people--the war situation has developed not necessarily to Japan's advantage, while the general trends of the world have all turned against her interest.

Moreover, the enemy has begun to employ new and most cruel bombs, the power of which to do damage is, indeed, incalculable, taking the toll of many innocent lives. Should we continue to fight, it would not only result in an ultimate collapse and obliteration of the Japanese nation, but also it would lead to the total extinction of human civilization.

Such being the case, how are we to save the millions of our subjects, or to atone ourselves before the hallowed spirits of our imperial ancestors? This is the reason why we have ordered the acceptance of the provisions of the joint declaration of the powers.

We cannot but express the deepest sense of regret to our allied nations of East Asia, who have consistently cooperated with the Empire toward the emancipation of East Asia.

We also thank the Soviet Union for its most recent support and friendship.

The thought of those officers and men as well as others who have fallen in the fields of battle, those who died at their posts of duty, or those who met death in other ways, and all their bereaved families, pains our heart night and day.

The welfare of the wounded and the war sufferers and of those who lost their homes and livelihood is the object of our profound solicitude. The hardships and sufferings to which our nation is to be subjected hereafter will be certainly great.

We are keenly aware of the inmost feelings of all of you, our subjects. However, it is according to the dictates of time and fate that we have resolved to pave the way for a grand peace for all the generations to come by enduring the unendurable, and suffering what is insufferable. Having been able to save and maintain the structure of the Imperial State, we are always with you, our good and loyal subjects, relying upon your sincerity and integrity.

Beware most strictly of any outbursts of emotion that may engender needless complications, of any fraternal contention and strife that may create confusion, lead you astray, and cause you to lose the confidence of the world.

Let the entire nation continue as one family from generation to generation, ever firm in its faith of the imperishableness of its divine land, and mindful of its heavy burden of responsibilities, and the long road before it. Unite your total strength to be devoted to the construction for the future. Cultivate the ways of rectitude, nobility of spirit, and work with resolution so that you may enhance the innate glory of the Imperial State and keep pace with the progress of the world."

'Kimigayo' resurfaced, stronger in tone and volume, the choral version seemingly carrying with it the sorrow and indignation of a nation.

President Truman opened his eyes and looked around him.

Many of his closest aides showed the tracks of tears on their faces; others showed huge relief.

All had relaxed as the tension had drained away with each word from the Emperor's mouth.

79

"Thank God for that."

The murmurs rose quickly and died away, as they all realised that Truman had something to say.

"Now, send orders to our Pacific and Asian units to stand fast. Act in self-defence only. Cancel all offensive operations across the board. Remain vigilant and accept no risks. You all know what we've discussed, so put it into action."

Most rose or moved to go, but Truman raised his voice, giving each man a moment's pause.

"None the less, let no man under your control drop his guard, and do not think that we are victorious, for we are not. One great evil has fallen, but one, the greater one, remains."

He stood and tugged his jacket into place.

"Remember this. Our victory over Japan will grant us some leeway with our public. Let's use it to the best of our ability, gentlemen."

The assembly spilt up as Truman sat at his desk, and prepared himself for the call to Churchill.

They tell us that suicide is the greatest piece of cowardice... that suicide is wrong, when it is quite obvious that there is nothing in the world to which every man has a more unassailable right than to his own life and person.

Arthur Schopenhauer.

Chapter 153 – THE RONIN

<u>1127 hrs, Monday 10th June 1946, Height 404, Baisha River, Zhujiawan, China.</u>

What was left of the Rainbow Brigade was gathered in defence of Routes 4 and 107, and the crossing of the Baisha River, protecting the approaches to Chenzhou.

Such as they could.

The Special Obligation Units were comprised of men who had given their all, and who had almost nothing left to give.

Four tanks were in camouflaged positions, overseeing the bridge south of Zhujiawan, one Panther on each flank, each with a small security force to protect it from stalking AT teams.

A Soviet T34m44, found abandoned during the great retreat, had been pressed into service, and formed the mobile reserve, complete with its own grape of infantry.

Centrally, the last surviving Shinhoto Chi-Ha supported the main infantry force, dug-in to oppose use of the bridge.

There was no explosive with which to destroy the structure, in fact, there was little of anything.

The three mortars had seven rounds between them.

Infantry weapons had one or two magazines available; those men with an extra clip or magazine said nothing, hoarding the means of self-protection.

The two Panthers had no machine-gun ammunition at all, and none of the best AP rounds.

It was a total miracle that the Panthers were still running at all, the German workshop engineers long-since departed into the next world. The remaining spare parts would barely fill a large suitcase, and no one was under any illusions that any breakdown would be terminal for the two remaining vehicles.

Cannibalism of wrecks and excellent work by the brigade's Japanese mechanics had kept the two Panzer Vs going, all be it the engine performance was a shadow of that it had been when the vehicles arrived with the Rainbow brigade.

Nomori Hamuda, long since promoted to Major and commander of 1st Tank Battalion, gave up Panther 'Masami', placing it in the capable hands of Captain, the Marquis Hirohata, whose own Panther had been lost the previous New Year's Eve.

Masami took the right flank, at the very western end of the defensive position.

Panther 'Ashita' and her commander, Sergeant Major Kagamutsu, took the left end of the line, the heavily camouflaged tank barely discernible from ten feet away, let alone to the enemy ground attack aircraft that constantly savaged the Japanese and Soviet troops in China.

Forty-seven kill rings adorned Ashita's barrel, a testament to Kagamutsu's command capabilities, as well as to the skill of her gunner.

Both Panthers had been topped off with as much fuel as they could take, which left less than one hundred litres available.

Out in front of the position, Sergeant Major Haro patrolled in a liberated Dodge 4x4, his old Marmon Herrington now a distant rusting memory.

Hamuda swept the approaches with his binoculars, seeing nothing but the occasional glimpse of a Chinese civilian going about their business.

He also swept the skies, conscious of the damage that the Yankee air force had inflicted upon his men.

His mind wandered…

'…Sakita'.

The popular Sergeant Sakita had been obliterated in his Panther tank, three enemy aircraft pouncing on the vehicle as it tried to cross a small bridge the previous January.

Bridge and tank had disappeared, and there was nothing left to salvage for an honourable burial.

There were so many names whirring through his mind, all comrades now departed, far too many to recall, although Hamuda conjured up many faces during whatever restless hours of sleep he could manage.

By his side, Yamagiri, commander of the surviving infantry, was tying a headscarf around himself, his face set in a vision of resignation, his signature sunglasses long since lost in the heat of battle for some godforsaken corner of China.

The Emperor's address had been listened to, as ordered by High Command, and caused wailing and tears amongst men who had given their all in the Imperial cause, only to see everything come tumbling around their ears because of weakness back in the home islands.

Hamuda didn't think it was an enemy fake, as some had decided once its' message was clear.

Whatever it was, the very idea that the Emperor would ever order a humiliating surrender was unthinkable...

Unimaginable...

Unfollowable...

In any case, the last survivors of the 3rd Special Obligation Brigade 'Rainbow' had no intention of surrendering.

Ninety-seven men had decided to continue the fight, knowing that they would not survive the day.

Fig# 181 – The Baisha River, Zhujiawan, China.

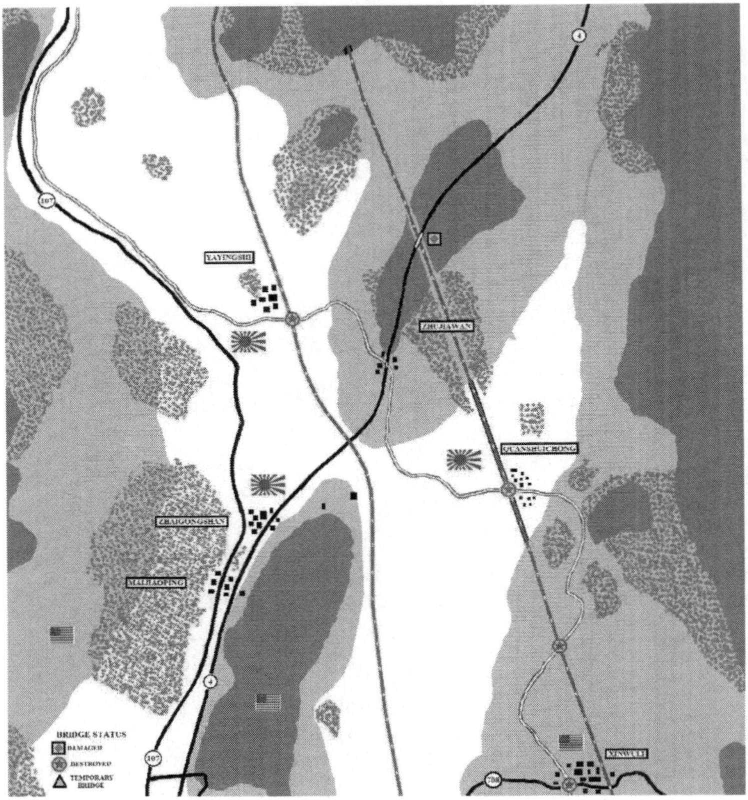

Haro had ordered his captured Dodge to pull into the animal pen on the side of Hill 402, a location well positioned above the roads, his ears having caught the betraying sound of tanks on the move.

Scuttling to the damaged wall that opened up to the roads that ran through the village of Zhaigongshan, he was horrified to see armored-infantry moving on foot through the rough lanes in the village, rooting out anyone they found, just in case of ambush.

Down Routes 4 and 107 came columns headed by halftracks and the big American Pershing tanks, again flanked by business like infantrymen.

As his radioman prepared the set, Haro made a swift calculation.

Sixty plus tanks of different types, but mainly the Pershing, equalled an enemy tank battalion or equivalent.

There were enough halftracks and other vehicles in sight to suggest a complete armored-infantry battalion plus change.

Fig # 182 - Opposing forces at the Baisha River, China.

OPPOSING FORCES AT THE
BAISHA RIVER, CHINA,
10TH JUNE 1946

**3RD SPECIAL OBLIGATION BRIGADE
'RAINBOW'**

**20TH US ARMORED DIVISION
CC 'B'**

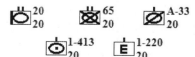

84

Haro took hold of the handset but stopped suddenly, as one of the leading vehicles started to talk, or at least, that was how it seemed to him at first.

A halftrack had been equipped with speakers, and an excited man fluent in Japanese loudly implored any troops listening to observe the will of their Emperor, lay down their arms, and declare themselves.

Neither Haro nor his radioman gave the propaganda any thought, and the NCO sent his contact report to Hamuda.

"Sunflower-seven, sunflower-seven to Buffalo, over."

Hamuda acknowledged, again seeking information with his binoculars as the contact report came in.

He found movement almost immediately, but waited until Haro had finished his broadcast.

"Buffalo to Sunflower-seven, fall back to the south and reconnoitre our southern flank to Zhoujiawan. Cross over the river and return once mission is complete, over."

"Buffalo, your message understood, Sunflower-seven over."

Hamuda was already thumbing the microphone, issuing orders to his meagre force.

They were simple orders.

Wait for the command to fire, fire accurately, and kill as many of the Americans as possible before the enemy killed them.

There would be no retreat.

The Dodge slipped quietly away, using the rise to mask it from the heavy column in Zhaigongshan.

However, it didn't mask the light vehicle from above, and a circling spotter aircraft called in a contact report to some Recon elements operating south of Hill 402.

Haro spotted the enemy pursuit as soon as it slipped out from behind a spur of high ground, the leading M8 Greyhound displaying more than enough speed to run them down in short order.

He issued a command and the dodge cut through the ground, sending clods of earth in all direction, as it made a swift right hand turn and headed towards the enemy force.

The MG34, his favourite weapon, salvaged from the wreck of his Marmon-Herrington, discharged the final thirty-five rounds left in its belt.

Fig # 183 - Baisha River battle.

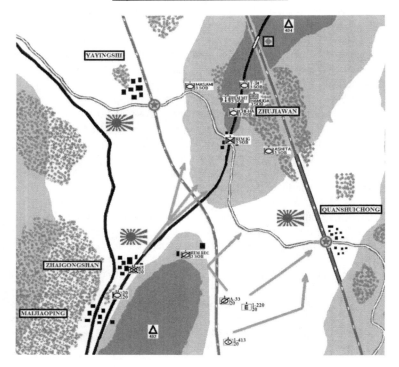

The rearmost soldier had no chance to add to matters before his head exploded like a ripe melon as two .50cal rounds transited the skull side by side.

Haro reached for his pistol but the impact of a .50cal round blasted his shoulder virtually off his body, the partially attached right arm flopping uselessly by his side.

Two half-tracks had moved out to the flanks of the Greyhound, and it was one of these that put a few choice rounds on target.

The driver felt the loss of power, as heavy bullets wrecked the engine, and then had other priorities as a .50cal passed through his left knee and travelled all the way through his thigh, splitting and destroying bone, until it exited through his backside.

Both men screamed as the Dodge coasted to a halt.

'Take no chances' was the very specific order issued by the Recon Battalion CO, and it was an order that the cavalry troopers intended to observe to the letter.

The six-wheeled Greyhound stopped thirty yards short of the disabled Dodge.

The driver, screaming with pain and indignity in equal measure, scrabbled for his rifle.

Haro, his right arm and shoulder flapping grotesquely as he stood up, waved his left hand, the contents of which were unclear to the watchful American soldiers.

The order was given, and the Greyhound's gunner fired the 37mm M6, shredding flesh and metal with a close range canister round.

1141 hrs, Monday 10th June 1946, Height 404, Baisha River, Zhujiawan, China.

The sound of heavy machine guns ended and a single heavier thump was the last sound of battle from across the river.

Efforts to raise Sunflower-seven were fruitless, and Hamuda correctly surmised that Haro and his men were dead, or worse, prisoners.

Thoughts of his comrades were swiftly brushed aside as enemy tanks and soldiers spilled out into the countryside across the river, the numbers growing every second he watched.

Snatching up the radio, Hamuda took in the situation, understanding that the final act was upon them.

He hesitated, the radio unused in his hand.

'Why am I waiting?'

The leading American tanks opened fire on the move, their shells arriving on the north bank in an instant, throwing up gouts of earth and vegetation.

"Buffalo calling, Masami, Ashita, acknowledge."

"Masami, over."

"Ashita, over."

"Buffalo calling, all units hold fire, except for Masami and Ashita, engage immediately, out."

The two 75mm shells flew over the battlefield and sought out an enemy tank.

Masami's round missed high, but Ashita's struck the turret of the lead vehicle.

The Pershing shrugged off the hit with no apparent effect.

An exchange of rounds followed, as the US tanks opened up on their now revealed enemy.

Behind them, the other Pershings, the remainder of the tank battalion, had drawn up on the edge of some raised ground, using the defile to conceal their presence and intentions.

Firing from fixed positions, their rounds flew straight and true.

The 'beauty' that was Masami came apart under numerous impacts, the German armour succumbing to the heavy 90mm strikes.

Hirohata was blasted out from the turret by the first impact, rising into the air like a faulty firework, his battered body falling into soft undergrowth, preventing further damage from being added to his several new injuries.

His crew died inside the smashed Panther.

Shells continued to strike Masami, as she refused to catch alight and reveal her death.

Eventually, one struck home and set her afire, but even then, the fire was gentle, almost as if the battle-scarred tank still fought to retain her dignity.

On the eastern end of the line, shells had chewed up the ground around Ashita, and three had struck her cleanly, but none had penetrated or caused her major harm.

Sergeant Major Kagamutsu engaged the tank battalion to his front, now supported by the T34, which Hamuda had called forward.

Hamuda saw the wave of leading tanks drop down behind a small rise the other side of the river.

They did not reappear.

He understood immediately.

"Buffalo, all units, all units. Relocate immediately, relocate immediately!"

His understanding was punctuated by the sharp crack of tank guns, and immediately reinforced by the bursting of smoke shells in and around all his defensive positions.

The rush had been a simple ruse, one he had fallen for... had no alternative but to fall for...

A machine gun nearby chattered, the desperation of the gunner marked by an increased wailing as his target drew closer, and closer.

Voices were raised, fear and indignation carried in the words.

"Aircraft! Yankee aircraft!"

'... *fakku!*'

"Buffalo, all units, Air attack!"

1157 hrs, Monday 10th June 1946, airborne over Baisha River valley, Zhujiawan, China.

In answer to the calls from the commander of CCB, 20th US Armored Division, two squadrons of Marine aviators were detached from the waiting queue of support aircraft, part of the Commanding General's plan to limit risk and reduce casualties when dealing with the last fanatical pockets of Japanese resistance.

Leading the way were VMF-312, a Marine fighter squadron riding FG-1 Corsairs, decked out with the distinctive checkerboard markings of their unit.

Three minutes behind them were the F8F-1 Bearcats of VF-191, working from a shore base whilst their carrier, USS Antietam, was away getting her bow welded back on after an encounter with an enemy mine.

The Corsairs attacked in line, not column, a deadly line that was three aircraft wide.

Sweeping in from over the top of the US ground force, the leading element selected one target each.

The T34, the Shinhoto, and 'Ashita'.

Each aircraft discharged six 5" HVARs, deadly high velocity rockets, universally known as 'Holy Moses.'

Not one struck its target, although in the case of the Shinhoto Chi-ha, two were close enough to kill it and its crew.

The machine-gun near Hamuda rattled out its final rounds, and to good effect.

The right wingman knew he was in trouble, and he struggled to get some height, pulling his damaged aircraft up and around to bail out over friendly ground.

The Pratt and Whitney power plant decided otherwise, and fuel lines let go, bathing the hot engine with rich fuel.

In a second, the nose fireballed and the wave of heat blistered 1st Lieutenant Cowpens' face.

Canopy back, he rolled the aircraft and fell out, his parachute grabbing at the air in an attempt to slow him sufficiently before impact with the ground.

Many in his squadron watched as the chute blossomed only moments before the screaming burden it carried hit the ground hard.

The anger that the pilots of VMF312 felt was all put into the attacks they made, the remaining aircraft repeating the line abreast attack, the fifteen aircraft making a total of five passes.

Impotent, Major Nomuri Hamuda watched as the T34 simply came apart under a number of hammer blows.

Miraculously, he saw a figure emerge from the wreckage, only to be consumed by a hail of high explosive as the next aircraft put his HVARs on the money.

The air attack coordinator, safely ensconced in his half-track, not far from Haro's original observation position above the village of Zhaigongshan, knew his trade.

In his own way, he was an artist, but a very deadly one.

The simple notations on his map, made during the initial contact, were all he needed to steer the two Marine squadrons into an accurate killing frenzy.

His only error was in assuming that the wreck on his right flank, trackless and smoking, had been knocked out.

Relaying his vectoring and attack orders to VF-191, he sat back smugly to await the destruction of the Japanese infantry element.

His ordered approach brought the F8F Bearcats up the river line, using the water to orientate themselves.

Three Pershings had already bathed the area in red smoke, as per his orders.

Fourteen Bearcats swooped on the smoke, each depositing a single M29 cluster bomb in turn.

The red smoke was replaced by a wall of sound, coloured yellow, white, and orange, as one thousand, two hundred and sixty 4-pound charges exploded in an area of three football pitches.

Hamuda's infantry were destroyed.

Many men died, ripped apart by high explosives or rapidly moving metal pieces.

A few men lived, spared by some fickle finger of fate, as the men around them were thrown in all directions like rag dolls, or simply destroyed in place.

A handful more lived, but wished it otherwise, their bodies and limbs torn apart.

More than one hideously wounded man took his own life, the desperate calls for help falling either on ears permanently or temporarily deaf, or those belonging to the dead.

Hamuda arrived, out of breath, his sprint from the command post punctuated by threatening but impotent gestures from his sword, trying to cut the enemy aircraft from the sky in his mind.

Since the US committed fully to the Chinese conflict, Hamuda had seen much of what the technology of the enemy could do to soft flesh, but he was still unprepared for what the charnel house that used to be his infantry position would throw before him.

In a daze, he moved through the unrecognisable pieces of his command, occasionally silently acknowledging a piece of a body

90

that bore some resemblance to a man he had shared rice with, or an NCO he had given orders to in battle.

He knelt beside the shattered body of a corporal, the man's face wiped away by one of the deadly bomblets, the same charge opening up his stomach and spreading the man's intestines around the hole like some macabre bunting.

The smashed chest rose and fell rapidly, the exposed heart and lungs damaged but still functioning.

The soft sound that emerged from the dying body was hideous, its animal-like tone leaving no doubt that what used to be a man was in the extremes of suffering.

Without a thought, Hamuda slotted his Katana into the man's chest, spearing the heart with a single thrust, turning his wrist immediately to open the wound.

The heart stilled instantly, and the man, such as he was, knew no more pain.

Hamuda rose and continued his walk amongst the misery.

A handful of men walked dazed, most zombie-like, their minds melted in a maelstrom of explosions, some moving with no purpose other than to move for movement's sake, others to reassure themselves that they still retained the ability.

One or two moved with purpose, seeking the living to offer assistance.

One such man found his Captain.

Yamagiri was quiet, his head bleeding from mouth and nostrils, injuries caused by blast concealed within his almost intact tunic jacket.

The sleeves hang tattily, absent material from the elbow down... absent flesh from the elbow down.

He sat on the stumps where once his legs had been, surprisingly little blood spilling from his wounds, the swollen ends partially sealing the awful wounds, twin tourniquets fashioned from webbing doing the rest of the life-saving work.

Hamuda squatted beside the destroyed man and held his shoulder.

Yamagiri smiled, the small act allowing a renewed surge of blood and detritus from his mouth.

"So, Major Hamuda... this is the end eh?"

Both listeners were incredulous that the man could speak at all, let alone coherently, and almost without any indication that he had been mortally wounded.

The young private wiped his captain's mouth clear of blood.

"Thank you, Saisho."

The soldier bowed his head respectfully.

Yamagiri made a study of examining himself, his eyes flitting from wound to wound.

"Major, it would appear that I'll not be making the last charge with you. So sorry."

"Rest, Hideyo, rest now."

The dying man laughed, clearly and crisply.

"No, I think not, Major. It's time to meet my ancestors."

Yamagiri looked at the bloody stumps of his arms, and turned his gaze back to Hamuda.

No words were needed, his mute request well understood.

Hamuda's silent reflection was interrupted by the sounds of approaching vehicles, the screech of tank tracks mixing with the revving of heavy engines, as Pershings and half-tracks moved towards the river crossing.

He stood and bowed deeply to the dead Yamagiri, using a piece of paper to wipe the remaining blood from his sword.

A number of survivors, nine in total, had gravitated towards their leader, arming themselves with whatever they could find, ready to offer a final act of resistance.

Two of the men were so wounded as to be unable to support a weapon of any kind, but they were determined to be in the charge.

The men organised themselves with the help of a Corporal, himself wounded and dripping blood as he walked the line.

Hamuda looked upon them; the last of the Rainbow Brigade.

The corporal brought the group to some semblance of attention, saluted Hamuda, and adopted the very best 'attention' position he could manage.

Something changed in his mind.

He would not die this day, nor would his men die in some grand gesture of fealty to the Emperor.

'Enough... we have all done enough.'

"Men... we have done our duty to the Emperor and our country... we have always done our duty... and done it well."

Hamuda turned and levelled his sword at the advancing armada of power.

"Our duty is clear..."

The sword swept savagely through the air as he turned back to his waiting soldiers.

"Our Emperor has today informed us of it, and you have all heard it."

The katana slid back in its scabbard. With additional drama, Hamuda extracted his Nambu pistol and tossed it on the ground in front of him.

"Our Emperor requires us now to endure the unendurable and limit any outbursts of emotion."

One or two of the battle-hardened soldiers wept openly as their commander gave them their lives back.

"We are commanded to devote our strength to the future of our country... and we will, men, we will."

Hamuda pointed at the pistol.

"With honour, and with my thanks, that of the Emperor and the Empire, place your weapons there... now... so that we may unite in the cause of our country and its people..."

One soldier looked near panic, the desire to immolate himself for the Emperor battling with the orders of his commander.

"Kitarane... Private Kitarane!"

The man snapped out of his trance.

"Lay down your rifle, private... our Emperor commands that you preserve your life for the good of and future of the Empire."

Kitarane dropped his rifle immediately.

"Well done... well done..."

Hamuda gripped the man's shoulder, the act bringing forth tears from both of them.

The rest of the weapons lay on the ground, the heavy atmosphere occasional punctured by a metallic sound as a grenade or a piece of ammunition joined the growing pile.

The military bearing had improved and the line was straight and more upright.

"Men... soldiers......... comrades... you are the finest troops I ever commanded... so... let us march with our heads held high... undefeated... ready to do what we must... endure what we must... and we will soon see Mount Fuji and our homes again!"

Spontaneously, the men threw their working arms skywards in unison.

"Banzai! Banzai! Banzai!"

A pair of eyes on the northern slopes on Height 404 was naturally drawn towards the sound.

"Here they come!"

Three half-tracks were over the bridge and they had fanned out swiftly, permitting men on foot to move up to support them.

"Sir?"

"Sergeant?"

"Orders were quite clear, Lootenant."

The young man hesitated.

"Don't look like they're doing a banzai to me, Sergeant."

The NCO looked at the new officer and spat demonstrably, a jet of tobacco juice clipping the top of the .50cal pulpit.

"How many banzai charges you seen, Lootenant Capaldi?"

The officer coloured up.

"None, as you well know... but they..."

"But fuck all, Lootenant. They wounded my brother and his mates on the canal with the games they play. Can't trust the bastards."

"But th..."

"And the orders were very clear, Lootenant."

Vincent Capalde, only a week with the armored infantry unit as a replacement for a well-respected officer on his way stateside with severe injuries, was out of his depth.

He looked at the small group of enemy soldiers, their leader holding a sword in his left hand as he led his men forward.

'Oh fuck it.'

"Fire!"

1224 hrs, Monday 10th June 1946, Height 404, Zhujiawan, China.

Captain, the Marquis, Ito Hirohata, could not feel his left arm, which, given its condition, was just as well.

When he was blasted out of the Panther's turret, he had broken it in three places as it connected with the inside of the cupola.

A fourth break occurred when he came down in soft vegetation, the mangled limb flapping across of bridge of wood, snapping noisily at the wrist.

His pain had increased and increased, amplified by the destruction of 'Masami', the loss of Hamuda's tank crew, and the obvious destruction being wrought around him by the terror fliers of the enemy.

94

His pain had disappeared in an instant as, above his head, an enemy aircraft was destroyed, causing the pilot to bail out.

The US Marine Corps' pilot landed heavily less than twenty feet away, and was immediately consumed by white silk as the parachute came to earth.

Curses and yelps of pain marked the man's efforts to free himself from the grip of the vegetation and the stifling presence of the deflated canopy.

Hirohata switched between watching the American lump struggling under a white screen, and the actions of his friend and commander, Major Nomori Hamuda.

He watched as Hamuda paraded his men, as they discarded their weapons, and as they gave three Banzai salutes.

He watched as they marched forward to observe the Emperor's wishes, and to surrender themselves to the unthinkable for the sake of the future of the Empire.

Cowpens struggled free, partially so, brandishing his Colt automatic in response to the howling that sprang from Hirohata's throat as the survivors of the Rainbow Brigade were machine-gunned to death.

A bullet flew past his ear, the pistol report lost in the heavy rattle of .50cals from the valley below, Cowpens' aerial prowess not matched by his handgun skills.

Hirohata's anguish turned to rage and he grabbed for his own pistol.

Cowpens had managed to jam his Colt, the mechanism snatching at the silk of his chute, jamming the slide half returned.

"Banzai!"

The Marine only had a moment's fear before the Japanese officer jammed the Nambu pistol in his face and pulled the trigger, blowing the side of the pilot's head off.

This shot was also lost in the echoes of the slaughter near the bridge, echoes that drew Hirohata back to examine the scene from his vantage point, his thoughts now changed from those of glorious death to feral ones of renewed hatred for all things Yankee, and of revenge.

As the marching soldiers were cut down, Kagamutsu slowly cranked the Panther's turret round, the blood of the dead gunner making his hands slip as he tried to point the 75mm at the lead halftrack.

Around him, the crew were out of the fight. As well as the gunner, the loader had also perished messily when whatever it was transited the tank, rising up from the front plate and bursting open the rear turret hatch, taking considerable portions of the gunner and loader with it. The two men in the hull were incapacitated and groaning with pain from their wounds.

It did not matter to Sergeant Major Kagamutsu.

All he wanted was revenge.

He manoeuvred the weapon slowly, laying it on the target he had selected, the one that had opened fire first.

The young armored-infantry lieutenant dropped over the side of the half-track, leaving behind the sounds of the heavy machine-gun being reloaded, and the self-satisfied drawling of his sergeant.

Regardless of what the orders had said, Capalde felt that he had just done murder.

The whoosh and explosion joined together in an instant, which immediately turned back and silent.

The half-track burst into flames as the 75mm shell struck home. The five dazed survivors, aided by other nearby soldiers, did their best to drag their comrades clear.

The dead sergeant was consumed by the increasing flames.

Across the river, angry American tankers turned their weapons on the smoking Panther and finished the job.

With the death of Kagamutsu and his men, the last resistance of the 3rd Special Obligation Brigade 'Rainbow' ended.

Capalde's Sergeant, and the other four men who died in the halftrack, were the last known ground force casualties in the war against Japan.

Earlier that day... 0455 hrs, Monday, 10th June 1946, Secret dock, Submarine Division One, Kannonzaki, Kure, Japan.

Lieutenant Commander Nanbu Nobukiyo bowed deeply to his commander, Rear-Admiral Sasaki Hankyu, OC Japanese Sixth Fleet.

"I envy you the opportunity these orders represent, Nobukiyo."

The Admiral nodded to his aide, who proffered the thick sealed file.

Nobukiyo took the file in both hands, repeating his stiff bow to the Naval Commander, and then to the 1st Submarine Division commander, Captain Ariizumi Tatsunosuke.

The formal party was there to see the two Sen-Toku class submarines depart on the last mission of the Imperial Japanese Navy.

Or, at least, the first stage of it.

The Sen-Tokus were the largest submarines in the world, built to launch an air attack on the Panama Canal, in times before the imminent demise of the Empire.

Inside the two submarines, other architects and key players in the grand plan were already concealed, their goodbyes having been exchanged in an innocuous building near to the dock at Kannonzaki.

On board I-401, Yoshio Nishina, the director of the Riken Institute and head of His Imperial Majesty's Nuclear Weapon research programme and Major General Michitake Yamaoka, overseer of the 'Imperial Institute of Sacred Knowledge', were safely stowed away, complete with numerous crates whose paper contents represented years of important research.

Lieutenant General Takeo Yasuda, Director of the Imperial Japanese Air Force's Scientific and Technological Team, and Professor Bunsaku Arakatsu, head of a special research team at Kyoto Imperial University, were similarly quartered aboard I-402.

Both were accompanied by numerous senior research staff from their own bailiwicks, as well as some important members of the Institute for Chemical and Physical Research who had been unable to return to the Institute's base in Hungnam, Korea.

Now they, the two huge submarines, and a number of lesser vessels, all had a crucial part to play in a secret mission to carry the battle into the heart of the enemy.

The mission had been planned sometime beforehand, but only Hankyu, Tatsunosuke, and the admiral's aide, Commander Iura, knew what horrors were about to spring from the Emperor's lips.

Which was why I-401 and her sister ship, I-402, were to be set loose, under strict radio silence, with orders to ignore all communications sent from any source unlisted on their secret orders, or any contact without the specific code exchanges.

Apart from their size and unusual carrying capacity, the two I-400 series had another singular quality, which set them aside from other undersea craft.

They carried enough fuel to sail nearly seventy thousand kilometres before needing replenishment.

This key fact brought them into Operation Raduga and delivered a key role for the Japanese Navy, one that the diehards in high places were determined to discharge, surrender or no surrender.

I-401 also carried three Aichi Seiran aircraft in her huge hangar, planes she could launch and recover whilst at sea.

I-402, outwardly identical, save for the forward catapult, carried no aircraft, having been fitted out as a supply submarine.

She had slid away from their base at Kannonzaki three days previously, and was nearly lost immediately.

The secrecy required for the mission meant that the local naval guard force was not informed, and the destroyer Hibiki attacked a submerged contact, only stopping when depth charges ran out.

I-402 was lucky to escape with a few damaged seals and shattered nerves, and made her way to her first rendezvous.

That took place in a covered inlet on the innocuous island of Okunoshima, where Japan had secretly constructed a poison gas manufacturing facility.

I-402's hangar contained a deadly mixed cargo of Lewisite and Mustard gas, but enough space remained for the next port of call, where the awful products of Units 731 and 516 could be loaded aboard, albeit with the utmost care and respect.

The fanatics intended to bring death and horror to their enemies, regardless of the surrender of their nation.

Continuing with the joint Japanese-Soviet plan seemed to be their best way of achieving their ends.

Revenge for their nation.

Salutes and bows exchanged, the crews of the two Sen-Tokus ran to their stations, readying the vessels for immediate departure.

As the sun rose into the morning sky, 401 and 402 slipped out of the hidden dock and descended into the cool waters, intent on making land in Manchuria.

Project Raduga moved forward.

No combat-ready unit can withstand the rigours of inspection.
No inspection-ready unit can withstand the rigours of combat.

John Joseph Pershing, General, USA.

Chapter 155 – DER WERWÖLFE

1200 hrs, Wednesday, 12th June 1946, Amstetten, Germany.

In many ways, 2nd Special Platoon, 16th Armored Military Police Battalion was a victim of its own success.

That success brought about a temporary detachment out from the US Third Army area, and temporary assignment to US Fifteenth Army, to assist with the increasing problem of Soviet stragglers.

Even then, Hanebury and his men had licence to roam as they needed to, which had brought them even further south, in pursuit of a small band of Soviet soldiery causing problems with the supply line.

None the less, whilst they enjoyed the freedom of operation, the assignment was no bed of roses.

Lucifer was fuming... no actually... worse than fuming.

Respect for rank had stayed his tongue as the new Lieutenant Colonel of the 7th's MP Battalion, fresh in from serving with a stateside training division, had inspected his special unit, and found it wanting.

Wanting in having the tyres blacked...

Wanting in having the paintwork immaculate and polished...

Wanting in everything pretty much...

The man even issued Hanebury with an ultimatum on the excessive weaponry carried by his vehicles, quoting regulations to justify his insistence at removing the additional means of waging war, in favour of the standard allocation of both weapons and ammunition.

Hanebury decided that he would do nothing in response to the written order that had been turned to ash in the brazier heating the unit's coffee; just ignore the man, and go straight over his head to 7th Armored's headquarters. He had a lot of stock there, given recent events, particularly as his boys had earned a bucket full of medals and praise for their work against the Soviet recon unit.

The unit had been assigned to the 7th Armored Division purely administratively, but the bird colonel had decided that meant they were under his purview, and had hunted them down for inspection.

When the man had gone, Jim Hanebury withdrew to his tent, reading the letter from his Air Force cousin for the third time, using Arthur's words to calm himself down sufficiently to appear approachable to his men.

Part of him envied the older man, roaming the skies and carrying the fight to the Japanese enemy.

But only for a moment.

Top Sergeant James Hanebury loved his boys, and his job, and besides, stooging around in the atmosphere was dangerous.

He smiled as he recalled the banter the two had exchanged the last time they had met, over two years previously.

Arthur was the man with the medals at that time, earned in the dangerous skies over Europe.

Since then, Jim Hanebury had acquired his own, with the 3rd Infantry and subsequently the 16th Armored.

He looked forward to discussing the family bragging rights the next time he and Arthur shared a cold one down at Ellie's Bar.

Folding up the letter, he slid it back into his pocket, silently wishing his cousin well, and calling upon God to keep him safe and away from danger, not knowing the danger was closer at hand for him than it was for Arthur.

1200 hrs, Wednesday, 12th June 1946, near Route 7312, one kilometre east of Bräunisheim, Germany.

The last of the Soviet soldiers was dispatched relatively silently, the noisiest part of the exercise being the rush of air as the unfortunate's throat was opened from ear to ear. The large soldier scrabbled and grabbed at his attacker, ripping the sleeve of the man's combat jacket, earning him a second slice of the blade, by way of revenge for a ruined uniform.

With few spoken commands, the assassins had closed on the slumbering soldiers, who had hidden in the woods above the road, dispatching all fourteen men in as many seconds.

Showing practised ease, the professional killers moved into action, some keeping watch, some taking weapons and food, and others dragging the bodies into cover.

Within two minutes, apart from the occasional trail of blood, the scene had been returned to nature and gave no indication of what had happened there.

A few hand signals were exchanged and the group blended back into the woods and were gone.

1232 hrs, Wednesday, 12th June 1946, near Route 7312, half a kilometre southeast of Bräunisheim, Germany.

Malicious eyes surveyed the scene and assessed the possibilities.

The ambulance, a Dodge WC54, was going nowhere, the driver buried deep in the engine compartment, his curses reaching the ears of the watchers with ease.

An army medic and a nurse stood outside the vehicle, sharing cigarettes with two men, clearly sporting tokens of their injuries, the white bandages fresh and clean.

Occasionally, one of the two medical personnel would take a close look at the other two passengers, men whose wounds were more serious.

What interested the watcher was the medical bag, and what it probably contained, for they had no supplies of their own, and two wounded men in desperate need.

The leader made his decision, understanding a second attack, so close together in time and location to the first, was a risk, but one he was prepared to take for the prize of medicine.

A flat-handed signal, followed by a curved roll of his hand, sent a group of efficient killers down the hillside, using the blind spot created by the bulk of the vehicle to close the distance at speed.

Back at their start point, two men sat behind Mauser sniper rifles, just in case.

The remainder fanned out to provide security in case other vehicles came to the party.

The doctor, nurse and two wounded men were too busy laughing to notice that the stream of swear words stopped in mid-flow.

Spilling blood, the driver's dead body was controlled as it flopped to the road, the killer wiping his knife on the man's jacket before running his hands over pockets in the hope of finding tobacco.

The nurse laughed in a high-pitched wail, and immediately died quietly, her squeal of fear stifled with a dirty hand and a blade in her heart.

The doctor turned in time to see his killer lunge, but felt no pain as the blade slid up through his armpit and into vital places beyond.

The wounded men both made a grab for the trophy they had insisted on bringing along with them.

101

Neither man made it to the SVT automatic rifle.

The snipers shot them both dead.

One camouflaged killer slipped aboard the ambulance and sent the two seriously wounded men to their maker.

The whole group was up and moving quickly, lent urgency by the sound of the two shots still reverberating around the valley.

The leader, struggling with a twisted ankle, gritted his teeth and moved past the site as his men threw the bodies in the back of the ambulance, having checked for anything of use.

The medical supplies were already safely in the possession of the second in command, and within minutes the bird songs started again, the killers having again disappeared back into nature.

1329 hrs, Wednesday, 12th June 1946, two hundred and fifty metres southwest of Bräunisheim, Germany.

Fig# 184 – Bräunisheim, Germany.

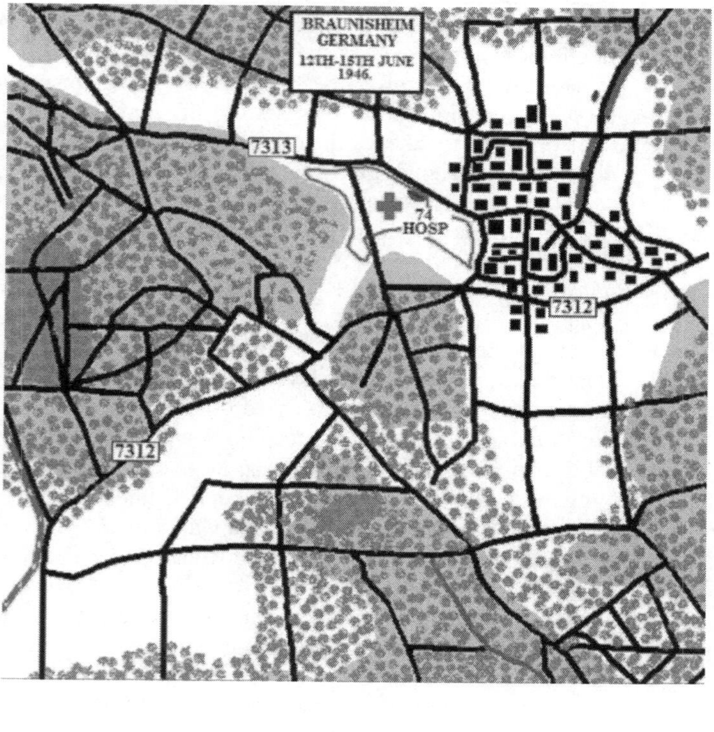

The group lay up on a height overlooking the area south of Bräunisheim, where they observed a US army medical facility at work, receiving and dispatching wounded in steady numbers throughout the day.

The need for medicines was still pressing.

There had not been enough in the bag... not enough painkillers, bandages, whatever...

The worst of the two wounded men was delirious now, the smell of his wounds carrying as far as his tortured groans of pain.

Two Russian prisoners, men who had been captured in the early stages of the new war, did their best to treat the injured men, but, in the case of Otto Jungling, SS-Sturmann, it was too little, too late.

A quick conference between the three senior men made two quick decisions. Firstly... they would move into the hospital and take what they needed the following night, just to ensure they didn't run into heightened security. Secondly...

The commander moved to the side of the young werewolf.

Taking a wet cloth from the more junior Soviet officer prisoner, he wiped the soldier's brow, leaning forward to whisper in the soldier's ear.

The moaning stopped immediately, and Jungling prepared himself.

A knife opened up both his wrists.

Lenz, showing remarkable and unusual tenderness, recited words known to everyone present, and held the dying man's hand until the life went from his eyes.

"Ich schwöre dir, Adolf Hitler, als Führer und Kanzler des Deutschen Reiches, treue und tapferkeit. Wir geloben dir und den von dir bestimmten vorgesetzten gehorsam bis in den tod. So wahr mir Gott helfe! Seig heil, Otto. Wiedersehen."

Patting the dead man's chest, he stood as quickly as his damaged ankle permitted, and ordered the two prisoners to bury the man where he lay.

Mikki and Nikki, their real names of Mikhail and Nikanor long since forgotten by their captors, set about digging a shallow grave for the cadaver.

There was not a day that went by without they wondered why they were still alive, as they had seen the Werewolves kill and murder their way through Southern Germany without compunction, hesitation, or scruples.

At first it had been the Red Army, but now, with the obvious reverses in fortune for the USSR, it was, apart from the occasional wandering group of Soviet soldiers, the Allies who received the full attention of SS-Kommando Lenz.

[* Der Eidformel der Schutzstaffel/The SS oath of loyalty - "I vow to you, Adolf Hitler, as Führer and Chancellor of the German Reich, loyalty, and bravery. I vow to you and to the leaders that you set for me, absolute allegiance until death. So help me God!"]

2310 hrs, Wednesday, 12th June 1946, near Route 7312, half a kilometre southeast of Bräunisheim, Germany.

The MP unit had spread out in professional fashion, covering the woods to either side, road front and back, leaving two vehicles to disgorge their crews and close upon the silent ambulance.

Hanebury's unit had responded to a possible sound of gunfire in the area, moving around the countryside until the lead element had spotted the medical vehicle sat on the roadside… bonnet up… silent… suspicious…

'Just not right.'

Hanebury waved his men to either side, eight men responding, moving wide of the ambulance, but keeping constantly focussed upon it.

Stradley moved forward with Corporal Gardiner close at hand, the both of them touting Thompson sub-machine guns.

Moving up to the rear of the ambulance, they exchanged silent gestures and determined their course of action.

Stradley held his weapon in his right hand and reached for the handle. Gardiner offset himself from the likely line of fire, just in case.

The door opened slowly, allowing light from the idling halftracks to flood the inside of the ambulance, revealing its awful cargo.

Hanebury and Rickard closed up immediately.

"Goddamned fucking massacre, Top. Even a fucking nurse, for God's sake!"

The First Sergeant cast his eye over the pitiful sight and could only agree with Stradley's assessment.

"Two shots reported, Roger?"

Rickard and Gardiner dragged out the first body, that of the driver.

"Not him."

With slightly more reverence, the two pulled the stiff body of the nurse from the vehicle.

The next body spoke volumes with its silence.

"Single shot in the head."

As did the next body.

"And again."

"The report said two shots... we have two here."

Hanebury's statement required no response.

The two NCOs moved aside as others from the unit closed in to assist.

"Bury them here, Top?"

"Not yet, Sergeant."

Jerry Ringold, the unit's unofficial medic, waited for the rest of the words to come.

"Set Bragg on that engine. See if he can get it going. According to my map, there's a hospital a'ways up the 7312 here."

A quick recheck of the markings suggested the ambulance did not belong to the unit on his map.

"If we can get it running, we'll take 'em there. Hustle Bragg up... I don't wanna hang around longer than necessary."

Hanebury and Stradley moved to one side, casting a professional eye over the dispositions and actions of their men.

"Thoughts, Rodge?"

"Bunch of commies bounced the truck... would have taken it, but it didn't work... killed them off to avoid detection... had to shoot a couple... they bugged out on foot, heading for Moscow."

Hanebury nodded, acknowledging some of it as true, but believing there was more to it.

"Maybe so, Rodger, but maybe not. The two guys shot... both wounded... but clearly lighter wounds than the other poor bastards on the stretchers."

Grabbing his chin, the First Sergeant thought aloud.

"Driver gets the chop, as do the doc and the nurse. The two stretcher cases too, but not the two guys... single shots... not pistol... distance shots I reckon, not close up... pistol or a knife would have been used."

He was on a roll now.

"No, distance... they grabbed for something, out of range of the knife guy... no, guys. The cover party did the shoot. Two shots, two kills... sniper rifles."

Stradley could now see the scenario as clear as Lucifer.

"Smacks of military organisation, not the raggedy arsed survivors we've run down of late."

Jerry Ringold strode up but waited for Hanebury to finish.

"Jerry?"

"Top, pockets rifled, medical supplies all gone. Quick deaths across the board. Single stab, cut, or bullet. Bragg reckons he can fix the engine easily enough... some worn cabling shorting out, that's all."

"Thanks, Jerry. If Bragg's sure, load the poor bastards up again."

Ringold doubled away.

"Rodger, watch over this. I'm gonna call this in."

Hanebury moved back to his vehicle, where Nave was waiting with a thermos of hot coffee.

"What gives, Top?"

Hanebury went through his deductions, in between sips of the real stuff, prepared just the way he liked it.

"So we going up there?"

Nave gestured to the hillside behind his commander.

"Nope. We're gonna get the ambulance going and take the bodies to the facility over at Bräunisheim."

He swilled back the last of the coffee, and gestured at the silent hillside behind him.

"Why would we go there anyway?"

Nave frowned in genuine puzzlement.

"You mean you haven't seen it, Top? See here."

Moving around the vehicle, Arthur Nave moved towards the wood's edge, his flashlight picking out marks that were now obvious.

"See here, Top. Many feet, spreading out from this point. There's a strange mark too... regular... like every other step distance, if you look close... like a dragging foot possibly?"

Hanebury looked closer, even prising the torch from Nave's grasp.

"Goddamnit."

"I only saw it cos I went for a pee, Top."

"Uh huh."

"Reckon it's where they come from, not went, Top."

"Same as... how many you reckon, Art?"

"Hard to say, Top. Reckon fifteen... twenty tops."

Hanebury was looking up at the dark wood, wondering if enemy eyes were upon him already.

He shivered involuntarily.

"Right, Arthur, get the vehicle started up."

In seconds, Hanebury was at Stradley's side, filling him in on developments.

106

His decision was assisted by the sound of a six-cylinder gasoline engine roaring into life.

"Rodger, change of plan…take your boys, get the bodies outta the ambulance… bury them quickly… right here… then take all the vehicles… leave me the ambulance… move down until you're clear of the valley to…," Hanebury picked a point on the map, "Here… and set up for all-round defence… and stay alert."

"And you, Top?"

Hanebury inclined his head towards the markings discovered by Art Nave.

"That's where the bastards came from. I'm going to quietly slip inside there with a section and see what we can find. Give us an idea of what we're up against here, cos I'm goddamned sure as I can be that this ain't renegade commies."

He pointed at the ambulance.

"That was organised, efficient killing."

From a distance, it looked like the entire platoon departed the scene, not that anyone was watching, save Hanebury and a dozen men who had slipped quietly into the woods.

He waited twenty minutes, keeping his men in check and silent, watching… waiting…

Nothing.

"OK boys, you two sit tight and watch that vehicle. Report anything to me. Rest of us… move it on out. Nave, you got point."

The small party picked their way forward, silently reversing the trodden path of whoever it was that visited themselves upon the medics and wounded.

It was nearly a quarter to one when Nave held up his hand, halting the silent advance in its track.

Everyone dropped to a knee and watched their assigned area for signs of trouble, all save Hanebury who noticed the summons and moved forward to Nave's side.

Even the studied whisper seemed like a church bell in the quiet darkness of the forest.

"This is where they camped, Top. See the flattened grass and undergrowth... fire circle... trimmed wood..."

Hanebury got the idea, and waved his men into a skirmish line, expanding outwards to embrace the modest clearing.

Whilst the men were shaking out, both he and Nave studied the area for booby traps, their torches flicking across the ground in front of them.

None were apparent but...

The two moved forward, assessing each step, checking the ground before they lay a foot down, moving apart... just in case...

Crack...

Hanebury froze, the faint sound and tremor of something breaking under his foot causing him almost panic with fear.

Almost... but his training and natural courage rose above the immediacy of his plight.

"Move away, Arthur, move away."

That his Sergeant was stock-still, and clearly tense, was enough for Nave.

"Where, Top... which foot?"

"Back away, Arthur."

"Not happening, Top. Which one?"

"Front."

Nave crawled gingerly, going flatter the closer he got to Hanebury's left boot.

Torch lodged firmly between his teeth, his knife was out and probing the area, seeking out whatever it was that had so spooked his commander.

Standing still is not normally a particularly draining exercise, but standing still when the slightest movement might send you and one of your men to Valhalla is as draining as it can get, and Hanebury, minute by minute, started to feel the strain.

His leg wanted to work, the muscle sought to get going, but he fought against it as hard as he could.

"Arthur, leave it now... my leg's got a fucking mind of its own here... move out, soldier!"

Nave hummed a response as he worked closer around the boot, scraping away earth and leaves and...

The laugh nearly made Hanebury lose it.

"What the fuck!"

Nave allowed the torch to fall away so he could talk.

"Err, Top... you can move your foot... it's clear."

108

Almost reluctantly, despite the urgent requirements of his aching legs, First Sergeant Jim Hanebury picked up his foot, revealing the cause of the alarm.

"Make a wish, Top."

The broken wishbone of some long since consumed fowl lay taunting Hanebury.

"Goddamnedsonofafuckingbitch!"

A couple of the others drifted in close, just to see what the fuss was about.

Hanebury's relief did not stop him from slapping Nave on the shoulder.

"Nice work, Arthur, but next time I give you an order, you better fucking obey it!"

Neither of them believed the harshness in his voice was anything other than relief.

Half the men moved through the clearing, whilst the others turned outwards and watched.

Hanebury was mentally rehearsing his report and citation for Nave's recommendation; chicken bone or no, the man had shown real guts and deserved his reward.

The man in question rummaged in a pile of wood nearby, his demeanour drawing Hanebury's interest.

"Shit!"

Nave jerked back, weapon at the ready, and immediately the whole group were primed and alert.

Nave beckoned the nearest man, and together they pulled some of the undergrowth away.

By the time Hanebury moved over to the site, enough had been exposed for his torchlight to reveal the last resting place of a group of slaughtered Russian soldiers.

Twelve... no... fourteen bodies, all bearing all the hallmarks of expert and quiet deaths... signs unfortunately familiar to those who had recently stood at the back of a certain US Army ambulance.

'What the fuck?'

That question went through a number of minds.

Nave leant down into the shallow grave and plucked something from the grasp of a large cadaver, whose neck had been sliced through twice, spilling the man's lifeblood in seconds.

The material was camouflage, of a type they had all seen before. Hanging from it was a thin strip of cloth, black with silver thread lines and inscription, made red by the product of the Russian's opened neck.

After cursory glance, Nave passed it to Hanebury, who examined at more closely.

"Sonofabitch."

Rickard moved closer, keen to see what was causing the commotion.

Handed the cloth by Lucifer, he spoke the two words aloud.

"Prince Eugene?"

Nave snatched it back with mock severity.

"Prinz Eugen, you illiterate chunk of Pennsylvanian dog's mess. Prinz Eugen... it's... it was an SS division. Don't you know anything?"

"I know you're gonna get my boot up your ass pretty soon, farm boy!"

The two often sparred, but now was neither the time nor place, so Lucifer descended upon them swiftly and mercilessly.

"Shut up!"

Control re-established, Hanebury spoke his thoughts aloud.

"So... this little bunch of bastards are a throwback... Nazis who'll kill anyone, commies, or us, come what may."

In a moment of clarity, Hanebury saw everything.

"Medical supplies... it's all about medical supplies. They hit the ambulance for its supplies."

His mind focussed... the enemy group had probably moved north... north... Braunisheim...

"Shit, they're after the hospital stores."

He beckoned Shufeldt forward with the HT set, dialling straight in to Stradley to issue a warning...

...that was neither sent nor received.

"Nothing... it's not working."

Handing the useless set back to Shufeldt, Hanebury worked off a little frustration.

"Work on it... get me contact with Pennsylvania-six-two pretty damn pronto."

Picking up his Thompson from where he had leant it, Hanebury pumped his fist and indicated the route of advance, sending the lead man out at increased pace, understanding that time was probably not his ally in the matter of the hospital and the SS unit.

0720 hrs, Thursday, 13th June 1946, near Route 7312, half a kilometre southeast of Bräunisheim, Germany.

The night had not been kind to the SS-Kommando, and Lenz was in a foul mood.

Whilst on guard duty, one of his men had blundered into an animal hole, hidden by overgrowing greenery.

His leg had slid into the hole and forward momentum did the rest.

The snap of the soldier's femur was like a gunshot, waking every man instantly.

With iron will, SS-Sturmann Jensen had not made a sound above a low groan, despite the fact that the sharp bone protruded from the back of his thigh like the shaft of a spear.

The injured man was made comfortable and the two Soviet officer prisoners set to his care.

In his mind's eye, Lenz imagined capturing a doctor, and having a proper medic to use the supplies he was intending to liberate.

With Jensen out of the equation, Lenz now had twenty-one men with which to conduct his raid.

According to his initial view of the medical encampment, twenty-one would be sufficient for a rapid surprise attack and withdrawal.

He spent the morning formulating his plan and the afternoon instructing his troopers on how best to carry out the night assault.

His planning was interrupted by a movement of vehicles, when four heavily armed Military Police vehicles swept into the camp.

Three pairs of binoculars turned instantly, focussing on the swiftly moving vehicles.

Their presence alarmed Lenz and his senior men, Emmering and Weiss, but the group soon sped off the way they had come and the medical facility returned to normal.

Lenz finished off his briefing on a hand drawn map, occasionally pointing towards the hospital to emphasise a point, and he was satisfied that the senior men of the Kommando knew the plan inside out.

The soldiers, dismissed to catch up on sleep, lay around in the undergrowth, as relaxed as only veterans can be.

Lenz swept the battleground once more, his binoculars seeking anything that he had missed, and he was satisfied that the plan was all in order.

Throughout the day, the occasional ambulance had arrived, deposited a desperate cargo, and left, all except the last one that had driven straight into the motor pool, where it was quickly abandoned by its driver.

Lenz took the opportunity offered by the growing sunset, and made himself comfortable, dropping off to sleep in an instant, whilst others watched and waited.

In Bräunisheim itself, the venerable rifle was once more on show, as its owner was called upon to describe deeds from another conflict, a time some thirty years beforehand.

The old bar had been destroyed by a combination of blows from the three times the village had changed hands since early 1945. Its replacement had been established in an old barn, across the main road from the village, but close to the US Army facility. The villagers were nothing if not resourceful, as the excellent location attracted off-duty US personnel, both men and women, and meant that American dollars were spent on consuming large quantities of German lager, both by those who were officially stood down, and those who sneaked out of wards without permission.

Holding centre stage amidst the music and laughter was a man in Imperial German Army uniform, one clearly well cared for and that still fitted him well.

Using the Gewehr-98 he had carried throughout World War One, Heinrich Raubach demonstrated the savagery of Verdun and the bitterness of the Argonne, the Pour-le-Mérite jumping at his throat with every mock thrust.

Three other WW1 veterans joined in, occasionally using the old rifle to illustrate their own suggestions on the finer points of bayonet and butt use.

Some of the American soldiers were fascinated by the old men's tales; others moved to enjoy peace and quiet away from such reminders of combat.

Raubach had fought with the elite Herwarth von Bittenfeld Regiment, part of the 13th Division of the Imperial German Army.

A man of great personal courage, he had been wounded on four separate occasions, and was one of only four men in 13th Division to hold the Blue Max.

On the occasion he had earned the award, Raubach had been field promoted and was an acting Leutnant, commanding the remnants of a company in the HvB Regiment.

Technically, as his substantive rank was Stabsfeldwebel and Spiess, he probably should not have received the prestigious medal, but it was 31st October 1918, and both the criteria and actualities of his award were lost in the German surrender.

The citation was made out for Offizier-Stellvertreter Raubach, and so the Pour-le-Mérite was awarded and immediately ignored by a nation cowed and quick to turn away from its military heroes.

Amongst his other qualities, Raubach was also a man with a keen eye and the ability to keep his mouth shut, and those qualities, married to his uncanny senses, had suggested that this night would be different to those that had gone before.

The things he had seen in and out of the hospital late on that summer's evening made him return to his house and pocket four strips of ammunition.

If his senses were correct... well... he intended to be prepared.

2320 hrs, Thursday, 13th June 1946, 74th Surgical Hospital, Bräunisheim, Germany.

Using infrared binoculars, Stradley surveyed the ground between the woods and the hospital site.

From within the complex, modestly illuminated, and busy with surgical shifts still working, other eyes, similarly equipped, were scanning the hills to the south, where smudges of heat had occasionally betrayed the presence of men.

Hanebury, once out of the ambulance, had made himself known to the 74th's commanding officer.

After a short conference, Lieutenant Colonel Brinkley agreed to the MPs riding shotgun over his unit until reinforcements arrived, and assigned some of his men to create a number of rifle squads.

Brinkley was very specific with his orders, forbidding any offensive action, and requiring Hanebury to act only in defence of the facility.

The hospital head of dentistry, Major Lewis Imerman, was de facto in charge of the overall defensive force, but no one, most of all the Major himself, felt otherwise than that Lucifer held the reins.

Hanebury's hardest job was persuading some of his new troops to go about their daily business without a care in the world.

He selected a large detail of men who knew their way around a Garand, and kept them close, sending the other 'less reliable' types to other parts of the perimeter.

With the dozen men that had arrived secretly in the ambulance, plus the rifle unit of belligerent medics, Hanebury had thirty men spread along the southern edge of the camp, some hidden, some revealed but seemingly inattentive to military matters.

He checked his watch as Shufeldt did the thirty-minute radio check with Pennsylvania-six-two, the faulty radio now working again.

Stradley's force was ready and raring to go.

Hanebury had discussed the likely tactical options, and each had a single code word that, once sent, would bring the heavily armed vehicles down on whoever it was that was sat on the heights above 74th Surgical Hospital.

2330 hrs, Thursday, 13th June 1946, near Route 7312, half a kilometre southeast of Bräunisheim, Germany.

SS-Kommando Lenz had survived longer than any other Werewolf unit; indeed, it was the only remaining unit of its type, filled with Nazi fanatics, still intent on taking the fight to any and all enemies of the Reich.

The Kommando had lost men along the way, and gained some too, but the unit was built around the granite core of its commander and two senior NCOs.

The same three-man group surveyed the camp, relying on moonlight and its own modest illumination to check the last details.

For all his professionalism and fanaticism, Lenz was a soldier first and foremost, and knew better than to ignore his gut instinct and the advice of senior men.

"Go on, Oberscharfuhrer."

Emmering had voiced concerns, unsupported by fact, without substance, but none the less very real.

"Can't put my finger on it, Hauptsturmfuhrer... it looks right... simple operation... but something feels very wrong."

Lenz concentrated harder, seeking something through his lenses to either confirm or deny the feelings of his senior NCO.

Feelings he shared.

"Unterscharfuhrer?"

Weiss was a man who had survived the worst the Soviet partisans could throw at him, and definitely a man to be listened to.

"He's right. Something doesn't sit right, Hauptsturmfuhrer."

He dropped his binoculars and leaned in closer to his commander, Emmering mirroring his closeness on Lenz's other side.

"Everything seems normal, but there is a tension there. I can feel it."

Emmering nodded his agreement and added his supporting view.

"It's there, Hauptsturmfuhrer. It seems differentto the last time we observed... there's a tension there... something's not right."

He lowered his voice even more.

"They seem to be doing the same routines that we have seen... I even think there's less people wandering around... village is quiet... the bar shut early... maybe that's a sign, Hauptsturmfuhrer."

The sound of an engine drew the three of them back to their observations.

An ambulance graunched its gears as it slowed to enter the north gate. The vehicle delivered its awful cargo and disappeared back off into the night.

A light went off in Lenz's brain.

"The ambulance."

His NCOs waited for further explanation.

"It's that fucking ambulance. The one that just drove in... didn't bring wounded... just parked up."

Emmering's brain lit up in response.

"And it came in from the south-east there... and..." his mind brought up something he had seen and not understood, "And the others... the ones that actually dropped off wounded, came in from the north-east and up the 7313... only the north-east and the 7313."

Weiss gave voice to his mind's immediate suggestion.

"The one we found?"

Lenz nodded, although Weiss didn't really see the acknowledgement of his question.

"It's a trap, has to be."

Both NCOs tensed ready for the inevitable string of orders.

Lenz, his heart set on the supplies and the possibility of a medic, dwelt on the matter for a moment longer, until his head took over and imposed ordered thinking.

'Too much of a risk. Verdamnt!'

He scrambled backwards, followed by the two NCOs, halting well below the ridgeline.

Dragging the zeltbahn over their heads, Lenz switched his torch on, applying a low light to the map he held.

"Right. We move away, and quickly. Unterscharfuhrer, organise your group and take the lead. Head...," he consulted the map and swiftly decided upon a destination, "South, staying within the

woods. I want us to be here... between Holzkirch and Lonsee...
before the sun comes up. Klar?"

"Zu befehl, Hauptsturmfuhrer"

"Go."

Weiss slipped out from under the zeltbahn and was already
lost in the darkness before Emmering got his orders.

"Rearguard... yourself and of your three men... the rest
come with me... you relocate to here...observe the camp for an
hour... then, or before, if you see movement... sit on this junction
here," he jabbed at the map, indicating a small crossroads in the
woods.

Emmering understood his task.

"Wait one hour there and then follow up quickly."

Lenz stifled a yawn, one of nervousness, not lack of sleep.

"We'll meet here, overlooking this valley. If you're being
pursued, move through the valley... be noisy if you can... and we'll
spring something on your hounds. Klar?"

"Alles klar, Hauptsturmfuhrer."

No further words were spoken, and SS-Kommando Lenz
melted back into the dark forest.

0007 hrs, Friday, 14th June 1946, 74th Surgical Hospital, Bräunisheim, Germany.

"Anything at all, Pennsylvania-six, over."

Hanebury strained to hear the reply, as Stradley tried to
keep his voice low on the radio.

"Negative since last report, Pennsylvania-six-two, over."

Major Imerman was singularly unimpressed. He had drawn
the duty for no other reason that he was rostered off medical duties for
that night.

The lack of sleep that came hand in hand with the
responsibility of command made him less than agreeable.

"So, a goddamned wild goose chase then, Sergeant."

Hanebury let it go.

"No, Sir. They're up there... no question... were up there.
Something spooked them. They musta seen something and they've
bugged out."

The MP NCO found himself suddenly unwinding,
convinced that he was right, and that the infiltrators had gone.

None the less, he could not bring himself to order a stand
down... *'request a stand down'* he reminded himself, as Imerman
made angry clucking noises off to his left.

The two MP forces remained waiting until 0315 hrs, when Hanebury made the decision, Imerman's presence a long distant memory, the dentist having, with Hanebury's blessing, retreated to his sleeping quarters before one o'clock.

SS-Kommando Lenz had had a close brush with the devil and, unknown to them, escaped certain death.

But Lucifer was not to be cheated, and laid his plans.

1102 hrs, Friday, 14th June 1946, 10, Downing Street, London, UK.

"I'm very sorry to hear that, Mr President, truly I am."

Churchill listened intently as Truman confirmed everything that had been reported about the state of public opinion in the States.

The backlash against the use of the bombs was huge, and still growing, and presently more active than the support for further use of the weapons.

"Yes, Mr President, I can only agree with you."

Both men were, in realistic terms, politically safe, or as safe as an incumbent politician can be when faced with internal revolts.

Churchill had been in power less than a year, and had been confirmed as leader for the duration of the Soviet War.

Truman had succeeded to the Executive post on the death of FDR, and the next election was not until November 1948.

However, the turmoil that had developed over the use of the bombs on Japan had taken their administrations aback.

Both had known that public opinion might not care for the images that appeared, although a large number just appeared from out of the ether, and most were not 'official' photos at all, but neither of them was prepared for the depth of feelings that washed over the Allied countries.

Horror and anti-war feelings on one side, 'they had it coming' feelings on the other.

More often, anti-war feelings were being expressed in every other Allied nation, and already the South American nations had expressed a desire to distance themselves fully from the Atomic strikes, up to and including withdrawal from the Alliance.

Opposition politicians found numerous bandwagons to jump on, citing the horrendous casualties suffered by the Allies and the latest developments in the technological arts of warfare, either as reasons to negotiate a peace and withdraw the troop, or to lay waste to Eastern Europe, all the way to the Chinese border.

Alongside the marches in protest or support of the three Atomic bombings were huge gatherings that called upon the leaderships to use the bomb or strike a deal for peace.

Politicians from Quebec to Buenos Aires, New York to Paris, across the spectrum of the Allied nations, spoke in terms of the inevitability of Soviet agreement to any terms the Allies would offer, now that the destructive capacity of the Atomic bomb was clear.

After all, as the French Prime Minister Félix Gouin stated openly, *'No sane leadership could possibly fail to see the likely effects of continued conflict.'*

Gouin had not had the benefit of meeting Stalin face to face, unlike the two men engaged in a secure telephone call, sat alone in their offices, thousands of miles apart, but joined in their mutual hatred of the idea of allowing Stalin's aggression to stand.

In the States, the growing movement to stop the war was still completely dwarfed by the calls to fully prosecute the war, and employ more bombs to bring it to a conclusion that meant the boys could come home, and that the Soviet Union was transformed into warm ash.

Most other countries, save Germany, were less enthusiastic.

Even the British laid back on a bed of tired stoicism, understanding that their nation must do what the nation must do, but without huge enthusiasm for either course, preferring whatever would be quickest and least costly, although Churchill himself understood precisely which course he wanted to take.

Truman wound up his report on the rioting that had cost nearly two hundred lives, and destroyed property and livelihoods from San Francisco to Buffalo.

The universal joys of the Japanese surrender had not survived the last month's heavy casualty figures from Europe, not for any of the Allied Powers The general public at home, democracy or no, had taken to the streets in protest. People had died in demonstrations supporting peace, as well as war, an irony wasted on few.

Except, perhaps, for the Germans.

There was no protest at the use of such devices, just the occasional call from some emerging politician or older but inactive elder statesman, seeking use of Atomic weapons against the Soviet Union, and the use of them immediately, a view which grew only within German borders.

Churchill listened, preparing his own message of gloom to his American friend.

"Quite, Harry, quite. For our part, you already know of the demonstrations in London and Birmingham. I regret that I have to add Glasgow and Edinburgh to that list. Regretfully, the former turned into a full-blown riot. Thirty-eight were killed before order was restored. Add that to those already lost and likely to succumb to their injuries, a round hundred deaths in a week."

He puffed on his cigar, ignoring the whisky that called to him, promising himself full access once this important call had been completed.

"De Gaulle has more problems, of course. Have you spoken to him, Harry?

Churchill laughed at the response.

"Yes, I know, but sometimes one had to perform one's duties, regardless of personal choice."

His response was well received and he risked another puff on his cigar.

His eyes narrowed as Truman added more fuel to the fire, listing the steady procession of ambassadors that either had trooped through the Oval Office or were still on the list to attend, all of whom sought cast-iron assurances that there would be no use against the USSR, in the east or west of the vast land.

He had his own list of visitations to relate, a virtual mirror of the lost of countries presently burning his ears.

The Polish, in particular, were caught between a rock and a hard place, as they had always rebelled against the use of 'special weapons' in Europe and, since the reports and interviews with survivors of the Japanese atrocities, railed against their use, period.

But they were also concerned that any deal struck with the USSR would leave them less of a nation than in 1939.

Truman finished his recitation of the disaffected nations and moved to personal comment.

"Not that we had any immediate plans to, of course, but there's no way, no how, we can employ any such weapon at the moment, Winston."

"I concur, Harry, but we can still proceed with our arrangement, can we not?"

It was something that Churchill had pushed for, agitated for, and that Roosevelt had constantly denied him.

Truman had acquiesced without too much effort on the British PM's part.

"Yes, Winston, that will proceed, given the inevitability of it all."

"Thank you, Mr President."

Churchill mentally ticked his 'want' list and, whilst the deployment of a British equivalent to CG-509, and shared mission status with an agreement on use of an atomic device, was important, there were other fish to fry.

He had noted that Truman made no announcements regarding Sweden.

"Harry, I had the Swedish ambassador here, and I think it's fair to say that we can expect no great assistance from them, openly or covertly, for the foreseeable future."

Truman had not had an inkling of that from either the embassy, or his own 'contacts' in the Court of Bernadotte, both home and away.

The situation was crystal clear to both the major Allied leaders.

What had been a general wish to avoid using 'enhanced' weapons on mainland Europe had grown into a public outcry across the globe, supported and encouraged by every single Allied power, all save Germany.

"Mr President... Harry... I believe we find ourselves at a turning point, one that we must consider very carefully."

Churchill leant back in his chair and closed his eyes.

"Our people have suffered a great deal, more than we had envisaged. Our prayers have not been answered, and we find ourselves, despite our stunning advances and domination of the sea and air, at a serious disadvantage. We both know that Secretary Stalin suffers from no such internal pressures and..." Winston added as an after-thought, "I daresay he has some hand in the domestic challenges and issues that beset us all at this time."

There was, as yet, no clue that much of their political discomfort was being orchestrated from a city many thousands of miles away.

He drew on his cigar as Truman offered his agreement.

"Unless we remove the shackles that have been imposed upon us, I see no alternative but for us to prosecute this war at a low level, until such times as the public furore passes over or lessens..."

Truman interrupted, putting his own no-nonsense interpretation forward.

"Indeed, Harry, we cannot have those sort of casualties again, and we both know that use of the Atomic weapons would have helped in that regard."

Churchill smiled at the response.

"Quite, nothing overt whatsoever... indeed... but, as agreed, we will continue to develop our own plans on the matter."

Churchill puffed furiously as the President of the United States spoke at length, nodding and making noises of agreement as Harry Truman set out the world as he saw it.

He finished and, with an intake of breath, Churchill crushed the cigar into the crystal ashtray with genuine strength and finality.

"Yes, I agree, Harry, and I suggest that our agencies work together to root out any agitators. I will clear my diary for the second week in July immediately. Chequers first, then off to France... I should think two days here will be enough, don't you?"

Churchill listened intently, chuckling to himself, Truman's wit surfacing in a comment about one of their close allies.

A knock on the door went unanswered, although the Prime Minister checked the mantle clock and knew exactly who was stood outside the double doors.

"Yes, Mr President. I think we must include everyone. I will have my staff make the arrangements to... yes... indeed... agreed... agreed... erm... I will think on that one until we meet face to face, Harry. Now, I'm about to set Second Army Group in motion. They're here now... yes... yes indeed..."

Churchill stood and eased his back.

"Come in!"

The door opened and the new arrivals were immediately greeted with an imperious hand, demanding silence.

"Yes, and to you too, Harry. Safe journey and Godspeed... yes, I hope so to... and goodbye to you, Sir."

He replaced the handset and swept up the whisky, all in one easy motion.

"Good afternoon. Help yourselves, gentlemen."

He indicated the decanter, but none of the four men wished for a spirit so early in the afternoon.

"Please, be seated."

They took their seats, arranged in a semi-circle facing Winston's desk, and waited to hear whatever it was that was so important that they had received orders to cancel everything and be here for one o'clock precisely.

Churchill, with a sense for the dramatic, refilled his own glass and resumed his seat, all to a backdrop of loaded silence.

They needed no introductions, either to the Prime Minister, or to each other.

They represented the very top of their professions, military men in the service of His Majesty.

Admiral of the Fleet and First Sea Lord Sir John Henry Dacres Cunningham enjoyed an excellent professional and personal

121

relationship with the Commander in Chief of the RAF, Air Chief Marshall Sir Charles Portal, 1st Viscount Portal of Hungerford, provided that the subject of Coastal Command was not raised, in which case they would fight for overseeing rights long into the night.

Both in turn had great respect for Alan Francis Brooke, 1st Viscount Alanbrooke, Field Marshal, and Chief of the Imperial General Staff, although the subject of an Army Air Force would spike Portal into reaction, and naval and marine amphibious forces was always guaranteed to make any meeting between Cunningham and Alanbrooke quite lively.

The three men turned their heads simultaneously, without a cue, and examined the fourth member present, a man with whom they had all had issues of varying subject matter, mainly caused by a combination of the man's abrasive manner, almost dismissive approach to opinions not wholly in support of his own, and total faith in himself.

Alanbrooke, in particular, had fielded more of the man's issues than most, and had been forced to placate more than one important ally, who had received a taste of the man's lack of tact.

"Thank you all for coming at such short notice."

Churchill turned to the fourth man.

"And I hope that you are fully recovered?"

"I am, Prime Minister, thank you."

Field-Marshal Sir Bernard Law Montgomery, recently created as 1st Viscount Montgomery of Alamein, settled back in his chair, wondering why he was present in such august company, but already imagining himself at the head of some huge enterprise, his natural place, given his undoubted superior abilities.

Churchill outlined the present political situation, adding in most of the matters recently discussed with Truman.

He wound up his delivery of the facts, moving them quickly into the area of resolution.

"So, as you can see, gentlemen, we have a singularly unpalatable set of choices. So, unless you can see another alternative that satisfies the aims and desires of His Majesty's Government and his allies, this is what it is proposed to do."

1517 hrs, Friday, 14th June 1946, Office of the Secretary General, the Kremlin, Moscow, USSR.

The meeting had opened with a briefing on the military situation in Europe, which had stabilised beyond hope.

The Allied armies constantly pushed and jostled, but there was no power, no great plan to their efforts. Almost as if it were fighting just to keep matters going whilst some other issue was resolved.

The Allied Air Forces were a constant thorn, but reducing the size of depots, moving more by night than day, and increasing AA defences, had all had an effect.

However, there was no disguising railway lines and huge bridges, so the infrastructure still suffered on a daily basis.

The increasing use of sunken bridges had helped greatly, but the supplies reaching the front line were still just about half of what would be needed if everything took off again.

None the less, the Military briefing, given by Malinin, was positive and upbeat.

The situation in the Far East was another matter, and some good units were to be sacrificed, as it was impossible to bring them back into Soviet-controlled territory before they would be overwhelmed by the victorious Chinese and Allied mainland troops.

However, connections with the Communist Chinese ensured that the rivalries of old would flare up again, and maintain confusion and instability in the region.

Handing over a much of their heavy equipment as possible, the Soviet units hoped to save as many of their qualified soldiers as possible.

The pledging of total support from numerous Japanese units who simply refused to surrender, increased the forces available to the Far Eastern Command.

The briefing ended with a victory, albeit an airborne one.

Soviet fighters had successfully intercepted a force of US bombers, en route from their bases in China to bomb something in the hinterland of the USSR.

Heavy losses, claimed to be over 25% of the enemy aircraft, were claimed by jubilant Red Air Force pilots, and, for the first time in memory, an enemy bomber force withdrew without reaching its intended target.

There was no hint of any US-led seaborne invasion, nor much possibility of anything of note of an offensive nature being constructed on the mainland borders of the Eastern USSR. Which meant that Soviet forces in the area could recover and make their own plans to tie in with the aims of Vasilevsky's targeting of US forces.

The increased feelings of optimism were bolstered further, by reports of events in the Ukraine, where nationalist resistance was weakening, assisted by the spread of hunger, as supplies dwindled and the agriculture suffered, frequently falling victim to the torch or similar deliberate destruction.

The projections of a poor harvest would be made more certain by positive interaction from the reformed POW units.

The Ukraine was becoming less of a problem, hour by hour.

And then there was the political instability in the Allied ranks. Plus, the Italian government agitating and criticising, the low-key condemnation of the Soviet incursion into their territory now completely forgotten in open hostility to the Allied presence in their lands, all thanks to a few well-placed sympathisers in their government.

Beria was beaming for ear to ear.

Stalin was as happy as a man could be.

The NKVD report lay unopened in front of the General Secretary, Beria being so anxious to pass on the latest news that he had recited it virtually word for word, pausing only to slake his thirst with tea.

The report was a gift from the god that neither believed in.

Mayhem, pure and simple, was assaulting the political leaderships of the united Allied nations, a group that, according to the reports emanating from agents, as well as free press sources, was becoming less united with every passing hour.

In an unlike-Beria fashion, the NKVD Marshal had not claimed the glory all for himself, conceding that there was a very real desire to sue for peace, stop using atomic weapons, and bring the soldiers home, even in the nations that had only a nominal role in the fighting.

Stalin could only imagine the pressures mounting on the politicians.

He chuckled.

He laughed.

He was unaware that the NKVD report deliberately understated the larger movement in America, the one that sought full and immediate prosecution of war with use of the bombs and everything that entailed.

Reaching out, he picked up a written report from Vasilevsky, one that had landed on his desk that very morning, the commander in chief's own addition to Malinin's presentation.

He wasn't so stupid as to offer it to Beria, he merely showed the front cover.

"I take it you've read this, Lavrentiy?"

"Yes indeed, Comrade General Secretary. Combined with Malinin's briefing, my own report, I think we can say that the political plan was done what we expected, can we not?"

Stalin nodded his agreement, and substituted the folder for his tea.

"So, now that Vasilevsky is in a position to enact his plan, I think the GKO should approve the immediate implementation of it."

It wasn't a question, and Beria never even thought to offer agreement or opposition.

A silence descended.

Beria, wallowing in excellent work by his agitators and agents, felt smug and knew he had gained ground in the eyes of his master.

Stalin merely imagined a face.

A thin face with a high forehead...

... glasses...

...thin lips...

...Truman's face...

"How he must be wriggling now, eh?"

Beria was startled out of his silence and looked at Stalin in query.

"I said, how that Amerikanski bastard Truman must be wriggling now, eh?"

"They'll sue for peace... it's inevitable... their democracy is their weakness... always has been, Comrade General Secretary. Their nations are weak... all of them, weak... but, even if they found someone with political resolve... they could never overcome this issue in their heartland..."

"Exactly, Lavrentiy, exactly... and that's exactly why we will win... because we have the will!"

Stalin checked the time, and found he had less than he thought.

"Right, Comrade Marshal. Let us proceed to meet with the GKO, have the Vasilevsky plan initiated, press on with our efforts in their countries, and push ahead with Raduga as quickly as we can."

He stood and pounded the desk with his hand.

"For the first time since those green toads stood at the gates of Moscow, and we drove them back, I know we will bring the world into a new Soviet era. It is inevitable, Comrade Marshal! Inevitable!"

The subsequent meeting of the GKO was buoyed beyond measure, the confidence of his Party leader enthusing each man, but also making him malleable to any proposition.

When the meeting broke up, the Soviet Union was set on a course that had the potential to divide the world for decades to come, and one that was aimed at destroying the major power bases of the United States and United Kingdom.

None who left the meeting room felt other than a new world era was about to start.

However, more than one had secretly thought that now was the time to seek an armistice, and secure all that had been gained, whilst the enemy was weak and confused by their inner wranglings,

Of course, none had dared to say so.

The tragedy of life is in what dies inside a man whilst he lives - the death of genuine feeling, the death of inspired response, the awareness that makes it possible to feel the pain, or the glory, of other men in yourself.

Norman Cousins

Chapter 156 – THE PAIN

1002 hrs, Saturday, 15th June 1946, Makaryev Monastery, Lyskovsky, USSR.

The Makaryev Monastery had been many things in its life.

Founded in the Fifteenth century, it had been a Monastery at its inception.

Fortified and secure, it became a centre for commerce, something that only terminated when it was burnt to the ground in 1816.

Brought back to life as a convent in 1882, it enjoyed some peaceful years until, 1929, the Bolsheviks ousted the nuns and converted the premises to an orphanage.

Passing through a number of interested parties, the premises were again taken over by the government, and became an important military hospital during the Patriotic War.

Much of the premises were turned over to the Lysovko College of Veterinary Medicine, retaining one complete wing for specialist treatment of one of war's most horrible injuries.

Burns.

He was still controlled by it… almost defined by it.

It was the ever-present focus of his mind.

No matter what wonders fell before his gaze, or what sweet sounds entered his ears, or tastes fell on his tongue, it was all-powerful.

It could be temporarily controlled or, more accurately, displaced in his mind and body by the soporific effects of the substances they gave him.

'Bless them.'

The doctors and nurses, sometimes the latter in tears, tended to his ruined body, washed him, fed him, and injected his raw flesh with all manner of medicines and analgesics, and had, by some miracle, dragged him back into the land of the living.

A land where living was defined by 'it'.

Pain.

'It' was pain.

He had been wounded before, even burned before, but never to this extent, and never endured the unendurable pain that visited itself upon him hour by hour, day by day.

He tried to use his mind to control it, seize hold of IT, the ruling force, subjugate IT, deal with IT, control IT...

... but IT was in charge and refused to take a back seat.

"Polkovnik? Polkovnik? It's time."

He shifted slightly and felt his skin crackle and stretch, the burns protesting at the smallest movement.

He groaned, his only outward concession to the agonies of existence that he endured every waking minute.

"Polkovnik, it's the doctor here. We've got to bath you today."

Yarishlov opened his eyes in momentary terror.

The previous bath had been to soak the bandages and dressings away from his tortured flesh.

In his world of pain, it ranked second to the actual moment in Pomerania, when he had started to burn inside his tank.

He could not bring himself to speak, but rather made himself less ware of the Doctor's presence, and focussed on the jab in his right arm, and the pulling in his other arm as the fluid bottles were changed.

At no time did he consider ending it all, not that he could have done in any case.

Yarishlov's purpose, his driving force, his obsession was pure and simple... to wear his uniform again.

The nurses cleared the way as the other occupants of the burns ward watched on, none of them so badly hurt as the much-decorated Colonel of Tank Troops.

Yarishlov was a hero in every sense of the word, feted by the Soviet state and Communist Party, and to see him laid low by such hideous wounds, was awful to behold.

Two of them, old soldiers who had served in the dangerous early days of WW2, threw up salutes as best they could, their own offerings of honour bringing pain to each individual, but both had heard of Yarishlov and neither would accept less.

The warm water lay waiting for him, and Yarishlov steeled himself, as the process had no painless sections in which he could invest and recover.

Hands gently grasped his sheets and he felt himself raised up slightly, the bed no longer taking his weight.

Whilst there was pain, it was lessened by the analgesia he had just been given and, unbeknown to him, the start of the body's best efforts at repair.

The warm liquid embraced him, not too cold and not too hot, and he was lowered beneath the water level, until the cooling fluid reached his neck.

The pain was lulled and calmed as one of the nurses used a piece of towelling to drizzle more liquid over his head, both over the burned area and the shaved section, bringing immediate relief to Yarishlov.

The team worked around him, ensuring every part was immersed or drizzled with water, and Yarishlov's sense of well-being increased.

That feeling went in a micro-second and the extremes of pain returned to claim him.

A scream immediately burst from his lips in response to an attempt to remove a dressing that had fused with his recovering flesh.

"NO! Not yet, Nurse! Leave it to soak longer... much longer. I'll be back in ten minutes. Leave it all until then."

Yarishlov heard the horrified apology of the young nurse, but had already decided to settle back and enjoy the ten minutes the Doctor had offered, and use it to prepare himself to endure the agony that was to come.

1632 hrs, Saturday, 15th June 1946, Freienwalde, Pomerania.

The prisoners were being assembled, as per the divisional commander's orders.

The small field was gradually filling up as the dejected soldiers arrived; shambling groups of Poles and British infantrymen, with a handful of Spaniards, all taken during the recent failed Allied attacks on the positions of 1st Guards Mechanised Rifle Division and her sister units of the newly reconstituted 2nd Baltic Front, the grouping tasked with halting and reducing the Polish landing incursion.

Kriks, sipping on the ever-present flask containing something of non-regulation issue, eyed Deniken with concern. The personality change that had swept over the young Colonel since the

129

loss of Yarishlov, and the heavy casualties infected upon his men in and around Naugard, seemed to have darkened the man irrevocably.

What had been a close relationship between them had quickly floundered, seemingly becoming more of something to tolerate for Deniken, a situation that was unusual for Kriks after his friendship with Yarishlov..

True to his word, he stuck as close to the 1st Guards' commander, or as close as the man's moods would allow.

He moved up to Deniken's side and offered the flask as a reminder of his presence and the good relationship they once had.

"No."

Kriks stayed close as Deniken moved forward to where the burial party had just completed its digging.

Other men moved forward to place fourteen men in the soil of Poland forever, men who were born and bred in Mother Russia.

Today was a bitter day indeed for the man that Yarishlov had seen as the future of his country.

As per his wish, Deniken assisted in carrying one of the bodies, that of his long-time friend, Vladimir Grabin, with whom he had shared breakfast, and now would bury, all in the same day.

The soldiers, without distinction of rank, spoke their piece over their dead comrades, heartfelt eulogies to men with whom the trials of a life of a soldier had been shared for months, and often, years.

More than one man shed tears as the earth was moved back into its former place, entombing the dead in its cold embrace.

A few prisoners watched dispassionately, some with understanding, some without comprehension.

A few, a very few, moved away from the site.

Deniken concluded his silent tribute to his close friend and made his vow, the mirror of the one he had given as the train carrying the hideously burned Yarishlov pulled out away from the station, and the one he had repeated on a number of similar occasions, when men under his command were forever confined in enemy soil.

He stood at attention and saluted the turned ground, holding his tribute long enough to repeat the names of those beneath his feet.

Taking a deep breath, he nodded to the waiting Captain as was the agreement on implementing his order.

Two DSHK machine-guns chattered into life, sweeping away those who had gathered to gawk at the internments.

Rifles and sub-machine guns joined in.

Kriks, horrified, shouted and screamed for a cease-fire.

A few men heeded his calls, but were quickly encouraged back to the killing by their own officer and NCOs, or, for a few, by the shouted threats of their divisional commander, Colonel Deniken.

Kriks rushed towards Deniken, screaming his protest.

"What are you doing, man? For the love of the Rodina, stop this madness! Stop it!"

Deniken turned deliberately, his eyes burning with fury and lacking any hint of reason.

He gesticulated at the bloody field in front of him.

"Those bastards put your friend... our friend... in a hospital or worse. They're responsible for this whole fuck up, all of it, so don't tell me to stop firing! I'll kill the bastards every opportunity I get!"

He turned and fired his PPd in the direction of the massacre, emphasising both his point and his lack of control over himself.

Kriks grabbed him.

"What are you doing, man? Stop this insanity! Have you gone mad?"

Deniken brought the sub-machine gun up, crashing it into Kriks' jaw and sending the Praporshchik flying.

"Serzhant!"

The nearest NCO turned and leapt to his Colonel's side.

"Arrest the Praporshchik, remove his weapons, and take him away."

Kriks mouthed a protest that was stifled in blood and broken teeth.

Detailing two men to the duty, the sergeant had the injured Kriks dragged away, as Deniken turned back to oversee the end of the killing.

Soviet soldiers picked their way through the littered corpses, occasionally halting to slide a bayonet home, or issue a coup-de-grace shot.

It is often said that there are always survivors from such massacres, but Freienwalde was an exception.

Seventy-two allied servicemen were executed on the orders of a man driven to the edge by personal loss.

The one man who could have saved him from himself lay in a peasant hut, under guard, being treated for his facial wound, and decidedly disinclined to have anything to do with the murdering colonel ever again.

[Modern day Chociwel was once called Freienwalde.]

The newly arrived units, two reinforced MP platoons allocated from the Corps command, had been assigned to the static defence of the hospital site.

In reality, Hanebury had recognised that the new arrivals were not up to the task of rooting out an experienced enemy unit and, for the matter, neither was the green Captain in charge.

The officer offered no opposition to Hanebury's continued command of the hunt, and accepted the passive role of his units with relative good grace.

The search had commenced early in the morning, when Hanebury led a reconnaissance cum assault on the positions in which they had observed the enemy the previous day.

With the exception of some excrement that might have been human, and traces of blood that could equally be so, the only certain indications of a recent human presence were suitable sized areas of grass that were slightly flatter than others… and a footprint.

The tell-tale marks of the metal studs declaring everything that Hanebury needed to know.

The birds had definitely flown.

Lucifer took the proffered HT set and contacted Stradley.

"Execute Alpha, Execute Alpha, over."

"Roger."

Plan Alpha was the only plan they had, but it had been put together to sweep up the area around the medical facility in the first instance, and then move outwards, embracing the likely area into which the enemy had melted. Trying to put themselves in the enemy's boots, Hanebury and Stradley had decided that the likely area was a large expanse of woodland that ran due south from Bräunisheim, extending some six kilometres, north to south, by five kilometres wide. They would move around the zone, watching out for signs and interrogating any locals they might come across, before methodically reducing the area down, although more troops would be needed to ensure success.

In any case, First Sergeant Hanebury had understood that he needed more help, so the armed medical staff, plus a handful of combat soldiers from amongst the wounded, were added to his force.

Utilising some of the new arrivals, he would be able to establish the picquets necessary for the plan.

He also had assistance from an unexpected but most welcome source.

Whilst not an official Kommando, a handful of German citizens had appeared, offering their services to the hunters.

Initially, Hanebury was perturbed that such things were public knowledge, but moved on immediately; he'd take all the help he could get.

Most of the score of Germans were ex-military, and wore their old uniforms, tactfully altered to remove certain 'devices' from a previous political era.

Most wore medals that marked them as combat veterans.

One had spent his life as a woodsman, and he was already positioned with Stradley's force, along with five of his compatriots.

Another six, including the two WW1 veterans, were kept within Hanebury's force. Initially, Lucifer's thoughts had been to reject the two 'grandfathers', but there was something about the older men, particularly the elder of the two, who proudly wore the 'Pour-le-Mérite' around the neck of a tunic that bore the insignia of the German Empire's 13th Infanterie Regiment.

The remainder were split between the units that would be deployed outside the perimeter of the hospital.

Hanebury's vehicles rallied below the height, and he got his unit mounted in record time, before they moved off, heading for their allocated line of march down Route 1229.

Stradley's force was already heading down the 7312, in the direction of Altheim.

1635 hrs, Saturday, 15th June 1946, the woods, one kilometre northeast of Lonsee, Germany.

Those that were the hunted had regrouped and concealed themselves on the side of a sharp rise that oversaw a small valley, some two hundred metres off the Ettlenscheisserweg, one kilometre north-east of Lonsee.

It was the rally point that Lenz had originally selected, and it proved an excellent spot for him and his men to hide up, although the lack of a close water supply was not in the location's favour. However, there was one only five hundred metres to the southeast, which made the site almost perfect.

Well-concealed by the thick canopy of trees, the undergrowth was lush and welcoming and, despite the numerous small paths used by forest workers, a large area away from the beaten track proved perfect for the Kommando to rest and recuperate.

The report from Weiss regarding the military presence in the camp, and the subsequent foray precisely to the position the

Kommando had occupied was met with silence, although every man was aware that their commander's decision had undoubtedly saved them from a difficult situation.

"Thank you, Unterscharfuhrer. I've set the guard... now get some sleep. We'll move to the southeast when it's dark."

Weiss' men needed no second bidding, and they soon joined the lucky ones from the main body, curled up on soft vegetation, and dreaming of a time when they could sleep in a bed with sheets and pillows.

The old man carrying the saw and axe stumbled and cursed. "Verdammt!"

Lenz, having taken himself off to one side, had fallen into a deep sleep, from which the man's shout had swiftly dragged him.

Gripping his PPSh tightly, he tried to orient himself, seeking the source of the noise, trying to establish the level of threat to his well-being.

Despite his years of service, his heart pounded, making a tangible sound in his throat.

Something broke underfoot, immediately jerking his head off to the right, where a man emerged from behind a large trunk.

He eased the Russian sub-machine gun out of the way and found the handle of his combat knife, a wide flat-bladed and double-edged weapon he had taken from a dead hand in Yugoslavia.

Silence was a key requirement of the Kommando, and he planned to kill the man without a single murmur.

The German woodsman stopped and examined a lofty trunk, clearly assessing everything about the tree.

Finally, he lit up a cigarette, and looked around to choose a felling path.

The man did a double take, noticing Lenz lying in the undergrowth.

Lenz placed a finger to his lips, and stood up, trying to appear as unthreatening as a man wearing a camouflaged jacket and holding a large knife can appear unthreatening.

The woodsman's eyes widened at the SS insignia apparent on Lenz's camouflage jacket, and the other insignia and medals clearly in display where he had opened the jacket up before falling asleep.

Lenz walked forward, looking around in case there was more than one.

"Kamerad, you are local?"

"Yes, yes, Herr Offizier... Bruno Weber... I live just back there..."

The woodsman turned his torso to point at his hamlet, less than a kilometre to the south, his eyes seeking something else in the undergrowth.

Sharp metal protruded from the side of his neck before the woodsman even suspected that Lenz had covered the three metres between them.

The entire blade had made the journey through the man's flesh, the metal buried guard-deep from one side of his neck to the other.

Taking the dead man's weight, Lenz carefully lowered the corpse to the ground as he continued to survey the area.

A figure rose out of nowhere, then another, then there were four.

The last one still kept his rifle lined on his target.

Unterscharfuhrer Uwe Weiss gestured at his men, and they spread out around the killing area, protecting their commander.

The rifleman relaxed and turned outwards, keeping his eyes focussed and his senses alert.

Weiss did not salute; the Kommando was well past such things.

"Hauptsturmfuhrer, you're unhurt?"

Lenz recovered the blade from the woodsman's neck, having to put a steadying foot on the head to get enough purchase to wrench it free.

"I'm unhurt, thank you, Unterscharfuhrer. Explain?"

"We didn't know you were there. We watched him... thought he was walking past, so I decided to let him go... then he didn't, and spotted you."

Weiss shrugged his shoulders.

"He made a bad decision."

Sliding the blade into its scabbard, Lenz could only agree.

Taking a last look at the corpse, he posed the real question.

"Bad luck for him... but will he be missed?"

It was a rhetorical question, his mind already made up to move the Kommando as soon as possible. That would depend on the balance of their physical needs against his interpretation of the likelihood of discovery.

There was also another factor to consider.

"How's Jensen?"

"He's feverish and the leg is undoubtedly infected, Hauptsturmfuhrer. Emmering's had to gag the poor bastard to keep him quiet."

Lenz took a moment to himself.

'He needs medical help... but what can I do...'

His face set.

'You will do what you must, of course!'

"Let's get back and get the boys moving. I want distance between us and this place as quickly as possible. Get your men to hide the body."

Lenz moved away, leaving Weiss to organise the disappearance of the evidence.

The three men made a reasonable scrape in the ground and dragged the corpse into it, shovelling the earth back again, and adding rocks and undergrowth for good measure.

Weiss admired the men's handiwork and decided that the body would not easily be found, at least not until they were well away from the area.

On the verge of leaving the site, he decided on one last look.

Immediately, his senses lit off, the senses of a combat veteran, honed in the hardest schools that war can offer.

He dropped to his knee, bringing his ST44 up in readiness, his eyes searching for some clue to the presence that he felt.

His men responded in kind.

Eyes moved from left to right, ears strained to catch the tiniest sounds, and bodies tensed, ready for immediate action.

There was nothing.

No sound.

No movement.

Nothing.

Weiss rose up and relaxed his grip on the assault rifle.

"I thought I heard something... obviously not. Let's go."

The small group moved off in military fashion, leaving the small space to the trees and the dead.

Peter Weber hardly dared breathe, the tears streaming down his face, but the grief he felt at watching his father murdered controlled, simply to preserve his own life.

He waited for what seemed like a lifetime before heading away, as best as his one leg and crutches would allow, heading to warn his family that the SS were back.

The Kommando was up and ready to move.

Lenz and Emmering finished a private conversation, and Emmering quietly called for the SS soldiers to listen, and detailed an order of march.

Weiss' men were given a few moments to police up their belongings and check their areas for giveaways of their presence, before Emmering ordered the move.

Lenz double-checked the area, finding nothing to betray their recent presence, and quickly moved on to catch-up.

He had debated killing Jensen. Indeed, most men in his position would undoubtedly have advised it, but something had softened inside of him, even if only towards his soldiers, and he had decided on another course of action.

He had sold it to Emmering with ease.

"They simply wouldn't expect it, Oberscharfuhrer."

Kommando Lenz headed north.

All except two men, who, with different orders, moved south.

1831 hrs, Saturday, 15th June 1946, St. Jakob's Kirche, Lonsee-Sinabronn, Germany.

Hanebury watched on as the pathetic attempts of the villagers failed to prevent the fire ripping through the heart of the fifteenth century church.

There was no point in detailing any of his men to assist.

The structure was as good as destroyed before he and his men had arrived, although he understood why the handful of men and women tried so hard to preserve the already damaged structure.

It was a community thing, something he could fully identify with.

Something drew his attention to a different sort of fuss, a one-legged man and a woman, grabbing people, shouting, apparently oblivious to the fire.

Clearly, the two had something serious on their minds, and Hanebury's curiosity was piqued.

137

During their sweep of the countryside, Jim Hanebury had engaged the veteran Heinrich Raubach in conversation, and had struck up quite a rapport with the old man.

He caught Raubach's eye and inclined his head towards the gathering.

Raubach understood immediately and strode off confidently. He was soon embroiled in a flurry of shouts and gesticulation, which mainly consisted of finger pointing at the woods to the north.

He returned quickly, his excitement lending him wings.

"The SS have been spotted."

He grabbed Hanebury's shoulder and pointed to the northern woods.

"In there, about a kilometre... they killed the young man's father... five of them... moved off heading north."

The First Sergeant grabbed his own jaw and looked at the woods, then back at the agitated gathering.

"We sure on this, Heinrich?"

"Certain sure. The boy's a Luftwaffe veteran... lost his leg in Normandy... he knows what an SS man looks like. They've gone back north."

Hanebury suddenly realised something he should have thought of previously.

'The ambulance... the hospital... they're desperate for medical stuff... shit! I've fucked up!'

"They're going back to the hospital."

It was simply a statement, requiring no response.

"Round the boys up, Corporal. Pronto."

Collier called the MPs back to their vehicles as Lucifer grabbed the radio.

"Pennsylvania-six-tw..." he started into a coughing fit as a change in wind direction ensured that the command vehicle was engulfed in rich smoke, "Pennsylvania-six-two, Pennsylvania-six, over."

Stradley responded immediately and took onboard the new information, and Hanebury's instructions.

To the northeast, his unit accelerated back down the road they had come, intent on resuming their over watch positions as quickly as possible.

After a quick exchange with Raubach, one of the Germans was dropped off to bring the villagers into some semblance of order, the man Raubach selected being an ex-Kriegsmarine Petty Officer with a level-head and a loud voice.

138

Within two minutes, Hanebury's men were back in the saddle and racing north.

The two SS troopers who had set fire to the church had long since vanished back into the woods.

1907 hrs, Saturday, 15th June 1946, 74th Surgical Hospital, Bräunisheim, Germany.

The radio had alerted the hospital defenders to the possibility... actually, the probability that the enemy was coming back their way.

The additional information that this was possibly an old SS unit left over from the last war caused a lot of concern.

Throughout the hospital complex, the defenders came alive and wished the sun to hang in the sky for a bit longer.

Most gripped their weapons more tightly, and they were right to worry.

SS Kommando Lenz had plunged back through the forest, determined to take advantage of any distraction started by the detachment sent south, and determined to get the medicines they needed, for the group, and for Jensen in particular.

During the march, Emmering and Lenz had discussed the possibilities of leaving the delirious soldier for Allied doctors to tend, but their ingrained comradeship, SS code, and lack of faith in any Allied good treatment, dictated that Jensen would be with them until the end, whichever end that would be.

Stealing a medic became a priority and, as they had moved back towards the hospital, they discussed how best to do the job.

Allowing his men to take a rest, Lenz and his two senior NCOs moved to a position from which they could observe the site, but avoided the position that they had occupied before.

Their previous plan had been to use the terrain and sweep around to the west, and it still looked good, although the obvious presence of alert armed men on the hospital's perimeter was an unwelcome change to cater for.

None the less, they were sure that whatever distraction Birtles and Kellerman had enacted in Lonsee-Sinabronn would keep any other elements looking in the other direction, at least long enough to do what they needed to do in Bräunisheim.

Lenz, Emmering, and Weiss had forgotten a couple of the simple lessons of war.

It is not a good idea for you to supply the answers to your own questions.

Things are not always what they seem.

Perhaps it was understandable, as the SS soldiers had been fighting everyone they came across since May 1945, killing Americans, Russians, and Americans again, as the armies see-sawed back and forth.

The Kommando had moved many kilometres from its starting point, and seen men lost throughout the fields and woods of Southern Germany.

Regardless of how tired they were, they were bad mistakes to make.

Time played its part in what happened next.

Speed was an issue, as in all military operations, but Lenz also wanted to be away as quickly as possible.

The attack would be timed for the initial hours of darkness, to allow them the maximum amount of time to escape the locale before enemy security units arrived.

Therefore Lenz elected to move his men to the assault point in the evening light; not ideal, but necessary.

From their final position, and with the twilight, they would be able to better assess the target and the approaches to it.

Using the terrain, he considered that he could move unseen, certainly by the defenders of the hospital complex.

Having let his men recover from the speedy move north, Lenz harried them into order and sent them scurrying up a roadside ditch, led by Weiss, with the rearguard commanded by Emmering.

Everything went smoothly until the ditch petered out at the junction of the lane and Route 7312.

The whole Kommando simply melted into the ditch, as hand signals made their way from man to man.

Lenz made his way forward, sliding in beside Weiss.

In whispers and using signals, Weiss showed his commander the problem.

Sat on the edge of the wood ahead, set into the rising slope, was a 'something' that had attracted Weiss' experienced eye.

Carefully, Lenz accepted the binoculars and homed in on the unusual construction, just in time to see a small movement, betraying the presence of an enemy.

Closer examination brought the sight of a .30cal machine-gun barrel… and a waft of cigarette smoke.

Lenz handed the binoculars back, and gently gripped his NCO's shoulder.

"Good work, Unterscharfuhrer."

Sparing a quick look at his map, and checking that his view of the terrain supported the printed information, Lenz laid a quick plan.

SS troopers Schipper and Zimmerman were given a quick brief and, having divested themselves of anything remotely military, disappeared back down the ditch.

The remainder of the Kommando stayed alert, eyes fixed on their surroundings... watching... waiting...

To the second, Schipper and Zimmerman emerged from the woods to the south of the US position, draped over each other, laughing and giggling, staggering like men who had enjoyed a little too much of what the local hostelry had to offer.

Lenz switched his attention to the enemy position, where three heads were now clearly defined, and all focused on the noisy new arrivals.

SS Hauptsturmfuhrer Lenz clicked his fingers once and, with a simple palm movement, sent death on its way.

Four killers rose and ran at top speed, reducing the distance between them and their targets rapidly, their crouched run less defined with each step forwards, their weapons held tightly, ready for immediate use.

The lead figure, Emmering, threw himself forward as a head appeared to turn, the American's mouth opening to shout a warning.

The rest of the murder squad fell upon the distracted GIs, and two seconds later, four beating hearts were forever stilled.

Like the professionals they were, the four SS soldiers took station in the position, scanning the countryside for threats.

The two drunks had 'sobered up' and met up with a comrade laden with their kit, the whole Kommando moving forward, across the road, heading for the relative safety of the woods.

The sound of the heavy engine reached all ears simultaneously, and the SS soldiers hit the ground, disappeared into whatever cover they could find, or continued to run for a distant position of safety.

It mattered not, and the annihilation of SS Kommando Lenz began.

1944 hrs, Saturday, 15th June 1946, Route 7312, southwest of Bräunisheim, Germany.

"Shit! They're the krauts! Let 'em have it!"

Hanebury grabbed the firing handles of the .30cal and let rip, the area around the bunker throwing up grass and earth as the bullets ripped through the air, and occasionally, flesh.

One of the four killers flopped to the floor, the top of his head waving like a bin lid over an empty skull cavity, the impact of three bullets sufficient to empty his head of anything remotely brain-like.

Emmering flew backwards, his left shoulder ruined by the passage of two more of Hanebury's bullets.

The M3 halftrack's heavier .50cal was working, and the SS Kommandos started to fall, as the gunner concentrated on those still running for cover.

Lenz screamed orders at his men, and then screamed in pain, as a heavy bullet blew his left hand off at the wrist.

A number of his men were down hard, but the others were starting to fight back, and the .30cal in the bunker position lashed out at the speeding vehicles.

Lewis Collier lost control of the command jeep as a .30cal and an SVT40 bullet struck simultaneously, one in each shoulder.

The jeep turned lazily and the front offside wheel stuck in a rut, rolling the vehicle and throwing the five occupants in all directions.

Collier's left leg was snapped as the jeep's windshield rolled across it, before the vehicle messily came to rest on top of one of the SS Kommandos' bodies.

Hanebury, weaponless and in pain, the bones of his considerably shortened left arm protruding through a shattered wrist, rolled for cover as best he could, as Schipper and Zimmerman tried to finish the job the crash had started.

Raubach, still in possession of his rifle, took a steady aim and put a round into Zimmerman's chest.

With a disbelieving look, he dropped to his knees, his chest welling with the vital fluids of life.

Unable to speak, he lost consciousness and dropped forward onto his face, almost like a man of faith at prayer.

He was dead before Raubach's second round threw him to one side.

Hanebury dragged himself in beside the old German, his face grimacing with pain.

Acknowledging his presence with a nod, Lucifer sought and found the radio, and quickly determined that it was of no use, its damage clear and very terminal.

He risked a look at the firefight and grunted with satisfaction as his remaining vehicles took the fight to the enemy.

A German dragging a makeshift stretcher was hacked down, falling backwards onto the man he was trying to rescue.

The casualty, undoubtedly the man who needed the medicines Hanebury concluded, tried to drag himself off the litter into cover.

The halftrack swept through the SS position.

Hanebury winced as first the heavy wheels and then the tracks flattened the wounded man.

Jensen did not die.

But he did scream... and scream... his abdomen and pelvis smashed and crushed by the halftrack's passing.

The Horch 1A had dropped off to one side, and its MG42, sounding like the proverbial ripping of cloth, ripped through three men in the tree line, killing each man with a minimum of four bullet hits.

Jensen's screams were still the loudest thing on the battlefield and, if anything, grew louder as more feeling returned to his shattered body.

Hanebury scrabbled around for a weapon he could use with one good hand. He found his Thompson, bent almost at right angles at the magazine port, its wooden stock split, making it unusable.

A Garand lay invitingly close, but was irretrievable, the weight of the jeep holding it in position.

One of the Winchester 12 gauge shotguns stuck in the earth like a marker, and Hanebury shuffled across to grab it, clearing the impacted earth from its muzzle to make it fit for purpose.

As he and Raubach were distracted, the Horch took some heavy hits, killing two of Hanebury's men, and causing lazy flames to work their way through the engine compartment.

Lenz moved as quickly as he could, dropping behind a piece of cover here or a corpse there, trying to get close to Jensen, who's tortured wails were increasing.

The halftrack's ma-deuce churned up the ground around his feet, ripping off a boot heel and taking a chunk out of his right calf.

The Kommando leader fell into an inviting hollow and, head in the earth, examined his options... option... to fight... surrender was not an option.

Half his men were down, if not more, but the enemy had suffered too.

The screaming from the destroyed Jensen grew deafening, and Lenz determined to end the soldier's suffering.

Sliding up to the edge of the hollow, he gripped his PPSh, steadier on the earth, and fired a short burst, shattering the wounded man's skull and neck.

Jensen died instantly.

Incensed, and close to losing control, Lenz rose up and yelled at his men.

Almost instantly, the SS soldiers got lucky.

Art Nave, driving the M3, took a bullet in the head. The ricochet hit the side of the vision slit and ploughed into his right temple. Nave went out like a light and the half-track drove into a tree, sending the occupants flying.

A Soviet grenade fell into the rear compartment, killing one MP and a German helper, and putting the rest out of the fight.

Lenz sensed victory, and urged his men forward.

Weiss, leading the surge, dropped to the ground, his ruined neck spurting blood with every weakening beat of his heart.

Trying to sit up, Weiss tried to shout at the men moving towards him, the very effort of turning his head causing his damaged jugular to give way, causing catastrophic blood loss.

His eyes glazed over and he died, his face still displaying a snarl as it thumped into the ground.

By the jeep, Raubach had missed the SS man he had selected as a target, and worked the bolt on his weapon, seeking to make sure of his kill with the next shot.

He ignored the stings as a bullet struck a wooden box from the jeep's load, sending splinters into his face, neck, and ears.

He breathed out and made sure the sight was on, and pulled the trigger with the calmness of a man who has seen all that war has to offer.

Oberscharfuhrer Emmering had just set himself up behind the .30cal as Raubach's bullet took him in the chest, robbing the SS NCO of his strength in an instant.

Julius Emmering fell back onto the body of the man he had recently slaughtered and, alone and scared, started the inevitable journey to darkness and the nothingness of what was to come.

Lenz saw his main man go down, hard on the heels of Weiss' death, and screamed in anger, putting a burst into the old German soldier, and sending Raubach flying with the heavy impacts.

Having killed Weiss and two others, Corporal Rickard turned his attentions to the lunatic enemy officer who seemed to be firing at the destroyed jeep.

The Springfield sniper rifle barked, and Lenz flew backwards with the impact.

Rickard sought other targets.

Out of the corner of his eye, he saw the shape and rolled instinctively.

The vengeful SS soldier responded with equal quickness, and grabbed Rickard's arm, slashing at the extended flesh with a cruelly sharp knife.

Rickard screamed as the blade bit and opened his arm almost to the bone.

The SS soldier rolled to slice at the American's exposed neck, his head coming to rest against the barrel of Rickard's Colt, which immediately discharged a single round that sent the German's grey matter over the earth behind him.

The dead weight of the body held Rickard in place, and he struggled hard to get back into the action.

Meanwhile, Lenz had reloaded, the empty magazine tossed carelessly to one side, the new 71 round container in place.

The six remaining SS Kommando soldiers, moved towards the Horch and halftrack, intent on carrying out Lenz's orders, namely to kill survivors and quickly grab anything of use.

Lenz himself went for Hanebury's command vehicle, the PPSh held one-handed, ready for any threat.

As Lenz moved behind the jeep, a new force entered the arena, one that swung the balance of firepower in favour of the MP platoon, and one that sealed the SS Kommando's fate.

The M8 Greyhound crashed through some modest hedgerow and started firing at the enemy to its front.

A halftrack quickly followed it, but moved out to the left flank, bringing its own .50cal into use.

A jeep and another half-track followed, completing the group commanded by Stradley, and effecting the reunion of Lucifer's platoon.

Schipper was first to go down, as heavy bullets hammered into his torso, flinging him aside like a rag doll.

The others quickly followed, with nowhere to run and nowhere to hide, they chose death, and death obliged them all.

Lenz watched as the remainder of his command was destroyed before his eyes, and his anger overcame him.

145

The PPSh lashed out at the halftracks, the jeep, and the armoured car.

Not without success.

Stradley took two rounds in the upper back, both of which punched out just below his collarbones. He dropped noiselessly onto the seat of the halftrack as it turned away.

Three others were hit by bullets from the vengeful Lenz.

The SS officer ducked behind the overturned jeep, stepping on the wounded Raubach.

Lenz straight-armed the sub-machine gun's butt into Raubach's face, smashing bone and teeth with real savagery.

Hanebury pulled the trigger, the muzzle of his pump action shotgun no more than eight feet from his target... and missed completely.

Holding the heavy weapon in one hand was tricky, and the motion of pulling the trigger, along with his fatigue, had been enough.

Lucifer prepared himself.

He had seen Stradley go down, and could only imagine how many of his boys had been lost to the piece of shit that now turned on him.

This was the man that had killed the medics...

Killed the Russians...

Set fire to the church...

Killed the old woodsman...

Killed how many countless others...

Lenz screamed at the American sergeant lying by the jeep and brought the PPSh up, aiming it in one simple manoeuvre.

He pulled the trigger.

A single bullet only, which took Hanebury in the midriff, causing him to moan with pain.

When Lenz had hammered the gun into Raubach's face, he had displaced the magazine enough to jam the feed of the next round, thus saving Hanebury's life.

Two bullets hit Lenz in the back, and he was thrown at Hanebury, ending up on his face right beside the wounded NCO.

Raubach had been responsible for the one that had entered Lenz's anus and burst out through his genitalia, ruining the SS officer for the rest of his tenure on life.

At the same moment, Rickard had put his own bullet through Lenz's back, destroying the right lung on its way through to the open air on the other side.

Hanebury moved himself up onto his elbows, and prodded the babbling German onto his side.

146

Lucifer looked at the man, the eyes still glowing with fanaticism and hate, even though death was rapidly approaching.

Shouts indicated more US troops arriving, as medics and other MPs from the hospital gained the field and started to tend to the wounded and dying.

A young medic stopped by Hanebury, who shrugged off the ministrations, intimidating the green soldier as much with his injuries as his scowl.

"Fuck you, Amerikan... fuck...," Lenz descended into a coughing fit, bringing fresh crimson blood to his lips.

Bringing his breathing under control, Lenz pushed himself upright, or as best he could, and spat bloody phlegm at Hanebury.

"Ich schwöre dir, Adolf Hitler, als Führer und Kanzler des Deutschen Reiches..."

Hanebury looked around, taking in the terrible scenes... of the medics tending to his wounded men... or covering those beyond help...

"Treue und tapferkeit. Wir geloben dir..."

Raubach fell back into unconsciousness, his face a bloody mess of flesh, bone and teeth...

"Und den von dir bestimmten vorgesetzten gehorsam bis in den tod..."

Lucifer's face went blank as his decision was made. His hand released its hold on the shotgun, and the Winchester dropped down through his fingers, his hand suddenly shifted from trigger to charger.

Not taking his eyes off Lenz, Hanebury made a sharp motion with his good hand, chambering a shell.

The charging of a pump-action shotgun has a very particular sound, one that carries no good news for anyone at the business end of the weapon.

None the less, there was no fear in Lenz's voice, or in his eyes... just hate... and malice... and fanaticism.

"So wahr mir Gott helfe! Seig heil!..."

Hanebury held the weapon steady as a rock, his hand back on the trigger, the muzzle placed nicely, balanced on the German's bottom lip and tongue.

It didn't make for clear speech, but Lenz still tried.

"Seeg Heeeiill..."

"Fuck you!"

The single report drew many eyes, and the young medic turned, took one look, and violently deposited the contents of his stomach over both the wrecked jeep and the unconscious Collier.

The muzzle of the Winchester stayed in place, supported by the lower jaw of what had once been a head.

Hanebury nodded, the gun slipping from his grasp as his strength suddenly sapped and he became light-headed.

"You'll kill no more of my fucking boys now, you bastard."

He dropped gently to the ground and passed into unconsciousness, his mouth trying to master more words for the destroyed corpse of SS Hauptsturmfuhrer Artur Lenz.

"Handy hock, you fucking Krauts"

The medical infantryman practised his recently acquired German.

The two men in brown looked at him with great concern as they slowly raised their hands.

"C'mon, you kraut fucks, handy hock!"

"It's Hände hoch, you idiot."

He looked at the MP Corporal and spat derisorily.

"Yeah well, what-fucking-ever, corp'ral…handy hock, you sons of bitches."

He looked back at the MP to see if his bravado was having an effect, but saw something else written large upon the man's face.

"Cover them… don't shoot them… ok?"

Not waiting for a reply, the MP was off at the run, returning quickly with a Sergeant from his unit.

"Reckon you're right at that, Smitty."

The senior NCO strode forward, addressing the taller of the two men.

"And who the fuck are you then, pal?"

His question was greeted with a blank expression, as Nikki could speak no English.

The sergeant turned his attention on the other man, conscious of something about the ragged uniforms that he couldn't quite work out.

"What's your name then, eh?"

Mikki, slowly dropped his hands, watched every millimetre of the way by a growing number of American onlookers.

"I are Mayor General Mikhail Gordeevich Sakhno."

He nodded towards Nikki.

"You am Polkovnik Nikanor Klimentovich Davydov."

Lenz had kept the two Soviet officers alive since the ambush in Ainau Woods, all those months previously, although they had expected death every single day.

The two were swept up in the move back to the hospital, where the wounded received the best of care, and the two former senior commanders of the 10th Tank Corps ate their first decent meal since August the previous year.

Army intelligence personnel arrived, and the two Soviet officers were quickly whisked away to another place, where impatient men waited with important questions.

[Author's note - The exploits of SS Kommando Lenz exceeded the efforts of any other Werewolf unit, or, as is often suggested, all other Werewolf units put together.

Without a doubt, the feat of keeping the unit active and fighting-fit was unique in Werewolf history, and SS Kommando Lenz proved a major thorn in the side of the Soviet forces in occupation.

However, true to his oath and mission, Lenz opposed all foreigners on his soil and, unlike a number of other clandestine units, waged war on Allied and Soviet soldiers equally.

Their war ended on 15th June 1946.

Only Emmering and Schipper survived the battle, although Emmering did not survive the night, dying of his wounds on the stroke of midnight, despite the best efforts of the hospital surgery team.

Schipper regained sufficient health to be tried for his membership of the SS Kommando. He was hanged as a war criminal on 24th December 1947 for his part in the murder of Bruno Weber, as witnessed by the man's son and heir, and for his collective responsibility for the slaying of ambulance personnel on the road to Bräunisheim.

Lenz and the rest of his men lie somewhere in the valley to the southwest of Bräunisheim, buried in an unmarked communal grave on the final day of their resistance.

The debate on honouring him and his troopers has now faded away, bringing no positive result for the family and friends of the fallen members of SS Kommando Lenz. A temporary effort, built near Ainau, was heavily vandalised within a week of its erection.

In the end, it would appear that their countrymen would prefer to forget the efforts of Lenz and his men.

The 2nd Special Platoon, 16th Armored Military Police Battalion, 16th US Armored Division was not reconstituted, and the surviving personnel found themselves distributed between the remaining units in the 16th Division.

Hanebury, Collier, Shufeldt, and Nave were all evacuated stateside, and none would ever actively soldier again, although Nave remained in service until the war's end, and Hanebury went on to a career in US law enforcement, achieving the position of Chief of Police before retiring.

In 2016, the surviving members of the unit will gather in the village of Bräunisheim for what will probably be their last reunion.

Corporal Arthur Nave [93], First Sergeant Richard Shufeldt [96], and Captain Rodger Stradley [96] are the last survivors of Lucifer's platoon.

Hateful to me as are the gates of hell, is he who, hiding one thing in his heart, utters another.

Homer

Chapter 157 – THE MASKIROVKA

1212 hrs, Monday 17th June 1946, the Black Sea, between Novorossiysk and Divnomorskoye, USSR.

The engineer looked smug and questioned the naval officer once more.

"Satisfied now, Comrade Kapitan?"

Captain Second Rank Mikhail Stepanovich Kalinin was partially satisfied that the site was clearly fit for purpose, and partially annoyed that he had not been able to wipe the constant smug look off the abominable civilian's face by finding it.

"It's well hidden, I'll give you that, comrade."

The obnoxious man chuckled and gave the order to put in to shore.

"We shall impress you even more when we get inside, Comrade Kapitan."

The launch moved close into the land, but Kalinin maintained his close watch, occasionally raising his binoculars to examine a straight line, or a curved one, anything that could give the base some form to prying eyes.

He saw nothing of note, save nature flourishing, untackled by man.

The boat grounded and the engineer led the way, splashing his way up to the beach, before turning to wait for Kalinin, the triumph of his achievement writ large on his face.

Kalinin dropped into the water and looked around him, assuming that the boat had grounded near to the site that was the object of the morning's search.

The old boathouse caught his eye immediately, as it had on the run in, and he used the proximity to examine it more closely.

It was simply an old boathouse.

Morsin, the engineer, waited patiently as Kalinin used the steadiness of the beach to scan the coastline to the north and south.

'Nothing.'

"Perhaps you would like to look from up there, Comrade Kapitan?"

Morsin indicated the hill and the rough stone steps set in its front edge.

By way of an answer, Kalinin set off with a will, determined to leave the civilian floundering in his wake.

Reaching the top first, the submariner took in his surroundings, first with the naked eye and then with the powerful naval binoculars.

He had been part of the planning of the facility, so had some idea of what he was looking for, the size and extent of it, but there was nothing even close... and yet here it was... apparently.

The engineer arrived, seemingly on death's door from his climbing exertions.

He placed his hands on his knees and took his time to recover, every second of which Kalinin used to find the damned facility.

Reluctantly, he dropped his binoculars to his chest.

"I have to say, Comrade Engineer Morsin, the camouflage is excellent. I cannot see it, I cannot sense it... there seems to be nothing at all of interest for kilometres around."

Morsin held up his hand as he gulped in volumes of oxygen.

"It is how we were ordered, Comrade. There... should be nothing to alert Allied observation, either from... the air or from the sea."

Kalinin nodded, happy that, wherever it was, the facility would not be detected.

"Fine, the job is clearly excellent, Comrade Engineer. Now, let us go and inspect the damn thing. Show me... where is it?"

Morsin laughed and pointed out to sea, slowly turning and sweeping his single finger across the horizon.

Enjoying his moment, he prescribed a full circumference before coming to a halt, looking at the naval officer, and pointing to the ground.

"You're standing on it, Comrade Kapitan."

Kalinin had seen the inside before, but only in drawings and a scale model that had long since been burned in the courtyard of the Black Sea Fleet's headquarters in Sevastopol.

In the flesh, the construction was more impressive than he had imagined.

Much of the work had been done during the interwar years and on into the Patriotic War when, given the impending demise of Nazi Germany and her cohorts, work on the special facility had been halted.

The imperatives and requirements of the new conflict, and, in particular, Operation Raduga, meant that the inoffensively named 'Vinogradar Young Communists Sailing Club' was reborn and work continued.

The whole floor area was flat, broken by two types of constructions.

Firstly there were steel pillars, rising to the rock ceiling, offering the additional support needed to the hewn rock curve that ran for nearly two hundred metres, side to side.

Secondly were the bays, six of them, each twenty metres wide and one hundred and fifty metres long, two dry and containing the parts of submarines under construction, the other four wet and ready to receive whatever was allowed to proceed through the huge doors that protected the entrance.

The six bays were slightly angled in, so as to present their openings at a better angle to the entrance.

Had Kalinin been able to work it out, he would have seen the old boathouse sat across the join of the two doors, obscuring their presence as had been intended.

The Captain moved around, observing the sections that had been transported from the Baltic to the Black Sea being put together by the best quality ship builders the Soviet Union could find.

The two type XXIs required no less than the best.

Elsewhere, the offices, stores, fuel tanks, and armouries that would make the base into an operational covert facility were being made ready by different but equally skilled men.

One tunnel was already guarded by NKVD soldiers, and Kalinin, lacking the necessary authority, was refused entry.

He did not push the matter, for he had seen what lay beyond in model form and had little need to see it in the flesh, at least not until it was occupied by the weapons of Raduga.

In the antechamber, to the side of the XXI berths, he could not help but admire the sleek forms waiting silently, their potential unrealised, their deadly task ahead of them, his part known only to him and a handful of others.

Morsin slapped him on the back, a comradely slap that Kalinin did not in the slightest welcome. None the less, he felt invigorated by what he had just seen, so he let it go with a smile.

"Beautiful aren't they, Comrade Kapitan."

The engineer looked up at the quiet sentinels and sighed.

"How I wish I had designed and built them. I'd have the Hero Award for it, I tell you. Anyway, they're ours and I'm sure that our glorious leaders have found a way to use them properly. Now... come... lunch with the facility commander awaits."

Kalinin turned away to follow in the hungry Morsin's wake, but risked one further look at the deadly weapons.

'One day soon, you will fly for the Rodina!'

He followed on quickly, leaving the silent V2s behind him.

1400 hrs, Monday 17th June 1946, Camp Rose, on the Meer van Echternach, Luxembourg.

Camp Rose was, as far as any enquiry would reveal, a medical staging facility, through which wounded men were returned to active units after additional training.

That was, in fact, its main job, and explained the comings and goings of experienced soldiers.

The camp spread itself down the west side of the lake, seemingly clinging to every open space from the forest's edge to the waterside.

However, there was another part, a secret part, that dwelt inside the woods and occupied a clearing that could not be observed by accident, and that clearing held the men destined to serve as members of Operational Group Steel, a joint US Army/OSS project.

The concept was to reinstate the ability of the US Army to project force behind enemy lines, and therefore train a unit of battalion size that could operate by itself, in conditions of low supply and support, and trained in stealth warfare and all that entailed.

To that end, the instructors were the very best, or worst, depending on who you asked, drawn from the SAS, Commandos, and US Rangers.

The group was so secret that it had not called for volunteers, but had quietly cherry-picked men from units across the spectrum of the US forces. Resistance from some unit commanders had met with secret and unimpeachable orders, supported by assurances of an unhealthy interest in their career progression, interest of a type not necessarily conducive to advancement.

One group of men recently arrived at Camp Steel was on parade, ready to be given some sort of idea what hellhole they had landed in.

The veteran soldiers, ranked from private to lieutenant, understood enough to know that, whatever it was, it would result in going in harm's way.

The array of divisional badges was impressive, with very few of the experienced European divisions being unrepresented amongst the one hundred and thirty men in the group.

As the murmuring rose, the paraded men were brought to attention by a sharp barked command, issued by a Commando RSM who clearly would not have their best intentions at heart.

The four lines came crisply to the correct position and all eyes followed the prowling RSM, whose moustache was waxed to points that almost reached his ears.

Having given piercing eye contact to as many of the 'yanks' as his time allowed, the martinet returned to the main office building and came to attention, throwing up the most immaculate of immaculate salutes to the emerging officers, who returned the honour as best they could.

The three men marched forward in easy style, coming to a halt in a triangle in front of the group.

The full colonel nodded to the RSM, who brought the men to the parade rest position, or 'stand at ease', as he shouted it.

"Men, thank you for coming here today. I know you're here blind, and had no choice. We were the ones with choice, and we chose each of you."

The colonel relaxed into his speech and put his hands on his hips.

"You ain't here to polish your boots or do rifle drill. You're here to learn how to soldier in a special operations unit. We ain't being put together for fun... we'll be used... and we'll be ready for anything the generals ask of us. Keep your noses clean... no old soldier tricks... the instructors know them all and probably invented most of them... work hard, train hard, fight hard. We'll ask no more of you."

He smiled disarmingly.

"Now, if any of you don't wanna stay after you've been here two weeks, then you'll be able to go back to your own units... no questions... but you won't be able to talk about this place or the men you leave behind. That's the deal and it ain't negotiable."

Coming back to a less relaxed position, he continued.

"Your platoon officers will now detail you to your new units, thirty-two men each, and then you will be assigned to a

155

barracks. As of now, you are men of Zebra Company, and the last company to be established in this battalion. Today, you'll settle in. Chow is at 1800. Your platoon officers will brief you on camp rules. There will be no infractions."

He smiled, the face suddenly becoming less friendly and welcoming.

"Reveille will be at 0530. That is all."

He nodded to the Commando NCO, whose voice literally made some of the combat veterans jump.

"ATTEN-SHUN!"

The colonel nodded in satisfaction and saluted the group, turning to his 2IC, who, in turn, saluted and took over.

"Right men. The following officers will come and stand in front of me. Lieutenants Garrimore, Hässler, and Fernetti."

The three selected officers doubled to the front and took up station as directed, each separate from the other by a dozen paces.

As further directed, they raised their hands and shouted a number.

"One!"

"Two!"

"Three!"

"Right men, when your name is called, fall in in column of your marker at the attention."

The Major consulted his clipboard and made a mark each time a man answered his name and fell in.

"Acron one... Ambrose three ... Barry three... Berconi two..."

The colonel watched through his office window, satisfied with the ongoing process, as he shared a coffee with the commander of Zebra Company, a man who he knew little of, but whose reputation had preceded him, a reputation much enhanced by the Medal of Honor that the Captain had earned in the early days of the new European War.

A handful of men remained to be called forward and the company commander took his leave, ready to go round each barracks and introduce himself.

"Rideout one... Rosenberg two... Ulliman one... Vernon one ... White two... Yalla three... Stalin two... fucking Stalin? You gotta be kidding me!"

A tough looking corporal doubled to the end of the second platoon line, his face set, having undoubtedly heard it all before.

The Major let it drop.

"1st Platoon," he extended his arm, pointing at an empty barracks, "That's your new home."

He repeated the exercise for the two other platoons and watched as they doubled away.

Hässler, as befitted his rank, pulled one of the two single rooms available.

After a short 'discussion', a senior sergeant from the Big Red One ceded the other single bunk to Master Sergeant Rosenberg, leaving a trail of bloody spots behind, his nose leaking the red fluid after receiving an argument-winning tap from Rosenberg forehead.

Having stowed his kit swiftly, Rosenberg made the short trip to the other room, stopping briefly to observe the men in the main bunk area, noting that they had sorted themselves and their kit out with the swiftness of veterans.

He entered without knocking.

"So, what does the First Lieutenant think about this fucking outfit, eh?"

Hässler shrugged and rolled onto the bed, testing the mattress.

"Beds comfy enough, accommodation is sound... lovely view, Rosie" he smiled mischievously and pointed at the window, through which green forest could be seen in all directions.

"If the bacon's good, I'd say we'll be fine here. It's what the bastards decide to do with us, or where they send us, that worries me."

"Same old shtick. Why always with the bacon, eh?"

Outside came a call they could not ignore.

"ATTEN-SHUN!"

They both went for the door and ran straight into the British RSM, whose unblinking eyes carved through them like a red-hot poker through butter.

"Get fallen in, Sergeant... you too, Sir."

The barracks was at attention, lined down each side, and the two friends joined the formation, every man's eyes fixed straight ahead and focussed on something a million miles away.

A slow but measured step broke the silence and, through their peripheral vision, they were aware that a shadow had entered through the end door, a shadow of some considerable size, for the light was all but removed as it came closer.

157

It was the company commander, in his best uniform, the Medal of Honor ribbon plain for all to see, giving him authority well over his rank of Captain.

In any case, the man was built like a mountain and was solid rippling muscle, and, as such, any confrontation was to be avoided.

"Ben Zona!"

The RSM was straight in Rosenberg's face.

"Did you say something, Sergeant?"

"No... err... well... yes, I did, Sarge... I mean..."

"You will call me Sarnt-Major. Call me sarge once more and I'll rip whatever bits the rabbi left you clear off... do I make myself clear, Sergeant?"

"Yes, Sergeant Major."

The RSM moved to one side, only to be replaced by the towering form of the company commander.

Hässler now caught the officer's eye and nearly followed Rosenberg onto the RSM's shit list.

The smile was wide and the teeth were white.

"Well, what we have here then? Don't I know you from somewhere?"

They knew better than to answer, and in any case, no answer was required by the man in front of them.

Tsali Sagonegi Yona of the Aniyunwiya Tribe, named as Cherokee by the Creek Indians, named as Captain Charley Bluebear by the US Army, and known, both jokingly and seriously, as Moose, was that man.

He had pleaded for a return to combat and, by dint of his award, had been heeded, and given a position in the new unit.

Bluebear had personally asked for Hässler and Rosenberg in his company, something that, again, he was not denied.

The pair of them had seen the things before but, as the Captain moved up and down the lines, the tomahawk and battle knife were in prominent positions on the webbing belt, and had the desired effect, the veterans who had heard of the combats at Rottenbauer and Barnstorf shivered involuntarily, as the man of legend walked up and down.

Charlie Bluebear had changed, the two could see that. It remained to see if it was into something they would like as much as the man who had boarded the aircraft all those months ago.

"Men, we have plenty time to get to know each other. There is much to do. Little time to do it. Weapons inspection at 1700. Sargeant Majah."

The RSM had long since stopped cringing at the Cherokee's efforts to say his rank, and simply saluted the departing officer.

"Right... you heard the man. Weapons inspection parade will be outside this barracks at 1700 sharp. Full kit. Any infringements will result in loss of privileges..."

RSM Ferdinand Sunday stopped and stooped, placing his face level with Corporal Zorba.

"Loss of privileges, in this instance, means forfeiture of access to the mess hall which, in your case, might mean you lose more fucking height, soldier!"

Zorba's eyes blazed but he kept his own counsel.

Sunday marched smartly to the entrance and turned, slamming his feet down like cannon fire.

"Dis-miss!"

The men set to cleaning their weapons, amidst chatter ranging from going AWOL, through to murdering the fucking British bastard.

Sixteen men missed their meal that evening, some for the tiniest infractions, but their comrades found enough space in their pockets to smuggle food back into barracks, something that did not escape the sharp eyes of either Bluebear or Sunday.

It was expected and desirable, the comradeship in adversity already pulling them together into a tight unit.

They would need every ounce of togetherness to get them through the rigorous training ahead.

1800 hrs, Monday 17th June 1946, CP, 71st Infantry Brigade, Lohmühlenstrasse U-Bahn station, Hamburg, Germany.

Brigadier Haugh was grim-faced.

There was no way he could wrap this attack up in pretty ribbons and pass it off as a cakewalk.

None of his experienced officers would buy it for a moment.

It would be a total nightmare.

71st Brigade had already taken a heavy hit, hammering through the Soviet defences as they strove to destroy the Soviet pocket and permit the port to begin resupplying the Allied armies.

In Wandsbek, they had ground to a halt, until Allied air forces took a hand, reducing the area in an attack of great ferocity.

159

Fig # 185 - Opposing forces at Hamburg 17th June 1946.

Opposing forces,

Hamburg, 17th June, 1946

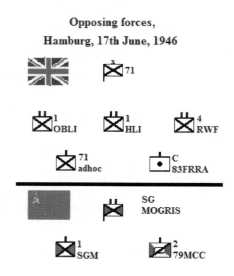

Fighting in Barmbek, Eilbek, Uhlenhorst, and Hamm drained the fighting battalions, although they gave a good account of themselves.

But it had been St Georg that had proved the costliest of all.

The 1st Oxfordshire and Buckinghamshire Light Infantry had been smashed in an unexpected combination of heavy defence and counter-attack, that left the battalion leaderless and below 40% effective strength.

The absence of their commander, Lieutenant Colonel Henry Howard, was keenly felt, and Haugh spared a silent moment to wish the badly wounded man well.

"Right, gentlemen. Thank you for coming. I know you and your men are tired, but we must press on, and Uncle Joe's boys are equally at their wits end, and without supply and reinforcement."

He leant over the map, encouraging the ensemble into the same action.

"The General wants us to have Altstadt under our control by the morning."

"Did he say which morning, Sir, only I have a request in for a spot of leave?"

The tired laughter gave everyone a lift.

Rory MacPherson was always a wag, but his humour had been slightly forced and deliberate on this occasion.

The 1st Battalion, Highland Light Infantry, had taken their own fair share of punishment.

His tam o'shanter was gone, replaced by a grubby bandage.

The product of the head wound remained on his only battledress, the rest of his private belongings somewhere in the divisional train outside of the German city.

His trews showed all the signs of having been trampled by rabid camels, but he was there and fighting fit, if not tired beyond words.

"Thank you for that, Rory. Alas, I will not have time for leave requests before this show kicks off. Now…"

Haugh drew a few lines on the map and added unit marks.

"I'm deliberately not going to use the waterside on this one. You all know why."

The last time the brigade had bared a flank to open water, it had cost them dearly, so Haugh was not having any repeat.

"Rory's jocks will take and hold this area, but you will anchor yourself on the Zollkanal to the left, and you will take and hold the Grimm Bridge here. No moving over Fischmarkt without orders. That's phase one. Phase two and you move up to here… and here. These bridges are long gone, but do watch out on the flanks in case. Cremon, up to Reimerstweite, that's end of phase two. Phase three… well, we'll call that as we see it, but I suspect that will be for another time. Clear, Rory?"

MacPherson checked his recall and nodded.

"Crystal, Sir."

"Your unit boundary will be Steinstrasse, and for phase two, Börsenbrucke, for which you also have responsibility."

"Terry, your special unit will take this line here, between Steinstrasse and Mönckebergstrasse. You have Mönckebergstrasse. No further forward than this park here for phase one, unless I order it. Phase two, liaise with the Royal Welch on your right, as they may need to manoeuvre, but I want your unit to hold the gap between the Jocks and the Welsh, no further forward than Johannistrasse. Understood?"

Major Terry Farnsworth was in charge of an ad hoc unit, drawn from the support services of 71st Brigade, and bulked up with two platoons of Ox and Bucks.

Haugh turned to the Welshman on his right.

"And you, Tewdyr… you get the prize, the Rathaus… for obvious reasons."

161

He brought the young Colonel in closer.

"See here. Do try and keep clear of Ballindamm, will you. As you move forward, the natural lie of the land concentrates you, giving you a frontage of less than a hundred and fifty yards when you attack the Rathaus itself... not that I need to tell you eh?"

Lieutenant Colonel Tewdyr Hedd Llewellyn VC, OC 4th Royal Welch Fusiliers, understood only too well, and for the briefest of moments, his mind went back to August 1945, when the cobbles and rubble had run red with the blood of hundreds of soldiers; German, Scots, Welsh, and Russian.

He shuddered involuntarily.

His commanding officer understood and slapped him on the shoulder.

"Perhaps lay a few ghosts eh, Tewdyr?"

Llewellyn nodded his agreement, although he actually suspected that he would simply acquire a few more.

1937 hrs, Monday 17th June 1946, CP, 4th Royal Welch Fusiliers, Hauptbahnhof Nord, Hamburg, Germany.

"Beg your pardon, Sir, but who came up with this fucking nightmare?"

Captain Gareth Anwill had also been present at the defence of the Rathaus all those months ago, and had a healthy respect for the area's defensive qualities.

"Well, Gareth, someone's gotta do it, and if you can think of anyone better qualified, then I'm all ears, trust me."

He let the statement hang in a quiet broken only by the occasional mortar round being slung at the enemy defences.

It had been sometime since the Red Army had replied, as their ammunition stocks were running low.

"Is there some reason we can't just sit them out, Sir?"

The other officer who had seen action on those fateful days made a fair point.

"Short answer is no. I put it to the Colonel myself, and got short shrift. We need this port up and running, and as quickly as possible. They might take weeks to jack it in, and the brass simply can't wait. Sorry, Malcolm, good idea, but non-starter."

Captain Reece withdrew into his shell.

Llewellyn detailed the general plan and then made his own mark on the orders, assigning routes, units, fire plans, support options, until everything that could be covered had been covered.

"We go at 2300 hrs. Any questions?"

Fig # 186 - Hamburg, Germany - unit dispositions.

2007 hrs, Monday 17th June 1946, CP, Special Group Mogris, the Rathaus, Hamburg, Germany.

In reality, the Red Army units opposing the 71st Brigade were a shadow of their former selves, undernourished, tired and low on everything, including hope; nowhere near as strong as Brigadier Haugh had been led to believe.

The Soviet defenders were on their last legs, drinking dirty water from the canal system and finding food wherever nature provided it, although it had been a long time since any self-respecting seagull or rat had come within killing distance.

In essence, they were dying, not as quickly as those who succumbed to artillery or bullets, but just as certainly.

163

Anton Mogris, once of 31st Guards Rifle Division, the Major who gave his name to the desperate groups of soldiers assigned to resist in this section of the crumbling defences, was out on his feet.

He washed himself in the seated position, his ragged uniform tunic set aside as he splashed water over his emaciated body, bones protruding and stretching white skin where any healthy man would have displayed pink flesh and nothing else.

"Report."

The runner had waited dutifully whilst his commander wiped the rivulets from his torso.

"Comrade Mayor, Comrade Kapitan Taraseva reports activity on her front. She suggests it's preparations for an attack down Rosenstrasse. She has ordered her unit to readiness and...err..."

"Spit it out, Comrade."

"Comrade Mayor, Comrade Kapitan Taraseva also asks if there is any ammunition or food available."

Even though the situation was dire, Mogris could not help but laugh aloud.

"Unfortunately, there is no food available to send forward. However, good news, Comrade Runner..." and Mogris leant across to a crate, extracting some items.

"I can give you these. Now, tell Comrade Taraseva that she is to hold her position at all costs, and send me word on any change. Is that clear, Comrade runner?"

The two grenades and four clips of rifle ammunition changed hands, and the runner left.

Mogris continued his ablutions calmly, understanding that his luck would run out today.

Having first served in the siege of Leningrad, he had seen combat constantly since then to the German defeat, and once again when the whole affair started over again.

His body carried the scars of a dozen wounds.

He dried himself fully and stood up, dressing in the tatty tunic jacket.

Pulling it into place, he ran his eyes over the awards that covered his breast, marks of a grateful nation, each one reminding him of the sacrifice of a hundred souls for places few had ever heard of.

'Enough.'

He tested his resolve.

"Enough!"

His mind was set and he strode out of the rubble and into the evening light, heading for his old friend's positions at St Jacobi's

Church, his two-man security section falling in behind him without a word.

"No matter what, Roman."

"They'll shoot you, Anton. You can't do this."

"I can and I must. These boys have sacrificed enough. If we had the bullets, the food, if we had fucking anything except bricks… but we don't."

He kicked out viciously at a brick that begged for his attention.

"I gave Taraseva the last two grenades… the last two grenades… and twenty rounds of rifle ammunition, Roman. How can we fucking fight against the capitalists with two grenade and twenty fucking bullets, eh? They have everything they need… we have nothing but our hearts and love of the Rodina… and I'll not see more boys sacrificed to this war… this… losing cause…"

Roman Sostievev held out his hands to calm his friend, and at the same time looked around, fearing a rush of NKVD troops to arrest them both.

"Don't talk like that, Anton… you've never talked like that."

Mogris shook his head slowly.

"That's because we would always win. Now, we can only lose, Comrade. We've no chance… and you know it… the Polkovnik knows it… hell, even Comrade fucking Stalin knows it!"

"You're set on this path then?"

"Yes, I must, Roman."

"What if I arrest you… here… right now?"

Sostievev fumbled for his revolver and made a play of threatening his friend with it.

"Then I'd resist arrest, Comrade Kapitan."

"Please, Anton, please. Do the memories of our comrades mean nothing to you?"

Mogris whirled and grabbed his friend by the lapels.

"They mean everything to me! Everything!"

He dropped his hands and opened the palms in a gesture of apology.

"Sorry old friend… yes, they mean everything to me… and I led them into battles when we had a chance to achieve… an

165

opportunity for victory... and they followed me because they knew I loved them and would do all I could to keep them alive!"

Picking up his battered old Mosin rifle, Mogris smiled at the comrade he had fought beside for so many years.

"I'll do what I can to keep them alive now."

Sostievev knew he could do no more.

They embraced and kissed and, in silence, said goodbye.

If Mogris was successful, then Sostievev would spread the word and ensure the defenders surrendered.

2158 hrs, Monday 17th June 1946, frontline positions of 1st Battalion, Highland Light Infantry, Springelwiete, Hamburg, Germany.

"I'm telling you, I heard summat."

The urgent whispered exchange stopped immediately, the sound of rubble shifting focussing the two men.

A voice drifted to them, carrying words they didn't understand.

"Ne strelyat... ya podchinyayus'... ne strelyat'."

The white rag that came into view was more understandable, although neither of the Highland soldiers were relaxed as it grew a hand, then an arm, and developed into a Soviet soldier.

"Don, get the corp up here, bleedin' pronto."

Responding to the Londoner's words, the other man slipped back to summon the corporal from his slumber.

"Stop there, my old china, stop right there."

Mogris didn't understand, so kept moving.

Fusilier Kent increased the menace in his voice, and this time Mogris got the message.

He remained still, holding the pillowcase aloft, until the Corporal arrived and took over.

The Soviet officer was quickly reeled in and frisked, losing his watch in the process.

2222 hrs, Monday 17th June 1946, CP, 1st Battalion, Highland Light Infantry, Steinstrasse, Hamburg, Germany.

"Sir... yes, sorry, sir, but this is important. I have a Soviet officer here who's surrendered to us of his own accord... I think he's the commander of the units facing us and he wishes to surrender his command."

The reaction at the other end of the field telephone clearly perturbed MacPherson.

"Yes, sir. He's a Major... a Major...Mogreece... looks like a veteran officer... yes, sir..."

In response to the question, the HLI commander reappraised the man stood opposite him.

"He looks the part, sir. My smattering of Russian helped, of course. Personally, I think he's genuine."

Rory MacPherson listened intently, continuing his examination of the prisoner, seeking some extra clue, some additional item that would decide his recommendation when the moment came.

The moment came far too quickly.

"In my view, he's the real ticket, sir."

Based on MacPherson's report, Haugh decided to risk accepting Mogris at face value.

His orders were clear on the matter, and left Rory no room for manoeuvre.

"Yes, sir, will do, sir. I will take a radio and report to you how it goes... immediately, sir... no time to lose, as you say. Goodbye, sir."

Within minutes of the receiver hitting the cradle, MacPherson and a handful of picked men were back at the frontline with a relieved Mogris in tow.

2340 hrs, Monday 17th June 1946, frontline positions, 2nd Company, 79th MC Battalion, Special Group Mogris, Hamburg, Germany.

"Let them approach... but be careful of tricks, Comrades!"

The small group, led by a beaming Mogris, moved closer to the Soviet positions.

Sostievev was ready to do his part, his fittest men ready to dispatch to all parts of the defence with orders to lay down their arms.

He concentrated on his friend and commander, the smile of relief broadcasting his relief loud and clear.

A wave of emotion washed over Sostievev, the feeling that they had done right by their men now stronger than the one that they were deserting their Motherland in her hour of need.

He raised himself up, revealing his position, and causing the handful of British to grip their weapons more tightly.

Mogris came to a halt and saluted his friend, who snapped to attention and returned the gesture.

"Comrade Kapitan Sostievev, do you have your men ready to deliver the message?"

"Yes, Comrade Mayor."

"Send them immediately. No firing, lay down your arms, accept the Allied soldiers will advance."

On cue, an HLI Sergeant ordered two privates forward with large sacks.

The contents represented more food than Mogris' unit had eaten in a week.

Mogris accepted the sacks with a nod and held them out to the nearest Soviet soldiers.

"Here, comrades, food. We will have food, and we will live to see the Rodina again!"

The cheer was strangled in the rush for the sacks, and the coherent frontline position disappeared into a feeding frenzy.

"Have your men spread the word, Comrade Kapitan."

The two formally saluted and Sostievev dispatched his runners.

MacPherson spoke into the radio.

"Yarrow-six, Yarrow-six, Wellington-six, over."

"Wellington-six, Yarrow-six, go ahead, over."

"Yarrow-six, Wellington-six, Singapore…say again… Singapore, over."

With that message, MacPherson set in motion a different sort of advance to the one that had been planned, one that would save lives, rather than take them.

2351 hrs, Monday 17th June 1946, frontline positions, 1st Company, Special Group Mogris, Hamburg, Germany.

Captain Malvina Ivana Taraseva listened impassively to the report of the exhausted man.

His heavy breathing replaced the sound of his words, but still Taraseva did not respond.

Her mind processed the information and elected to respond by way of action.

The knife was out and slid into the man's chest before he could offer a protest.

"You traitorous dog! All of you, traitorous dogs who deserve death!"

The runner was long past hearing, his eyes glassy, and his ears unreceptive to Taraseva's rage.

She yanked the blade free, permitting the dead man to fall.

"Comrade Starshina, get them ready. The Allies are coming!"

2352 hrs, Monday 17th June 1946, frontline positions, 4th Royal Welch Fusiliers, Brandsende, Hamburg, Germany.

"Listen you fucking monkeys… and listen good. If I ever… ever… find out who took a dump in my rucksack, I'll have his bollocks off in a jiffy."

The sniggering left Corporal Keith May in no doubt that the perpetrator was present.

A spent force, his bullying ways no good in present company, he tried to ponce a fag from the nearest smoker.

"Here, six-six, give us a fag will yer?"

It was a Welsh regiment, and there were so many Jones', Davies', and Jenkins' that each man had a number, which rapidly became his standard name.

Lance-Corporal Ian Jones, the six-six in question, shrugged his shoulders.

"I'm out, Corp."

It was a lie, but he didn't care.

"Simmo, cough one up now, there's a mate."

"This is me last one, Corp."

"Fucking hell, will someone one spring me a smoke… please?"

Davies one-four decided to cut the whining short, and a woodbine flew across the gap.

"Oh ta, one-four, very decent of you."

Ensuring that his rotund frame was properly concealed behind the counter of the ruined tobacconists shop, May flicked his lighter and drew in the pungent smoke.

"Fags out, you bastards."

May looked at the Sergeant as if he was a member of the Spanish Inquisition.

"I've just lit the bastard, Sarge."

"Well, fucking unlit it, Corp'ral. We're getting set to go now, boys. Change of plan. Rupert'll fill us in shortly."

The sergeant, Jones nine-five, dropped down next to his brother, Jones five-nine, and stretched his legs, easing the aches and pains of the day's exertions.

The 'Rupert' arrived within seconds, bringing with him the wonderful news of the Soviet surrender.

2nd Lieutenant Gethin Jones lit up a celebratory cigarette as he explained the plan and the delay, May giving Jones nine-five the evil eye as he relit his own battered offering.

Close on Gethin Jones' heels came the most hated man in the Fusiliers.

Major Stephen Monmouth-Kerr, or as he was known to pretty much everyone…Wayne.

The general description offered by his men tended to include the words 'posh twat', 'arrogant' and, perhaps most unforgivably, 'useless'.

'Wayne' had decided to move forward with the first wave, perhaps to acquire some of the glory that his old military family had been steeped in, as he was so fond of telling his subalterns whenever they stood still long enough.

Most thought it was simply to find some item around which he could concoct a story of great valour.

The assembled soldiers shared a common thought.

'Twat.'

As the seconds passed, the men of 1st Platoon readied themselves.

The support gunfire from 83rd Field Regiment had been cancelled, although the experienced gunners were waiting… ready just in case anything went wrong.

0000 hrs, Tuesday 18th June 1946, frontline positions, 4th Royal Welch Fusiliers, Brandsende, Hamburg, Germany.

"Right-ho, Lieutenant. Move your platoon forward. Chop-chop."

Gethin Jones rose swiftly and waved his sten.

"Come on then, boys… after the Major now."

The younger officer deferred to the company commander, and Major Monmouth-Kerr suddenly found himself outside his comfort zone and in front of his men.

Taraseva held the flare pistol close and automatically checked above her to ensure she could get the last flare up through the ruins.

The gap was sufficient and she smiled, wondering if the single green flare she had left would be enough for her needs.

170

It took her only a moment to understand that there was nothing she could do, even if it wasn't, so she contented herself with calming those soldiers around her.

"Wait, Comrades… wait… wait…"

The Major managed to find a torturous route to scramble through, but still hit the paving of Brandsende ahead of the others.

His bravado increased and he encouraged the men forward with his revolver, the ice white of its lanyard waving about as he pointed at the men around him.

"Come on, Sergeant. Get a move on… no hanging back, man."

Jones nine-five's look was lost in the darkness of the night and he bit his tongue, halting the retort at source.

Jones five-nine leant in closer as he hauled himself over a large lump of masonry.

"Come along, nine-five, stop skulking now, you old gont."

The sergeant aimed a swing at the back of his brother's head, which was as easily evaded as it was expected.

"Shut it, you little bastard. Show some respect for your betters."

Instinctively, he put out a hand to help his younger brother over the next obstacle.

"I'll do that when I find someone better, nine-five."

The younger soldier received a less than helpful push towards the final barrier in their stealthy advance across the small street.

Left and right of them, the men of A Company were doing the same, and the entire company had now left the safety of the ruined buildings that had formed their defensive position.

Fusilier Cornish, the 1st Platoon number one gunner, had established his post back in the same buildings, and his Bren gun moved gently from left to right as he scanned the dark rubble ahead for threats.

The two Jones brothers moved apart and Sergeant Jones 95 found the unit's unofficial medic, Davies one-four, on his shoulder.

"Something's wrong, Sarge."

Jones' arm shot up, and those around him stopped and dropped as low as they could, the effect rippling outwards in both directions.

Fig# 187 – the Battle of Hamburg

"What, one-four?

Only the Major failed to stop, and he moved slowly forward to the threshold of some unidentifiable building.

Turning around to order some soldier to proceed inside before him, Monmouth-Kerr suddenly realised he was alone and quite exposed, which was not a very satisfactory state of affairs for him, and he went to move back, intent on ripping some poor unfortunate off a strip.

As Davies one-four explained his feelings on the absence of any display of surrender from people supposed to be surrendering, the matter was spectacularly resolved.

Captain Taraseva saw the line of advancing British drop to one knee, which alarmed her.

The leading man, clearly an officer, suddenly turned his back and moved back, displaying unusual urgency.

'Blyad! They know we're here!'

A green flare exploded overhead, drawing nearly every eye.

Less than a second later, all hell broke loose.

Major Monmouth-Kerr was the first to die, literally coming apart as a burst from a DP28 took him from the small of the back to the top of his head, spreading his blood, guts, and brains over the unfortunate Gethin Jones.

Two of the bullets also hit the Lieutenant, and he dropped to the street, his shoulder and neck penetrated by the DP rounds.

Bullets slammed into the rubble around the Welshmen, claiming victims with ricochets as much as direct hits.

Sergeant Jones sustained such a wound in the rump of his ass; painful, nothing more.

Jones six-six took a direct hit in the mouth that detached his complete lower jaw, but, despite the horrendous gaping wound, still managed to make his animal-like screams louder than the growing firefight around him.

Most of the wounds were upper body and head, and the Royal Welch suffered badly in the opening exchanges.

Jones nine-five, the senior man for yards in any direction, quickly decided to get the hell off the street.

He shouted in all directions, gaining the attention of the men around him.

"Grenades... grenades!"

He waved a Mills bomb in all directions to emphasise his point.

Those who could see, grabbed for their own little bomblet and readied themselves for the orders.

Sergeant Jones grimaced as the nearby Fusilier Simpson took a ricochet in the side of the head.

Davies 14 was on hand, and quickly started work on the nasty wound.

Jones nine-five pulled the pin, holding the Mills in plain sight. His actions were mirrored along the line.

He ducked as a round clipped his helmet, cursing inwardly at his own stupidity for raising his head out of cover.

Using his other hand, he held up three fingers.

Allowing the lever to spring clear, he dipped the grenade arm in a clear fashion, counting out the three seconds, before raising himself up and sending the deadly charge into the rubble, aiming at the flashes of weapons to his front.

His grenade arrived with a number of others.

The sharp cracks of the detonations were all Sergeant Jones nine-five needed.

"Charge! Up and at the baaarrrssstttaaarrrdddsss!"

He was moving immediately, in fact two grenades went off as he rose, and he plunged forward into the ruins ahead of him, followed by a tidal wave of fusiliers, yelling anything that came to mind, and firing as they charged.

A number of the Soviet defenders had been killed or wounded by the grenades, and most had ducked instinctively.

Some were out of ammunition already, others had some left to use.

A few fusiliers fell on the run-in, but most slammed into Taraseva's defensive line.

Corporal May stumbled as he tried to leap the barricade.

The bayonet took him in the throat, missing everything vital but transfixing him to a door that lay on the floor.

He scrabbled at the blade, slicing the flesh of his fingers.

The female mortar corporal, screaming in her fear, pulled the trigger as she remembered she had once been instructed, almost blowing May's head off his shoulders.

She, in turn, took a rifle butt in the side of the head, as Corporal Robinson came up on her blind side.

The young girl was dead before she toppled over the barricade and onto May's corpse.

The Royal Welch outnumbered the defenders, and were in a lot better physical condition, but some of the Soviet troops had earned their spurs on the streets of Kharkov against Hitler's SS, and were not easily shrugged aside.

Jones five-nine and Steven eight-five found themselves suddenly isolated and opposed by a group of dreadfully thin soldiers, who fought with the desperation of experienced men.

An entrenching tool just failed to remove Steven's head, clipping the ear, cutting in to the hairline, and sending gobbets of blood in all directions.

A knife ploughed a furrow in Jones nine-five's thigh, but the perpetrator received short shrift, the butt of the Enfield rifle hammering into the man's throat, wrecking everything vital in an instant, and dropping the veteran soldier to the ground.

A glancing blow knocked Steven eight-five's rifle from his hand, shattering the thumb and two fingers on his right hand.

Incensed, as Steven was a boxing champ within his battalion, he clubbed his adversary with a fist on the top of the head, sending the man to the floor.

He dropped onto the insensible man's chest knees first, breaking a number of bones, and punched him four times in the face for good measure.

The dying man spouted frothy blood with each breath, and Steven eight-five transferred his attention elsewhere.

Ignoring the excruciating pain from his right hand, he dragged a soldier off Jones five-nine, the Russian having pinned the younger Jones brother to the rubble where he tried to throttle the life out of him.

Grabbing up a British pudding bowl helmet, Steven slammed the edge into the back of the man's head, breaking bone and driving the rim into the skull cavity.

The two Welshmen were suddenly reinforced, and soon the small knot of enemy resistance was overcome, mainly with fatal consequences for the Soviet soldiers.

The fighting stopped as quickly as it had started, and the Soviet positions were in fusilier hands.

Part of the buildings was burning, illuminating a modest space, within which a handful of men gathered.

Lieutenant Gethin Jones had been brought forward, purely for his own safety, and Davies one-four used the light to check his handiwork.

Mike Robinson carefully laid the body of Fusilier Simpson on the old table, the killing wound apparent on his forehead.

Sergeant Jones nine-five organised the survivors of first platoon into some sort of order, and then took time out to see to Gethin Jones, and to inform him of what had come to pass since the officer had been taken out of the equation.

All of this was observed by Captain Malvina Ivana Taraseva, as best she could, given her predicament.

She had been one of the first casualties of the engagement, taking solid hits from the Bren gun of Fusilier Cornish.

Her left breast, left shoulder, and left arm were all wrecked by the passage of the heavy .303 bullets.

She then received shrapnel hits from the deadly Mills bombs, a number of pieces of hot metal taking her low in her groin and legs.

Her ginger hair was much redder on her left side, where blood continued to squirt and pulse.

Covered with gore and with limbs set at unusual angles, the British had clearly assumed she was dead and had ignored her.

Her one good limb was her right arm, and in it she held one of the F1 grenades that Mogris had sent her.

Moving carefully, so as not to attract attention, she used her teeth to pull the pin and gently, pressing the grenade to her surviving breast, allowed the lever to detach without the normal noise that marked its separation.

She then threw the grenade into the fire-illuminated area.

Jones five-nine extended his flask to his brother, its contents decidedly non-regulation.

"Not bad work for an old bastard, Sergeant, even if I do say as part of the family like."

Jones nine-five moved to take the offered drink and then shouted, pushing his brother out of the way.

The men around the small area tensed and sought threat in the area round them, only Sergeant Jones having seen the real threat arrive in their midst.

"GRENADE!"

He threw himself forward, his body landing to cover the deadly object, to absorb its blast and deadly metal, the man's instinct being to look after his boys, come what may.

His brother, Jones five-nine screamed.

"NOOOOO!"

The UZRGM fuse could be set from zero to a hair under thirteen seconds, not that anyone knew what it was that lay under their sergeant's body.

Time stood still as the fusiliers scattered for their lives.

Silence.

Disbelieving silence.

Incredulous silence.

A silence broken by the voice of Sergeant Carl Jones nine-five, a voice that showed the strain of his predicament.

"Right... ok, lads... get everyone moved away... shar...," his voice broke slightly with the stress of the situation, "Look sharp now... look fucking lively, you gonts."

He reverted to insults to regain his composure, and was successful, accompanying the effort with deep breaths.

"Robbo, let me know when everyone is safely outta the way, man."

"Sarge."

Robinson checked and waited whilst the wounded Gethin Jones was placed behind cover.

"Sarge... we're all clear."

Jones nine-five braced himself and, almost as if performing the longest press-up in the history of man, slowly pushed himself up and off the grenade.

When he was sure he was clear, he moved to examine it, not daring to touch it, but purely using eye contact.

He took a quick look around and determined a safe area, his decision to throw the device into a quiet corner taken in spite of himself, his hand now shaking with approaching shock.

Taraseva watched on, incredulous that the grenade had not killed a number of the capitalist swine, incredulous that the thing had not even exploded, and incredulous that the grenade was now in the air and heading straight back at her.

The hunk of metal struck her in the centre of her stomach and dropped into the bloody remains of her lap.

The F1 did not explode. It could never explode, as the spring had long since seized within the fuse casing.

Taraseva had not known that it failed to explode, the moment it struck her coincided with the closing down of her system due to blood loss.

The unconscious woman passed quickly into death as the enemy celebrated the incredible escape of their NCO.

"You stupid, stupid bastard!"

"Fucking hell, Sarge... I mean... fucking hell!"

The words of congratulations, surprise, horror at his act, or whatever, were all accompanied by slaps and handshakes.

For his part, Carl Jones had drained completely of any colour, and had even accepted the lit cigarette that someone had stuck in his hand, taking a deep drag before he remembered that he didn't actually smoke.

Second Company troops moved forward, their brief to advance to contact, as Soviet officers and NCOs, escorted by men from the Fusiliers and the HLI, fanned out through the Soviet

177

defences, yelling out in their native language, calling upon the last defenders to surrender.

Llewellyn, accompanied by a horrified Mogris, arrived in the front line to establish what exactly had happened.

Satisfied that the bloodbath had not been caused by his own men, the Royal Welch's CO assigned Captain Thomas, one of his headquarters officers, to help in sorting out 1st Company's organisation, and headed off in the wake of 2nd Company.

Elsewhere in Hamburg, similar incidents had taken place, some resulting in nothing more than silent surrender, others in tragedy.

None the less, by the time that the dawn gathered the ruined city in its warm embrace, the Soviet resistance had ended, with most Red Army soldiers in organised captivity. A handful of diehards held out, but were quickly rooted out for blessedly few casualties amongst the British divisions.

By the time that the evening stars became viewable, the vast majority of the Soviet force were enjoying the first decent food they had seen in weeks.

Hamburg was retaken, and would not change hands again.

2nd Lieutenant Gethin Jones refused to be taken to the casualty clearing station until he had made a report to Captain Thomas.

Two days later, Thomas' report was on Llewellyn's desk, where it was read and endorsed.

The report flew past a number of officers, rising in rank, before it made its way to London, and those who would decide on its contents.

Jones nine-five had no idea.

The sword was a very elegant weapon in the days of the Samurai.
You had honor and chivalry, much like the knights, and yet it was a
gruesome and horrific weapon.

Dustin Diamond

Chapter 158 – THE WEAPONS

2303 hrs, Thursday, 20th June 1946, Ul. Rostovskaya, Sovetskaya Gavan, Siberia.

One vessel had fallen to roving US aircraft from some anonymous carrier, the crew and cargo of I-15 now resting on the bottom of the Sea of Japan.

The sister AM-class submarines, I-1 and I-14, had made it through to their destination, and they rendezvoused with their larger friends off the coast of Siberia, before, in pre-ordained order, they silently slipped into the facility concealed on the bay north-west of Sovetskaya Gavan.

Although not a permanent structure, the Soviet engineers had dedicated their best efforts to developing it secretly, building it bit by bit, almost growing it as part of woods and modest rocky escarpments into which it blended perfectly.

By 0312, the four Japanese submarines were safely ensconced in their berths. The single empty dock reminded the submariners of the absence of I-15, the silent water drawing more than one reluctant gaze for a former comrade, or, in two instances, in memory of a lost brother.

The important Japanese technical personnel left hurriedly, their documents following swiftly in their wake.

Half of the harvest from Okunoshima was unloaded, the general plan being that one half of the products of Japanese research and development of mass killing weapons would be taken by rail, the other half would move by submarine

Everything had arrived at Sovetskaya Gavan without loss from air attack, something that had not been anticipated, and so the loading of the dastardly products of Units 731 and 516 would take much longer than had been expected.

Vice-Admiral Shigeyoshi Miwa, the overall mission commander, arrived and was greeted by the temporary commander, Lieutenant Commander Nanbu Nobukiyo of the I-401.

Pleasantries exchanged, the two occupied an office in the facility and, with the other submarine captains and their No 2s, explored the mission to the smallest degree, Miwa's additional information contributing to a sense of excitement amongst the experienced submarine officers.

Miwa introduced two new men, vital to the plan.

The two naval personnel, equipped with the necessary language skills were quickly excused and transferred to I-401; one ensign with Greek ancestry and a Lieutenant Commander who had previously been an attaché in Ankara, although the officer had been invalided out of the Naval Air Service, blinded by some wasteful tropical disease contracted on Borneo.

Their part in the plan would come much later.

The presence of two emotional-less Kempai Tai officers and their men was considered unnecessary and provocative to the professional submariners, but Miwa did not order them from the room, simply to stand to one side.

They acknowledged with a nod and stepped back.

He returned to his briefing.

The details of the extended mission in full cooperation with their ally, one that would harness the incredible range of the Sen-Tokus, were impressive, particularly for a nation on its knees.

The journey would be long and fraught with danger, but the planning had been extremely thorough, with back-up plans available where assets permitted.

Some of the other vessels involved were anonymous or of no import, at least as far as the Allies were concerned.

The I-353, a tanker submarine and the Bogata Maru ex Kreigsmarine merchant vessel, hastily converted to an auxiliary submarine tender, both now serving solely one purpose; the refueling and resupply of the four submarines of Operation Niji.

Other innocuous vessels had a part to play along the route of advance.

The Nachi Maru and Tsukushi Maru, two submarine tenders, now ostensibly under Allied orders, were ready to respond when needed.

Even the Hikawa Maru no2, a respectable hospital ship, had a part to play in ensuring the mission's success.

However, when the Niji unit was round the Cape of Good Hope, friendly berths and supply would be much harder to come by.

But not impossible.

The last intelligence received from a South African agent indicated that the U-Boat supply dump at the mouth of the Ondusengo

River in South-West Africa, had not yet been discovered. Figures available from the days of the Axis Alliance indicated that upwards of two thousand, six hundred tons of fuel oil were still concealed within the rolling sands.

The Sen-Tokus could make their destination without refuelling, but the two AM class could not, even if all the rendezvous' in the Indian and Southern oceans went as planned.

When Miwa was satisfied that the briefing was complete, and the men who would carry out the mission were fully on board and enthusiastic, he dropped his bombshell.

Nodding to the Kempai-Tai Major, he indicated that the tape recording should be played.

Miwa called the room to attention.

The strains of 'Kimigayo' rose from the single large speaker, and Miwa saw the stiffening and deference that swept through the assembly. A minute passed before the music ended and a disembodied voice declared the identity of the coming speaker.

Shōwa-Tennō... the Mikado... Emperor Hirohito.

"To our good and loyal subjects. After pondering deeply the general trends of the world and the actual conditions obtaining in our empire today, we have decided to effect a settlement of the present situation by resorting to an extraordinary meas..."

There were tears.

Many, many tears.

Eyes flashed fanatically, wet with tears, shed for the Empire and for the dishonour of it all.

Eyes shed tears for departed comrades, their loss now clearly in vain.

Lips trembled as emotions battled inside the rigid bodies, each man dealing with the unexpected... the unthinkable...

The words were absorbed, their meaning clear, and the anthem marked the end of the speech and the dreams of a nation.

Miwa spoke softly.

"So, there you have it."

He walked forward smartly, and stood before the Kempai Tai commander.

"You and your men will now leave. My officers and I have much to discuss."

The Major looked confused, as this was not what had been discussed.

Miwa continued, in an assertive and formal fashion.

181

"Shōsa Harrimatsu. You will both leave now to allow us to talk. There is no need for your services. Remain outside this building to preserve our security. That is all."

The Major bowed and ordered his security force out, eyeing the assembly with suspicion and still not totally sure why he had agreed to the Admiral's request... order.

The instruction was more than it seemed, which only he and Miwa understood.

The door closed and Miwa turned back to the group.

"Our Emperor has spoken, and to all of us that is a divine order that cannot be disobeyed."

He walked slowly around the room, weaving in and out of the men that were stood rigidly at the attention.

"But I fear that our Emperor has been misled... lied to... put in a position, a protected and uninformed one, from which he has no knowledge of the truth and actual events!"

He stopped in front of Itaka, the commander of I-1, a man who had lost two brothers aboard the battleship Yamato during its suicide mission.

"It is unthinkable that he would order us to stop fighting now, when so many have given their lives willingly for him... and for the glory of the Empire!"

The words went home and found a fertile resting place in Itaka's mind.

In other minds, the words also found a receptive resting place and, as Miwa continued to move through the assembly, he saw resolve in each man's eyes.

Stopping in front of Nobukiyo, the Admiral delivered his final statement on the matter.

"In the light of the obvious deception played upon the Emperor, I see no alternative... no honourable alternative whatsoever... but to continue with the mission that he had entrusted us."

His eyes burned deeply into those of Nobukiyo, almost inviting a challenge to the veracity of his words.

"We have been entrusted with a special task, one of significant importance to the Empire and its Allies. One outside the normal remits of our glorious navy. There has been no recall... no coded message halting our endeavours... no indication that we are not expected to proceed and discharge our duty to the Emperor."

His eyes hardened, and the fanatical Admiral delivered his bottom line, moving his face closer to the man who could make all their efforts count for naught, Nobukiyo's personality and cult

182

following amongst the submariners giving his opinion a weight well above his rank, especially if it came to obeying the spoken word of the Mikado.

"It is our honourable duty to undertake this mission regardless, for the Emperor. There can be no other conclusion."

Nobukiyo remained silent, his mind in turmoil, dragged in two directions by the words of his Emperor and the words of the Admiral in front of him.

The delay was an age, or seemed it, but Nobukiyo resolved the issue in his mind and bowed stiffly.

"Hai."

Miwa nodded in relief and spoke softly, his hand grabbing the submarine commander's shoulder.

"Hai... hai..."

He regained his composure and swung round to face the majority.

"Then we are decided."

Raising his arms vertically in the air, he screamed with a combination of national fervour and relief.

"Banzai!"

The rest of the room followed him a triple repetition of the salute.

"Banzai! Banzai! Banzai!"

Outside, Major Harrimatsa relaxed and thumbed the safety catch on his Browning 1910FN, indicating that his men could also now relax.

Had they but known it, the submarine officers had experienced a brush with death.

1101 hrs, Friday, 21st June 1946, Camp 1001, Akhtubinsk, USSR

There was something about the Russian psyche that made the Volga a serious national asset, over and above the physical barrier it represented.

When the Germans had marched into Mother Russia, it was at Stalingrad, on the Volga, amongst other places, that the invincible Wehrmacht had first floundered.

The Soviet capacity to produce the weapons of war had been carted over the large river, and installed in the Soviet hinterland, where it was safe, and could not be reached.

It was in the heart of every Russian, an inspiration and source of pride, and Camp 1001 was protected by its flowing waters.

Men from a number of important sectors of the Soviet war machine had flown into the small airbase at Akhtubinsk on the east bank of the river, looking for a number of special requirements to come together in one place, a search they had embarked on immediately the Germans had beed turned back.

Fig # 188 – Camp 1001, Akhtubinsk, USSR

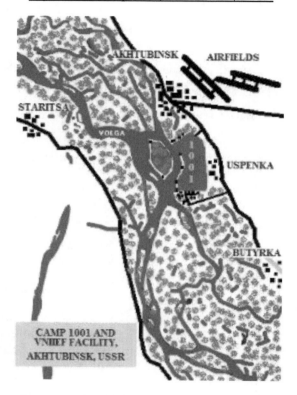

Representatives from the office of the People's Commissariat for Ammunition, the Ministry of Middle Machinery, and the VNIIEF moved around the insignificant corner of the Soviet Empire, finding that their checklists were being rapidly satisfied.

Electricity, environment, concealment, access… the factors were satisfied on all counts, and more.

The preliminary reports cited the satisfactory and favourable elements of the site.

With all interested parties in total agreement, the decision was quickly reached, and the development and relocation plan was presented to Stalin and the GKO.

In a nutshell, a huge secret facility was to be constructed in the area but its existence would not be announced to their Allies.

If it became known, then it would simply be a POW facility full of German POWs.

By the time the German War was over, the nature of Camp 1001 had changed, and work started anew on enhancing its facilities.

When the Allies started their attacks on Kremlyov, Vannikov proposed shifting the entire project to Akhtubinsk, and concealing it with a large population of Allied prisoners, who could also be used as a work force for further expansion.

The facility would be declared as a prison camp to the Allies and Red Cross, in order to avoid any unnecessary deaths or, as Vannikov suggested, 'to use their soft natures and regard for life against them.'

Colonel General Boris Vannikov, the People's Commissar for Ammunition, was glowingly positive about 1001 and the facilities it promised, and promised quickly, the vast majority of underground work having been completed some months previously.

Within the large site, there would be sub-facilities, where Soviet engineers and scientists would continue the work of the Soviet Atomic programme.

The assembly of all major components parts would be done within Camp 1001, and the waterway provided an excellent means to transport the larger items from their own factories, and in a disguised way, which was had been one of the deal clinchers.

For the months to come, Allied intelligence had absolutely no idea, and continued to bomb both the real and distraction sites set up throughout the USSR, whilst 1001 grew and became operational.

At 1101hrs on Friday 21st June 1946, the last electrical connections were made, meaning that every research and manufacturing facility was now functioning.

NKVD Lieutenant General Dustov received the confirmation over the phone and immediately sought a connection to Moscow.

His head of security, Colonel Skryabin, arrived to confirm the report.

After the telephone conversation with Vannikov, Dustov and Skryabin decided to wreak havoc with the readiness company by way of a surprise test of their response.

By the end of the drill, the base was short one NKVD Captain, who found himself waiting at Akhtubinsk for the next aircraft to Siberia, and the readiness company had a new commanding officer, who understood fully the value of being efficient and swift in all he did in future.

1209 hrs, Saturday, 22nd June 1946, Château de Versailles, France.

It had been a hell of a morning and, as Saturday afternoon arrived, it got no better for the commander of the Allied Armies in Europe.

Eisenhower settled back, his flow of orders now ceased, the men and women of his staff dispatched to sort out the crisis in Southern Germany, where Soviet pressure had actually jolted some of his units back, the first real losses in territory since the March offensive began.

Devers had been upbeat, but Ike had seen through the bravado, despite the concealment offered by the telephone, understanding the concerns that had built up, day after day, as US casualty rates grew.

Eisenhower had decided to blood more of the Allies, and his orders to Devers and other commanders committed the South Americans and Spaniards like never before.

Ever conscious of the political need to reduce casualties amongst the main players, Eisenhower had been judicious in the use of his British, Commonwealth, and US soldiers, and had successfully reduced casualty rates, offset by a drudgingly slow advance and higher consumption of the chattels of war.

And yet, the last few weeks had seen an increase in casualties; stiffer resistance, more counter-attacks, thicker minefields, heavier use of air assets, all in areas of American responsibility.

Whilst Soviet resistance was fierce everywhere, it seemed more targeted, more resilient, more pro-active in zones where US troops were in the majority.

The figures were developed and, when Ike had last spoken with his commander-in-chief, he had suggested the possibility of a defined attempt by the enemy to increase US casualty rates.

The reasoning was as clear to the military minds in Versailles as it was to the political ones in Washington.

The United States Army was being deliberately battered to increase casualty rates and influence political opinion at home.

It was a dangerous time for the Allied armies, and matters got a whole lot worse in short order.

Answering the phone, Ike acknowledged General Bradley's greeting and reached for a cigarette... and stopped dead.

"Say what? Say that again, Brad."

Eisenhower grabbed a small map from his desk, all that was to hand to interpret Bradley's words.

He listened without interrupting, seeing everything in his mind's eye, as Bradley's words fell onto the map in his hands, illustrating an unexpected horror.

"When did it start?"

'Ten hundred hours.'

"At three points..."

'Yes, Sir.'

Eisenhower examined the map and saw opportunity mixed with the threat of an unprecedented Soviet counter-attack.

"Kassel?"

'No reports of activity, Sir.'

"Can you firm that up, Brad? Get some air up to examine it, I want to know if that's the secured pivot of this attack, clear?"

'Yes, Sir. Are you thinking of using the French?'

Bradley had read his mind.

"Yes, Brad, I am. We know the enemy are weak, and if this the all-out effort you suggest, it will be limited in form. If they are anchored on Kassel, as seems likely, we move the French in behind them... cross the river at...," a ring-shaped stain from a long-since consumed mug of coffee temporarily defied his efforts to read the name, "At Hann Münden... on the Fulda River."

Eisenhower relaxed enough to light his cigarette and delivered his instructions slowly and precisely.

"Right, here's what we do. I'll assemble my staff and take another look at the whole shooting match. You get some more recon in place, and get me what I need to make the decision."

He took in more of the calming smoke, mixing it with the comfort of applied activity, before delivering the rest of his orders.

"Have your boys work the problem too, just to make sure. Meanwhile, prep the French for a rapid deployment and assault to the southeast, aimed at crossing the Fulda at Hann Münden, isolating Kassel, and driving into the rear of the forces attacking into your front. Any questions, Brad?"

'How much time you looking at, Sir?'

Ike consulted the clock and did the calculations.

187

"I want firm information in hand by fifteen hundred, and no later. I want boots on the road and a firm plan before sixteen hundred comes and goes, clear, Brad?"

'Yes, General. I'm on it already. I'll call as soon as I have anything firm.'

Exchanging the normal pleasantries, the call ended, and Eisenhower was straight on the phone again, calling his planners to order.

The Soviet attack presented a huge opportunity to break the stalemate in front of Bradley's Twelfth Army Group, and to do so with limited loss of American lives.

By sixteen hundred hours, a huge portion of the French First Army was on the move or about to move. The reconnaissance photos and reports supported the notion that Kassel was the hinge, and that crossing the Fulda to the east would bring unprecedented dividends.

Fig # 189 – Organisation of the Legion Corps D'Assaut, June 1946.

BASIC ORGANISATION OF THE LEGION CORPS D'ASSAUT						
	UNIT	TANK	INF	INF	ART	ENG
GROUP NORMANDIE	1ST LEGION DIVISION CAMERONE	1CDA	1 RDM	5 RDM	1 ART	1 ENG
	3RD LEGION DIVISION ALMA	2 CDA	3 RDM	7 RDM	3 ART	3 ENG
GROUP LORRAINE	2ND LEGION DIVISION TANNENBERG	5 CDA	2 RDM	6 RDM	2 ART	2 ENG
	4TH LEGION DIVISION SEVASTOPOL	3 CDA	4 RDM	8 RDM	4 ART	4 ENG
GROUP AQUITAINE	5TH LEGION DIVISION AUSTERLITZ	6 CDA	9 RDM	7 RTA	5 ART	
	LEGION INFANTERIE GROUP		2 LE	3 LE		3 GENIE
GROUP RESERVE	CORPS RESERVE TROOPS	4CDA	11 RDM	15RDM	6 ART	5 ENG
EX-WAFFEN SS TROOPS			FRENCH FOREIGN LEGION OR FRENCH COLONIAL TROOPS			

1209 hrs, Monday, 24th June 1946, Holzhausen, Germany.

The shell that had chopped Lavalle down had also reaped a full harvest amongst the Normandie officers and headquarters staff that had accompanied him.

Bittrich, returned to something approaching rude health, had been spared, but every other man from the score or so members of Group Normandie's headquarters were either dead or wounded.

Lavalle was not badly hurt, but the blood loss from numerous minor shrapnel wounds was a problem that required attention, so he was loaded on to an ambulance, together with five other casualties, one of whom expired as his litter was slid into place.

Fig # 190 – The Fulda, Germany.

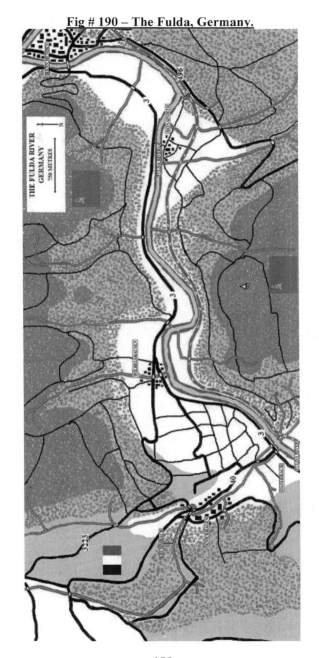

The French officer had come to visit the headquarters of Camerone, in order to assess for himself the disaster that had befallen the best unit in his command.

As the ambulance sped away, the phone rang shrilly.

The duty officer answered and recoiled at the harsh voice that assaulted his ears.

"Mon Général… Général Molyneux for Général Lavalle."

The telephone changed hands and Knocke spoke calmly and clearly.

"General Molyneux. Knocke here. I'm afraid that General Lavalle has been wounded and is on his way to hospital."

'Which makes you in command, or is it that idiot Bittrich. I will send a decent replacement officer as soon as possible. Meanwhile, you will renew the attack at once. Follow the plan and attack again. I want Normandie over the Fulda and defending the crossing point at Hann Münden immediately. You're already behind schedule!'

"I regret that's not possible, General Molyneux. It will take some time to get Alma online, and Camerone has just taken a bad beating because of those damn mortars and anti-tank guns."

'You have mortars! You have guns! Use them, Général Knocke, or I'll find someone who will. Now, get your troops moving and get me my bridgehead. The eyes of the world are upon us, man!'

Knocke surveyed the men around him, who had heard the ranting voice on the phone, and who all listened in disbelief.

"Herr General, Camerone has just taking a beating. The division's lead elements sustained over thirty percent casualties in less time than we've been on the telephone. We walked into intense minefields we didn't know about, were shot at by anti-tank guns that apparently don't exist, and were cut down by shells from mortars the enemy supposedly don't have any ammunition for."

'So, a handful of casualties turns you into a frightened sheep. Develop a fucking spine, man! Whoever gave you a French uniform needs their fucking head examined!'

"I think you need to calm yourself, General. There's no need to panic. We will cross the Fulda, but it will require more planning and more time."

'Shut your mouth, Knocke… just shut your useless German mouth and listen to me.'

The officers of Normandie saw a change in the facial expression of their most illustrious officer, one that they had never seen before, and one that made them see Knocke in a new light.

"I… am… listening… Herr… General."

190

The controlled fury did not transfer itself into the ears of the Frenchman so intent on carving his own mark on the proceedings.

'I am ordering Group Normandie to renew the attack immediately. Brush aside this resistance and take the river bridge at Wilhelmshausen. Discharge these orders or face courts-martial, Général.'

The silence seemed to last for a thousand years.

"No."

'Repeat that?'

"I said no."

The silence was marked by a buzzing in the Legion officer's ear.

'Say that again and I'll have you arrested and shot. Now, repeat your orders immediately.'

"General Molyneux... I refuse your idiotic order. I will not attack again. It's suicidal and the order of a man out of touch with the realities of the moment. We're neither prepared nor organised for such an attack. Come here yourself, if you wish... but I'll not lose another man to your madness."

Molyneux turned white with fury, his knuckles white as he gripped the receiver tight.

He shouted so loud that every man in the tent could hear his vitriolic outburst quite clearly.

'Merde! Who else is there to receive my orders? Who is there that can fucking soldier and act like an officer in the French Army! Lavalle, give me Lavalle! Give me a French officer immediately!'

The phone in the Legion headquarters changed hands, Molyneux's voice carrying loud and clear to the handful of men assembled in the command centre.

"Mon Général, St. Clair here. Général Lavalle has been wounded and is not on the field. Général Bittri..."

'I don't want that useless German bastard either. Who is the highest ranking French officer there... right now?'

He had been going to say that Bittrich had disappeared and could not be located,

St. Clair looked around him and found he didn't like the situation he found himself in.

"I am, mon Général."

'Right, St. Clair. You will take immediate control of Normandie, and have that SS imbecile Knocke arrested. I want the attack renewed immediately. The plan is sound... follow it to the letter! You will take and you will hold the bridge at Hann Münden, so

191

that the rest of the Corps can move forward. Do you understand your orders, St. Clair?'

"I understand your orders, mon Général. I regret, but I'm unable to carry them out."

Molyneux nearly passed out with rage, his brain so assailed with the thoughts of such incompetence and clear mutiny on the part of his officers that his reason, what little of it he had been able to call on, left completely.

'Cochon putain! Arrest yourself! Arrest everyone! I'm coming immediately! I'll have you all shot! Merde! Shot I say!'

The phone went dead.

At Corps headquarters, Molyneux raged at anyone and everyone, all efforts to calm him down failing badly.

Assembling a platoon of military policemen, Molyneux delivered a pep talk, emphasising the treachery of the ex-SS officers who they were about to arrest and shoot.

He climbed aboard his vehicle and the entourage swept out of the Legion Corps headquarters in the cloister of St-Maria-Himmelfahrt, Warburg, speeding up rapidly, intent on consuming the twenty-five kilometres to the frontline as quickly as possible.

In the Citroen staff car, Molyneux continued to work himself into a frenzy.

St. Clair handed the receiver back to the duty officer.

In a tent full of silent and incredulous men, there was a feeling of total shock... almost despair.

"We are to arrest ourselves. He's coming forward to take personal command. He's gone fucking crazy!"

No one who had heard anything of the heated exchange could argue against St. Clair's view.

Knocke, with a face like thunder, moaned as the medical orderly continued to tease at the piece of shrapnel in his forearm.

"Then we must act immediately."

He held out his hand imperiously for the telephone handset.

"Get me General De Lattre immediately."

As Knocke waited for the call to be put through, a damaged Aardvark was towed past the tent, its mesh screening mangled and blackened.

Knocke doubted that the crew had come away unscathed.

Close behind the towing vehicle came a battered Wolf, which slithered to a halt and permitted a smoke-blackened figure to dismount.

The new arrival threw up a casual salute to his commander and made his report.

"Brigadefuhrer," Uhlmann had not yet bothered to master the French ranks, "I'll need two hours to sort my regiment out... ammunition and fuel... spare crews... we took a heavy hit. Here's my initial report."

Uhlmann handed over the hastily prepared document, and then proceeded to recite the basics from memory.

"I have thirty-six dead, one hundred wounded. That Aardvark," he pointed at the disappearing trailer, "Is probably the only thing we'll salvage off the battlefield at the moment. I've lost two of the Panthers for now, although mine only lost a track, which is why I borrowed this little beast."

The Wolf showed the signs of heavy action, clear silver scrapes where machine gun bullets had pecked away at the armour, and two larger scars where something bigger had come close to ending its life.

"All four of the aüfklarer Antilopes are gone. Heavy losses amongst the crews."

He gratefully accepted a mug of coffee and a cigarette.

"Three Hyenas are gone, plus my support infantry took a hammering."

He remembered something he should have said earlier.

"Krause is dead. His Felix took two solid hits... burned out."

Another old campaigner was gone.

Uhlmann paused whilst Knocke shook his head and grasped his Panzer commander's shoulder.

"Anyway, it's all in the report. We walked into a fucking firestorm, Brigadefuhrer. What went wrong? Why didn't we know about what we were facing?"

Knocke gave a shrug, the telephone still pressed to his ear.

He covered it with his hand and spoke softly.

"An intelligence failure,... a reconnaissance failure, Rolf. Someone simply didn't do their job. We will find out... yes... yes, I want to speak directly to General De Lattre... no... you will get him on this line immediately... that is an order... now!"

Knocke turned his conversation back to Uhlmann.

"We will find out in time, but for now, we need to find a weak spot and plan for another attempt. Our beloved Molyneux is on his way up here to lead us to victory, although we're all under arrest for disobedience of his orders."

Rolf choked on his cigarette.

"What?"

"He wanted us to attack again... same plan... no reorganisation, just attack again."

Uhlmann exchanged looks with St. Clair and the rest of the officers present.

He opened his mouth to speak but Knocke cut him short.

"General de Lattre? General Knocke here.... no... I'm afraid not, Herr General. I'm reporting a defeat... we were stopped dead by a large enemy force that we didn't know about... no... no, not there. No... we didn't get that far, Sir... Route 3323, one kilometre west of Wilhelmshausen... heavy... roughly forty percent of my lead units and," Knocke looked at Uhlmann as he examined the report, taking Uhlmann's shrug as confirmation, "And unusually high casualties amongst the unit commanders. It'll take some time to get my men back on line for another attack, and we'll need to revise the plan. Also, General Molyneux has ordered our immediate arrests and is on his way here to ensure matters are carried out to his satisfaction."

Knocke listened intently, nodding to a man many kilometres away, occasionally humming a positive response.

"Yes, Herr General. General Bittrich is out of contact at the moment, but I'll confirm his temporary position as soon as I contact him. My commanders think it'll be two hours before we can get back into the fight. We will have a plan by then. You'll have your bridgehead, General de Lattre... but... th..."

De Lattre butted into the conversation, understanding the issue that needed to be addressed.

"Yes, I understand that order, General."

Those watching saw a smile declare itself.

"No, I do not need you to repeat that order, Sir."

The smile broadened further.

"Yes, Herr General. Thank you and goodbye."

He handed the telephone back and slapped Rolf on the shoulder.

"Get your men ready to renew the attack, Rolf. I will get you some decent information, so we know what we are up against here. Now go."

Opening his words to the whole group, Knocke continued.

"We will make our own plans. We'll commence at 1500, so officers group here at 1400. Find General Bittrich immediately; let

194

him know he has command of Normandie until Lavalle is back in action."

He clapped his hands, chivvying his staff along.

"Now, we must move quickly. I want the latest reconnaissance photos, reports from the last action, everything here, on my desk, before I finish this coffee, kameraden."

The officers and men moved in all direction like a bursting star.

Camerone, wounded and stung, would return to the field.

1313 hrs, Monday, 24th June 1946, Holzhausen, Germany.

Bittrich had been found and was in control of Group Normandie, his absence caused by nothing more sinister than a vehicle breakdown that kept him out of the loop during the vital time.

Hitching a ride on a passing supply truck, Général de Brigade Willi Bittrich, or as he was now, by De Lattre's recent order, temporary Général de Division arrived ready to apologise for his lateness.

The loss of Lavalle, albeit temporary, was not something he had anticipated, but the ex-SS officer was up to the task and took up the reins immediately.

He, Knocke, and senior staff officers were poring over the map and latest reports when Molyneux's entourage swept into the site, changing the atmosphere from one of confident preparation to that of suspicion and threat.

The Frenchman strode into the command tent and stopped at the table, his face dark and malevolent, silently waiting for some recognition of his status and presence.

Bittrich obliged by calling the assembly to attention, throwing up a salute, and starting into a formal report, one that was cut short with malice.

"Herr General Molyneux, I have taken command of Normandie and…"

"Shut your mouth! Just shut your mouth right now! I'll deal with you later!"

Molyneux slammed his hand on the table, sending pens and documents into the air.

His hand shot out, a single gloved finger holding a magnificent polished ebony cane, trimmed with elegant silver settings, pointing out the two main targets for his malice.

"You, you… you… fucking useless German bastard!"

Knocke stood silently and expressionless.

195

"And you, you traitorous pig!"

St. Clair blanched and his face showed his anger and contempt.

"Why are you still here? I ordered your arrest! Capitaine!"

The officer commanding Molyneux's troops stepped forward, ready to do his General's bidding.

"Capitaine, detain that... and that," he pointed at the two Legion officers with all the contempt he could muster, "And if they resist, you may shoot them out of hand."

Captain Maillard relished his instructions more than anyone realised, except Molyneux, who had selected him purposefully and, perhaps, Plummer, who knew everything there was to know about anyone in the Corps headquarters.

Maillard's extended family had suffered huge loss at the hands of the Waffen-SS in the atrocity at Oradour-sur-Glane in 1944.

That no one present had been anywhere near the massacre was of no consequence.

To him, all SS were to be hated and exterminated.

Plummer was not present to enact De Lattre's long-standing instructions, having already absented himself due to the death of a family member.

Had he been there, what came to pass might never have occurred.

The atmosphere in the command post went from suspicion and threat to one of extreme danger for all concerned.

The four men positioned behind Maillard tightened their grips on their Mulhouse manufactured ST-45s*.

It said a lot about Molyneux that he had allocated the modest supply of the excellent new assault rifles to his rear headquarters before sending any to the front.

The muzzles of the ST-45s present in the tent moved from side to side, menacing the assembled legion officers.

Three people entered the command post, aware that something of importance was happening.

The leading officer, De Walle, quickly assessed what was happening and moved to interject, but a head gesture from Molyneux ensured that one of the ST-45s was focused purely on the 'Deux' General.

"Keep very quiet, Général de Walle, and you may well come out of this with your rank intact."

Molyneux returned his attention to those around the table.

St. Clair was extremely agitated, and the sadistic Frenchman derived great satisfaction from the sight of the decorated officer, albeit clearly a coward and traitor and not worthy of his awards, visibly cowed by his presence and under his thumb.

He derived much less pleasure from the sight of Knocke.

Stood erect at parade ease, face set in a passionless mask, the useless German bastard had not moved a muscle.

"Capitaine, I believe that one needs some encouragement."

Maillard stepped forward and, in one easy movement, slammed the butt of his assault rifle into Knocke's midriff.

Hard.

The veteran soldier folded instantly, firing liquid from his mouth as his stomach rebelled at the treatment.

Bittrich protested, his shouts stopping any further harm to the gasping Knocke.

"Molyneux! What the hell do you think you're doing, man?"

Molyneux's face betrayed his total pleasure at the circumstances he presently found himself in.

"Clearing out this nest of vermin... cleansing this formation so that it consists solely of those who will fight for France... removing traitors..."

He walked slowly round the table until he was next to the collapsed Camerone commander.

"This piece of shit disobeyed my direct orders, and he should think himself lucky that I don't have him shot right here... right now!"

He released the stick from under his arm and slid the black ebony shaft under Knocke's chin, pulling the distressed man upright.

"You will not walk away from this one, you German bastard."

Perhaps it was the fact that there was no perceived threat from this particular officer... perhaps it was a matter of gender... certainly, it had to be because one of Molyneux's entourage knew who she was...

Molyneux became aware that all was not well and that the pressure in his throat was probably caused by the cold business end of a handgun, pressed hard into his flesh by a beautiful woman with cold and deadly eyes.

"Touch Général Knocke again and I'll blow your head... mon Général."

The military title she delivered to him could not have been delivered with less respect and more venom.

Something about the woman stilled Maillard and his men.

They now understood something that they had previously completely missed.

The beautiful woman with the curvaceous form and long curly hair was a person not to be crossed, something her eyes announced to everyone she made eye contact with, even Molyneux, who was suddenly very afraid.

"So... how do we resolve this? I can pull the trigger and we'll be rid of you and your stupidity forever, or I can step back, and leave you to withdraw."

Maillard offered his own suggestion.

"You can surrender that weapon to me and hope that the courts-martial will be lenient to you, Commandant."

He used Anne-Marie's rank with more deference than he felt, as he had already assigned the bitch to his list of traitors ripe for destruction.

"That will not be necessary, Captain."

Knocke spoke, his pain evident in his clipped words, pulling himself back upright to deliver his message.

"Under orders given to me by General de Lattre de Tassigny less than one hour ago... I must inform you that you have been relieved of the command of the Legion Corps D'Assaut... effective immediately that I delivered his order to you. You will return to your former headquarters and wait for further orders to arrive. You will no longer issues orders, but will be afforded the privileges of your rank, until such times as your fate is decided."

Ignoring Molyneux's blustered rebuttal, Knocke switched immediately to Maillard, licking a tinge of blood from his lips before he spoke.

"General de Lattre was specific about any officers presently under your command..." the veteran tank officer splutter and coughed, a mixture of spittle and blood causing concern amongst those around him, "...They are to be permitted to return to their duties, in the full understanding that they have acted under orders that they believed to be fully lawful. There will be no repercussions... so long as the response to this command is total and immediate."

Maillard was a man in turmoil.

His natural hatred for the ex-SS around him was bolstered by the presence of the French General who had issued him with definite orders.

On the other side of that, was the presence of a gun at the throat of that same General, and the orders that the German bastard had just passed on from De Lattre...

'... from De Lattre?'

198

"Show me these orders."

Knocke could not, and said so, and explained why.

He turned to the communications officer, seeking reconnection with De Lattre's First Army headquarters.

The attempt quickly proved in vain, the General not being available to take a further call.

"So, we have a problem, Capitaine... I need to plan an attack to break through the enemy positions ahead. I can't do that while you stand there with your guns, refusing the orders of the Army commander."

Knocke left that hanging for a moment, hoping to reinforce that message with the silence.

"I have no order... just the words of someone I came here to arrest."

Maillard left off the bit about the swift courts-martial and inevitable sentence that had been loosely discussed with the vengeful Molyneux.

In his mind, the single most important factor was the automatic pistol rammed into Molyneux's throat, held there firmly by a woman who clearly knew how to use it... and would do so without a second's hesitation.

De Walle held up his hands in a placatory gesture.

"Gentlemen, we're all military men here," which was the first of his lies.

"There is a war to prosecute, so let's find an arrangement that will allow us to do so properly, and without duress."

Eyes swiveled to him and gave him their full attention, all save Anne-Marie de Valois, who kept hers firmly on the men with guns drawn.

"We clearly have an impasse."

To Maillard, he spoke firmly, but with an even voice.

"You have acted under orders from authority and, as Général De Lattre's orders state, shall not come to harm. So there is no pressure on you to act precipitously in any way."

He looked at his 'Deux' comrade.

"My colleague has acted as she believes correct in the circumstances that have presented themselves. I know her... and know she will not hesitate to remove the Général's head from his shoulders."

That was definitely no lie.

De Walle looked at his watch, gauging the time of the events he knew were in operation.

"Might I suggest the following compromise until we can get definite instructions from higher authorit..."

"I am high authority, De Walle, I a..."

The pistol pushed just a little harder.

"With regret, Général Molyneux, I think we have yet to have that point decided."

The Frenchman wisely decided to await the rest of De Walle's proposition.

"I believe we should place our weapons away from use, clear the headquarters of unnecessary personnel, and get about the process of organising a successful attack."

Everyone, except Molyneux, understood that the words had been directed mainly at Maillard.

De Walle decided on a different tack.

"Perhaps, Capitaine Maillard, it would be appropriate for you to remain in here, purely as an observer? Retaining your firearm as befits your rank. Similarly, I think Commandant De Valois will remain in comparable state."

The reaction was slight but noticeable, and the wily intelligence officer knew he had his man.

"Général Molyneux, I would suggest that we all refrain from unhelpful threats and orders... and that... for the moment... you remain purely in an observer's role... whilst we make the greatest possible efforts to ascertain the present circumstances."

Restricted by the recently increased pressure on his windpipe, Molyneux wisely decided to give solely a curt nod.

Turning to the assembled Legion officers, his eyes took in Knocke's bloody lips and grey face.

"I trust that is satisfactory to you all."

His eye gave the slightest of winks.

Bittrich moved forward carefully, picking up the disorganized sheaf of intelligence photos.

He brought the men of Normandie back to business.

"Perfect... now let's move on with the war, gentlemen."

A wave of relaxation and relief swept through the command tent, the last sign of which was the sudden absence of the pistol at Molyneux's throat.

The martinet General turned to De Valois and, staring at the female officer as evilly as he could manage, spat a threat with his most venomous voice.

"Regardless of what happens here, you will pay for that. I will have my day with you, Commandant."

Anne-Marie leant closer, and her tone gave greater weight to her words than Molyneux ever thought possible, and he felt the sudden return of fear.

"I'll be ready, mon Général... I won't be stood open and vulnerable so you can just strike me down with a rifle butt or your cane... I'll be prepared... so... when it comes to it... we'll see who will have their day with whom."

The beautiful face contained the eyes of the Grim Reaper.

De Walle coughed.

"Commandant De Valois, stand down if you please."

She held Molyneux's gaze for three seconds longer, then relaxed her posture, slowly removing the weapon that had reappeared at his throat and bringing it down to her side.

The Frenchman rubbed his neck, the presence of the muzzle, even though absent, still seemingly apparent and urgent on his flesh.

Uncharacteristically, although perhaps not surprisingly, Molyneux moved to the table in silence, ready to observe the planning in progress.

Bittrich nodded to him and set about the task of regaining the initiative.

[*Author's note – For RG purposes, the French designated the refined ST-45 as the CEAM m46. I have retained the former German nomenclature for ease.]

1400 hrs, Monday, 24th June 1946, Holzhausen, Germany.

The atmosphere had gradually calmed down, although occasionally it would rise to a little peak, most often with an outburst from Molyneux, mainly objecting to part of the military plan. His contribution ended each time with a simple gesture or cough from De Valois. No more was required.

However, the plan was finished and the unit commanders arrived to receive their brief, all having been tactfully intercepted outside by De Walle's men and apprised of the unusual circumstances they would find inside.

The briefing commenced, with Bittrich laying down the overview.

His words were cut short by a kerfuffle at the entrance, and, like the Red Sea opening to Moses and the children of Canaan, the officers moved aside to let De Lattre enter, accompanied by two very agricultural looking NCOs.

The salutes were numerous and impressive, all of which were returned with a single simple gesture as the commander of French First Army took centre stage.

Molyneux went to speak, but a hand stopped him on the intake of breath.

"Wait please, Général Molyneux. You will have your opportunity later."

"Général, I must insist! I..."

"Later."

"I must insist!"

De Lattre paused and looked at the red-faced officer and immediately decided to change his plans.

"Very well then. We'll get this out of the way immediately."

De Lattre held out his hand and one of his staff officers swiftly slid an official document into it.

"This is your transfer to the Foreign Ministry in Paris, effective immediately. You will go straight there, and report to the Minister who, at my suggestion, will assign you to the Ambassador's diplomatic staff in Senegal, in the role of special military advisor. I envy you this opportunity to serve France."

Molyneux took the orders like a man in a trance, read them, and still didn't manage a word by way of reply.

"Now, Molyneux, we have work to do here. We wouldn't want to keep you from your important assignment, so if you don't mind, we'll move on. Bonne chance."

Turning to the nearest man, De Lattre continued, ignoring the barely concealed grins on a number of Legion faces.

"Capitaine, you will remove yourself from this command post and wait outside. Consider yourself under my direct orders until further notice. Am I clear?"

"Yes, mon Général!"

Maillard saluted and left immediately, following in the trail of the disgraced Molyneux, not knowing what his future might bring.

Finally, De Lattre turned to Anne-Marie De Valois, his face softening in an instant.

"You may also leave, Commandant De Valois. I will wish to hear your version of these sorry events once I have finished here."

He turned away to the table, the sounds of the departing disgraced Molyneux and party fading as he concentrated on the maps and notes before him.

"You are unwell, Général Knocke?

He had spotted the man nursing a clearly tender stomach.

202

"No, thank you, Sir, I'm fine."

"You don't look fine."

Knocke brought himself more erect, controlling his reaction to the growing pain in his stomach.

"Honestly, Herr General, I'm fine. The plan…"

De Lattre shrugged as only a Frenchman can shrug.

"Mes amis, I regret… this plan… it will not come to pass. I bring news of change."

Over the next thirty minutes, the new plan was discussed and the Legion's attack was modified.

1525 hrs, Monday, 24th June 1946, Holzhausen, Germany.

The Legion artillery had been raining down for twenty minutes, sending death and destruction all over the Soviet front and rear line positions.

Fig # 191 – Allied Order of Battle – the Fulda River, 24th June 1946.

ALLIED FORCES,
FULDA RIVER, GERMANY,
24TH JUNE 1946.

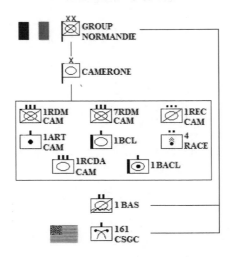

The leading echelons of Group Normandie had already enjoyed a spectacular display by medium bombers and ground attack aircraft.

Smoke, fire, and explosions from the air raid melded with the additional destruction wrought by the Legionnaire's guns.

At 1525 precisely, mortars commenced throwing smoke shells downrange, bathing the area in front of the Soviet line in chemical smoke.

The recently arrived US 161st Chemical Smoke Generator Company started churning out large volumes of concealing smoke, which was carried in the right direction by the gentle and cooperative breeze.

Late to the field, Knocke had ordered one of his infantry companies to help with setting up the generators.

The African-Americans and the Legionnaires were wary of each other at first, but had soon found how to work together.

The M2 generators had been readied in record time, in purpose-built positions, complete with spare oil stocks, as the black Americans and ex-SS troopers worked and sweated side by side.

Fig # 192 – The Legion's second battle on the Fulda.

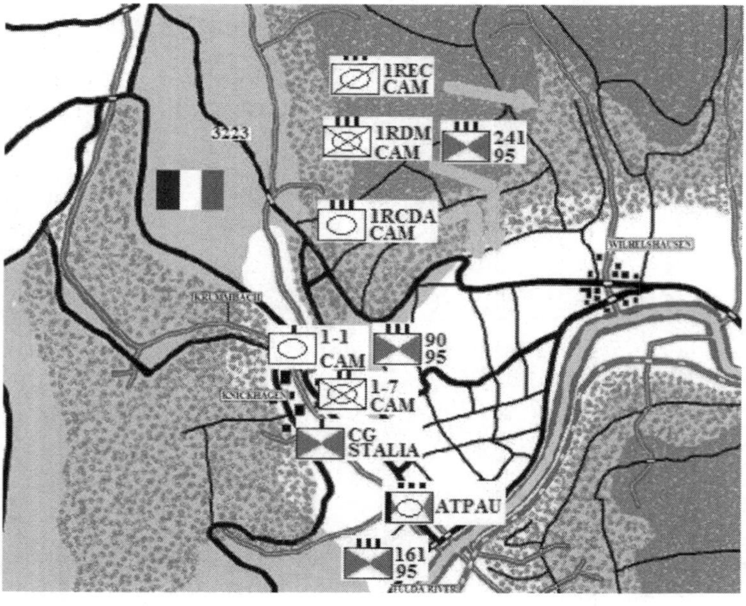

204

Many a legionnaire had pockets stuffed with Luckys or Chesterfields, and in return, the 161st soldiers had secreted bottles of cognac or calvados.The Legion artillery switched from HE and fragmentation to add their own smoky contribution to the mix.

The perfect gentle easterly ensured that the Soviets could hardly see their hand in front of their face.

Nervous Red Army soldiers, sat astride Route 3223, started firing at nothing but a waft of smoke, convinced that the devil incarnate was upon them.

At 1530, soldiers and gunners from Camerone fired back, aiming blind into the smoke, but with the advantage of having marked many targets before the smoke engulfed the battlefield.

The plan moved ahead like clockwork, as elements of the 7e Regiment du Marche launched a noisy diversionary attack against Fuldatal, to the south of the main defensive positions around Route 3233.

Centrally, a battalion of the 7e RdM, supported by some of Uhlmann's tanks, kept up a steady fire through the smoke screen, which was ably topped up by the smoke generators and indirect fire from support weapons.

Their job was to pin the defenders in place, suggesting a further advance, but actually keeping their heads down in the hasty positions they had assumed.

It was the attack of 1er Regiment du Marche, supported by a hard wedge of the 1er Chars D'Assaut, both units from Camerone Division, which had the task of breaching the enemy defensive positions.

Moving fast and light, two battalions of Camerone's 1st Regiment du Marche pushed into the woods to the west of Holzhausen, negotiating the brooks and streams that were commonplace, running between the roots of the tall trees.

With them came the Wolves and Hyenas, the converted tanks ready to knock down any heavier support that the assaulting foot soldiers might encounter.

Close behind the lead elements came the reserve 3e Bataillon and the majority of the 1er Régiment Étranger de Cavalerie, Camerone's small reconnaissance unit.

The flank attack slammed into modest Soviet positions in the woods northwest of Wilhelmshausen and quickly overran the distracted defenders.

In the handful of hand-to-hand combats that occurred, the Soviet defenders were quickly overwhelmed, their continued physical decline a huge contributory factor to the one-sided close quarter fighting.

The 1er REC and the reserve battalion, the 3^e/1er RdM, quickly followed through and led off, striking northeast towards the bridge at Wilhelmshausen, seeking to capture it intact.

2^e/1er wheeled to the south and drove into the rear of the main line defences, supported by half of the Wolves of 1er Regiment Char D'Assaut, who quickly scored successes when they overran a redeploying company of 100mm anti-tank guns.

1er/1er mopped up and secured the area, suffering a few casualties rooting out diehard Soviet soldiers.

7e RdM reported unexpected success in their diversionary attack, so Knocke, not one to miss an opportunity, ordered them to drive on through Fuldatal and seal off any escape by the Soviet forces to his front.

Bittrich had already placed the 1er Bataillon Amphibie Spéciale at the disposal of the Normandie commander, and the unit was swiftly dispatched to cross the river at Fuldatal and drive up to Wilhemshausen, thus taking the bridge from both ends.

A map reading error brought the 1er BAS into the column of units destined to move through Knickhagen, some kilometres north of where Bittrich had intended them to be.

The disaster of the first action was quickly washed away by the success of the second, and the mood was lifted throughout Camerone and the rest of Normandie.

The main Soviet defences crumbled and the reports quickly filtered back to the command post.

The Soviets were running.

Knocke ordered the smoke generators stopped, the artillery and mortars were called off, and his main force was prepped for an immediate advance, pending confirmations that he had already asked for.

Such was the euphoria of the moment that no one noticed his pale features, the sweat running down his face, and the controlled breathing of a man in pain.

He sat down heavily, holding his stomach, finally attracting attention.

"Mon Dieu! Ernst!"

"Ernst! Mein Gott!"

De Walle moved swiftly for a big man, Bittrich similarly for a man not wholly well, but neither was quick enough to stop the now unconscious tank officer topple off the chair, face first into the leg of the table, adding a nasty facial wound to the ruptured stomach that Maillard had inflicted with his butt.

Bile and blood passed Knocke's lips.

The shouts of alarm summoned the security detail, whose commander immediately dispatched four men in search of medical assistance.

Bittrich wobbled on his feet, as his recent illness declared itself again, and was assisted to a chair to await the medics' arrival

For a sometime to come, the collective eye was off the ball.

1554 hrs, Monday, 24th June 1946, Knickhagen, Germany.

The Legion units were backing up as they tried to flood down Route 3233, and some enterprising commanders sought to bring their men to the field by alternate routes, ones outside their orders but that offered the promise of speed of advance.

The commander of the 1er Légion Étrangère Batallione de Chars Lourds informed headquarters of his intent by radio, but the message was one of those that was somehow lost in the kerfuffle of Knocke's collapse.

The heavy tanks of the 1er BCL drove forward, complete with their infantry escort company, and leading the 4e Légion Étrangère Roquette Anti-char Équipe, taking the track that would link up with the minor Route 40, allowing the entire force to move through the valley and on towards the river plain and the main road north.

Backed up behind them were the amphibious transports of the 1er Bataillon Amphibie Spéciale, miles away from where they were supposed to be.

95th Rifle Division had had a bad war, and, despite receiving reinforcements at the end of the cold winter, the formation was a division in name only.

None the less, it had still performed well against the advancing Allies soldiers, so well that the Third Army commander had, uncharacteristically, pulled it out of the line for some rest in a quieter area… on the Fulda.

Fig # 193 – Soviet Order of Battle – Knickhagen on the Fulda River, 24th June 1946.

SOVIET FORCES, FULDA RIVER, GERMANY, 24TH JUNE 1946.

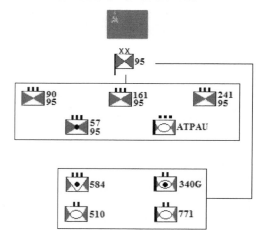

At least, it had been quiet until the legionnaires of Normandie arrived.

The men of the 90th Rifle Regiment were presently being driven from the field to the north of Knickhagen.

Part of the 161st Rifle Regiment, the most savaged of the division's main combat units, was fleeing northwards in front of the advancing 7th RdM, apparently aware that their only route to safety lay in Wilhelmshausen.

However, part of that same unit, Combat Group Stalia, was still in position within Knickhagen and its commander, the eponymous Major Stalia, had very specific orders on two matters; namely holding his position at all costs, and his responsibility towards the special unit under his protection.

In essence, the attached ATPAU, Army Tank Prototype Assessment Unit, field tested new vehicle designs under combat conditions, a risky but worthwhile venture, at least to Soviet eyes.

However, its presence in Knickhagen was an error, and the unit found itself in dangerous surroundings, too far forward and in danger of being cut off.

None the less, the experimental weapons were there to fight and prove themselves, so preparations were made to do just that.

Under no circumstances were the ATPAU vehicles to fall into enemy hands, something that Stalia understood both from his colonel, who had informed him his life hung on successfully discharging that order, and from the straight-forward statements by one of the heavy tanks' commanders, a no-nonsense senior NCO called Kon.

His particular vehicle was an IS-IV with a difference, upgunned to deal with the new Allied tanks that were expected to make an appearance in the summer of '46.

With a huge 130mm main gun, new gearbox, upgraded suspension, and twin all-new engines, the IS-IVm46/B was virtually a new tank, and, as such, needed a field test with the specialists in the ATPAU.

There were two of these huge beasts, both manned by experienced Soviet tankers.

Alongside them was the experimental SPAA troop, consisting of two of the extremely new BTR-152, known as the ZSU-12-4, based on the latest transport development, the Zis-151 truck, and two ZSU-12-6, a recycled KV or IS-II tank hull, mounting the all-new four and six barrel DShKM heavy machine-gun mounts respectively, something hastily thrown together to help counter the ever-present ground attack aircraft on the modern battlefield.

The approach of the Legion armoured spearhead committed the IS-IVs to closer combat than Kon would have liked, but they were there and could not shirk the task, so the two behemoths waited in hull down positions, ready for the moment to strike.

The battlegroup paused north of the Krummbach Bridge whilst an evaluation was made.

The smaller bridge that would have taken the group straight across the Osterbach and onto Route 40 was considered hardly suitable for the lighter vehicles, and most certainly incapable of carrying the Tiger IIs of 1er BCL.

A small composite unit from the 1er Régiment Étranger de Cavalerie led the way, detached purely to satisfy the heavy tank unit's reconnaissance needs.

Part of that composite took the southern route, intending to move parallel to the main force, but on the eastern bank of the Krummbach.

The rest went ahead of the main body.

The leading Camerone vehicle, a recently acquired and quite battered SDKFZ 251/D half-track, still sporting the partially obscured insignia of the panzerjager abteilung of 2nd Panzer Division, turned the corner, stopped, and disgorged its squad of grenadieres.

The soldiers moved apart and swept down the hedgerows, making for the nearest houses, all the time chivied by their unit commander, who was, in turn, chivvied by Hubert Hertz, the commander of the Heavy Tank unit.

Fig # 194 - Action in Knickhagen, Germany.

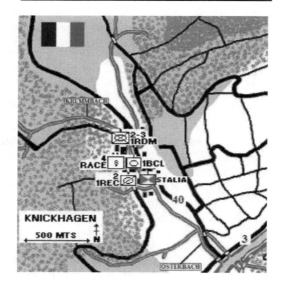

Time.

On the battlefield, time can be as much of a killer as a champion, the absence of it, or the urgency in trying to gain it, often leading to disaster.

In the case of the Legion units traversing Knickhagen, the latter case held sway, and the imperatives of time meant that things were not as they should be, were not done as they should have been done, or were overlooked.

210

A kubelwagen took up the point position on the junction of Sudholzstrasse and Vor dem Wiedehagen, closely supported by a jeep with a .50cal mounted.

An Opel Blitz truck disgorged more men, who swept deeper into the village, hastily ensuring that no Soviet heroes lay in wait with a panzerfaust or Molotov cocktail.

The axis of advance was down Sudholzstrasse, heading to secure the bridge at the junction of Osterbachstrasse.

In a building adjacent to the kubelwagen, soldiers prepared to defend the stairs. Stalia's men held their breath as the Legionnaires swept through the ground floor, sparing only a cursory look up the half burned dog-legged staircase.

A terse radio message interrupted the search and the leader, a new NCO, drove his men on, eager to please his unit commander, who had demonstrated confidence in him with the recent promotion.

The error was repeated elsewhere.

In the butcher's shop, a vicious firefight broke out, as a group of Legionnaires found some enemy hidden away in an attic room.

The exchange was brief, and the Soviet soldiers were killed to a man, grenades doing most of the grisly work, as well as setting fire to the old shop.

The small fight was repeated in a few other places, and with the same result.

Anxious to get the tank officer off his back, Felix Bach pushed his recon troopers harder, transferring the pressure from above to his men up front.

The men obliged, and hurried through their duties, quickly reporting the road and main bridge clear.

"Panzer marsch!"

Hertz, buoyed by the quick work up front, whirled his arms at his subordinate tank commanders, speaking into his intercom for the benefit of his crew.

The King Tiger leapt forward as the driver let the clutch out too quickly.

Hertz was thrown forward, but managed to steady himself, although he did smack his nose with his own hand, causing his left nostril to spout blood and his eyes to water.

His Porsche King Tiger preceded the three Henschel versions in line, the column led off by the Staghound armoured car.

Close behind the heavy tanks came infantry support in lorries, and between the two an M-16 moved forwards, its crew scanning the skies in case the Red Air Force made an unexpected appearance.

The 4ᵉ RACE was next in line, with the rear brought up by a platoon from the infantry element.

The two Tiger Is had moved off the road and remained north of the Osterbach whilst an oil leak was being dealt with on one of the vehicles.

Both Tiger crews were taken by surprise at the quickness of the recon unit's work, and worked fast to try and tack themselves onto the rear of the column, as soon as the fault had been found and fixed.

Stalia waited and watched, both concerned and buoyed by the sound of approaching heavy tanks.

His troops had a motley assortment of weapons at their disposal, from a PTRD anti-tank rifle, through a pair of US bazookas, three panzerfausts, and a few crates of Molotov cocktails. The fire discipline of his hidden troops was superb, and the leading echelons moved past unhindered.

Hertz's tank, leading when it should have been nowhere near the front of the column, moved up to and past Stalia's concealed position, the familiar shape of the deadly tank bringing back more than one awful memory for the troops of 161st Rifle Regiment.

The Staghound moved over the bridge and positioned itself on the junction of Route 40 and Burgstrasse.

Behind it, the Porsche Tiger II moved onto the bridge.

Hertz's eyes still ran with moisture, his stinging nose provoking the reaction.

Perhaps, had he been able to see clearly, then the extra height he enjoyed from being in the huge tank's cupola might have made a difference, and he might have seen something deadly, and what came to pass might have started a different way.

But he couldn't, and he didn't, so did not see the cable that everyone had missed.

Stalia clapped his hand on the shoulder of the NCO waiting, the tension of the moment causing the Corporal to yelp with surprise, even though he still managed to twist the handle on the captured German Glühzündapparat 37 detonator, sending an electrical pulse down the cable to the explosives underneath the Osterbach Bridge.

Underneath Hertz's tank, the demolition charge of two hundred kilos of US military explosive did just what explosive is supposed to do, propelling energy waves in all directions, many of them upwards.

The bridge rose, taking the seventy-seven ton tank with it, reaching an impressive height before gravity resumed control, returning the lump of metal to ground.

The tank slammed into the riverbank, nearside first, and rolled onto its top, messily flattening the upper portion of the insensible Hertz, who had somehow remained within the cupola.

Whilst not as demonstrably deceased as Hertz, the rest of the Tiger's crew were equally dead, slain by concussion and hard impacts with the unyielding metal of the tank's interior.

The destruction of the bridge was the signal for mayhem to commence, and all along the route of advance, Soviet troopers revealed themselves, raining down death and destruction on the stalled Legion column.

Two of the other King Tigers took numerous hits and both added smoke and flame to the confusion, some of the escaping crewmen screaming as fire took hold on their clothing.

The surviving King Tiger shrugged off Molotovs and a panzerfaust hit, and pushed off the main road, meting out fire and destruction in the direction of anything that looked like a threat.

All along Osterbachstrasse, legionnaires were dying, as hidden pockets of resistance sprouted bullets and grenades.

But the ex-SS troopers reacted swiftly, and mounted assaults on the known and suspected positions, quickly reducing half of the resistance at the end of the bayonet or with a sharpened entrenching tool.

The physically weakened Russians stood little chance in a battle of strength, and very few of the Legion's soldiers died in the swift hand-to-hand combats that ensued.

Surprisingly, some Soviet soldiers raised their hands, seeking life over sacrifice and, perhaps more surprisingly, the Legion soldiers, for the most part, accepted their surrender.

Some ex-SS soldiers, most often those with dead or wounded comrades lying around their feet, chose a quicker and more vengeful resolution.

At the rear of the column, the infantry platoon deployed and swept forward, supporting the aggressive moves of the trapped main force and the recon elements that had survived the ambush.

The soldiers of the 4^e RACE, mainly unaffected by the attack, secured their own area and, under orders, waited for further developments.

The commander of the 1er BAS decided to remain where he was, set his unit for all round defence, and sent a messenger forward to establish what was going on, all as he struggled with finding his whereabouts on the map.

Casualties dictated that the Battle Group's command had switched to the officer commanding the Second Company of 3^e/1er RDM.

Captain Durand had grown in stature since the early days of the Legion Corps, when he had distinguished himself during the relief of Stuttgart, and had risen immediately to the challenges of his enhanced duties. It was he who was responsible for ordering the assaults and movements that saved the small battlegroup, and ensured victory in the brief but intense battle for Knickhagen.

The infantry of 3^e/1er RDM overcame Stalia's men in less than thirty minutes, enabling Durand to report Camerone's right flank clear up to and including Knickhagen.

Rolf Uhlmann, temporarily thrust into the spotlight as Camerone's senior surviving officer, pushed the rest of the division hard towards Wilhelmshausen and the bridge they needed to hold.

Things started to happen and, unusually for the Legion Corps, they started to go wrong.

The lead elements of the 7^e RDM ran into more mines in unusual numbers as they moved north of Fuldatel, approaching their crossing point on the Osterbach.

Part of the way was marked by dead Soviet soldiers, men felled by their own mines in their haste to escape.

Uhlmann, aware that the 7e and its supporting elements would, at some time, move across his front, did not receive the report of their delay, neither did the divisional headquarters relay it back to him, as commander on the ground.

The 1er Bataillon Amphibie Spéciale came under fire from mortars across the river, causing the unit to scatter and lose cohesion.

Camerone's artillery were tasked with plastering the area east of the Fulda River, keeping enemy reinforcements away from Wilhelmshausen and its vital bridge, denying their support to the under-pressure 1er BAS, the stalled 7^e RDM, or the elements of Camerone advancing north of the Fulda.

Uhlmann ordered the 1er BAS to reform and prepare to force the Fulda east of Knickhagen.

As a stopgap measure, Uhlmann ordered the remaining heavy tanks of the 1er BCL to position themselves on the two hundred metre line, north of Knickhagen, and do what they could to support an assault crossing, should the commander of 1er BAS be able to mount one.

Acting both with and without orders, 4ᵉ RACE followed the heavy tank unit onto the height.

4ᵉ's orders had been to accompany the tanks, so, in that regard, they were correct to move off in pursuit.

However, those orders had been issued under different circumstances, and divisional staff officers assumed that the anti-tank unit remained at Knickhagen, and marked their maps accordingly.

The men of 1ᵉʳ BCL and 4ᵉ RACE were also unaware that the 7ᵉ RDM had been stopped dead by mines to their southwest, their last orders simply stressing to avoid friendly fire against units coming up from Fuldatel.

In the defence of the staff personnel and leadership involved, Wilhelmshausen had started to develop into a major engagement, as considerable Soviet forces were well dug in on the outskirts and inside of the small town, calling more and more of Camerone's limited assets into the fight.

Elements of the division, mainly based around the bulk of the 3ᵉ/1ᵉʳ RDM, sought out the tracks and paths on the southern slopes of Height 346, intent on crossing the Mühlbach to the north of Wilhelmshausen, to try and turn the right flank of the solid enemy resistance.

They, in turn, ran into more trouble, as more mines and well-sited defensive positions chewed up the advancing legionnaires until they were down to a yard-by-yard slugfest.

To the north, Alma had similar problems on the road to Reinhardshagen, where the main approach ran through a pass heavy with Soviet defenders intent on staying put.

The exchange and receipt of information almost collapsed under the strain, and many staff officers, normally proficient and professional, underachieved in their roles.

With devastating results.

Kon had waited on the reports from the group he had sent to check on Knickhagen.

They reported that the enemy force had come to a halt and was making no identifiable efforts to move on.

With an enemy formation halted and in the open in front of him, Kon had resisted the temptation to go at it hammer and tongs, remembering the responsibility the ATPAU tanks represented, although the commanding Major had been all for an immediate assault.

With the enemy force in Knickhagen stalled, an assault on the units to his front was possible.

Leaving two of the SPAA vehicles with the security element to watch their rear, safe in the woods in which they had been concealed, Kon led the two IS-IV variants into the attack, flanked by the deadly ZSU-12-6s.

Each IS had a grape of infantry on board, purely to watch out for any infantryman with an eye for glory and an anti-tank weapon in his hand.

1644 hrs, Monday, 24th June 1946, open ground, north of Fuldatal, Germany.

Fig # 195 – Battle at Knickhagen – Soviet counter-attack.

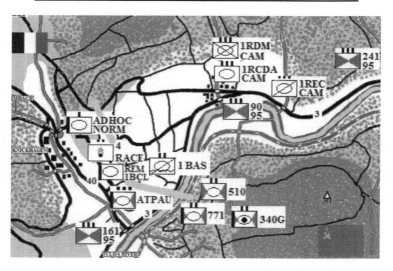

The 1er BAS had moved to the river line but had yet to cross, as building Soviet fire stopped them dead.

Above them, the surviving tanks of the 1er BCL spotted forces moving up from the southwest.

"Hold your fire."

216

The crews of the three tanks, concealed in over watch positions, expected to see the 7e RDM move north from Fuldatal, so saw exactly that.

The men of the 1er BAS expected to see the 7e RDM come up the road to the south from Fuldatal, so saw exactly that.

Except they weren't the friendly troops of the 7e RDM, but the ATPAU moving down upon the stalled amphibious troops, tank guns silent in an effort to not attract attention and get in close enough for the ZSUs to do bloody work.

The senior man, a weary ex-Obersturmfuhrer from the Frundsberg Division and commander of the last surviving King Tiger, took an extra deep draw on his cigarette and exhaled as he spoke into the command net, informing them of the arrival of the lead elements of the 7th Legion Infantry Regiment.

"Ritter-one-four, out."

He took another long draw, unaware that his report had triggered consternation in Camerone's headquarters.

7e RDM's radio sprung into life, requesting a situation report; the reply added to the confusion at base, as the whole unit was still stalled south of the Osterbach.

"Ritter-one-four, Ritter-one-four, Anton, over."

"Anton, Ritter-one-four, go ahead, over."

"Ritter-one-four. All units Rotkopf are stalled at point seven, repeat, all units Rotkopf still at point seven. Confirm identity of units to your front immediately, over."

Lieutenant Laurenz threw his cigarette away and brought up his field glasses, this time using them to actually scrutinize the force that had appeared out of the trees, rather than just for a cursory examination.

"Scheisse!"

In his anger, he thumbed the throat microphone heavily.

"Anton, Ritter-one-four, force to front is Soviet armour and infantry, engaging, over."

He switched channels immediately.

"Achtung! All units Ritter, enemy to front. Engage immediately, out."

His ears were filled with the acknowledgements of the other tank commanders and the shouts of his own crew, as the gunner and loader made their reports, and the driver revved the Maybach engine, making sure he was ready for any movement order.

217

The amphibious unit suddenly had more to worry about than the desultory fire coming from the woods to their front.

Voices were raised in alarm as some soldiers identified the oncoming vehicles as enemy, or, more accurately, as not of the Legion.

Kon, sensing his discovery, ordered all vehicles to open fire, selecting a large amphibious vehicle as his first target.

The 130mm shell demolished the LVT, leaving precious little to mark its existence, and nothing in the slightest bit recognisable of the men who had been aboard it.

The other IS-IV managed to miss, the shell streaking through the target-rich area and ploughing into the ground a few hundred metres beyond.

Either side, the ZSUs commenced sending streams of heavy calibre bullets into the throng, cutting men and vehicles to pieces with the volume of fire, each DShKM mounting capable of flinging over three thousand rounds per minute at its enemies.

The noise was tremendous, but still not enough to mask the passage of high-velocity shells overhead.

Incredibly, the Legion tigers all missed with their first shots, the armour-piercing rounds serving only to announce the presence of unsuspected enemies on the western heights.

Kon, conscious of a lack of heavy opposition to his front, ordered the two IS-IVs to swing left, leaving the ZSUs to finish up the massacre of the amphibious unit.

To add to their problems, T34s slid out of the trees into firing positions, adding weight of shell to the streams of heavy machine gun bullets.

Kon could still see nothing on the heights and knew the enemy would get another shot in before he could use the advantage offered by his 130mm.

'There!'

The muzzle flash gave him a point to concentrate on, and his sight revealed enough for him to fire at.

"Gunner, target tank, gun left eight degrees, range six-five-oh."

The turret whirred briefly.

"No target."

"The hedge, comrade, look at the hedge."

The 'hedge' spat another shell downrange, and the white blob quickly grew large in both commander's and gunner's sights.

The clang was tremendous, but the shell failed to penetrate and, for the observers, flew spectacularly skywards, disappearing from view.

"Identified... firing..."

The vehicle almost staggered, losing forward momentum, as the huge 130mm flew back in its mount.

The shell missed.

Kon examined the lie of the land.

"Driver, move left... to that heap..."

The IS-IV slipped in behind the pile of something unmentionable, clearly the by-product of a thousand livestock.

The breech on the huge gun clanged shut.

Another shell struck the turret front and, again, deflected off without causing noticeable harm.

"Identified... firing..."

The 130mm tank version of the Soviet naval gun had been refined, with deeper rifling, an improved breech, an auto loading mechanism, and superior optics, making it potentially, the best gun on the modern battlefield.

Its weakness was in its ammunition, which failed to measure up to the potential offered by the huge gun.

None the less, the armour-piercing shell punched through the frontal plate of the Tiger I, exploding inside the tank, level with the right ear of the driver.

The Tiger came apart spectacularly, as the internal explosion set off other forces, ripping open the fifty-six ton tank like it was a balsa wood model.

The Soviet tankers celebrated their victory, halting only when another shell hammered into their frontal plate, causing many of the internal lights to fail.

'Time to move.'

"Driver, move out left... head for the road... then full speed into the trees."

Kon saw a way to get round the flank of the enemy, moving back towards the ZSUs he had left to cover his rear.

Laurenz completed his radio report and returned to fighting his tank.

"Leave that one, target, tank, left two degrees, range six hundred."

"On."

"Fire."

The 88mm struck the IS-IV on the front plate, but the tank was expertly angled, giving the heavy tank the maximum protection, and another shell disappeared into the ether with no lasting effect.

To Laurenz's left, the surviving Tiger I scored a direct hit on the nearest ZSU.

The IS-based ZSU-12-6 stopped dead, its engine wrecked by the passage of the tank shell, and was immediately abandoned by its crew, who sought cover from the vengeful Frenchmen of 1er BAS.

In an instant, the other ZSU realised its predicament, and dodged back behind a line of small trees.

The desperate manoeuvre did not save it, as the Tiger hit the gun mount with an armour-piercing round, smashing metal and flesh, and creating a mist of deadly metal fragments that claimed more lives.

The severely damaged ZSU made off, jinking to avoid further hits.

It escaped, aided by the fact that more Soviet armour was presenting itself on the east bank of the Fulda River.

Laurenz heard the squawk box alert him to the presence of someone outside the tank, and lifted the handset, leaving his gunner to fight the tank.

It was the deputy commander of the 4e RACE.

"Laurenz, we're set up and ready to engage. Just making sure you aren't going to move forward if we start sending our wasps down the hill."

Nothing could have been further from his mind at that time, so Laurenz was able to reassure the Lieutenant.

The single Pak40 attached to the RACE lashed out at the assembling T34s, without success, and attracted a volley of shots that, while they missed, unnerved the crew for some time to come.

'Assembling? They're assembling... for what?'

Laurenz's mind idly debated what he was seeing, as well as the problem of the 'whatever the big bastard was to his front', and the other one that had skipped off to his right.

Ending his exchange with the anti-tank officer, Laurenz decided he had to do something about the missing tank, and switched to the local net.

"Ritter-two-one, Ritter-two-one, Ritter-one-four, over."

The terse acknowledgement was accompanied by the sound of the other Tiger's 88mm firing, and the howls from the successful crew.

To his front, the damaged ZSU was hit again, and this time started to burn.

"Ritter-one-four, Ritter-two-one receiving, over."

He quickly checked and could see no sign of the missing Soviet tank.

"Ritter-two-one, that other bastard disappeared off to the right and into the woods. Take your tank and knock him out. Keep him out of point five at all costs... and don't let him get behind us, over."

"Roger, Ritter-one-four, Ritter-two-one, out."

Laurenz stuck his head out and watched the old Tiger I back out of its position, angling away behind a stand of trees.

The roar of a passing heavy shell brought him back to reality, and he resumed command of his tank, only to be struck momentarily dumb by the sight in front of him.

'What the...'

The T34s were moving forward in columns, four lines moving up to the east bank of the Fulda... and across the water...

Laurenz had heard of them before, but this was the first time he had seen them first hand.

He yelled at his gunner.

"Target tank, left four, range seven hundred, hit them in the water... hit them in the water!"

He switched to divisional net and made his report.

"Anton, Anton, Ritter-one-four priority one. Enemy tanks crossing the river at..." he checked the map and reeled off the reference quickly, returning his eyes to the spectacle of medium tanks driving over water.

"At least four, I repeat, four underwater bridges in place. Enemy forming for a counter-attack. Need urgent orders and reinforcements, Ritter-one-four, over."

Nineteen T34s of 510th Separate Tank Regiment swept up to and over the river, descended quickly upon the savaged remnants of the amphibious unit, and sent men and machines to hell in a deluge of metal.

Behind them, a dozen IS-IIs of the 771st Heavy Tank Regiment, early models reclaimed from the Polish Army, moved out into the open, intent on following the T34s across the river.

One smoking tank sat, seemingly floating on the surface of the Fulda, where the King Tiger's gunner had picked him off, the crewmen similarly appearing to run on water, as they escaped the inevitable second killing shot.

Laurenz went for the radio again.

"Anton, Ant…"

The world went red… orange… white… there was even a purple of sorts.

His mind failed to comprehend the situation as it struggled to complete the important task, not realising that a 130mm armour piercing had taken the lives of two of his crew, scattering their body parts and sharp metal throughout the interior.

Laurenz continued to speak into the microphone as the hatch beside him sprung open and his loader, decorated with the detritus of the hull gunner and driver, garnished with urine and faeces where the huge impact had loosened the man's bodily control.

The loader rolled into the rear compartment, squealing with shock and terror, adding to the surreal feelings in Laurenz's mind.

He continued to report the appearance of the Soviet heavy tanks, without comprehending that no-one could hear him, and that parts of the radio set were now embedded in his stomach.

The gunner, resembling something medieval and malevolent, emerged next, his cheek laid open by something sharp, exposing the ivory bone of his jaw.

He shouted as best he could, but his words fell on ears controlled by a distant mind.

He kicked the loader.

"Give me a hand for god's sake!"

The action of his mouth caused blood to pulse from the open wound and triggered severe pain.

The loader looked vacant and the gunner knew he was on his own… and he also knew he had little time.

Wiping the tears from his eyes, he placed his arms around the exposed upper body of his commander and pulled.

Laurenz came up and out much more easily than he had anticipated, probably because the tank commander was much lighter.

His left leg was missing its foot, and his right leg was gone from just above the knee, with both thighs smashed and bloody.

Even as he was dragged across the rear deck, Laurenz continued to send his full report over a radio net that only existed in his shocked mind, until blood loss claimed his conscious thoughts and he departed to a darker place.

Meanwhile, his killer moved closer.

On the ridge, whilst Laurenz and his tank were both still intact, the 4ᵉ RACE engaged.

The X-7 Rotkäppchen was an ugly beast, but troop trials in the latter stages of the previous conflict had shown that, in skilled hands, it could take out anything on the battlefield.

Provided the operator was on the top of his game.

The Legionnaire, once Oberscharfuhrer Peters of SS-Kampfgruppe Dora-III, and considered a master of his craft, waited as the mobile launcher was moved forward, clearing the undergrowth in which the unit had concealed itself.

From the moment the rocket left its cradle, Peters would have roughly seven seconds to make the corrections to the wire-guided missile's flight and bring it into contact with his chosen target; the lead IS-II.

Accelerating quickly, the X-7 Rotkäppchen's speed rose to over one hundred yards a second.

Peters realised he had missed his initial target so, calmly, made the smallest of corrections, sending a signal down the guiding wires.

The tail fins acknowledged, altering the course sufficiently to hit the third heavy tank in line.

The small rocket packed a powerful punch, and the penetrative ability of the hollow-charge warhead exceeded the thickness of the IS-IIs armour by some considerable amount.

One other X-7 struck home from the first volley, two more going off elsewhere, seemingly with minds of their own.

No sooner had the rocket left its cradle, than the support crew grabbed the wooden frame and set a new X-7 in place, attaching more cabling, and finally pushing the whole assembly back into place.

By the time the well-drilled crew had completed the task, nearly a minute had passed, during which time the Soviet armour swept closer.

A single T34 came apart spectacularly, as the 75mm Pak penetrated the medium tank's hull armour, setting off ammunition in its passage through the compartment.

Some of the surviving amphibious troops caused distraction, but, in the main, the ridge ahead became the focus of the Soviet drive.

The concept had been to lure the Allied force into overcommitting at Hann Münden, trying to cramp the advance with stiff resistance.

It might have succeeded, but for the astonishing successes in the defence of Wilhelmshausen, and the unforeseen attempt to cross the river directly in front of the underwater bridges and the secreted Soviet tanks and infantry, east of the Fulda River.

The Red Army tankers pressed home their attack, intent on driving up the ridge and severing Route 3233.

Preparing to send his fourth rocket down the hill, Peters suddenly jumped as something moved at the very edge of his peripheral vision.

The IS-IV had slipped out of sight once Laurenz's tank had been silenced, and had also slipped from the consciousness of the rocket operators, each assuming another had destroyed the threat.

The threat in question manifested itself once more, having crept up a tree-lined track that ran parallel to Route 40.

Shouting at the others, Peters waved his hands, sending signals about the new target.

The two crewmen leapt forward and repositioned the rocket so it was pointing roughly at the huge enemy tank.

The flight was brief.

It was also unsuccessful.

The trailing control wire snagged on a low bush and parted, pulling the X-7 sufficiently to the left to ensure a miss, the smoky trail serving only to mark out where the shot had come from.

Attempting to recover the trolley, the two crewmen were both wounded by a burst of machine-gun fire, which also rendered the mount unusable.

Both men rolled away as best they could, fully expecting the follow-up shell that swiftly arrived and turned the wheeled wooden mount into splinters no bigger than matches.

Neither of them had managed to roll away far enough from the monster shell, and both received more wounds in the process.

Peters dropped back into cover, hoping the hedge would save his life. Despite the hopelessness of the task, he took a firm hold of his Walther pistol and waited to see what the IS-IV did.

What it did was surprise him by staying put.

The act was forced upon the leviathan as a Legion AP shell struck the front idler and separated the track in a spectacular display of sparks and flying pieces of metal.

Peters looked around him as best he could, and saw evidence of friendly armour on the field of battle, albeit the nearest of which was a smoking Panzer IV chassis, whose unrecognisable upper works lay behind it, where the impact of a 122mm shell had deposited it, by weight of shell alone.

The sound of tank cannon rolled over the battlefield, as Legion armour arrived to blunt the Soviet advance.

Uhlmann had dispatched part of his own 1er CDA back to come into the northern flank of the thrust, and sent seven AFVs from the 1st Bataillon Anti-chars Lourde to protect the direct route to the important road.

It was the first major combat for the new SPATs, and great hopes rested on the three Schwarzjagdpanthers, the upgunned production version of the Jagdpanther, kitted out with the lethal 128mm gun and increased armour protection.

It differed from the Einhorn because it possessed the new drive train, whereas the Einhorn used the older Maybach engine and had no transmission revisions. The Einhorn's engine was placed under greater stress, with the additional weight of the heavier gun and applique armour, potentially increasing reliability issues and reducing speed. However, the payoff of survivability and greater killing power had tantalised the Legion, and the handful of einhorns were considered to be amongst its most potent weapons.

However, the brand new Schwarzjagdpanthers were a cut above even them, outperforming the old but excellent field convertion Jagdpanther in all departments.

The surviving two Alligators engaged the T34s immediately, scoring hit after hit, although not every hit resulted in a kill.

The Schwarzjagdpanthers took on the IS-IIs and halted the heavy tanks in their tracks, sometimes literally.

The 128mm shells were more than capable of penetrating the thickest of the IS-IIs defensive armour, and the attacking Soviet tanks started to fall back as more of their number were smashed to a halt.

Some crews even abandoned their vehicles without attempting to withdraw, their morale suddenly broken by the new arrivals and the sights of battle around them.

Peters screamed and screamed at the nearest tank, or more accurately the commander of the Schwarzjagdpanther, who had his head out to survey the battlefield, but who was unable to hear the words of warning.

The IS-IV stopped and made the minutest of adjustments, before sending a 130mm shell smashing into the side of the SPAT.

The impact scattered the road wheels and severed the track at top and bottom points, rendering the vehicle immovable.

Abandoning their crippled vehicle, the slowness of the IS-IVs reload saved the panzerjager crew further wounds, although the turret machine gun sped them on their way as they quickly sought cover.

A Legion shell struck the IS-IV.

Peters held his breath, waiting to see what happened, but the Soviet tank merely moved off, seeking a different position from which to enfilade the Legion flank.

The IS took up a text book angled position and fired, or at least Peters thought it did, although the shot, if it happened, was lost in the most violent explosion he had ever witnessed.

The fire took hold of the experimental tank in the briefest of moments, and no one escaped the brewing tank.

Fascinated by the sight and sound of the jet of flame that rose from the blasted open hatches, he was distracted by a movement beyond the smoke and flame.

Although he didn't recognise the type, he knew it was a friendly vehicle by the colour scheme and markings.

Peters moved quickly away from his hiding place to help the wounded members of his rocket crew, leaving the victorious Einhorn to find a position from where it could visit more mayhem upon the retreating Soviet tanks.

The battlefield started to quieten, with only the occasional whoosh of an X-7 or crack of a tank gun to mark the end of the Soviet attempt to cut Route 40.

Whilst the battle had raged on the banks of the Fulda River, a smaller but equally deadly game of hide and seek had been played out in the lanes in and round Knickhagen.

A deadly game in which there could be only one winner… or two losers.

1700 hrs, Monday, 24th June 1946, south of Knickhagen, Germany.

Kon called for the driver to pull in behind a small barn, the brick and wood structure probably slightly smaller than the tank that attempted to hide behind it.

Whilst he intended to run his tank into the flank of the Legion hillside positions, Kon did not intend to fall foul of any forces in Knickhagen.

He slipped out of the turret and clambered onto the roof of the dilapidated barn, gaining a little extra height.

Had he seen anything in and around Knickhagen, then his options would have been greatly reduced, as would his area of operations.

A fleeting glimpse of an enemy vehicle moving back towards Allied lines made him feel that the forces opposite him had quit the village and that the way was clear.

But he had not got to survive the battles on the Russian Front by making assumptions, so he planned accordingly.

Kon decided to drive further up Route 40 and take a right before the village, far enough away as to not risk tangling with any anti-tank soldiers or armour that might be present.

The arrival of his infantry grape, panting and wheezing, brought a smile to his face. The man had jumped off when the tank engagement first started, which he could not blame them for.

However, he needed them now and he beckoned the commanding NCO to join him on the roof. Pointing out the outskirts of Knickhagen, describing what he expected of the NCO and his men, Kon detailed the initial plan to the red-faced Starshina commanding the ten man group.

The infantry NCO dropped back down onto the deck of the IS-IV and encouraged his men to climb aboard.

They broke out cigarettes as they waited for Kon to finish his reconnaissance, hands emerging from the turret hatches to share in the looted US tobacco.

Kon had nearly finished his sweep when something caught his eye… *'what's that?'* … he stared hard… *'I swear there's something there'*… but there was nothing there… his eyes burned through the lenses of the binoculars, seeking an answer to the question… but there was nothing… *'Are you sure?'*… had been nothing… *"Really sure?'*… nothing at all… *'Nothing at all. Shit but I'm getting jumpy'*…

He slid off the roof and dropped into the cupola, all in one graceful movement.

"Driver, move up, turning right onto the track."

227

Köster held his breath, not daring to risk the slightest of movements of his chest, resisting even the urge to blink as he braced himself against the small tree trunk in order to reduce the possibility of movement to nothing.

He could sense the unknown enemy's eyes seeking him out, boring into the lush green undergrowth around him.

Time stood still, and seemingly an age passed before the man disappeared from sight, and the process of respiration could resume in safely.

Through his own binoculars, Köster had seen the very distinctive headwear of a Soviet tanker, and he knew that the ramshackle building hid the object of his search; the enemy tank.

Slipping back into the small copse, he turned and ran as fast as he could, to where Lohengrin sat waiting, purring like the pedigree cat she was.

Climbing on the front glacis, he paused to brief Meier.

"He's there... down in the valley... cautious tank commander this one...not just coming in with all guns firing... we must be careful with this fellow, Klaus."

"Did you see the bastard, Rudi?"

"No... it's hidden behind a farm building... but I saw the tank commander out having a recon... he'll be coming up this way shortly. We need to reposition."

Köster hauled himself up onto the turret and quickly dropped inside, where he slipped on his headset, connected up, and growled a few orders to Lohengrin's crew.

The Tiger I backed up and then swung off to the right, seeking a position of cover.

Having selected a convenient patch of trees and undergrowth. Köster was taken aback when the chosen lump of greenery spouted streams of heavy calibre bullets.

The hidden ZSUs burst from cover and charged, seeking to get close enough to find some way of disabling the Legion tank and flee the field.

"FIRE!"

Jarome shouted automatically, acting without orders, simply needing to kill the thing that filled his sights. The shell slammed straight into the hull front of the rushing KV based AA tank.

No one was more surprised than Jarome himself when the shell ricocheted downwards into the earth, failing to stop the tank's rush.

Schultz slammed another shell home.

Köster called the target.

Jarome fired the gun.

The ZSU staggered under the impact and slowed perceptibly, but did not stop.

Soviet crew men appeared, smoke issuing from the tank's innards as they popped their hatches.

They rolled off the moving tank and sought cover, leaving the dead driver to ride his tank forward, until the impact with a reasonably sized tree was enough to stall the engine and let the lazy fire slowly consume vehicle and undergrowth at leisure.

The other ZSU took a different course, one that spelt danger for Lohengrin and her crew.

The driver pressed his accelerator to the floor and drove hard at the Tiger, intent on ramming the vehicle, as his uncle had done at Prokhorovka in 1943, although, unlike his uncle, he intended to live.

Jarome lost the target, Köster didn't realise what was happening, only Wintzinger and Meier could really see the intentions.

Wintzinger was speechless and could only manage to fire his machine-gun, hoping to ward off the approaching ZSU.

Meier shouted into the intercom.

"Traverse the gun full right now! Brace yourselves!"

The Tiger swung to the right as the KV bore down on it.

The manoeuvre saved Lohengrin from substantial damage, the call to move the gun preserved the tube from harm.

Instead of hammering into the offside leading edge and shattering the track and sprocket as the Soviet tanker had hoped, Meier's move had presented the flat front of Lohengrin to the flat front of the KV chassis.

The impact was still tremendous and, despite the warning, the crew were flung around.

The squeal from Wintzinger was drowned out by the awful shattering of his radius and ulnas in both arms, as the braced limbs failed to halt his forward momentum, disintegrating simultaneously in the mid-forearm area.

His scream was cut short as his head smashed against the metal, rendering him insensible, and unable to feel anything when the KV rose up onto the Tiger's front plate and drove the machine-gun into his throat with deadly force.

Meier, shaken but in charge of himself, gunned the engine and continued pushing forward.

Köster, Schultz, and Jarome all had matching nosebleeds, plus Schultz had the makings of the darkest and widest of black eyes, following a coming together with Jarome's elbow.

229

The graunching of metal was incredible, but quickly stopped, as the Tiger stalled and the KV stuck fast.

Meier restarted the engine as Köster decided to risk a look.

He immediately saw three shaky figures rolling off the ZSU, all seemingly intoxicated.

Grabbing his pistol, he fired at them, putting one down hard, and adding extra speed to the wobbly withdrawal of the others.

"Back her up, Klaus. Quick as you can."

Supervising the manoeuvre, Köster spared a look in other directions, praying not to see a dark shape in the undergrowth.

The graunching started again, and the KV chassis slid off for the briefest of moments before clinging to Lohengrin like a child to its mother.

"Stop! Whoa!"

Köster waited until the motion ceased and then rose up out of the cupola, sliding across the turret roof to have a closer look at the problem.

It was easy to see what was causing the Soviet tank to hang up.

The impact had displaced one of the bottom plates, and the lip was now sat proud of the rest, and had hooked onto the top of Lohengrin's glacis.

He had left his comms attached, so whispered into his microphone.

"Klaus, I'm still on the turret, so nice and steady. Ease forward about six inches."

The engine note changed and the vibrations showed that Meier was gently slipping the clutch.

The weight held the KV in place for the briefest of moments until the engine overcame the resistance and Lohengrin pushed gently under the hull.

"Good... whoa... enough."

The Tiger stopped and the engine tone dropped off...

...and another engine tone reached Köster's ears.

"Scheisse! Engine off!"

His instincts, honed to a razor edge in combat all over Europe, understood the situation immediately.

He slid quickly backwards and held his hand over the top of the gunner's hatch, demanding that it be filled as quickly as possible.

"Smoke grenade... quick... no one moves, no one fucking breathes."

The grenade hit his palm, and was up and primed in the blink of an eye.

He dropped it underneath the KV's hull and those inside heard it roll and bounce down the front of the Tiger, before the silence indicated it had hit the ground.

No one dared move... they hardly dared breathe...

The sound of the heavy growling transformed into the distinctive sound of heavy diesel engines labouring to propel something large at high speed.

Cursing his head position, Köster used every ounce of his self-control to avoid moving for a look at whatever it was, although, in his heart, he knew it was the enemy tank.

The chemical smoke was intrusive, making his eyes smart and disturbing his attempts to breathe softly.

Fuel leaking from the damaged ZSU was ignited by the grenade's heat, adding burning fuel to the list of worries.

On reflection, it probably saved them, as the smoke grenade petered out very quickly, and a light breeze sprang up, shifting the product of its labours away.

Köster staved off a cough with the greatest of difficultly, all the time feeling fear test his bladder and bowel control... knowing how exposed he was... how vulnerable he was... how they all were...

"Slow down... gunner... mark your target... enemy tank right four degrees... close range... hold your fire..."

The IS-IV slowed and Kon stuck his head out of the hatch, straight into the line of sight of the infantry NCO, who waited for orders.

"Wait a moment, Comrade. I need you up there."

He shouted into the tank.

"Tank halt!"

The IS-IV came to a swift halt and Kon made a decision.

"Comrade Starshina... two of your men... quickly run up there and toss a grenade inside the fucking thing. I'd put a shell in it, but I've none to waste."

Ammunition stowage on the IS-IV, like all IS series vehicles, was at a premium, and Kon was not prepared to waste one on a dead tank.

Two soldiers dropped off the tank and sprinted to the destroyed Tiger, light smoke bathing the front of the vehicle, and a

231

darker, more pungent variety, wafting slowly from the open turret hatches.

Inside Lohengrin, Schultz held a steel helmet containing a few oily rags, all of which were lazily burning, the crew's effort to help paint a convincing picture of the Tiger's destruction.

The sound of someone climbing on the tank meant that Schultz moved slightly to one side and was replaced by Jarome, his Beretta-35 handgun held ready to obliterate the face of anything stupid enough to look inside the turret.

Having been reminded forcefully of the need for speed, the rifleman simply primed his grenade and dropped it into the open hatch, rolling quickly away and onto the ground.

The two soldiers ran away as fast as their legs could carry them, intent on putting distance between them and the likely effects of the grenade in a vehicle filled with ammunition.

Both men stifled a squeal of terror as a grubby hand dropped a deadly egg grenade into their laps.

Schultz, unable to think of anything better in the micro seconds available, turned the helmet over and forced it down over the grenade, dropping his body on top of the stahlhelm.

There was not even time to utter a prayer.

The grenade exploded, firing Schultz upwards into the breech of the 88mm, snapping two of his ribs and adding more injury to his head and face, knocking him out in the process.

His leg broke as he was forced upwards and the limb was left behind, caught up under the gunner's seat. Something had to give, and his tibia and fibula conceded the unequal struggle. His unconscious state prevented the inevitable screams of pain.

The blast scattered the remnants of the burning rags, sending fiery sparks in all directions, some through the open hatch, adding to the evidence of an explosion for the watching eyes at the IS-IV.

"Driver, move forward… follow the track."

The IS-IV leapt forward, almost sending three of the riders flying.

"Remember we have passengers, Leonid!"

Kartsev was an impeccable driver, but the new clutch configuration was, in his own words, a bitch from hell.

Leaving the two 'dead' tanks in its wake, the IS-IV moved on towards the outskirts of Knickhagen, now totally abandoned by the Legion and home only to a few hardy German residents.

Köster decided that he could now breathe again and risked a gentle movement of his head, catching the last moment of the IS-IV's presence before it disappeared from sight.

His sigh of relief was audible to those inside the tank, and brought forward a rush of words loosely based around two themes.

"Has the bastard gone?"

"Max is hurt bad!"

Köster stuck his head into the turret and winced at the sight of Schultz's mangled leg.

"That's got to fucking hurt!"

Jarome, who was figuring out how best to move the insensible loader, could only agree.

"He's out for now, so best we get him moved before he comes round or they'll hear his screams in Berlin."

"Dolf, keep an eye open whilst..."

"He's out cold. Broke his arm at least in that impact."

"Right... Klaus?"

"Ok, I'll do it," and the hatch opened up enough for the driver to look out for approaching trouble.

Köster slipped inside the tank, careful not to step on anything that might object.

He and Jarome managed to organise the broken leg and propel the loader up and out of the turret, where Jarome fished some medical equipment out of the turret bin.

"Right, let's drop that heap of Russian shit off our beautiful Lohengrin, and get out of here quick as we can. Anything, Klaus?"

"Nothing. Engine sound has disappeared, so either he's close and silent or moved off. It went bit by bit, so I think he's gone away."

Acting on instinct, Köster made the call.

"Start her up, Klaus. On my mark, slow reverse, full left."

The Maybach roared, and those that could, even Jarome, spared a look in the direction that the huge Russian tank was last seen.

Nothing.

"Ready?"

"When you are."

"Three... two... one... mark."

The engine note changed and Meier put the tank into hard left reverse.

Köster watched as the displaced plate desperately tried to hang on to the Tiger's glacis, but the extra angle of the left turn meant that it failed.

The plate slid free and the ZSU came away, dragging some of the protective mesh with it.

"We're free... steady back and let the bastard slide off us."

Klaus Meier controlled the ZSU wreck nicely, reversing slowly, and the Russian's tracks gently came to rest on the ground.

"Free."

"Right. That makes me the loader, but first, I'll help Hans on the engine deck."

"Quick check of the tank, Klaus. I'll keep an eye open. Once you're happy, see what you can do for Dolf.'"

Every now and again, Köster spared a look back at the man working on Schultz. He didn't envy him the task of sorting the loader's leg out into some sort of shape, but it had to be done, even though they were taking too much time.

He ducked his head inside and grabbed the MP-40, checking it automatically.

Köster stuck his head back out of the cupola.

"We're going to have to drop him off... first chance we get."

Jarome nodded as he finished up tying the shattered leg to the good one.

"I've given him morphine... should take the edge off when he comes round."

"Hans, leave him now. Just make sure he isn't going to roll off. Check out the gun and make sure we're ready to work."

The gunner had been inside the tank for less than a minute.

"Verdammt! Rudi!"

The finger pointed out the damage.

The hydraulic traverse unit, mounted on the turret floor, had taken a few hits from the grenade.

"Can you rig it?"

"Nope... it's fucked. Unit needs replacing."

"Hand traverse?"

The wheel was spun, but Jarome felt it needed more effort than normal. None the less, the turret moved smoothly.

"Bit stiff, but fine."

"Stiff but fine will have to do."

"Good. Stay there while we move up to that building," he pointed at an old barn, "Then we'll shift Max into it and move off after that Russian bastard."

Meier reported he was happy with the tank; he'd packed some of the new silver scars with mud just to make them less noticeable.

He was less happy with Wintzinger, who was conscious, but not with it.

An ampoule of morphine sent Adolf Wintzinger back to a quiet and restful place.

"Move off left... head to that barn... remember Max and Dolf are on the back."

The driver dropped into his seat and put the Maybach into gear.

Lohengrin eased herself forward and made the short trip to the barn.

Max Schultz was quickly moved into a comfortable spot, whereas Wintzinger required more effort to extricate from the front of the Tiger.

The two injured men safely hidden away, Köster moved the Tiger back towards the suspected position of the IS-IV.

The radio simply refused to function, despite no apparent damage, so they were technically blind to the events on the ridge.

A quick check of the map suggested the most likely route for the Soviet leviathan, the Burgstrasse out of the town being perfect for bringing the enemy tank out on the flank, or even behind the forces defending against the river attack.

Lohengrin set off as fast as Meier felt comfortable with, until Köster called for a right turn and the Tiger moved off.

Having swapped sides in the turret, Köster observed through the loader's hatch, using his binoculars.

Meier's voice piped up in his ear.

"Oberscharfuhrer, if I might ask a question?"

"As if I could stop you, Comrade Driver."

The normal start of an exchange over, Meier posed the question that was on his and Jarome's minds.

"Given that there's just three of us, why in the fucking name of the devil's drawers are we still going after that big bastard?"

It was something that Köster himself had been giving some thought.

Not that he felt his friend deserved a sensible answer.

"Because we are heroes, Ritterkreuzträger Meier. It is expected of us."

Jarome saw the opening.

"In which case, Oberscharführer, I should be permitted to leave. I don't have the Ritterkreuz."

"You were recommended for one, so you're in, like it or not."

That the statement came from Meier caused the gunner to scoff, and his right foot lashed out, catching Meier's shoulder sufficiently to display his feigned 'annoyance'.

"I've been assaulted by a junior rank, Rudi. What sort of fucking tank are you running here?"

"You deserved it for being disloyal to your only friend. Shitty drivers are all the same... and ten-a-pfennig, so... if you don't want to be assigned to the petrol column, I suggest you stop annoying our efficient gunner and know your place."

The humour died away in an instant.

"Come right... I want to go up that grassy slope there... I think we can do that... agree?"

"No problem."

The Tiger moved onto the new course and took the grassy route with ease.

"I'll give you ten-a-fucking-pfennig drivers. It's you tank commanders that are cheap and nasty... with your nice Ritterkreuz, all shiny and unspoilt because us drivers do all the work whilst you put brilliantine in your hair and pose for the photographers."

Not for the first time, the subject of Köster's photo shoot was used against him.

After Hangviller, Köster had been photographed and interviewed by 'Voir' magazine. The subsequent edition contained no clue to his former allegiance, but simply talked of the efforts of the French Army and, in particular, the Foreign Legion, in stemming a huge Soviet counter-attack.

The picture had been edited, for 'security purposes', removing all but clearly French insignia and rank markings, and the accompanying story held little resemblance to the events of that cold January day.

That did not stop Köster getting stick from anyone who knew anyone who had heard someone tell the story they had heard from someone else.

Basically, everyone with a pulse and the ability to work their mouth.

"I sense your next application for leave may fail."

"I haven't asked for any leave."

"Excellent."

Köster started humming the funeral march.

"Bastard."

Jarome decided to stay well out of it.

Suddenly, it was back to business.

"Take her left into that scrub. I want to take a look around."

Lohengrin disappeared into the greenery.

The infantry group had waved Kon and his tank forward, no resistance, no mines, nothing in place to bar the way.

'Almost too good to be true.'

He reasoned the matter out.

This was not a set defence, the enemy had only recently arrived.

No time to do anything much by way of preparing a defence.

The battle was fluid.

An organised ambush wasn't likely.

More likely was an encounter with something moving up or back…

'Or sideways… or up its own ass…'

Kon laughed.

Such was the nature of battle.

"Right, driver, move up slowly. Stop by that wall and let our infantry comrades remount."

The IS-IV moved forward.

With all the soldiers back on their perches, Kon order the heavy tank to move up the road.

Jarome and Meier had taken a few moments to check out more of the tank.

Meier was happier than the gunner, who discovered that the foot pedal linkage to the coaxial had been neatly severed by a piece of grenade.

He had also caught his foot in the blast hole in the metal floor, the pain growing by the second.

His continued assessment of the damage was cut short by the breathless arrival of a red-faced Köster.

"Bastard's coming up the road on the other side of this wood."

He quickly grabbed the map and ran his finger over it, lifting information from it and forming a plan.

"We can't go through the wood... too much noise... skirt it to the right but he may get in position and raise hell before we can intercept. Klaus, move off around the wood to the right... quick as you can."

He tucked the map away in one of the clips that had housed the ready use main gun ammunition.

... which reminded him.

"Gun is loaded?"

"Yep. Forty up."

Which meant that an AP-40 APCR tungsten-cored shell was in the breech, the best tank-killing round the Tiger possessed.

Perversely, the AP-40 had been in shorter supply in the previous war than it was now, with few Tiger Is in service, the round could be allocated in greater numbers, mainly from Allied-held dumps of captured aummunition.

Meier used all his skill to bring the tank up to the required position, as quietly and quickly as he could.

"This will be no place for your men, Comrade Starshina. Drop off here and watch our tail, just in case someone comes up the hill after us."

The infantry grape dismounted and moved back to cover the rear.

Kon ordered the IS-IV forward.

Moving up to the edge of the tree line, he looked in front of him and saw what was often labelled as a 'gunner's dream'.

Enemy vehicles and guns, all looking the wrong way.

Ever the veteran, Kon checked around, sensing a something that worried him, and looked straight down the barrel of a large calibre gun on a very familiar chassis.

"Driver back! Now! Gunner target right forty!"

The IS-IV lurched back.

"FIRE!"

Köster stood away from the breech, ready with another AP40, although he knew that Jarome would not miss... could not miss.

Nothing happened.

"FIRE!"

"I can't fire. Something's wrong."

"Back up... for fuck's sake, back her up now!"

Lohengrin's gearbox protested but held, and the Tiger made a sudden lurch backwards.

A 130mm shell gently kissed the top of the glacis plate and passed close enough to the side of the turret to sear the paintwork with the heat of its travel.

Köster stuck his head out to check the rear.

"Back left, hard down, keep up the speed, stand by to hit the woodwork!"

The rear of Lohengrin swung into the stand of trees, smashing two small trunks flat without a hint of trouble, before coming up against a more worthy and decidedly thicker opponent.

Meier changed down to a lower ratio reverse and kept up the pressure.

The tree gave up the fight, and the Tiger tank disappeared into the small wood.

"Lucky bastard moved just as we fired."

"Never mind, Oleg. We have other company. Target, tank, front, right eight degrees."

Whatever it was, it died.

The 130mm shell made a mess of it, sending armour plates and other pieces of wreckage flying in all directions.

A shell spanged off the turret, small in calibre and of no threat to the IS-IV.

"Recon vehicle crossing right to left…"

Kon resisted the challenge.

"Ignore him… target… tank. Left five degrees."

Morozov could not see the target until a flame blossomed from its gun.

The 128mm APCR struck the gun mantlet and flew off to the left, ploughing through the trees.

The ATPAU crew knew they had been lucky.

Morozov had fired back, but his shell had either missed or had no effect. If it was the latter, then they were in even bigger trouble.

'What is that thing?'

"What the fuck is that thing, Roman?"

"Never seen one before, but I know I don't fucking like it. Driver, back off down the slope. We'll try another way."

The IS-IV reversed.

The deadly Einhorn waited for it to reappear.

Jarome found the severed electrical cable quite quickly, and rigged a workable repair.

"It'll keep, just don't catch it when you're loading."

"Good work, Hans."

Köster returned to thinking through the problem.

"It's not coming. That other gun was a one-twenty-eight… either a Pak or the Einhorn… he'll have fucked off."

Köster was not canvassing opinions, merely talking aloud.

"If he's the steely type he seems to be… well, he won't be running… he'll be trying to do the job…"

The map revealed a track through the woods they were hiding in.

"He'll need to stay below the ridgeline… he'll move to the north… and try to come up this side of that lane… right, Klaus… take her out and right… follow the tree line until you find a track on the right… turn down it and make best speed… got that?"

"Jawohl, Oberscharfuhrer!"

Köster laughed.

"Ten-a-Pfennig drivers, I shit 'em!"

Lohengrin lurched forward and out of cover.

Köster was technically correct in his reasoning, but incorrect overall, as he didn't understand the full nature of the circumstances.

Kon would have taken the fight on further, but his brief was already exceeded, and the safety of the experimental IS-IV was of greater concern to him.

His map was an old German military one, which was far superior to the ones his own leadership expected him to fight with.

"There's a track... through the woods... we'll use that... signal the grape to get back on the tank."

Morozov stuck his head out the turret and waved at the infantry NCO. The soldiers bolted back towards the IS-IV, keen to leave what was clearly a tank-rich environment.

Kon spoke into the intercom.

"Leonid, as soon as the infantry are back on, we'll move off... head towards the woods down this road... when you get to the trees, turn left and follow the tree line... the track will be on the right... about sixty metres or so... straight in and out, as quickly as we can... downhill and to the right... I'll reassess then."

The track was overgrown, and visibility was not great, hardly enough to remain on the track as far as Klaus Meier and Leonid Kartsev were concerned.

The two tanks entered different ends of the one hundred and fifty metre long track at almost precisely the same moment.

What happened would, much later, be described as a replication of a joust of old, with two armoured knights charging each other, flat out, with lances raised.

The foliage receded, permitting both tanks to see each other.

The gap gave little time for anything but a snap shot.

The IS-IV shot first, Morozov firing purely on instinct.

The muzzle flash from the 88mm overwhelmed his vision, and the immense clang on the ISs turret indicated a hit.

The screams from outside indicated that things had gone badly for the infantry clinging to the heavy tank.

The 130mm had screamed inches over the top of the Tiger's turret.

Kon and Köster now shared half a second for a decision on a matter of life and death.

They both decided on the same course of action.

"Ram!"

Kartsev and Meier were mirror images, huddling in their driving positions as they accelerated towards the other steel beast, conscious that nothing good was going to come of the collision.

"Hang on!"

The gun tubes rubbed briefly as the distance closed and the tanks smashed into each other, nose to nose... but not quite.

The track was uneven, and the piece of dirt on which the Tiger raced raised itself slightly, whereas, under the IS-IV it fell away, creating a difference of roughly a foot or so, but a foot was enough to give Lohengrin the advantage; that, and the Russian tank's angled bow.

The height difference allowed the Tiger to rise up on the front of the IS, its momentum driving the fifty-six tons of metal underneath the huge 130mm barrel, causing it to deflect and bend, and rendering it useless.

The impact was less jarring than that with the ZSU in many ways; certainly less destructive on Lohengrin's crew.

The same could not be said for the IS-IV and her servers.

Hero of the Soviet Union Sergeant David Kolesnikov, experienced a nano-second of abject terror before the heavy breech of the 130mm was displaced, mashing his torso against the steel turret wall.

Death was instant.

Sergeant Oleg Morozov had no such luck.

The displacing trunnions sent metal work flying in all directions, and one piece smashed into his forehead, opening up the skull and revealing its contents.

His screams echoed through the huge tank and he clawed at Kon, covering him with blood and other less savoury matter.

Kartsev, closest to the point of impact, was unharmed, but reduced to tears by the sound of Morozov's suffering.

"Kill him... for the love of God... kill him..."

He became almost unhinged by the screaming, the animal-like squeals of suffering.

Morozov was flailing around now, his sightless eyes betraying him as he clashed with the internals of the tank.

The snap of his arm as he smashed it against the breech was like a gunshot.

Kon, his dislocated shoulder preventing him from reaching for his revolver, could not help the dying man.

Metal started to squeal, adding its awful sound to the pitiful Morozov's, and Kon tried to clear his head, realising it had to be the enemy tank moving off.

He had nothing to fight it with, but he would ram it again if he had to.

The screaming ceased in an instant.

The wounded gunner had dashed his head against the turret side and driven a small bracket into the exposed soft tissue.

Still he did not die, but death would embrace him within minutes, and do so quietly.

Kon looked through the vision block on his cupola.

"Leonid... we need to ram him again!"

The engine turned over, but refused to start, sending black clouds out the rear and causing the four surviving infantrymen to cough and splutter.

Enough was enough, and the broken riflemen headed into the trees, intent on escape.

Kon pushed himself upwards, his shoulder sending shivers of pain through his body.

The object of his attention, the 12.7mm DShK machine-gun, had a curious curve to the end of its barrel, enough to render it inoperable.

"Ram the bastard! Ram the bastard!"

"Comrade Starshina. The engine's dead. We can't move."

The Tiger... Kon recognised the type now... sat there, its own engine turning over, gun barrel pointed at the IS-IV, and his counterpart revealing his eyes over the top of a hatch cover.

"Mudaks!"

Kon lapsed into silence before speaking in a softer tone.

"Can you get out, Leonid?"

The clanging sound of metal reached Kon's ears.

"Yes. My hatch is fine, Comrade."

"Then I order you to make your escape, Leonid. Move!"

The driver pushed himself up slowly, not wishing to break the uneasy truce that seemed to be in place.

He moved up onto the turret and looked at Kon.

"And you, Comrade? Are you coming?"

Kon smiled and coughed a little blood.

"I think I have some unfinished business, Leonid. You go… I'll be along as soon as I can."

The driver nodded and rolled off the turret, slid onto the track and was immediately lost from sight.

Which left Kon with a dislocated shoulder and probably more, stood in the turret of a disabled tank, and facing a Tiger tank without a working gun to his name.

'Hardly fucking ideal.'

He laughed, and again the blood came.

"It won't fire!"

Köster looked at Jarome's hasty repair and it still looked intact.

"Again!"

The frustration was tangible on both their parts.

"It won't fucking fire!"

"Scheisse!"

Köster pushed himself up and out, again cradling the MP-40 for protection.

The driver climbed out of the enemy tank and spoke to the figure in the turret, before rolling off and disappearing into the woods.

Clearly, the big Russian tank was crippled, its gun clearly destroyed and the crew abandoning her.

The possibility of capturing the prize suggested itself to Köster.

"Get the gun working as soon as. I'm going to have a look at that bastard over there. Klaus, cover me."

He was up and out before the surviving crew could raise any objections, although the decision seemed rather foolish as mortars shells started to drop nearby.

Running in a crouched position, Lohengrin's commander reached the IS-IV and scrambled up the same front armour his tank had risen up on a few minutes beforehand.

The marks of its presence were clear to see.

The enemy tank commander had dropped out of sight as soon as he saw the Legion NCO approaching, but popped up just as quickly, almost earning himself a face full of 9mm parabellum.

A blank face greeted Köster's request for 'hands up.'

"Ruki Verkh! Ruki Verkh!"

His time on the Russian Front gave him enough experience to remember the Russian words.

The Soviet tank commander raised one arm, pointing at the other and grimacing, his mind full of the knowledge that this was one of the hated SS, masquerading in the uniform of France.

Köster nodded his understanding, whilst he wondered how the man could still smile with his tank smashed around him and dead soldiers all over it.

There was something in the man's eyes...

Something fatalistic...

Something that spoke of duty done...

Something that gave him a moment's concern...

The smell hit him, the slightest waft of some sort of burni...

Kon's smile turned to alarm, as he understood that the German legionnaire had recognised it for what it was.

"You fucking bastard!"

Köster threw himself backwards, not caring where he might land, desperate to get away from the demolition charge the Russian had set.

He failed.

The IS-IV exploded before Meier's eyes, his vision shot by the bright colours as the internal charge wrecked the big tank.

He retained enough sight to see the heavy turret rise into the air and crash back down onto the burning hull.

Meier and Jarome were up and out of 'Lohengrin' in an instant and hit the track almost at the same time, moving forward in search of their commander.

They found him quickly and, in some ways, wished they hadn't.

Naked as the day he was born, save for his boots, Köster was bleeding from a number of wounds, and burnt all down his left side, the side that was nearest the tank as he had twisted in mid-air.

"Oh fuck... Rudi... Rudi... can you hear me..."

Jarome felt for a pulse as Meier slid his hands under Köster and took a hold.

"We've got to move away from that thing," he nodded at the burning tank, the fire growing more intense by the second.

The wounded man groaned as they dragged him further away from danger.

245

"Don't stop. Let's get him up on the tank while he's out."

Although both men were almost exhausted themselves, they managed to get their commander up on the Tiger's rear.

"Right... you do what you can. I'm gonna back out quickly. We've got to get him to a sani quickly."

Meier moved up and into his position as Jarome did what little he could with the already depleted first aid kit.

The engine roared and Lohengrin started the journey back, Meier steering by memory, and occasionally feeding the two men on the rear into thicker over hanging branches.

Lohengrin got the three of them to the main road, Route 3233, and then stubbornly refused to go any further, both transmission and the Olvar gearbox deciding that enough was enough for one day.

They flagged down the first vehicle that passed.

It belonged to Commandant Emmercy, OC of 3e Battalion, 1er RDM, and he immediately ordered his medical team forward and, once Meier had pointed out the correct spot on a map, sent a party off to retrieve the two wounded from the barn on the outskirts of Knickhagen.

The three tankers were whisked off to the temporary aid station, quickly established in Wilhelshausen, where the wounded of both sides were being brought, to live or to die, depending upon the skill of the surgeons or the fickle finger of fate.

Emmercy came himself and gave them the bad news, as both Schultz and Wintzinger were gone by the time his men reached the old barn.

It was a sombre pair that received the news of Köster's survival, albeit in the short term.

Time would tell... risk of infection... shock... the non-committal explanations seemed endless.

Their own wounds treated, the two lay down and were asleep in seconds.

Around them, the ex-SS legionnaires of the Camerone Division, Legion Corps D'Assaut, bled and died, or survived, as the surgeons or fate dictated.

Whilst the battle was technically won, the cream of the Camerone had been blooded, much equipment had been lost, and the impetus of the advance spent and lost in a disorganised and hasty repelling of the Soviet counter-attack.

Molyneux's interference, combined with the loss of Knocke and Bittrich early on, were certainly problems, but not so much that what happened subsequently could not have been... or as the investigation stated, 'should have been avoided'.

Whilst superior skill at arms had been a factor in holding the tide, not one of the senior Legion officers doubted that they had been lucky to come away with the division basically intact, and that there were lessons to be learnt across the board.

It had been a sobering experience for all, not the least for Uhlmann.

His efforts had borne fruit, and he received many plaudits for his quick thinking. In the continued absence of Knocke, he continued as temporary divisional commander, and now faced the difficult task of stitching Camerone back together.

Although, personally, I am quite content with existing explosives, I feel we must not stand in the path of improvement.

Winston Churchill

Chapter 159 – THE HAPPENINGS

1417 hrs, Saturday 29th June 1946, Château de Versailles, France.

"Thank you all for coming."

Eisenhower stubbed out his cigarette and took a deep breath.

"Gentlemen, yesterday I was handed a report from Intelligence. A copy of that report is on the desk in front of you."

Some of the assembled generals went to pick up the folder but Ike raised his hand to stop them.

"Please... look later. For now, I'll give you the bare bones."

He nodded at Hood, who lifted the cover off a display board, whose figures lay stark and unequivocal, supporting Eisenhower's next words.

"The Red Army and Air Force are deliberately targeting US troops."

The losses of the US Army in all areas were twice that of every other Allied nation put together.

Each of the US commanders present had known he was paying a price for the slow slog across Germany, but had assumed that his own situation was, on the whole, no different to the other forces in Europe.

McCreery examined the losses besides his own and grimaced.

His British Twenty-First Army Group had lost nearly twenty thousand men across the board, since the winter broke, and the advance could continue.

Alexander's Italian Group had suffered twelve and a half thousand casualties, and the French eight thousand.

The German Republican Army had suffered the most of all the non-US forces, with thirty-two thousand casualties overall.

Sixty-three thousand US servicemen had become casualties in the same time period, of which just over twenty-three thousand now lay in the earth.

It was Devers that piped up first.

"Sir, the figures you have put before us are accurate?"

"They are."

"So, in the last three months or so, the US Army in Europe has sustained just under ten percent of the casualties the entire US forces suffered in the period '41 to '45?"

Devers went straight to the heart of the matter, earning a few nods from most, and a 'goddamn' from Patton.

"Yes, General."

Eisenhower rose and went to the board, and Hood stepped back to allow his boss full access.

The Allied Commander tapped the bottom line with studied violence.

"Sixty-three thousands of our doughs… let me put that into perspective for you."

He turned, selecting Bradley for eye contact.

"In the Normandy landings and breakout, the total dead the Allies suffered is calculated as between forty-five and fifty thousand."

His finger wagged over the assembly.

"And we all knew we were in a gutter fight then, didn't we?"

Bradley certainly had.

"The US forces alone have sustained approximately 50% of that number of dead since we commenced our attack."

He left that hanging for a moment.

"So, it is Intelligence's view… my view… that the Red Army is deliberately targeting US forces, over and above our Allies."

The men in the room were not unintelligent and needed no more pointers to reach a conclusion.

None the less, Eisenhower supplied it, just in case.

"It's a political move, for sure. They're trying to knock us out of the war by using public opinion against us."

Alexander sought the floor, and Ike motioned that he should speak, using the moment to find and light a cigarette.

"So, by bumping up the resistance to your forces, and inflicting as many losses as possible on your soldier boys, the Russians hope to get the American public to rebel against the war… and make your politicians bring the boys home?"

"Yes, Field Marshal, I believe that is their intention."

"Is that possible, Sir?"

Eisenhower went to reply, but the exclamation of Lieutenant General Mark Clark beat him to the punch line.

"You've seen the demonstrations on the news reels, Sir. You bet your goddamn life it is, Field Marshal!"

Bradley went and grabbed a cup of coffee, starting a minor migration for refreshment.

Returning, he slid one in front of Eisenhower, who acknowledged with a friendly pat on the arm.

The room quietened down again.

"Does the President know, Sir?"

Eisenhower checked his watch.

"General Marshall is presenting him with a copy of that folder as we speak. I have told General Marshall that we will come up with some sort of plan to counter this Soviet ruse, and communicate it to him as soon as possible."

He took a belt of the strong coffee.

"So, gentlemen, what do we do about this?"

The end result was less than satisfactory, *'particularly to George'*, which was not unexpected.

Increased commitment by the other nations, including the South Americans who were presently less than happy with the Atomic weapons use in the Pacific.

The military sticking point was that offense offered advantages, and many, vociferously led by Patton, believed that attacks should be increased, not curtailed.

Eisenhower countered with the fact that the politicians would probably not see it that way; the American public certainly wouldn't.

The air war was to be intensified closer in to the front line, giving enemy field formations additional attention to reduce their effectiveness even further.

General Juin, the French Army's Chief of Staff, had readily agreed that France should shoulder more of the burden, and proudly stated that his country would put more divisions into the line, relieving a number of US units.

Similarly, Generaloberst von Vietinghoff promised more from the ever-increasing German Republican Army.

By the end of proceedings, Eisenhower at least felt he had a plan to present to General Marshall, one that Truman could see would go some way to reducing American casualties in Europe.

Marshall had already mooted that the proposed invasions of Northern China and Siberia would probably be put on hold indefinitely, with a huge effort to supply and rearm Chinese Nationalist forces likely to be proposed instead.

After the meeting had broken up, Ike took a few quiet minutes to himself, draining the last of the coffee pot and finishing his last cigarette.

The board once more drew his eye.

'Sixty-three thousand... goddamned Russian sonsofbitches...'

He drained the cup and left.

1617 hrs, Sunday, 30th June 1946, Sankt Georgen an der Gusen, Austria.

The attack was carried out by 30 Squadron, SAAF, their B-26C Martin Marauders considered more than capable of dropping the Sankt Georgen Bridge into the flowing waters of the River Gusen.

The Marauders lined up their target, well below their normal bombing height of ten thousand feet, and flew straight in from the west, and straight into a wall of flak, thrown up by a Bulgarian anti-aircraft unit that just happened to be in transit and hiding in the worst possible place for the South African airmen.

Both the second and third aircraft were hit, but pressed on, smoke announcing both their passage and difficulties.

More flak rose up, snatching at the medium bombers, and fourth aircraft simply vanished in a flash, small pieces cascading over the Austrian countryside.

Martin Marauder 'Ouballie", coded B-N, the seventh in line, took a shell directly in the port engine.

It did not explode, but caused enough damage to turn the whole engine compartment instantly into a roaring inferno.

Pieces of the engine flew in all directions, one fatally so for the pilot and co-pilot, both of whom had their chests ripped open by the same whirling piece of metal.

'Ouballie' rolled left, and lost height rapidly, describing a fiery arc through the midday air. The remaining five crew members screamed out their final seconds, unable to escape from their aircraft, dying instantly as the B-26C slammed into one of the hills that surrounded the picturesque Austrian town, in an area previously known as Gusen-II, part of the Mauthausen concentration camp.

The remainder of 30 Squadron completed their mission.

Three aircraft had been lost, a heavy price to pay for destroying something that the Soviets would probably temporarily rebuild overnight.

The burning wreckage of Marauder B-N warranted a guard detail, and three reluctant soldiers stood sentry over the glowing remains until the following morning, when what they discovered ensured that the sleepy town of Sankt Georgen an der Gusen woke to a very different day.

0727 hrs, Monday, 1st July 1946, site of the wreckage of B-N, Sankt Georgen an der Gusen, Austria.

"Right, Yefreytor, show me."

The Bulgarian corporal, terrified by the presence of a Soviet Major, and one from the NKVD no less, pointed towards the entrance that had been exposed by the crash and subsequent detonation of the Marauder's pair of thousand pounders.

He had the presence of mind to send his junior man to report their discovery, which report had brought immediate attention from the Soviet security service.

"Here, Comrade Mayor… we made the entrance a little bigger."

The Bulgarian corporal pointed again, just to make sure that the Major understood that the modest opening was actually the one that had caused all the excitement.

"Stay here, Comrade… when my men turn up, tell Kapitan Lapitin to join me inside."

Understanding that he had been dismissed, the Bulgarian saluted and beat a hasty retreat, much to his own relief.

The NKVD officer switched on his torch and slipped inside.

"Comrade Mayor?"

"Comrade Lapitin! Here… look at this!"

Major Voronin was the unexcitable type… normally.

But this was not 'normally'.

Not by any stretch of the imagination.

"Comrade May…"

Lapitin's jaw hung open as the torch beam flicked from him to a row of aircraft fuselages, all marked with the Balkenkreuz of Nazi Germany.

"This way… I need your help… quickly…"

Voronin led off hurriedly, almost losing Lapitin in his haste to get where he was going.

Almost as quickly, he slammed into the back of his Major, who had stopped at a solid steel door.

Voronin shone his torch on a sign.

"Look… stromgenerator… help me with the door."

Lapitin's German was not very good, and he understood the signage more by the graphics than the words.

The two of them heaved on the locking handle, and were greeted by a response.

Inside the room was clean and tidy, and smelt of oil.

They examined the silent generators, wordlessly, thoughtfully, deciding what to do next.

Voronin made the decision, having wisely checked that the generator was connected to a vent.

"Let's get one started."

The task was quickly performed, and it was a testament to German engineering and maintenance that a machine that had lain undisturbed for over a year started smoothly and without issues.

"I think this one here," Voronin announced, more for his own benefit, as he threw a large switch.

Nothing.

Lapitin found the wall switch and flicked it warily, bathing the generator room in yellow light.

"That's a lot of generator for so small a light, Comrade!"

The light was also creeping through the door jam.

Both officers approached the steel door and pushed it open again.

They were rewarded by light everywhere they looked.

And everywhere they looked they saw things… things with the Balkenkreuz… or the swastika… or…

"Blyad!"

As they walked on through the huge tunnels, the contents became more and more bizarre.

Aircraft…

Large rockets…

Small rockets…

Sealed rooms with heavy duty vision panels containing solid metal chests marked with the symbols of death…

The two officers, motivated by greed and curiosity in equal measure, opened one, striking off the heavy duty padlocks.

Lapatin opened a heavy casket and ran his fingers over the object it contained.

Whatever the metal was, it was clearly not valuable, so they closed the lid and moved on, sealing the room back up behind them.

Fuel vapours of some sort assaulted them as they moved deeper into the unknown, the odours making them both light-headed as they moved past that particular storage tunnel.

Starting to feel sick, the two men decided they had seen enough to make an exciting report to their commander, and returned to switch off the generator.

Voronin posted a full NKVD security detail to secure the underground site, and the two returned to Sankt Georgen to telephone a report to Voronin's superior officer.

Both men were blissfully unaware that from the moment they had let greed overcome natural caution, their lives were forfeit, and that they had been fatally wounded. Their wounds made no marks, left no trace, at least not yet, but they were deep and deadly, and neither would see Christmas or his family again.

The metal they had uncovered was valuable in a very different way.

1132 hrs, Tuesday, 2nd July 1946, the Kremlin, Moscow, USSR.

The briefing on the welcome increase in Italian Communist partisan activity was concluded before Stalin turned to acknowledge the woman officer's presence.

"We are thankful that you have been spared, Comrade Nazarbayeva."

Unusually for Stalin, he actually meant the words of sympathy he offered the injured GRU General.

The flight she was on had come under attack from Allied fighters, fast jets by all accounts.

The speed differentials had saved the Li-2 transport aircraft at first, and then the escort rallied and drove off the enemy jets, but not before the fuselage had received a number of hits, and Nazarbayeva had her arm slashed by a piece of flying debris.

254

The meeting had commenced at the allotted time and was already in full swing when she arrived.

A folder containing the latest military production and training figures was thrust at her and she quickly came up to speed on events behind the lines as the briefing continued.

Production and training were good, although the manpower pool was smaller than ever.

The problem of getting new equipment forward remained and losses were still running high due to Allied air intervention, but less so to partisan activity.

Enough higher quality weapons were getting through to make a difference, although she had seen a number of military reports that suggested priority should be given to ensuring adequate deliveries of standard ammunition, qualified replacements, fuel, and food, rather than the latest weaponry.

Three other folders lay silently in front of her position, containing information on the briefings that had already taken place.

She had missed the latest update on the Ukrainian uprising but was, in any case, fully aware that it was almost totally suppressed now, the ex-POWs keen to display their prowess and renewed commitment to the Motherland. The file held no real secrets for her.

She had also missed the Army position on the events in Europe, and how the plan to inflict more casualties on the US forces seemed to be succeeding. Again, Vasilevsky had ensured she had been kept fully informed along the way.

Malinin, standing in for Vasilevsky, tapped the folder containing the latest production figures for oil and coal, suggesting she might like to look at it.

She cast her eye over it, not sure if she liked the figures or not, but was quickly distracted by the discussion on armaments, and the extremely positive statements about the new weapons, particularly tanks and aircraft.

As normal, she divided every figure by a half, but still the projections were every bit as impressive as the current values.

In her mind, Nazarbayeva pondered the addition of the POWs to the order of battle…

The urgent knocking at the door cut through everything, except Stalin's indignation at the disturbance.

"I said no interruptions…"

Stalin's anger turned to curiosity in an instant, the sight of a red-faced NKVD Lieutenant-General holding an armful of files enough to stop his tirade in its tracks.

"Comrade General Kaganovich?"

255

The Deputy Head of the NKVD, recently promoted for his part in the prevention of assassination attempt on Stalin, spoke quickly.

"Comrade General Secretary, my apologies, but I knew you would not wish this information kept from this meeting. It is of vital interest and I believe you should see it immediately."

Kaganovich held a folder out, and it was greedily accepted by the Soviet Union's leader.

The NKVD General knew better than to hand out any more folders, even though Beria held out a demanding hand.

Stalin looked different, his face coloured by shock or excitement.

"This is confirmed, Comrade General?"

"No doubt, Comrade General Secretary. Those numbers are from a very quick examination. I have asked for a fuller report as soon as possible, but there are other issues, as you can see."

Stalin hadn't.

"Other issues? What other issues?"

Kaganovich went from memory.

"Middle section on page four, Comrade General Secretary. Perhaps…"

He approached Stalin and leant to whisper.

"Perhaps Comrade Kurchatov or Comrade Polkovnik General Vannikov could assist you better than I, Comrade General Secretary?"

Whilst Stalin did not fully understand the specific section of the report, he understood the significance of the two names, which, of course, immediately added to his understanding of the report.

"Show me…"

Stalin moved to the huge map of Europe, a clean one, unencumbered by the normal plethora of military markings.

His eyes roved Austria, seeking the location of this incredible news.

The rest of the ensemble closed in around the Soviet leader, who waited expectantly for a clue as to where Sankt Georgen an der Gusen was.

The General Secretary puffed on his pipe, sending out a thick cloud that caused more than one of those nearby to cough.

His thick finger tapped the map roughly where he thought Sankt Georgen to be.

"Comrade Malinin," he waited until the CoS of the Red Banner Forces of Soviet Europe stepped forward, "Assure me this position is secure."

Malinin, being Malinin the efficient, had brought details from Chuikov's forces to the front of his folders the moment he saw the attention being given to the area around Linz.

"Where exactly is the location, Comrade General Secretary?"

Kaganovich helped Stalin out.

"Sankt Georgen an der Gusen, Comrade Polkovnik General."

Malinin did some swift calculations, a soft snort betraying some slight amusement, a snort that drew unwarranted attention.

"Something funny, Comrade?"

"No more than a coincidence, Comrade General Secretary. The nearest enemy forces are roughly one hundred kilometres away...," he leant forward to mark the spot with his finger, "As of 0800, Marshal Chuikov reports American forces here, at Sankt Georgen im Attergau."

Despite the official view of religion within the Communist state, the importance of St George was not lost on any of those present.

He was, after all, the patron saint of Moscow, were they to acknowledge such things.

"Ensure that 1st Alpine preserves this location at all costs, Comrade Malinin."

He stepped away from the map, moving people aside by his presence alone, puffing on his pipe and thinking aloud.

"We have an opportunity here, and we must seize it with both hands."

He nodded at Kaganovich, indicating that he could distribute the files he was holding.

"From preliminary reports, there are a great deal of items to bring away... and much to be learned by studying certain other pieces in the caves."

He sat down heavily, bringing an ominous sharp protest from the chair.

"There is no time to lose."

Most people in the room were nose down in the file, either trying to understand the enormity of the find, or working out the logistics of transporting that many aircraft and missiles.

Only a few fully appreciated the real significance of the middle section on page four.

Nazarbayeva did, and moved closer to Stalin.

"Comrade General Secretary."

"Speak, Comrade."

"I am aware that Comrade Polkovnik General Serov is in Austria. Given his track record, perhaps he should be ordered to the location immediately?"

Beria almost hissed at the GRU General, but confined himself to volunteering more information on Serov, the man who had secured uranium oxide and scientists at the end of the German War, a man better placed than most to understand and recover the secrets contained within the caves at Sankt Georgen an der Gusen.

"Comrade Polkovnik General Serov is in Austria acting on new information discovered by my department," both Nazarbayeva and Kaganovich looked at the NKVD Marshal, both knowing that he had just lied.

"Serov is at Lake Toplitz, controlling recovery operations. We have had reports that the Germans secreted items in the lake at the war's end."

Beria fished in his briefcase and brought out a report on the matter, one he had previously had no intention of producing in front of the GKO, until his hand was forced by the woman who, unknown to him, had made the discovery in the first place.

Some days beforehand, Nazarbayeva informed Kaganovich and, at his suggestion, had conceded that Serov was the best man for the job, and passed responsibility to Beria's department, something her new relationship with the Deputy Head of the NKVD made much easier.

"And has Toplitz yielded anything of note, Comrade Marshal?"

Beria shrugged.

"So far, some office equipment, printed paper work, administrative records... some gold..."

"Send Serov to Sankt Georgen immediately. I want his first report on my desk by the morning."

Stalin tapped his pipe out into his hand and disposed of the remnants, allowing Toplitz to move to the back of his mind in favour of Sankt Georgen, where luck had provided the Soviet Union with an opportunity not to be wasted.

The discussion on the new discovery was brief.

From initial reports, it seemed likely that an underground facility over a million square metres had existed under their noses for months.

The initial appraisal of the contents was mind-boggling.

...Factory equipment and jigs for producing some of the Reich's finest technological miracles...

... High-octane fuel in the millions of litres...

258

… And Heinkel 162, the Salamander, or so-called People's Fighter, most seemingly in flying condition…

… Dozens of V2 rockets… with pristine launcher vehicles and associated ephemera…

… And other rockets of all shapes and sizes, complete with blueprints and notes…

… And crates… even sealed rooms …

… Crates and sealed rooms bearing the markings of German scientific research on that most secret of developments…

A veritable Aladdin's cave for a Motherland outclassed and outgunned in everything but fighting spirit.

Nazarbayeva's small briefing on the latest intelligence developments included an unsubstantiated report that the British Field Marshal Montgomery was back on the active list, and that he had been seen in, of all places, Tehran.

Even though the 'rumour' was accompanied by credible reports of increased Allied naval and air activity in the Arabian Sea and Gulf of Hormuz, nothing could dampen the enthusiasm of the GKO and military men, and few attached any significance to the information, although Beria made a mental note to check his own reports to see if anything supported the woman's claim.

The matter was set aside and the briefing moved on to the reports of Donitz's ill health.

Stalin and Beria remained when the others had left, the politicians and military all clearly buoyed by the collapse of Ukrainian resistance, the political and military successes against the USA, and the wonderful news from Austria.

Sipping his tea, Stalin stared his NKVD chief into submission.

"So, Lavrentiy… Montgomery."

Beria felt relief. He had expected a completely different question.

"An irrelevance at first glance, Comrade General Secretary… but the woman seems to think it important."

"She's rarely wrong."

Beria smarted at the words, even though he knew them to be true.

"I will have my men work to discover the truth of this but… my first thoughts are maskirovka, nothing more."

"Explain, Lavrentiy?"

"He is an icon for the British, but he was badly wounded, and, according to my last reports, had not recovered enough to even walk unassisted."

Stalin lit a cigarette, not taking his eyes of the NKVD boss. "Recent information?"

"Two weeks old, no more, Comrade General Secretary."

"So… probably maskirovka… a cheap move for them… no assets needed to try and make us move resources to the southern borders."

He accepted the tea that Beria had poured and greedily consumed it.

"None the less… watch the situation closely, Lavrentiy. Liaise with Comrade Nazarbayeva too."

Even though the cup was raised to Beria's lips, it didn't mask the automatic snarl that formed at the mention of the GRU general's name.

Stalin changed tack pouncing on something he had noticed earlier.

"So, what do you have to tell me about Toplitz, Lavrentiy?"

Beria had made the right noises for the rest of the briefing, but his mind had still remained firmly on the Toplitzsee, for reasons presently known only to him and Serov.

Stalin had spotted the change in his man, and now gave him no way out.

He bought himself a moment by carefully placing the bone china cup and saucer back on the table.

"Comrade General Secretary, I did not wish to proceed further in front of the others. The matter of Toplitz will require some… err … delicacy of thought, so I felt I should inform you… and only you… in the first instance."

From behind his raised cup, Stalin managed a strangled '*go on*'.

"Comrade General Secretary, the printed material so far recovered reportedly equates to roughly five hundred million pounds of counterfeit British currency…"

The conversation continued well into the evening.

A large number of dignitaries had gathered to witness the demonstration, and many were already suffering in the relentless heat, the sun beating down on all, regardless of status or rank.

After a briefing in Westdown, a convoy of vehicles had taken the entourage to the firing range, where they waited for the short display to begin.

A small fire had been quickly extinguished, probably started by the sun's rays striking some long abandoned glass fragments.

Those with an experienced eye had spotted the targets and the intended killers, successfully identifying all but the sleekest of the enemy vehicles placed downrange.

These consisted of captured tanks; an IS-II, IS-III, the huge ISU-152, and the mystery beast.

At the firing line sat two more familiar types; an Archer SPAT and a Centurion.

The latter was the very latest effort from the British Tank industry, a revised mark III, armed with the 20-pounder main gun and improvements to the Meteor engine.

But today, it was all about the gun…

… or rather, the shell.

Charles Burney had developed his shell in the 1940s, initially as an anti-concrete shell that was intended to be effective against the legendary German fortifications of the West Wall and Siegfried Line.

Lieutenant General Sir Sidney Chevalier Kirkman, GOC Southern Command, was the senior military man on parade, supported by a plethora of officers and experts from the Tank Corps and Cavalry regiments, all men who had ridden the steel beasts into battle.

A handful of politicians were there to be suitably impressed and sign off on the project, if the military men thought it was the resolution to the problems the armoured force was starting to encounter.

As per the briefing, the Archer kicked off proceedings, speeding an APDS shell downrange.

The gunners had been picked for their skill, and the shell struck true, penetrating the IS-II.

This was no surprise to the tankers amongst the observers, the capabilities of the shell being widely understood.

The Archer next took on the IS-III, successfully hitting the stationary tank three times and, as expected by the veterans, had no effect whatsoever at that range.

The ISU-152 succumbed first shot, the APDS core easily slicing through its armour.

Finally, the Archer took on the mystery tank, revealed now as one of the latest T-54 Soviet battle tanks, captured in Poland.

The shell failed to have any effect.

Two more hits produced the same result.

There was a twenty-minute break whilst a small group of tank officers rode out to the targets and quickly inspected them.

On return, they hastily passed on their findings. The tanks that had been hit and penetrated might not have been knocked out by the small shell, something that was a known problem, and another reason that the 17-pdr was starting to fail to measure up to the modern battlefield.

The new Centurion Mk III took on the IS-II with its 20-pdr gun... then the IS-III... ISU-152... and finally the T-54.

One shot each.

One hit on each.

The whole group travelled out to the targets.

The excitement at what they found made normal conversation impossible.

Each vehicle showed the signs of an external explosion but there was no evidence of penetration.

Mainly because the armour had not been penetrated.

However, to a man, the experienced tank officers concluded that each vehicle would have been knocked out of the fight and its crew killed or wounded as a result.

Burney explained the principle as easily as he could.

HESH.

High-explosive squash head.

The shell struck the armour plate and squashed, spreading wider as it flattened itself.

The base fuse set off the charge once the shell had spread itself over the target's defences.

A simple concept that had been found to work extremely well against all sorts and thicknesses of armour, relying not on penetrative capability, but on shockwaves hammering through the metal and spalding pieces of the tank's armour off on the inside, sending whirling lethal pieces through the interior, pieces that were particularly unforgiving to soft objects like tank crew.

262

Inside each tank, wooden dummies had been placed to perform crew functions.

No dummy was without severe damage from flying debris, and some were simply matchwood.

By using a shell already developed and adding a few refinements, Burney had given most British tanks the capacity to kill the latest enemy tanks anywhere they could be found on the modern battlefield.

HEAT ammunition, a hollow-charge shell using the Monroe Effect, was becoming more commonplace in vehicle ammunition inventories, but the rifled main guns meant that its performance declined, the effect lessened by the spinning effect of the rifling.

HESH did not suffer any problems with rifled weapons; indeed, it was enhanced as the spin enabled the shell to squash further, and more effectively, increasing the area it affected.

Burney remained behind with two of his technicians, waiting for the old Bedford truck to arrive.

Moving down to the eight hundred yard marker, the civilian engineers set up the 3.45" RCL.

The recoilless rifle went through its paces, although it missed its target twice, earning the firing technician considerable harassment at the hands of his friends.

Burney and his men knew the weapon worked, but they were there to examine the new changes to the gas venting system, a problem that had delayed the weapons inclusion in matters in the Far East.

Twenty shots later, eyes examined the breech, precise measurements were taken, and calculations made.

For Burney, it was a very successful day.

The value of his HESH shell had been fully appreciated by people who mattered, and his RCL modifications appeared to have overcome the wear issues, which hopefully meant that British infantry would soon have a weapon capable of dealing with the biggest of the enemy's tanks.

A very successful day indeed.

1321 hrs, Sunday, 7th July 1946, the Rathaus, Aachen, Germany.

The Council of Germany had relocated to Aachen as soon as was practicable, the act of installing the political machinery in a German City considered vital for national pride, and far outweighing the disadvantages of the lesser facilities afforded by the ruined metropolis.

The connotations and mystique of the ancient Roman city, its links with Emperor Charlemagne, and its history as a crowning place for German Kings, lent further weight to the decision to install the council within Aachen's town hall. Damaged during the previous war, hasty repairs had made to make the old building tenable enough for move the politicians in.

That had been fourteen days previously.

Today, the comings and goings of politicians and military men had been interrupted by the physical collapse of Franz von Papen.

Almost a week to the day after Donitz had succumbed to a serious gastric problem, resulting in some complicated and extended surgery, Von Papen had fallen down the Rathaus stairs, having suddenly complained of feeling dizzy and nauseous.

Whatever his internal issues were, the broken leg and deep head wound would have been enough by themselves to remove the aging politician from office for some time to come.

In the White Hall, the former Mayoral office, the convened Council of Germany, or what was left of it, had just made a decision.

That the decision was made without any consultation with the Allied powers was a matter of unease for some, a pre-requirement for others.

The result was that Germany would have a new leader and his appointment would be presented to the other allies as a fait-accompli.

The newly elected head of the German Republic stood.

"Kameraden, I thank you for this privilege, and for giving me the chance to lead our country forward into better times. We will continue to support our new allies, and restore Germany's lost honour, through the blood of our soldiers and the sweat of our people."

Inside, the latest German Chancellor felt elation that months of planning had finally come to fruition, that ideas and concepts had finally become a reality, and that he and his closest associates were now in a position to bring forward the agenda of unfinished business; one of restoring Germany to her rightful place on the world stage, and of destroying communism.

"I pledge myself to the pursuit of victory by the quickest and most practical route, and in restoring peace to our great nation. Thank you."

Acknowledging the polite applause, Albert Speer resumed his seat and enjoyed the moment.

1812 hrs, Sunday, 7th July 1946, Versailles, France.

"Sons of bitches... goddamned sons of bitches!"

Patton said what was on all of their minds.

What was supposed to be a gently paced meeting and dinner had turned into a frantic exercise to get a radio, and the grabbing of an interpreter so they could understand the words of the new German Chancellor.

Eisenhower sat with his finger steepled, pressing the tips to his lips, failing to mask a face like thunder.

Bradley and McCreery were struck dumb.

Alexander had excused himself for a moment, and was probably ranting into the mirror in the well-appointed rest room.

Eisenhower finally broke his silence.

"I'm not clear what the President will think of this, but one thing's for sure... it isn't what he signed up for."

He silently sought a view from McCreery.

"The Prime Minister certainly won't be happy, Sir."

Bradley put it all into a few words.

"Doesn't matter, does it? They've railroaded the lot of us. The Krauts've presented us with a situation, and we can't back out of it. They know... heck, we all know, we need them more than ever now."

Whilst the casualty figures were better, the US forces were still taking the lion's share of hits from the Red Army.

Ike's eyes narrowed.

"They agree to take on more of the front line, releasing our forces, and in so doing actually increase their importance to the Allies. Then, within days, this happens...Brad?"

The Twelfth Army Group commander clearly had something to say.

"Sir... Donitz went too, remember? Suddenly... without warning... there and then gone... and he was Von Papen's natural successor..."

Bradley's voice trailed off as his mind went deeper into what he was suggesting.

265

All the heads nodded, wondering if there was something they weren't seeing here, a something that looked and smelt rotten.

Alexander walked in with a worrying thought in his mind, his own concerns having been reinforced by the last few words he had overheard.

"General, if Papen had gone first, and then Donitz, the successor, had followed, it would have looked rather bad... but this way round, the move from chancellor to chancellor is... well... less questionable at first sight and... err... somewhat smoother and..."

"Hold on one cotton-picking minute... are you seriously suggesting that the chancellor and his deputy have been removed by something other than coincidence?"

Alexander held Ike's stern gaze and gave his reply a moment's further thought.

"General Eisenhower, sir ... I think that puts it rather well."

The commander of the Allied Armies sought the feelings of his commanders and, to a man, they all felt something was not right.

Before Eisenhower spoke to members of the darker arts, in order to establish what was known of the personal and political rivalries within the German Council, he posed a question that no-one could really answer.

"Why?"

That question travelled to all the political centres aligned to the Allied cause, and remained unanswered, the suspicions of conspiracy purely guessed at, and with no proof of any type unveiled.

Churchill and Truman growled down the phone at each other, but found no comfort in their discussion.

Both subsequently rang Speer to offer their congratulations and support, whilst each, in their own way, sounded out the man who had been thrust upon the Allied cause as leader of the increasingly important former enemy.

2301 hrs, Sunday, 7th July 1946, Sankt Georgen an der Gusen, Austria.

NKVD Colonel General Ivan Aleksandrovich Serov was a man on a mission, empowered by those at the very summit of the state apparatus, and therefore not a man easily brushed aside.

Objections and objectors had come and gone, his authority supreme in the face of all-comers.

No matter what, his mission had priority, and it was the inventory of special items that were carefully and secretly loaded on nondescript vehicles, ready for the long journey back to the Motherland, regardless of the other plans for use of the transport network.

Having considerable experience with such things, especially with his overseeing of the removal of the German uranium ore from Oranienberg, he knew not to rush matters, but applied calm urgency.

The heavy metal caskets containing the radioactive material came in for extra special handling.

Serov's authority had also brought forth numerous Red Air Force night fighters, circling four distinct separate areas, three as a maskirovka.

In the dark skies above Austria, aircrew from many nations stalked and killed each other, unaware of what was happening under the hills beneath them.

At great cost, the Red Air Force kept the Allied efforts away from Sankt Georgen an der Gusen and by morning, Serov was gone, and the continuing recovery effort was left to junior ranks.

Such victories for the Soviet pilots were hard won, and rarely won a second time.

On a rugged outcrop above the site, a small group of silent soldiers had spent the previous day observing the goings-on, and they had reported back all they knew to their Allied commanders.

Their report ensured that the following day and night brought forth the power of the Allied air forces, as waves of bombers struck numerous targets in the hills around the Gusen River, many specifically guided in by the SAS team operating behind the lines, men who had first come to understand that something important was happening in the valleys.

Much of the recently discovered German equipment was destroyed, either on transport vehicles, or as they lay waiting to be removed to safety.

Live V2 warheads added to the damage with their secondary explosions.

Marshal Chuikov, with overall responsibility for removing the treasures from the huge network of caves, sought a different way to rescue the remaining assets, especially the high-octane fuels that were stored in large quantities.

The removal work ceased temporarily.

1203 hrs, Monday, 8th July 1946, the Rathaus, Aachen, Germany.

"Thank you, General von Vietinghoff."

Having passed on everything of the previous day's meeting, von Vietinghoff saluted and left the room.

Speer exchanged glances with Guderian.

"They are showing weakness, when all that is needed is strength."

Guderian nodded sagely, but held his tongue, allowing the new Chancellor his head.

"We must accelerate our plans, bring matters forward, in case their weakness drops to unimaginable levels, Feldmarschal."

"We are doing everything quickly, Herr Kanzler, but it takes time to assemble an army, especially when our former enemies are the ones supplying much of the resources."

"Yes, I do know that, Feldmarschal. Our output of tanks and guns is rising steadily, now that we're receiving the minerals of war, and the French are contributing decent numbers too... albeit unwittingly... but I do understand that you'll not have all that you need quite yet."

Speer went to the window and observed the everyday life of Aacheners in the square outside his window.

"We must be careful not to alarm our friends."

"They'll need us to be strong, Herr Kanzler."

"Yes they will, and we'll be strong, not for them, but for us."

Speer moved swiftly back to his desk.

"I want you to implement this plan immediately."

Guderian knew which file Speer held out to him.

"We don't have enough tanks and guns for the men we have, Herr Kanzler, so why bring these men into our thinking right now?"

Speer laughed.

"Well, for one thing, they are good at what they do."

Guderian could only concede that point.

268

"Secondly, why on earth would we let the useless French have them?"

The second point was conceded in turn.

"Herr Kanzler, you are sure you want to name them in this way?"

"Feldmarschal, I'm told by a number of your generals that these men are not Heer, but other forces, so we'll grant them the distinction of being a force that has its own identity, and is not Heer, eh? In fact, much like it was before."

Guderian accepted the file and slid it into his briefcase.

"Good day, Herr Kanzler."

The Field Marshal clicked to attention, and left the modest office, with orders to harvest as many ex-Waffen SS soldiers as possible, and bring them together under the control of the newly-formed 'German Legion'.

He knew exactly where he would start.

1303 hrs, Tuesday, 9th July 1946, Camp 1001, Akhtubinsk, USSR.

The Red Cross inspection was in full swing, and the chief inspector left no stone unturned.

"Colonel Skryabin, it is against the convention to have military facilities within the environs of a prisoner of war camp."

The NKVD officer choked back his contemptuous reply and opted for one more studied and placatory, just as his orders dictated.

"Inspector Diviani, this facility is not for military production of any kind, but for humanitarian purposes. We intend to install equipment to produce bandages and dressings, nothing more. Prisoners must not be idle, but we understand your requirements, even though we are not signatories."

The status of the USSR with the Geneva and Hague conventions had been a matter of contention since Germany marched her troops into the Motherland at the start of Operation Barbarossa.

None the less, the Soviet Union had suddenly permitted widespread access to its prisoner of war camps and hospitals, where Red Cross officials uniformly reported barely adequate nutritional provision but generally adequate accommodation in the former, and excellent standards of care in the latter.

Inspector Diviani had chosen his team with care, and no little direction from his own GRU masters, ensuring that two of his group had affiliations with Allied intelligence groups, and would report back on exactly what they saw at the vast new camp on the Volga, that being exactly what the Soviets wanted them to see.

As the Red Cross team walked the huge camp, they found no clues as to what would go on in any of the buildings they saw, or indeed, what was presently going on underneath their feet.

"Who's he?"

Dryden took the briefest moment to check out the civilian observer, quickly returning to concentrate on the open wound in front of him.

"Damned if I know, Hany. Hold that steady now…"

A concrete fence post had fallen from a cart and smashed a German POW in the leg, messily dragging the soldier's calf muscle off the bone.

It looked a lot worse than it was, and the new equipment that graced the medical facility helped greatly, not that Hamouda and Dryden had abandoned their old tried and trusted collection of pieces.

The civilian moved forward, until a growl from Dryden stopped him in his tracks.

"I don't care who you are, but not one bloody step closer."

"Apologies, Doctor, but my time is limited. I am Benito Deviani of the Red Cross, here to inspect this camp's facilities and ensure you are being well treated."

Dryden looked at his Egyptian friend and silently invited him to take over cleaning the gaping wound.

He stood back as Hamouda got to work.

"Well, Mr. Deviani, it's fair to say this place is a palace compared to where we've been before."

He noticed Skryabin's eyebrows raise and understood the warning they represented.

"Are you well treated, Doctor…err…"

"Apologies… Leftenant Commander Miles Dryden, Royal Navy. My friend here is 2nd Leftenant Hany Hamouda, late of the Egyptian Army. Yes, Mr. Deviani, we're well treated, certainly better than we have been previously."

He looked Skryabin in the eyes, falling just short of deliberate and overt defiance.

"Need a hand."

Hamouda muttered a religious invocation as he searched for the source of the sudden bleeding.

'Rahmatic ya Rab.'

Dryden was back on the job in seconds, forgetting the audience.

The Red Cross team moved on, leaving the medical team to their trade.

Diviani continued his tour, finding himself steered towards the camp's new showpiece medical facility.

When the intelligence agencies received their reports, Camp 1001 lost any importance in the overall scheme of things, and the documents were archived.

There was no hint of the importance of the facility on the Volga.

1306 hrs, Wednesday, 10th July 1946, mouth of the Ondusengo River. South-West Africa.

The San, Etuna Kozonguizi, was an old man, so old even he had forgotten how many seasons he had suffered. The wiry bushman had seen all that Africa, and in particular, the 'Land that God made in anger' had to offer.

His dwelling was mainly made up of parts of the ill-fated ship, the Eduard Bohlen, plus pieces from numerous other vessels that had floundered on the unforgiving coastline.

It was covered with skins from the seals he had killed over the months, as much to retain the early morning dew as a source of water as to provide shelter from the interminable sun.

Kozonguizi lived a simple life…

… that was until 1306, when his normal daily routine was disturbed by the arrival of a man-made leviathan.

Armed with his spear, the old bushman sat on his receiving stool, awaiting the arrival of the 'visitors', who were now splashing in the surf as they struggled with their dinghies.

The metal whale had disappeared as soon as the four boats had taken to the water.

Instinctively, Kozonguizi's eyes strayed to the rock promontory on the mouth of the river, where he had discovered many

271

precious items, some of which he had taken for himself, and some he had bartered for some of the luxuries of life. Many other things still remained there.

He instinctively knew that these 'visitors' had returned for their treasures.

Gripping his spear more firmly, the old bushman straightened his spine and examined the leading man battling his way up the sand with studied disinterest... the clothing... the hat... the sword...

'Strange man...'

The leader shouted in a strange tongue unknown to him... not Khoisin, the click language of the desert people... nor Afrikaans, with which he was reasonably familiar... nor English...

Waving his sword in the direction of the rocks, the nearest man encouraged the others with him to greater efforts, all the time keeping his eyes fixed upon the old native, assessing the threat and planning his approach.

It was something in the voice, the imperatives of the unknown language, which carried warning to Kozonguizi's ears.

That and the body language of the approaching man, a body clearly preparing for action.

Despite his sixty-two years, the San was still fit, his roving days curtailed only by the foot injury he had suffered on sharp rocks, his reactions and strength still present in abundance.

The sword swept through the air, slicing only the space he had previously occupied, whilst the spear drove home into the man's chest, stealing his life in an instant.

Drawing the shaft clear, Etuna Kozonguizi waited stoically for his death, his spear dripping with the blood of a Kaigun daii; a Lieutenant of the Imperial Japanese Navy.

The old man died well.

['The Land that God made in anger' is modern day Namibia.]

1316 hrs, Wednesday, 10th July 1946, mouth of the Ondusengo River. South-West Africa.

"It will be for the Commander to decide. Place our leader in the shade for now, and cover him well."

The Sub-Lieutenant directed two of his men to tend to the remains of the landing party's commander.

272

He spared a kick for the corpse at his feet, the dead African's eyes still wide open, even in death.

"Now, we must complete our glorious task."

He waved the German instructions to emphasise his point... and perhaps his own value to the mission... as he was now the only German reader left.

Even though there were instructions in Japanese, the original technical manual for the fuel pumps and hose systems were in German, and more thorough than the Japanese versions.

The plan of the site revealed the location of everything they needed, and the shore party from I-1 set to work with a will, determined to have everything ready for nightfall.

1556 hrs, Wednesday, 10th July 1946, at sea, off the Skeleton Coast. South-West Africa.

The distant throbbing of multiple propellers had first alerted the submarine to the presence of something large and powerful bearing down on them.

According to the chart, the surface contingent of the special force should be well out to sea, some hundreds of miles to the west, if they were sailing to plan.

The submarine commander discounted friendly ships as a possibility and came to periscope depth to see what was creating the immense noise band directly north of him.

It took a few incredulous sweeps of the periscope to confirm what the multiple sounds suggested.

"Down periscope. Take the ship to one hundred and thirty metres."

"Hai!"

Commander Nanbu Nobukiyo, his promotion to Kaigun chūsa bestowed in Manchuria, moved to the chart table.

The Sen-Toku creaked as it dropped further into the waters of the Atlantic, still carried northwards on the Benguela Current, which had lowered fuel consumption for all the vessels in his tiny fleet.

His first officer waited on further commands.

"Starboard thirty. One-third speed. Silent operation."

"Hai!"

The orders were repeated and I-401 swung towards the shore of Africa, and away from the armada of Allied boats.

"I didn't see any aircraft, but we'll take no chances whatsoever," Nobukiyo announced to no-one in particular.

"There must be two hundred ships up there... at least... all kinds... warships... fat merchantmen... I even saw three aircraft carriers... at least three..."

Many eyes swung towards their captain, hoping for attack orders.

But none were forthcoming.

"Such a shame our mission is so secret. We must let them pass... but..."

Nobukiyo slipped into silence.

He examined the chart again, not for his own course and destination, but to gauge that of the immense convoy that had borne down upon the Japanese submarine force.

His first officer, Lieutenant Jinyo, waited quietly, knowing his commander would confide in him when ready.

"Jinyo, we must operate secretly... but I feel obliged to report this huge enemy movement... somehow..."

Dropping back onto his elbows, Nobukiyo drew his second in command closer.

"This convoy is heading round the Cape and into the Indian Ocean... I'm convinced of it."

"To the home islands, Commander?"

He shook his head.

"No... I think not... no... I see three possibilities."

He drew a fine line on the chart.

"To reinforce their Chinese lackeys in some way, either by invasion or reinforcement... not invasion though... no... that cannot be... the enemy has enough assets already in theatre... so..."

A second line went all the way up and through the China Sea... to Siberia.

"Here... which would trouble our new friends... but again... their Pacific assets could do the job."

Jinyo nodded, but stayed silent, although he knew where this was leading.

"So, it is here, I think."

The line went from the Atlantic, round the Cape, across the Indian Ocean, traversed the Arabian Sea, and culminated in the Persian Gulf.

He looked up at his experienced man and saw a question in his eyes, and encouraged him to speak.

"Suez, Commander. Why not through the canal?"

Nobukiyo smiled.

"Good question. You didn't see what I saw. Some of those vessels wouldn't fit, I think. But, in any case, I think it's secrecy.

274

Remember all our wartime briefings on what went through the Suez Canal into the Indian Ocean? Always very precise. Never wanting for detail?"

"Hai."

"Look at the course this immense fleet is sailing."

He tapped the chart and created a dotted line.

"Well off shore… away from prying eyes. They don't want to be discovered and reported about."

"You certainly must be correct. Commander."

"I think we must warn our new allies that the enemy is about to attack their vulnerable belly."

He circled the regions of Georgia, Armenia, and Azerbaijan with great gusto, and added a firm arrow striking into the hinterland of the Soviet Union.

"I agree, Commander, but how can we do that without endangering our secrecy?"

Standing slowly upright, Nobukiyo placed the pencil with great care and eased his back with both hands on his haunches, letting his mind work the problem in silence.

The silence was assaulted by the growing propeller sounds of the huge armada.

Two minutes passed before he leant back on the chart table again, drawing Jinyo back into a soft conversation.

"It can be done… will be done… and all we need is one man prepared to do his duty for the Emperor."

Dropping his voice to a whisper, he explained his plan.

0356 hrs, Thursday, 11th July 1946, mouth of the Ondusengo River, South-West Africa.

There had been a number of interruptions to the preparations ashore, as Allied coastal command and naval aircraft made numerous appearances, shepherding their charges southwards, on the lookout for anything that might pose a threat.

A Hudson V of the SAAF surprised the shore party in the process of assembling the fuel hoses, but it did not have eyes for the land, and they were not seen.

I-1, and then I-14, had gorged themselves on the fuel secreted there for the U-Boats.

They had no need of the torpedoes and heavy calibre ammunition stored there, at least, not at that time.

Whilst the torpedoes were compatible, the 88mm and 105mm main gun ammunition was not, but all would help with Nobukiyo's plan.

Whilst not part of the plan, both the Sen-Tokus arrived at the site.

I-401 and her sister submarine did not close to top up their tanks, as soundings indicated that the depth had decreased from that marked on their charts.

However, Nobukiyo did bring his vessel closer to land and risked a quick meeting with the other boat commanders, mainly to advise them of his discovery and beliefs, and discuss any changes to their operational plan.

He also sent one man ashore, charged with a special mission.

The volunteer's comrades sought and received permission to come on deck.

Smartly lined up, the eight men saluted their comrade and swung softly into the Japanese martial song, Umi Yukaba.

If I go away to the sea, I shall be a corpse washed up.
If I go away to the mountain, I shall be a corpse in the grass.
But if I die for the Emperor,
It will not be a regret.

Ensign Ito Kisokada tried to control his tears, not shed for what he was about to do, but for those who stood in front of him, honouring him with their song.

He failed, and his emotions overcame him when he realised that Nobukiyo and Jinyo were also stood erect, saluting him, and adding their voices to the anthem.

It was the proudest moment of his short life, and he saluted as correctly as he could.

Taking his leave, he made sure his equipment was secured in the small dinghy, and allowed himself to be slipped slowly off the casing and into the water.

His comrades again struck up with Umi Yukaba, bringing his tears back. Digging the paddle into the sea, he moved himself away towards the beach, and his date with destiny.

Forty-eight hours to the precise minute that he had said goodbye to the shore party, and become the only occupant of the beach around the mouth of the Ondusengo River, Ensign Kisokada checked his radio for the hundredth time, confirmed the frequency, and flicked the transmit button.

He sent the message five times as ordered and waited, seemingly for an age, before two overlapping five-letter acknowledgements came back.

His mission discharged, Kisokada switched off the radio and slumped, no longer driven by the need for service, or the mission with which he had been entrusted.

Driving himself out of his temporary melancholy, he grabbed the radio and took it to the rocky promontory, where he placed it next to the reasonably comfortable seat he had constructed out of shell boxes and other stores.

Before he made himself comfy, he took his rank markings, personal effects, and his identification tag, consigning them all to the weighted bag he had been given for the purpose, strode into the water, and hurled the bag as far as he could into the flowing waters of the Ondusengo.

Returning to his seat, he examined the crystal clear starry display, and his mind drifted to his home village, where he would often gaze at the night sky.

He poured a healthy measure of the German brandy for himself, and lit one of the cigarettes that had been liberated from the German stockpile.

Life was good, and Ensign Ito Kisokada was now at peace and soaked up the cold breeze coming in from the dark sea.

He flicked his lighter one more time and used the light to apply the pliers just as he had been shown.

Twice he squeezed the tool before settling back again to savour his pleasures.

The Asbach brandy and rich smoke stole his senses.

He smiled at the images he conjured up; his ancestors images, those of his wife and daughter, and of his comrades, both dead and alive.

The two British-made pencil fuses silently did their work, the cupric chloride eating through the retaining wire, which, when destroyed, would release the striker that impacted the percussion cap.

The No 10 Pencil fuse performed its allotted task with great efficiency and, only seven seconds over the ten minute setting, ensured that the stars were surpassed in their brilliance, if only for the briefest of moments, as the former U-Boat replenishment point evaporated in fire and light.

As per Nobukiyo's plan, nothing of note was left, least of all a recognisable Japanese radio set.

Kisokada's body travelled in all directions, none of which pieces were recognisable as human, let alone as one of the Emperor's subjects.

In a few days, his stripped bones were simply unremarkable additions to the thousands of remnants already blanched by the sun all along the Skeleton coast.

Kisokada's transmissions had been received in Groblershoop, South Africa, and in Mbour, Senegal, from where communist sympathisers ensured that the important message was forwarded down the line of communications to their political masters in Moscow.

The arrival of Nobukiyo's information caused consternation in the Soviet ranks, and Red Army forces in the Caucasus were immediately put on alert.

Sympathetic observers on the Cape also added their own information, which did everything to confirm the radio reports that originated from God knew where.

Combined with the reappearance of Montgomery, the presence of a huge troop-carrying fleet suggested exactly that which the Japanese submarine commander had suspected. What had been suspected as a ruse previously now clearly had 'meat on the bone', forcing the GKO to make dispositions in response.

In turn, the loss of some assets changed a few of Vasilevsky's plans, although he persuaded Stalin and his cronies to enable the movement of some ex-POW units to the new theatre, dispatching the equivalent of one full field army to the southern front within hours of receiving the news.

No sooner had that decision been made than a high-level report from still friendly Japanese assets indicated a mass sailing of vessels that could suggest a seaborne invasion somewhere on the Pacific coast of the Motherland.

Combined with the noted increase in air raid frequency in Siberia and all points east, the possibility was difficult to ignore.

In fact, impossible.

Some more NKVD units were stripped from interior duties, resulting in an increased severity and savagery from those who remained behind, anxious to prevent any further rumblings of discontent amongst the various states of the Union.

The remaining Soviet military and NKVD forces in the Ukraine, if it was possible, increased their harsh treatment of the civilian population. The Red Air Force used the opportunity of the revolt to experiment with their own newly developed cluster and napalm-like munitions, using the villages of the Ukraine as a risk-free environment in which to judge the effectiveness and abilities of their weapons and newly-trained aircrews.

Starving Ukrainians were slaughtered in their thousands.

Many Red Army soldiers of Ukrainian origin were arrested and either executed quietly, or found themselves in newly formed Shtrafbats. Others were left in place and watched closely.

The GRU and NKVD in the south and east were hounded by Beria and Kuznetsov, each anxious for confirmation, and each anxious to get it before the other.

They in turn were harassed by Stalin, who reminded them of the price of failure.

Is it possible to succeed without any act of betrayal?

Jean Renoir

Chapter 160 – THE BETRAYALS

1600 hrs, Friday 12th July 1946, House of Madame Fleriot, La Vigie, Nogent L'Abbesse, near Reims, France.

Their lovemaking had been prolonged, passionate, but controlled, as they took advantage of the extended absence of Madame Fleriot and the girls, away in Reims, visiting one of Armande's friends.

Now almost healed, Knocke was convalescing in Nogent L'Abbesse.

Anne-Marie had insisted on taking control and doing all the physical 'work', citing his surgery and doctor's orders.

Group Normandie, and therefore Cameron and Alma, was out of the line refitting as best they could, given the limited resources that were made available to the Legion.

The knocking on the front door grew more and more insistent, and Anne-Marie slipped into a robe, knowing that such a racket would probably spell bad news for one or both of them.

She opened the door and saw Jerome the butler shuffling faster than the norm, implying that either the Russians were at the gates of Paris, or there was a lack of claret in the cellar, each equally as horrendous a proposition to the old man.

"What is it, Jerome?"

"I do beg your pardon, Mademoiselle, but there is a Legion officer here. He insists on speaking with the Général immediately. Says it's extremely important… regarding 'La Legion'."

He spoke the last two words with studied reverence.

"He'll come down shortly. Show the … did he give a name, Jerome?"

"A Colonel Haffily, Mademoiselle."

"The Général will be down soon. Show our guest into the drawing room, Jerome, and please attend to his needs. He is a personal friend."

She closed the door and dropped her robe to the floor, moving around the room naked, collecting Knocke's clothes.

"Ami? Where's the fire?"

"Haefali is here, Ernst. There's a problem with the Legion."

280

"Albrecht!"

"Général Knocke."

He made eye contact with the delectable woman.

"Mademoiselle De Valois, enchanté."

"Colonel Haefali."

Knocke shook Haefali's hand and ushered him to a chair, nodding to Anne-Marie who, by previous arrangement, disappeared off to organise some light refreshment.

"Where's the fire, Albrecht?"

"We're losing men, Sir."

"What? We're out of the line... what's happening?"

"We're losing men. Deserting. One moment they're in barracks, the next they're gone... not just one or two, but dozens... they just disappear without trace."

"They desert? My men? My soldiers?"

The idea was preposterous.

"Yes, mon Général."

Haefali leant forward and dropped the volume of his words.

"Yesterday we found out why, mon Général."

De Valois slid back into the room and took up a seat away from the exchange.

"It's the damned Boche."

Haefali suddenly realised what he had said.

"My apologies, mon Général. The men are deserting back to the German Army. There's a new force being formed, one for the ex-SS soldiers, one that means they can fight under their own flag, not the flag of France."

"But, they gave their oath... as legionnaires..."

Haefali shrugged.

"They are still legionnaires, but German ones now. The German Republic is forming its own German Legion."

"How's this happening?"

"We only found that out yesterday too. Some of the latest men to join have been encouraging the soldiers to move back to the German Army, acting as agent provocateurs. From what we understand, some of our German officers have received letters, offering positions and rank within the new force. Certainly, I've had sight on one received by Rolf Uhlmann"

Knocke and De Valois' heads swivelled as one, and they stared at an envelope on the mantelpiece, an official looking letter,

281

posted from Aachen, that had been left unopened and deliberately placed there for opening at the end of Ernst's convalescence.

They had squabbled about it, but Anne-Marie had her way, and the letter was placed behind the picture of Capitaine Bernard Fleriot, Armande's late husband.

Knocke nodded and the envelope was quickly recovered and slipped into his hands.

"A letter like this?"

"From Aachen?"

"Yes."

He slipped his finger into the loose flap and split the paper.

Having read it, he passed the letter to Haefali, who consumed the words that leapt from its lines, comparing them to those lodged in his memory.

As he went to speak, Jerome arrived with coffee and sandwiches, so Haefali used the opportunity to re-read it.

As the butler left the room, he offered the document back to Knocke.

"Exactly the same, except the final offer, Mon Général."

Knocke hummed a response and offered the letter to Anne-Marie.

She declined to read it.

"Just tell me what it says."

"The new German Republic offers me the rank of GeneralMaior... and command of the 1st Legion Panzer Division."

Haefali went to speak, but Knocke cut him short.

"GeneralMaior eh?"

He smiled at Anne-Marie.

"You know I must go back to the Legion, Ami. Right now."

"Yes, Ernst, I know."

He leant forward and took his coffee, which encouraged the others to follow suit.

"Colonel Haefali, will you be fine to travel with me in an hour?"

"Yes, mon Général."

"We must get back and stop this flow, or we will have no Corps to command."

"So, you're not going back to your own, mon Général?"

Knocke's laugh rang through the drawing room and out into the garden beyond.

"Indeed I am, Albrecht. I took an oath. I'm a legionnaire until the day I die."

Haefali stood with Knocke, and the two exchanged handshakes.

"Legio Patria Nostra, mon General."

"Honneur et Fidélité, Colonel Haefali."

1021 hrs, Saturday, 13th July 1946, Château de Versailles, France.

Churchill finished his delivery and resumed his seat, the silence deafening in its totality, the faces of those officers seated around the meeting table revealing real shock... horror... almost tangible pain.

The British Prime Minister and the American President had rehearsed this moment, the former delivering the information as eloquently as he could, the latter ready to deal with the inevitable cries and wails of military men.

Even in their wildest thoughts, the two men had not conjured up what came to pass.

Eisenhower was drained of colour, as were most of the others who had heard the incredible suggestion.

General Emilio Esteban Infantes y Martín, the new Spanish liaison officer, simply rose from the table and moved to an alcove, turning his back on the scene of the betrayal.

McCreery simply sat rigidly still, his fierce eyes burning into those of his own political leader, carrying as much contempt as he could possibly project.

Churchill, a man previously his idol, had transformed into a pariah with a few words.

General Juin, the French CoS, said nothing, his face twitching with anger and disbelief in equal measure.

Bradley's mouth started to move, the jaw working up and down, but no recognisable sounds emerged.

Walter Bedell-Smith poured himself a glass of water, and quickly followed it with a second full measure. The dryness that temporarily robbed him of speech simply refused to go away.

Amongst the military hierarchy present, it seemed that only von Vietinghoff was unaffected by the incredible proposition, remaining impassive and without movement.

There was a blur of movement and the sound of ripping cloth.

Patton's epaulettes skittered across the table, one falling into Truman's lap.

"Mister President," George's control was as magnificent as it was unexpected, "If that really is your order, you can keep those, 'cos I'll go to goddamned hell before I obey that order."

Eisenhower stood at speed, holding out his hands, one directed at the fiery Patton, the other, more surprisingly, palm first towards his commander-in-chief.

"George, sit down and shut up."

That was as about as abrupt and out of character as Eisenhower had been in living memory.

He turned his full attention to Truman.

"Mr President, is that your order, Sir?"

Harry Truman removed his glasses to buy himself a moment, the display by Patton having fired up his Missouri soul.

"General… that is our considered opinion, an opinion we've just set out before you… as a proposal… a suggestion."

Truman looked around the room, seeking as much eye contact as he could, whilst Churchill was engaged in his own silent exchange of glares with McCreery and Alexander.

"As yet it is not an order… but it may well become one… may need to become one. That's the purpose of this meeting."

Patton rose to tackle the thing head on, but was again waved to his seat by a clearly upset Eisenhower, who wanted to say his piece.

"Sir, let me put my cards on the table right now. If you do make it an order that we withdraw our troops from Poland, and that we leave our Polish allies there to survive with only logistical support… well… my own epaulettes will be lying aside General Patton's, and you'll have to find someone else to run your goddamned war!"

Truman rose and leant forward, his hands on the table in front of him.

"Let me make this clear, General. Presently, we're asking, not ordering. The Polish enterprise has not been successful, and we have recreated another Anzio in all but name."

That was a fair point, and the similarities had been painfully clear to all those with the right level of knowledge and recollection of 'Operation Shingle'.

Truman leant back, making himself appear less aggressive.

"Gentlemen, the domestic political situation presents us with certain imperatives. Things at home have changed since the furore of the Soviet betrayal. I don't need to tell you that the casualty figures are horrendous. There are riots… civil unrest across the spectrum of our Allies."

284

He gestured Eisenhower to resume his seat, leading by example.

"As Prime Minster Churchill has said, the Polish excursion served some purpose, but now solely seems to consume men and supplies holding a bridgehead. There is no intent or capability to exploit it and, according to your reports, it is of minimal use pinning down Soviet assets."

That was indeed the finding of a report that Eisenhower had submitted not a week hence, so he could only give the briefest of nods in agreement.

Churchill took up the baton.

"General Eisenhower, we believe the Poles, with supply from us, can hold the ground more than adequately. If circumstances change, we can return and exploit their labours another day. If they cannot, then we will do our best to pluck them from danger. Undoubtedly, the forces we withdraw would presently serve us better in the main line... the removal of the Allied units from the bridgehead would reduce strain on our supply... release air and naval assets for other tasks... as the President has alluded, the wildcat has once more become a stranded whale."

Churchill had famously used the same description on the inactivity of the Anzio-Nettuno landings in early 1944.

"With respect, Prime Minister, had we withdrawn then, we would not have left an Allied nation's soldiers behind to die or surrender."

"You make an excellent observation, General Eisenhower, and, as I said, if it became necessary, we would advocate recovering as many of our brave Polish Allies as possible."

Politicians' speak rarely rested easily with military men, and that particular sentence certainly did nothing to reassure them.

Eisenhower baulked at the first thought that came into his mind, sending the reference to Gallipoli to the deeper recesses of his mind, deciding that dragging up a World War One Churchill failure would serve no purpose.

"There's no way that we can make a full evacuation of all forces in the Polish bridgehead. The safe extraction of our own forces would require considerable forces left in situ to cover any withdrawal, probably requiring all of the remaining Polish forces, and probably even some of our own assets to ensure success. That's just unacceptable."

There was a rumble of agreement from the Generals around him, with only George Patton's *'you're goddamned right, Ike'* understandable.

"Surely, Prime Minister... Mr President.., you can't ask us to abandon the very nation with whom the British allied themselves, and ultimately committed to war to preserve?"

Truman bristled.

"General, it's not a question of abandoning. If we withdraw from the landing we can consolidate elsewhere. Yes, we will have to leave some men behind... that is regrettable."

He nodded at Churchill.

"At Dunkerque, the British accepted that some brave men would have to remain in order to preserve the safe escape of others. Poland would be no different an..."

"With respect, Mister President, the situation would be wholly different. The British were forced to flee... we would be exercising choice to withdraw... and from a position of military strength... a choice that would spell death to thousands of our Polish allies... and possibly even undermine support for our cause with them and other nations."

"According to your own report, we can hardly call our Polish excursion a position of strength, General."

"It's hardly the same as Dunkerque, Mister President. As we stand, we ain't going to be overrun or pushed into the sea. It's only an order like you're proposing that'll make that a possibility!"

Realising he had just closed down on his boss, Ike rose and held out both hands in a placatory gesture.

"Sir... Mr President... I understand that the domestic political position in many of our homelands is not positive... and we have taken steps to reduce the effects of combat on our home populations... but if we stand back from Poland now, we will be sending out negative messages in all directions, not just to Georgia in the States, but also to Georgia in the east... a message that might make them believe that we are weak and lack the will to succeed."

He looked around the room, checking that everyone present was cleared for what he was about to say.

"We have yet to fully understand how successful Operation Atlantic has been. Surely that must make a difference?"

Atlantic, the attempt to lure Soviet forces to their southern borders, appeared to have affected Soviet thinking, and intelligence and reconnaissance both indicated a movement to the south, but nagging doubts existed as to whether it was a genuine move or one designed to convince the Allies their plan had worked.

Truman took a deep breath and wiped his hands across his face.

When Churchill and he had discussed the Polish matter at Charters, it had seemed a lot simpler, but now, in the presence of the military commanders, the waters had been well and truly muddied.

Churchill cleared his throat and extracted one of his cigars, using the moment to bring peace to the room, his puffing the only sound until he exhaled and stood slowly.

"General Eisenhower, you make your point eloquently, and I think that the President and I can understand the risks present in what we have presented for discussion."

The lessening of importance, the lower weight in the words, were not wasted on any of the men listening.

"But, I think we can agree that the present predicament cries out for remedy… for action… for a decision on how to proceed, rather than allowing the status quo to slowly fester and reduce our options in the future."

Churchill drew in the rich product and exhaled noisily.

He stood, carefully placing the Cuban in the crystal ashtray, clearly buying a moment to weigh his reply carefully.

"We… the President and I… do not believe we can trust to the success of 'Atlantic', much as we pray for it. Any benefits from its fruition may not become available until long after the Polish Bridgehead has been resolved… and not necessarily resolved in our favour."

He grabbed his lapels, in the style he adopted in the house, when addressing his nation's parliament.

"Inactivity is inexcusable in the face of the incompleteness of the Polish mission. Success was ours, initially, but since we have simply permitted the whole landing and exploitation to become nothing more than an irritating boil to the Communists, and a significant drain on manpower and resources for us."

He puffed on his cigar before resuming his classic pose.

"Gentlemen, the situation cannot endure… must not endure… which is why President Truman and I are here. If not this suggestion, what? What would you have us do? There is no option for inactivity in Poland. We must either do something positive, or withdraw… and we simply cannot… must not… rely on some unsupportable vision of unprecedented success from Operation Atlantic to cloud our vision… our decision making… and our unpalatable duty."

Churchill took a deep breath.

"Now, what are our options? General Eisenhower, you have said that to further reinforce the bridgehead is a fool's errand. So we have no option to expand operations. We are left with a choice between status quo or reduction, unless you can bring some new idea before us."

Winston resumed his seat, drawing on the rich Cuban cigar and carefully avoiding sending any of the smoke in Truman's direction.

"Breakthrough to 'em, Prime Minister. Give us the word and we'll smash through the goddamned commies all the way to Warsaw."

Patton's simple reply avoided the issues that had first steered Churchill and Truman down the path of contemplating withdrawal.

"General, that is not an option as things stand."

Truman expected no rebuttal, but it came anyway.

"Yes it is, Mister President. Use the bombs, and we will carve our way through the bastards like a hot knife through butter."

Truman made a display of anger, slapping his hand, palm down, on the table.

"No! We cannot! How many times do I have to tell you all? The use of those weapons in Japan has caused so many problems for the Alliance! To use them here, unilaterally, without political consultation, would almost certainly ensure the end of support for our cause from too many nations to count."

Alexander got in before George Patton had time to draw breath.

"Then, Sir, have a consultation. Lay it out before our Allies. Tell them we need to use these bombs to succeed. Tell them the alternatives if we don't use them... if we lose... sir."

"The process would be a waste of time, Field Marshal. We have had deputations from numerous nations, stating their clear position on further use in the Far East, let alone in mainland Europe. No, no, no. it's not happening. Find us another solution to the Polish problem."

George Patton could control himself no longer.

"No! No! No! Can't you see it, Mister President? The Commies have orchestrated it all, goddamn them. All of this crock of shit... this... this... anti-bomb thing."

He strode round the table and went up to a map of Europe.

"We got bombs... let's use the damn things... hit 'em hard, where it hurts... here... here... here... destroy their will to fight."

'Blood and Guts' virtually punched each spot on the map as he marked out his preferred targets of Moscow, Leningrad, and Chelyabinsk.

"General Patton, please sit down."

288

"Sir, you gotta understand that all we need to do…"

"General Patton, sit down."

Eisenhower rose to interject.

"George, com…"

"The hell I will… the HELL I will! We're in possession of the goddamn means to end this thing and lack the goddamn spine to do it! My God, what'll history think of the men in this room, eh? Commanders of the greatest army ever assembled, with the best weapons, and best soldiers, and no goddamn balls to use it!"

Truman virtually flew out of his chair.

"Sit down, General Patton!"

"The hell I goddamned will!"

Eisenhower shouted.

"George! Enough!"

Patton turned to him, his eyes ablaze, and with no pretence of control.

"Ike, you see it. You have to goddamn see it! We've the tools and this sonofabitch won't do what's needed to be done."

Truman flushed with colour and stood rock still, exuding white hot anger, a feeling of something wholly unpleasant, a something that stopped even the mad as hell Patton in his tracks.

"You, General Patton, are hereby relieved of your command. You, General Eisenhower, will have this officer placed under arrest, awaiting proper disposal by courts-martial."

Patton went from white anger to realisation in a split second.

He opened his mouth, but Eisenhower closed him down immediately.

"General Patton, stand down."

Ike nodded towards the door that had flown open in the middle of the furious exchange, a door now filled with three gun-toting MPs who had wondered if World War IV had commenced in the meeting room.

"Captain."

The MP officer strode forward, into the centre of more military and political muscle than he had even seen in his lifetime of service.

"Sir."

"Arrest General Patton and escort him to his quarters in this building. You and your men will stand guard on his door and he is not to leave, or be allowed to see anyone, until I personally relieve you. Is that clear?"

The Captain nodded, the orders crystal clear, but the reasons lost on him.

"George... George..."

Patton, shocked and stunned, turned his head from the silent Truman to his field commander.

"Sir?"

"General, surrender your sidearm to the arresting officer."

"What?"

"Your gun, General Patton... give the man your gun."

Patton retrieved the Colt.45 revolver with the distinctive stag horn grip from his holster and passed it to the waiting MP, who moved it on to his sergeant like it was a hot coal from hell itself.

"Now... please... go with this officer, General."

To everyone's surprise, George Scott Patton did exactly what Eisenhower ordered, without so much as a word or a look back.

The silence in the room was deafening and laden with a disbelief akin to having witnessed the arrival of aliens in their midst.

Von Vietinghoff coughed, drawing all eyes to him.

He rummaged in his briefcase.

"President Truman, Prime Minister Churchill, if you are looking for options, there is something that the German staff have been looking at for some time, something that might provide you with the alternative you seek."

He divided his paperwork into four section, one for each of the politicians, one for Eisenhower, and the final copy, surprisingly for most, for the Frenchman, General Alphonse Juin.

The men in the room felt their pulses slow as the German general restored normality, as best it could be restored.

All except Truman.

He accepted his copy in silence and resumed his seat, his hands still displaying the tremors of anger that had taken hold of him moments beforehand.

Those observing the scene noticed him bring himself under control and the body relaxed. They then noticed the name on the folders, and immediately those with a sprinkling of the German language felt some understanding of what it might contain.

'Fall Erwachen Riese'

Operation Awakening Giant...

Less than an hour later, thoughts of abandoning the Polish bridgehead were but distant memories, and the basic plan that was Erwachen Riese had approval to be developed into the major operation it represented, an operation that required the German Army to take up the offensive and become the major instrument of prosecuting the ground war against the Communist forces in Europe.

Military minds that had sought a resolution were calmed and encouraged by the developments, and the potential of the German plan.

Some of those minds failed to recall previous thoughts on recent German activity and intentions.

Von Vietinghoff had played his part to perfection.

"Mister President?"

"Yes, General?"

"What are we going to do about George?"

"He's finished, General Eisenhower. End of. I cannot let that go."

Ike opened his mouth to protest and closed it just as quickly.

Truman was right.

"He's been our finest, Sir. A hard man to replace... a hard-charger...hot-headed for sure... but it's stood us in good stead a number of times..."

Truman looked directly into Eisenhower's eyes as he gently grasped his commander's arm.

"I cannot let that stand... you do understand that, Ike?"

Eisenhower replayed some of the expressions from the moment that the peak had been reached. The faces of Allied officers struck dumb that such a display should be performed in front of the US President... on the US President.

"Yes, Sir. He'll be hard to replace."

Truman squeezed Ike's arm once more.

"Yes and no. You have a pool of talent... none like George, that's for sure, but you'll find someone to do the job. But do understand this, General... he's finished. Finished."

"Yes, Mister President."

"Thank you. Now, lead on, General. I'm told that the lunches here are excellent."

Battle is the most magnificent competition in which a human being can indulge. It brings out all that is best; it removes all that is base. All men are afraid in battle. The coward is the one who lets his fear overcome his sense of duty. Duty is the essence of manhood.

George S. Patton

Chapter 161 – THE MATURATION

0930 hrs, Monday, 15th July 1946, Fulda, Germany.

The US artillery opened fire, sending shell after shell into the Soviet positions to the east of the ravaged town.

Fulda was in ruins, smashed to pieces as the forces of East and West swung back and forth over its bricks and mortar.

It had changed hands eleven times in the last fortnight, as determined Soviet counter-attacks smashed into the US defensive positions, only to be thrown back out again by equally determined American ripostes.

There were no civilians left in the town, leastways, none alive, although an exploding shell occasionally revealed a corpse or some body part left over from previous battles.

The last occupation of Fulda had spent much of the 65th US Infantry Division's offensive capability, and two of its three regiments were moved to the flanks to regroup and absorb replacements.

Bemused officers from the 260th and 261st Regiments of the Battle-axe Division found less than the required number of men available to fill the holes left by dead and wounded men, and many of those that were available came from non-fighting trades.

The 259th Regiment, nearly at full strength and not worn out by weeks of heavy fighting, was moved up to hold the centre ground in and around Fulda. They were made very aware that it was ground hard won, and that they were not to let it go.

Elements of the 15th US Armored Division slipped across the Fulda River and into the frontline positions, called forward to help them hold it.

A lot had happened to Nathaniel Parker in the new war, some of it to his benefit, but much not.

The man who had caused so much trouble during his time at the Haut-Kœnigsbourg Colloque had changed, was less pushy, less inclined to run off at the mouth, and more wise to the ways of war.

It would also be fair to say that he was still considered to be an ass by those above and below him, but for different reasons than back in 1945.

His command, C Company, 361st Tank Battalion, was one of two tank formations committed to the east bank of the Fulda River.

Fig # 196 - Plan of attack on Height 493, Fulda, Germany.

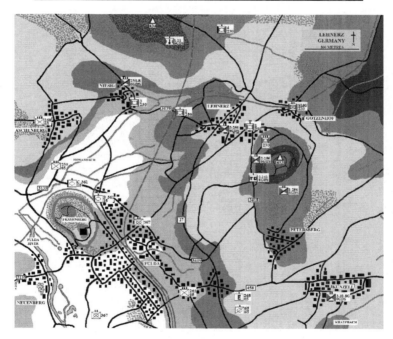

The combat reports of the 65th Infantry indicated that the Soviets used their armour up front in their defence and counter-attacks, and Major General Lindsay McDonald Silvester, commander of 15th Armored, had ordained that he would put some of his best armour up front as a counter, especially as the anti-tank and tank destroyer support units were still recovering after being chewed up some miles to the south.

293

There was another reason for the deployment of B and C companies up front.

The tanks were slow, especially off-road, so Silvester kept the more manoeuvrable Easy Eights back to react to events, leaving the heavy Super Pershings to lie closer to the enemy.

Leastways, that had been the plan, but orders from Corps made him swing into action and, given the time scale, the General had no choice but to employ the two heavy tank companies in the attack.

Parker checked and rechecked his map, reassuring himself that his memory was good, and that he understood the task assigned to his unit.

Infantry from the 259th Regiment of Battle-axe Division were to lead off, ensuring that they held the heights on the left flank of the advance, striking quickly through Niesig and up the main northern height that over looked the valley, namely Height 434, a wide area covered with the tress of the Michelsrombacher Wald.

Fig # 197 – Allied order of battle, Lehnerz and Height 493, Fulda.

ALLIED ORDER OF BATTLE LEHNERZ AND HEIGHTS 434 & 493, GERMANY, 15TH JULY 1946.

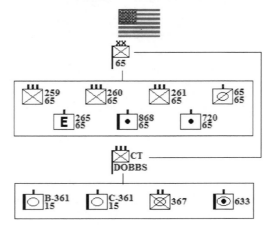

294

A combination of combat engineers and recon troopers were tasked with acquiring Künzell, securing the southern flank.

Once that was achieved, Parker's tank company was to advance in support of the left flank of the 367th [Colored] Armored Infantry Battalion, which was tasked with capturing and holding the vital height 493, from where the entire area could be overseen.

His initial requirement was to capture and hold Lehnerz, but he would take orders from the Lieutenant Colonel in charge of the Armored-Infantry, so the new Parker, more tactically aware, capable, and responsible, had also studied the area north and east of Height 493, just in case he had to go in harm's way there.

Happy with his understanding of the battle to come, he emerged from the turret of the monster tank, swinging up his binoculars to take in any sights of the battle being fought in and around Niesig.

Smoke and dust obscured his vision, but he could decipher enough of the battlefield to understand that the progress was good, something immediately reinforced by the crackle of the radio, announcing the start of phase two of the 259th's advance, as well as reporting minimal casualties.

"Crew report."

"Driver, everything good, Major."

"Gunner, no problems, Sir."

The four men had no issues, and neither had he expected any, but it paid to be sure, and you could never check too much.

"Father, did you check the squawk box?"

"Yes, sir, Major, sir. Dawn check, sir."

The new and painfully young addition to the crew was keen and efficient, but somehow Parker felt he wasn't going to quite fit in.

"Check it again, father."

Lawrence Priest pushed open his hatch and dropped to the ground, smiling at his nickname, seeing it as a sign of acceptance from the experienced men, who, for their part, saw it as nothing more than ragging the new boy.

The telephone burst into life, marking a successful test of the vital communications tool.

"OK, father, Get back aboard."

Following procedures, Priest moved quickly round to the front of the tank, from where the driver could see him, before clambering back up the front plate and dropping into his hull gunner position.

Soviet counter-fire, nowadays rarely effective, made its presence known amongst the advancing 259th's infantrymen, a blossoming orange ball indicating where some vehicle had taken a devastating artillery or mortar hit.

Over the radio, the warning order gave everyone the heads up to be ready to move.

Dewey, the gunner, popped his head up through the hatch and produced a packet of cigarettes, using a hand gesture to seek permission.

Parker nodded and Dewey lit two, slipping one between the commander's lips, receiving a grunt by way of acknowledgement.

Sucking gently on the 'Old Gold', the harsh unfiltered smoke drying his throat, Nathaniel Parker checked Height 434 again, sensing rather than seeing the progress of the lead infantry elements. He looked again to the south, but had no view of the progress towards Künzell.

The radio crackled with an urgent report from one of his commanders.

Turning to face the direction the captain's unit was placed, the rising smoke confirmed the seriousness of the fire that had started to engulf one of his heavy tanks.

'Fucking artillery got lucky, goddamnit.'

It was an inauspicious start to the attack, a near miss having started a fire in the engine compartment, but the captain moved his command to another tank, kicking out the incumbent sergeant and leaving him to sort out the fire fighting and repair of the command tank.

Ears accustomed to the sounds of battle suddenly prickled at the changes ringing around the fields and houses.

"That's high-velocity shit."

"Damn right, Art, something…"

The radio assaulted his ears, calls for help and warnings scrambling with each other for priority and airtime.

An organised attack had suddenly gone completely pear-shaped.

"Brandy-two-six, Brandy-two-six, all units Brandy. Prepare to move forward. Out."

The useless soldier that Parker had been was now a serious asset, and the asset instinctively knew that the 259th's doughboys had run into trouble.

No order came.

Parker waited.

The combat seemed to be intensifying.

As one, he and Dewey threw their dog ends away and exchanged simple nods.

The gunner dropped into the tank and called for APCR in the gun.

"Brandy-two-six, Brandy-two-six, all units Brandy...advance."

B Company and its support units moved forward.

The 259th had moved past Niesig and were in the valley between the village and their final objective when all hell broke loose.

Mines had been the start, and then a handful of anti-tank guns.

The infantry pressed on until Soviet tanks came into play, at which time the fight became uneven and assault quickly turned to a desperate fight to preserve the units.

Soviet mortars switched targets to heap more hurt on the bogged down GIs, and casualties started to mount.

Bazookas knocked down a few of the T34m44s, but not enough, and the lead elements of the Battle-axe Division were suddenly in danger of being overrun.

Parker swung his first platoon more to the left flank, with orders to support the infantry as soon as possible, the recon elements assigned to his company pushing hard, trying to get information for him as to what the hell was happening to the soldiers of the 259th.

All hell broke loose in short order, and Parker became quickly aware of a swarm of enemy tanks on his left flank.

The Super Pershings of his 1st Platoon were engaging, and their 90mm guns immediately made themselves felt against the inferior enemy armour.

Halting to fire, the first shell from each tank drew blood from a target in the valley and immediately the officers and men of the 259th felt the pressure ease, as the T34s went quickly through the gears to high speed, jinking to avoid the deadly guns that could kill them with impunity.

But the Soviet commander did not lack courage, and his orders brought his tanks closer and closer to the Super Pershings of 1st Platoon.

He also committed his ace in the hole, his own upgunned tanks, the hasty marriage of the ubiquitous T34 and the 100mm.

The design was not without faults, but the gun was deadly against all but the most superior armoured of targets.

297

Unfortunately for the Russian tankers, the Super Pershing was just that.

The single version to see action in the previous war had benefitted from extra armour plate welded on in the field, be it boilerplate or recovered pieces of German tanks.

The production versions were born with all the armour they could ever need, but paid the price for their virtual invulnerability with slower speeds and manoeuvrability.

The armour on the hull and turret front approached 200mm thickness and it, and other additions on the hull and turret sides, were spaced, to reduce the effectiveness of hollow-charge weapons, particularly the Panzerfaust or Soviet equivalent, a weapon that still brought sleepless nights to most Allied tankers.

One of the Soviet copies of the lethal weapon dispatched the lead M5 recon tank as it picked its way forward, the tank commander in mid-report with his own commanding officer, a radio message that stopped abruptly and would never be resumed.

The light tank smoked briefly and then the fire came, hounding three of the crew from their refuge behind the knocked-out vehicles. It took less than a minute for the tank to become a cauldron and then explode as its ammunition gave up the struggle against the heat.

Soviet infantry helped the running tankers on their way with bursts of DP fire.

The T34m45/100 tanks were at the rear of the enemy push, taking time to engage, making sure of their shots.

A solid lump of metal struck the front of Parker's tank, and deflected away, missing his head by no more than three feet.

He felt the gut-wrenching assault of fear and strove to control his stomach, determined to keep his meal down, fighting against the attempts of his system to throw up.

Another shell came close, throwing earth and debris up other the tank.

He vomited, sending his egg and bacon breakfast down the side of the turret and onto the top armour, following it up quickly with the rest of the meal plus coffee.

Wiping the remnants from his mouth, he keyed the mike.

"Driver, move left. Wall and tree. Put us in behind the wall a-sap. Gunner, target, left twelve, range twelve hundred."

Dewey moved the long-barrelled 90mm into the right line, adjusting as the tank moved into its firing position.

The movement stopped and he waited for the rocking of the suspension to stop.

"Target tank, on."

"FIRE!"

The breech flew back into the turret as the powerful gun sent its deadly missile down range.

Dewey never celebrated his kills for reasons best known to him, but Parker's whoop let the tank crew know that their shell had gone home to good effect.

In fact, Dewey was something of a mystery to the rest of the crew, bar Parker, who had the advantage of having read the man's file.

He suspected he knew the reasons behind the gunner's aloofness, but had never tackled him on the subject of what had actually happened at Arracourt in September '44, and the story behind the Silver Star and Purple Heart Dewey had been awarded.

He never wore the ribbons and evaded any questions when asked about his family, life, or history, save to confirm he had seen combat with the 4th Armored before arriving with the 15th.

All Nathaniel Parker really needed to know about the man was his gunnery skills, and Dewey was as proficient as they came.

"Target, tank, right two, range thirteen hundred."

"On."

"FIRE!"

Another armor-piercing, composite rigid tank-killing shell went from muzzle to target in the blink of an eye.

The old Model44 T34 disintegrated under the hammer blow.

"Driver, move right and forward, hedge line."

The Super Pershing clipped the stonewall as it moved, destroying the corner in an instant.

Parker instinctively dropped himself into the turret as a flurry of mortar shells arrived, adding to the destruction of the old wall and its surroundings.

He smiled to himself and raised his head enough to sweep the enemy positions with his binoculars.

There was...

He concentrated.

'Well I'll be...'

Parker saw something important.

Allowing the tank to find its cover, he whispered into the mike.

"Command tank, right three, range fourteen hundred, Chinese fucking laundry...see him?"

The gun swung gently.

"Nope... ah... yep... fucking sneaky bastard!"

The tell-tale aerials of a command tank were tied down and the T34 was camouflaged by the simple but effective use of washing draped around it.

Dewey made a small adjustment.

"On."

"Fire."

The Soviet tank company lost its commanding officer.

Fig # 198 – Soviet Order of Battle, Height 493, Fulda.

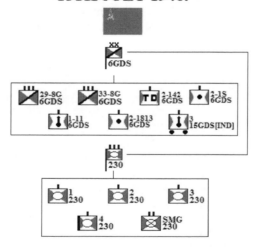

230th 'Zhitomir' Independent Tank Regiment had lost more than a company commander to the lethal 90mm's of the Super Pershings, its first company T34s mostly burning and smoking in the valley where they had first sprung a surprise on the Battle-axe infantrymen.

The Zhitomir Regiment was not at full strength, but had received reinforcements from units broken up by casualties, and touted an impressive order of battle for a Soviet armoured unit at this stage in the war.

Major Yatzhin, a veteran of Kursk, Bagration, and the final days in Czechoslovakia, commanded a mixed force of T34s, as well as an infantry company and the remnants of a heavy tank unit, whose IS-IIIs now lay in wait for the US advance.

The Cossack General commanding had sent more cavalrymen from the 6th Guards Cavalry Corps to help with the defence of Heights 434 and 493.

The tank Major ensured his own defences on 493 were fully prepared, and ordered the newly arrived horseless cavalrymen to thicken up his defence, and retained his own SMG unit as a reaction force to seal any breach.

Yatzhin's command tank was dug-in on the slope of Height 493, from where he observed the slow but sure advance of the American heavy tanks.

Puzzled that the artillery had slackened off, Yatzhin contacted the Artillery liaison officer, only to discover that the artillery battalion had been attacked by aircraft and was repositioning…

… what was left of it…

He still had a company of Katyusha up his sleeve, but their value against heavy tanks was limited.

The American juggernaut crept closer.

"Gunner, follow the lead one on the road there. Stay on target."

He flicked the radio switch to his unit's frequency and thumbed the mike.

"Kukhnya-Zero, all units Podval, Uchitel-Zero, Kukhnya-Two and Kukhnya-Three, hold your fire… hold your fire…"

He released the mike button and spared a milli-second's thought for the commander and men of Kukhnya-One, whose men and machines lay blasted in the valley to his right.

The moment passed and he returned to his mental picture of the battlefield, imagining his tanks, and those of the broken heavy tank regiment, the handful of anti-tank guns, and the infantry… and the mines.

"…Hold your fire…"

The mines had been provided from stocks liberated from the former Nazi army, Type 43 Riegel bar mines in large numbers, notorious for their sensitivity and instability due to corrosion in the wiring, a fact attested to by the engineer unit that had laid them, which had lost three valuable men in the process.

The mines were another reason that his artillery had avoided the valley floor, not wishing to set off the sensitive devices before they had a chance to play their part.

"...Hold your fire..."

The large enemy tanks were still progressing, seeking new targets to their front, occasionally halting to fire and pick off a survivor from his First Company.

"... Hold your fire..."

A shell sent from the side of Height 434 achieved success, struck the side of a Super Pershing's turret and deflected perfectly into the hull armour.

The turret leapt skywards, driven up by the huge force of the explosion, killing the entire crew instantly.

Vengeance was swift, despite the best efforts of the T34 to move back to cover.

Three 90mm shells transformed it to scrap metal within seconds.

"...Hold your fire..."

The destruction of the T34 was a signal to the GIs of the 259th, and they rose up as their officers and NCOs screamed at them, pushing hard to get out of the valley and up the slopes to their target.

This surge encouraged Parker to push his men harder, and he urged his two platoons to move forward quicker.

"...Hold..."

Yatzhin held his breath, sensing the moment approaching.

Above the sounds of battle, the crack of exploding Riegel mines reached his ears. Shifting his binoculars, he quickly spotted an enemy tank, its tracks both shed, disabled, and bereft of cover.

To its left, another tank, one track gone, desperately tried to make some move to the nearest cover.

"Fire!"

More Riegels exploded before the first volley arrived, disabling a total of six of the heavy tanks.

Two of the disabled Super Pershings became kills as 100mm and 122mm shells arrived on target, although it was the 100mm missiles that did the damage, the 122mm HEAT shells being defeated by the spaced armour they struck.

More HEAT followed before the IS-III commanders realised their error and reverted to solid shot.

Even when disabled, the Super Pershings were a tough nut to crack, and soon Yatzhin's casualties started to mount.

He reverted to tactics of old, used successfully against the waves of panzers at Kursk.

"Kukhnya-Zero, Kukhnya-Two, Kukhnya-three, advance immediately, close down the range, out."

He took the acknowledgements before contacting the IS-III unit.

"Kukhnya-Zero, Uchitel-Zero, hold position, out."

The IS-IIIs were mainly positioned on the eastern side of Height 434, oriented to the south and south-west, still perfectly placed for over watch of the US advance.

Yatzhin watched with pride as his two companies responded immediately, using the speed of their T34s to close down the distance, bringing the enemy closer, intent on reducing the effectiveness of their thick armour, and hoping to take advantage of the enemies' slow speed and low manoeuvrability.

Just as he had been taught, and just as had proved successful at Kursk.

A roar overhead broke his moment of self-satisfaction.

"Blyad!"

Some new enemy aircraft swept overhead and dropped cluster munitions on the top and reverse slopes of the height opposite, and he knew he his force had just been badly hurt.

His AA defences were inadequate, and the second wave of aircraft attacked, easily putting their munitions right on target.

The third wave of aircraft, recognisable as P-47 Thunderbolts, swept lazily overhead, and bathed the Soviet defensive position with the now traditional application of deadly napalm.

He keyed the mike, sending an order to the Guards mortar unit, who in turn released their Katyusha rockets, turning the valley in front of Height 424 into a bloodbath, and hammering the second echelon of the US infantry attack.

True to their doctrine, the Guards Mortars started the process of rapid relocation before the last rocket left the rails.

Another order brought whatever artillery and mortar fire available to bear upon the stranded tanks of the US tank company to his front, where he determined to give his advancing T34s the best possible chance at success.

The screams pierced Parker's concentration and he instinctively turned his head, just catching the red mist aftermath left by a mortar shell that destroyed two men working on the track of a nearby Super Pershing.

He had made a command decision.

Threatened by the advance of numerous enemy tanks, he should have withdrawn, but too many of his tanks had been disabled by mines, and to withdraw meant leaving them to be overrun and knocked out.

So, Nathaniel Parker elected to stay and fight, moving his remaining running tanks to the left flank.

His reasoning was sound.

He moved to cover the flank of the infantry, ensuring that the advancing enemy tanks had to deal with his unit first. Parker also gave at least part of his unit better angles on the approaching enemy vehicles.

He also hoped to move around the minefield, opening up his manoeuvre possibilities.

With the courage of desperate men, the disabled Pershings started to claim victims amongst the jinking T34s.

"Move up, nice and slow, stay tight."

The group of seven tanks obeyed, moving ahead of their stranded comrades, changing the angles as Parker knew the move would.

The lead T34 responded, changing direction and hurtling towards his group, exposing a larger target to attack from the side.

The disabled Super Pershings needed no second invitation.

A shell went straight through the target, apparently without causing any real damage.

A second shell brought the now smoking tank to an immediate halt, and the crew abandoned under fire from coaxial machine guns.

A flash overhead heralded the arrival of more air support, and the smoking tank disintegrated as two rockets hit it flat on, sending metal in all directions.

The IS-IIIs commander, call sign Uchitel-zero, called his vehicles to cease fire, thus avoiding attracting swift retribution from the air.

The handful of static and mobile flak weapons available to the Russian force did what they could, and that was next to nothing, the nearest thing to victory a minor damage hit on one of the latest attackers, a Thunderbolt, which lost part of a wingtip as it wheeled away from delivering its rockets.

A clang announced a direct hit on the hull of Parker's tank, but the solid shot soared skywards as the heavy plate resisted its attention.

Soon, the smell of faeces and urine reached the turret crew.

'Father' had lost control of both bowels and bladder with the fright of the impact.

No one said anything.

They had all been there before themselves.

Parker's manoeuvre had worked, after a fashion, as the advancing tanks concentrated more on the running vehicles than those disabled in the minefield, which meant that the stationery vehicles enjoyed easier shots on their enemy.

The aircraft circled the battlefield, seeking employment, but conscious of the close proximity of the two armoured units.

Impatient, as only airmen can be, the USAAF pilots welcomed the unexpected arrival of some Mikoyans, and pursued the terrified Soviet pilots as far as they could.

It was an error.

Yatzhin seized the moment.

"Kukhnya-Zero, Uchitel-Zero, open fire on the mobile group immediately. Kill them all! Out."

The silent IS-IIIs had been tracking their targets, waiting for the moment of release.

With the advantage of height, they fired, and their AP shells angled down on the Pershings, negating much of the slant of their armour.

"Fuck! Incom…"

Parker recoiled from the hatch and tensed as the white blob ate up the distance from tank to tank in the briefest of moments and arrived before he completed his warning.

Kerangg!

A wave of heat and sound assaulted every member of the crew.

Kerangg!

A second shot struck home.

Screaming…

"Shut the fuck up, father!"

It wasn't father.

It was Middlemass, the driver, who had broken both ankles as the heavy shell had struck the front hull and the shock wave had travelled through all things metal until finding his vulnerable bones tensed against the pedals.

Kerangg!

The screams stopped and the metallic tang of blood and bone filled the inside of the tank.

The solid shot had punched through the plate and ploughed through the screaming driver on its way into the floor pan.

It did not explode.

Parker knew he was hurt, the blood flow down his head quickly impairing his vision, but not enough for him to fail to notice he no longer had a cupola.

The whole thing had been stripped away by the first hit and he had daylight above him.

"Everyone ok? Talk to me!"

Acknowledgements of different types came back from all but Middlemass, with only Dewey sounding in control of himself.

"I'm on, Major."

"Take 'em out. I can't see a fucking thing."

The 90mm sent its reply towards its tormentors, but the IS-III it struck proved resilient.

Kerangg!

Another shell struck the front upper edge of the turret and disappeared off into the remains of the German village, doing further mischief amongst armored infantrymen waiting to advance,

"Gun's fucked! Major, the gun's fucked! No elevation."

The barrel had dropped dramatically, pointing to the ground and it refused to respond to any adjustments.

The external stabiliser springs had been carried away, and the shock wave had done other damage to the gun mount.

Parker immediately knew the right thing to do.

"Shit! Abandon tank!"

Needing no second invitation, the four survivors bailed out.

Four became three as Rogers, the loader, took a bullet in the back of the head and dropped lifeless on the engine grilles.

The IS-IIIs were in the ascendency, and another of Parker's tanks erupted in a storm of orange and red.

Parker checked his remaining two men, neither of whom were wounded, one of which was terrified out of his skin.

Leaving Dewey in charge, the blood-covered Major Parker sprinted to the nearest tank and dropped in behind it, liberating the handset to the squawk box.

On the inside of the tank, the young Lieutenant was wholly glad to receive orders to withdraw, and lost no time in passing the instructions to the survivors.

Parker moved away and watched as the remnants of his mobile force worked their way backwards... still engaging... still fighting... face to the enemy.

He nodded in silent praise at the way the three tanks worked as a team. Pulling out his Colt automatic, he ran back to where he had left his two crewmen, but found the position empty.

A quick scan revealed no clue as to their whereabouts, but he had other fish to fry in any case.

The sound of aero engines made him look skyward, and he was rewarded with the sight of the returning aircraft, who immediately renewed their attack on the Soviet positions, including the IS-IIIs who now started to suffer casualties.

Leaping from rubble to rubble, hole to hole, he moved closer to the nearest surviving disabled Super Pershing, intent on organising the resistance or salvaging what he could of the unit, whichever needed to be done.

Gauging the distance to the rear of the disabled tank, Parker made the final sprint and flopped onto the ground in its shadow.

Underneath him, a Type 43 Riegel bar mine sensed the pressure. Normally it would not have been enough to detonate, Parker's weight being less than the designated one hundred and eighty kilos down force.

However, that did not matter to the unstable mine.

Four kilos of TNT exploded in an instant, spreading parts of Parker over the rear of the Pershing, and numerous points beyond.

1030 hrs, Monday, 15th July 1946, Fulda, Germany.

Yatzhin, dismounted from his tank, watched in a rage as his second and third companies withdrew in disarray.

His rage was not aimed at his poor soldiers, who had given all they could, but at the Allied airmen, who once again had saved the day for his enemy.

He swivelled his binoculars and exercised a stufied calm as he noted the smoking ruins of all but four of the IS-IIIs, most destroyed by the enemy aircraft that continued to circle the battlefield.

Just to confirm his recollections of the swift but merciless air attack, he sought out the blackened and smoking hole on the side of Height 424, the site of the sole success against the fliers who had plagued his command.

A single Thunderbolt had succumbed to his AA defence, and had driven straight into the hillside.

Yatzhin dropped the binoculars to his chest and took a deep breath to clear his mind.

His orders had been discharged, and the enemy assaults on the two key heights had been repulsed, the Cossacks on Height 424 having recaptured the high ground when the tanks in the valley had started to withdraw.

However, he had lost the majority of his command in the process, and a second push by any substantial enemy force would carry them through and beyond his positions in a matter of a few moments.

The US artillery started up again, harrying his withdrawing tanks, as well as bringing discomfort to the cavalrymen repairing their positions on Height 424.

He envied the matériel available to his enemy, his own supply situation tenuous at best, at worst a nothingness that forecast solely disaster for the Red Army.

Yatzhin snorted, totally without humour, assuring himself that the only reason he would have a full load of ammunition on his tank was that he now had less tanks to supply.

"Blyad."

"Comrade Mayor?"

"Nothing, Comrade Praporshchik, nothing."

"Right, pack up and prepare to move back. I'm returning to my tank."

Neither he, nor the Praporshchik, or the rest of the headquarters group heard it.

None the less, it was very real.

The shell had been fired by an M43 Self-propelled gun, sporting a heavy M115 8" howitzer.

It was the first shot the unit had fired that day, and the most effective.

The two hundred pound shell struck directly on Yatzhin's command tank, sending vicious pieces of sharp metal in all directions.

The Major felt as if he had been kicked in the belly, but his attention was mainly drawn to the Praporshchik, who simply fell into four large loosely connected pieces, as shards of metal scythed through his body.

The screams and wails of those hit by life-taking metal filled his senses.

A wall of flame washed over him as his smashed tank and crew were immolated before his eyes.

The shock wave lifted him up and sent him flying backwards, smashing through something that could only have been

308

another human being, before he came to rest in a bush thirty yards from where he had been standing.

Still he felt no pain, but he was fascinated by the silver-grey entrails that spread from his riven stomach back down the path he had just been thrown.

His belly had been sliced open, as neat and precise as if done by a top surgeon, allowing his stomach and organs to come tumbling out and drag in the earth.

His back started to protest first, a number of teeth and parts of a jawbone buried in his kidney area, pieces of the young radio operator he had smashed into during his rearward flight.

And then, like a tidal wave, the pain came and robbed him of his senses.

Yatzhin screamed...

...and screamed...

...and screamed...

He was still screaming when the medical detail recovered his intestines, washed them clean with water, before bagging them as best they could, and carrying the hideously wounded officer away.

What happened at Fulda, and around Lehnerz and Niesig, was a microcosm of the American front.

A battle that produced nothing but dead and maimed men, smashed equipment, expenditure of supplies, and little to show for it militarily, save for a few feet of ground, one way or the other.

In just over an hour of combat, forty-eight tanks, six anti-tank guns, twenty-nine assorted vehicles, and one aircraft had been destroyed or put out of action.

Combined casualties amounted to six hundred and seventy dead, with a similar number wounded.

The Soviet plan to inflict casualties upon the Americans was working, as the US generals knew only too well.

The Red Army's own casualties were horrendous, but the USSR did not suffer from the diseases of freedom and democracy, as Stalin was want to put it.

Despite the losses, Fulda was insignificant in the greater run of things, or so it seemed, because one particular loss proved to be the catalyst for significant events in the American capital.

Some weeks later, well after the battle, the family of Sergeant Art Dewey received the confirmation that he had been killed in action, his remains, and those of Priest, eventually found amongst the smashed rubble of Lehnerz.

They were one of many families that received such notifications in the month of August 1946.

The difference was that Arthur Lawrence Dewey was the son of Thomas Edmund Dewey, Governor of New York and the defeated Republican presidential candidate in the '44 election, a man who was an established anti-intervention politician, a man now in mourning, and a man supplied with the full facts of the pointless nature of his son's death in front of Height 424 near Fulda.

A man who developed a thirst for retribution, and a specific idea on how it could be achieved.

And so it was that a relatively unimportant battle became a pivotal point in the European War or, more accurately, the political war at home.

1123 hrs, Wednesday, 17th July 1946, Magdeburg, Germany.

Lieutenant Colonel Konstantin Djorov listened impassively to the instructions of his air controller.

Returned from his test pilot role to command of 2nd Guards Special Fighter Regiment, he now led the most capable fighter unit in the Red Air Force and, if things went as was hoped, he would shortly have an opportunity to lead them into combat for the first time in their new guise.

The 2nd, or to give it's the full honorifics, 2nd Guards Special Red Banner Order of Suvorov Fighter Aviation Regiment, comprised two groups of aircraft, amounting to forty-seven craft in total.

Four companies of jet fighters, two of ex-German Me 262s, and two of MiG-9s, were lurking high above the city of Magdeburg, favouring a position slightly to the south-west.

Waiting…

1125 hrs, Wednesday, 17th July 1946, approaching Magdeburg, Germany.

At twenty thousand feet, the 20th Schwerekampfstaffel of the DRL's 8th Schwerekampfgruppe was approaching its assigned target, the fifteen US-manufactured B32 Dominator bombers in perfect formation and untroubled by the modest flak that was thrown at them.

Two Jagdstaffels of late model ME-109K fighters flew above them, waiting for any Soviet interceptor response.

Behind the first wave came the second, a mish-mash of British four-engine heavy bomber aircraft, from the Vickers Windsor, Short Stirling, to the Handley-Page Halifax. The 22nd Schwerekampfstaffel brought another nineteen bombers to the party.

A further two squadrons of fighters shepherded their charges on the approach run to the Magdeburg rail yards, the target for today's modest raid.

The DRL bombers reached Aschersleben, and turned hard to port, lining up their approach on a north-north-east course, to bring them directly down the line of the recently repaired marshalling yards.

Soviet flak was virtually now virtually non-existent and no aircraft were lost from home base to a point east of Sülzetal... where an easy mission suddenly became a bloodbath of monumental proportions.

1133 hrs, Wednesday, 17th July 1946, skies above Sülzetal, Germany.

"Attack pattern one. Dive, dive, dive!"

Lieutenant Colonel Djorov led his group of MiG-9s directly into a frontal attack on the approaching bomber formation, closing from above at an incredible speed, despite throttling back to gain more 'time on target' for his weapons, one 37mm and two 23mm cannons.

Despite his skills and experience, Djorov only managed the briefest of bursts before he was through and past the first wave of bombers.

His followers also failed to exact the price of their surprise attack, although one of the Dominators gradually fell from height, its flight deck flayed by shells and occupied only by warm meat.

The DRL protective fighters, ME-109Ks of the 5th Jagdgruppe, swarmed down, angry at being caught unawares and keen to protect their charges, and found themselves suddenly fighting for their lives as the Me-262 group, led by Oligrevin, the Regiment's 2IC, fell upon them with gusto.

With more time on the 262, the Soviet pilots judged their ambush better, and four of the 190s came apart under the concentrated fire of the cannon each 'Schwalbe' carried.

Two others fell away smoking, with no more aggressive intent, each pilot concentrating on just staying airborne.

The MiGs came back round in a wide arc, bleeding off more speed.

Djorov lined himself up on a Dominator, its rear defensive .50cal machine guns already spouting tracer in an effort to put him off his approach.

The veteran pilot eased his jet fighter into position and judged his burst to perfection.

Shells chewed into the starboard wing and fuselage with dramatic effect.

Whilst the spar did not fail completely, the damage was such that it bent. The right wing kinked upwards, ensuring that the large aircraft transformed from an aerodynamic beauty into a useless piece of spiraling metal within seconds.

The crew screamed their lives out as the aircraft's G-forces ensured they rode it all the way into their native soil below.

Above, Djorov flicked into another attack line and managed a half-second burst at another target, before his speed carried him away from the increasingly desperate German airmen.

His flight sent another four Dominators falling from the sky, their heavy cannon shells doing murderous work with flesh and metal alike.

One MiG flew through a cone of defensive fire and simply exploded in mid-air, no piece larger than a manhole cover surviving to drop to the ground.

Behind the leading flight, the DRL Me-109s and Red Air Force 262s fought in isolation, the defensive fighters with nothing to do but fight to preserve their own lives, the Soviet Schwalbes intent solely on their own mission of destroying the escort.

Five destroyed Dominators became nine, as Djorov led his men in for a side attack.

Whilst Djorov learned that the larger silhouette was an easier target, he also learned the hard way that it unmasked more guns, as the pass ensured two more of his aircraft were lost, one in a huge fireball that left an orange and black rainbow as it fell away, and the other simply stopped flying through a storm of heavy bullets, its wounded pilot trusting to his silk to return safely to terra firma.

The highest ranking German bomber officer called off the attack, and the Dominators turned to port, closing in even tighter for self-defense, whilst their radio operators screamed for support, for anyone... anything close by that could come and save them from massacre.

Djorov turned his flight's attentions to the other enemy heavy formation, bringing his men around the fighter melee and into another frontal attack.

The results were better and, despite the loss of two more of his aircraft, four bombers went down hard, with another two smoking badly and falling out of formation.

As agreed previously, Oligrevin had detached some of his fighters to deal with any escort that the second wave might have, and these 262s found themselves embroiled in a fight with 262s of the DRL, only the third such encounter recorded in the new war.

From the euphoria of fighting and destroying the outclassed ME-109s, the Soviet pilots suddenly found themselves in the situation of fighting pilots with more experience than them in their aircraft, and with jets that were better maintained, fueled, and conditioned. They had barreled headfirst into the 200th ZBV Jagdgeschwader, a squadron of elite German pilots with more jet fighting experience than any other such group in the world. Jet tangled with jet, but the DRL pilots had the upper hand from the start.

Djorov kept his MiGs focused on the bombers, but instinctively understood that he had little time before the yellow-nosed aircraft overcame his cover and started to attack his unit.

He also understood that he would be outclassed, but applied himself to the task of bringing down the enemy bombers, rather than contemplate what was to come.

Olegrevin was fighting for his life and could spare little time for the niceties.

"Yaguar-krasny-odin, Yaguar-belyy-dva, they're all over us…we can't cover you."

He instinctively thumbed the firing button as a shape flashed across his nose from left to right.

"Mudaks!"

He missed, which was fortunate, as the white and red tail of a friendly aircraft became apparent.

"MUDAKS!"

However, he held his line and managed to land a few shells on target, the pursuing DRL aircraft taking vital damage in its port turbojet, causing it to spin away, out of the fight.

He also missed Djorov's reply as his cannons roared again, missing an enemy aircraft adorned with the evidence of scores of kills, its evasive manoeuvre seemingly well beyond his own understanding of the 262's abilities.

'Blyad! This one's a real ace!'

Olegrevin turned as tight as he dared, intent on trying his hand again, but the enemy pilot guessed his intent and performed a sudden climb and tight turn, accompanied by a loss of forward momentum that defied the laws of physics, a manoeuvre that took him unawares. It was almost as if the ace deliberately stalled his aircraft to drop off speed in an instant.

The Russian overshot and found himself the hunted.

Rolling to the right, he dropped his starboard wing and did a roll around, coming back upright in a left-handed dive.

A fluffy cloud proved a momentary haven, and Olegrevin pulled up as hard as he dared, with right stick and pedal, intent on turning the tables on his enemy.

…Which enemy was still on his tail.

'Mudaks! Job tvoju mat!'

Tracers flashed past his cockpit, close enough that he felt he could lean out and catch the deadly cannon shells in his hat.

He spun away, using his right hand turn to advantage, feeling the forces push him hard back into his seat.

Johannes Steinhoff, commander of JG200, had one hundred and eighty-eight victories to his name, and was perturbed that number one-eight-nine was proving so difficult.

From the kill markings on the enemy jet, the man was clearly an experienced pilot, but such was Steinhoff's confidence and self-belief that he had expected to down the Soviet airman with much less of a fight.

His last burst had missed, although it must have shaved the Schwalbe's cockpit.

The red and white tailed jet threw itself into a breakneck right diving spin.

Fate took a hand, and Steinhoff had to shift his stick to the left rapidly, as two enemy aircraft closed in on a collision course.

"Scheisse!"

Narrowly missing the leading enemy, he swung around in a long port turn His eyes sought out his worthy opponent, but failed to find him.

Another target suggested itself, and Steinhoff flicked back into the vertical and pulled on the stick, walking his shells from tail to nose.

The enemy 262 simply fell apart as its integrity was compromised and forward air speed did the rest, ripping open the fuselage.

Steinhoff ignored the pilot as best he could, as the man, clearly missing a leg, fell out of his disintegrating aircraft and disappeared out of sight.

'*189.*'

He heard the thuds.

He knew he was in trouble.

A piece of debris from the Soviet aircraft had entered his starboard intake, and the JUMO turbojet began the brief and spectacular process of tearing itself apart.

Steinhoff was floating free of the dying Schwalbe before he knew it, his razor sharp instincts again preserving him.

Before his chute had properly deployed, the JUMO disintegrated and his aircraft fireballed and plunged to the ground.

This was the thirteenth time he had been 'shot down', but only the second time he had taken to a parachute.

He had little trust in them, and watched his canopy suspiciously as he floated gently to the ground.

Djorov sent another DRL Halifax out of formation, its port wing awash with fire, pieces falling off, further reducing the crippled heavy bomber's ability to stay airborne.

He and his MiGs had downed seven of the bombers, but he had lost three of his own pilots in the process...

... and worse was to come.

With his MiGs low on fuel, he called his regiment off, but disengaging was not possible with the enemy 262s intent on revenge.

"Yaguar-krasny, Yaguar-krasny, disengage, Odin, out."

"Yaguar-Odin, Yaguar-dva, over."

As Djorov moved away from the remaining heavy bombers, he listened to Olegrevin's brief status report.

"Belyy-Dva, you must disengage now! Disengage now!"

"Odin, we're trying to but..."

Above Djorov's head, something turned orange and exploded.

"Dva... Dva... Belyy-dva, come in..."

The radio died.

Olegrevin felt the thuds as something chewed away at his aircraft. Whilst the response was slightly less than normal, he evaded with a tight port turn.

In front of him, an enemy 262 was in trouble. Instinctively, he sent a burst into the damaged jet and was rewarded with an instant fireball.

Just in case, he yelled his orders into the radio, but he expected no reply, and there was none, as he was sure that the radio was the original of the burnt electrical smell that assailed him.

The enemy fighter ace was nowhere to be seen, and he realized that suddenly the sky had become less busy.

Olegrevin's eyes flitted from aircraft to aircraft, but all he saw were the red and white tails of his regiment.

Below and heading north-east were the MiGs of Djorov's group.

In the distance, he could just about make out the remnants of the 109s that had escorted the first group of enemy bombers.

As he double-checked that no hostile aircraft were still in the vicinity, he made a loose count of his aircraft, and came up short by seven.

'Nearly a third... fucking bastards... the fucki...'

His eyes saw and sent the images to his brain, which took a little longer to understand.

He thumbed his useless mike, despite himself.

"Yaguar-belyy, Yaguar-belyy, enemy aircraft diving... break left... break left!"

Even as he shouted uselessly, Olegrevin worked both pedal and joystick, breaking away from the rallying aircraft of his regiment, reasoning that if his men couldn't hear him, they would at least follow his movements and realise that the enemy was upon them.

Below him, Djorov had been momentarily distracted counting his own aircraft, finding five missing, before his eyes strayed back to the 262 group... and what was diving on them.

"Yaguar-belyy! Yaguar-belyy! Enemy aircraft diving... break left... break left!"

'More jets... Blyad!'

Steinhoff, nursing a sprained ankle, found a position from where he could observe what was happening above.

His Walther was kept close to hand, just in case some nosey Soviet soldier came on the scene.

He didn't know who the new arrivals were, but he had no doubt that it was the head of the DRL's fighter units himself, flying with the newly established 'Squadron of Aces', a unit constructed around experienced men that nearly rivalled his own for total kills and missions flown.

Steinhoff's professional eye took in the small details that escaped most other watchers, instinctively understanding which of the black blobs was flown by an expert, and which was likely to fall in the vicious dogfight that was developing.

The 'Geschwader von Asse', as the new unit was officially named, or 'Asse Geschwader' as it was more simply known by its pilots and ground crew, was easily gaining the upper hand, the Soviet fighters already low on fuel and ammunition, and the pilots tired by the intense combat they had already experienced.

Steinhoff sniggered to himself, remembering the AG on the side of the General de Jagdflieger's Me262, standing not for 'Asse Geschwader', but just for the legend's name.

Adolf Galland.

He shaded his eyes, seeking some sign of the great man in the skies above but the aircraft, all of the same type, were indistinguishable from each other, so he could not even celebrate when an aircraft here and there staggered and fell from the sky.

Steinhoff grasped his pistol tighter in sympathetic alarm for his comrades, as he watched some of the strange new Russian jets rising up into the fray, but relaxed quickly as he examined their movements and swiftly concluded that they were undoubtedly second best in aerial combat with the superior 262s.

He shouted at the blue and white battleground above.

"Come on, leutchen. Knock the communist bastards out of the sky."

None the less, the arrival od the Sukhois gave the enemy some breathing space, and two distinct groups formed, that comprising the enemy making off and diving as quickly as they could, the other group, quickly reformed, headed off to the southwest.

Steinhoff frowned, wondering why the DRL aircraft had yielded such a strong position, not knowing that the 'Asse

317

Geschwader' had been recalled to respond to a heavy Soviet ground attack mission on German frontline units near Göttingen.

He watched the 262s depart at high speed, and then similarly dwelt on the Soviet departure, all the time noting, with satisfaction, the pall of smoke rising from Magdeburg.

His satisfaction turned to ice water in his veins as something metal touched the back of his neck.

A gravelly voice, seemingly hell bent on destroying Steinhoff's native language, asked a simple and direct question.

"So… who the fuck are you, sunshine?"

Steinhoff talked and the four men listened, whilst six others, similarly attired, waited in the shadows and hedges, looking the other way.

Even though the men wore no recognizable uniforms, they were undoubtedly professional soldiers, and men who would kill him without compunction.

What he very quickly appreciated was that his life hung in the balance, so he produced his documents as quickly as he could, and sought permission to remove his bland jacket, revealing his proper uniform and awards in all their glory.

The speaker raised an eyebrow, but otherwise gave no sign of any reaction.

Weapons remained trained upon him whilst the officer, he was clearly in charge, examined the paperwork.

"Right-ho, boys. He's one of ours."

A hand offered up the documents, and remained, waiting to be shaken.

"Sorry about that, Colonel, but we can't be too careful. Titus Bottomley, Major, SAS. You're lucky we're here. There's an absolute cartload of Uncle Joe's boys down the road there, and sure as eggs is eggs they saw you come down. We have to move, and move now. Sarnt Cookson."

An arm whipped around around Steinhoff's shoulder and the German found himself propelled by an irresistible force, belying the British NCOs modest size.

"Arsch!"

The ankle sent a shockwave up his leg, working his mouth on arrival at his head.

"Sorry… my ankle."

Bottomley took a quick look and turned towards a fallen tree trunk.

"Hold, Cookson. You're injured, Colonel?"

Steinhoff managed to confirm the ankle problem through gritted teeth.

"Settle him down there, Sarnt. Corporal Tappett, have a quick shufti at this fellow's ankle, there's a good man. We need to be gone in two, so shake a leg."

The tree trunk separated into two pieces, and the mobile part moved forward and knelt in front of the incredulous Steinhoff.

In under two minutes, his ankle was bound tightly and two tablets had travelled down his throat, effective painkillers flushed down with a gulp of water.

Whilst that was happening, Bottomley consulted with another man who had emerged from a small bush, establishing the line of march and movement orders with his second-in-command.

Tappet interrupted respectfully.

"Major, he's good to go, but not too fast, Sah. It's a nice sprain, to be sure."

Tappett received a slap on the shoulder by way of thanks and acknowledgement.

"Hang with our guest then, Corporal, if you please."

Without further ceremony, Bottomley circled his hand around his head and motioned with his hand.

Steinhoff gave up counting when he reached forty men that emerged from their concealment, and realised that these British soldiers were, if nothing else, extremely adept at the art of blending into the countryside.

"Right, Colonel, we've a few miles to go, and precious little time to do it in, so do please try to keep up."

Bottomley's German had improved so much that the pilot understood it had all been part of the deception.

He had heard of these SAS soldiers, but had never expected to encounter any, let alone rely on them for his life.

"I'll do my best, Major. Lead on."

The binding was good, and Steinhoff followed the main body on their journey back to Allied lines.

As they made their way steadily away from the site of his landing, the DRL officer took in more of his new 'comrades', their tatty clothing and unkempt appearance not in keeping with their lithe and professional movements, and their obviously well maintained array of weapons.

Despite still being behind Soviet lines, he knew he would be kept safe and return to his Geschwader in safety. Clearly, these Britshers were all that their reputation promised, so Steinhoff fully understood that he was surrounded by a group of extremely competent professionals, for whom the art of warfare came as easy as falling off a bike.

0703 hrs, Thursday, 18th July, 1946, Av. V. Lenine 2445, Lourenco Marques. Mozambique.

Sergei Tomaschuk was not an early riser at the best of times, and this was most certainly not the best of times. The previous evening he had enjoyed the Lourenco Marques hostelries and consumed considerable quantities of the local libations, rums and beers mainly, and his all three of his heads were paying a terrible price for a few hours of pleasure.

The hammering on his door roused him from his agonies, and he determined to destroy whoever it was rousting him well before his time.

The door flew open as he wrenched on the handle, only for his plans to change immediately, when he found that his torturer was none other than the NKVD resident, who stood waiting impatiently.

"Comrade Tomaschuk, eventually. Good morning. You have two minutes to get ready."

Grassovny clapped his hands to chivy his number two along and walked in, throwing open the curtains to allow the early morning sun to stream into the modest bedroom.

Outside, the USSR's embassy compound was quiet and going about its business as normal, unaware of the urgent matter that had woken the NKVD's top man in Mozambique, and brought him to the door of the Naval Attaché and deputy head of the NKVD| section at such an unearthly hour.

Looking much better than he felt, Tomaschuk stepped out of his bathroom, resplendent in the uniform of a Red Navy Captain of the 2nd Rank.

Grassovny again clapped his hands, as much in approval of the metamorphosis as to underline the importance of his mission.

"Right, Comrade Kapitan, let us go."

Grabbing his cap, Tomaschuk hurried after the disappearing NKVD man.

Catching him up on the stairs, he asked the first of his many questions.

"Where are we going, Comrade?"

"To the docks, Comrade Kapitan, to the docks."

"The docks? What's happening?"

"It's the English."

"What?"

"They've landed soldiers!"

Eight minutes later, the two Soviet officials were in a nondescript building, overlooking the harbour.

It did not need an expert eye to understand that British soldiers were swarming all over the docks, and that two grey painted transport ships were tied up at the quays, with what appeared to be a large warship hovering outside the port entrance.

"So... you're the sailor. What are we looking at, Comrade Kapitan."

Tomaschuk knew one for certain, and three by class, so was confident in his answer.

He started with the vessel disgorging soldiers.

"The nearest vessel is a transport, and American one. It's what they call an attack transport, a ship that delivers troops straight onto a beach or into the war zone."

Grassovny continued to stare through his binoculars as he asked another question.

"How many men?"

"Two thousand or so, Comrade Grassovny."

"Four thousand at most then."

"At the least, Comrade Grassovny."

"Why do you say that?"

"The second vessel serves a similar purpose. I can't remember its type right now, but its capabilities are roughly the same. In any vcase, I say four because there's only berthing for two vessels at the moment. There may be others below the horizon."

Grassnovy understood and inwardly lauded his man's understanding.

"And the warship there?"

Tomaschuk moved his head to confirm his first impressions of the enemy destroyer.

"A British J-class destroyer. I can find out which one, but I doubt it makes a difference. The smaller vessel is an ocean-going tug."

As if responding to an unheard order, the two men moved their binoculars to observe the larger warship, gently moving around outside of the harbour.

Grassovny waited patiently, and gasped audibly as another enemy vessel became apparent.

"Blyad! There's two ships out there."

"Yes, so I see, Comrade. The nearest one is a light cruiser, again British... Arethusa class I think... which means she's either Arethusa herself, or Aurora. The others were sunk by the Germanski."

"And the very big one?"

He drew hard on his memory of the relevant silhouette books and intelligence sheets, and could only come up with one thought.

"It's an Essex class aircraft carrier. Over that I can't be specific. They all look alike, but the Amerikanski have plenty of them."

"Amerikanski?"

"Definitely, Comrade. They have given none to the British that intelligence knows of, so it is Amerikanski."

'Blyad... that complicates things...'

A cough from the doorway drew their attention, and a nondescript black man greeted their gaze.

"Well, Mutumbu? What did you discover?"

"Their ship is unwell, Mestre. They get permission to dock and make better very quickly."

"And the soldiers?"

"The soldiers are allowed ashore to walk their legs, Mestre. No guns allowed."

He had noticed the lack of weapons, so that fitted.

"Good work, Mutumbu. Now get your boys working hard. I want to know who they are and where they're going within the hour."

The African nodded his head and was gone.

Both Soviet intelligence officers returned to examining the view, processing the latest information and comparing it with what they were seeing.

Less than an hour later, the additional information was to hand, and both prepared urgent reports for Moscow.

1952 hrs, Thursday, 18th July 1946, Office of the General Secretary, the Kremlin, Moscow.

"Come in."

Lavrentiy Beria strode in, clutching two folders, both containing distressing news.

He nodded to Isakov, whom he had not expected to be present, and suddenly realised that he had been beaten to delivery of one revelation by the Admiral of the Fleet and commander of the Red Navy.

"Ah, Lavrentiy. You too have news from Mozambique, I take it?"

"Yes, indeed, Comrade General Secretary."

Beria handed over the relevant folder, which contained all the reports concerning possible Allied movements to the Gulf, not just the latest information from Lourenco Marques.

The latest message tied in perfectly with the one Isakov had presented a few minutes beforehand.

Placing the folder on the desk, Stalin resumed tugging gently on his pipe, studying the words in silence.

He pointed the stem at the paperwork.

"So, we now have hard words… direct knowledge of this movement of Allied ships… and better information on where they are going."

He tapped the naval report, if for no other reason than to annoy his NKVD boss.

"A carrier, a cruiser, a destroyer, all escorting two vessels… a single damaged ship into harbour. What does that imply?"

Isakov understood the question was for him.

"That they have great strength, Comrade General Secretary. To allocate such a force… it's not for such small assets… not for small a mission… it suggests a much larger force to hand, one with a surfeit of strength and numbers."

Beria took the opportunity as Isakov drew a breath.

"The, ah, special report from East Africa suggested over two hundred ships, Comrade General Secretary. Without that report we could probably suspect some sort of maskirovka, but that report was quite specific."

Stalin and Beria both, demonstrating full agreement.

The General Secretary took up the analysis.

"And now, we have this information. A ship develops a fault and puts into a port, seeking to repair. This time on the other coast of Africa. It carries these soldiers…," he looked down to remind himself, "These... 63rd Royal Navy soldiers... British soldiers in an Amerikanski ship, supported by capital ships, British and Amerikanski... all supposedly heading north-east."

He drew on his pipe and spoke directly to Isakov.

"Heading to Bushehr?"

"Yes, it would seem so, Comrade General Secretary."

"And we have no naval assets with which to interfere?"

"None at all, Comrade General Secretary."

Beria realised he had extra information and raised his hand.

"Comrade General Secretary, the soldiers. My agents identified at least one senior officer from the British Fourth Corps, a unit we previously had included in their maskirovka operation."

"Second Army Group?"

"The same, Comrade General Secretary. It would appear possible that the transition from maskirovka to real units has taken place."

"Montgomery."

Beria nodded, allowing Stalin to cross the 'I's and dot the 'T's himself.

"So, this fleet of ships contains soldiers of their previously non-existent Second Army, on their way to join up with the British hero Montgomery, so they can attack into our territories in the south, and threaten our oil and mineral supplies."

Neither senior man chose to speak, leaving a heavy silence in place, the ticking of the clock all-pervasive.

Stalin sucked pensively on his pipe, his mind working hard, his eyes narrowed in cunning as he worked the possibilities.

"Still think this is a maskirovka, Lavrentiy?"

"I believe it was when we first evaluated it, Comrade General Secretary. A cheap one, centered around sending the wounded Montgomery to Persia."

"And now?"

"If it is maskirovka, then it is anything but cheap. Moving all those ships is a monumental task, is it not, Comrade Admiral?"

Isakov started, unexpectedly dragged back into the discussion.

"Simply staggering, in resources and complexity, Comrade Marshal."

Beria nodded in acknowledgement and pressed ahead.

"And we now have confirmation of real soldiers, and ones previously thought to exist in name only, as part of their ghost army maskirovka. Comrade General Secretary, if this is maskirovka, then it is on a huge scale, and beyond what we have previously accepted as their skill level. That being said, I would like more time to develop better knowledge of their strength, but I understand that you must act immediately, for the sake of the Motherland."

Beria kept the smug look off his face, knowing that he had just danced nicely around committing himself fully, and handed full responsibility to his leader.

Stalin puffed away, understanding that to do nothing would be unforgiveable.

He picked up the telephone and waited for the briefest of moments.

"Summon the GKO immediately. Nine o'clock. No excuses."

Replacing the receiver, Stalin looked at the old timepiece, almost as if seeking confirmation of his decision.

Something made him hesitate.

"There's something else, isn't there?"

The second folder came into Stalin's possession.

He read it slowly, his eyes widening, so much so that Isakov felt the need to enquire of the contents of Beria's other folder.

"From one of the observation posst we and the Japanese established on Tsushima…"

The pain was written all over Isakov's face, the island having given its name to a terrible defeat that the Imperial Navy inflicted on Russian forces.

"It's a siting report from the Senbyomakiyama station, Comrade Admiral. I have sent a copy to your office for verification. The numbers seem a little off, but the observer is a member of your navy, and seems adamant."

That the man in question was also an agent of the NKVD was left unsaid.

"When, where, and how many ships, Comrade Marshal Beria?"

A huge sigh escaped Stalin's lips, and he raised his hand to prevent Beria from saying any more, continuing to skip read loud enough for the other two to follow.

"Yesterday… between Tsushima and the Korean coast… heading northeast… and… this… this figure is accurate, Comrade Marshal?"

"I believe so, Comrade General Secretary. The report is not specific, but the officer in question is extremely reliable and not easily rattled. I have no problem believing his figures."

Which was as committed as Beria ever got.

"Then we have a fleet of over three hundred vessels, from merchant vessels to aircraft carriers, sailing in the direction of the Sea of Japan."

He rounded on Isakov.

"First Mozambique!"

He smashed the folder down hard, making both men jump.

"Now Tsushima!"

The second folder followed the first.

"Do they really have those assets, Comrade Admiral?"

Isakov needed no thinking time.

"Yes, Comrade General Secretary, they do."

"Then I suggest you get your Pacific Fleet to do something about these bastards!"

He rammed his finger into the report from Senbyomakiyama, just to emphasis his point.

Stalin turned swiftly to the NKVD boss.

"Move more of your assets to the eastern borders immediately, Lavrentiy. Get us more information from whatever source you can. Work with the GRU. We need hard facts."

He leant forward and picked up the telephone again.

"Get me Marshal Vasilevsky immediately."

Late that evening, an urgent report passed across Beria's desk and into Stalin's hands, one that confirmed the arrival of the vehicles and men of the 4th Australian Armoured Brigade in Southern Iran.

The following day, further large scale movements of Soviet forces began, sending additional forces to the newly established Caspian Front, and more on the longer journey eastwards, to Siberia, and the shores of the Pacific.

So, whilst thousands of Soviet soldiers moved south and east, taking with them valuable equipment and supplies, the reports on their deployment filtered back across No Man's Land, or were garnered from the indiscreet whispers and gripes of overworked logistics officers.

They arrived before incredulous eyes, presenting themselves to the men who had developed and sold the 'big' idea.

They, in turn, proverbially rubbed their hands in glee, almost needing to pinch themselves that the deceptions seemed to have worked as they did.

All in all, it was a stunning coup for Allied Intelligence, and a maskirovka of epic proportions.

It had required a show of strength, and that was delivered by a host of warships and merchant shipping, all to demonstrate real power, although, for Iran, the vessels carried only a naval infantry division, an Australian armoured brigade, and a few reduced size headquarters units, all of questionable fighting value.

The Pacific fleet contained more substance, with the alternative of putting their amry and marine unist ashore in a number of places.

In the event that the ruses were discovered them they would have, if nothing else, caused the Red Army to consumed large quantities of its POL reserves.

And there was always the option of changing the two ruses into something more substantial at a later date.

But for now, the Red Army sent much-needed units south to meet the threat posed by Montgomery's force, and east to counter the seeming invasion of Siberia.

So, whilst Soviet attention was split, all Allied eyes turned back to Europe, and to the area of operations for 'Awakening Giant'

1002 hrs, Friday, 19th July 1946, Makaryev Monastery, Lyskovsky, USSR.

Pain was still ever-present, but with the combination of his body's resistance and painkillers of all descriptions, Yarishlov managed to get through each hour with hope preserved.

The skin grafts were agony, but he had contributed so very little of his own flesh to cover the huge burns, with most of the material coming from the corpses of other unfortunates, whose skin was harvested and refrigerated, for use by those whose capacity to donate from their own undamaged flesh sites was far outweighed by the damage they had sustained.

By such means did Yarishlov receive treatment that started to repair the deadly work done by the burning T-54.

The baths, the operations, the dressings, the times when his raw flesh was left deliberately exposed, the awful moments before his painkillers were due, and the effects of the previous doses had long worn off; each brought their own particular brand of hurt.

At his insistence, Yarishlov's dress uniform was placed on a stand in full sight of his bed.

It was there to remind him of his goal... to motivate him to conquer the challenges ahead.

Having just had his analgesia, the pain was removed and he studied the uniform, drawing inspiration from it and, asd always, his eyes lingered on the Hero Award.

Testing his fingers, he constantly thanked his creator that they had not been badly damaged, he became aware of the approach of a visitor, and was delighted to see it was Kriks.

"Stefan!"

"Polkovnik!"

He went to embrace his commander and friend, but hesitated, not knowing where to hold and where to avoid.

"It's difficult to find somewhere. Here, take my hand."

Yarishlov extended his right hand, the bandages hiding the loss of his little finger and part of the fourth.

Having shaken hands, Kriks leant forward and kissed his friend on both cheeks in the Russian way.

"It's good to see you, Sir."

Yarishlov laughed.

"Forget that crap, old friend. For the Motherland's sake, call me Arkady."

"That will come hard, but I will try... ah... Arkady."

"So how are the boys?"

"Out of the line at the moment, which is how I got away to see you."

"And?"

The pain was now evident on Kriks' face too.

"In a fight on the ground, we were always ahead. You know the boys... you trained them, Polkovnik. But their aircraft have become worse, if that's at all possible."

"Losses?"

"Most of our losses were in the battle you were wounded in, and an engagement three days afterwards. We launched a counter-attack and ran into dug-in enemy tanks and anti-tanks guns. We held our own, even made advances, but their aircraft came and we lost many of our vehicles."

Yarishlov asked again.

"Losses?"

"Half of our boys are in the ground or in a similar position to yourself, Comrade."

Yarishlov grimaced with the pain of his thoughts.

328

"We're out of the line and getting some replacements. Some of the new lads are promising, but they're all raw, and... well..." Kriks looked around, checking who was in earshot, before leaning forward and whispering the rest of his response, "... the Army seems like it's fishing in the bottom of the pond now."

Yarishlov managed what counted for a grin.

"Last time you said that, we were facing Hitler Youth and Volksturm. Those bastards did alright."

He moved in even closer.

"The peasant spirit's there, but little else. And it's different for our soldiers now, remember? The Germanski were fighting for their homes and families. What are we fighting for, eh? You said yourself, the war is lost. And our boys are now fighting for what? We started this fucking mess, Comrade Polkovnik, and we're fighting in Germany for soil we've shed blood on twice already."

A nurse ventured into the ward, and busied herself with some enamelware.

Kriks changed his tack.

"The new boys are a scrawny bunch, not a scrap of fat on any of them... some have even been released from the Gulags to serve... others come straight from the hospital sick bed... probably about one in every five will make a combat soldier."

He leant back and found a chair, all the time looking around to see who might have heard.

"I heard our prisoners of war were being given a chance to serve the Motherland again, Stefan?"

Kriks nodded and took a seat.

"If it's so, and I doubt it, then they are being used elsewhere, not as qualified reinforcements for units like ours. So our strength gets watered down all the time, as good men die and boys take their place."

The nurse moved to tend to the nearest patient, making them change the subject.

"Anyway, Comrade Polkovnik. How are you doing?"

Yarishlov spared Kriks the gory details, understating the seriousness, talking up the positives, and concluded with his returning to uniform.

"Well, that's great news, Comrade Pol... Arkady... really it is. And when you return to service, remember to get me transferred."

Something in the tone made Yarishlov frown.

"Is there a problem, Stefan?"

329

The nurse disappeared as quickly as she had arrived, and Kriks wrung his cap in his hands, in a very 'peasant' way, clearly uneasy about the matter he had just been cornered on.

He considered his words very carefully.

"Comrade Deniken has changed, Arkady."

Yarishlov understood his man, and decided on a different approach.

"Unless you've changed, I expect you have something warming in your possession, you old rogue."

Kriks smiled the smile of the guiltless and protested his innocence, whilst fishing in his bread bag.

Again he checked the small ward for nosey people, but the patients were all asleep, and there were now no members of staff to see or hear him.

He slid something under his friend's pillow.

"Later... and for medicinal purposes only, of course."

The protest died on Yarishlov's lips as another bottle was produced.

"This is for now," and a bottle of Goldwasser was broached and poured into two cups that magically appeared from the same bread bag.

"Na Zdorovie."

The toast was whispered and two throats suffered under the assault of the Polish liqueur, laced with flakes of 22-carat gold.

The liquid assault was repeated.

"Fucking hell."

Yarishlov coughed his way through swallowing the second shot.

"Hideous... give me another."

The two friends smiled their way through five shots before a halt was called, albeit temporarily.

Whilst a sense of well-being filled Yarishlov, partially from the liqueur and partially from the visit of his old friend, he had not forgotten his question, and posed it as easily and blandly as he could.

"So what is young Deniken up to then, eh?"

Kriks, loosened by the alcohol, was less reluctant to hold his tongue.

"He's gone mad... really... totally changed. No longer the happy boy we met all those months ago... yes... still efficient as an officer... but he's lost his humour."

Kriks grabbed his face and pulled on the skin, feeling wretched.

330

"He's had prisoners shot... executed for no great reason. He was very angry when you were wounded... he took it out on some prisoners. It happens, of course. But it continues... he's still doing it. It's like you getting hurt has transformed him into some sort of machine... he works, he eats, he sleeps, he has no time for me, not like you did... like he used to."

He checked the ward again.

"Remember how he used to be with his soldiers, eh? Always smiling... he knew their names... would sit down with them for a vodka and a cigarette... not now... not now..."

"What have you said to him? How did he respond?"

"He dismisses me. He won't talk about anything except the unit and the needs of the war. I mention you and he blanks me. I bring out a bottle and get told to go and drink it elsewhere."

"Does he not talk to you at all?"

"Once he did. Although it was brief and he was very controlled. He was very angry."

"About?"

"You getting wounded, the men who were dying in this 'stupid war'... his words, Arkady, and the fact that all the dying and suffering was for nothing."

"Is that what he said?"

"That's what I remember, Comrade Polkovnik."

Kriks sat up and increased the volume of his voice, acknowledging the approaching nurse as he warned his friend of her presence.

"Visiting time is over, Comrade Praporshchik. Sorry. Comrade Polkovnik, time for your bath."

The two shook hands again.

Yarishlov held his friend's hand as firmly as he could.

"Remember, Stefan... he's a good man. Stay with him and help him all you can. When I'm fit, I'll send for you. Now..." he shook hands with great sincerity, "... Away with you. Give him my best, and ask him to come and visit me soon. Look after him... and look after yourself. The Motherland'll have need of us all when this war is over. Good bye, old friend."

Kriks croaked an emotional goodbye, and was chivvied away by the arriving senior nurse, who understood a lot about front line soldiers, and used that knowledge to locate and confiscate the bottle stowed under Yarishlov's pillow.

Some of the world's greatest feats were accomplished by people not smart enough to know they were impossible.

Doug Larson

Chapter 162 - THE HILL

1002 hrs, Saturday, 20th July 1946, Hemmendorf, Germany.

The assault had been going on for over an hour, and the engineers leading the attack had only just secured their river crossing.

The Saale was not the widest or deepest of obstacles, but it had proved to be one of the bloodiest in the war so far, as the pioneers of the 266th Division and 3rd Korps attempted to cross in the face of fierce Soviet resistance.

Both battalion commanders were down and on their way to the rear, broken men, in spirit as well as body.

Losses amongst the remaining officers and senior NCOs were huge, as they struggled to push their men forward, exposing themselves to the greatest dangers and, too often, paying the price.

But the valiant men of Pioniere-Bataillon-266 had finally gained a foothold and had started to remove the barbed wire and obstacles that posed a risk to the follow-up forces, backed up the soldiers of 3rd Korps' own assault pioneer unit, the 903rd.

The bridging engineers waited patiently, in no hurry to expose themselves to the maelstrom of shot and shell that transformed the waters of the soft flowing Saale into a blend of the finest liquids Germany had to offer; the water of her mountains and the blood of her sons.

More tanks were brought up, their massive guns providing direct fire support as the Soviet commanders counter-attacked, desperate to throw back the Germans and destroy their tenuous hold on the east bank.

The men of the Red Army died in their scores.

German artillery, combined with air support, hammered front and rear line positions incessantly.

The men of the Red Army died in their hundreds.

The bridging engineers were sent forward, ordered to construct their bridges even though still under fire.

Men were killed and men were wounded, but the structure quickly took shape.

More pioneers made the short journey across the Saale, and rienforced the bridgehead.

Infantry followed, as the lead companies of the 897th Grenadiere Regiment made their way over, clinging to the developing structures or using the flotation devices they had been given or made from materials to hand.

Another hasty Soviet counter-attack drove into the men clinging to the bank, and floundered in close quarter fighting. The clearly weakened and less fit Red Army infantrymen failed to gain an upper hand, despite their superior numbers, and fell back in disarray, pursued by fire from the German soldiers, whose numbers grew steadily as more men crossed the bloody waters.

Soviet mortar fire increased in tempo, but was less accurate than usual, although men still died as hot metal penetrated their flesh.

To the southwest, more men of the 897th were pushing against the defenders of Salzhemmendorf. Pushing none too hard, as per orders, hoping to pin the defenders in place, rather than push them out, as the plan was to pinch off the small salient before pushing further into Germany.

The lower half of the pincers was still silent.

Half a kilometre north of Ockensen, the two watercourses, the Saale and Thüster Beeke, were less of an obstacle, being of considerably less width at that point than at Hemmendorf. It was here that 3rd Battalion, 899th Grenadiere Regiment, temporarily assigned to the 897th, waited for the order to attack.

"Get them ready, Hermann. It won't be long."

"Will do. Still no sign of anything to my front. I hope the recon photos are right."

Hermann Keller left that hanging.

The phone buzzed softly as Von Scharf, some metres away in his battalion command post, wished for the same thing.

"I suspect there'll be something up there, and we've catered for it, Hermann. But whatever it might be, it won't be a lot. Just keep that rogue Schneider and his radio close, and we'll deal with whatever challenges us today."

Keller smiled, seeking out the sleeping figure of his radio operator.

"Never doubted it, Herr Hauptmann."

"Hals-und beinbruch, Hermann."

"Hals-und beinbruch, Herr Hauptmann."

Two minutes later, the phone rang again.

"Attack immediately, as per plan."

1029 hrs, Saturday, 20th July 1946, the Saale, Ockensen, Germany.

"Vörwarts!"

The men of Seventh Company rose up as one and pelted forward to the edge of the small watercourse, immediately welcoming the cooling liquid as it rose up their legs to waist level.

Newly fledged Stabsfeldwebel Keller, popular NCO and the sole Ritterkreuzträger in the regiment, pushed his men hard, wishing them out of the exposed area and into the uneven ground beyond.

Fig # 199 - Allied Order of Battle - Height 462, Marienhagen, Germany.

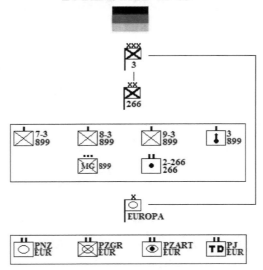

334

The trouble with the assault was obvious to every man who had sat waiting to advance. The whole of their initial movement was overseen and dominated by a huge hill, Height 462, from which they expected fire to descend at any moment.

"Quickly! Push on quickly!"

Keller's cry was taken up by all the NCOs of Seventh Company, although the now veteran soldiers of the 899th needed no encouragement.The men had all developed the crouching run that marked veterans from new soldiers, their jinking low advances intended to throw off the aim of any defenders ahead.

Mortar shells started to arrive, a few at first, and then more, and the first grenadiers fell.

Keller's company pushed forward hard, and escaped most of the shrapnel, the occasional man dropping as a light defence was offered by the handful of Soviet infantry occupying Height 462.

Those grenadiers following the lead company fared worse, as the majority of the mortar shells landed amongst them.

They went to ground, isolating Keller's men, who kept plunging forward, intent on getting as close to the hill top as they could.

Height 462 had once been covered with lush green trees, but three separate heavy battles over two years had converted it to a barren landscape, the occasional ruined stump belying its former beauty.

Keller forced his men on, and they started up the gentle foot slopes, moving from shell hole to shell hole, inexorably closing on the defenders.

Von Scharf saw the danger and shouted orders down the radio, encouraging the other companies to rise up and follow Keller.

They did not, the maelstrom of shrapnel made worse by more mortars being targeted on their positions.

"Koenig-five-three, Koenig-five-three, Koenig-one, over."

Through the steady crumps of mortar shells, von Scharf recognised Keller's voice.

The radio operator acknowledged.

"Koenig-five-three, keep on going. I'm bringing the rest of the kompagnies up behind you. Push hard and don't stop, over."

"Received, Koenig-one. Do it quickly, enemy fire is increasing the closer we get to the top, over."

'Scheisse!'

"We're coming. Koenig-one, out."

Gathering his battalion headquarters troops around him, he rushed forward, determined to shake the companies loose of their hidey-holes, and get support to Keller.

Back with his weapon of choice, an MP-40, von Scharf led his battalion troops, sweeping up stragglers from the lead companies as he went, accepting losses from the lessening mortar fire, in order to get as close to Keller as possible, and as quickly as possible.

Some men hugged the bottom of shell holes, feigning injury or working on a real one; some lay in ready-made graves, ready for the clearing parties to come after the battle.

But, in the main, von Scharf swept up the reluctant grenadiers and drove them up the hill towards the crest, where it was obvious that Keller had closed with the enemy.

1107 hrs, Saturday, 20th July 1946, Height 462, near Marienhagen, Germany.

It was all over by the time that von Scharf and his cohorts arrived on the peak, the only work being done by Keller's men being that of first aid to wounded, or repairing damaged positions.

The dead of both sides lay where they had fallen, not presently a priority.

The battalion commander dropped into the command position and slapped his friend on the shoulder.

"I'm surprised you aren't on the way to Berlin by now."

Keller turned to face him.

Von Scharf recoiled in mock horror, even though the injury did look nasty.

"Ouch! How did you get that?"

Keller's eye was turning purple and black, and getting worse by the second.

The Stabsfeldwebel pointed at his ST-44, leant against a rickety table, almost placed in the corner like a boy being disciplined in the classroom.

"Self-inflicted, Herr Hauptmann. Can't even bolster my wound tally. Caught that fucking thing on the wooden support there, fell over... got the butt straight in the optic."

Von Scharf failed to keep a straight face.

"Sorry, Hermann... I mean..."

He took the flask that Keller offered, a Russian one, which meant he prepared his throat for some fiery content; it was greeted solely with water.

"How many did you lose?"

"Doing the numbers now, but my belief is seventeen dead or still lying back there wounded."

Von Scharf nodded, surprised that the butcher's bill wasn't much higher, something that Keller understood.

"Me too, Herr Hauptmann. You?"

"More than that, for sure. I don't know yet. Anyway, what have you done to get organised here?"

The officer moved out of the bunker in order to study the position with his senior NCO.

Keller reached for the offending ST-44 and, with studied care and a look of hatred for the vertical wooden post in question, moved out through the narrow entrance after his commander.

The two walked the position as best they could, stopping in suitable cover to make observations of the surrounding hills and the valley below.

The frontage of the hill was nearly four kilometres, so the tour took some time, but the general defence plan had been decided beforehand, and needed little alteration, so the landsers of the 899th got themselves setup quickly.

Von Scharf and his officers had requisitioned, as well as obtained by various other less straight-forward means, extra machine-guns for their platoons, and Von Scharf himself had 'borrowed' an ad-hoc machine-gun platoon for his headquarters.

Even though their task was complete, and all they had to do was hold the hill and pin the enemy in place whilst other forces, north and south of the diversions moved around and bit off the salient, Von Scharf and his men were intent on taking no chances.

Parties were organised to scour the slopes for casualties, and to recover weapons and ammunition.

Abandoned Soviet equipment was policed up and stockpiled.

The German mortar platoons were called forward and, once they had toiled up the hill with their weapons, would be directed to positions that had been, until recently, occupied by their Russian counterparts.

Von Scharf settled into his bunker and accepted the scalding coffee offered to him, reading through the message pad to pick up a sense of the battlefields around him.

It made surprisingly poor reading.

Even though everything in sight was a diversion, there had been an expectation of some advances, but there were next to none worthy of the name.

'Except us… and the pioniere boys…'

"Koenig-one, Koenig-one, Koenig-five-five, over!"

Fig # 200 - Position of 3rd Bataillon, 899th Grenadiere Regiment, on Height 462, Marienhagen, Germany.

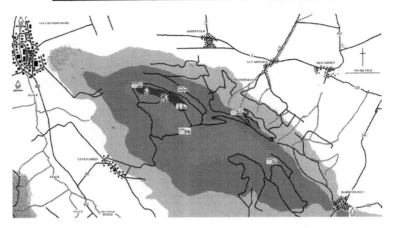

The tension in the voice was not masked by the gentle static that troubled the radio waves.

The radio operator responded.

"Koenig-one, enemy counter-attack forces spotted moving south from Hoyershausen. A force has detached and is heading towards our position, over."

Koenig-five-five, Oberleutnant Hubert Aschmann, the 9th Company commander, was a relatively unknown quantity and was clearly rattled.

"Tell him to continue to monitor and report."

Whilst the radio operator sent the message, Von Scharf gestured to a nearby Feldwebel.

"Hanson... take two men and get over to Nine Kompagnie."

He took the older NCO by the arm, leading him to the entrance of the bunker.

"Keep an eye on things for me. Aschmann sounds rather... err... worried."

Hanson understood perfectly and was soon jogging away with two men in tow.

"Koenig-five, Koenig-five, Koenig-five-three, large enemy force to our north. Tanks and infantry... counter-attacking against the bridgehead. Large enemy infantry force heading our way, looks like just under a full battalion, over."

'That can't be right... surely... but it's Keller...'

He grabbed his submachine-gun.

"Kasper, look after things here. I'm going to Keller's front to see for myself."

The Leutnant saluted casually and returned to logging the contact information on the battalion tactical map.

Kasper Janjowski was a former POW, once of the 340th Volks-Grenadiere Division, captured by the Americans during the Battle of the Bulge.

Whilst he bore solely the Iron Cross Second class, he exuded a confidence and calmness that had ensured he was quickly trusted by those around him.

He was also the smallest officer any of them had ever seen, being only a cigarette paper over one and a half metres.

In Von Scharf's absence, he forwarded the new contact reports to Regimental Headquarters, where the news was greeted with a mixture of alarm and scepticism.

A report from 8th Company added to the growing feeling that something worrying was about to happen.

1204 hrs, Saturday, 20th July 1946, Height 462, near Marienhagen, Germany.

"Where's the fire, Hermann?"

Keller said nothing, but hastily ducked into a small trench that led from his command position, gesturing for Von Scharf to follow.

Keeping low, the two moved quickly along the earthwork and into a covered observation post, from where two further trenches led off, one to a position occupied by a machine-gun crew who were clearly alert and ready for action.

Gently pulling aside part of the foliage that camouflaged the position, Keller invited his commander to take a look. Although the sounds of battle had been growing the closer he had moved to the edge of the hill, he was still surprised by what greeted his eyes.

"Verdammt!"

"Like I said, Herr Hauptmann, they're hitting the bridgehead units... and winning as I see it. Look to the right and you'll see the bastards who have us in mind."

"Hurensohn!"

As they were alone, Keller felt duty bound to indulge in some humour.

"I love you too, Herr Hauptmann, but now is not the time."

Von Scharf stayed focussed on the large movement of infantry.

"The mortars'll be ready soon, but I suggest we don't provoke them for the moment…"

He looked at his friend, "Just in case it's not us they're after."

In truth, there was little chance that they intended to go around the 3rd Battalion, and both men knew it.

"Well, at least we'll discharge our mission, Herr Hauptmann. Consider the enemy suitably distracted by our presence. High Command never mentioned that there were thousands of the bastards, and that they were full of fight though, did they?"

Von Scharf coughed politely.

"Cigarette?"

He took the offered smoke, checking that the bunker would disperse the smoke without drawing attention to their position. It was a Soviet bunker, so he didn't expect a problem. The Russian knew how to build a bunker fit for purpose.

He returned to view the goings-on on the Saale.

"Mein Gott, the bridges are down, they're cut off!"

Two kilometres away, the situation had changed dramatically.

"The bastards have organised a counter-attack damned quickly…"

He left the though hanging there as his mind came up with another possibility.

Keller's eyes narrowed as the evidence of his eyes also suggested something extremely unpalatable.

"Mein Gott… it's not a counter-attack, Hermann. We've only walked into a fucking Soviet assault force."

The two took to their heels and headed back to Keller's command position, Von Scharf issuing orders on the way.

Pausing to shake hands, the two went their separate ways; Keller to get to his radio and send out the warning, Von Scharf to get back to his headquarters and get ready to organise the defence of Height 462 against a mixed armoured and infantry force much larger than had been anticipated.

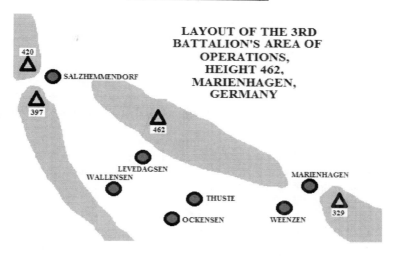

LAYOUT OF THE 3RD
BATTALION'S AREA OF
OPERATIONS,
HEIGHT 462,
MARIENHAGEN,
GERMANY

1204 hrs, Saturday, 20th July 1946, the Stadtpark, Gronau, Germany.

That enemy force was better known as the 11th Guards Tank Corps, a veteran formation that had suffered less than most from the privations of winter and poor supply.

The Corps had also been no more than lightly engaged since the early months of the war, and was at nearly 80% strength, considerably more than most major frontline formations in the Red Army.

Von Scharf and Keller were right.

From their position, they had the benefit of seeing the real Soviet strength, something that was denied to the units dying on the Saale or fighting in Salzhemmendorf.

The intended distraction attacks had blundered into the waiting 11th Guards, whose own attack was scheduled to start that evening, once the sun had disappeared.

A reconnaissance mission by USAAF aircraft photographed nothing unexpected in the area, a testament to the well-known Soviet skill at camouflage, often referred to as 'the ability to hide an elephant under a postage stamp.'

Von Scharf called in artillery as best he could, but a dedicated team was needed, and he asked for one to be sent forward immediately. German efficiency was such that a suitable observation section was quickly dispatched to join 3rd Battalion on the top of Height 462.

In the German rear, controlled panic ruled, as some staff officers redirected units to bolster the centre, whilst yet others pushed the pincer formations harder, sensing an opportunity.

Seven kilometres from where von Scharf had his headquarters, another bunker, secreted within Gronau Park, contained the commanders of 11th Guards Tank Corps, gathered together to review the attack plan, and now employed in responding to the unexpected German incursion.

The Corps Commander, Major General Amazasp Babadzhanian, had only just finished agreeing a fire plan with his artillery commander, Major General Mikhail Solukovtsev, when he saw the opportunity presenting itself.

"Comrades! Comrades!"

The hubbub in the bunker died away and the harried staff officers all turned to face their boss.

"Impress upon every officer... every soldier... we have an opportunity here. We can inflict huge losses on the green toads... but only if we attack hard... attack quickly... and do not stop. I'm convinced we can roll these bastards all the way to our first objective," he tapped the map down the length of the heights between the Saale and the Ilse. "And probably beyond... but we must push... and push hard."

Babadzhanian slammed his balled fist into his palm to emphasise his point.

"We have some air cover, but not enough, so make sure our AA assets stay tight," he directed his comment generally, but his gaze was fixed on the Colonel in charge of the AA regiment.

"Now, leave 44th Tanks to overcome the river crossing, and implement the attack plan at," he paused, looking at his watch, "1220. Move!"

To the untrained eye, it would have seemed that the command post descended into organised anarchy in seconds, but Babadzhanian understood that all was well, and his powerful corps would soon be crushing the hated Germanski under the tracks of their tanks.

1215 hrs, Saturday, 20th July 1946, Height 462, near Marienhagen, Germany.

The Third Battalion was engulfed in a man-made storm of fire and metal, as the Soviet artillery pounded the height with a regimental barrage, with numerous mortars adding their own brand of death to the party.

Men dug deeper, even as the artillery arrived and, now and again, claimed them and their comrades, the illusion of safety offered by the cool earth occasionally shattered by the explosive force of a Russian howitzer shell.

The telephone line had been laid, but was already useless, severed by some unseen strike.

The signallers were out, braving the storm of shells, seeking the break, the radio useless for reasons unknown.

A Soviet Guards radio unit hidden, west of Bantein, jammed the channels, furthering hampering the German defence.

Which meant the Von Scharf and the Third were on their own.

Their supporting artillery had ceased fire, unable to receive fire instructions from the OP group that had arrived, firstly because the radio was jammed, and subsequently because a Soviet fragmentation shell scattered a number of their bodies over the summit of Height 462.

By running cables through the trench system, the battalion signallers had enabled communication from the companies to the battalion command post, and it proved a godsend almost immediately.

"Herr Hauptmann. Seven Kompagnie."

Scharf grabbed the handset and ducked, all in the same motion, as dust and earth shaken from the ceiling fell around him, the large calibre near-miss enough to shake the sturdy bunker to its core

"Scharf."

"Herr Hauptmann. We have three companies of infantry forming up at the bottom of the slope. I'd say they are about set to charge."

A nearby shell made Keller duck instinctively, as pieces of bark dislodged from the reinforcing tree trunks in the ceiling cascaded down like confetti on a bride.

He missed Scharf's question.

"Say again. I can't hear you."

"Do they intend to flank?"

343

He was conscious that Keller's men held the edge of the height, but that their position curled back on itself for the smallest distance before there was no defensive force.

"Not how they're set up, Herr Hauptmann, but I'll keep watching. Perhaps send two squads to position there, just in case?"

Von Scharf battled against his instinct to support the Seventh Company.

"Nein. I need the reserve here, under my command. Ninth Kompagnie has infantry and panzers entering Marienhagen as we speak, and Eighth has a similar force as you to its front. Just watch that flank, Keller. I'm relying on you."

There was a pause.

In the distance, von Scharf could hear the distinctive sound of MG-42s.

"They're attacking now. Not flanking at the moment. Direct assault. Signing off."

Keller was gone before he could respond, and, in any case, the telephone came to life in his hands as eight and nine companies reported their own problems.

More defensive machine-guns opened up as the height came under full attack.

The soldiers of the Second and Third Battalions, 27th Guards Motor Rifle Brigade, were less than enamoured with their allocated task. Trained to ride into battle alongside their armoured comrades, they were now committed to footslog up a hill manned by their traditional enemy, well-armed with automatic weapons.

None the less, they were Soviet Guardsmen, and they charged forward.

Babadzhanian accepted that he would lose some of his supporting infantry whilst he overcame any resistance on the hill, but he could not move forward with it in enemy hands, and felt the risk of waiting for an ordinary infantry unit to arrive was one he was not prepared to take.

His motorised infantrymen started to pay the price for his decision, the machine-guns of the 899th Grenadieres cutting down men half a dozen at a time.

Von Scharf, with limited mortar ammunition, held his fire until he could decide where the greatest threat was, and ended up not firing them at all, as the Soviet attack ran out of steam halfway up the slope.

"What's happening, Aschmann?"

"They've gone to ground, Herr Hauptmann... well... mainly so. My left flank reports that the enemy attacking them have dropped all the way back to the valley. Centrally, we've stopped them cold, about a third of the way up. They found it more difficult to come up from Marienhagen, but the bastards are still clinging to the slope there."

"Casualties?"

"A few hundred of them for sure, my own presently unknown, and very few from the infantry attack. It's the damned artillery and mortars that's hurting us. I had nineteen casualties before the attack. I'll tell you the firm figure as soon as I know, Herr Hauptmann."

Von Scharf wondered if he had been wrong to mistrust Aschmann. He sounded in control.

"Keep me informed, and keep up the good work, Oberleutnant. This hill is ours, and I intend to stay here, come what may. Alles klar?"

Half of his conversation had not arrived with Aschmann, as a mortar shell severed the cable precisely halfway between the two posts.

"Aschamann?... Aschmann?..."

He tossed the handset to his signalman.

"Verdammt... repair party!"

The two remaining signallers looked at each other, having only just returned from a dangerous spell outside looking for a break in the line to Eight Company.

"Somewhere between here and nine, menschen. Keep your heads down, but get it fixed quickly. It's very important and I'm depending on you."

He patted each on the shoulder as they gathered up their kit and, without a word, disappeared off into the barrage.

Von Scharf dropped onto the sawn-off tree trunk that served as a stool and lit a cigarette from the butt of his radio operator's hand-rolled offering.

He dispensed with the cigarette holder, given the circumstances.

"Scheisse!"

They both gave voice to the word, as a shell landed adjacent to their position, bringing down more stone and earth, and shaking everything around them.

Drawing on the comforting smoke, von Scharf looked at his watch.

'1243...scheisse! Is it only 1243?'

The field telephone announced itself through his thoughts.

"Bataillon... ja... ja... Herr Hauptmann, Stabsfeldwebel Keller."

The receiver changed hands.

"Scharf."

"Herr Hauptmann, the enemy are gathering for a second attempt. A large panzer formation drove past us, with panzer-grenadieres and... I'm not totally sure, to be honest... but it seems to have progressed beyond Salzhemmendorf and almost to Heights 397 and 420."

Von Scharf consulted the battalion situation map before replying.

"What's that you say? Are you sure, Hermann? There was a full bataillon of the 897th moving through there, with armoured support."

"No, I'm not sure, Herr Hauptmann, but I do know that it certainly looks like there's fighting going on to the west of Salzhemmendorf."

"Are they coming round your flank yet?"

"No, Herr Hauptmann. That's another reason why I think they've gone straight over the river. Nothing is developing to the south of Salzhemmendorf, which it would do if they had been stopped, don't you think."

"Ja, sound thinking. All right. Get me better information as quick as you can. Anything else?"

"Nein. We'll hold, Herr Hauptmann."

"Get me more information, Hermann. Out."

Lighting another cigarette, he contemplated sending some of his reserve to the left flank of Keller's company, but held himself in check.

'I need facts... what's going on... what the fuck is going on...'

It was then he realised that he had two cigarettes in his grasp.

He laughed inwardly and hoped that the other occupants of the bunker hadn't noticed.

'I'm getting far too old for this shitty mess.'

Fig # 202 - Soviet Order of Battle - Height 426, Marienhagen, Germany.

SOVIET ORDER OF BATTLE
MARIENHAGEN, GERMANY
20TH JULY 1946

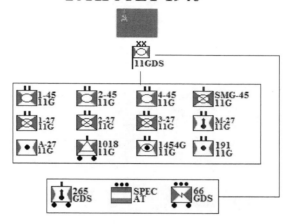

Lieutenant Colonel Vesnin knew exactly what was going on, and he held his leading platoons in check whilst his plan was put into place.

Resisting the standard shouts and threats from his Brigade Commander, he had withdrawn the units on his right flank, and sent them to move quickly around the base of his position, in order to extend and strengthen his left flank.

Careful examination of the heights, through a convenient shell hole in the roof of the west tower of Marienhagen's evangelical church, led Vesnin to believe he had spotted the end of the enemy defensive line.

Lacking men to exploit his discovery, he did the next best thing by holding back his second attack, and allowing the withdrawn units to concentrate where he felt the enemy line no longer existed.,

Even as his supporting artillery and mortars redoubled their efforts to wear down the defenders, he could hear the sounds of small arms fire from elsewhere on the height, indicating that the other battalions were already into their own attacks.

Tanks of the 45th Guards Tank Brigade assigned to bolster his force, opened direct fire on the German defenders.

'Hurry up, Dushkin... hurry up, man!'

No sooner had he thought the words than, as agreed, Major Dushkin sent a single blue flare skywards, which initiated a full-scale attack by all of Vesnin's force.

He checked his watch.

'1257.'

Fig # 203 - Soviet second assault, Height 426, Marienhagen, Germany.

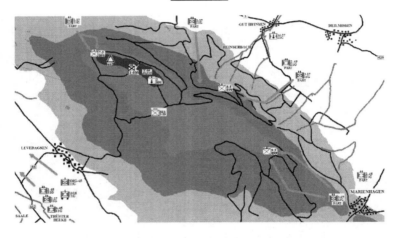

"Send a message to the Polkovnik. I'm attacking and expect to turn the enemies flank. Route 240 will be open shortly."

His aide scurried away, leaving Vesnin to ponder the scene developing in front of him.

1300 hrs, Saturday, 20th July 1946, Height 462, near Marienhagen, Germany.

"Scharf."

"Herr Hauptmann, I need reinforcements. The enemy's attacked again, but on a broader front. They're nearly around my right flank, and will get between you and me if they're not stopped."

"Calm down, man."

Von Scharf didn't wait to see if there was more.

348

"Where are the lead elements now?"

"Nearing the trench lines… not quite in grenade range… I need more men, Herr Ha…"

"Spread your men to the right, Aschmann. Don't let them get round you."

"I can't, Sir… I simply can't. I've nearly a Bataillon to my front. If I spread out further, I'll be overrun."

Von Scharf made a snap decision.

"Hold your positions, Aschmann. That's an order. Help's on its way."

Within two minutes, Hauptmann von Scharf had gathered a group of twenty-two men and placed them under the command of Janjowski, who was dispatched towards Aschmann's right flank.

As he watched the group dash off, he recognised the two signallers returning, one favouring a leg that had been clipped by shrapnel.

"All done, leute?"

"Yes, Herr Hauptmann. Three breaks in all."

"Good effort, damn good effort, Kameraden," he slapped each man enthusiastically on the shoulder, "Damn good effort. You're hurt, Finze. Bad?"

Gefreiter Finze shook his head.

"Just a clip, Herr Hauptmann. Nothing to trouble the sani with. A decent coffee'll make it go away."

Von Scharf poured two.

"Catch your breath, Kameraden. Thank you again."

He held out his cigarettes, which the two exhausted signallers accepted gratefully.

He turned to the operator.

"Get me Keller."

Von Scharf stood over the situation map and waited for the handset to arrive in his hand.

"Keller, this is Scharf. I've just sent some men to bolster Aschmann's right flank. It seems the enemy has moved around and threatened to roll around him. I suggest you watch out for the same."

"Already on it, Herr Hauptmann. I sent a small group to the west as soon as I had some spare men… but the bastards are coming again."

"Different attack?"

"No, Herr Hauptmann, still coming straight up the slope, as before… slower, and using the cover better. They'll get closer this time, of course."

"But you'll stop them, of course. Anything else from Salzhemmendorf?"

"Not yet, Herr Hauptmann. Too much smoke and dust, but the enemy artillery's pounding the high ground, which would support my thoughts."

"I've had no runner... the radio's not working... for all I know we've been ordered off this hill already."

Keller said nothing, whilst von Scharf silently debated his options.

It didn't take long.

"Unless I hear otherwise, we're staying on this damned hill, klar?"

"Alles klar, Herr Hauptmann."

"Keep an eye on your flank, and whatever's going on at Salzhemmendorf. Let me know if there is any change. Hermann... you can hold, yes?"

The chuckle was almost masked by exploding artillery shells, but it was none the less there.

"Zu befehl, Herr Hauptmann."

Janjowski's small unit arrived at the perfect time and in the perfect place.

They crashed straight into the back of the Guardsmen preparing to storm along Aschmann's trench line, intent on rolling it up from one end to the other.

Leading the way, Janjowski used his Gewehr 43 to good effect, dropping three men with bullets before he slammed the butt into the throat of a confused NCO.

The rest of his men crashed into the backs of the Soviet troopers, dealing out death and wounds without reply.

Major Dushkin, caught in the act of writing a message for his commander, was knocked to the ground by a falling body, and then pinned to it by two bayonets.

He screamed his life away until his lungs filled with blood and he screamed no more.

It took less than five minutes for Janjowski's force to rout the Soviet flankers, five minutes in which Aschmann's line waivered, bent, and suffered, but held fast.

Grenades flew in both directions, and the sharp cracks of the deadly little missiles were often accompanied by cries of anguish from wounded men.

Janjowski established a part of his force and moved on, intent on finding Aschmann and understanding what was going on.

He found the Oberleutnant in the centre of his line, surrounded by dead and wounded enemy, issuing orders, and occasionally pausing to shoot a target that presented itself amongst the retreating enemy, and doing so in a way that immediately impressed the headquarters officer.

"Aschmann! Thank God you're alive! What happened here?" he gestured at the pile of Soviet dead, at least a score of which had penetrated the large depression in which Aschmann had established his forward command post.

"It was fucking close I can tell you!"

Although clearly pumped up and running on adrenalin, Aschmann retained enough composure to quietly chat with the men around him, asking after a wound here, offering encouragement there.

"Are you ok?"

Aschmann patted himself down, seeking a wound.

"Seems so, though God only knows how, Kasper. It was only Feldwebel Spatz, my signaller, and myself in here when these bastards charged in."

Aschmann bent over and touched the shoulder of the dead NCO, lying face down in a huge puddle of his own blood.

"God, but Spatz fought like a mad dog... so did Fischer... I swear he bit one man's throat open."

There was such a wound on one corpse, but Fischer was long past confessing to inflicting it.

"And you, Hubert?"

"They are untermensch... vermin... so I treated them as same..."

At Aschmann's feet was an MP-40 and its spent casings.

In his right hand was a Luger, and in his left, a Hitler Youth dagger.

Both had a smattering of blood and matted hair smeared over them.

He realised what Janjowski was looking at, and examined the contents of his hands.

"I killed my share of the bastards, Kasper."

Suddenly, Aschmann started to shudder and shake, as shock set in and dropped him to his knees as instantly as a rifle bullet.

351

Jankowski sent his Corporal to check further along the line, squatted next to Aschmann and lit a cigarette, forcing it between the shaking man's quivering lips.

Nearby, one of his men started rummaging through the Soviet bodies, throwing items of military interest onto a growing pile, until he found what he was looking for, and handed it across to Janjowski.

Nodding in appreciation, the Leutnant undid the flask and poured some of whatever it was down Aschmann's throat, causing a violent reaction of coughing and spluttering.

"And again, Hubert. Get some more down you, man."

Moving across to the field telephone, Janjowksi spun the handle.

"Janjowksi here. I must to speak to the Hauptmann."

"He's not here, Herr Leutnant. He's gone to Seven Kompagnie. The bastards've broken through on that side, Herr Leutnant. He said if you contacted, to use your judgement. Stay there if you are needed, or get back fast and reinforce Seven Kompagnie if not."

"OK…"

His words trailed away.

He stood carefully, with the handset still to his ear, and looked around, listening for the sounds of renewed combat, only just appreciating that the enemy artillery and mortars had all but ceased.

He felt happy that the situation was restored but for Aschmann…

"… if the Herr Hauptmann contacts you, let him know I 'm sending my force back to him with orders to support Seven Kompagnie. I am staying here to assist Nine Kompagnie until I'm not needed. Alles klar?"

"Alles klar, Herr Leutnant."

Tossing the handset on to the ground, Janjowski summoned two men to him.

"Gefreiter, take the men back, fast as you can. Seven are in trouble… go straight there. Leave me five men. Klar?"

The man acknowledged and disappeared, summoning his group to him.

The other man, a wounded Unteroffizier, waited patiently for his orders.

"Can you walk, man?"

"Jawohl, Herr Leutnant."

"Right, come with me, and let's put our defences back together."

352

Whilst the two toured Ninth Company's positions...

...Whilst the pioneers withdrew over the Saale...

...Whilst Grenadieres of the 897th clung to the slopes of Heights 397 and 420...

...Whilst reinforcements sent by Oberstleutnant Bremer were bogged down under artillery fire at Ockensen...

...Seven Company was fighting for its life.

1331 hrs, Saturday, 20th July 1946, Height 462, near Marienhagen, Germany.

Keller moaned and pressed his fingers to the sticky hole in his arm.

The bullet had passed straight through without hitting the bone, but it bled like a burst dam, and hurt like hell.

The man who fired it had been almost cut in half by a torrent of fire from a friendly weapon down the slope.

Schneider, his Mauser across his knees, tied a dressing to Keller's arm, inducing a squeal and a threat to remove part of the signaller's anatomy.

"Calm yourself, Stabsfeldwebel. Unless I miss my guess, this'll mean the Wound Badge in Gold for you."

The sounds of fighting were not abating, and the dressing was hastily done.

Rising up, Keller immediately bundled Schneider to one side.

"Granate!"

The explosion threw earth and stones over the pair, but no more than that.

Keller was up and moving instantly, his MP-40 sweeping two running Guardsmen off their feet and sending both tumbling back down the slope.

He paused and looked over his lines, and it was immediately obvious that the enemy were almost on top of his men, with only a few places where the assault had withered away in front of the trenches, those mainly being where the 34s and 42s had plied their trade.

An egg grenade loomed large before his eyes and he swung his weapon two handed, deflecting the charge away far enough that it was of no concern.

More Soviet infantrymen rushed up the slope, and he dropped low, steadied his weapon, and emptied his magazine.

Two still came on, one leaking vital red fluid, and Keller instantly knew he had no time to reload.

One of the two went down hard before he heard the rifle shot in his ear.

Schneider worked the bolt to chamber another round.

"Fuck! Watch out!"

Schneider rolled away as two more Russians loomed out of the trench to their right, and a burst of fire did nothing more than disturb the earth where he had been kneeling the moment before.

The Kar-98k spat another bullet, clipping the enemy submachine gunner, but the second man was on Schneider before he could reload.

The signaller screamed in pain and terror as the bayonet lunge tore through the material of his tunic, slicing the flesh down to his collarbone.

He shoved with both hands, and his rifle struck the enemy's weapon, giving him enough leverage to separate himself from his assailant.

The enemy soldier, his face a mask of fear and concentration, lunged again, but Schneider deflected the attack easily, pushing the weapon off to the left of his body, allowing him to jab his rifle butt forward in an attempt to knock the teeth out of his opponent's ugly face.

The man ducked his head, and the metal butt plate clanged against the metal of the guardsman's helmet.

They drew apart again, taking up a stance with their weapons to the fore, seeking an opportunity to attack.

In the corner of his eye, Schneider could see Keller throttling the life out of one enemy soldier, his MP-40 crushing the man's windpipe, the soft skin split by both by the action of the rear sight and the man's clawing nails.

Keller's mouth emitted an animal-like snarling as humanity was brushed aside for the most basic of instincts; survival.

'Scheisse!'

Schneider yelped as he realised his attention had wandered, albeit for the shortest of moments, and the Russian had seen the opportunity.

Instinctively, he sucked in his stomach and twisted, sensing the passage of metal the smallest of distances from his flesh.

The Russian overbalanced and stumbled forward.

Schneider jabbed opportunistically, and the muzzle of his weapon punched into the man's chest.

354

Had his bayonet been fixed, he would have won the duel there and then, but, although winded, the Soviet infantryman was still in the fight.

Rolling away, the Russian lost his grip on his rifle, and desperately looked for a weapon.

Schneider worked the bolt of his rifle and blew the man's throat into a bloody mess of shattered flesh.

Keller had finished disposing of his opponent, and took the time to put another clip in his SMG, before he dropped to one knee and sucked in as much air as he could.

"You alright, Stabs?"

Keller, panting like a greyhound, gave Schneider a baleful look.

"Think so…"

The NCO stood on shaky legs and tried hard to control his breathing.

Something he saw did it for him.

"Mein Gott! Quick!"

Schneider followed the suddenly sprinting NCO, and found himself at the nearby machine-gun position.

Trying not to stand on the moaning gunner, or in what was left of the loader, the signaller grabbed the ammo belt of the MG-34, ready to feed it through his fingers.

Keller pulled the trigger, aiming at the body of Russians he had seen charging into one of his platoon positions.

The weapon leapt into life, but most of the first burst went wildly overhead.

Leaning more into the butt and controlling his heavy breathing, Keller brought the gun back on target and swept the line of guardsmen with a veritable tempest of bullets.

Over half of the enemy were bowled over, buying time for Keller's platoon to gather themselves and step forward.

Rifles and sub-machine guns fired virtually point-blank and, for good measure, a couple of stick grenades added to the slaughter.

Schneider added another belt to the length as his NCO looked around for further threats.

He had no need to look far, a full platoon of heavily armed guardsmen suddenly emerging from a defile to the right of his position.

"Gun right", shouted Keller, as he dragged the weapon around.

The belt snagged and nearly parted the links, but Schneider reacted just in time.

Settling the bipod, Keller took aim and let rip.

The air above the Soviets filled with 7.92mm, missing every man.

"Scheisse!"

They had seen the machine-gun and dropped into cover immediately before the fire erupted from the machine-gun post.

"Need more ammo!"

"Then get it!"

Keller fired two to three bullet bursts down the slope, hitting nothing, but successfully pinning the enemy platoon in place.

Between each burst, he looked around the position, seeking more ammunition… and spotting…

'Stielhandgranate!'

He sent the last of his bullets downrange and made a decision.

Schneider had already disappeared in search of more ammo belts, so Keller discarded the weapon and grabbed the grenades one by one, arming each with a simple tug on the cord, and sending them downhill to explode amongst the bushes and rocks where the enemy platoon had gone to ground.

The second one sent a man flying into the air, performing a lazy somersault, even in death.

All six flew through the air and landed in the general area of the enemy platoon.

Schneider, bleeding from a nasty ear wound, flew back into the position, and spilled the contents of one ammo box on the parapet.

Thrusting the tab through the receiver, he prepared the MG-34.

Having grabbed the dead loader's rifle, the Stabsfeldwebel was firing at targets, real and imagined, hoping to keep their heads down for as long as possible.

The silence from the machine-gun emboldened the guardsmen and, under orders from their commander, they rose up and charged.

"Urrah! Urrah!"

Schneider clipped two belts together as his company CO grasped the gun and settled his cheek on the wood.

The gun burst into life, jerking and wagging from side to side, as Keller sought to put as many bullets on target as humanly possible.

The Soviet soldiers fell in numbers, but pressed hard, gaining ground, even in the face of the lethal storm Keller was creating.

"Barrel!"

The one in the gun glowed a dull red, and Keller made the instinctive decision to change it rather than jam the weapon.

He'd spotted a spare near the grenades, so grabbed it instantly, flicking the catch on the gun, and accepting the burns to the tips of his fingers.

The hot barrel dropped free as he manoeuvred the gun.

He inserted the new, all the time watching the enemy get closer, again enthused by the weapon's silence.

Schneider clipped two more belts together, adding them to the belt already in.

"Go, go, go!"

Keller needed no second bidding and dropped the leading man with a burst that nearly decapitated the Soviet officer.

The guardsmen screamed in anger and their legs pumped hard, closing down the distance as quick as they could.

"Urrah!"

The MG-34 cut many of them down, but the others just kept coming.

Had he had the time to comment, Keller would have ventured that it was the bravest charge he had ever seen.

The gun jammed, Schneider's inexperience finally coming home to roost as he twisted the feed.

Six Russians remained, full of fight, and with vengeance in their hearts.

Keller picked up the discarded MG barrel, feeling enough heat to know that he was damaging his fingers, and brought it down on the fingers of the first rifleman into the position, breaking bone and splitting flesh.

The man howled and dropped his weapon, whilst somehow also aiming a punch at his opponent's face, a punch that missed as the hot barrel crashed into the side of his head, and the Guards Corporal lost further interest in the battle.

Schneider struggled to pull his Walther from its holster and only managed a single shot before he was bowled over by a flying Russian.

Keller tried to brain the next man, but lost his grip on the barrel, which flew away harmlessly.

He ducked under a flailing rifle butt and punched the man hard, almost bending him in two, as his solid fist combined with the soldier's forward momentum to bring about a telling blow.

A glancing blow struck his wounded arm and felled the Stabsfeldwebel, as another enemy came at him from the side.

Keller and Schneider were now both down, and both on their backs in the gun pit with enemy soldiers gaining the advantage.

The signaller flailed with his legs, trying to find some leverage to push his assailant off.

He screamed in pure agony as another enemy stamped hard on his left leg, the snap as the bone parted louder than any gunshot to the ears of those battling in the gun position.

His opponent gained the upper hand and Schneider started to pass out as the hands restricted his throat more and more.

Keller took a heavy blow to the forehead, as his enemy head-butted him, although fortunately not with enough accuracy.

His eyes watered with the stinging pain, and Keller realised that his arm wound was leaking blood once more and had started to surrender its strength.

His right hand was on the Russian's jaw, so he grabbed a moment's opportunity and twisted on the heavy bone.

Whatever he did, it visited excruciating pain on the enemy soldier, and the man fell back, clutching his face in his hands, only to be replaced by the latest arrival in the gun pit.

Keller could only scream and protect himself with outstretched arms as the guardsman lunged with his bayonet.

Von Scharf ran as fast as he could, understanding that even a second's delay could lose them the position, and therefore, the height.

It had been the absence of communication from Seventh Company, combined with the sounds of a battle growing more frantic by the second that had drawn him.

Grabbing every spare man he could find, von Scharf arrived just as the Soviets were on the verge of success.

His men moved left and right, hammering into the groups of enemy who had invested the summit, whilst others dropped into position and opened up a heavy fire on the guardsmen still toiling up the slope.

The intervention tipped the balance in favour of the defenders, and most of the enemy started the process of falling back, leaving half their number behind, in one way or another.

However, von Scharf only had eyes for the cameo in front of him.

Keller's scream was superseded by that of the enemy rifleman, as a burst of sub-machine gunfire stitched across his shoulders.

He continued to squeal with pain as he dropped face first onto Keller with his lifeblood draining away and his useless nerveless arms unable to do anything to stop the bleeding.

Next to Keller's confused form, the metal butt plate of a Mauser smashed into the side of a guardsman's skull, and a rough kick directed the dead body away from falling on top of Schneider.

The position was suddenly only occupied by the men of 3rd Battalion, save for the dead of both sides.

Von Scharf beckoned to three men.

"You two man this weapon... you, get at least four cases of ammunition here immediately. Move!"

Other hands grabbed Keller and Schneider and pulled them out of the gun pit and, with surprisingly more care and reverence, recovered the bodies of the two-gun crew.

Less reverently, two Soviet bodies were pushed into place to temporarily strengthen the position; the other enemy corpses were sent rolling down the hill.

Only the occasional shot interrupted the conversation back at Keller's forward position.

"You look like shit, Stabsfeldwebel."

Aching in places he didn't know he had, Keller intended no humour.

"I feel like shit, Herr Hauptmann."

A sanits arrived and went to work, the grey-faced Schneider getting first use of his medical bag.

A simple dose of morphine put the signaller out for the count, allowing the orderly to straighten and splint the ruined leg.

Keller and von Scharf shared a tug on the former's water bottle.

"Cigarette."

359

Keller had lost his manners, but it didn't matter, and his commander pushed a lit one between his lips.

"Want to give me a verbal report for now, Hermann?"

It was meant as a light-hearted comment, but fell on stony ground.

'The bastards attacked... we shot the bastards... strangled the bastards... the bastards fucked off.'

Keller rejected the idea immediately and went for the simpler option.

"Not quite now, if that's alright, Herr Hauptmann."

Neither man said any more, and they withdrew into the satisfaction of a cigarette and the unadulterated pleasure that a survivor draws from post-battle silence.

1530 hrs, Saturday, 20th July 1946, Height 462, near Marienhagen, Germany.

The Soviets had tried again, but got nowhere near their previous high-water mark.

The attack had simply petered out.

It actually hadn't existed in front of Eighth Company's positions at all, and von Scharf had decided to risk reconstituting his reserve force by pulling men from the Eighth to form it.

His main problem now was ammunition and water, one he was addressing by stockpiling weapons and ammunition from the dead of both sides, as well as scavenging for anything drinkable or edible amongst the corpses.

Von Scharf also risked a small party to take all the empty water bottles they could find and head back to the river in the valley behind them.

He consumed a pack of dry biscuits, washed down with some acidic red wine, and surveyed the battalion situation map, seeking out any weaknesses that he might have previously missed.

Reports from his companies showed differing fortunes for the Soviet advance.

Heights 397 and 420 were quiet. According to Keller's 2IC, the Soviet attack formations had withdrawn back to the Saale, and in some cases, to their starting positions.

The only aircraft seen in the skies overhead were now Allied, although they had shared the space with a number of Soviet aircraft for a short and violent period of time.

Honours were even as both sides lost three aircraft each, but the sky belonged to the Allied air forces.

To the south, messages from the recovered Aschmann told of heavy fighting in Weenzen and southern outskirts of Marienhagen itself, although there appeared to be nothing more troublesome than enemy stragglers for Ninth Company to concern itself with.

The presence of friendly aircraft had even put a stop to the enemy mortar and artillery work so, for the first time since they had taken the height, the men of Third Battalion were not under fire from anyone.

Most casualties had been evacuated, save for walking wounded like Aschmann, or the seriously bloody-minded 'I'm not going anywheres' such as Keller.

The former was recovered from his momentary psychiatric lapse and, with his senior NCO, was examining an object of interest in the enemy positions.

"Gas cylinders? Some sort of field kitchen?"

Aschmann snorted.

"No chance... really... no chance. On their side... on such a low frame work... only one man... don't see that at all, Oberfeldwebel."

The two dropped back into silence, observing the curiosity that had appeared a few minutes earlier, slipped into a position almost unobserved, served by three men, two of which had melted into cover to the rear of the 'thing'

"Tell you something, Herr Oberleutnant... whatever it is, that man is in an ambush position. Look at where his 'cylinders' are pointing... where he's covering."

Aschmann concentrated hard.

"You've a good point there, Oberfeldwebel. If I was going to position an anti-tank gun, I'd find no really better position, Behrens. He's covering the approaches to Marienhagen, plus the cross route there, Route 462 and Route 240."

He forced his eyes onto the binoculars.

"But it's not an anti-tank gun, is it, Behrens... is it?"

"No, Herr Oberleutnant."

Aschmann coughed and spat a gobbet of something unwelcome over the edge of his position.

"So what in the name of God and all his sainted triangles is the shitty thing eh?"

"Perhaps we should ask the old sweats, Sir?"

Ninth Company had two men who, allegedly, had accompanied Marshal von Blücher onto the field of Waterloo, so long was their war service.

361

"Go and grab the elderly gentlemen, Oberfeldwebel. Let's see what they have to say, eh?"

Two minutes later, Stabsgefreiter Arturs flopped noiselessly beside his company commander.

"Herr Oberleutnant?"

Aschmann pulled the binoculars away and passed them to the wizened infantryman who, according to his records was forty-nine, but looked roughly twice that.

Pointing across the valley, Aschmann brought Arturs attention to the 'thing'.

"To the left of that stone ruin... on the down side there... see it?"

"No, Herr Oberleutnant... I... ah, yes."

"And?"

"Field kitchen?"

"We've decided not, Arturs. Not seen one before?"

"I've seen most that the communists have to offer. Not seen one of those before... mind you... it's set up in a beautiful position, Herr Oberleutnant... lovely field of fire."

Confirmation of his and Behrens' thinking was of little use without knowing what it was.

"Thank you anyway, Arturs. Return to your platoon. Thank you."

The old Stabsgefreiter returned the binoculars and saluted.

He passed his older friend on the way back.

"It's a field kitchen, but play dumb, Roland. You're good at that."

Roland Freiser took a playful swipe at his old comrade.

"Fuck off, boy."

He was a mere three months older than Arturs.

"Seriously. I've no idea what the bastard thing is. Asch is worried about it though, so it won't take too much to get a rise out of him."

The two parted, leaving Freiser's 'bullet-loading swine' comment floating in the widening gap between them.

Freiser dropped into the earth alongside Aschmann.

"Reporting as ordered, Herr Oberleutnant?"

The binoculars changed hands again, but the sound of heavy engines and the crack of high-velocity guns distracted both men.

Snatching the binoculars back, Aschmann found the source.

362

"Our panzers are advancing. King Tigers and Panthers! They should make short work of the communists!"

Suddenly all smiles, he forgot the initial problem, concentrating on the nine heavy and medium tanks as they rolled forward in two lines, rolling down the road from Thüste, driving towards the enemy at Weenzen, occasionally stopping only to pick off an enemy tank here and there.

"Was there something you wanted, Herr Oberleutnant?"

Brought back to subject number one, Aschmann pointed towards the 'thing' and explained the problem.

Binoculars to his face, Freiser found first one, then quickly two more of the 'things'.

"Fucking hell!"

"What? What's that you say, man?"

"I can't pronounce the name but I know what they are... and there's three of them. The panzers are in trouble, Herr Oberleutnant. We've got to stop them before they get too close. Those bastards are deadly!"

"What are they?"

"They're rockets... Hungarian anti-tank rockets. Saw some in use when I was with the Feldherrnhalle in Budapest. No fucking prisoners with those things. They'll make mincemeat out of the panzer boys, no problem, Oberleutnant."

He turned to look at his commander and saw nothing but horror on Aschmann's face.

The officer thought fast.

"Get on to Bataillon. Tell them what we have, and that I'm going to try and stop the panzers. Oberfeldwebel Behrens!"

As he waited for the NCO to appear, Aschmann rummaged in the battalion chest.

"Herr Hauptmann?"

"Behrens... they're rocket launchers, according to Freiser. I want them under fire immediately... tracer rounds... try and let the panzers know the enemy's set up there."

He paused as he lifted out the signal pistol.

"If the mortars had any ammo, I'd direct them onto it... them... there's three apparently. I'm going to try and stop them another way."

He found the flares.

"Tell the Leutnant that he's in charge. Now get to it!"

Behrens was away like a flash as Aschmann slid the first flare into the pistol, and pocketed half a dozen more.

He moved back to Freiser's side.

363

"Any more, Stabsgefreiter?"

"Not sure, Herr Oberleutnant. Three for certain… that's what I can see. I remember the things used to engage up to about a kilometre or so, less to be certain. I think our panzers are still beyond that."

He clicked his fingers as a memory surfaced.

"Buggiveters… they're called Buggiveters…*"

He turned to look at his commander, but saw only a pair of heels as Aschmann was up and out of the trench. Running down the slope with his SMG in one hand and the flare pistol in the other.

He was still watching Aschmann as a burst from a DP28 chewed up the earth around the running man's feet, before it was professionally 'walked' into the target.

The Oberleutnant went down hard, and stayed down.

[*Buggiveters = Buzogányvető, Hungarian AT rockets]

1530 hrs, Saturday, 20th July 1946, slopes of Height 329, southeast of Marienhagen, Germany.

Vesnin was fuming, and his bad temper grew with each hit on a tank of the 45th Guards.

"You say you can hit up to twelve hundred, so fire, Mayor, for the Motherland's sake… can't you see that the tankers are getting hammered out there?"

The AT unit commander shook his head.

"They'll have to make their own arrangements, Comrade Alezredes Vesnin."

He used the Hungarian rank deliberately.

"I'll not risk my unit until I know I can hit what I aim at."

Vesnin bit back his reply, as his briefing on the Hungarian-designed Buzogányvető rocket system had been quite specific.

'…the Mace unit commander is a veteran who knows what he's doing. Assist as he sees fit, allow him to do his job, and protect the rocket systems and crews at all costs…'

Major General Babadzhanian had been so invested in this unit that he had bothered to send a written message specifically to Vesnin, under whose command he had placed the Special unit.

"When?"

"Eight-hundred."

Vesnin made the calculation and came up short by nearly one hundred metres.

"And these things'll kill their King Tiger?"

"No problem, Comrade."

That was a claim and a half to Vesnin, but he held himself in check, grimacing as one of the supporting ZSUs exploded violently.

An enemy barrage pounded the top of Height 329, completely missing the launchers concealed on the northwestern slope.

He could keep his mouth shut no longer.

"That has to be in your range now, Comrade Mayor!"

Not removing his eyes from the special sight, Major Sárközi sighed audibly, like a parent at an overly questioning child.

"I need all five maces in range, or we'll lose our advantage, Comrade Alezredes."

That made sense, and Vesnin kicked himself for not thinking of it.

'The man knows his trade remember!'

A scream betrayed some injury to the covering infantry force, two platoons of his guardsmen had been laid out in front of the launchers to provide security.

Another scream penetrated Vesnin's brain to the core, one originating from Sárközi, as the Hungarian gave the order to fire.

The five 'Mace' launchers sent their rockets downrange as one.

Accelerating to two hundred metres per second, the Mace rockets ate up the battlefield and hit home.

Spectacularly.

Each hollow-charge warhead was capable of penetrating three hundred millimetres of armour, if the rocket warhead presented perpendicular to the armour plate.

The King Tigers and Panthers all had angled armour, so some penetrative power was lost.

Not enough to preserve some of the targets.

One King Tiger shrugged off a glancing frontal hit, its crew unharmed, but suddenly petrified beyond words.

Another one, a Henschel version, was struck on the flat turret plate.

Everyone died as the metalwork simply disintegrated and flew in all directions.

Similarly, the nearest Panther took a turret hit and came apart in a violent explosion.

The rear turret hatch cartwheeled away, the heavy piece of metal covering the short distance to the command Panther tank in the blink of an eye, where it wiped through the head and shoulders of the unit commander.

The foremost King Tiger lost its nearside track and half the drive sprocket, which halted its forward movement in the blink of an eye.

The second volley of missiles were already in the air and the disabled King Tiger was struck again. It burst into flames, knocked out whilst the crew were still working out what had happened in the first instance.

The leading King Tiger, spared when the 'Mace' targeted at it struck a tree trunk, had turned to present an angled front, but lurched down into a hole at precisely the worst possible moment, enabling the second rocket to strike its armour at the perfect angle.

The 215mm hollow charge warhead ignited and focussed its penetrative force on a spot precisely forty centimetres below the driver's episcope, easily cutting through the thick armour, and similarly through the chest cavity of the panzer crewman next in line.

The huge tank started to burn lazily, and the crew quickly evacuated, only to fall foul of vengeful guards infantrymen, who mowed them down with unconcealed relish.

With all four King Tigers and two panthers knocked out, Vesnin was elated.

"One more volley and you'll have wiped out the lot, Comrade Mayor!"

"No time for that, Comrade. We're moving."

"What? You've got them beaten. Fire again!"

"No."

'The man knows his trade remember!'

Sárközi shouted at his men, winding his right arm in a circular motion,

Each launcher had a crew of three, and was set on an old Maxim machine gun mount.

The entire set-up was manhandled away at breakneck speed; the Hungarians understood the urgency of the situation.

"I suggest you move swiftly, Comrade Alezredes. There'll be a barrage shortly."

Vesnin knew why they had relocated, but still wondered if the Hungarians should have taken another shot.

'The man knows his trade remember!'

He followed Sárközi and his senior NCO as they sprinted away with arms full of equipment, trailing wires as they ran for safer ground.

Behind them, the Panzer unit's Speiss, the senior NCO and all that was left of the command structure, howled into the radio, firing

366

off coordinates at the same time as he tried to direct his driver on how best to get his Panther into cover.

The veteran of many a battle did both admirably, and saved himself and his crew, and also provided accurate details to the waiting artillery.

Shells crashed down on the ground that Vesnin and the Mace launchers had occupied a few minutes beforehand, and he knew that the Hungarian had been right.

He was also man enough to say so.

"Good call, Comrade Sárközi. You live to fight another day, whereas I would have killed the rest of them, and my corpse would have been decorated with the Red Star."

The wiry Major turned away from watching his men set up their launchers again and nodded curtly, accepting the statement for what it was.

"We bloodied the fascist's nose for them. There was no sense in throwing away my men and rockets in a gesture, Comrade Alezredes."

In the valley, 45th Guards Tanks rallied and drove hard at the surviving Panthers, but overextended themselves, and found the rest of Von Hardegen's Panzer Brigaden Europa waiting for them.

The surviving T34s streamed back through Weenzen, and didn't bother to stop at Marienhagen.

It was not until Dunsen that the Guards Tank Brigade Commander managed to bring order to the chaos and halt what could only be described as the total rout of his unit.

Vesnin left the Hungarian special anti-tank company to its own devices, understanding that, no matter what he thought of fighting beside turncoat troops, they knew their trade and were solid soldiers.

He arrived in Marienhagen, where chaos reigned supreme.

Wiping his eyes clean of the dirt of battle, Vesnin reread the radio message script, the general retreat order almost unbelievable in the light of the successes of the Mace unit, and the heroics and sacrifices of his men on Height 462.

He screwed up the paper and closed his eyes.

Overhead, the sound of aircraft made him open them again, and the reports of exploding bombs and the whoosh of rockets seemed almost to taunt him, to remind him of his impotence and his inability to resist, against both the enemy air force and the General's order.

'*Blyad!*'

"Mayor Dushkin!"

His staff all looked at him, but only the Praporshchik spoke.

"Comrade Mayor Dushkin died on the hill, Sir."

'*Blyad! I'm losing my mind!*'

"Yes… he did. Right, get me second battalion immediately. We're pulling back to another position."

No matter how he said it, they all knew it was an ignominious retreat.

1602 hrs, Saturday, 20th July 1946, Bruggen, Germany.

265th Guards Mortar Regiment received its own orders, which were twofold.

The second part relocated them some kilometres to the east, where they would set up and get ready to support the defence of Hildesheim.

The first part involved firing its BM-8-36 weapons at a relatively small area nearly five thousand five hundred metres away.

The Regiment was not at full strength, few Soviet units were, but it still possessed enough power to make life distinctively uncomfortable at any point in the line that it brought its weapons to bear.

Twenty-nine launchers, mounted on Zis-6 trucks, discharged thirty-six rockets each, the whole firing process over in less than thirty seconds.

One thousand and forty-four rockets were in the air at the same time.

The Regiment was well skilled at relocating, a skill much needed by the Soviets since the Allies had totally perfected their counter-battery fire techniques.

1604 hrs, Saturday, 20th July 1946, Height 462, Marienhagen, Germany.

The grenadiers of Third Battalion had relaxed, the unexpected setback of the loss of the panzers at Weenzen the only negative in sight.

From their lofty perch, it was clear that the German Army had sundered the enemy lines, in spite of the unexpected presence of some prime Soviet formations.

368

The Saale had been forced and troops flowed over three bridges, not now to bait the enemy into staying, but to pursue a force in total retreat.

The jaws of the pincer were working hard to close around 1st Guards Tank Army and its supporting cohorts, but the retreat of the forces that faced 3rd Korps meant a change in the situation.

Ordered now to press hard on the units to their front, 3rd Korps moved on rapidly, staying as close in contact as possible, not giving the Soviet soldiers a chance to stand and fight.

Meanwhile the jaws were redirected, ordered now to take a much larger bite out of the Soviet frontline forces.

The 266th Infanterie Division was allocated to the second echelon, all but the 899th Regiment, which was, as had been promised, left to police the newly won ground.

By Bremer's order, Third Battalion were left alone, without any orders, save to rest and recuperate on their hard-won ground.

The same hard-won ground that interested the 265th Guards Mortar Regiment.

Leaving all his units in the hands of subordinates, Von Scharf had assembled his commanders for a combined briefing, debriefing, and general 'how are you' session at his command post.

With no incoming fire, and a constant stream of friendly aircraft overhead, the bare hill seemed almost like a paradise, compared to recent places they had served.

The bright sun almost seemed to gather itself to launch stronger rays, so a feeling of well-being grew as the senior men took time for a drink and a cigarette in the warm embracing summer air.

Keller lay flat on his back, his hands across his face, preventing the intense light from penetrating his eyelids, or more accurately eyelid, as his swollen face had completely closed one eye.

Von Scharf felt comfortable enough to produce his trademark cigarette holder, and was, when not puffing away, relating some portion of the recent battle to Behrens, who in turn enlightened his commander as to how Aschmann had been badly wounded.

Janjowski chatted with Erich Horstbeck, the fresh-faced commander of Eighth Company, who didn't look a day over sixteen.

The impression never survived further examination of the man's uniform, his impressive array of bravery and other awards

369

evidence of a great deal of time spent in violent proximity to the enemy.

A member of the 44th Hoch- und Deutschmeister Division, the quiet unassuming Viennese had started the war as a private soldier and ended it as an Oberleutnant, decorated with most awards the Reich had to offer, save the Ritterkreuz and any type of wound medal.

The latter was nothing short of a miracle for someone who had served the six long years of WW2.

Horstbeck was enthusiastically displaying his left forearm, the rent flesh, the clotted blood, the ripped sleeve bringing him joy, rather than pain.

"Finally Kasper...finally! Wound badge in Black for certain!"

Janjowski immediately rained on his parade.

"That's not an insect bite, is it?"

"Eh?"

"Looks like an insect bite to me."

"It's a bullet wound... went straight through, hit some rock... came back into me here and took this chunk out."

Horstbeck used his other hand to detail the passage of the single bullet.

"Right...fine... keep your hat on... I will accept that, despite the fact that it clearly looks like an insect bite... but my point stands. Regulations clearly state that the wound must be either sustained from frostbite, air raid, or hostile enemy action."

Horstbeck's eyes narrowed.

"What are you saying?"

"I understand that Oberschutze Köttler has confessed to missing a shot on an enemy and accidentally wounding you."

"What?"

"Not enemy action I'm afraid, Rupe... sorry and all that... but these things come across my desk...can't possibly sign off on it."

"You bastard! You utter bastard!"

He aimed a swipe at Janjowski, who fell off his log avoiding it.

His laughter spread throughout the assembled commanders, who had, one by one, stopped to listen to the exchange.

Horstbeck sprang to his feet.

"I swear you lot conspire against me, just because I'm a veteran soldier with more experience than all of you rogues put together."

The laughter spread.

Janjowski stuck his head over the fallen tree trunk.

"Still looks like an insect bite to me."

He dissolved into laughter once more.

Horstbeck threw his cap at the face of the laughing man.

With mock severity, Janjowski wagged his finger.

"A clear case of assault on a fellow officer. Disgraceful... all because I'm not falling for your weak attempt to secure a decoration!"

"You utter schwein! Herr Hauptmann! I'm being victimised!"

Von Scharf was incapable of adding any words to the conversation, as he descended into a laughter-induced coughing fit.

Janjowski tossed the cap back to Horstbeck and sat back on the log, holding up his hands in mock surrender.

"However, Herr Oberleutnant, with the correct inducement, I might... err... turn a dark eye to your clear attempt to gain laurels not due to you."

Horstbeck played the game.

"You total schwein, Kasper, or should I say, fucking Judas! This wound was sustained on the field of battle whilst I and my soldiers valiantly held back the Slavic hordes... unlike you... sitting in the safety of the battalion bunker counting pencils and paperclips!"

The laughter was raucous, and just what they all needed to wash away the memories of hideous combat.

"It isn't me that writes the rules, Herr Oberleutnant... I'm sorry, but there is little I can do... unless..."

"Unless what...eh? Unless... hold on!"

Horstbeck almost exploded.

"You want the pepper vodka!"

"What an excellent suggestion, Herr Comrade Starshy Leytenant. I accept."

"You asshole... I'll piss in it before I..."

Some new sound made Horstbeck stop in his tracks.

"ACHTUNG! Take cover!"

The echo of his words was replaced by the sounds of rapid movement, as the veterans threw themselves in all directions.

The sound of scrabbling bodies was, in turn, superceded by a familiar and very dreadful sound, as the first of one thousand and forty-four Katyusha rockets streamed out of the sky.

Height 462 disappeared in a deluge of high explosives.

"That is the latest situation report received from Generalfeldmarschal Guderian, Sir."

"Excellent, General. Thank you."

Ike gestured von Vietinghoff to a chair and poured two coffees.

"So it seems that this coincidence will reap some advantage for your forces, General?"

Von Vietinghoff accepted the cup and saucer with a nod.

"Very much, General Eisenhower. Their assault elements made our initial running difficult but… according to the report I have just passed to you, it seems we have routed the units that were to attack us and, as a result, their front line has collapsed in three places."

He took the opportunity to take a sip of the excellent fresh brew.

"The initial pocket area has been redesignated, and the Feldmarschal privately believes we will bite off much more than the First Guards Tank Army."

"Good news indeed, General."

They lapsed into silence as the coffee called to them.

Eisenhower was the first to break it.

"General Vietinghoff… I just wondered if you could help me with another matter."

"Most certainly… if I can, Herr General."

"The movement of German forces into our frontline… well… it seems a little slower than we had anticipated. I want to be able to tell my President that the plan is on schedule. Political pressure at home, of course. You understand."

"Of course, Herr General," he said.

'Not really,' he meant.

"Another coffee?"

Eisenhower swept up the dirty ware and returned with a fresh set, filled to the brim.

"Thank you, Sir. General Eisenhower, I believed that General Bradley was in liaison on this matter?"

"I've not been in direct receipt of any definitive further information since our last joint meeting, General Vietinghoff."

"Then my apologies for our mistake. Some units were delayed in moving forward as they needed time to finish conversion to the newer weapon systems that are becoming available. Somewhat perversely, it seems the more experienced men require more input…

overriding their previous training is how it's been put to me...
anyway, the units are moving and some are already in position, ready
to exchange with troops from General Bradley's Army Group."

Eisenhower concealed his sigh of relief.

"Then I can report to the President that the process is on
track?"

"Most certainly, General Eisenhower."

Von Vietinghoff smiled broadly... disarmingly...
concealing his thoughts.

'... *in both senses of the word, Herr General.*'

Those that I fight I do not hate, those that I guard I do not love.

William Butler Yeats

Chapter 163 - THE MEDALS

2228 hrs, Monday, 22nd July 1946, Schloss Hartenfels, Torgau, Germany.

Nazarbayeva was still in her office, the one she had occupied since the headquarters of the Red Banner Forces of Soviet Europe had relocated from Nordhausen to Torgau, a relocation speeded up by the victories achieved by the new German Army.

She had ordered copies of a number of relevant reports and they lay before her, spread all over a huge trestle table that served as her desk, map table, and dining station.

The paperwork all concerned German forces, and she was trying to develop her own picture of what was happening, independent of the one her staff kept constantly updated.

There was a general suggestion that the DRH was of growing importance to the Allied cause, and the fact that they were spearheading the latest Allied effort could be interpreted as supporting that.

The British were reasonably quiet, with limited gain attacks here and there where their forces held sway.

The Americans were also quiet, even the cowboy Patton keeping his units in check.

One report had piqued her interest, despite its age.

Italian sympathisers had started to notice that German formations, those that had 'monitored' the line between Italian National forces and the Allied rear, were being or had been replaced with the soldiers of other Allied nations.

She skim read the group relating to the new Italian boundaries.

'... Uruguayan infantrymen...'

She flicked another page up.

'... Argentine soldiers and artillery...'

Nazarbayeva frowned and rubbed her eyes with her free hand.

'... Brazilian riflemen... frontline soldiers... experienced soldiers... interesting...'

The knock on the door made her jump, so deep was her concentration.

"Come!"

"Good evening, Comrade General. I was about to be relieved, but this message came through. It concerns your present problem."

He held out the two-page document.

Nazarbayeva accepted it but didn't examine it, but instead dropped it on the table in front of her and stretched her back and arms.

"Sit and tell me about it, Comrade."

"Rufin has the other report. He's just cross-referencing some information, and then he'll bring it straight to you."

He leant forward, looking for a particular item from the selection in front of him.

He couldn't see it.

"The report from Schwalmstadt, Comrade General?"

She found it instantly.

"Yes... the German forces seen moving southeast. We felt that it was most likely to be those French SS Legion units."

"Based on what we knew then... yes. Some of them were around Kassel of course, but our information was interpreted as being the rest of the Devil's bunch."

She looked at Poboshkin expectantly.

"We were wrong."

Another knock made them both jump.

At Nazarbayeva's insistence, Major Rufin waited whilst Poboshkin finished, although she understood he had important news.

"A second report from Schwalmstadt indicates that the flow of 'German' units has increased, probably three divisions worth...and includes all arms, from tanks to postal services."

He pointed Rufin at a stool.

"Comrade General, our man has been counting carefully, and the figures make disturbing reading. Bear in mind, we have had excellent intelligence on their forces... or thought we did anyway... and believed we had identified all their known armoured formations with what I might now call their main body... Guderian's Army Group."

"Go on."

"The latest fighting has revealed these known tank divisions still to be with Guderian's force, so...," he checked the report to make sure he was accurate,"... where did the Germans get over three hundred tanks and self-propelled guns from?"

"Well, we knew that devil Speer was getting their industry working again, so tha…"

"Apologies, Comrade General, but that's not the point. The point is that these are confirmed German tanks, nowhere near the Guderian group, and certainly not the SS units of the French Army.

"They're new?"

"Most definitely, Comrade General. Our man had identified the latest Panther II models, which we know are not supplied to the French, or anyone else for that matter, only for German Army use."

"You've convinced me. And?"

Poboshkin ceded the stage to Rufin.

"Comrade Mayor General, I have two reports, one of which came in earlier today, but that has just come to my attention."

He slipped a copy of the first to both senior officers.

"This is from an agent in Washington. Low-level, works within their USO service. The report details memoranda exchanged between the US War Department and his organisation, trying to organise a huge entertainment operation to provide shows to troops in five newly stablished centres in Germany."

Nazarbayeva looked up from the document, concentrating on Poboshkin as he reeled off the details.

"We don't know where they are, Comrade Mayor General, but the list asks for a few of their celebrities by name… their major players… names like Hope, Crosby, Dietrich, Adler, Laurel and Hardy… but it's the numbers, Comrade Mayor General. The request is for eighty plus entertainers across the five sites, two shows a day… it's a huge operation."

"And the point would be… who's going to watch them?"

"Indeed, Comrade Mayor General."

"I see this is old news, and that these camps should have been in place a week ago…"

She lapsed into the silence of intense thought.

"Polkovnik?"

"Comrade Mayor General, I think we could possibly think that the German Army units seen at Schwalmstadt were not all that were on the move southwards… and that the Allied plan is to relieve some of the pressure on the Amerikanski by replacing them in the front line… with German troops."

She nodded and picked up the lead.

"Which would mean that the plan to target the Amerikanski is working… it can only be casualties that's causing them to replace with German units… no…no…" Nazarbayeva wagged her finger at no one in particular, "... they could be recovering units to get ready for another offensive? Possible?"

"It's possible, but not likely, Comrade Mayor General."

Nazarbayeva waved her hand.

"Just for now, we will all stick with Comrade."

The two men nodded.

"So, why not likely?"

"We have seen none of the normal pointers that indicate an Amerikanski attack. Admittedly, our intelligence is greatly limited, and much of it delayed by circumstances... and photo reconnaissance a thing of the past, but... there are no indications of increased rail traffic, no missing units... certainly none of the usual suspects when it comes to their attacks... air activity is within the norms... brutal as ever... but there is nothing of the normal pattern of increased attacks on our logistic routes behind the front target areas... I have seen nothing whatsoever to suggest an Amerikanski attack... not in Germany... not in the Alps, Comrade."

Nazarbayeva shook her head to emphasise her words.

"Something simply isn't working here... it doesn't make sense... if... and I stress if... the Amerikanski are being replaced in the front line by Germans, that means either our plan is working or they are getting ready for another attack. Yet we have reports of the gathering of huge forces in the Pacific... Amerikanski in the main... to attack our eastern coast... it doesn't make sense."

"No, Comrade."

She pointed at a display on the wall that listed their known information about Persia.

"And Montgomery and this huge convoy with British soldiers, plus whatever else, are about to come together to threaten our southern borders... and yet the British and their Dominion forces have adopted a passive stance, the same as the Amerikanski... are the Germans taking over from the British too?"

"We have no suggestion of that, Comrade."

"We had no suggestion of that... and maybe we simply weren't looking properly... find out," and she gestured to the phone.

Whilst Poboshkin made a swift telephone call, she rapped her knuckles on the table to attract the other man's attention.

"Comrade Rufin, we need some liquid assistance in the thinking process, if you please."

Within two minutes, a large bottle of Asbach had arrived and its contents were already burning three throats.

"If the British are staying in place, it might suggest that the manpower reserve they created from their POWs has been directed

377

into reinforcing their European fortunes... if not, then maybe the available soldiers are those seen in this convoy."

"I understand, comrade... but you're suggesting we've fallen for a huge maskirovka... the Pacific... Persia... all created to disguise the weakness of our enemy?"

"If the green toads are replacing the Amerikanski, and there is no hint of any renewed attack, then we can only assume that the leadership's plan to weaken them has reaped its reward... and then it becomes easier to assume that the Pacific movement is a maskirovka."

The room echoed to solid knocking and opened to allow Pinkerova to bring the information that Poboshkin had requested.

He offered the folder to Nazarbayeva, but she held her hand up, preferring to keep her own thought pattern going strong.

"English and German troops arriving in Denmark... nothing unusual... possibly a second armoured brigade added to their 6th Division in Northern Italy... possibly also the reconstitution of their 8th Armoured Division in Holland... the report suggests the amalgamation of two existing brigades..."

"Nothing to suggest matters either way then, Comrade?"

Poboshkin's eyes had narrowed, and his pursed lips told a different story.

"Comrade Pinkerova, bring me the file on enemy formations destroyed since August 45. Thank you."

Nazarbayeva's eyebrow raised, and her aide placed a pencil around three names on the report he had been reading.

"And why they are a problem?"

The requested file arrived and Poboshkin quickly found what he was looking for.

"47th is brand new. Totally brand new."

He returned to checking the sheet.

"The 15th was utterly destroyed in the early days, mainly in and around Lübeck."

He passed the report over.

"The 51st Division was decimated in and around Hamburg, reinforced, and again totally gutted during the battles south of Bremen, especially at Barnstorf and Diepholz."

Nazarbayeva gestured at Rufin, encouraging him to refill the glasses, adding Pinkerova to the drinking circle.

"5th Division is back in the line... relieving 38th Division... but..."

He rifled through a sheaf of paperwork, his memory screaming something vital at him, something he couldn't quite hear...

couldn't quite understand... and then he found the paper and it clicked into place.

"5th Division was worn down badly by our forces, and our intelligence suggested it would be broken up to flesh out other divisions. This has been a British practice. And yet... 5th Division is back in the line... and covers the same area as the 38th Division, a unit that was at relatively full strength, which..."

"...Which suggests that the 5th is also... or might suggest that there is an opportunity for our ground forces if it isn't... but I think not."

Nazarbayeva stood and held out her glass.

"Finish your brandy, Comrades. No one leaves this building until I have the answers to these questions."

She knocked back the final dregs of the Asbach and slammed the glass on the table.

"One... estimated strength of individual British formations now, compared to lowest point... plus, say November and March for most."

She moved on quickly.

"Two... all reports on British and Dominion units to be reviewed... looking at physical strengths, reinforcements, time out of the line, all the factors that will help us here."

Poboshkin was taking notes and added a couple of extra specifics.

"Three...estimated strength of the new Germanski Army... POW numbers... break it down into Italy and the main force... estimated numbers elsewhere, of course. I want to know exactly what we do know... and what we don't know. Start on the basis of underestimation, remove such 'estimates' and start with fact, fact, fact.'

She smacked her palm on the desk three times to emphasise her words.

"The Fascists have put one over on us, I'm convinced of it."

Poboshkin shifted uncomfortably, knowing he had played a major part in any mistakes.

Rufin shifted uncomfortably, without words reminding Nazarbayeva that there was an outstanding matter.

"Four, contact Moscow for any reports on home political pressure on the military of our enemy... indications of a lack of resilience, especially the Amerikanski."

"Five... five... reports on Allied offensive activity in the Pacific. Simple enough.

379

The telephone rang.

"Nazarbayeva."

She listened.

"No, thank you, Comrade Leytenant. Tell my driver I'll be staying here tonight."

Replacing the receiver, she paused for effect.

"Six... I'll attend to six personally, Comrades."

Poboshkin raised an eyebrow, seeking information.

"Through my personal contacts, Comrade Polkovnik."

He understood fully.

"Comrade Rufin, what else do you have, before we set to this task?"

"The Germans, Comrade Mayor General. It's a stupid little report of no consequence... or so it seems... but I think it might help you in this moment."

She examined the paperwork and smiled.

"Medals?"

"Yes, Comrade Mayor General. These four firms produced medals for the Nazi pigs and, it seems, are about to do so for the new Germanski government."

"So I see... but what exactly am I seeing?"

"I quickly checked the register of destroyed German infrastructure, and those four are the only facilities that survived intact enough to start any sort of production, except for some still within our lines."

"So these four are the only German firms available to make their medals?"

"Yes, Comrade Mayor General."

"I see. Continue, Comrade."

"That message has been transposed from the original German to Russian."

"Yes?"

"Here is the original German report."

She compared the two quickly, not absorbing the content.

"Fine... my German's a little rusty, but that seems to be accurate."

"No, Comrade Mayor General, it isn't. Comrade Pinkerova is our language specialist."

He passed another two pieces of paper to the woman officer, copies of the original documents, but held up a hand to stop her proceeding, and turned to Pinkerova

"Do you agree with the additional notations, Comrade?"

Pinkerova examined the extra notes and nodded her agreement.

"Yes, Comrade. They are correct."

Rufin returned to addressing the wider audience.

"As you see, Comrades, the report speaks of an order from their Army Headquarters, sent to those four manufacturers, an order for new medals in the new style. It is broken down into replacements for existing awards, what they call de-Nazification, and for new awards."

Nazarbayeva hid her impatience well, just not well enough, and Poboshkin picked up on it... and acted on it.

"For the Motherland's sake, man, get on with it!"

Rufin's ruffled feathers were obvious, but he pressed on.

"Comrade Mayor General, it is estimated that the Germanski awarded some four million second class medals in their whole war, from 39 to 45. They have asked for roughly two and a half million for replacements which, I have reasonably assumed, is because many holders were killed."

He cut Poboshkin a look and continued.

"The figures for first class awards and the Cross also seem to tally nicely. Each company is asked to produce a quarter of the awards, so that would be six hundred thousand of the second class award each."

He accepted the two reports back from Pinkerova and set them before his commander.

"Here's the original, which lays out the replacement medal requirements... and here's where it states about the new requirements. The medal is apparently different in both cases. Our problem lies in the translation."

He pointed at both as he read the upside down words.

"It was mistranslated, Comrade Mayor General. Instead of saying that these four companies produce a quarter of four hundred thousand new style second class awards, or of the higher medals... it actually says each..."

"What?"

"The Germanski High Command is ordering over one and a half million new Iron Cross second class medals to award its soldiers."

"Mudaks!"

All eyes turned to Pinkerova, who went the very brightest of bright reds.

"Apologies, Comrade Mayor General!"

Nazarbayeva laughed and smiled.

"I agree. Mudaks! They think they'll need them. Comrade PodPolkovnik, concentrate on the Germanski first. I want answers to the questions that this poses."

She held up the mistranslated report.

"Comrade Mayor Rufin. The Motherland thanks you... and I thank you. Well done. Now, get the staff up and in... if they've gone off duty... are on leave... sick... no excuses... everyone gets on with this now. Go!"

Her officers split like a bursting star and she was alone with her thoughts almost immediately.

Taking a moment to steady herself, Nazarbayeva picked up the telephone.

"Communications office."

"General Nazarbayeva here. Get me a secure line to Moscow... office of the NKVD Deputy Chairman..."

The communications personnel did their work efficiently and within a few seconds there was a voice at the other end of the line.

"Mayor General Kaganovich's office, Polkovnik Oberunov speaking."

"Comrade Oberunov. General Nazarbayeva here. I need to speak to the General immediately."

"I'm afraid he left orders not to be disturbed under any circumstances, Comrade Mayor General."

"I understand your reluctance, Comrade Polkovnik. But I assure you that the deputy chairman will want to take my call."

Aware of the developing relationship between the GRU and NKVD generals, Oberunov made a judgement call.

"Are you in your office, Comrade Mayor General?"

"28284... we relocated to 28284. The military exchange will route properly."

She used the code number for Torgau, rather than the name, just in case.

"Wait by your phone please, Comrade General. I will contact the deputy chairman immediately."

The phone went dead and she slid it back on the receiver, wondering if she should have had the Asbach... and equally pondering if she should have another.

The shrilling of the telephone ended the mental struggle.

"Nazarbayeva."

"Comrade General, Kaganovich here, still dripping from the steam bath. What's so important that you track me down so mercilessly?"

She told him.

He reacted appropriately.

"Blyad!"

He then told her something she didn't know.

"Mudaks! And that information is how old, Comrade Kaganovich?"

"This afternoon. I was having it verified before I arranged to meet you prior to the Saturday briefing."

"But your gut feeling is that it's correct?"

"My source has never been wrong yet."

"So it is all about the Germanski then."

"Maybe not all, but certainly it appears we might have underestimated them. What will you do?"

"When will you confirm this all by?"

"Hopefully by tomorrow, day after at the latest."

"As soon as I have everything in order here, I'm getting on the first plane to Moscow. The GKO will need to see this... and to understand it... I'm not going to trust it to a telephone call."

"No, you're correct not to. I will pursue my verification and let you know as soon as I have it... or not... as the case may be."

"Thank you, Comrade Kaganovich. I'll keep you informed."

"Tread carefully, Tatiana. Goodbye."

The click underlined the statement, and Nazarbayeva stared at the inanimate object, seeking further clarification... which was clearly not forthcoming.

She gently seated the handset, treating it like an unexploded bomb.

"Comrade Poboshkin!"

Her aide appeared in the doorway, and Nazarbayeva waved him to a seat.

"Number six has proved... err... interesting... and supports our theory. Comrade Kaganovich is confirming the information right now. It appears that the British are having a service of thanksgiving for the end of the Japanese conflict, on Sunday... this Sunday... July 27th."

"Right..."

"Kaganovich's agent is a British policeman... their London police force... he has seen the dignitaries list..."

"Let me guess, Comrade... might it contain numerous senior commanders of the American forces that we have as possibly being replaced by Germanski units?"

"Not quite, Comrade, not numerous... all."

"What?"

383

"According to Kaganovich, the list specifies senior officers from the 12th Army Group... every corps commander, army commander, except that ass Patton, plus Bradley, Eisenhower, and even Bedell-Smith."

Poboshkin was speechless.

"Eisenhower and Bedell-Smith... well... they can get by without them... but taking out nearly every other senior commander. Even if they leave experienced second in commands in charge... well... it's without precedent."

"Not if the Americans are out of the line..."

He paused as his mind flicked a switch.

"Or if the attention of our army is going to be focussed elsewhere."

"As we suspected, Comrade, the two things are interlinked. We have all missed the probable expansion of the Germanski forces, and it is they who are going to launch the attacks now, a situation we have contrived by the success of the Vasilevsky plan to target the Amerikanski."

"Now we know what to look for, I'm sure we'll find more evidence, Comrade Mayor General."

"We better had, because I'm flying to Moscow tomorrow, and I want to take as much proof as I possibly can."

"Then I'll get back to my desk... if there's nothing else, Comrade?"

"Get me everything you can, Andrey Ivanovich. Everything you can."

2028 hrs, Tuesday, 23rd July 1946, the Duingerwald, east of Folziehausen, Germany.

The patient's eyes flickered, implying that he was waking up, something that immediately prompted the nurse to summon the doctor.

Emaciated by the after-effects of disease and the terrors of the Russian Front, the medical Captain limped over and examined the medical miracle that was Hubert Aschmann.

Punctured in a dozen places, Aschmann had received the largest quantity of blood anyone in the experienced German medical facility could remember.

He was now without some God-given parts of his body, such as spleen, a portion of liver, part of his intestine, a thumb, an ear lobe, six teeth, and a testicle.

384

Bordered in red, the tag still affixed to the shredded remains of his tunic, informed anyone with half an eye that he had been close to the end, as if the state of the tunic itself was not enough evidence of his luck.

"Well, Herr Oberleutnant, you've been one hell of a lucky man."

As he spoke, the doctor examined the wound sites, each revealed in turn by the beaming nurse.

"No infection... none whatsoever... testament to the pharmaceuticals supplied by our Allies... and the diligence of our nurses, especially Agnetha here."

Her smile broadened with the clear recognition of her efforts by the unit's top battle surgeon.

Speech for Aschmann was a studied affair, although he managed unexpected clarity.

"I'm thirsty."

A glass of water magically appeared and the nurse held his head to allow him to savour the cold fluid.

"Thank you. How long have I been here, Doc?"

"Two days, give or take a minute or two. Nurse, I think this needs more frequent dressing."

"It will be done, Herr Hauptmann."

Aschmann looked extremely concerned, as Doctor Grüber had been fiddling with items of great importance to the as yet unmarried man.

"Calm yourself, Aschmann, don't look so glum. It will still all work and will be hardly noticeable... provided our nurse gives the area the attention it deserves."

Agnetha Folstein blushed heavily.

A noise behind the two clinicians grew into raucous laughter, and quickly drew out the different side of Hauptmann Grüber.

"Silence! What the hell do you think this is, a Scheisse kindergarten? It's a hospital, now shut up or I'll sign you off and send you back to fight the communists!"

The laughter dropped to sniggers immediately, sniggers that grew in volume until they manifested into the bandaged personas of Janjowski and Von Scharf.

"I'd watch this one I were you, Nurse Folstein. He's a terror... and still available. I can protect you, of course."

Aschmann laughed at Janjowski's humour and went to playfully punch his arm, but failed miserably.

"Lie still, you fool!"

385

Hubert Aschmann took some time to examine his left arm and realised it was immobilised.

Grüber answered his question.

"You lost the thumb, and both the hand and arm are broken. Nothing dramatic, Oberleutnant, just messy, so I wanted it all immobilised... so there it is. Everything will work... given a little time, of which you'll have plenty."

He looked at the two waiting officers and decided on discretion.

"I'll leave you three to it... but Nurse Folstein's word is law, and if you give her any trouble, then I'll hear about it. Klar?"

They mumbled their responses through smiles and waited until the Doctor had left the bedside.

Aschmann coughed a greeting, and felt pain shoot through his body.

"Steady, Hubert. I know you're pleased to see me but stay calm, man!"

Another bout of coughing brought Aschmann time to conjure a response.

He first worked his jaw to make sure he would manage the words he had selected.

"Up yours, Kas."

Janjowski sat on the bed, contrary to ward rules, resting his damaged leg, whilst Von Scharf placed an inflatable ring on a folding chair and lowered himself onto it with great care.

He caught Aschmann's quizzical eye.

"If you say one fucking word, it'll be the penal bataillons for you."

Janjowski made a great play of hiding his mouth from view, but stage whispered so that even his words penetrated the bandaged head of a 'Berlin' Division Grenadier officer at the end of the ward.

"Hit in the ass. Can you believe it, eh? Managed to get all of his towering bulk into cover, but left his little button up so Ivan could put some shrapnel right on the bull's eye."

Von Scharf growled playfully.

"There are vacancies for Leutnants as well as Oberleutnants in the penal units... remember that before you flap your lips."

"Excuse him, Hubert, he's very tired."

"Shut up, you schwein. How are you feeling, Aschmann?"

He could feel the stitches pull as he talked, so tried to move his jaw less.

For some reason, his companions ignored the resulting unintended comedy voice.

"Like shit to be honest. What happened on that fucking hill?"

"They hit us with a full regiment of Stalin's Organs. We lost a lot of good boys."

Their humour turned to silent regret as silent faces came into their minds.

"Keller?"

Von Scharf shook his head, displaying a smile that split him from ear to ear.

"He's on another ward here. There's a communal area where you can take in a cigarette and a drink... non-alcoholic of course... I ran into him there this very morning. He's well... well... as well as can be expected. He got it in the back and legs. Not serious apparently. Schneider's here too."

Even though it hurt, he made sure his words were pronounced clearly.

"He did well in the battle, Herr Hauptmann. I'll write him up as soon as..."

He went to hold up his left hand... and remembered he couldn't.

"As soon as I've learned to write right-handed."

"From what I hear, everyone did very well... except some idiotic swine who decided to go on an Olympic sprint just because he was pleased to see the boys in black grace the battlefield."

Aschmann was on the cusp of biting, then realised his commander was simply baiting him.

"I confess... the excitement of seeing the death or glory Hussars simply overtook me, Herr Hauptmann."

Serious for a moment, Von Scharf eased his damaged posterior and leant forward to squeeze Aschmann's shoulder.

"It was a good effort, Hubert. A damn fine effort."

That it had failed was also true, but not because of a lack of effort or a lack of bravery on Aschmann's part.

"Anyone of the other rogues here, Herr Hauptmann?"

"Hauptmann Sauber is here. Not good. Part of our regimental headquarters was moving up and got caught in the barrage. I've heard that Bremer was badly wounded... not sure about that. Sauber's very chewed up. Oh, and that Signaller Finze is here too. He'll be getting a write-up from me... one of many."

Janjowski pulled out a notebook and showed it to Aschmann.

387

"Without any testimonial from you or your company, I've already got seventy-six recommendations down here…"

Von Scharf cut in.

"I decided that Kasper needed gainful employment, so he's collating all the reports for the Third Bataillon, seeing as most of it's in the facility."

There was no real humour in his statement.

"Third was flayed by the rocket strike. With those we lost repelling the attacks, the Bataillon is combat ineffective. In fact, there's a rumour going round that the whole division is going to be broken up."

"Why?"

"After we got swatted off the hill, the rest of the division got bogged down in some heavy fighting to the east. Shitty stuff, from what we hear. There's quite a few of ours in here from the other units. Tales run from Soviet counter-attacks with waves of tanks, horrendous artillery, down to a terrible error by our RAF friends."

"English bastards!"

The words were spat from the mouth of a bandaged man in the bed across from Aschmann.

He said no more and dropped back onto his bed, exhausted by the small effort.

"From what we hear, RAF ground aircraft dropped fire bombs and high-explosive all over the 897th's assault elements and the Feldersatz-Batalion. Over four hundred killed and many, many wounded. Stopped the attack in its tra…"

"We shot down four… four of… of the bastards though…"

The bandaged man again collapsed, this time expressing blood and mucus with each convulsion.

Folstein arrived from nowhere and tended to the dying man.

They watched as an injection was administered, bringing peace to the tortured body.

Von Scharf stood gingerly.

"Anyway, Hubert. I feel the need to stretch my legs. I'll drop back in later. Rest up and get yourself better, Kamerad."

Janjowski also took his leave, and the two continued on their rounds of the wounded survivors of Third Battalion, a process that took a lot less time than they had hoped.

As a result of an investigation into the circumstances surrounding the battle on and around Height 462, the loss of the panzer force, and the high casualties sustained by 266th Infanterie Division, no blame was laid on any of the senior DRH officer.

The commanding officer of the typhoon wing that inflicted the horrendous casualties on the 266th, two of the squadron leaders, the ground attack sector commander, and the RAF forward liaison officer were all put before a courts-martial, where only the FLO was acquitted.

The German Council received a written apology from no lesser person than Prime Minister Winston Churchill, hand-delivered by Tedder, with endorsements by Eisenhower and himself.

The 266th Infanterie Division was disbanded, and its personnel spread between other units, preserving them in their integral company and battalion formations where possible. Von Scharf's Third Battalion was not allocated to any new formation but, by the direct order of Guderian, was saved from disbandment, and preserved as a special purpose unit until further notice.

Oberst Bernd Freytag von Loringhoven, after a painstaking process of sifting through numerous reports, submitted a list of recommendations to Feldmarschal Guderian, which was signed off with relish.

When those named on the list were fit enough, there was a a formal parade and presentation, to honour the new recipients of the Knight's Cross, and other medals and awards.

The actions and courage of Hauptmann Werner von Scharf, 47th Recipient of the Knight's Cross, Oberleutnants Hubert Aschmann and Erich Horstbeck, 48th and 49th recipients respectively, Leutnant Kasper Janjowski, 50th recipient, and Gefreiter Gustav Schneider, the most junior rank to receive the award in the new DRH and its 51st recipient, were honoured in the extended ceremony, where the conduct and bravery of one hundred and fourteen Third Battalion soldiers was recognised.

However, before anyone else would received their awards, pride of place went to Stabsfeldwebel Hermann Keller, 1st recipient of the Oak leaves to the Knight's Cross of the new German Republic, who became, as a result, the most highly decorated NCO in the DRH.

Once the ceremony was over, the officers, NCOs, and men of Third Battalion gathered together as comrades to remember lost friends, celebrate new awards, and drink to their own survival.

It was, perhaps, a sign of the undaunted fighting spirit and comradeship of the survivors of the Battle of Height 462, that the noisiest and most raucous celebrations accompanied toasts to the award of the black wound badge to Erich Horstbeck.

"It's a father's duty to give his sons a fine chance."

George Eliot

Chapter 164 - THE SCIENTISTS

1109 hrs, Thursday, 25th July 1946, Arzamas-2510, VNIIEF Secret Facility within Prison Camp 1001, Akhtubinsk, USSR.

Colonel Skryabin looked on at the smoking ruins of the VNIIEF medical facility, one of the few parts of the secret complex that was above ground.

Whatever had caused the fire, and first indications were some sort of ignited gas leak, the damage was catastrophic, both to the clinic and to the staff that ran it.

All the senior medical staff were confirmed dead, either by dint of their corpses being recognisable, or, as was more the case, by items on the destroyed and charred corpses being known to those few medical workers who were not on duty at the time of the explosion.

Whilst the fire did not burn for long, the lack of an organised firefighting response meant that it consumed everything of note, even though his NKVD troopers turned their hands to the task and performed valiantly.

Three of them had excruciating burns, sustained during forlorn rescue attempts.

His deputy's suggestion held merit.

"Very well, Comrade Durets. But have each man guarded... and each of the prisoner staff... there must be no conversation, am I clear?"

"Perfectly, Comrade Polkovnik."

Major Durets saluted and set to the task of organising the transfer of the wounded medical staff and NKVD soldiers to the POW medical facility which, although not up to the standard of the VNIIEF clinic, would suffice in the interim.

The door flew open without warning, causing Surgeon Lieutenant Commander Dryden to leap and spill his tea.

The protestations died on his lips as he saw what the NKVD guards were carrying.

"Over here... put him here..."

The words almost stopped in his throat, as if they were avoiding being exposed to the sight that fell before his eyes.

'Oh my God... how is this porr man still alive...'

Of course, everyone in the camp had heard the explosion but, with the apathy of those without hope, had thought little of it.

Now the after effects of it lay on the couch under Dryden's gaze.

"Major Durets... I'll need analgesia..."

The Russian looked blankly at him.

"Pain killers..."

The blank look remained.

Thinking quickly, Dryden fished in the medical bin, retrieving a small empty phial of some substance that he had used during an operation the night before.

The Russian language was as much a mystery to him as English was to Durets, but the label was clear.

The NKVD Major called an NCO to him and issued his orders.

As the soldier left, more casualties arrived.

Hamouda accompanied the second stretcher, and worked away at the throat of whatever it was that the rescuers had pulled from the fire.

The Egyptian tapped an item on the belt of one soldier, whose first thought was to strike the prisoner down.

Further taps made Hamouda's needs clear, and the NKVD trooper reluctantly gave up his bayonet.

The blade opened up the casualty's neck, and the rush of air was loud enough to be heard by all.

Hamouda grabbed a note pad and ripped the card backing from it, fashioning a large V-shape, which he inserted into the wound to keep the airway open.

As he did so, the man died, the combination of fluid loss and shock too much for life to continue.

The room was filled with guards, casualties, and the POW staff, something which was making effective work very difficult.

"Hany... triage... those with a good chance stay here... others... mess hall."

The Egyptian Lieutenant nodded and set to work, suddenly appointed arbiter of life and death.

For every casualty retained in the main room, two were sent to the dining room.

Dryden's eyes nearly came out of his head when the NKVD NCO returned with more pain-killing drugs than he had seen since being taken captive all those months ago.

He grabbed a handful of what were very clearly opiates of US manufacture.

"Collins! Collins!"

The big NCO moved to his side quickly.

"Get those into the dining room... tell Lieutenant Hamouda to do what is necessary, understood."

"I'm on it, Sir."

Julius Collins took most of the remaining opiates to the dining room, where Hamouda quickly set to work easing pain and suffering and, with extra administrations, moved the casualties quickly to the next life.

1829 hrs, Thursday, 25th July 1946, Prison Camp 1001, Akhtubinsk, USSR.

Dryden and Hamouda were exhausted, as were everyone concerned with the care of the injured.

Skryabin had visited twice during the hectic times and, unusually for the NKVD commander, had left them alone, resorting to observation alone.

Durets remained throughout, even assisting on two occasions when hands were needed and rank was not in question.

Only one casualty had returned from the dining room to the main room, whereas three had made the reverse journey.

The dining room was now a temporary morgue, housing seventeen badly burned bodies.

Five others lay under observation, most with some chance of clinging to life.

The medicines that had suddenly become available to Dryden and his team staggered them and, as they fought to preserve the lives of their enemy, old habits died hard, and many items simply vanished, squirreled away for a time when the Soviets were not so beneficent.

Skryabin returned, this time with four guards and a man in a white coat, a man clearly in pain.

One of the NKVD commander's men was there to translate.

"Doctor, this man is from our farm facility, where he tends the experimental livestock. He fell off a ladder and broke his arm.

393

Polkovnik Skryabin demands that you fix him so he can return to work."

That wasn't quite what the man said, his English letting him down in places, but Dryden filled in the gaps and changed a word or two.

Gesturing towards a chair, the naval officer rummaged for a pair of scissors and started to cut away the coat and shirt surrounding the open fracture.

The man remained silent, despite what must have been excruciating pain.

Exposing the wound site, Dryden, flush with pain relief, elected to administer a modest amount of morphine.

It brought immediate relief to the silent man.

As Dryden sized up the wound, he became aware that he was under intense scrutiny from the NKVD Colonel, more so than usual… and that, in fact, the scrutiny was equally split between him and his charge.

Dryden, a lover of who-dun-its, especially the likes of Sherlock Holmes, had his senses aroused by something that was clearly not as it was suggested.

As he gently moved the broken limb, he realised that the hand he held was clean and soft, and not the hand of a farm worker, even one responsible for experimental livestock…

'… whatever they may bloody be!'

His mind started to check off a few things that he started to understand were a little out of place.

The casualty smelt of soap.

He was reasonably well fed.

Hair was groomed.

Clothes were of reasonably good quality.

Dryden's mind started to deal with all that information and then found something that puzzled him. He realised that the injured man was not looking at the wound and what the doctor was doing, but was instead watching Skryabin like a hawk, whilst trying hard not to look like he was watching Skryabin like a hawk.

'The plot thickens.'

Dryden bought himself some more time by examining the breathing and pulse of the casualty. He noticed something else about the man, something that grew from a query into a certainty.

He was Jewish.

'Well kempt… clean… Jewish… obviously someone important enough to warrant the attention of Skryabin… what the bloody hell?'

A soldier had walked in and reported to Skryabin, momentarily distracting him.

At lightning speed, the casualty's other hand had shot out and back, unseen by anyone save Dryden.

The wound required traction and the two doctors worked together to prepare to pull the broken bones back into place.

Topping up the morphine with a further dose, Dryden lapsed into English to tell the casualty what was happening.

"We're just going to straighten your arm now, old chap. Shouldn't hurt too much."

The man looked at him and then at the place his hand had briefly touched in that unguarded moment.

The injured man whispered with a mix of fear and urgency.

"Just get it out, Vrach, whatever you do, just get it out."

A Nagant nuzzled the side of Dryden's head before he could even think of whispering a questioning reply.

"No more talking, Dryden. Just mend him."

Skryabin's words were repeated by the soldier with the English language skills, but it was the lunatic colonel's finger on the trigger.

Hany and he pulled on the limb and despite the morphine, the man gave a shrill cry and passed out.

With the arm purged of dead material, wound stitched, and partially in plaster, the 'livestock handler' was taken away, leaving Dryden and Hamouda time to sit down for the first time since the whole invasion of their hospital had started, or in Dryden's case, second time, counting the visit he had just made to the lavatory, where he found the cigarette butt in his tunic pocket.

Three guards remained in the main room, but they seemed only alert and concerned when the POWs interacted with the injured, paying little or no attention at other times.

A simple ploy had determined that none spoke English, so the two men spoke in whispers over their second cup of tea of the day.

Dryden put forward his theory.

Hamouda could only shrug and admit that he missed it.

"I didn't notice, to be honest. He seemed just like everyone else here."

Dryden laughed, drawing a gaze from one of the NKVD soldiers.

The gaze moved one and the naval officer leant forward and lowered his voice.

"You should read more Conan-Doyle, Hany."

"Find me one and I'll read it."

'Fair point.'

"Anyway... listen in... the bugger passed me something, but I'm damned if I know what. But when we were about to set his arm, he looked at me and said 'get it out, get it out'."

He sat back and swigged the last of his tea, feigning relaxation when he was anything but.

"Whatever it is, it's bloody important to him... but it's gobbledygook, makes no damned sense at all."

Julius Collins and Murdo Robertson walked in, having just organised the cleaning and layout of the dining room, now that the cadavers had been removed by a POW work detail.

"Ah, RSM. Will you and Collins please be so kind as to watch over our charges for a little while? Lieutenant Hamouda and I are going to get some air. We won't be long... just round the building, so we'll be at hand if needed."

Robertson swung up his trademark immaculate salute.

"No problem, Sah. We'll look after 'em for ye."

Out in the warm evening sun, the day took on a new complexion, and the two settled down to bask in the rays, or that was what they intended to look like.

Dryden produced the cigarette butt, which clearly had been unravelled previously, despite his best efforts to make it look like a normal discard being recycled.

Hamouda examined the message which, as far as he was concerned, might as well have been in Urdu.

'AKNEPSU-65AB141/63RK29-29U532...'

"A map reference... library filing code... shipment information?"

"No idea, Hany, but it was important enough for him to give it to me, and for him to break his arm deliberately to do it."

"What?"

Dryden accepted the message back and rewound the cigarette butt as he spoke.

"On the wound, there were the marks of a patterned sole. He never fell off a ladder, Hany. His arm was stamped on,

396

deliberately… and he's no farm hand either. He was brought to us through choice… I could see it in his eyes. He's Jewish, well kempt, clean and well-fed… as out of place here as a pork sausage in a synagogue… sorry, no offence."

The Muslim officer smiled, used to such unintended slips.

"Then we must get his message out."

"How… and to whom."

Dryden laughed.

"The latter is easiest, as there is an address further on… you missed it, didn't you."

They paused as two NKVD guards strolled round in a relaxed fashion.

"The former is the hard part."

Actually, it wasn't.

2242 hrs, Thursday, 25th July 1946, Arzamas-2510, VNIIEF Secret Facility within Prison Camp 1001, Akhtubinsk, USSR.

They waited until they were alone before speaking.

"Sorry, my son. I'm so sorry."

"It had to be done, father. Enough already."

Passing a cup of cool water to his injured son, the senior man, owner of the foot that had broken the arm, sat down beside him.

"Well?"

"The Englishman appeared intelligent enough… he's a doctor after all."

The son's face split with the broadest of grins, as did that of his father, Doctor Jakob Steyn.

"Thank you, Professor David. Praise indeed."

"I'm sure he understood. Anyway, we've done what we can with the opportunity the fire presented. Let's pray to Hashem for success."

"Indeed."

The two fell into silence and pleaded with their God for success, and, as always with Jakob Steyn, thanked the creator for the mercy he brought by reuniting him with the son he thought long dead.

The two Steyns were now part of the VNIIEF project and vitally important to its advance.

This they both knew, and worked as slowly as they could possibly do, aware that discovery of their low cooperation level would sentence the other to death, something that they were constantly reminded of when Soviet scientists needed work done, or experiments created.

German intelligence had prematurely promulgated news of each man's death, in order to remove them from Allied thinking. It was an oft-used ploy. In this case, it also served the Soviets well, given that many German camp records had long since been destroyed.

Whilst there had been nothing but silence as they made their intonations, both men felt their prayers had been answered, and took to their bunks believing that Hashem would lend a helping hand.

1009 hrs, Friday, 26th July 1946, Prison Camp 1001, Akhtubinsk, USSR.

Another Red Cross team arrived, unanticipated, unexpected, and inconvenient.

None the less, they were admitted to the camp, and saw the site of the fire, and the temporary morgue containing those who had perished.

They also visited the survivors, believing the living and the dead to be prisoners.

Conversation with Dryden and Hamouda, or any of the orderlies, was discouraged, and more than once an NKVD arm came between a Red Cross official and an inmate.

One low-level clerk was making notes for the inspector leading the mission and Dryden saw an opportunity.

Using only eye contact, he conveyed a message to Collins, who nodded his understanding.

The metal dish clattered to the floor and sent its contents flying.

Every eye was drawn, and none observed the glass phial being dropped into the open case.

Twenty minutes later, the inspection of the hospital over, the case and its precious contents were mobile to another two nearby POW camps, the first just outside of Verkhiny Baskunchak, and the second at the airfield from which they were due to fly home that very afternoon.

2229 hrs, Friday, 26th July 1946, Grossglockener, Carinthia, Austria.

At precisely 1600, the Lockheed Constellation transport aircraft, sporting distinctive Red Cross markings, and guaranteed safe passage by all belligerents, took off from Akhtubinsk air base for the non-stop flight back to Geneva.

The Red Cross inspection team settled down for the nearly seven and a half hour journey to Switzerland.

Six and a half hours later, the aircraft drove into the highest peak in Austria.

There were no survivors.

1058 hrs, Saturday, 27th July 1946, Schloss Hartenfels, Torgau, Germany.

"Come."

The door to Nazarbayeva's private rooms opened swiftly, and Poboshkin almost tumbled through the opening in his haste to inform his commander.

"Good morning, Comrade General. I hope you slept well?"

The words were said in such a way as to be different to the normal morning pleasantries.

"I did, thank you, Andrey, and from that, I assume that you hold something of great importance."

Wearing only a crisp white shirt and loose trousers, Nazarbayeva looked every inch the Russian mother, albeit prettier than most.

"I certainly do, Comrade General."

"One moment."

She poured tea for them both and sat at her small private desk.

"Proceed, comrade."

Poboshkin slid one of the folders in front of her.

"The staff have worked through the night and prepared this document."

He sat down at Nazarbayeva's invitation.

"We revisited every report, cross-referenced everything, and what you see is our best effort at predicting the present level of their forces."

The front cover had announced that the folder contained the intelligence assessment of the DRH.

Nazarbayeva raised the cup to her lips but never made it the full distance, as the words and numbers she was reading washed through her eyes and penetrated her brain.

The cup made it back to the saucer and she flipped through the pages, took in the information and built a picture that all was not as it had seemed, and that their worst fears had been realised.

She skipped to the last page, where the report contained the customary summary sheet.

399

"Mudaks!"

Poboshkin, sipping his tea, could only nod in agreement.

"I have to ask, Andrey... the staff worked this all up on the basis of information we already had?"

Her inference was obvious.

"Yes, Comrade General, but with the different interpretations that our suspicions aroused. There was some fresh information, but most of this we already had... we'd just not interpreted it correctly... well... we had, but differently."

She held out a conciliatory hand.

"The best was done at the time. Now is a different time and," she closed the document and tapped her fingers on it, "We have done our best again."

She rose and poured more tea, selecting an apple and a pear from the small display.

Tossing the apple to her aide, she sat back down.

"Help yourself when you've finished that one."

She bit into the pear and savoured the fresh flesh and juices.

"You're sure about these figures?"

Poboshkin gave a little shrug.

"As sure as I can be, Comrade General. I took presentations from the staff on their interpretations, and all seemed founded in logic and backed by a great deal of fact. I've signed off on the report, and believe it is our best estimate of the German field army."

That it was twice previous estimates was the enormous stand-out point.

"Andrey, I'm struggling to understand how our estimates could have been so far out. What's the factor here?"

Again he shrugged.

"We saw what we wanted to see... or possibly, what they wanted us to see. As ever, Comrade General, we're restricted by our lack of reconnaissance, loss of agents across Europe, and their increasingly effective maskirovka."

"Example please."

"One of those we have highlighted is the arrival of a large number of troops by ship, probably from Amerika. It had been assumed that they were returning German prisoners, and that they would take time to integrate and get ready for combat. The information we had at the time supported that view, Comrade General."

Poboshkin flicked through his notebook.

"We had a report from 1st Red Banner Front that suggested one of its prisoners was from that convoy. He was part of a German unit fully equipped with Amerikanski equipment. Review of our information seems to suggest that from arrival to capture, the German prisoner was in Europe for less than six days. The report was flawed, so I sent off for the medical examination file on the prisoner."

The notebook rustled as he found what he was looking for.

"That report came in last night, and detailed a medical examination of five German soldiers taken prisoner by 1st Red Banner on that date, and at three separate locations. I explored that further and established that they came from three different formations, all equipped with Amerikanski weapons."

Nazarbayeva tossed her pear core at the bin, the metallic ring punctuating Poboshkin's words.

"The physical health of the soldiers was exceptional... I use the physician's word, Comrade General... exceptional. Well fed, well developed, and in the peak of health."

"So that would suggest that the Germanski were trained and converted outside of Europe, and arrived combat-ready."

"Yes, Comrade General."

"Another example please, Andrey."

"At least three camps that we had identified as being rehabilitation centres for Germanski soldiers were, in fact, military training sites. Our loss of assets on the ground damaged our understanding, Comrade General."

Her silence drew him on.

"It seems likely that there has been some confusion in identifying troop nationalities... uniform... weapons... vehicles... the normal initial pointers are all confused as it appears the Amerikanski have handed over a lot of equipment, much more than the NKVD and our own reports indicated."

She could only smile at Poboshkin's weak attempt to fend off some of the inevitable blame that would fall on GRU-Europe.

"Could we have done better, Andrey?"

He needed little time to think.

"Yes, Comrade General... most certainly we could have done better... but our efforts and interpretations were sound at the time, all save one distinct problem that we have, unfortunately, repeated."

She drained her tea and licked her lips slowly, knowing what her man was about to say.

Nazarbayeva said it for him.

"We have underestimated the Germanski powers of resilience again, haven't we?"

Poboshkin nodded gently, as if not saying it made the error less weighty.

They sat in silence, sharing their thoughts only with themselves, avoiding eye contact as both minds sought out the bottom line.

Nazarbayeva spoke first.

"Well, the responsibility is mine, and mine alone. Make twenty copies of that report. Have them ready for twelve. I'll decide what I'm doing by then. Thank you, Andrey... and thank the staff from me. I'll speak to them shortly, but for now, I have other things to attend to. Leave me that," she grabbed her copy of the report, "And get things moving straight away. Thank you, Comrade."

Poboshkin took his leave and closed the door.

Nazarbayeva picked up the phone, hesitating momentarily as she decided whom to call first.

She elected the practical approach, not the political skin-saving one, and spoke into the receiver in reply to the Communications officer's question.

"Get me Marshal Vasilevsky urgently."

Her previous dealings with Marshal Vasilevsky had been pleasant and professional, her most recent conversation had been less so, and she didn't blame the harassed commander of the Red Banner Forces of Soviet Europe one little bit.

To be disturbed on his rest day with the news that the German field Army was probably twice its reported size was something guaranteed to wreck his day, and he vented his spleen on the hapless GRU officer.

Regaining control, Vasilevsky apologised, and made notes from Nazarbayeva's reading of the report.

The call ended in strained fashion.

Her next call was to Stalin himself, and went even worse.

The General Secretary ranted and raved down the line, so much so that Nazarbayeva had to hold the receiver from her ear to prevent lasting damage.

She was ordered back to Moscow immediately, and left in no doubt that her career, probably life, was in the balance.

Within seven minutes of ending the call, her recently appointed deputy, Major General Nikita Olofurov, was in her quarters, and was given verbal orders to take her place until further notice.

Nazarbayeva didn't care for Olofurov for a number of reasons.

His awful bad breath had been the first, that he was Beria's man was the last, knowledge for which she was indebted to Kaganovich, the deputy head of the NKVD, who had revealed the true nature of the man's appointment.

Within another minute, Lieutenant General Dustov, the NKVD liaison officer with the Red Banner Headquarters, presented himself in her quarters, informing her that he had been expressly charged with placing her on the next flight to Moscow... and more.

Dustov had only just returned to duty following wounds sustained during the Allied Heracles mission against Nordhausen.

However, although he felt distinctly uncomfortable with his orders, and despite his personal admiration for Nazarbayeva, he intended to carry them out to the letter, a fact attested to by the two SMG equipped soldiers at his back.

Nazarbayeva had found time to quickly dress in her full uniform, but found time for little else, as Dustov was insistent that they leave for the airfield immediately.

Poboshkin arrived with the requested copies of the report and placed them in her briefcase.

"Are there any orders, Comrade Mayor General?"

Olofurov went to speak, but realised that the aide was addressing Nazarbayeva.

She smiled at her man's display of loyalty.

"None, thank you, Comrade Polkovnik, except to ensure the staff keep working. Thank you, Andrey."

Her use of his name made his chest swell with pride, as it was a deliberate public airing of her own loyalty to her aide.

Dustov broke the moment unceremoniously.

"I have orders for you too, Polkovnik Poboshkin. You are to accompany us to Moscow... immediately."

Poboshkin exchanged a confused look with his commander, before gaining control of himself.

With all the major players now in place, Dustov discharged his duty... reluctantly.

"General Nazarbayeva... Polkovnik Poboshkin... by order of Marshal Beria, commander of the NKVD, I arrest you both on suspicion of treason against the State, collusion with the enemy, and military incompetence. Hand over your weapons immediately."

He nodded to his two soldiers, who moved forward to accept the officer's side arms.

"I am instructed by Marshal Beria to shoot both of you on the slightest sign of non-compliance with my instructions."

Without any further instruction, another two NKVD soldiers appeared and seized the two pistols, plus Nazarbayeva's briefcase, as ordered by Dustov.

"Now, with regret, Comrade Mayor General. If you please."

He indicated the door, the party marched off, moving a few steps closer to Moscow.

1238 hrs, Saturday, 27th July 1946, Private Dacha of the Deputy Head of NKVD, Kuntsevo, Moscow.

"Kaganovich."

The deputy head of the NKVD as less than happy, the sounds of two giggling women reaching his ears from the bedroom, where he had planned to spend the day enjoying their charms.

His plans changed in a few words.

"When?"

He looked at his watch, the only thing he was wearing at that time.

"Quickly, man... why?"

He listened as Rufin spoke of the German Army report, and what had transpired when Nazarbayeva telephoned Moscow.

"But she's the Secretary's favourite... why would he..."

Rufin spoke over his master.

"What?"

In Torgau, Rufin repeated his information slowly and with more detail.

"One of our own officers overheard the arrest, Comrade Leytenant General."

Rufin was sufficiently switched on to use Kaganovich's new rank, something that went straight over the General's head as he waited on confirmation of what he had first heard.

"The arrest was made on the direct orders of Comrade Marshal Beria, of that I am absolutely sure, Comrade Leytenant General."

He redigested the information, and still found it unpalatable.

"And Olofurov?"

"Strutting like a peacock, Comrade Leytenant General."

"Keep an eye on him. Who's replaced Poboshkin?"

"No-one as yet, Comrade Leytenant General, but I would expect that Comrade Orlov will be nominated, He's just returned from a prolonged sickness absence, so will be considered untainted. He would be my bet."

Kaganovich thought for a moment.

'At least he isn't Beria's man.'

"You were right to ring me. Good work, Comrade Rufin. Keep it up and keep me informed."

He replaced the receiver gingerly, unhappy that his day of cavorting was over pretty much before it began, but more unhappy that a key element in his planning was now at risk.

He lifted the telephone again and gave a clipped instruction.

"Good morning, Comrade Marshal. I need to see you urgently."

He looked at his watch again.

"13.30 will be fine. Usual place? Thank you."

He tapped the telephone a number of times.

"Have my driver and car report to me here for thirteen-hundred."

Kaganovich ended the call without another word, or even waiting to hear a response.

He reflected quickly on how he would pass on the news, and tried to anticipate what the man would say.

Floundering on both points, Kaganovich busied himself making his excuses to the twin sisters, Sonia and Ludmilla Laberova, as he dressed himself informally, as best suited the intended surroundings for his meeting with VKG.

1500 hrs, Sunday, 27th July 1946, United States Embassy, Grosvenor Square, London.

Ambassador Winant had long since finished describing how the pretty garden of the embassy had been converted back to a habitable space after the departure of the British WAAFs and the barrage balloon called 'Romeo' that they crewed.

The US Army senior officers had listened dutifully and, one by one, had drifted away, until Winant himself found other distractions, leaving the most senior men to their own company.

As usual, Eisenhower was smoking like a chimney, feeding his incessant craving for nicotine, something he had avoided during the formal lunch in the main residence.

405

Gerow and Simpson had finished their discussion on the recent rumours from home and were drinking coffee in silence.

Bedell-Smith was making a few notes in his diary, recording his thoughts on the service of celebration at Westminster Abbey, and on the unfortunate waiter who spilt a water jug over the Argentinian Ambassador's wife.

Eisenhower had overheard some of the discussion on the stateside rioting, and ventured an opinion to Bradley who had naturally migrated to his side.

"Seattle, San Francisco, Detroit, Chicago, Boston, New York... all with curfews... Abilene and Charlotteville half burnt to the ground by reports... scores dead and wounded. What the hell is going on, Brad?"

"The war has become unpopular for sure, either for its nature or the way it's being fought, and certainly because of the casualties we've sustained... well... that's a lot for the folks back home to stomach. Not sure about Abilene, but sure as eggs is eggs, the families in Charlottesville lost a lot of their kin when the 29th Division got hammered... an awful lot of their kin."

The 29th US Infantry had attracted an unenviable reputation as the highest casualty rated combat unit in the US Army, bar none. Its recent return to the front had resulted in the virtual destruction of its 115th Infantry Regiment and the 29th Reconnaissance Troop, and clearly the flood of telegrams back home had agitated an already unhappy civil population.

"Our casualty figures were on the way down, Brad... and now the Germans have replaced most of your boys in the line, they will continue on down."

Ike leant forward, keeping his words for Bradley alone.

"Cutting down on infantry attacks, bumping up artillery and air work... it's reaping benefits, of course... but we're less effective. Let's hope the Germans can get things moving for us... and the British..."

Both men knew that McCreery was about to launch a limited offensive, one for a more political reason than any military one.

Churchill wanted to be seen to take some of the load alongside the German Army, and so a limited operation in Northern Germany had come into creation.

"Mind you, the Brits have their own problems."

He alluded to the recent demonstration which, whilst peaceful and respectful of the celebration, had thousands gathered outside the cathedral, complete with damning signage and loud voices, both condemning the continued war and the loss of sons, brothers, and fathers.

The previous day's unfortunate shooting of seven demonstrators in Glasgow was not yet known to them.

Bradley took a sip of his drink and sat back in the comfortable garden chair.

"Do you think the President will ever use the bomb on the Commies?"

Eisenhower lit another cigarette from the stub of his present one.

"I think he'd secretly like to. Heck, no. Of course he would, He dropped it on the Nips, didn't he? Use of it would ease the casualties, which in turn would ease pressure at home, of course."

He left some of his reply out.

Bradley filled in the blanks.

"But would it work, for a start eh? Where would they target? Industrial, political, military?"

"You got that right, Brad, plus, the President seems to feel any advantage gained from using the bomb would be lost in additional political err... disharmony between the Allies, and even worse, more demonstrations at home."

"Really, Ike? There were rallies, hasty and hot words for sure, but worse than of late... worse than Abilene and Charlottesville?"

Eisenhower accepted a sweet pastry from an immaculately turned-out waiter, waiting until the man had moved away before continuing.

"From what George told me, there's virtually no one left undecided any more," he spoke of Marshall, the Army's CoS, "The anti-bomb movement is growing fast, fuelled by these damn pictures of horribly burnt children... you've seen the things... heard the stories... they've had an effect at home and it's not getting any better. The pro-bomb lobby is growing even faster, fuelled by rhetoric from people like the Governor of New York, Edmund Dewey. He lost his boy at Fulda, and he's taken it bad. He's become a focus for the 'By all available means' movement, and he's been doing a damn fine job of it, from what George believes. Actually, all over the States, crowds are being whipped up by politicians, either for their own beliefs, or with another agenda, George wasn't sure which at times, but whipped up they all are. Anyway, we have our new rules of combat and the President has taken the bomb off the table... for now anyway."

Bradley finished up his pastry and rubbed his hands to clear the last residue of crumbs from his fingertips.

"So… we get to fight the goddamn war with people at home trying to drag the carpet out from under us or push us into precipitous action… without being able to use the Army as it should be used… either without the best weapon our experts can provide us with or encouraged by others wanting us to chuck it indiscriminately at anything that has a red star on it… and all as we try to work side by side with a bunch of Allies whose commitment to the cause wanes with each passing day, Britain and Germany excepted."

"And the French, Brad. De Gaulle's rock solid and, from what I understand, is for dropping the bombs all over the Russians tomorrow…"

Bradley interrupted.

"…but his people think differently, as we've seen in Marseilles and Bordeaux. They seem to be sick of the war and just happy to have their country back, whereas the Brigadier wants to put France back in the major league with a display of military muscle."

Eisenhower looked around him before adding to Bradley's comments.

"Which doesn't seem to be happening. Apart from De Lattre's army, there's precious little else of substance available, despite the promise of another hundred thousand bayonets!"

Bradley snorted. His opinion of French promises and, for that matter, the French leader were well known.

He leant forward to catch Eisenhower's softer delivery.

"Internal problems like the Bordeaux and Marseille riots have caused a lot of problems. Lots of lower level stuff happening throughout France as we know. French morale simply doesn't seem to measure up to De Gaulle's ambitions. Anyway, De Lattre's boys are pretty good and have stayed in the line with the Germans for now…"

Eisenhower grinned.

"Not that I need to tell you that. Sorry, Brad."

Bradley raised his coffee cup in mock salute and fired a rare shot of humour at his commander.

"Age gets us all in the end, General."

Eisenhower laughed and joined him in sampling the excellent coffee.

"I'll drink to that, Brad."

"Don't spill it now."

"Damn Missourians… bane of my life."

They laughed, the double meaning understood, and lapsed into comfortable silence.

*The stern hand of fate has scourged us to an elevation where we can
see the great everlasting things that matter for a nation; the great
peaks of honour we had forgotten - duty and patriotism, clad in
glittering white; the great pinnacle of sacrifice pointing like a
rugged finger to heaven.*

David Lloyd George

*Heroism on command, senseless violence, and all the loathsome
nonsense that goes by the name of patriotism - how passionately I
hate them!*

Albert Einstein

Chapter 165 - THE BRITISH

0803 hrs, Sunday, 28th July 1946, office of the General Secretary, the Kremlin, Moscow, USSR.

Stalin's face remained straight, emotionless, and showed no reaction to Beria's words.

"Both her and her aide have been questioned regarding this clear failure. I confess, Comrade General Secretary that, as yet, they have not incriminated themselves... no more than the written evidence of their shocking failures," he picked up the folder that Nazarbayeva had been given by Poboshkin the previous day, producing it like a barrister in court, as irrefutable evidence of guilt.

He placed it carefully back on the desk.

"Further questioning will bring more evidence, and I'm absolutely sure she was involved with the traitor Pekunin."

Stalin reacted with studied calm.

"She killed the traitor Pekunin... and there has never been any proof of her involvement with whatever he was planning. You've looked and come up with an empty hand."

Beria polished his glasses furiously.

"I will find it, Comrade General Secretary..." he corrected himself quickly... "If it's there, I **will** drag it out of her."

He emphasised 'will' very deliberately.

Stalin rose and tugged his tunic into place, making Beria automatically stand in his presence.

The dictator walked around the table and stood directly in front of his NKVD chairman.

"So, Lavrentiy, let me understand this matter clearly."

He counted off the points on his fingers one by one.

"I ordered the woman back to Moscow to account for her actions... to me... **to me**... yet you decided to have her arrested in her own headquarters and escorted back to here... and then place her in your basement and interrogate her before I've had a chance to question her?"

"Yes, Comrade General Secretary."

"Sit down."

Stalin walked to the window and exercised silence as only he could; a silence full of menace and ill portents.

"Your obsession with her is well known."

He turned and made an unexpected concession.

"We have both brought death to the door of her and her family... for the good of the Motherland, of course."

Menace returned as quickly as it had faded.

"But you have arrested her for treason, and there is not a shred of evidence for that accusation... NOT ONE!"

He leant forward and spoke in a softer tone.

"Unless your own investigation was faulty... or you have kept something from me, Lavrentiy?"

"Just because there is no evidence yet, doesn't mean I won't find any, Comrade General Secretary. With her detention, I can now employ more tried and trusted methods which, I'm sure, will produce the results we need."

"You need! Your obsession has overcome your reason, Lavrentiy."

He resumed his seat and picked up the folder.

"These errors... these mistakes in understanding the full situation... you made the same errors... you did. Should I have you arrested, Comrade Beria?"

The polishing stopped in a heartbeat.

"We followed some of the GRU assumptions... that is regrettable, but there is no hint of any treachery from me or my department. We are loyal to you and the Motherland."

Beria was flustered and it showed.

"They are the same thing, Comrade."

"Yes... yes, indeed, Comrade General Secretary... indeed."

"So, we have Nazarbayeva arrested and in the Lubyanka for doing exactly what your own service did, and your justification is

410

an unproven... but fully investigated... suggestion... your suggestion... that she might have been linked to Pekunin's treachery... the same Pekunin that she executed on my orders... and, in the process of discharging those orders, was badly wounded."

Stalin lit his pipe as Beria's normally sharp brain realised there had been an error and he had overplayed his hand.

Inside he cursed himself for acting too quickly, but he had sensed the opportunity to rid himself of the bitch once and for all.

'Stick with the plan, you fool... just stick with the plan.'

"I understand your view, Comrade General Secretary, and I can assure you I acted in what I thought were the best interests of you and the Motherland. As ever, you have identified an error in my haste to be of service. I apologise."

Stalin raised his eyebrows, for no other reason than to view the squirming of his NKVD chief more clearly.

He held out an unexpected olive branch.

"None the less, there have been failings within our intelligence services, have there not?"

"Yes, Comrade General Secretary, and I have already acted to deal with the ones in my department."

"How?"

"Three of my senior officers have already confessed to failures in their systems and management of those under their command. They have been executed on my orders..." he took a quick look at the ticking clock, "...Seventy minutes ago, Comrade General Secretary."

"As efficient as ever in dealing with those who have transgressed, Lavrentiy."

The sarcasm in Stalin's voice was noted.

"None the less, GRU have failed in their duties, as you say, and examples must be made. You have shown me the way."

Beria's insides churned at his own unusual ineptitude in understanding how things would work out.

"Comrade Nazarbayeva, as with you, cannot be held responsible for this fuck up. You have found those more worthy of punishment within the NKVD. I'm sure similar culprits can be found within her headquarters."

Beria nodded.

"So, we understand each other, Lavrentiy?"

"Yes, Comrade General Secretary."

"She's important to the Motherland. Play your games as you always do, but never go over my head in regard to this woman again... never... ever."

411

"Yes, Comrade General Secretary."

"Now, attend to her release, and the other details."

Dismissed by no more than a look, Marshal Beria left Stalin's office smarting from both Stalin's words and his own failure, and with a reinforced hatred of the GRU bitch.

1223 hrs, Sunday, 28th July 1946, office of the General Secretary, the Kremlin, Moscow, USSR.

Nazarbayeva stood at full attention in an immaculate uniform, the only inklings that all was not how it should be were the split lip, bruised cheek, and some missing medals, the result of an enthusiastic questioner who decided that ripping the awards from the woman's chest was an excellent pre-cursor to slapping her around.

Stalin stood and walked around Molotov to where she was standing, embracing the still shocked GRU officer, and kissing her on both cheeks with seemingly genuine warmth and affection.

"Please, sit, Comrade Nazarbayeva. Tea?"

She did as she was told, but declined the tea, for fear of dribbling the hot liquid down her tunic through lips that had still to recover their feeling.

"I wanted you back in Moscow to answer for the errors of your department. You know I had to do that, Comrade General. But I did NOT..." he slammed his hand on the desk, making Nazarbayeva jump, "... Did not order your detention, nor did I have anything to do with that."

He pointed at her injuries, both those to her person and her pride, the missing Hero Award making him react in an unexpected fashion.

He fished in his top drawer.

"Comrade Mayor General, as an apology, I ask you to please accept this medal in the stead of the one you have mislaid."

He moved around to her side of the table yet again, and she stood as he pinned his own award on her tunic, repeating the hug and kiss routine with an equal amount of genuine affection.

"Sit."

He resumed his seat and leant forward, wringing his peasant hands, almost in a show of supplication.

"Comrade Beria did what he thought was correct, although excessively so. He'll apologise to you in due course."

Beria had declined to be present for the reinstatement of Nazarbayeva, citing pressing department reasons, an excuse Stalin had accepted for expediency's sake only.

412

Molotov was only there for unconnected reasons, but took the opportunity to stow away a few snippets to relay to Beria later.

"A brief investigation has established that the blame was not yours, and you have been exonerated. I hope you'll continue to serve Mother Russia to the best of your abilities, Comrade Nazarbayeva?"

"That has always been my only concern, my only duty, Comrade General Secretary."

"Excellent. Then this matter is behind us, in part at least."

He pulled out the file on the DRA.

"This... this abomination cannot be permitted to happen again, are we clear, Comrade Mayor General?"

"Yes, Comrade General Secretary. I apologise. We should have understood the information better, and armed you and Marshal Vasilevsky with more accurate details."

Stalin held up his hand, halting her immediately.

"Enough. Errors have been made, those responsible punished, lessons have been learned. We will move on, Comrade. The NKVD also repeated those errors," Stalin could not help himself but to crow just a little, "Something of which I reminded Marshal Beria when he had you arrested."

Nazarbayeva nodded, still too in shock to really understand the point.

Her mind, fuzzy and indistinct, suddenly melted through the haze and focussed on one point.

"Those responsible, include me, Comrade General Secretary. That is in my report."

He looked at the document and nodded like a sage of old.

"Ah yes, true, Comrade Nazarbayeva. But its author was another, and clearly the initial responsibility was his. His confession under questioning was sufficient."

"Sufficient..."

"Sufficient for prompt action, Comrade Nazarbayeva. Now, let me not keep you. Take two days to recover... there is a suite for you in the Hotel National... enjoy some rest and return to your duties reinvigorated. Organise yourself, and then take some leave with your husband. I will ensure he's available."

She had only really comprehended the initial words.

"Comrade General Secretary, may I ask what prompt action has been taken?"

He had never really expected not to tell her everything, so was ready to answer the inevitable question.

413

"Polkovnik Poboshkin confessed and was executed this morning."

He picked a list out of his second drawer.

"Of your staff, the following members confessed to deliberately sabotaging intelligence efforts and presenting you with false information, for which treasonable acts they have paid in full... Polkovnik Poboshkin, Mayor Ergotin, Kapitan Guvarin, and Mladshy Leytenant Pinkerova. You were badly served by your staff. Choose your replacements wisely, Comrade Mayor General."

Nazarbayeva's mind was in a whirl and she couldn't think straight.

Most of her staff... almost all of her inner sanctum... gutted by the NKVD and the wrath of Beria.

'Andrey... loyal Andrey...'

In her grieving mind, a happy and smiling face replaced that of her now dead aide.

'Maya... innocent... what a brain...lost... betrayed...'

Stalin interrupted her melancholy.

"Comrade Nazarbayeva... Comrade Nazarbayeva!"

She shook herself free of it all.

"Apologies, Comrade General Secretary. I... err..."

"Yes, I know. It must come as a shock to learn of their betrayal... it always does when the closest of your circle fail you, Tatiana."

She missed the sarcasm in his voice completely, and Molotov's muted but nonetheless very real reaction.

"Comrade Nazarbayeva, I will arrange movement orders and leave for you and your husband at Sochi, and will ensure that my private dacha is made available for your use."

Stalin stood and extended an arm towards the door, indicating that the female officer should now depart.

"Now, Comrade Mayor General... go and rest at the National, then enjoy your leave and return to your headquarters reinvigorated and ready to serve the party and Motherland."

"I'll not let the Motherland down, Comrade General Secretary."

She saluted smartly and was gone.

Stalin looked at the closed door and his eyes narrowed.

He kept his thoughts to himself.

Breaking away from them, he turned to Molotov.

"Right, Vyacheslav, the Italians, and the Greeks?"

1333 hrs, Sunday, 28th July 1946, south of Neu Matzlow, Parchim, Germany.

The attack hadn't so much faltered as simply run out of steam logistically.

The Red Army had put up heavy resistance, mainly infantry, artillery, and anti-tank guns, and they had been overrun eventually by a combination of British artillery, RAF ground attack aircraft, Guards tanks, and, as normal, the poor bloody infantry.

The Battlegroup based around the 2nd Battalion, Grenadier Guards had ground to a halt in the rough ground overlooking the ex-Luftwaffe air base at Schwerin-Parchim, just under five hundred metres to the east.

Fig # 204 - The battleground of Parchim and Spornitz

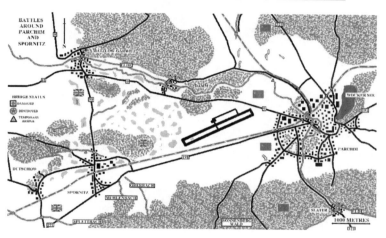

Here the Centurions found themselves with no visible enemy to stop them driving on, but with no fuel in their tanks to allow them to take advantage of the situation.

Additional pressure was unwittingly brought to bear upon the headquarters officers by the presence of Colonel Jacob 'Bunty' Hargreaves, recently arrived from divisional headquarters to check on progress and report back on his best view of how the attack could be pushed ahead.

The Battalion commander, Lieutenant Colonel Keith, and his staff, were turning the airwaves blue in their quest to find the missing fuel column, with little success.

415

A simple map reading error had deprived the Grenadiers of the necessary fluid of armoured warfare.

Meanwhile, the battalion adjutant was up with 'B' Squadron, the point unit, organising the siphoning of fuel from other vehicles in order to keep the drive going.

Fig # 205 - Limit of initial Allied advance, Parchim, Germany

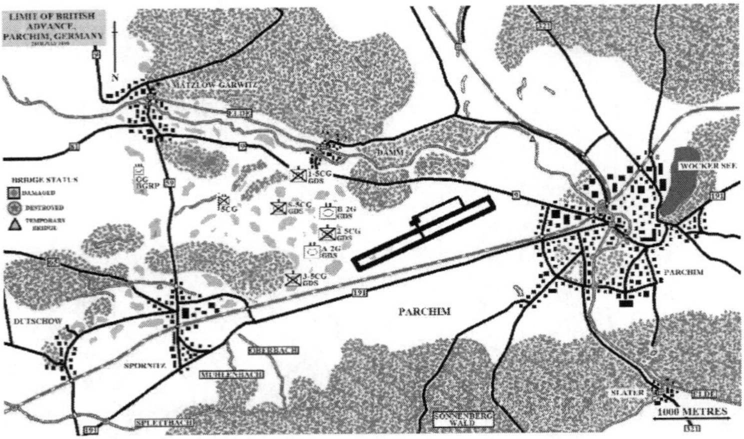

Acting Major Heywood passed on the Colonel's orders to 'A' Squadron, who reluctantly gave up half of their petrol, leaving enough for modest manoeuvre, and the rest was greedily consumed by the Centurion IIs of 'B' Squadron.

2nd Grenadiers had taken further hits since the battles around Lützow, and had been withdrawn as soon as the front had been stabilised.

'C' Squadron, until recently removed from the battalion for recuperation and for training with the new ammunition type, was on the road somewhere to the west, carried on M19 Diamond T transporters.

The Grenadiers' Centurion Is had all gone, and Centurion IIs now filled their ranks, as best they could, although insufficient numbers were available because of decidedly avoidable delays. Back in the home country, the decision to commence production of the new but untried Mark III had inadvertently crippled production of the Mark II, and arguments flared, which served neither the war effort nor the manufacturers, stuck in intransigence until Churchill himself stepped into the quarrel.

Eventually, the Mark II production lines were restarted and the proven vehicle, still equipped with the ubiquitous 17-pdr, started to flow from Britain to the continent in modest numbers, but never enough to satisfy the all-consuming modern battlefield.

The Mark III production line produced a few vehicles before some defects were detected, specifically with the gun stabiliser and mount, ensuring that the appearance of good numbers of the 84mm bore QF 20-pdr-equipped universal tanks were delayed.

The first versions, hurried across the English Channel, were greedily accepted into service. On Saturday 26th July, the first Mark III in action, crewed by men of the Irish Guards, destroyed five Soviet tanks outside of Ludwigslust, two of which were knocked out whilst on the move.

The stabilised 20-pdr, excellent power train, and upgraded armour protection made the Centurion III a formidable adversary.

There were just not enough of them.

Fig # 206 - Allied Order of Battle - Parchim, Germany.

ALLIED FORCES
BATTLE OF PARCHIM
28TH JULY 1946.

GG
BGRP

2GG
GDS

5CG
GDS

2WG
GDS

55RA
GDS

755
CBRS

'B' Squadron pushed on, screened by recon troopers from 2nd Welsh Guards, and supported by the mechanised companies of the 5th Battalion Coldstream Guards, leaving a disgruntled 'A' Squadron in hull-down positions to their rear.

Some of the Coldstreams rode on the flank tanks, providing close infantry support, should Soviet infantry try to interfere with the

Guards' advance. Their M3 halftracks had also yielded up the contents of their fuel tanks to keep the Centurions on the move.

The left flank troop took advantage of the good going offered by Route 9, and moved ahead of the main body, under orders, intent on securing a modest military bridge that aerial reconnaissance photographs had revealed.

It was set over the River Elde, which formed the northern border of the Battlegroup's advance, but offered opportunities for opening another line of attack on Parchim itself.

The engineer bridge also marked the most forward positions of the 10th Guards Army, positions the Red Army had been ordered to hold at all costs.

Fig # 207 - Renewed advance at Parchim, Germany.

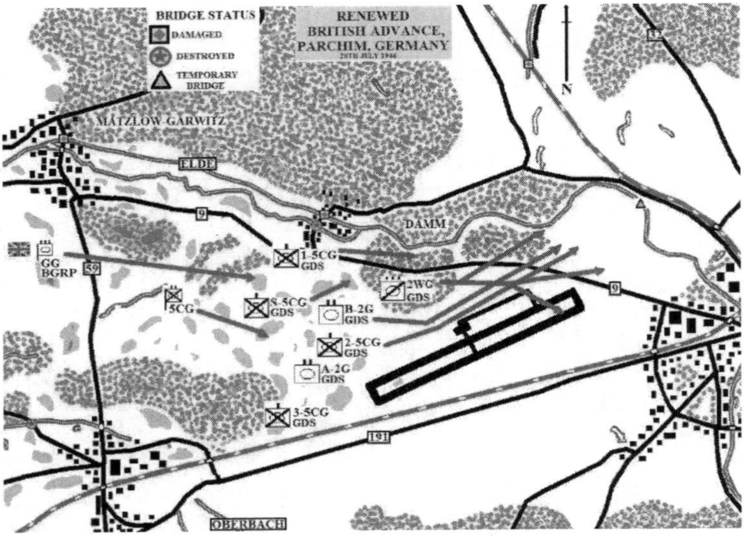

1413 hrs, Sunday, 28th July 1946, Elde River crossing, Parchim, Germany.

As the enemy force approached, the commanding NCO steadied his men.

"Wait, comrades… wait… the leading one's nearly to the mark."

A seemingly innocent broken road sign marked the location of the mines.

He pulled the stock of his favourite weapon tighter into his shoulder.

"Wait, lads…"

The Staghound armoured car staggered as the ground erupted under its rear wheels, the front set having failed to set off the teller mines concealed in a diamond pattern in the dusty track.

Pulling the trigger, the Soviet NCO sent a heavy calibre bullet into the body of the officer extracting himself shakily from the turret, the signal for his unit to open fire.

The Welshman's upper body literally flew apart as the 14.5mm round transited it.

Behind the smoking armoured car, the tanks started to manoeuvre as the Coldstreams deployed into cover and started to fire back.

The PTRS rifle cracked again, and this time the AP bullet penetrated the hull front, catastrophically wounding the driver as he attempted to lever himself out of the hatch.

The man barely had time to scream before his heart exhausted the supply of blood.

Around the Praporshchik, DPs, Mosin, and SKS rifles sought out the deploying infantry; across the river to their backs, two anti-tank guns duelled with the Centurions, and lost.

Within seconds of each other, the two D-44 85mm guns had succumbed to direct hits, despite their excellent concealment, something that was let down by poor ammunition, the smoke from which marked their hiding place as effectively as a brightly-coloured marker round.

Their only 'success' was to knock a track off one of the Centurions.

Across the river, a Maxim machine gun started its own contribution and sent a stream of bullets into a running group of Coldstreams, sending nearly half flying under heavy impacts.

A purple haze started flowing across Praporshchik Yuri Nazarbayev, one that presaged no good whatsoever.

'Fuck. The bastards've marked us.'

"First section back! Over the bridge! Move, Comrades, move!"

The men needed no second bidding, for they also knew what would follow the purple smoke.

Twenty men virtually flew back to the water's edge adjacent to the bridge's end, and moved quickly across underneath the structure, where a cunning walkway had been concealed.

419

None of the First Section was even wounded, and they dropped into prepared positions and commenced firing again.

The Soviet plan calculated that, if the defenders clung tight to the bridge, then they would be preserved from what usually followed the purple smoke.

That problem still remained for Yuri Nazarbayev and his remaining guardsmen.

"Let's go, Comrades! Back! Back! Quickly!"

The man next to Nazarbayev rose and immediately fell, his face ruined by something solid.

Bubbling and squirting blood from a face that was beyond repair, the young guardsman thrashed around in pain and fear.

Nazarbayev grabbed the man's straps and dragged the heavy body as best he could.

A Sergeant joined him, and together they moved the wounded man quicker and ate up the distance to the bridge, and its illusion of safety.

Fig # 208 - Soviet defensive positions - Parchim, Germany.

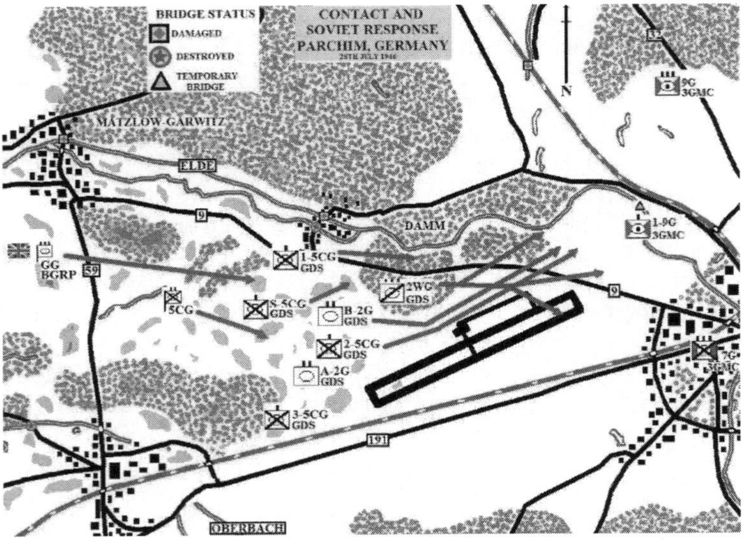

A sound burned through the numerous cracks of tank cannon, bursts of machine gun fire, or the screams of wounded men, a sound known to each and every Soviet soldier… a sound that carried nothing good for them.

The first aircraft screamed down upon the battlefield, its new noisemakers bringing fear to the hearts of even the most steadfast of enemy. In truth, often to those the aircraft were supporting too.

The Beaufighter Mark VI gracefully drove itself straight into the ground, killing two nearby Coldstream Guardsmen, and never having fired its guns or loosed off a single rocket.

The next three aircraft put their ordnance right on the target markers, RP-3 rockets and cannon shells ploughed up the target and transformed the flat ground into a moonscape of whirling earth and stones..

Second Section were already underneath the bridge, encumbered with three wounded, but none the less, still full of fight.

Nazarbayev reported to the captain in charge before returning to his men.

They were old comrades, and there was no ceremony.

"Comrade Kapitan, Third platoon withdrawn, four casualties."

"Keep your head down, Yuri. Wait 'til I blow it, and then give the Capitalists shit."

Guards Captain Nauvintsev took a moment to watch the veteran hobble off, a turned ankle preventing Nazarbayev from striding around the battlefield in the manner for which he was renowned.

"Comrade Starshy Leytenant, test the circuit."

The engineer officer nodded to the designated man, and the circuit was duly checked.

A nod sufficed as a report that all was well.

"Comrade Kapitan Nauvintsev, the circuit is…"

The first of the Coldstreams mortar rounds dropped fair and square into the centre of the pit in which they were concealed.

Nauvintsev was catapulted into the sky as just over two pounds of high explosive killed every other man in the pit.

The veteran Captain dropped from the sky.

His scream carried across the battlefield as his battered body fell on hard ground, breaking more of his bones.

Another 2" mortar round sought him out, picked him up, and threw him at the small bridge, where he was transfixed by the guardrail. The modest diameter timber poked out from his chest and held him upright on his knees, his broken legs at awkward angles to his front and side.

Nauvintsev could make no noise, not move an arm or leg. All he could do was kneel exposed on the battlefield as his lifeblood ebbed away from numerous wounds, none more hideous than the penetrative wound, where the solid timber had pushed bone and lung out of the ragged exit would.

But he stayed conscious, his mouth working, trying to form a word, a scream... a something.

The agony subsided, as if some unseen doctor had filled him with pain relieving chemicals, and the dying officer found himself becoming aware of the battlefield.

Behind him, not that he could turn and professionally examine the work of the enemy, the British tanks and infantry were closing down on the bridge as the surviving three Beaufighters circled over friendly territory, ready to return to avenge their leader.

In front of him, his own guardsmen fired steadfastly, despite the growing casualties caused by the nasty little British mortars and direct fire from the assault force.

A stray bullet clipped his left elbow, its passage a matter of indifference to him.

He felt no pain whatsoever.

Almost clinically, he watched his men die one by one, a rifle bullet here, a tank shell there.

His mouth worked but no sound came out.

'The bridge, Yuri... blow the fucking bridge.'

On cue, the Praporshchik rose up and was immediately felled.

Incapable of even a gasp, Nauvintsev willed his man to rise again.

Nazarbayev staggered to his feet and started to move towards the shattered pit.

Nauvintsev watched fascinated, as his predicament enabled him to observe a battle in a way he had never been able to before.

Relieved of his own duties by his wounds, the Captain could see how his men fought and died, the bravery of some, the cowardice of others, his whole military career set out in one microcosm of combat in an unimportant corner of Germany.

'Blow the fucking bridge, man!'

Something whacked into Nazarbayev's shoulder and spun him around, and probably saved his life, as tracer bullets split the air he had been running through a fraction of a second later.

Again, the NCO rose, albeit slower and with more care, his right shoulder bloody and rent.

He covered the remaining short distance in a half roll, half crouching effort that kept him safe from further harm.

That he dropped into the messy remains of the Engineer officer was unfortunate, but he had no time to rid himself of the unfortunate man's organs and entrails.

The detonator was intact, but one of the wires was clearly broken.

"Job tvoju mat!"

Setting the detonator straight, Nazarbayev looked for the other end of the wire.

A bursting shell threw a load of earth and stone over him, and caused him to shrink onto the bottom of the hole.

Up again, he risked a look over the parapet and saw that the British were closer than he had anticipated, and…

"Mudaks!"

His officer… his veteran commander…

"Mudaks!"

The virtual corpse's eyes burned into his, issuing orders without words so that, even at distance, the iron will of Guards Captain Nauvintsev made itself known.

Nazarbayev managed a nod and, had he not returned to the task of finding the broken wire, he would have seen the nearest thing possible to a smile form on the broken face of his leader.

He followed the intact wire up to the edge of the pit, and over it, attracting a burst of fire from the nearest Centurion.

He ducked down, gripped the detonator in his good hand, counted to three, and propelled himself up and over the edge, dropping into a piece of dead ground on the side away from the enemy.

Working his way round, the shoulder wound increasingly inhibiting him, Nazarbayev found what he was looking for, but the broken wire end lay in plain sight, in an area exposed to enemy fire.

Without a thought, the NCO threw himself forward and grabbed at the end with his wounded arm, the pain of the impact with the earth almost enough to push him into unconsciousness.

He landed badly and smashed his face into the detonator, and opened up his top lip virtually to his nostril.

He scrambled for the wire end and stuck it between his teeth, biting down hard as he pulled on it, instantly stripping the insulation off a two-inch section.

Nazarbayev repeated the exercise with the other end, joined the two together in rough fashion, and readied the detonator.

The smile that he saw on Nauvintsev's face was one of pride and of sorrow, an expression that he acknowledged with a nod, before he twisted the detonator and sent a small current down the repaired line.

The demolition charge ignited, destroying the bridge, killing or wounding the three Coldstream Guardsmen closest to the bridge, and terminating Nauvintsev's existence.

On the British radio net, all hell broke loose, with Scipio-six, the 2nd Grenadier's commander, hunting down information like a hungry hound.

Blenheim-six, A Squadron's commander, was on the airwaves, desperate to get the fuel with which he could move forward and bolster the assault.

Maj Godfrey Eben Pike DSO MBE, OC B Squadron, confirmed the loss of the bridge, called for more support, bridging engineers, more infantry, more everything.

'Bunty' Hargreaves took notes but could offer nothing tangible as yet, leaving Lieutenant Colonel Keith with only words of encouragement.

"Corunna-six, Scipio-six, you've done well so far. Sit tight and cover the airfield area to the south and river ahead. Blenheim will be moving up directly. Alma's forty minutes out. Over."

"Scipio-six, Corunna-six, understood, but I'm low on sherry. Any news on that delivery, over."

"Corunna-six, Scipio-six, not as yet. Just sit tight, Corunna. Out."

Pike tossed the headset into the bottom of the armoured car in disgust.

"Bugger, bum, balls! How in the name of blazes can I fight a bloody war without petrol for my tanks, eh?"

Lance Corporal Devenish wisely kept his mouth shut and concentrated on the gauges in front of him, noticing the distinct lack of 'sherry' in the dingo's tank.

"Right, Devenish, get me over to the left flank there, and quick about it."

Pike determined to take a personal look at the destroyed bridge, in order to assess if there was any mileage in getting a bridge layer up.

Within a few minutes the idea was but a distant memory, and 'B' Squadron were in the fight of their lives.

Colonel Hargreaves hastily conferred with Keith, and the two parted, one to fight the battle as best he could, the other to bring up as much as he could by way of reinforcements.

Keith spared a moment to watch Hargreaves' Morris quad bounce away, but quickly returned his focus to the battle in front of him.

1410 hrs, Sunday, 28th July 1946, Parchim, Germany.

"Excellent, Viktor Timofeevich. When?"

"Almost immediately, Comrade Polkovnik General... moment..."

Removing the telephone from his ear, Viktor Obukov, commander of 3rd Guards Mechanised Corps, accepted a written report from his deputy, Major General Golov.

"Blyad. Casualties?"

"Not many guns, but they have to move. It will take time, probably nearly an hour, Comrade."

He nodded by way of reply and spoke rapidly into the telephone.

"Comrade Polkovnik General, my artillery has been attacked and disrupted, but I'm going with the plan anyway. The Capitalists have stopped for a reason, and I'm going to exploit it. We attack at 1415."

"Objective?"

The words slipped easily from Obukov's mouth, but both men knew the doing would be harder than the saying by some considerable distance.

"Spornitz by direct assault... then I shall feint towards Ludwigslust, but centre my main efforts on moving northwards through Matzlow, and fall upon Schwerin. The opportunity to encircle the enemy forces north of my Ninth Brigade is too much to ignore, Comrade Polkovnik General."

The silence on the phone was penetrating as Kazakov, commander of 10th Guards Army, assessed the possibilities.

In his headquarters, he ran his fingers over the situation map, reading the ground, the forces... the possibilities.

"I agree, Comrade Obukov. Comrade Marshal Bagramyan will be informed, and I'll submit an urgent request for all the air cover we can muster. We've an opportunity here, Comrade. I'll send some more support to your units south of the Elde. I suggest that you keep 9th Guards Brigade in place as a hinge. I'll prepare our forces to their north for action in support of you, once you head for Schwerin. Have your staff get the written operational plan to me immediately."

"Yes, Comrade Polkovnik General. Now, we'll give the bastards something to think about."

425

"Damned right. Now, set to it, Comrade. I'm going to speak to frontal headquarters immediately."

The connection was terminated and both men, separated by fourteen kilometres of telephone cable, set about their tasks with renewed enthusiasm.

Fig # 209 - Soviet Order of Battle - Parchim, Germany.

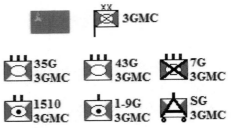

SOVIET FORCES
BATTLE OF PARCHIM
28TH JULY 1946.

1420 hrs, Sunday, 28th July 1946, Parchim, Germany.

With the speed and accuracy of veterans, the gunners of the 1510th Self-Propelled Artillery Regiment reacted to their hasty orders and put down a barrage on the advance British elements; their 152mm shells caused havoc with tankers and infantrymen alike.

An HE shell from one of the monster ISU-152s found no resistance worth the name when it smashed into the turret of a Centurion II, the kinetic force alone sufficient to drive the top armour down into the turret space, where it easily won the battle between flesh and steel.

Even though the shell failed to explode, the 2IC of 'B' Squadron and his crew were messily removed from the equation in the blink of an eye.

At the rear of the advance group, another Centurion was tossed onto its side by two near misses, leaving none of its crew capable of evacuating the tank, as their bones shattered and disintegrated when bodies smashed into immovable metal.

Major Pike, his head bleeding from a close shave, screamed into his radio in vain, not knowing that it was the source of the burning smell that was just about recognisable over the metallic smell of blood from his scalp wound.

Despite mounting casualties, the Coldstreams and Grenadiers steadied themselves and waited for the inevitable.

Fig # 210 - Soviet counter-attack, Parchim, Germany.

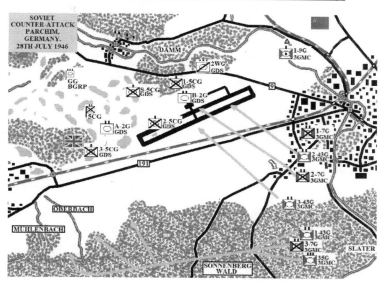

2nd Grenadiers had driven straight into the divide between the 7th and 9th Guards Mechanised Brigades.

The latter was set on the defensive, still understrength from its exertions during the initial stages of the Allied offensive.

The 7th was a different proposition, nearer full strength, and Obukov had, with some other units of the 3rd Guards Mechanised, nurtured and kept them safe for the right moment.

As far as Colonel General Kazakov was concerned, that moment had come, and Obukov set loose his best remaining troops in a counter-attack intended to destroy the British resistance to their front, and retake Schwerin.

Leaving the 1st Battalion in Parchim and its environs, the remainder of the 7th's motorised infantry components struck out, 2nd battalion straight out of Parchim and across the airfield, 3rd Battalion moved through the woods to the south, intent on occupying Spornitz in the first instance.

2nd Battalion was supported by elements of the 43rd Guards Tank Regiment, equipped with a mix of 85mm and 100mm equipped T34s.

The 43rd's commander intended them to rely on speed rather than ability in a stand up fight, and his unit acted accordingly.

The 3rd Mechanised Battalion moved alongside part of the 35th Guards Tank Brigade, whose 1st Tank Battalion, although greatly reduced, possessed some quality T-54s alongside the venerable T34m44s it had started hostilities with.

The remaining part of the 35th Guards Tanks was conserved, held behind the 1st Tank Battalion, ready to drive in between the lead British units and the second echelon and develop the route to Schwerin.

Although equipped solely with T34s, both m44 and m45 models, Lieutenant Colonel Sarkashian, the 35th Brigade's commander, had preserved his most experienced men for the difficult exploitation phase of the attack, and he was confident they would open the road to his final target.

Elsewhere across the battlefield, a leavening of SP anti-tank guns were held back, ready to provide support should a particularly difficult situation arise, and SPAA assets moved carefully forward, ready to provide close support when the inevitable fighter-bombers arrived.

Along with the artillery and mortar support arraigned against it, 2nd Grenadiers and 5th Coldstreams suddenly found themselves in the fight of their lives.

17-pdr shells crossed the battlefield, 85mm and 100mm shells passed them on the other track, all set against a back drop of artillery and mortar strikes, called in by harassed officers on both sides.

In the main, the 85mm shells proved ineffective against the Centurions.

A number of tanks were hit but, apart from soiled underwear, little damage was done.

The 100mm shells were a different matter.

One Guards troop commander was still screaming his joy at registering a fourth kill in as many minutes when a 100mm solid shot smashed through the hull of his tank, creating a whirlwind of bone and gristle, and leaving him suddenly alone.

Unable to recognise anything human about the things around him, the young subaltern screamed in horror and pushed himself up out of the cupola, desperate to escape the horrors of the tank's interior.

He quickly added to them, when his headless corpse flopped onto the turret deck, his head removed by a passing shell.

As the Soviet attack flowed along the south bank of the Elde River, the Coldstream infantry started to give ground, firing as they went, leapfrogging backwards from positon to position.

Encouraged by Nazarbayev, the soldiers of the 9th took them under fire and pinning a number in place as best they could, which permitted their attacking comrades to get closer and closer.

Perhaps understandably, some excitable soul in the lead Soviet assault unit mistakenly took Nazarbayev's men under fire, which forced them to take cover more effectively than any attempts by the British Guardsmen to their front.

The lead elements of the 2nd Battalion started to dismount and move into foot assault on the small knots of resistance they encountered.

Although Sarkashian's guardsmen had suffered many deprivations during the long winter and the supply shortages, they were decidedly fitter than most frontline Soviet soldiers, and their assaults swiftly overwhelmed the Coldstreams, whose choices were clear; surrender or die, and the British Guards were not minded to surrender.

'B' Squadron's tanks stood and died, or reversed, often with the same result, as, not for the first time, numerical superiority started to overcome technology.

Godfrey Pike, his radio now repaired, did all he could to try to reorganise his battered force, all the time ensuring that Lieutenant Colonel Keith understood the perilous position his command was in.

'A' Squadron was also engaged, but was hampered by its inability to manoeuvre. Using speed alone, Soviet tank units closed down the range between vehicles, and both British tank squadrons found themselves fighting at ever reducing range, as 43rd Guards Tank Regiment charged forward, in spite of its own grievous losses.

British artillery opened up and managed to reduce the odds even further, but the Soviet's understood that getting in close was of benefit in more than one way, and the British artillery would inevitably cease to prevent friendly casualties.

A number of passes were made by Allied ground attack aircraft, but only two attacked, the rest unable to make sure who was who, and fairly chose not to add their ordnance to the maelstrom below.

To the south, a large force of Soviets slipped past the British positions, moving through the largely intact Sonnenberg Wald, and closing on Spornitz virtually unopposed.

The southern force commander, Sarkashian himself, ordered the advance out of the Sonnenberg Wald, and his tanks crossed the almost dry Splettbach. Part he sent barrelling straight at Spornitz, to run parallel with the Oberbach and Mühlenbach. Part he sent further westward, with orders to circumvent Spornitz, pass to the east of Dutschow, and occupy the junction of Routes 65 and 59.

1456 hrs, Sunday, 28th July, 1946, Route 59, Dütschow, Germany.

"But my orders say Spornitz, Sarnt-Major."

"Your orders are out of bloody date, Sir. Listen to that…"

Charles pointed in the direction of whatever hell was being stirred up to their west.

"I take your point, Sarnt-Major, really I do, but… I say…"

With exasperation rather than respect, CSM Charles interrupted the transport officer's words with a raised hand.

"Sir. Will you help us dismount?"

"Not here, Sarnt-Maj…

Charles spun his finger in a simple sign, and the Centurion's engine burst into life.

The transport officer went nearly blue with the indignity of it all.

"No! That won't do… won't do at all! Stop that!"

Charles, his back towards the elderly man, waved his hand once more and Lady Godiva III dropped into gear and drove backwards off the trailer.

"My God, man! I'll have you arrested! I mean to say… what the blazes?"

One of the Diamond Whites came apart in a violent explosion.

The tank crews present recognised the crack that had preceded the arrival of a high-explosive shell.

'Enemy tanks!'

Other transporters were slowly coming to a halt behind the lead vehicles that had, until a few moments ago, held Charles' own tank.

The tanks of 'C' Squadron has been caught on their transports, and were at great disadvantage.

"Captain! That's why your orders are out of sodding date! We need the tanks off the bloody trailers… NOW!"

He shouted at the engineer officer.

"Lieutenant Ansell! Can you keep the bastards off us long enough to get the tanks off? As best you can!"

"Will do. Good luck!"

Ansell shouted at his men, pointing towards the ruins of Dutschow.

The men, engineers from 14th Field Squadron RE who had travelled up in company with 'C' Squadron, needed no second invitation and charged towards the hard cover offered by the rubblised remains of Dutschow.

Leaving the shocked transport captain to work things out, CSM Charles climbed aboard his tank, intent on buying some time for the rest of his squadron to unload.

"Up that rise to the left... in behind that old building... fucking sharpish, man!"

The Centurion's Meteor engine purred as the tracks gripped the grass and pulled the fifty-two ton tank up the small incline.

The destroyed building proved to be a superb firing point, one from which the Soviet attacking force was revealed in all its glory.

Fig # 211 - The arrival of 'C' Squadron, Battle of Parchim, Germany.

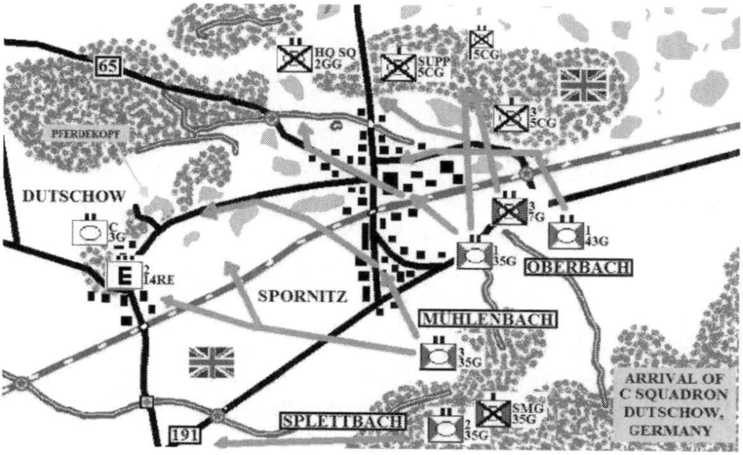

"Fucking hell! The whole of fucking Uncle Joe's three-ring circus is out there!"

Patterson was confronted with the original 'target-rich' environment.

431

Charles was momentarily stunned into silence, a silence broken by Wild's laconic observation.

"Are you lot planning to use that fucking gun or what?"

The side of a T-54 proved an irresistible target.

"Target tank, right two, moving right to left, range, thirteen hundred..."

The tank commander's instructions fell away as Charles knew his sabot round was no good at that distance.

Although he knew the answer, he had to check.

"What you got up the spout, Pats?"

"APC."

"Good enough. You got 'im?"

"Nope. He's stopped behind cover, Sarnt-Major."

"Roger... target tank... right two... range twelve-fifty."

"On... he's a command tank..."

"FIRE!"

The 20-pdr swept back in its mount and the APCBC shell sped down range.

"Fuck it!"

"Again!"

Charles moved his cupola to examine the rest of the battlefield, and saw the deploying tanks and infantry splitting, some on the original axis, others moving towards the debussing members of his squadron.

"Kill him quick, Pats."

Again, the big gun spat a solid shot at the enemy force.

"Got the bastard!"

One of the T34m45s ground to a halt, its engine smoking as flames licked around the compartment.

Charles called the new target.

"Traverse right, Pats. There's a gaggle coming out of the woods. Line of tanks... new type... see them?"

"Yep. I'm on."

Charles examined the enemy vehicles.

"They're the new 54 type I think."

Patterson gave a murmur of agreement.

"Beefy, change to HESH next."

"Sarnt-major."

"Still on, Pats?"

"Yep."

"FIRE!"

The gun rocked back.

"Hit! Don't think we killed the bastard though."

432

"Again."

Silverside had slid one of the new shells into the breech.

Patterson made his adjustments.

"Same target, on."

"FIRE!"

The APCBC shell hadn't killed the T-54, but it had damaged it by jamming the turret in the forward position.

Quickly working the problem through his mind, the commander decided to alter course towards a small rise where he could take cover and evaluate the damage.

The HESH shell arrived and made his efforts immaterial.

It struck on the turret, roughly two foot to one side of the main gun.

The thin shell casing collapsed and the explosive filler spread like a lump of dough, all in a fraction of a second. A base fuse did the initiation of the explosives and the shock wave was dispatched through the armour plate.

On the inside, the wave detached, the technical term was spalled, three pieces of the inner armour surface.

The smallest piece of metal was five centimetres across its largest section, the biggest piece nearly twenty-three centimetres at its widest point.

The three 'missiles' mowed through the tank interior, not discriminating between equipment and man, and reducing both to instant wreckage.

Death was swift and the insides of the T-54 was bathed in the fluids of men who were literally chopped to pieces.

Practice with the HESH rounds had revealed an unusual problem, in that there was often no tell-tale revelation that the target had been killed; no penetration evidence, no smoke and flame, no crew abandoning.

The problem posed a question. To fire again, risking a wasted shell, or find another target, risking leaving an adversary still operational?

Charles made the call.

"Target, left one, T-54, stationary."

Patterson found the tank just as its gun spouted flame.

The enemy shell roared down the side of Godiva's turret, missing by no more than four coats of paint.

"On!"

"FIRE!"

Another HESH, another messy end for four sons of the Rodina.

The radio waves were full of the voices of 'C' Squadron officers and NCOs, their own tanks driven off the trailers and almost ready for combat.

The tell-tale sound of a 17-pdr cannon indicated that at least one of them had got into a firing position.

The Soviet force split yet again. The T-54s sought positions of cover from which to engage the British tanks at distance, the T34s and halftracks advanced, jinking as they came, trying to close the range as quickly as possible.

Soviet artillery also joined in, as Sarkashian directed his final concealed artillery unit into destroying the threat to his own flank.

Unfortunately for him and the Soviet artillerymen, one of the latest British CBR units was positioned just south of Matzlow-Garwitz.

The much-improved ground radar system was a few steps ahead of the AA radar that had proved so successful in locating Soviet mortar units.

Counter-battery fire was fast becoming a major tool in the Allied armoury, reducing the effectiveness of one of the Red Army's strongest arms even further, by causing artillery to reposition quickly or risk catastrophic loss to incoming artillery.

The 755th Counter-Battery Radar Section, temporarily attached to 55th Field Regiment, Royal Artillery, had the very latest technology and the skill to use it appropriately. In this instance, the 755th proved extremely effective.

Their four sets were laid out in the approved manner and quickly fed back information to the waiting battery commander. Using accurate maps, combined with the radar data, the likely position of the enemy guns was extrapolated, and the artillery Captain dialled in his guns in a matter of seconds.

His battery of 25-pdrs, kept silent for one purpose and one purpose only, was quickly brought into action, and it pumped shells into the sky at an alarming rate, and with great accuracy.

1510th Self-Propelled Artillery Regiment's last two batteries were caught as they moved off to an alternate firing position.

Whilst only two of the monster SP guns were knocked out or disabled, the real losses lay in ammunition vehicles.

The ZIS-6 and Gaz-AAA supply trucks had moved off as soon as the firing had commenced, but had been restricted by a bottleneck, that had nicely concentrated the vulnerable vehicles.

A single 25-pdr shell turned one ZIS into a fiery projectile, which in turn smashed into two other trucks, as well as sending some of its cargo of projectiles flying in all directions.

The chain reaction was impressive, and within a minute a dozen trucks and their precious cargoes of munitions were either ablaze or destroyed by the numerous explosions that followed.

Further 25-pdr shells added to the indignities wreaked upon the Soviet artillerymen, including the artillery commander and his staff, who were stood transfixed by the horrors in front of their eyes when a British shell landed roughly six foot behind the irate Lieutenant Colonel.

What was left of him was propelled into the growing inferno that was his supply column.

The leaderless artillerymen elected to move back, rather than sideways, and withdrew from the battle without further contribution.

Not that Charles and his crew really noticed their absence, as the Soviet T34s charged closer, covered by the T-54s to the rear.

1502 hrs, Sunday, 28th July, 1946, Dütschow, Germany.

"On."

"FIRE!"

Charles had switched to the oncoming T34s, and the APDS shell struck its target directly on the driver's hatch, destroying the Soviet tanker before going on to create havoc inside the model 45 tank.

"He's dead. Target tank, left two, range four hundr…"

Like a sledgehammer hitting a bell, a T-54s shell clanged off the turret and flew skywards, deflecting off the leading front edge just above were Patterson was pressed to the gun sight.

"Fuck!"

His face jerked away as the power of the strike pushed the sight into his face, something that hurt despite the soft rubber edging.

"Bastard…"

He spat blood, some from his gums, some running down from one nostril.

"You ok, Pats?"

"Fine."

He reseated his face on the rubber surround and found the target.

Another enemy shell sped past Lady Godiva III, closely followed by one that ploughed into the ruined wall that provided them with much of their cover.

"C'mon gunner. Driver, standby to move."

"On."

"FIRE!"

Another APDS shell burrowed into a Soviet tank, although the T34 seemed to shrug it off like no more than a mosquito bite.

"Again!"

Another Centurion did the job for them, and much more impressively, as the Soviet tank simply came apart with a massive bang and flash that left only the basic chassis and half the body in place.

"Driver, reverse."

The Centurion moved back off the mound and into cover.

"Ammo?"

"Eight sabot, seven HESH, ten BC, full load of HE and Canister."

Charles hummed a response to Beefy's precise reply and made a decision.

"Lads, I'm going after their 54s. We're the only 20-pounder here, so it's up to us to take the buggers on."

He checked his vision blocks again, noting even more of 'C' Squadron deployed in line and engaging the Soviet charge.

He grimaced as one Centurion took a fatal hit, smoke and flame immediately belching from its open turret hatch.

'Shit!'

"Driver. Move left, take the road through the village."

Lady Godiva swung quickly and accelerated, the upgraded engine carried the fifty-two tank forward with ease.

Racing down Dorfstrasse, Charles warned Wild well in advance.

"Take the next road on the left, Laz. Don't lose us a track now or I'll have your guts for bloody garters."

Charles levered himself up into the cupola and took some deep sucks on the slightly fresher air outside the confines of the turret.

The tank slowed and Lazarus Wild negotiated the turn into Querstrasse with ease.

"Laz, at the end of this road, take it right and get me to the top of the hill there, reverse side approach, stop short of the summit, ok?"

The map notation stated 'Pferdekopf', whatever that meant.

The standard mumbled acknowledgement came back.

Charles stooped down and tapped Silverside on the shoulder.

"Pass me the Sten, Beefy."

The tank's sub-machinegun and two mags were quickly handed up.

"Tank halt."

Laz brought Godiva to a gentle stop.

"I'm going to recce the top of it. Make sure you stay below the summit 'til I wave you up. Commander out."

Charles dropped to the ground, already running, knowing he had to get his tank back into action as quickly as possible.

Wild held the Centurion below the skyline as ordered, and the three of them took the time for a crafty cigarette.

Patterson risked a look out of his hatch and, off to the left, he watched the close battle in Spornitz between the T34s and some tanks from his battalion.

'C' Squadron had three tanks knocked out from what he could see, but the wreckage of the Soviet tanks went as far as he could see, the 17-pdr equipped Mark IIs more than holding their own against the 85mm and 100mm guns of the enemy.

He was brought back to earth in a second as a long whistle attracted his attention.

Charles was waving at Wild, encouraging him to bring the tank forward.

The idling engine took the strain and pulled lady Godiva III the last few yards to the summit.

Wild followed the hand signals, favouring the right side, and immediately saw what Charles had planned, and nosed the tank into a scrape on the top of the mound, a lovely piece of natural cover that left only the turret exposed.

Some trees completed the ensemble, making it a superb firing position.

Charles was up and in before Wild could take the engine out of gear.

"Right, Pats. Hold your fire for the mo. There's a few of the buggers set along the main road line... not the main road... the other one behind it... range about two thousand I reckon."

"I'm on it, Sarnt-Major."

437

"HESH up?"

"Yep, Sarnt-Major."

"None to waste, so make them all count. We'll stay as long as possible… it's a great position… stay ready, Laz… you fit, Pats?"

"Reckon so, Sarnt-Major… left to right seems best… suit?"

"Do it. Don't wait for me."

Patterson took a deep breath and concentrated on his sight, his mind working at high capacity to get things just right.

"Firing."

The 20-pdr sent a shell across the battlefield, seeking out a T-54 that was partially concealed in a hedgerow.

The shell struck home and the process of death commenced, as layers of the internal turret armour whirled around inside the confines of the steel box, converting tender breathing flesh into something resembling the contents of a chef's mincing machine.

The turret whirred a few inches to the right and Patterson repeated the process.

This time the process of dying was more abrupt and recognisable, as something inside the target surrendered catastrophically to the high-speed metal scabs, blasting the turret up and behind the destroyed tank.

The Centurion's gun was already on the next target and a third HESH went downrange.

"Fuck!"

The shell struck short, making a small cut in the road, before bouncing up and over the target.

Charles was understandably nervous about any artillery fire, and made sure Wild was ready to move in an instant.

The 20-pdr spoke again.

"Oh for fuck's sake!"

Patterson had missed for a second time, this time over the top of the enemy's turret, an inch over, but an inch was enough.

The tree to the Centurion's left splintered as it surrendered to a direct hit. The heavy trunk fell across the front of the British tank, adding to the concealment without inhibiting its ability to fight.

Charles chose to stay silent, not wishing to break Patterson's concentration.

Silverside chose a different course of action.

"Get it fucking right or the next round will be loaded up your fucking jacksy, sunshine."

Charles slapped the back of Beefy's head, part in jest, part to relieve his own tension.

"Firing."

The HESH went home and the enemy tank was silenced.

As was the next, again in more identifiable fashion, as smoke issued from the open hatches.

The driver escaped from his vehicle, the colour of his battledress drastically altered by the brief events inside his vehicle.

Miraculously unhurt, the man ran as fast as he could, trying to escape the images that were locked into his brain.

"Last HESH."

Beefy's announcement confirmed the countdown each crewman had been making.

The final HESH shell did no more than smash the right track off a T-54.

"Driver, reverse."

Lady Godiva III moved quickly out of the scrape and onto the reverse slope, stopping out of sight, and allowing the whole crew to take a much-needed deep intake of air.

"Good effort, Pats."

The gunner was less than enthusiastic.

"Not fucking good enough, Sarnt-Major."

Patterson reflected on it for a second.

'Four out of seven, plus a disabled… at two thousand… that's pretty fucking good actually.'

"Should've done better."

"Fucking right you should 'ave."

This time, both Charles and Patterson aimed blows at the grinning Silverside.

"Right, let's move around to the right. Laz, take her round on this path… nice and slow."

The Centurion rotated on the spot and moved around the side of the hill.

Charles sniffed the air and narrowed his eyes; the whole sky seemed to be changing colour and disposition in front of his eyes.

"Storm coming I reckon, lads."

He switched his eyes back to the front and saw the enemy tank moving gingerly through the ruined buildings.

"Bloody hell! Tank halt! Gunner, target tank, left two, range three hundred, ass shot."

Patterson found the T34 quickly, its vulnerable rear pointed towards them as it tried to manoeuvre for side shots on the British defensive line.

An APCBC shell slammed through the engine compartment, sending burning fuel across the road and into the ruined house beside the tank.

"There's another, Pats! Left two, next to the burning lorry ... behind the wall there!"

The two Soviet tanks had somehow manoeuvred themselves into excellent firing positions on the left flank of the Grenadier's defensive line.

The second tank sent a solid shot crashing through the side of a Guards' Centurion, smashing the engine into worthless scrap.

The crew abandoned swiftly, but took machine-gun fire and dropped out of sight.

Meanwhile, aware that there was an unknown but deadly threat to its rear, the other Soviet tank drove through the side of a wooden barn in an effort to conceal itself.

The attempt failed as another solid shot followed it into the barn and instantly turned the vehicle and building into a fireball.

"Driver, right, down the slope to that fence, then left to the road."

Following Charles' instructions, Lazarus Wild dropped Godiva down the slope and moved her left at the fence.

"Bring her up to that building and stop next to that smashed up Morris, Laz. I'm going to recce again."

He grabbed the Sten again and was up and out of the tank.

No sooner had his feet hit the dirt than Charles was clambering back up the glacis plate.

"Tank action left... three of the bastards!"

He dropped in through the rotating turret, leaving the Sten on the roof out of the way.

"Three T-34s in line, Pats... going like shit off a stick... take the first one and we'll shift position. Ready to move, Laz."

The 20-pdr was trained on the leading edge of the slope.

Patterson waited.

No one dared breathe.

Nothing, save the electric air and the steady patter of large raindrops.

"They must've seen me. Back up, Laz, fast as you can, straight line, no messing!"

The Meteor engine dragged the Centurion backwards, gaining speed.

Charles stuck his head out the turret and grabbed at the Sten as he twisted to check the route behind.

"Little left-hand down, Laz... excellent... keep the pedal hard down... more left... good..."

Charles' plan was to go the other way around the hillock and come in behind the enemy.

440

It was a good plan but, as is the case with good plans, they are sometimes thought of by the other side too.

"SHIT! Laz, hard right, tank action front, fire when you bear, Pats!"

The first of the T34s had come round the slope and Lady Godiva was showing it her vulnerable backside.

As she swung, the enemy tank fired.

The sound of metal striking metal was unmistakeable, and they all prepared themselves...

... but it was not their time.

As Godiva had swung, the 85mm shell had just missed the turret proper, but smashed through the crew bin on the rear of the turret, destroying much of the possessions the men had managed to acquire since they had lost their kit at Lützow.

"Straighten up, Laz!"

Charles corrected the turn and the tank continued surging backwards, aimed for a gap between two houses.

Despite being on the move, Patterson took the shot, placing his faith in the new stabilisation system.

"Firing!"

The shell hit but bounced off, defeated by the T34s angled armour.

"Tank halt!"

Charles hadn't given the order, and his first reaction was to tear a strip off his gunner.

"Firing!"

The shell ran inch perfect, struck the advancing tank under the gun mantlet and penetrated the turret mount, knocking the heavy lump of metal backwards.

Aided by a bump that raised the front of the Soviet tank, the entire turret slipped off the chassis, neatly cutting two of its crew in half on its travels.

As the turret slid to the ground, a huge flash marked the start of a summer thunderstorm.

The roll of thunder that followed indicated that the heart of the storm was close by.

The rain descended like a burst dam, immediately reducing visibility to a few yards.

Charles closed his eyes, mentally conjuring up the images of the enemy tanks.

"Driver, left turn... down the track... slowly... gunner, turret right six. Don't wait for my order... engage on sight."

441

Lady Godiva III moved down the track, its dirt already turned to mud by the torrential downpour.

Charles, eyes glued to his optics, opened his mouth, as a dark shape grew into something more tangible.

The 20-pdr lashed out and the dark shape became light as fire consumed it.

"Nice one, Pats. Prepare to engage to front. Driver... take the tank right... pass down the right of that burning tank... on the other side of the hedge... not too close."

The Centurion moved to the right and dodged behind the hedgerow as Patterson brought the turret to the inline position.

Charles was gambling that the other enemy tank would avoid the fire and would use the hedgerow for cover, placing the vegetation between it and the growing illumination of its comrade's funeral pyre.

He was partially right.

A shell struck the front glacis of Godiva, smashing the spare track links housed there and burrowing into the armoured plate.

The Centurion's armour won the battle and prevented full penetration.

Faced with the imminence of death, Wild lost control of his bladder.

"Driver, reverse, angle front! Where's the bastard at?"

No one answered Charles.

Another shell streaked past the wounded Centurion, missing high and wide down the right side.

Wild spotted their tormentor.

"He's in the fucking hedge, Pats! Left two... see 'im?"

The tank lurched as Patterson fired and stabilisation system failed to compensate in time, sending the shell into the ground twenty yards short of the enemy vehicle.

The Soviet tank stayed still, the tank commander electing to give himself the best chance of a kill whilst risking his own by being an easier target.

"Jink, Laz, for fuck's sake jink!"

The 100mm shell missed the nearside front by a whisker, a small manoeuvre by Wild undoubtedly saving his own life.

However, it didn't miss everything.

Firstly, the shell hit the top of the last but one road wheel, which deflected it slightly upwards, again deflecting off the drive sprocket, which altered the shell's course once again, and it nearly vertical, punching through the track before it exited through the nearside exhaust system and flew skywards, still in search of more resistance.

Laz Wild instinctively touched the brakes, which imposed enough strain on the damaged track for it to separate.

Not that anyone needed to be told, Wild shouted automatically.

"Track's gone!"

Patterson held his breath and fired.

His aim was true and the Soviet tank commander's gamble with his and his crew's lives failed.

Charles stuck his head out of the cupola and grimaced, as the driving rain and increasing flashes of lightning made vision difficult.

He could see nothing, except the shattered remnants of the exhaust system.

"Laz, make an assessment. I'll cover you. Commander out."

He pushed himself up into the driving rain, and immediately felt chilled to the bone, as his uniform provided little protection against the elements.

He dropped into the mud and took a quick look at the damage.

Wild moved past him and knelt in the quagmire, running his hands over the shiny scars that marked the enemy shell's progress.

His assessment was short and sweet.

"Workshops job, Sarnt-Major. Sprocket's cracked... track's well shot... exhaust's non-existent... plus, there's summat else... not sure what... but the engine don't sound right."

Charles concentrated and realised he could detect a rhythmic knocking that was not normally present.

Lazarus Wild volunteered a little more information.

"So long as the engine holds out, we can move on the spot, but we ain't going nowhere, Sarnt-Major... not without proper kit to mend this feckin lot."

The coaxial machine gun cut through their conversation, and Beefy emerged from the turret, exposing his considerable upper body to the elements.

"Sarnt-Major! Looks like some of their infantry bastards are on top of the hill where we were earlier. Pats thinks he saw a bazooka or summat like it. Can we move?"

Charles shook his head as he turned to view the high ground they had vacated.

The shape was barely discernible in the rain.

443

He saw no movement, but sensed they were there.

A bullet came out of nowhere and pinged off Godiva's side armour.

"Right, Laz... back in the tank with you. Not healthy out here."

Both men clambered back into the tank, dripping water everywhere as their uniforms rid themselves of the rain.

"How many, Pats?"

"Saw three for sure... next to that felled tree trunk just off the top... one with what looked like a bazooka... took a chance burst... don't think I hit the buggers... went to ground and ain't showed their noggins since."

"Load canister, Beefy... can you pepper the spot with a shotgun round, Pats?"

"No problem, Sarnt-Major."

"Do it."

Patterson gave himself a little more elevation and the breech flew back as the 20-pdr's purpose-built canister shell sent its deadly little projectiles into the general area around the tree trunk.

Even through the rain, both Patterson and Charles saw a red mist as at least one enemy suffered a telling hit.

Four men rose up out of nowhere and ran in all directions, desperate to escape a second shot.

The .30cal followed two of them, chasing at their heels, as Patterson walked the coaxial into their defenceless bodies, putting both men down.

"Didn't see your bazooka man, Pats."

His reply was lost in a horrible sound from the tank engine, one that was immediately followed by silence, as Laz Wild killed it to prevent further damage.

As the sound of the Meteor died away, the storm reasserted itself, and the wind and constant battering of heavy drops created a soft and comforting sound that, had they not been in the middle of a battle, would have sent Godiva's crew to sleep.

The sharp crack of a 17-pdr to their right announced that friendly vehicles were now closer than before.

Charles stuck his head out of the cupola and swept the hillside with his binoculars, seeking something, finding nothing.

A growing sound of distress caught his attention, and he lowered the binoculars in time to see an Allied Mustang fighter, belching smoke and flame, sweep low overhead, the pilot clearly desperate to find somewhere to land his crippled aircraft.

A few seconds later, the sound of an explosion betrayed the unfortunate American's failure, although the rain and storm kept its location a secret.

Charles shook his head, wondering how many men had already died this day.

He wiped his eyes and resumed looking for...

"Infantry to front, 11 o'clock, Pats, hit the bastards quick!"

The turret whirred to the left but the rocket was already in the air.

The Soviet version of the panzerschreck was every bit as deadly as its German forebear, but only if it hit.

The rocket sped past as the main gun flew back on its trunnions once more, Patterson electing to put a canister shell on the target instead of using the coaxial.

The three-man crew and their weapon were utterly destroyed, the heavy ball bearings wiping through man and metal without feeling any resistance.

Even through the rain, it was an awful sight.

"Fucking hell! I mean... fucking hell!"

Wild had his head out the hull hatch and had the closest view of the carnage created by the canister shell.

He dropped back in out of the rain and added the contents of his stomach to that of his bladder.

Silverside, the only man who had not seen the after-effects of the canister shell, went to lighten the obvious tension.

"'Ere Sarnt-Major... seeing as wee'm unable to keep a tank for more'n one bleedin' punch-up nowadays... do yer think if this one's totally fucked, we may not get another fucker, and they'll have to send us home?"

Charles laughed without too much humour and stuck his head back out of the cupola, announcing his views into the intercom.

"Buggered tank or no, the Gods of War ain't finished with us yet... not by a long chalk, Beefy."

As if by reply, the Gods of War decided to redouble their efforts at creating the perfect thunderstorm, as the lightning and rain took over their every sense.

1559 hrs, Sunday, 28th July 1946, Friedensstrasse, Spornitz, Germany.

Less than an hour had passed, but much had changed for both sides.

445

Lieutenant Colonel Sarkashian was part apoplectic with rage, part stoical in the face of the inevitable.

His driver had received both barrels for crashing into a friendly tank, despite the fact that he had been stationary at the time, and the other tank had cornered at the highest possible speed.

Under a tarpaulin, Sarkashian knelt down at the side of his command tank with his 2IC and examined a damp map.

"Vadim, we're fighting here, but the situation is unclear."

He circled Dütschow, where his lead elements had been stopped by another British tank force arriving on trailers. Information had stopped flowing from the commander some while ago, and Sarkashian had sent out reconnaissance teams to establish what was going on.

They had yet to report back.

"Behind us, the British have withdrawn into the area south of Neu Matzlow and our boys cannot shift them back further."

Guards Major Vadim Rozhinsky nodded, seemingly more concerned with keeping his cigarette dry than contributing to the discussion.

However, looks were deceiving, and he tapped the map with a decided flourish.

"That may be our opportunity then, Comrade PodPolkovnik. We're already around them. Perhaps we should strike into their flank up this road." He screwed up his eyes to better make out the detail, "...Route 59 will take us further behind them, and then turn right onto Route 9 and we have them by the balls."

"Maybe, maybe not, Vadim. I have no knowledge of what is here... at Matzlow... and the units I sent out to scout our left flank have not reported in."

Rozhinsky understood the dilemma and put it into words.

"So, if you advance to isolate the British here, you risk exposing the flank to whatever may be here, or whatever defenders the enemy has in Matzlow... and there has to be something there, yes?"

Sarkashian nodded.

"Also, the situation in Dutschow is unclear, and we may have an enemy mobile force to our rear?"

Sarkashian took a long drag on his cigarette, trying to see a solution.

"The solution seems clear to me, Comrade PodPolkovnik."

"Enlighten me, Comrade Mayor."

"We cannot advance at this time, for fear of losing everything we have already paid for with the blood of our soldiers.

Information is key here, and this fucking storm isn't helping either side, but I think it hinders us more here, even if it is keeping their fucking aircraft off us for the moment."

Rozhinsky took a final puff and threw the dog end into a large puddle.

"So I think we must send out more probes... find out what we face..."

Sarkashian interrupted after adding his own cigarette butt to the rainwater.

"And if we let the British force escape, when we could've encircled and destroyed them?"

Rozhinsky shrugged as only the Russians can shrug.

"Whatever you do will be criticised, Comrade PodPolkovnik... this you know. So perhaps the decision should be one that you know won't endanger your soldiers and make sure they're ready to fight for the Motherland on another day?"

A heavy burst of rain made conversation momentarily impossible, as the tarpaulin resounded to the constant strikes of heavy rainfall.

It gave Sarkashian time to think.

He found many reasons to support his decision.

"We will stop here until I get better information as to what is to my flank and ahead. This will also enable us to restock our fuels and ammunition... and for our artillery to reorganise itself."

Sarkashian was still smarting from the loss of his valuable artillery reserve, a major contributing factor to his perception that his attack had, thus far, failed to properly progress.

The thunder was supplemented by a growing Allied artillery barrage, fired blind at likely areas of concentration or routes of advance.

A drenched signals officer slipped under the tarpaulin.

"Comrade PodPolkovnik. Comrade General Golov on the radio, demanding a situation report on the attack's progress."

Lieutenant Colonel Sarkashian shared a silent look with his 2IC.

"Relay my orders to all units, Vadim. Send out more patrols... get me information that I can use to make a better plan. I'll speak to Golov. He'll understand."

They shared a quick salute and went their separate ways.

As it happened, Golov was not at all understanding, but the advance had stalled for a number of reasons and, eventually, the plan was abandoned as Allied reinforcements arrived, all set against the back drop of one of the worst European storms in living memory.

By the time that night arrived, it had not yet abated, and kept many a soldier awake into the small hours.

One soldier who managed to find the solace of sleep was rudely awakened by his commanding officer, who produced a priority air transport order and documentation guaranteeing two full weeks leave in Sochi, the Soviet holiday resort on the Black Sea.

Whilst his mind was full of questions, Yuri Nazarbayev assumed it had something to do with his wife and, in any case, refused to look a gift horse in the mouth.

Within twenty minutes, he was on his way, leaving the harsh realities of war and the bloody stalemate that was Parchim-Dutschow behind him.

0053 hrs, Monday, 29th July, 1946, Hotel National, Moscow, USSR.

Nazarbayeva, her mind cloaked in a protective wrapping of vodka-induced carelessness, opened the curtains and sat watching the display.

Overhead, Allied bombers plied their trade, as they visited the Soviet capital with thousands of pounds of high-explosive and incendiaries.

Below, the anti-aircraft batteries sent shell after shell into the sky, seemingly without any reward, save that their bark boosted the resilience of the Muscovites who cowered in their cellars and shelters.

Moscow had seen the war up close before, but of late, the Allied visits had become more numerous, and more devastating.

Advances in radar technology meant that their cargoes could be laid more accurately, even in the darkest and cloudiest of nights, something that Soviet repair engineers understood only too well, as the factories, offices, and worker's accommodations suffered heavily over the weeks.

But not the Kremlin.

The decision had been made not to target the Soviet leadership.

Nazarbayeva's nakedness was constantly illuminated by the flash of gun or bomb, but she swiftly concealed it as she elected to dress herself and take to the balcony, the better to see what damage was being wreaked upon her Motherland's capital city.

The attack abated markedly, and she went out into the cool air expecting the illuminations and firing to fall away.

But the second wave of bombers arrived, and the battle was joined again.

She enjoyed the cooling breeze, so took a seat and poured herself another drink.

Poboshkin's face flashed through her mind and she raised her tumbler to his memory.

A flash, larger than most, caught her eye, and she was treated to the spectacle of a large burning bomber falling from the sky with all the grace of a dead pigeon.

Instead of toasting her dead aide, she made a small gesture, offering her drink up to the men who were dead or about to die in the fiery fuselage.

She refilled the exquisite crystal tumbler and paid tribute to Poboshkin, raising her glass to his memory before sending the fiery liquid down her throat.

And then, in turn, to each of the other members of her staff, claimed by Beria's orders.

She quickly tired of the display and the alcohol, and the bed drew her into its embrace... and sleep came...

... a sleep with lost faces...

... a sleep with vivid memories...

... a sleep with awful demons...

... a sleep with unexpected questions...

0948 hrs, Monday, 29th July 1946, Vnukovo Airfield, USSR.

The DC-4, an original USAAF VIP transport version that had been captured intact during the early stages of the new war, held twenty-two souls, not including the crew.

Decked out as a military hospital plane, it had plied its trade without a single incident for months, despite frequently encountering the enemy aircraft that roamed deeper and more freely into the Soviet heartlands.

Not that a single casualty had ever been carried in its comfortable interior.

The markings remained in place purely to protect the important passengers.

As the modern transport aircraft taxied out to start its take-off, Nazarbayev eased her damaged foot out of her boot, feeling the relief immediately, and looked around her, assessing her travelling companions.

She recognised the sole naval officer, but wasn't sure from where and when.

449

Putting him to the back of her mind, knowing that trying to recall the man would occupy her later, she examined the others, who were mainly military men.

Some she had exchanged nods with, acquaintances from meetings in the Kremlin and elsewhere.

Some she had exchanged nods with, but was none the wiser as to their identity or role.

Nazarbayeva suddenly realised that the man in front and to her right had turned round and was looking directly at her.

"May I, Comrade Mayor General?"

He indicated the seat directly across the aisle from her.

"As you wish, Comrade Leytenant General."

The old man repositioned himself, allowing Nazarbayeva to weigh him up... his decorations... his difficulty in moving... his shortness of breath.

He flopped into his seat and extended his hand.

"Gurundov... Vassily Gurundov... People's Commissariat for Foreign Affairs."

"Nazarbaye..."

"I know who you are, Comrade."

The man chuckled warmly, putting Nazarbayeva strangely at ease.

"Everyone knows who **you** are."

He coughed and retrieved a handkerchief from his pocket, wiping away something unpleasant.

Unbidden, he offered up an explanation.

"Lungs are shot... Eastern front in the first war... German gas attack... still killed my fair share of the bastards though."

He wiped again, as he was racked with another bout of coughing.

"Think the bastards will do for me soon enough."

The handkerchief disappeared and the conversation died as the engines ran up to take-off power.

Neither of them spoke until the ascent was complete, and the 'hospital plane' was set on its course to Rostov-na-Donu.

Gurundov fished in his pocket and brought out a flask of vodka, pouring two measures in the modest silver cups, and offered one to the female GRU officer.

"Let us toast to your successes and victory for the Motherland, Comrade Mayor General."

Nazarbayeva shook her head.

"To victory, Comrade General Gurundov. My successes have not been great of late."

"A setback... happens to all of us... but... as you wish... to Victory!"

They knocked back their measures, which amounted to hair of the dog for Nazarbayeva.

"You have done your best for the Motherland. Comrade Nazarbayeva, and Comrade Stalin understands that. Otherwise, why would he permit you and your husband to spend two weeks in his most favourite place in the whole Motherland, eh?"

Nazarbayeva's eyes narrowed.

"I'm sorry, Comrade Leytenant General, but how do you know that? I only found out myself some hours ago."

Gurundov chuckled again, holding out his hands, palms first, in a silent admission that he knew what he knew.

He added an explanation to calm the clearly worried GRU officer.

"I work for Comrade Molotov... as an... err... unofficial advisor on military and other matters. I'm not really a General... well... not any more. I was once, but after the war I travelled the world in search of something that would help my lungs."

He poured another measure for them both and continued.

"I visited many countries, without great success. This brought me to the attention of the Commissariat and I was asked to... um... advise and consult... you could say spy for them."

Gurundov smiled disarmingly, but Nazarbayeva's suspicions were aroused.

"But you're not Comrade Molotov's official military liaison officer, that's Com..."

"No... you're right... I'm not."

He extended the flask again, and she accepted the refill.

"In many ways, I'm in your line of business. I gather information for Comrade Molotov... on matters that affect foreign policy. I report to no one but him, and owe no affiliation to anyone but him... and, of course, the Motherland."

"I had no idea, comrade."

"Excellent. That's the way I like it, Comrade Nazarbayeva."

"So, why are you travelling to the Black Sea, Comrade Gurundov?"

He knocked back his measure of vodka and considered his words carefully.

"The sea air is good for my lungs, and Comrade Molotov has secured a dacha at Sochi, which he has graciously permitted me to use for a restorative break."

451

She waited for the rest of it.

He decided to invest in the woman, to display trust… to remove her suspicions…

He lowered his voice and leant forward.

"Also, I am here to help with part of Project Raduga. I know you are aware of this project."

Nazarbayeva simply nodded her understanding, although hearing the name of the Soviet Union's most secret operation whispered by someone she had known for less than thirty minutes was a considerable shock.

"The aircraft will make a quick stop at Novorossiysk, where myself and Captain Kalinin will alight and leave you to continue your journey. My language skills, amongst other of my talents, are apparently needed. I won't be in Sochi for a few days yet, but I will call on you when I arrive."

Nazarbayeva's brain accessed a memory… of a naval officer waiting outside Stalin's office… and who had accompanied him at the time.

She married the visual recollection with the live image of the Red Navy Captain sat three rows up.

'Captain Third… no… now Second Rank Mikhail Stepanovich Kalinin… submarine commander… Stalin's birthday… atomic weapons… what was his name… Nitina… no… Nishina.'

She took a chance.

"Language skills. Japanese, I assume?"

Gurundov smiled without smiling, remembering that the woman in front of him was not to be underestimated.

"Very perceptive of you, Comrade Nazarbayeva."

"So is there a problem with Raduga, Comrade Gurundov? I've heard nothing."

"That's because it's only just come to light, Comrade."

She waited to be enlightened further, but Gurundov did not volunteer anything further.

"Another?"

He produced the flask once more.

"Thank you, Comrade Gurundov. Shall we drink to the success of your mission, whatever it may be?"

He grinned from ear to ear and put her out of her misery.

"Let us drink to our allies, and that they recover their commitment to the cause."

He went to knock back his vodka, but realised that the woman had not moved.

452

Even with her urgent whisper toned down, Nazarbayeva failed to mask her concern.

"There's a problem with their commitment? They're absolutely essential to the project."

He waved the empty flask at nobody in particular, solely to highlight the gravity of his next words.

"Yes, they are, and at the moment, Raduga is dead in the waterfor a number of reasons... one of which is because 'they' have doubts."

"Then we must remove those doubts and reinvigorate them, Comrade. If I can help, then don't hesitate to ask... please."

"Thank you, Comrade. We may well need you, but in any case, I'll see you at the dacha, once my work is done."

The unequivocal statement was bound to draw a comment.

"That's twice you've said that, Comrade Gurundov, almost like that's part of your mission."

His chuckle held less humour third time around.

"In a very real sense it is, but not part of the mission entrusted to me by the GKO."

She passed back the silver cup, accompanying it with a look that required an answer to the question it posed.

"Comrade General Kaganovich has asked me to spend some time with you, on matters too delicate to be openly observed."

"Comrade General Kaganovich?"

"But yes... shall we say... err... I don't just report to Comrade Molotov?"

Some small sense started a fire in her brain, which stoked up to a raging inferno of thought processes, which quickly resolved into a single intense blazing memory fighting its way to the front of her recognition.

"Gurundov? The name is familiar to me for some reason, Comrade General."

"My brother was Filip Karlovich Gurundov... a hero of the Soviet Union. He was killed by fascist tanks at Kharkov in 1943, along with his oldest son Alexei Filipovich. Perhaps that is where you have heard the name, Comrade Nazarbayeva."

He noticed the look that fell across her face.

"Comrade?"

"So... you are Vassily Karlovich Gurundov?"

"That is so."

'VKG.'

She made her move quickly.

"Have you ever been to Krakow, Comrade General?"

453

If he recognised the attempted pass phrase, Gurundov hid it expertly behind a mask of confusion.

"I once spent Christmas there. Wonderful place."

"There's nothing like Christmas in Krakow."

Nazarbayeva hardly dared breathe.

Gurundov nodded.

"Comrade General Nazarbayeva."

It took her a moment to realise that the words had not come from Gurundov.

"Yes?"

"Peltsov, Commander of the Southern Special grouping. I was wondering if I could pick your brain for any further information about the Allied threat?"

She looked at Gurundov who simply shrugged in acceptance.

"The Motherland's needs must come before small talk. We will continue our conversation another time, Comrade Mayor General."

Gurundov moved away as quickly as his damaged body would allow him, and Peltsov dropped into his place.

Nazarbayeva stared at the departing general's back, willing him to turn and speak, or even simply mouth the response she sought.

'Except May Day in Moscow.'

Gurundov turned.

'Go on, old man, speak the words… now… just mouth them…'

The old general smiled and found a seat in which he could silently drop off to sleep.

Peltsov's enquiries were pertinent, and she answered them as best she could, occasionally stealing a glance at the lolling head, and wondering what he had been about to say.

The plane was diverted from Rostov-na-Donu airfield, for unexplained technical reasons that an Air Force colonel confided were likely to be Allied aircraft visiting the facilities again, and the DC-4 was descending to Novorossiysk before Peltsov had finished his questioning and note taking, leaving Nazarbayeva no chance to renew her conversation with Gurundov.

He left the aircraft without any further chance to speak to Nazarbayeva, save a small nod and goodbye, and the old man made the short walk to the security compound, where he joined the small convoy that would take the road from Novorossiysk to the Vinogradar Young Communists Sailing Club, as it was known locally.

The DC-4 climbed into the air once more, taking a combination of happy military personnel to a well-deserved break in Sochi, and disgruntled military personnel who had yet to arrive at Rostov, their final destination.

Plus one GRU General whose mind whirled with questions and possibilities.

1539 hrs, Monday, 29th July 1946, Grossglockener, Carinthia, Austria.

It had taken some time for the team to reach the area, and even more time for them to find anything resembling a modern transport aircraft.

But they found it, none the less.

There had never been any hope of survivors, for the Grossglockener was a cold and forbidding place, even in summer, so even if a body had been lucky enough to survive the impact, the environment would be bound to triumph.

And so it had proved, as the wreckage, spread over a large area, yielded only the frozen-rigid corpses of those long dead.

The 'rescuers' moved quickly around the site, seemingly more concerned about personal possessions and baggage than recovering the mortal remains of the Red Cross personnel.

The leader spoke into his radio.

"C'mon guys, hustle up. The rescue teams are about two hours out, and I want to put plenty of snow between them and us."

Throughout the area, his men, clad all in white, rummagedg through the wreckage and recovered all sorts of material, stowing the contents of their labours in large rucksacks.

Papers, files, containers… anything that had intelligence value.

"Cap'n!"

Morris Snyder turned to the source of the shout.

Farrah, the unit's radio operator, waved him closer.

"According to our top cover, they're in the next valley up… closer than we thought, Cap'n."

Snyder looked around him and worked the problem.

His briefing had been clear.

*'Command's orders are simple. Get to the wreck as quickly as possible and recover as much intel as possible. Make it as anonymous as possible, but certainly **do not get discovered**. The possibility of recovering injured has not been discussed and you should use your own judgement. Rememver, the mission comes first…'*

455

He looked at the map and confirmed in which valley the recon aircraft had spotted the rescuers.

The aircraft was ostensibly working for the rescue effort, but was actually observing for the small team of experienced skiers and mountaineers from the elite 10th US Mountain Division.

"Green, Red, over."

"I hear you, Red."

"We have twelve minutes tops, Green. I want your squad ready to lead off in ten. Clear."

"Roger."

William Green drove his men harder.

"Red, Blue, over."

"Receiving."

"Blue, hustle 'em up. You got ten minutes. Check over by that big boulder", he pointed so that Sergeant Berry could see where he was talking about, "There's all sort of shit over there, Blue, over."

"Roger."

Red Snyder watched as Berry sent some of his men towards the unexplored area, and returned to Farrah.

"Get that info firmed up with the birdmen, Corporal. I ain't getting jumped by a bunch of civilian do-gooders."

He lit a cigarette and watched his men redouble their efforts.

Eleven minutes later, the thirty-man group moved off, now also burdened with a lot of materiel from the dead Red Cross party.

Files, briefcases, loose papers… anything that could be of value.

1701 hrs, Tuesday, 30th July 1946, Karup Air Base, Denmark.

It was the hottest day of the year so far, a fact that needed no announcement to the men who disembarked from the C-69 Constellation.

The aircraft, one of the most modern in the USAAF transport fleet, had been crammed full with specialist personnel, enacting a command decision to move the maximum number of qualified bodies, in order to expedite the operations of Composite Group 663, the most secret operational bomber unit in Europe, bar none.

The eight-hour flight had tested the resolve of even the most resilient of men, and the aroma that accompanied them as they stepped down did not go unnoticed by the reception committee.

Colonel Jens Lauridson of the Danish Air Force, base commander at Karup, led the delegation that received the American airmen and ground crew.

"Colonel Banner?"

Behind the sunglasses and huge cigar lay a tired and unhappy man.

None the less, he tried to be polite.

"Colonel Lauridson?"

They shook hands warmly, although the Dane felt unclean from the moment he touched flesh.

"I suggest that we get you and your men cleaned up first, Colonel?"

"You'll get no goddamned resistance from me on that one, fella."

"Have your men follow this officer", he beckoned an Air Force Captain forward.

The man beside Lauridson coughed politely.

"Apologies, Wing Commander. Colonel Banner, this is Wing Commander Cheshire... Colonel Banner."

The two shook hands.

Banner's eyes were immediately drawn to the array of ribbons on the man's tunic, including the highest his country had to offer, but he was also aware that the eyes that assessed him were tired, almost lacking in light.

"You're my second in command I think, fella."

"Indeed, Colonel Banner. I command the RAF contingent here. Perhaps we should postpone further introductions until you and your men have a chance to eat and rest."

"I'm all for that, fella."

Banner turned to his weary crew.

"Ok, listen up, boys. We're gonna get ourselves cleaned up and get some chow. This Danish officer will show you the way. No duties for tonight. Just get your gear stowed away. Best behaviour or I'll know why. I'll issue orders during the evening. Dismiss."

Cheshire observed the disorganised display with some disdain, but kept his own counsel, although he caught Lauridson sending him a quiet look.

'Was this man really the best the Americans had for the mission?'

It would surprise Cheshire no end that he would one day refer to Colonel Gary George Banner as probably the finest officer he had ever met.

457

Eternal Father strong to save,
Whose arm has bound the restless wave,
Who bids the mighty ocean deep,
It's own appointed limits keep,
O hear us when we cry to Thee,
For those in Peril on the sea.

William Whiting.

Chapter 166 - THE STRAW

0934 hrs, Wednesday, 31st July 1946, the docks, Swinemünde, Pomerania.

"Is that wise, Sir?"

"Well, unless you want to get your boys off and make way for proper fighting soldiers, I guess it's all we have, Crisp."

There was no insult, only humour, although McAuliffe's resilience was being tested heavily.

"Wouldn't it be better to wait... see what the navy comes up with, Sir?"

"This withdrawal has been planned down to a tee, Colonel. The Spanish are in your old quarters as we speak. You and the 327th have nowhere to go back to. In any case, the trains'll be waiting at Lübeck. Waiting for both your troopers and the 327th boys. Navy's let us down... couldn't be helped... that's the way it is, son. If we pack 'em tight in your boat, we'll get both of you to the trains and back to Mourmelon a-sap."

On cue, they both turned to examine the crippled Haskell-class attack transport, USS Allendale, from whose superstructure smoke still rose lazily.

An accidental fire, according to the ship's captain, but one that deprived units of the 327th Glider Infantry their ticket home.

McAuliffe received a written report with a grunt, read it, and handed it across to Crisp.

"So, navy say they can definitely squeeze you all into Kingsbury. Let's get it done, Colonel. It won't be for too long. Just make sure your boys give the 'Bulldogs' enough room for them to stand up and cock a leg to pee, ok?"

"I hear that, Sir."

The 327th had taken a pounding during its time in Pomerania, losing their commander, Bud Harper, injured in the initial stages. They then suffered the loss of the replacement regimental commander to Soviet mortars on the final day of their exposure to front line action.

Which left Acting Lieutenant Colonel Griffin Field in charge, a man with whom Crisp had an excellent relationship, following the bloody slugfests at Wolin.

"Liaise with Field and get 'em stowed away so that Kingsbury can get away by midday, Crisp."

The harbour at Swinemünde was capable of taking only two decent sized vessels, much of the ports facilities having been damaged by the Allies, then the Germans, then the Russians, and finally, the Allies once more.

McAuliffe acknowledged Crisp's salute and set his mind to the next problem, which had doubled in complication with the damage to APA-127 USS Allendale, which vessel was now occupying one of his two berths.

Determined to put a 'burr under the arse' of the ship's captain, McAuliffe strode off down the dock, followed by harassed staff officers who were better equipped for organising an airborne assault than a seaborne evacuation.

101st had been denied an aerial return, the increased number of Soviet jet aircraft cited as one reason, the constant presence of transports delivering Spanish and Polish units another, although rumours about shortages of transport aircraft through to fuel abounded.

Still, as McAuliffe had quipped to his senior officers, it was a lovely time of year for a cruise.

1017 hrs, Thursday, 1st August 1946, the Oval Office, Washington DC, USA.

Truman stood at the window, his brain full of facts and assumptions, statements of intent and promises, some of which were historical, and some of which had been dramatically set out before him by the small group of men sat silently behind him.

'Ban the bomb…use the bomb… send more troops… bring the boys home…'

He rammed his hands onto his hips and set his jaw, examined his reflection and scowled at himself.

He turned round and slammed his hand on the desk.

"Goddamned censure? Is he really expecting us to believe that?"

459

"No way, Mister President, but Governor Ellis is talking about it just the same. Moreover, at the moment, he's the only one that's talking openly about it, Mister President, but others are following suit behind the scenes, stirring the pot."

"Say that again, John."

"It's not just Ellis that's talking up censure as a way of making you use the bomb and bring the boys home. Sure, Georgia's taking the lead, but South Carolina, California, Florida, Michigan, Virginia, New York, and Texas are close behind. Not counting the few on the other side of the argument, who are also rumbling on the matter... I mean those who are tentatively backing the application of pressure to withdraw... either way, there is a ground swell of heavy muscle that is taking a stance against the way you are running this war."

"On what grounds?"

"Mister President, on the grounds that you are failing to prosecute the war to the fullest extent and endangering American lives and the safety of the American nation by not so doing."

"What?"

A session intended to discuss the changing situation in Britain and Canada had become something entirely different.

John R. Steelman, White House Chief of Staff, was the bearer of the bad news.

Truman resumed his seat and looked at each man in turn.

"Gentlemen, before we go any further with this session... has any of you brought me good news?"

The silence was heavy with meaning.

"George?"

George Marshall prepared himself to heap more bad news on top of it.

"Mister President... I have some figures here..."

"One moment, please. Henry?"

"I'm afraid not, Mister President."

Henry Stimson had anything but good news to deliver.

Truman looked directly at James Byrnes, Secretary of State, and pursed his lips in a silent request.

"No, Sir. I am the bearer of bad tidings."

Truman heard them all out, taking the latest casualty figures from Europe badly, the total American casualty figures since December 1941 now approaching two million, including a staggering total of six hundred and seventy thousand dead, two hundred and sixty-five thousand in the period commencing on August 6th 1945.

460

Considerably more than half the number that had died in the previous four years of war.

He winced as Secretary of State Byrnes relayed messages, ranging from concern to outrage, from heads of state or ambassadors, most accompanied by threats to withdraw direct support from the Allied cause.

Stimson and Marshall added to the sense of foreboding with their appreciation of the military situation, and the likely effects of continuing the struggle.

Stimson, in an attempt to be upbeat, played the technology card, talking of new tanks, new guns, new aircraft, all being made available to the boys on the front line, but nothing he said could hide the truth.

The Unites States capacity to wage war was intact, but the political situation was confused, with rival camps wanting peace or use of the bombs, entrenched polar opposites who wouldn't budge.

Truman spoke to no-one in particular, simply giving voice to the turmoil in his head.

"So, all it's gonna take is one single thing, one tragedy, one lost battle, one effective speech, one more bloody demonstration on an American street. That's probably now all that is needed to bring it all crashing down around us, one way or the other."

"Use the bomb, Mister President."

Only Byrnes refrained from the call.

Steelman led the baying for its deployment.

"If the Allied nations are going to fall out, then to hell with it. Use the bomb... use it now... stop the rot spreading... stick one on the Communists and we will have all the public support back behind us... talk of censure will disappear because it'll shut up the 'go for broke' lobby... people will see that our boys will prevail. If you prevaricate and the Allies start falling away, that'll obviously give the anti-war movement steel in their backs and create more issues."

"No."

"But Sir, we must d..."

"I said no. We will not use the bombs and fracture the Allied cause. Without a strong Allied group, the Communists will prevail, if not now, then at some time in the future. I will not pass on that legacy to the world. I will NOT! We WILL maintain the Allied grouping at all costs. Am I clear on that point, gentlemen?"

There was little to be unclear about.

The meeting terminated with no further decisions, save to diplomatically massage the Allies, pressurise the Canadians as nicely as possible, and to sympathetically and publically support Churchill in his struggle against public discontent the length and breadth of the United Kingdom and beyond.

It was also decided to review the military plan and reduce US exposure to the barest minimum.

Truman enjoyed a moment's solitude before the door opened and one of his secret service agents stuck his head around it.

"Sir, your eleven-thirty is still waiting."

Truman looked at the clock and grinned momentarily.

'11.50. Let the man wait a while longer.'

Truman grinned at his own thoughts.

'Petulance isn't your style, Harry. Let him have his say.'

"Thank you, Raoul. Please have him shown in."

Thomas Edmund Dewey, Governor of New York, strode in, with the two NY senators, James M. Mead and Robert F. Wagner, close on his flanks.

Truman shook hands with the three men and motioned them towards seating.

"So, my apologies for the delay. How may I help you, gentlemen?

Dewey took the lead.

"That's simple, Mister President. You can either fight the goddamned war with every weapon God has given you, saving the lives of countless American boys along the way, or you can resign and let someone with the cojones take the lead. Which'll it be?"

Within fifteen seconds, members of the Secret Service charged into the room, expecting to find a huge mob out of hand, such was the violence of the short conversation.

Truman and the three politicians did not part on good terms.

2357 hrs, Thursday, 1st August 1946, eight kilometres northwest of Darsser Ort, the Baltic Sea.

Crisp had been asleep since just after nine pm, the blissful experience of not having to make decisions and not having to worry about the day-to-day business of commanding a parachute infantry regiment, had brought the deepest sleep he had experienced since two nights before the jump into the blackness over Pomerania.

Unusually for the two and a half thousand men shoehorned aboard, sleep took precedence over craps, poker, or simply horsing about, as almost every man, glider infantryman or paratrooper, used the opportunity to store valuable sleep away.

462

The gentle tenors of the waves lapping at the hull, and the rhythmic sound of the throbbing Westinghouse turbine, brought kind dreams to each and every man, as the USS Kingsbury's single screw carried them further away from the war.

Four miles ahead, a number of technical problems plagued the commander of HMS Jason, a Halcyon-class minesweeper, as his equipment again failed him.

Acting Lieutenant Commander Harry Layland Dudley Hoare chased his crew in all directions, but they simply could not restore full operation. One of the kites had decided to dive to the bottom, and the winch that could recover it had simply given up the ghost.

Hoare radioed the Commodore, but the man railed against anything that could mean delay, and simply told the minesweeper officer to 'sort it out'.

The Commodore, anxious to preserve his sailing schedule, ignored Hoare's recommendation to transfer some north side work to one of the other minesweepers, and decided to press on regardless, citing the complete absence of any mines on the journey to Swinemünde and, thus far, on the return.

Which meant that L3 'Frunzenets', sunk on 10th December 1945, would reach out from her watery grave and claim yet another Allied vessel.

2357 hrs, Thursday, 1st August 1946, eight kilometres northwest of Darsser Ort, the Baltic Sea.

Colonel Marion Crisp was lifted from his bunk and deposited with perfect precision on the bunk on the other side of the cabin, much to the displeasure of the occupant.

Griffin Field moaned in pain and clutched at his stomach, where Crisp's hard buttocks had announced his soft landing.

Marion Crisp rolled off the injured man and immediately realised that he simply continued to roll across the floor of the cabin, heading back the six feet to the bunk from which he had been thrown.

His hands pushed out, stopping him from clattering into the metal supports.

"C'mon, Griff, move your ass… the ship's listing."

He grabbed at the winded Field and virtually dragged him to the door.

It refused to open.

Field, recovering slowly, lent his shoulder to the effort.

463

The door shifted a little, not enough to permit them to leave, but sufficient for the smoke to enter the cabin.

"Again!"

Crisp threw himself against the unyielding metal and bounced off.

"Again!"

The two men hit it together and the movement encouraged them.

Another three blows brought enough of a gap for Crisp to call a halt.

"Let's go… you first, Griff."

The Acting Lieutenant Colonel squirmed through, closely followed by Crisp.

The smoke was denser now, and moved thickly through their throats and lungs, bringing about racking coughs.

"Fresh air… this way… follow me…"

Crisp grabbed Field's hand and followed the memory image in his head, and found the stairs up immediately.

As the pair climbed towards the next level, a tannoy announcement cut across the growing sounds of men under duress.

Whilst many of the words were somewhat distorted by some sort of damage issue, the message was absolutely clear.

"Attention all hands! Attention all hands! Abandon ship. Abandon ship!"

The two officers emerged into the darkest of nights, now transformed by the severe fire that was claiming the ship around them.

"We've got to organise our boys… calm them down and do this orderly… get some control…"

Field nodded and plunged towards a group of his own soldiers massing at the ship's side.

The Kingsbury shuddered and lurched a few feet further over, enough to send men flying off their feet and hurtling into others, creating more struggling forms.

Searchlights from other vessels also lit up the scene, and help create the surreal sight of soldiers and sailors illuminated in dancing shades of diamond white and orange.

An explosion opened up the deck in front of Crisp, and he was picked up and thrown into dark sky.

His unconscious form dropped into the cool waters, surrounded by men desperate to stay afloat… desperate to survive.

At 0006, before a single rescue ship could get close enough, USS Kingsbury APA-177, rolled over into the Baltic, nine minutes to the second after she had hit 'Frunzenets'' mine.

464

Fig # 212 - The voyage of USS Kingsbury, APA-177.

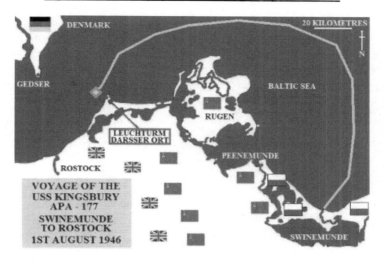

1847 hrs, Sunday, 4th August 1946, the Guards Club, London, England.

Sir Fabian John Callard-Smith, VC holder, MP for Wroughton, and retired Coldstream Guards Colonel, read the report in silence, seeing familiar names in every paragraph, some alive and soon to be honoured, others lost to the insatiable machine of war.

Across the small table sat his friend and confidante, the Right Honourable Percy Aston Hollander MC and bar, formerly a major in the Irish Guards, who was reading the same document, an insider's report that recorded the efforts and exertions of the Guards units of His Majesty's army.

"Good Lord... Bunty's gone west. Poor Janette... we must go and visit as soon as possible... poor old Bunty."

Percy Hollander shook his head at the news that another of the old school had lost his life in the new war.

Whilst he hadn't served with Jacob 'Bunty' Hargreaves, he knew of the man by reputation, one often enhanced by anecdotes from Callard-Smith, who had shared a bunker with him for many months on the Western Front in 1917-18.

"All through the last lot, only to die in some crabby corner of Krautland... damn and blast... damn and blast..."

"Wasn't he divisional staff, John?"

465

Callard-Smith nodded and offered up an explanation immediately.

"Never one to sit at the back though. Never. Bound to have been up at the front. Looks like he was with the Coldstreams up the sharp end when he copped it... lots of Coldstreamers got the chop on the same day... 28th July... around Parchim... not just Coldstreamers either... seems like the Grenadiers got a bloody good dusting too."

Aston nodded, concern at the loss of so many members of the Guards Brigade written large on his face.

Squires, clubman and an ex-Coldstream Guardsman himself, moved towards the pair as quickly as his disability would allow.

"Colonel Fabian... Major Percy... The Sunday Evening News, sirs."

He passed each a copy of the London newspaper.

"Dreadful business, Sirs... dreadful."

The headline screamed at both men.

'BALTIC DISASTER - THOUSANDS DEAD'

They quickly consumed the bare facts, grimacing at the numbers involved.

"I say, poor sods."

"Quite, Percy. Squires, two more scotches please, there's a good chap."

The clubman nodded and hobbled away to distribute more of the freshly printed newspapers on his way back to the bar.

The murmurs grew in the smoking room, as more eyes acquainted themselves with the disaster.

Percy's eyes clouded over with painful memories as he read one word.

"Mine, so they say... nasty bloody things. Brother Clarence was lost to the nasty bloody things... on the Irresistible, off Gallipoli in '15. Nasty blighters."

"I remember, Percy. Johnny Turk used a lot of the horrible things off the peninsular. Did for a few of our matelots. So damned impersonal."

Callard-Smith dropped his gaze again and immediately took a sharp intake of breath.

"I say...101st... those boys saw an awful lot of fighting... an awful lot of fighting."

Both men dropped their newspapers down so they could look at each other.

"The God of Battle, eh, Percy?

Hollander snorted. A confirmed atheist, he believed in no such thing, but he understood what Callard-Smith meant.

'All that fighting ... from D-Day to Poland... and killed by one of those nasty bloody impersonal things when out of the front line.'

"Tragic way for a soldier to go, Fabian. Bloody tragic."

"Quite. Still... over two thousand American dead in one foul swoop... that's certainly not going to go down well on the other side of the pond, is it?"

"Most certainly not. The common American will either want the boys home yesterday, or will be baying for Uncle Joe's blood like a hound on the scent."

When the news reached the states, and families from Oregon to Maine became aware that one of their most prestigious units, the 101st US Airborne, had suffered grievous casualties in such a random manner, the result was very much the latter.

Tuesday, 6th August 1946. Editorial piece, First edition, Washington Evening Star.

President Truman's constant failure to employ the full range of weapons from the armoury of liberty cannot be underestimated. He has cited, on numerous occasions, the need to ensure that the coalition of Allied forces remains cohesive, and names the opposition to further use of certain weapons, prevalent amongst those Allies, as the chief reason for staying his hand.

This publication accepts that the use of those weapons, and we must be clear that we are speaking of the new atomic bombs so recently deployed against the Empire of Japan, will bring about horrendous loss of life and suffering, both at the time of deployment and, it has been suggested, long into the futures of those subjected to its use.

Whether or not the President is correct about the Allies' discontent, and the threat it poses to our coalition of freedom, we must consider the situation in its fullest context.

We, America and our Allies, have been subjected to the vilest form of attack; an unprovoked aggression and betrayal of our nations by one country, supposedly friendly, and one so recently allied with us in that great crusade against the armies of oppression and aggression.

467

The peoples of the Soviet Union and its allies have, by their act of unparalleled perfidy, laid themselves open to our wrath, and we should not feel shackled by the undoubted superiority of our technology, not feel shackled by its totally destructive nature, and certainly not feel shackled that it would visit hell on earth upon the enemy. Whilst we can only accept that there will be casualties amongst the innocent, with whom the guilty will inevitably surround themselves, we have to understand that this nation, this alliance, has at its disposal the means to end this war, and possibly all wars to come

What appears to be lacking is the will to use it, a stance excused by the interpretation of how others might react; how others may 'view' such a use.

This publication offers the following clarifications to assist the President in deciding on the right way forward.

This great nation of ours has made prodigious sacrifices on the altar of freedom, and none more so than in this latest and most costly of wars. Our casualties, counted since Pearl Harbor to the fall of Berlin, numbered roughly two million, dead, wounded and missing. That number has recently risen to over two and a half million.

That means that many hundreds of thousands of Americans have succumbed to injury or death, or are missing, since the enemy rolled across the divide last August.

Recent events in the Baltic have claimed the lives of two and a half thousands of our youngest and finest, men from the Screaming Eagles Airborne, men who had experienced countless battles from the Normandy shores to the green fields of Poland.

This single incident represents one of the greatest losses of life in the history of the United States military, and to what end?

In just under a year of the new war, combined with the bloody echoes of the now concluded war against the Empire of Japan, this nation has sustained these unprecedented levels of loss, knowing that freedom is never free, and that we must fight to preserve it from tyranny, wherever it is to be encountered. We, as a people, have come together in support of our soldiers, sailors, airmen and marines. We have provided the weapons and fuels of war, and answered every weighty call that government and honour have placed upon our shoulders. Our armed forces have an expectation; we, here at home, have an

468

expectation, that our administration will do everything within its power to end the war as soon as is possible, and for the minimum loss of life and limb amongst our sons, husbands, fathers and brothers. Actually more than that. Our armed forces and public alike have the absolute right to demand that our administration will do everything in its power to end the bloodshed, and ensure that as many brave American boys as possible return from the combat zone.

Our valiant Allies will unquestionably understand and embrace that demand, for it is also their sons, their husbands, their fathers and their brothers that will profit from a speedy conclusion to this conflict.

We have the means to end this war, and set in place a peace that could last for a thousand years.

There is no satisfactory argument against it; against the inevitable saving of American and Allied lives, so this publication demands that President Truman employ the new atomic devices, and that he bring our loved ones safely back home.

1423 hrs, Tuesday, 6th August 1946, the Oval Office, Washington DC, USA.

"And there are no more… definitely no more?"

"No, Mister President. We believe that there were upwards of two and a half thousand soldiers on that ship, plus the crew of five hundred and one… from which we have confirmed seventy US Navy survivors, and one hundred and thirty-seven paratroopers."

"Two hundred and seven men… that's all?"

"Yes, Sir, but I urge caution. Some of those boys won't make it."

"Good God. I've a recommendation on my desk for another presidential citation for those airborne boys. Now I'm going to have to write a tribute to their lives, and try and convince folks that these brave boys gave their all in the service of our nation… how in the name of God do I do that? Eh?"

"The British fouled up, Mister President. Their minesweepers didn't do their job."

Truman gripped the desk so hard his fingers went white.

"You can make that the last time you say that, George."

George Marshall relaxed his posture in acknowledgement of the rebuke.

469

"These things happen, and I will not pillory our allies… is that clear? This was an enemy mine… it killed our boys… that's all our people need to know. Anything else, we keep in house. Is that absolutely clear, gentlemen?"

The responses reassured Truman and he relaxed.

"Ok then. How are the people taking it, John?"

Steelman couldn't wrap it up in any way, and simply passed over the first edition of the Washington Evening Star, accompanying it with one word.

"Bad."

Actually, it was much worse than bad.

The editorial was pretty good, Truman had to admit, but it was also damaging to him and his administration, laying out the awful loss sustained by the 'Screaming Eagles', and asking for what had they died, undermining much of Truman's intended speech in a few lines of well-thought out print.

The setting out of the arguments for use of the bomb were well-known and well made, and Truman knew he would have a hard time rebutting the points, as he tackled the maintenance of the Allied Alliance head on, citing the cost in American lives of propping up the ailing group, with figures, awful figures, that showed how much blood America had spilt in the doing.

"We've the heads up, as a courtesy only, from the nationals… they're running the same editorial themes nationwide."

The Chief of Staff sat down heavily, his day having been spent in exhausting damage limitation…

'… failed damage limitation…'

Truman waited whilst the others in the Oval Office consumed the story and the editorial.

The final face looked up and he continued.

"Well, one thing's for sure. Our lives got a little more complicated. George, do everything you can for those poor boys… living and dead… I want them all brought home straight away… straight away, y'hear me."

Marshall nodded, knowing it would be a simple enough matter.

Dead men were easier to transport than the living.

"Now, gentlemen, what can we do to fix this mess?"

At 7pm Eastern Standard time, President Truman spoke primarily to the nation, although his words were broadcast around the globe, words addressing the wider issues of the conflict, words intent on specifically addressing the non-use of the bomb.

He also spoke intimately about the losses the country had sustained, with particular reference to the tragic events surrounding the 101st's recent history.

Truman spoke for thirteen minutes, bringing spirit and passion to the cause he held so dear.

Having laid out the facts as he saw them, he appealed to the heads and hearts of the people, seeking support and understanding for the position of his administration.

His entourage followed his delivery word for word, the text agreed by all lifted from the pages of script to roll off Truman's tongue, delivered in the President's inimitable style.

The speech in general, and bombshell at the end in particular, had already been discussed with Churchill, De Gaulle, and even Speer. The Allied leaders understood and were, in general, in agreement,

But then the entourage started to shuffle their papers, seeking the missing page, as words hit their ears that did not come from the speech... simple words that came from Truman's heart.

"For nearly five years now, the free world has looked to us, seeking inspiration and guidance from the leadership we bring, and the sacrifices we are prepared to make in the name of our country's values... make in the name of maintaining freedom for all."

"This leadership is best delivered by a country and people united behind its common conviction, a belief in the righteousness of the cause to which it is committed."

"I appeal to you, my countrymen, to further journey with me... to produce the materials of war... to send them across the oceans... to support our troops in the prosecution of this war... a war not of our making."

"We cannot do this shackled by doubt, be it doubt about the sacrifices this nation and our young men are making, or doubt about how best to bring an end to this conflict, an end that best serves the needs of the world."

"Yes, we have the technology... the aircraft, the tanks, the ships... and yes... we have the bomb... and we have all seen its terrible effects. Some Americans oppose its further use, others encourage its profligate use... both views have merit... and both have their issues."

"The world has been horrified by the images and reports that have sprung from the hands and lips of survivors."

"The bombs are the ultimate weapon of war, but they are horrible weapons and, quite rightly, we should think long and hard before using them again. Perhaps... it may be... that this display on Japan might ensure they are never needed again."

Truman paused and gathered himself.

"As your President, I ask this of you. Understand that I will not shirk from their use, and would not hesitate to order such a use right at this moment, should it be prudent to do so... but... at this time... it is not."

"There are wider issues here, for we must convince the free world, and carry them with us before further employment. We cannot just expect the people of this planet to fall in line with our way of thinking. To do that would be arrogant at the very least."

"Our Allies baulk at further deployment of these weapons and we must, and will, listen to their concerns... and assuage them as best we can... and not deploy them until we can carry the world with us, in wholehearted agreement that their use is just and proper."

He eased his collar with a swipe of his finger.

"That is the assurance I have given to the leaders of the Allied nations, and one I reiterate here... now... in front of you all."

"There is a weighty proposition that our refusal to use these weapons might be misunderstood, and might give comfort to our enemies. This is an argument I have heard, and can understand... but one I also disagree with."

"Our enemies have seen that we have the will, and will not shirk from their use, should the circumstances be right."

"On 16th April last year, I stood before Congress and made the following statement."

Truman produced a small piece of paper that contained a verbatim of the passage he wished to remind his people of.

"And I quote... *It is not enough to yearn for peace. We must work, and if necessary, fight for it. The task of creating a sound international organization is complicated and difficult. Yet, without such organization, the rights of man on earth cannot be protected. Machinery for the just settlement of international differences must be found. Without such machinery, the entire world will have to remain an armed camp. The world will be doomed to deadly conflict, devoid of hope for real peace.*"

"My fellow Americans, that is the crux of it all. We must... and we will... defeat the Communists... wherever we find them, and we, as a nation, and I, as your president, am as committed as ever to

472

that end. But we must maintain the Alliance, and create a stronger organisation. By using the bomb unilaterally, without the agreement of our Allies, we risk sundering the very base of the organisation that we need to construct to ensure that peace will flourish for our children, and all the children that come after."

"Constant vigilance will be the price that we, as a world, will pay for our future liberty and freedoms."

'Here it comes...'

"To that end, today, I announce that we will formalise and strengthen our international Alliance under a new title... the North Atlantic Treaty Organisation... a grouping that will bring the nations fighting in this conflict together, unified under the umbrella of an organisation conceived by free peoples, for the purpose of maintaining freedom for all."

"As soon as is practicable, I will travel to Europe and meet with the heads of state of our Allies, and together we will bring forth the new organisation, NATO, born out of our common desire to combine all our peoples in the defence of liberty and freedom."

"I humbly pray to Almighty God that you, the people, will embrace this new organisation, and permit America to lead the world to peace and prosperity."

"Good night to you all, and may God bless America."

The morning newspapers and radio programmes were less than enthusiastic, hardly addressing the formation of NATO, instead focussing on the failure to employ the bombs and the 'weak' excuses the President had cited.

Around the world, the press was generally more accepting, and there was a slight change in attitude towards the bomb, now that the views of the US president were laid bare.

However, it was in Moscow that the reverberations of Truman's words made most impact, and the interpretation of them started, imperceptibly at first, to crystallise divisions in the hierarchy of the Soviet State, although, in truth, there was only one interpretation that really mattered, and his was that there was a weakness to be explored and exploited.

In Stalin's unchallenged opinion, the formation of NATO was considered almost an irrelevance.

Battles are sometimes won by generals; wars are nearly always won by sergeants and privates.

F.E. Adcock

Chapter 167 - THE PHOTOGRAPHS

1545 hrs, Wednesday, 7th August 1946, Bad Nauheim Air Base, Germany.

Two weeks previously, a Mk XI-PR Spitfire of the USAAF's 14th Photographic Reconnaissance Squadron, had overflown Auschwitz-Birkenau in Poland, one of a number of missions trying to ascertain the nature of the present occupants of the former Nazi death camp.

Photo-interpretation had been done, but the evidence was still not there, although unconfirmed reports from the ground indicated that there were a leavening of Allied POWs and political prisoners from amongst the 'liberated' Poles, the POWs located mostly in the brick-built Auschwitz site, a former Polish cavalry base.

The killing machines, the huge gas chambers and ovens that had been the despicable heart of Birkenau, had been demolished by the retreating Germans in 1945, in a desperate attempt to hide the monstrous crimes they perpetrated there.

The Soviets used the remaining facilities to keep their undesirables in one place, and a burgeoning camp developed.

Photo-recon birds visited regularly, and the intelligence interpreters steadily built up a picture of what was happening.

One such interpreter looked long and hard at the latest photos, no more than three hours old, and found an itch he couldn't scratch.

There had been a short delay whilst the camera was recovered from the wrecked Spitfire. Its damaged undercarriage had lost the unequal struggle to support the aircraft's weight and collapsed the photoreconnaissance bird onto the grass, which had trenched and flipped the aircraft over in the middle of the strip, where it had burned merrily until the firemen put out the flames.

The pilot, showing incredible presence of mind for a man with a broken arm and a cannon shell fragment in the nape of his neck, had managed to extract the camera before fire claimed it.

His bravery meant that the latest pictures were preserved, setting in motion a string of events with far-reaching consequences.

Despite the fact that a break was called by the unit's officer, the sergeant, whose job it was to interpret the new images, wandered around the huge filing system and pulled the previous shots, and, for good measure, the two missions before.

He laid them out across the desk, sat back, and examined the major differences whilst seeking the subtle ones.

His thoughts were disturbed by the appearance of a mug of coffee.

"Whatcha got, Pete?"

"Not sure, Hank... not sure."

He picked up the first set of photos.

"The camp... same as ever... a few extra shadows on the ground... more people... but nothing of note."

He leant over and retrieved the next set.

"You did the interpretation on this set, Hank. A few extra lorries... that train in the main compound... but nothing to write home about. Except a couple of civilian lorries with a load of pipes on."

Hank couldn't remember the set of photos particularly, but if that's what his report said, then that's what he had seen.

He checked the photo and stirred a memory as he looked at the loaded lorries parked openly on the banks of the river.

"Oh yeah... I questioned the square blocks... I remember now... concrete mountings... so I was informed."

Peter Manning picked up the set dated 23rd July and offered them up.

"I did the interpretation on these. The only thing of note was the lorries with the pipes on board... look to the west of the main camp... up by the Vistula there..."

Henry Childs put the lens to his eye and sought out the lorries in question.

"Yep... I see them. More lorries this time. Lots and lots of pipes... more mounting blocks... the call was what?"

"Extra water to the camp, seeing as it was expanding. Seemed logical as they started at the river."

"Fair enough, Pete. And they signed off on that ok?"

"Yep."

Hank offered the set back, but Pete Manning kept his hands still.

"Anything else you see there?"

475

Clearly there was something to be seen, so Hank took his time.

"Staff car at the main building?"

"Nope."

"New construction at the top end of the camp?"

"Nope."

"Go on then."

"Look at the woods to the west, those either side of the river."

Hank compared the pictures.

"It's summer, what do you expect, Pete? Things grow, pal."

"And this one?"

He handed the most recent picture over.

"Shit. Where's the river gone?"

In the previous comparison, Hank had spotted the flourishing growth, by the simple fact that, from above, the river width appeared reduced.

The final picture showed no river, implying that the trees had grown so much as to cover over the water completely... or...

"Netting?"

"Look at the tones... pretty much spot on... but not quite."

"So you're thinking what?"

"I'm thinking they've camo'ed it up for a damn good reason. That's not all. In the woods itself... there's a difference here and in tone here... look."

There was. An almost imperceptible one, one easily missed unless the eye was trained and keen.

"Over here... in the camp... what do you see?"

"That's easy... logs..."

Hank's voice trailed away.

Two minds worked the problem.

"That's trunks from at least eighty trees right there. Would make a noticeable hole in the woods in one place. Even if they're just thinning out, we'd see something... but in any case... if you want lumber, just take it from the edge nearest you, eh?"

"Good point, Hank. Now, try this one on for size. Where are the pipe trucks now?"

"Still by the riv... hey, hang on... why are they up there?"

"And where's the turned ground. There isn't any, and we'd see it for sure."

"Damn right we'd see it so..."

Henry Childs' eyes narrowed.

"You gotta theory, don't you?"

476

"Yeah. Pull the lieutenant in, cos I think he's gonna wanna hear it too."

The officer sat patiently listening as his men expounded their theory, occasionally looking at the pictures and trying to see things through their words.

The arguments were there.

The theories were supportable.

The evidence was open to interpretation, but that was their job, and it could make sense.

"Hold it right there, boys. You sold me. I'm going to drop this in front of the Colonel a-sap. Give me the photos."

He took up the offered evidence.

"Good job, both of you. Come with me in case I get anything wrong."

The Squadron Commander listened impassively, carefully examining the photos and listening to the Lieutenant's explanation of what the two sergeants had discovered... thought they had discovered, the devil's advocate in his brain reminded him.

As with most things, there were alternate explanations that he could offer, but the Lieutenant Colonel held his peace and let the young man continue.

Everything was thoroughly laid out for him to understand.

He could see everything clearly, and knew where his boys were coming from, so still held himself in check.

Up to the moment the Lieutenant addressed the pipe lorries' present location.

"Why there? That's away from the camp."

"Sir, it is our belief that the Russians are laying the pipes in the water itself. Laying them against the current would be tricky to say the least... laying them with it is much easier...we can get some expert opinion on that, but it makes sense to me... which is why the lorries are there, heading away from Birkenau... or should I say the woods... and downstream to Bierun Nowy... here."

His finger pointed at a small staging area that had been interpreted as a barge landing point, built by the local population to replace the town one destroyed by a combination of fighting and bombing.

"We haven't had time yet, Sir, but I'm willing to bet that we'll find barges docking at this point regularly over the last week or so... maybe more... and that we don't see anything of note move into the town."

The Lieutenant Colonel nodded his head, took off his glasses, and pushed himself back in his chair.

Filling his pipe, he ordered his own thoughts before speaking.

"So, Lieutenant, what exactly's your bottom line here. Reach as much as you figure you need to, but tell me what you and your boys think's actually happening here?"

He exchanged looks with the two sergeants, who could only offer silent encouragement.

"Colonel, Sir, we think that the barges are being used to transport fuel. They've taken terrible hits on their fuel, even though they went to smaller dumps a while back. We've caned them on the roads... and on the railways when they've tried that... makes sense that the Commies would try water."

"Go on. Lieutenant."

"The pipes are not water pipes... they're fuel pipes, and they run from that little landing stage all the way to the woods. Our guess is that the little hut there is the pump that shifts it upriver."

The Colonel's puffing was increasing with each word.

"My guess... sorry, our guess is that the blocks are actually weights to hold the pipe down. A quick estimate puts it at four blocks to one section of pipe."

He produced the photos that best showed the canopy of the woods.

"See here, Sir. The river is all but gone and, even though it's summer, the trees ain't gonna grow like that... and here... and here, Sir... the difference in the canopy. Our bet is that is netting, clever job, but not quite clever enough."

He pointed to the pile of lumber in the camp, emphasising the fact that a work party was pulling one immense piece of timber from the direction of the woods.

"Where's the hole these trees came from, eh? Why not take from the edge nearest you? Remember the trick they pulled before the war, where they hollowed out forests and created railway sidings and rallying points for huge formations? Our bet is they're doing something in those woods, and a something to do with hiding their fuel supplies, Sir."

The Lieutenant Colonel drew heavily on the rich smoke, nodding his head gently as his eyes moved from piece of evidence to piece of evidence.

"OK, Lieutenant. You sold me. I'm gonna get this up the line. Good work, boys, damn good work."

1005 hrs, Thursday, 8th August 1946, 8th US Air Force Headquarters, Chateau de Foulze, Bourgingnons, France.

Lieutenant General James Doolittle had been up and working since five, and had decided to take advantage of the lovely morning and take a mind-clearing walk by the River Seine, which ran through the bottom of the extensive gardens surrounding the Chateau de Foulze.

His aide hunted him down there, and produced a document set that had travelled through the night from an airbase at Bad Nauheim.

Gesturing his aide to take a seat, Doolittle examined the report and the photographs, seeing exactly the picture that the Colonel's words were trying to paint.

"Hot damn. You read this, Sam?"

Samuel Greenberg had, and was as excited as Doolittle.

"Sam, by God but we're gonna hit this place, but not yet. If this is a policy change by the Commies, I want another appreciation done, actually a hell of a lot of 'em… looking at potential sites where the fuckers might've pulled this on us elsewhere. If this is a change, we'll get the all we can find in one hit."

Mind clear and focussed, Doolittle led off at high speed, keen to get the orders out.

Two days later, the Allies had identified a possible four additional locations where a similar ploy might have been used.

The five missions were all aimed at targets near large civilian life risks, or camps such as Birkenau, calling for precision strikes, rather than brutal area bombing.

The Soviets actually only had four such sites, and were relying on maskirovka to keep them safe.

By midday on the 11th August, four fuel storage sites and a large field hospital were destroyed by Martin Marauders and Mosquitoes from the RAF, USAAF, and the Armee de L'Air.

479

Had the planners and crews understood the full ramifications of what they had achieved, they would have celebrated into the next month, rather than the next day.

1604 hrs, Thursday, 8th August 1946, Headquarters of the Red Banner Forces of Soviet Europe, Schloss Hartenfels, Torgau, Germany.

The four senior officers were enjoying a lighter moment, sampling the local pastries and enjoying tea in the sunshine of an idyllic summer's afternoon.

Malinin regaled Nazarbayeva with stories of how the Germans once kept bears in the castle's moat, whilst Vasilevsky contented himself with humming one of his favourite folk songs, in between bites of a nameless but delicious sugar coated something.

Tarasov, the recently appointed CoS of the RBFSE, simply enjoyed the sun.

Their sojourn was disturbed by the noisy arrival of Atalin, Zhukov's loyal Colonel, bearing a report of great significance.

"Comrade Marshal... Comrade Marshal..."

Vasilevsky broke out of his idyll.

"Polkovnik Atalin. Is it some news from Comrade Zhukov?"

Atalin enjoyed Zhukov's complete trust, and was often used on sensitive missions, such as the one he had recently discharged by bringing Vasilevsky a private letter from the ailing Marshal.

"No, Comrade Marshal. It has come from your communications officer. I said I would deliver it to you in person."

He handed over the sheaf of papers.

Vasilevsky's face went white as he read each in turn, attracting the full attention of those around him.

"Thank you, Comrade Atalin. Please, prepare yourself to fly out to Moscow almost immediately. Get some food inside you. There will be little time for rest from now on."

The Marshal stood and acknowledged Atalin's salute.

"Comrades, with me."

He strode off towards his office, increasing his speed with every step, his face going from white to thunderous as the implications of the latest reports bored further into his thoughts.

"All of it?"

"All of it."

"Job tvoju mat!"

Vasilevsky would normally have smiled at the woman's outburst, but there was precious little for the commander in chief of a crippled and immobilised army to laugh about.

He turned to Tarasov and rattled off some requirements.

'Fuel state of operational armies and fronts.'

'Fuel reserve held locally by each front.'

'Fuel marked as 'in transit' and not allocated.'

'STAVKA fuel reserve.'

'Fuel awaiting delivery to RBFSE.'

'Fuel consumption minimums for the army.'

'Anticipated fuel available from the Motherland over the next two weeks.'

Nazarbayeva watched as Malinin made some rough notes, summoning figures from the deeper recesses of his mind.

Tarasov departed at speed to seek out the information his commander in chief required, save the existing fuel stocks, which Malinin relayed from his notes.

"Comrade Marshal, from memory I believe that 1st Baltic last held 0.6 stocks at local level, 1st Red Banner 0.3, 2nd 0.6, 3rd 0.7, 1st Southern 0.8, and 1st Alpine was 1.2. All front reserves were at 0.5 as of yesterday evening."

Vasilevsky nodded, knowing that Malinin's recollections were probably good enough, but that a military front with a stock of 0.3 refills of its vehicles was as close to unable to properly manoeuvre as it could get under present circumstances.

"And of course, Comrade Marshal, that does not account for the inevitable losses that will come from enemy activity."

"You bring joy, as ever, Comrade Malinin. STAVKA reserve... we must have some of that released."

Nazarbayeva, horrified that Vasilevsky did not know what she knew, had her own bad news to add.

"Comrade Marshal, I can tell you that STAVKA reserve is virtually non-existent."

Vasilevsky closed his eyes, hoping that he had misheard the shocking news, but could not avoid asking the question.

"Explain please, Comrade Nazarbayeva."

"I've made an error, Comrade Marshal. I thought you would know? I am... err... aware that STAVKA fuel reserves have been denuded to enhance the supply to the front, in order to maintain reasonable supplies for your intended operations against the Amerikanski forces."

He sensed there was more, and there was.

"I'm also informed, by a very reliable source, that projections for output from our new sources are very much at the optimistic end, and that we should expect some delays before any reasonable flow is achieved, and then it will most likely be no more than 60% of what has been claimed, at least for the foreseeable future."

NKVD second in command Kaganovich had shared the gloomy revision with Nazarbayeva during their last meeting, amongst other snippets, confirming that a number of things were not as they seemed to be.

Vasilevsky stood up, and the room's occupants automatically came to attention.

He walked to the situation map, a smaller version of the main operations room map, but as up to date.

The silence was broken by a cursory knock and the entrance of Tarasov.

"Comrade Marshal. These are a quick set of initial figures. I have my men working on a definite set, but these should be reasonably accurate enough for you to see the situation."

The Marshal accepted the swiftly typed document, and consumed the information without comments on the typing errors.

No errors could hide the enormity of the problem that leapt off the page, and he expressed himself like a peasant.

"Job tvoju mat!"

He passed the paper to Malinin.

The normally calm and collected officer simply drained of colour and re-read the damming figures.

Vasilevsky stuck out his hand, seeking to look again, hoping to find some crumb of comfort.

There was none.

"I must travel to Moscow as soon as possible. Comrade Tarasov, I want firm figures within the hour. Comrade Nazarbayeva, I would ask you to accompany me with your own latest reports. Comrade Malinin, we must conserve our resources as much as possible. You know what needs to be done. I'll leave it all in your capable hands."

Malinin nodded, understanding the mission Vasilevsky was about to undertake.

"Comrade Marshal..."

"Mikhail Sergeyevich. The army is my responsibility. This mission is my responsibility. Your orders are to preserve the army until such time as we have the means to resume the fight properly."

Nazarbayeva was shocked to hear the words, even though she had grasped the implications of the Allied bombing missions.

"Comrade Marshal... you mean that you will recommend abandoning our offensive against the Americans? Resorting to defence only?"

He looked at the GRU General with sad eyes.

"No, Comrade Nazarbayeva. I will recommend that, in order to preserve the Red Army, we find a political settlement at the earliest possible opportunity."

When you have got an elephant by the hind legs and he is trying to run away, it's best to let him run.

Abraham Lincoln

Chapter 168 - THE UNTHINKABLE

1000 hrs, Friday, 9th August 1946, Andreyevsky Hall, the Kremlin, Moscow, USSR.

The meeting had been organised for the lavish surroundings of the Andeyevsky Hall, for no reason other than the normal meeting places were either being redecorated following a small but damaging fire, or were unsuited for the larger gathering that had been brought together for a purpose now defunct, as Vasilevsky's arrival and insistence on a meeting with the GKO had made all other matters irrelevant.

The absence of the big metal detectors meant that each officer was subjected to the most thorough search, although the guard commander had ensured that a female officer was present to search Nazarbayeva, something she did with female reserve and genuine respect, all down to apologising for having to remove Nazarbayeva's boots.

Inside the portion of the hall set aside for the briefing, two of the commander-in-chief's staff, both volunteers who understood the risk, had set up the presentation, as directed by their leader.

Zhukov had been briefed within an hour of Vasilevsky's arrival at Vnukovo airfield, but, by agreement, would remain silent.

Beria had been unable to supply Stalin with the precise nature of what had exercised Vasilevsky so much, and could only offer up the recent enemy air attacks of fuel depots, or the German penetration, as possible reasons for the hasty arrangements.

When the commander of the Red Banner Forces of Soviet Europe gave his presentation, he quickly covered the situation at the front, painting it as it was, without frills, and without exaggeration, something that all noticed, and something that all felt augured badly for what was to come.

"Comrades, whatever the situation we face at the front, and in our echelons, and rear lines... and even into the Rodina herself... the situation that presented itself to me yesterday has brought about the most terrible harm to the Motherland's cause."

He turned to the elderly Colonel and nodded.

484

The man, one useless arm tucked in his pocket, whisked the cover away and the ensemble were confronted by a map, simple in its notations.

Vasilevsky took a sly look at Zhukov, who remained impassive, but silently wished the condemned man well.

"Acting on the decision by STAVKA, we centralised our major fuel resources in four well-disguised locations, fit to service the battle fronts in Europe."

He extracted a file, a copy of which was being distributed by his second assistant, a Major whose two sons lay long dead on the battlefield of Kursk.

Stalin's eyes never left Vasilevsky, seemingly unaware of the document offered up to him.

Beria took it for him, and placed it gently in front of the pre-occupied dictator.

"Comrades, you will see from this file that my responsible senior officers discharged their orders to the fullest extent, and exceeded the standards set within the STAVKA order. The standards were rigorously checked, and diligent security was provided by significant forces provided by NKVD Leytenant General Dustov."

Vasilevsky took a sip of water to ease his rapidly drying throat.

"As directed, we created these facilities adjacent to large well-known sites, but in secret, and under heavy camouflage. We avoided direct support from AA units, in order to not draw suspicion on the areas."

"I concentrated virtually my entire frontal fuel reserve within these four facilities."

The dawn of realisation started to spread in the minds of the more able members present.

"Comrades, I regret to inform you that yesterday afternoon... American, British, and German aircraft destroyed virtually the entire fuel reserve of the Red Banner Forces of Soviet Europe, leaving me only with the fuel held at Front Level, and any fuel in transit, minus wastage that will inevitably accrued, given the Allied mastery of the air."

Vasilevsky suddenly realised that no one was looking at him.

All eyes were on Stalin, whose eyes were very firmly burning with anger.

"What's this? WHAT... IS... THIS? You're given simple instructions and fail to carry them out, and all of a sudden it's the fault of STAVKA?"

Vasilevsky looked at Zhukov for support, and remembered that there would be none coming.

"No, Comrade General Secretary. The reasoning was sound. Our air assets were able to concentrate for interceptions without drawing attention to the locations, as was predicted. Distribution from those sites that were fully established and operational was excellent, and losses in fuel supplies due to fixed site attacks dropped dramatically."

"And yet they were attacked, Vasilevsky... destroyed!"

"Yes, Comrade General Secretary."

"How can this be....eh... how can this have happened if you and your fucking officers were so fucking brilliant... so fucking diligent at discharging STAVKA's fucking orders!"

"We do not know... I do not know, Comrade General Secretary. There must have been a flaw in the execution... some security lapse... but all four were struck within ten minutes of each other... plus there was an attack on a medical facility... one that was a mirror of the other attacks... so I believe that they thought it was also a fuel depot... which makes me think that there was an error that they spotted with all five sites."

"So, an error with your efforts to discharge the orders of STAVKA?"

"The troops undertook the orders to the letter. The NKVD inspection teams found nothing to fault at all four fuel sites...nothing, Comrade General Secretary."

"And yet, the fuel the Motherland entrusted to you is no more, Comrade Marshal."

"Yes, Comrade General Secretary."

"Comrade Beria, do you have these inspection reports to hand?"

Of course, Beria did and produced them from his briefcase.

They supported Vasilevsky's assertion as to the excellence of the entire projects.

Stalin gave them a cursory look and almost tossed them back to the silent Beria.

"So, Comrade Marshal. You've managed to lose the fuel for your army. Have you come here to propose an end to offensive action?"

"No, Comrade General Secretary."

"No?"

"I've come here to propose much, much more."

486

A murderous silence stilled everything in the room. Even the grandfather clock seemed reluctant to tick in the presence of such violent, quiet anger.

Stalin drained the last of his chilled orange juice, produced a cigarette, and lit it, all with the gusto of a silent screen actor... combined with the focus and concentration of an executioner.

Those watching and listening held their collective breath.

Beria saw the opportunity and pounced immediately.

"Comrade General Secretary... perhaps we should hear from the GRU on this matter, as Comrade Nazarbayeva is well-placed to be able to comment on the situation."

It was not intended as a snub to Vasilevsky, but that didn't stop the Marshal seeing it as such, and a real enemy was made.

"Indeed. Comrade Nazarbayeva. The GRU's position on events?"

"Comrade General Secretary, I can only agree the figures as stated by Comrade Marshal Vasilevsky. The fuel situation is grave beyond comprehension. What seemed like a good idea has not proven to be so, and the army is now crippled because of it."

Vasilevsky tried to interrupt but was cut short by the angry Stalin.

"Shut up... Comrade Nazarbayeva, your accusation against STAVKA aside, is there any indication from the enemy regarding attacks, reactions to our own efforts, or anything at all to support the Marshal's notion of cancelling any offensive action, retreat, or whatever it is he intends to recommend... shut up!"

His hand shot out, emphasising his words, as Vasilevsky again tried to speak.

"Comrade General Secretary, I do not know what Comrade Marshal Vasilevsky intends to suggest to the GKO. I am not privy to his inner thoughts."

Usually correct but, in this instance, it was a lie, as she had been party to the discussions in Vasilevsky's office.

The brief silence decided Beria, and he helped her along the path of self-destruction.

"So what would you suggest then, Comrade Nazarbayeva."

Stalin turned to chew lumps off the head of the NKVD for interrupting, but stopped himself and, wishing to hear the reply, turned back to the woman GRU officer.

"Speak, Comrade Nazarbayeva. You should know that I will listen to views honestly given in the service of the party and the Motherland."

No one present was under any illusions that some views were simply too honest to deliver... and live.

"Comrade General Secretary, I'm not a strategist like the Marshal or yourself, but the matter seems clear as clear can be to me."

Stalin laughed, and a few other dry throats joined in, more out of nerves than appreciating the humour that Stalin had found in her words.

"Then please, Comrade Nazarbayeva, make it all clear for me... for us..."

He waved his hand over the assembly, neatly depositing a large lump of ash on Beria's tunic.

"Comrade General Secretary."

She turned to Vasilevsky.

"Comrade Marshal, do you have the figures on fuel stocks held ready for review?"

He nodded, first to her, and then to the major, who dragged a cover off a display stand.

Vasilevsky spoke slowly and evenly.

"Comrade General Secretary, these figures represent the last fuel available to the Red Banner Forces, from those held at battalion level, all the way to Front stocks."

Stalin nodded and returned his gaze to Nazarbayeva, ignoring the figures on the display.

She thumbed through her own folder, as those who needed them reached for their glasses.

All absorbed the awfulness of the figures in front of them.

"Red Banner Forces, in the person of Marshal Vasilevsky, had no reason other than to assume that the STAVKA fuel stocks had been maintained at the stated combat levels. I was previously aware, and reported this problem to him on Friday evening during a senior officers meeting. At that time, regretfully, I informed Marshal Vasilevsky that that is not the case, and that STAVKA fuel reserves have been slowly fed into the main supply system, denuding stocks to a critical level."

"A critical level means what... in layman's terms, Comrade?"

Stalin's voice showed a strain previously undetected, hidden as it was, by white-hot anger.

"Comrade General Secretary... STAVKA stocks are presently at 8% of combat norms, to plus or minus 1%."

"Go on, Comrade."

Vasilevsky piped up quickly, and was as surprised as everyone else that Stalin didn't stop him in his tracks.

488

"The situation is dire, Comrades. The worst the Red Army has faced since the Revolution. The resolution may be unpalatable, but I can see no alternative, unless the wisdom and acumen of this assembly can find a resolution not obvious to this old soldier."

Stalin held up his hand, stopping Vasilevsky before he could swing back into his presentation.

"Comrade Zhukov? You've remained silent, but you will have an opinion... maybe even a solution?"

"Comrade General Secretary, I have an opinion only. An acceptable solution is not yet apparent to me. There are only ways of coping, in the short term, ways that would be heavy on our ordinary soldiers, who would have to carry out orders on foot, and unsupported by our powerful all-arms forces... orders that would cost many their lives. We have no fuel to attack. We have no fuel to manoeuvre. We have no fuel to..."

"Yes, yes, yes. Very good, we have no fuel. You, the Victor of Khalkin Gol, surely you can find a solution here?"

He exchanged looks with Vasilevsky, who had been elected as the sacrificial lamb, the one to put the dramatic and unpalatable solution to Stalin and the political leadership.

"Hah!"

Stalin misinterpreted the silent exchange between the two marshals, seeing it as weakness and a lack of courage to deliver the bottom line. He knew someone who would have the necessary 'balls of steel'.

"It seems my military leadership lack the courage to inform us of their opinion. Perhaps you have the strength to tell us in their stead, Comrade Nazarbayeva?"

"It is not my place, Comrade General Secre..."

Stalin flew into an immediate rage, hammering his hand on the table to emphasise virtually every syllable.

"It is your place if I command it, woman!"

Nazarbayeva recoiled in horror.

Beria smiled as discreetly as he was able.

'At last... at last!'

"Comrade General Secretary, as you order."

The 'Hero of the Soviet Union' in her took control, and all of a sudden the beautiful woman set her jaw and changed into the soldier who had fought and killed in the Crimea many years before.

"The Red Army cannot attack. It cannot manoeuvre. It is, to all intents and purposes, immobile. There is no fuel for tanks, for lorries, for staff cars, for anything. Even fodder is in critically short supply but, as many of the horses have been eaten by hungry soldiers, that is less of a problem."

She moved forward, standing closer to Stalin, on the cusp of a respectful distance, but closer than most normally dared to wander.

"GRU intelligence suggests an increasing German Army, probably taking over many of the duties of the Amerikanski, which in turn will relieve pressure on their President. It seems the green toads again relish the prospect of fighting us, now they are backed up by the industrial might of our capitalist enemies. I'm sure that the NKVD opinion will agree with ours."

Beria suddenly found himself the centre of attention, and didn't enjoy it at all.

"The NKVD reports are roughly in agreement with the GRU suggestion, Comrades."

Attention switched back to Nazarbayeva.

"The Ukrainians have been subjugated, but the drought has hit the harvest hard, as has the fighting, and we stand on the edge of further supply problems, all of which will be undoubtedly increased by Allied air actions. Historically, we lose a huge proportion of all supplies long before they reach the front, but we have seen more problems occurring with inner distribution since enemy bombing raids started to spread further through the Rodina, despite the gallant work of the Red Air Force."

Colonel General Repin, the Air Force deputy commander, nodded in acceptance of her words.

"Set against that inevitability, we will not be able to feed and provision our troops or our people."

"Militarily, we cannot order our soldiers to move back without abandoning most of our equipment."

Nazarbayeva had heard those words in Vasilevsky's office the previous day, so they were easy to employ.

"Also, regardless of what we seem to see in the Allied press, I believe that their politicians will inevitably order use of the new bombs against the Rodina. I see it as inevitable that they will use their bombs on us, bombs to which we have no answer, and can offer no response of our own at this time... unless I am missing some exciting developments within our own programmes?"

Kurchatov fidgeted uneasily as most of the eyes in the room shifted to him.

His headshake was enough for Nazarbayeva to continue.

"So, we find ourselves with no ability to move our armies. No definite guarantee that we can supply our armies enough of the basics to give them a fighting chance against the Allies. Foodstuffs will be limited before the Allied aircraft increase our supply problems, not just for the military, but for the Rodina as a whole. Our industry and infrastructure continue to suffer at the hands of their bombing force. And then there is the question of these new weapons. Our own special weapons programme is unable to offer anything of value at this time, whereas theirs is available, and can transform large sections of the Motherland to ashes virtually at will. It seems clear to me what must be done here, Comrade General Secretary."

She waited for a response, holding the leader's gaze as his face changed colour and his eyes blazed.

"So, Comrade Nazarbayeva, your opinion as to what must be done is what exactly?"

Standing erect, ramrod stiff, and every inch the Soviet hero, Nazarbayeva delivered the damning words.

"Comrade General Secretary, I believe that you must seek peace, or lose the army, and the war; it is that simple."

The collective intake of breath was audible.

Stalin moved forward, until she could smell the orange juices still clinging to his moustache.

"Say that again?"

"I believe you must make peace, Comr..."

Stalin moved with incredible and unexpected speed, landing a vicious slap across Nazarbayeva's face, and sent her reeling back against Vasilevsky, who caught and steadied her.

"So... there we have it... and I thought you had steel... that you, above all others, had the backbone to succeed... to win against all odds."

Nazarbayeva the soldier moved back to her previous position in front of the dictator and stood her ground.

Throughout the room, there was genuine horror and shock at what had happened.

Stalin's eyes were still burning wildly, but Nazarbayeva gave him direct eye contact, despite the growing bruise across her left cheek and the gentle drip of blood from her nostril.

Even Beria had a grudging admiration for the courage that she displayed.

'Balls of steel.'

"Comrade General Secretary, the Red Army is the instrument of the Party... of the State... and it must be protected, for without a functioning and strong army both could flounder."

She instinctively wiped a run of blood from her chin, too late to stop a pair of red spots appearing on her shirt collar.

491

She pressed her index finger to the Hero Award on her jacket.

"This award was given to me because I refused to give in, at a time when all seemed lost. I understood then… and understand now…"

Nazarbayeva checked herself, realising that her own voice was rising with anger.

She continued in a more controlled fashion.

"I understand when I cannot win, Comrade General Secretary, and also when I must do what is unpalatable to avoid losing."

Vasilevsky moved forward with a napkin and offered it up as the blood started to flow more readily, her own anger still rising and causing her blood pressure to rise.

"I am yours to command, Comrade General Secretary, and you may beat me, or worse, as you wish. But that will not change a single fact here. To preserve the army, and therefore the party and state, peace must be sought. In the short term, there is no choice. It will buy time… perhaps enough for Comrade Kurchatov's weapons to become available, but certainly time that will help the army recover. At this moment, we cannot win, Comrade General Secretary, but we can… we must… avoid losing."

She wiped a run of blood and, as she did it, she saw a lessening in the dictator's tension, his body relaxing in some small measure.

"Comrade General Secretary, you have done this before, in a different way. You bought time in the struggle against the Germanski, signing an unpalatable pact with them, all for the benefit of the Rodina. You saw then that it was the best way to protect the party and state… saw what many others could not. I'm sure you will see it again… here… in these circumstances."

Stalin said nothing as he resumed his seat, a nothing that clearly signalled a reduction in the tension.

Nazarbayeva's left eye started to lose full vision, as swelling and bruising acted.

None the less, she held firm and waited.

They all waited.

Finally, Stalin pointed a finger at Vasilevsky.

"Marshal? Does your opinion correspond to that put forward by the GRU?"

Kuznetsov, the GRU head, briefly considered stating that it was not his opinion but, wisely, the GRU chief thought better of it.

Vasilevsky moved forward and stood beside Nazarbayeva.

492

"Comrade General Secretary... unless you and the GKO have some device, some plan, some strategy that is hidden to me, I can only agree that a peace, even a temporary one, is the only way to preserve what we presently have and hold."

Stalin blanked Vasilevsky and turned to Zhukov.

"And you, Georgy Zhukov, Marshal of the Soviet Union... the victory bringer... what is your opinion on this grave matter eh?"

He too moved forward, flanking the GRU general.

"I agree, Comrade General Secretary. Unless you have some brilliant plan that is not known to me, the only course of action to preserve our army is to seek a truce."

Beria whispered something under his breath, an inaudible something that clearly was not in agreement with the three officer's view.

However inaudible, Stalin heard it and turned on him in an instant.

"Comrade Marshal Beria, we'll hear your alternative plan shortly. For now, keep your views to yourself. Summon your men."

Beria moved to the telephone and, in response to his words, the door opened and in walked Colonels Sardeon and Sarkisov.

"Comrade Beria, have your men detain these five officers in this building until otherwise ordered. If any of them try to leave, they are to be shot immediately."

Beria simply had to nod, as both colonels had heard Stalin's words.

Supported by a squad of NKVD troopers, they escorted the military group from the hall.

Stalin refilled his glass and took a healthy swig of the chilled juice before speaking to the silent group of grey-faced men.

"Comrades... speak."

1444 hrs, Friday, 9th August 1946, Andreyevsky Hall, the Kremlin, Moscow, USSR.

Half expecting to be shot, the three were greatly relieved to be ushered into the Andreyevsky Hall once more. The two junior officers, having not been included in the orders delivered to Sardeon and Sarkisov, were left behind under armed guard.

Sat facing them were a grim faced GKO, some clearly more angry than others.

Zhukov led the trio in, and immediately wondered which of these men would stand as his accuser, and condemn him for his treachery to the Motherland.

493

He took a position of attention and wondered what marvel of manoeuvring these politicians had conceived to extricate the Red Army from the morass of their own making.

Vasilevsky and Nazarbayeva took station beside him.

The answer was delivered quickly, and in an unexpected fashion.

Beria sent his two henchmen away with a dismissive wave.

"Comrade Marshal Zhukov... perhaps Comrade Beria acted precipitously... an unfortunate set of circumstances."

Beria looked wide mouthed at his leader for the briefest of moments, before he recovered his poise.

"Comrade Vasilevsky... you and Comrade Zhukov have presided over this debacle... this abomination... and yet, perhaps, you are not wholly to blame. The GKO has decided to give you both the opportunity to recover our confidence."

He looked directly at Nazarbayeva, who returned his gaze with eyes burning in defiance, albeit one was closed by the swelling of her cheek.

"And you, Comrade Nazarbayeva... you and your prized organisation seem to have failed to properly arm us with the information needed to avoid all these... these... disasters," he waved at the European situation map, "As has the NKVD..."

Beria blanched but offered no protest, probably because it was totally true.

"...But you have mostly been efficient in your duties and, in this most recent instance, spoke clearly, and... no, in all instances... you have spoken in the best interests of the Party and the Rodina as you have seen it."

He went as far as he felt he could.

"What happened was regrettable, Comrade Nazarbayeva."

Which was more than Comrade Stalin had ever gone before.

And, as far as the leader was concerned, that was that, and he moved on.

"It has been decided that the Red Army needs time to recover from the unfortunate and adverse prevailing circumstances that have recently robbed it of a portion of its capability."

The military men understood face-saving politicians speak when they heard it.

"We will use the present circumstances to seek a truce, during which we will renew our forces, sow political discord throughout the Allied nations, and wait for the most favourable time to continue with our overall plan."

494

Stalin sought eye contact with the head of the Soviet Union's atomic programme, and found it, before Kurchatov broke it by dropping his gaze to pretend to search for something vital amongst his papers.

"Given some of the recent difficulties with Operation Raduga, we propose to halt all special actions, and use the time to enhance and refine our own programmes... all the better to ensure greater success when the plans come to fruition."

Zhukov took a quick look at Isakov, who understood the enquiry that flowed from the Marshal's eyes.

'The Japanese?'

Isakov could only give the smallest of shrugs before Stalin's voice overrode their quiet exchange.

"However, it is vital that we negotiate from a position of maximum strength, so... to that end... the Red Army will maintain its operational effectiveness at all times, using whatever means are at its disposal to ensure that we have the best possible military platform from which to contrive a temporary cessation on the best possible terms."

Vasilevsky and Zhukov groaned inside, knowing that those words would mean the deaths of countless more soldiers.

"We entrust that task to you both."

A single nod each was all they could manage.

"Now, let's get down to planning this maskirovka."

2155 hrs, Sunday, 11th August 1946, Dybäck Castle, Sweden.

The initial moves were entrusted to the Foreign Ministry, with Molotov taking the lead, and to the GRU, or, more specifically, to Nazarbayeva.

From her office, a message went out, one that travelled by diverse means before arriving in Sweden.

Per Karsten Tørget, head of Swedish Military Intelligence, enjoyed a glass of fine wine as he waited for the mystery to be solved.

He checked his watch, estimating that it had been nearly an hour and a half since the cryptic call from Lingström.

'Soon this little secret will be explained.'

No sooner had the thought developed than the sound of urgent feet reached his ears, as a pair of boots hammered on the floors of the main hallway, bringing his number one double agent closer.

He responded to the knocking and Lingström admitted himself, clearly bursting with something extremely important, a

495

something that Tørget's sharp mind had failed to work out whilst he sat waiting for his prodigy to arrive from Copenhagen.

"Well, you look like you have a story to tell, Överstelöjtnant. Sit."

Lingström did so and took a deep breath to control himself.

"Speak, Boris. What has got you so excited eh?"

"Överste, I've received a message from my Russian masters. I am to report back, as a matter of extreme urgency, on any information that I can gather on the Swedish position regarding anything related to a direct approach that will be made to Minister Undén tomorrow."

"The Minister for Foreign Affairs? Are they threatening us or asking for an alliance... either way, they can go to hel..."

"Neither, Överste. They will be seeking our help... the government's help..."

"And what do they mean by that then?"

"Hägglöf was summoned to see Molotov in Moscow today, and the envoy has reported back to Minister Undén, indicating that Soviet Ambassador Kollontai will present herself tomorrow with a genuine proposal... one that the Soviet Union hopes that Sweden can both broker and oversee."

"In Loki's name, spit it out, man!"

"The Communists are seeking a truce."

Tørget's mind rejected a number of replies, instead sending messages to his mouth to stay firmly closed.

Lingström used his boss's silence to expand on his bombshell.

"The Soviet Foreign Ministry will be sending a high level delegation to meet with Minister Undén, at which time they'll seek Sweden's help in organising a face to face with the Allied leadership, under the chairmanship of Undén, in order to broker a ceasefire in place, and to negotiate terms for a permanent peace."

Tørget rose, so Lingström automatically stood and came to attention.

He resumed his seat as his commander waved him to relax.

Topping off his own glass, and wetting a new one for the bringer of such incredible news, Tørget returned to his seat, offering the glass of vintage Bordeaux to Lingström.

"Skol!"

The glasses clinked together and taste buds were assaulted by the fine wine they contained.

"Remind me... you have been contacted why?"

"I'm to report back on anything that seems disingenuous… any sign of treachery… any activity behind the scenes that might undermine the process."

"Maskirovka?"

Lingström took a gentler sip of the wonderful red before replying.

"I'm not being risked… I'm not being asked to do anything actively… just to report back on the… err… genuineness of proceedings… and of course, anything I hear on the bargaining position of the Allies, once talks get underway. I don't sense anything here but a genuine approach to end the war."

More wine flowed before Lingström added a codicil.

"Whatever their reasons may be, Överste."

Tørget savoured the taste.

"Indeed… whatever their reasons may be."

The delegation, headed by their unconventional ambassador, Alexandra Mikhailovna Kollontai, laid out the bare bones of the Soviet Union's approach to Sweden, expectations and wishes, hopes and fears, and emphasised the trust that the Rodina had in Sweden's impartiality.

Despite the physical change and slight speech impediment that a stroke had inflicted upon her, Kollontai managed to eloquently convey the essence of the message she had been tasked to deliver. Alexandra Mikhailovna was a consummate politician, and her sincerity was appreciated by Östen Undén, Swedish Minister for Foreign Affairs.

Undén, already pre-warned by Tørget, confirmed that the Swedish Government would be only too pleased to assist in brokering a full and meaningful peace in Europe, and would offer safe passage and guarantees of safety to all persons attending.

Kollontai was not fazed by the fact that Undén had clearly known of the Soviet approach, and known sufficiently in advance for the Swedish government to have discussed and developed an official position, although it would figure in her report.

She was not privy to the advance 'work' of the GRU.

The Soviet Ambassador continued with her request.

"The people of the Soviet Union would also request that the government of Sweden makes the initial approach to the Allied governments through diplomatic channels, without directly revealing that we have instigated this process... but to do so in such a way as to offer to initiate a dialogue, and to mediate all discussions as an honest broker, and to work with both sides to bring about a lasting peace. We would be most grateful if that could be seen to be a matter that Sweden has been proposed to us, and that we are prepared to be a party to."

Undén was unprepared for the suggestion, and held his tongue as he worked the issue in his mind, deciding if it was disingenuous, a plain lie, an inaccuracy, an acceptable mechanism, or any one of a number of labels he could think for being a party to a statement that was not wholly the truth.

He was a politician, so he quickly found a compromise that he could live with.

"I believe that my government will, in the spirit of bringing about this peace, represent that the idea as ours, and ours alone. After all, I'm sure the rest of the world will be grateful for our leadership in the matter."

Kollontai smiled, knowing that Undén was already imagining real advantage for his country, by way of trade agreements and similar kudos.

"So, Minister, are we agreed?"

"I speak for my government in this matter. We are agreed."

They nodded, stood, and shook hands, understanding each other perfectly.

0624 hrs, Monday, 12th August 1946, the Guards Club, London, UK.

"Sir Stewart."

"Hmmm?"

The knocking continue again.

"Sir Stewart."

The head of MI-6 summoned himself from the depths of his dreams with great reluctance, the previous evening's entertainment, in the company of Percy Hollander, having broken well into the new morning.

"Yes...what?"

"Sir Stewart, there are two gentleman to see you, Sir... said it's extremely important... wouldn't take no for an answer, Sir Stewart. One is a colonel, the other a naval officer...I'm sorry, Sir, but they were most insistent."

Sir Stewart Menzies looked at the bedside clock and frowned.

"I'll be there directly, Squires."

"Very good, Sir Stewart. I took the liberty of installing the gentlemen in the terrace area, and of providing them with tea, Sir Stewart."

"Right ho, Squires."

Menzies swung out of bed and headed for the sink, intent on blasting away with the cobwebs with cold water.

It didn't help much, but would have to do, the reason behind someone... two men, he corrected himself... hunting him down at the club at this early hour was intriguing him. More to the point, decidedly bothering him.

Menzies slipped back into his uniform and checked himself out, and finding his appearance on the right side of satisfactory, he descended to the terrace.

"Good grief, Val... Sir Roger," he nodded, "What on earth has got you two out of bed at such an early hour?"

Valentine Vivian, second in command of MI-6, gestured towards a concealed table, laid with the accoutrements of an early morning breakfast.

Dalziel poured three teas as Vivian handed over a hand written report.

"Rush job?"

"Yes, Sir... you'll see why."

Menzies read the first message.

"Good grief! The blazes they are! The Swedes? They're brokering a peace deal? Why on earth ha..."

"Sir, the second report, Sir."

Vivian helpfully reached forward and pulled at the edge of another document.

"From Tørget, Sir Stewart."

The message from the head of Swedish Military Intelligence made all things clear.

"Good grief. I mean... good lord, Valentine."

"Quite, Sir."

"Thoughts? Sir Roger?

Dalziel opened the palms of his hands outwards.

"Quite clearly, we have, on one hand, a document that states that Sweden intends to offer its services to broker peace talks between the Allies and the Soviet Union as soon as is practicable... on its own soil... guaranteeing safe passage et al. And then, on the other hand, we have our friend Tørget informing us that this whole idea is a Soviet one, and that Sweden is agreeing to appear to propose it, so as not to weaken the Soviet bargaining position."

"But if the Soviets are proposing it, that must mean they are in a dire position... much worse than we believed... otherwise..."

"Otherwise why would they make such a proposal, Sir?"

"Indeed, Valentine."

They sat in silence, sampling the tea, thinking of the ramifications of the proposal... and the requirements of their profession.

"If we inform our politicians, they'll reveal what we know. They won't be able to help themselves. Is that a problem?"

Vivian answered Menzies' question with a question of his own.

"How could we not inform our leadership, Sir Stuart? Their negotiating position will be much stronger if they know it was the Soviets who suggested these talks."

Dalziel added his own views.

"Sir Stuart, clearly there are none of our assets to protect, just Tørget's wish that we are discreet with the information because of his own issues."

Vivian chuckled and spoke to no one in particular.

"Discretion and politicians do not mix."

Menzies smiled and raised his cup in acknowledgement.

"I understand Tørget's concern. He's protecting his country's reputation... maybe even possible that he has an asset of his own... but mainly to protect Sweden from any accusations."

Dalziel set his cup and saucer down gently and made a suggestion.

"Sir Stewart, perhaps it might be prudent to inform solely the Prime Minister at this time. He can decide how best to let our American cousins in on the secret, which, I suspect, would be directly to their president. Between them, they would decide the position that the negotiators would take. No need to advertise the knowledge of the Soviet weakness openly."

"My thinking exactly, Sir Roger."

Breakfast arrived.

'Blasted kippers!'

"We took the liberty of ordering breakfast for you, Sir Stewart. I remember you enjoyed the kippers at Rossahilly House.

'No I bloody well did not!'

"Thank you, Sir Roger. Splendid choice."

They hammered out the details of what would happen next over buttered kippers, poached eggs, and toast.

'Blasted kippers!'

0719 hrs, Monday, 12th August 1946, Chequers, Ellesborough, UK.

"Sir?"

"Inches?"

David Inches, Churchill's butler, had interrupted the Prime Minister and his wife at their breakfast, something that was not done lightly, certainly not at Chequers.

"Sir, Madam, apologies for disturbing you at your breakfast. Sir, I have taken an urgent message from Sir Stewart Menzies. He is coming to see you here, this very morning, Sir."

Winston frowned, remembering that he had an appointment with the same man later that afternoon, so something had clearly upset the apple cart.

"Did he say why, Inches?"

"No, Sir, nothing at all, but he did sound somewhat... err... enthusiastic... actually quite excited, Sir."

"Thank you, Inches."

The butler closed the door with due reverence.

'Menzies excited?'

"Pass the conserve, please, my darling."

He accepted the raspberry conserve from Clementine, though his thoughts were elsewhere.

'Last time he was excited, Adolf had shot himself.'

0950 hrs, Monday, 12th August 1946, Chequers, Ellesborough, UK.

"Sir, Sir Stewart Menzies."

"Thank you, Inches. Do come in, Sir Stewart."

"Thank you for seeing me at such short notice, Prime Minister."

Churchill chuckled.

"My butler felt that you bore exciting news, so how could I not, Sir Stewart."

Menzies sat in the chair Churchill indicated.

"A moment, if you please."

On cue, the door opened and Inches delivered a small tray containing the makings of a cup of tea.

"Shall I pour, Sir?"

"No, Inches, I need the exercise. Thank you."

Churchill poured two cups and passed one to the head of MI-6.

501

"So, what great news has brought you here in advance of schedule?"

As Menzies spoke, there was no visible reaction from his political master.

Remaining uncharacteristically silent, Churchill almost froze in place as the incredible and most unexpected development was slowly unfolded.

Menzies fell silent, but still Winston stayed quiet, sipping his tea with great studiousness, almost as if the resolution to the turmoil taking place in his brain could only be found within the brown liquid.

"And this is all confirmed, Sir Stewart?"

"The information comes from a wholly reliable source, Sir."

"Wholly reliable?"

"Yes, Sir. I have no doubt that the Swedish offer to mediate will be delivered to you by the Ambassador from the Court of Bernadotte this very day."

"And the other matter that you have yet to inform me of? What is that, Sir Stewart?"

Menzies smiled, not realising that he had been quite so transparent.

"Your nose for matters has not failed you, Prime Minister. I have information, from the most reliable of sources, that changes everything but, I hasten to add, Sir, that my source has asked that his report be limited to the very highest echelons of the Allied leadership."

"I understand. Proceed, Sir Stewart,"

"Sir, my source states that the whole move towards a peace conference is not authored by the Swedes, but by the Soviets themselves."

"Good grief."

"Quite. He's asked that we do not reveal that we know it is a Soviet driven initiative, to avoid embarrassing the Swedes, who , I have no doubt, intend to secure some rather splendid agreements and concessions from the USSR for their part on the process."

"Your contact is Swedish, of course, and is it possible that he might be the contact that has previously been of great service to the Allied cause, Sir Stewart?"

"It is indeed, Sir."

"Then I agree, but it will have to be shared with the leaders. The President, De Gaulle, even Speer, they have to be told so they can understand the strength of our bargaining position."

"I understand, Sir, but I must request that they are informed personally, and asked to adhere to the strictest secrecy on the matter."

Churchill nodded by way of agreement.

Standing, the Prime Minister indicated that the meeting was over and that his drive to get moving had taken over.

"I will inform the President immediately. Thank you for bringing this to me in timely fashion, Sir Stewart."

"My pleasure. Thank you, Sir."

By magic, the door opened and Inches appeared.

"Sir, an urgent message has just arrived from the Foreign Minister's office."

Churchill and Menzies exchanged smiles.

Inches waited, expecting the head of MI-6 to leave, but Sir Stewart held his ground as Churchill tore open the envelope with undisguised anticipation.

After a moment's silence, he looked up with a beaming smile and nodded, confirming its contents to the spymaster.

"Thank you again, Sir Stewart. Inches, please see Sir Stewart out and have my appointments for this afternoon cleared between three and four."

As he moved into the hall beyond, Menzies caught the words, knowing they were as much for him as Inches.

Picking up the telephone, Churchill arranged for a line that connected him directly to Truman.

He calculated that the time in Washington was just after five in the morning and prepared an apology for waking up his American friend.

The apology was unnecessary.

Tørget had sent a message to his own American contact, Sam Rossiter, who, in turn, had given his boss the heads-up.

Major General William Donovan, head of the OSS, had woken Truman some thirty-two minutes before Churchill's call disturbed the President's train of thought.

"Mr President... apologies for the early morning call. I have some news that simply couldn't wait."

"I was just about to ring you, Prime Minister. You have the same news as I, I don't doubt. It seems that our Swedish friends have pulled one out of the hat."

"Yes, Harry. Can I assume you know the other bit?"

"You certainly can, Winston."

"So how do you wish to proceed, Harry?"

503

"Well, I'm going to be on the first flight I can get organised after I've met with the Swedish ambassador. I assume you will be seeing the ambassador in London?"

A negative noise stopped Truman's flow.

"No, Harry, he's forced himself into my afternoon schedule at Chequers."

"When is that?"

"Three o'clock."

"Ten o'clock here. Coordinated delivery. So, I think we meet up in Versailles... apprise the leaders... I'm thinking De Gaulle, Franco, your Dominion leaders, as tight a group as possible."

"Speer?"

"Don't suppose we have a choice on that one, do we?"

"I don't think we do, Harry."

"So, we get them all in a small room and tell them... and tell them they can't talk about it to anyone... and then politicians being politicians, the whole shooting-match is through their delegations within the hour, and probably in the press within the day."

"I understand that only too well, Harry, but we have no choice in the matter. We cannot exclude our major Allies, otherwise the new alliance, for which we striven so hard, will be placed at risk."

"You're right, but I still have an itch about the Germans."

"We have no choice, as I see it. After all, if we're to take advantage of this, we need them to know the full situation, which will also encourage them to give operations their fullest commitment."

"Operations, Winston?"

"Harry, we have to. The Soviets are weak and vulnerable... coming to the table has revealed that, as we know that they, not the Swedish, have commenced this process. Something we have done has precipitated this. We must find out what it is and exploit it fully. Clearly, General Eisenhower and his staff must be consulted and, equally clearly, some of them will be included in the circle that know the full situation, but we simply cannot pass up on the opportunity that now presents itself."

"Attack them... yes, I do see... yes, you're right. Where?"

Churchill took a deep puff on his cigar, something that Truman detected despite being thousands of miles away.

"Everywhere, Mr President. Everywhere."

Stalin waited as the telephone connection was made, and observed his Foreign Secretary making a few annotations on the basic document that had been agreed as the basis for negotiations with the enemy.

A voice drew him back from the sight.

'Zhukov.'

"Comrade Marshal, good morning. The Allies have agreed to attend the Swedish talks."

He took a gentle pull on his cigarette as Zhukov asked his questions.

"As quickly as possible, Comrade Marshal. Minister Molotov intends to travel to Sweden as soon as the corridor of safe passage is arranged and confirmed."

He nodded at the words his ears deciphered.

"Yes, you must, Comrade Marshal. If the capitalists smell weakness, then they will place great pressure on our forces, as well as harden their negotiating position... neither must happen, we are clear on that, Comrade Zhukov?"

He waved his hand to remove the ash that had tumbled down his tunic top, and stubbed out the offender before quietly waiting for the man on the other end to stop talking.

"Yes, yes, Comrade. You and Vasilevsky have our complete confidence. I understand tha..."

An aide had slipped in unnoticed and placed a small report in front of the General Secretary. He cut across Zhukov's request for more fuel.

"Let me stop you there. There is no more fuel. Use what you have wisely. I've just been informed that the safe passage is confirmed, so Comrade Minister Molotov will be in Sweden today. That should mean that formal talks could begin tomorrow morning."

Zhukov asked the burning question.

Stalin gave him the answer that had been agreed.

"The 19th at the latest. The Red Army must maintain its fullest efforts until then. That is the absolute imperative of this situation, and you must not fail the party and the Rodina. Implement the operations as planned tonight, Comrade Marshal."

He put the phone down without hearing the Marshal's parting words.

Molotov sensed Stalin's eyes on him and looked up from the document.

"So, Comrade, the Red Army stands ready to do its duty, and it'll buy you time to negotiate from a position of strength. The 19th, Vyacheslav, you've 'til the 19th."

An honourable peace is and always was my first wish. I can take no delight in the effusion of human blood; but, if this war should continue, I wish to have the most active part in it.

John Paul Jones

Chapter 169 - THE DIALOGUE

<u>**1100 hrs, Wednesday, 14th August 1946, Camp Vár conference facility, Lungsnäs, Sweden.**</u>

Military Airfield 16 at Brattfors had been declared as the receiving airbase, with safe flying zones and fighter escorts provided by the Swedish Air Force.

As each delegation landed, the Allied transport aircraft outnumbering those of the USSR by four to one, the Swedish Army whisked the great and powerful away in an armed convoy, quickly covering the fifteen kilometres to the hastily constructed Swedish Army facility on the banks of the Lungen at Lungsnäs.

Whilst adequate, the site lacked many of the creature comforts to which the senior politicians were used, a deliberate choice on the part of the Swedes, who felt such absences would spur the delegations to quicker agreement.

The Swedish Minister for Foreign Affairs, Östen Undén, called the room to order with a gentle knocking of a gavel, the agreed sign of his authority over the powerful assembly.

"Ministers, ambassadors, generals, good morning. Sweden and the world thank you for attending this meeting place, and for your assertion that you all come here with good intentions and a wish to seek a swift, proper, and enduring peace."

As he spoke, Undén nodded at the dignitaries as eye contact was made with each in turn, switching from one side of the huge table to the other, so as not to seem to favour either one group or the other.

"We have come together in a camp named after the Goddess Vár, the goddess of promises and agreements. For the sake of all our peoples, it is my fervent hope that she brings us her wisdom and guidance."

Undén took a deep breath.

"Now, shall we begin? Sweden proposes an immediate ceasefire in place whilst these meetings are conducted."

The Swedish were dumbstruck that Allies and the Soviets were in full agreement, although more dumbstruck by the vigorous and total rejection of the idea, as both sides spoke at length, refusing to be militarily constrained during the peace talks.

Molotov ceased his diatribe and resumed his seat, leaving a silence which Undén broke.

"So, gentlemen, your position is that, whilst we sit here in earnest talks to bring peace to the continent, neither of you can bring yourselves to stop fighting in any way, meaning more and more young men will die as words are thrown back and forth across this table? Minister Molotov, is there no room to accept any cessation in the fighting at this time?"

"No. That is the position of my country, Minister Undén. Until an agreement that is satisfactory to the Soviet Union is ratified by our leadership, there can and will be no truce."

Undén turned to the Allied delegation.

US Secretary of State James Byrnes shook his head to emphasise his words.

"Absolutely not, Minister Undén. The Allied nations will not permit any truce to come about until this meeting has produced a result that brings about peace, and the start of the process of the restoration of freedoms for the people and nations of Europe."

The Minister for Foreign Affairs' sigh was audible.

"Very well. We will take a short break for refreshment and consultations, and return back here for midday. We will then hear your initial basic negotiating positions before we take lunch."

He banged the gavel, ending thirty-nine wholly unsatisfactory minutes, during which the two enemies had been in complete agreement, but only that the killing should go on.

1155 hrs, Wednesday, 14th August 1946, Hofbieber, Germany.

"Well, perhaps someone ought to tell the sonsofbitches that they ain't gotta any goddamned ammo, cos from where I'm fucking sitting, seems they got a whole goddamned lot it, and they ain't afraid to chuck it our way, Sir."

Major William S Towers. Acting OC 3rd battalion, 359th Infantry Regiment, was on the field telephone, apprising his regimental commander, Colonel Bell, as to events in the front line, a front line that Towers and his men had occupied that very morning, relieving the tired soldiers of the 357th US Infantry Regiment from his own division, ready for an assault on Height 444 to their immediate front.

To emphasise Towers' point, something extremely large landed nearby, bringing screams from some unfortunate.

508

"That's probably one of their two-oh-three howitzers, Sir. Lots of other stuff too."

Fig # 213 - Hofbieber, Germany.

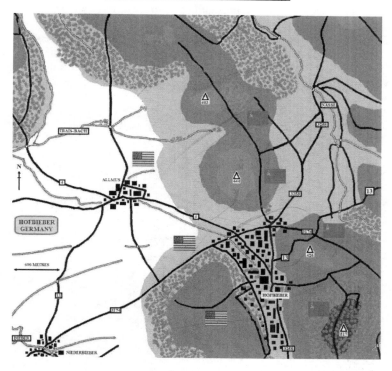

Towers stuck his head round the opening to the bunker and saw a pair of medics scurrying towards the growing sounds of a man in extremis.

"Well, Sir, either they're fixing to bug out, and don't want to carry the weight, or they're fixing to come calling, and I don't see the commies bugging out any time soon."

The acting Battalion CO grimaced as a shell plunged down and tossed the two medics skywards, not whole bodies, but enough to be recognisable as once human beings.

"I'm taking casualties, Sir. They're not slacking off at all, and it's nearly an hour now. What are m…"

Bell interrupted with a question of his own.

"Yes, Sir. Our arty is firing back, but obviously they ain't getting the job done, 'cos there's no slackening off by the commies... none at all, Sir."

Behind Towers, the radio crackled into life, carrying an excited voice barely distinguishable over the sound of automatic fire on the airwaves.

The same sound carried across the battlefield and reached Towers' ears, indicating that the enemy were pushing forward.

Fig # 214 - Soviet attack, north of Hofbieber, Germany.

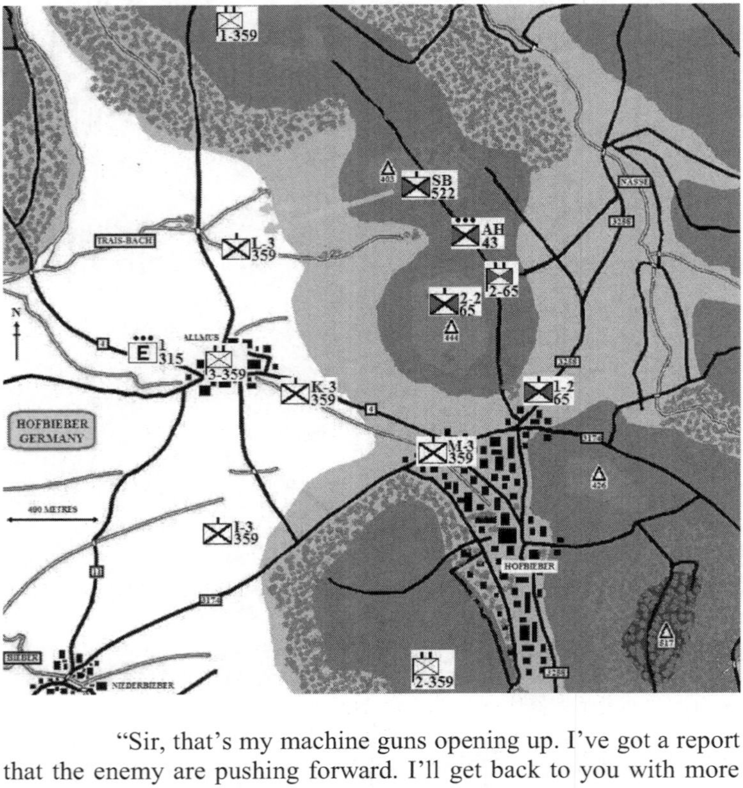

"Sir, that's my machine guns opening up. I've got a report that the enemy are pushing forward. I'll get back to you with more information when I can... yessir..."

Towers tossed the handset onto the table and grabbed his new weapon, a M1A3 Garand, a weapon improved by some modest remodelling of the stock, and the ability of firing twenty rounds from one magazine.

510

3rd Battalion had turned over all their M1s whilst they were out of the line, so Towers knew that whatever it was that was coming down the ways was about to plough into a US infantry battalion with unprecedented firepower.

Whatever it was…

1207 hrs, Wednesday, 14th August 1946, Hofbieber, Germany.

The heavy .50cal Brownings were doing murderous work amongst the advancing Soviet infantry of Shtrafbat 522, and were then joined by their .30cal smaller brothers.

Towers could not help but admire the courage of the advancing soldiers, whilst at the same time baulking at the stupidity of it all.

At least their advance had brought an end to the incoming artillery.

"Time to see what these beauties are capable of, Remington. Your call, son."

Towers dropped into a firing position as the Captain gave the order to fire.

Love Company's weapons spat their bullets across the shrinking divide.

Towers actually didn't reload, instead watching as the attacking force almost melted in front of his eyes.

"Holy Mother of God!"

Captain Remington, a non-contributor to the slaughter by dint of his personal choice of a Thompson, had simply and incredulously observed the whole Soviet attack come apart before his eyes.

"Didn't think you were a believer, Harry?"

Remington could not take his eyes off the sight.

"I'm not, Major, but I've never seen anything like it."

"Me either, Harry… me either."

A sound started rising from the US positions, one of celebration, a sound not unlike that heard on the battlefields of a civil war some eighty years beforehand, from men in blue on Cemetery Ridge, Gettysburg, or others, clad in grey, from behind the stone wall on Marye's Heights at Fredericksburg.

Men were yelling and whooping, raising the new Garands in the air, and celebrating the rout of a large enemy force by inflicting the heaviest of casualties.

"Get 'em back under control, Harry. The artillery'll start back up directly. No sense in losing any of the boys, just cos they're fired up."

"Sir, Major..."

Remington bounded up from the firing position, shouting at his NCOs to bring about order, and for the most part, failing.

Towers, dropped his magazine out and inserted another twenty rounds worth into his beautiful new weapon of war.

'Ain't you a thing of beauty.'

"Get me the Colonel on the horn."

Towers continued to examine the bloody field until a telephone was shoved towards him.

"Thanks. Sir? Colonel Bell, Sir, We stopped them absolutely dead in their tracks... literally... the firepower of our new rifles just hacked them apart. As good as a full company of ma deuces on heat. The attack was probably two full battalions... it just melted, Sir, just melted away."

The artillery resumed, albeit lighter than before.

"Yes, Sir, I agree. Yessir."

Two men looked at two wristwatches two miles apart.

'1220.'

"Soon as, Colonel. Yessir, 1240."

Again, he tossed the handset down.

"Tell all company commanders. We will go with our straight assault option, commencing 1240. Get the message out now."

His staff scurried in all directions.

Towers grabbed his binoculars and quickly surveyed the carnage to the front of his battalion, before switching to view the almost bare hilltop that was Height 444.

Bell had ordered that 3rd Battalion make the assault as soon as possible, to make the most of the shock and disorientation of the failed assault.

As he watched, US artillery started to put a mix of high explosive and airburst on the positions that he intended to occupy shortly.

1240 hrs, Wednesday, 14th August 1946, Hofbieber, Germany.

"Let's go! Move your goddamned arses!"

Third Battalion's L Company rose up with great energy, buoyed by their recent success, and rushed forward.

Some spared a glance at their grisly handiwork, where bloody groups of Russians lay in lines or clusters, slaughtered by a

512

combination of the machine-guns and the volume of fire from the new Garands.

Third Battalion's own mortars started putting down fire on Height 403, a lower promontory to the northwest of 444, the target for Love Company, who led off first.

Fig # 215 - US Forces at Hofbieber, Germany.

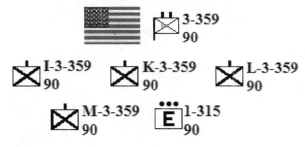

ALLIED FORCES, HOFBIEBER, GERMANY, 14TH AUGUST 1946

The other two companies, King and Mike, would push straight at Height 444 itself, leaving Item Company and a reinforced platoon of 315th Combat Engineers to fill the trench line behind them.

First Sergeant Micco, commanding the leading platoon, pushed his men hard, despite the light resistance so far encountered.

The Soviet mortar fire seemed so much less effective than normal, even though they were used to the much lower enemy fire volumes by now.

Towers, despite the fact that a battalion commander shouldn't really be up the sharp end, brought his small command group with him, and trailed along behind the soldiers of Love, his former company.

Occasionally, he would see a wounded man or a corpse, and know the man's name, remember the man's voice, or what brand of cigarette the man smoked.

A groan caught his attention, and a pair of legs came into view as he moved towards it.

'Oh my God!'

Fig # 216 - Third Battalion's attack on Height 444, Hofbieber, Germany.

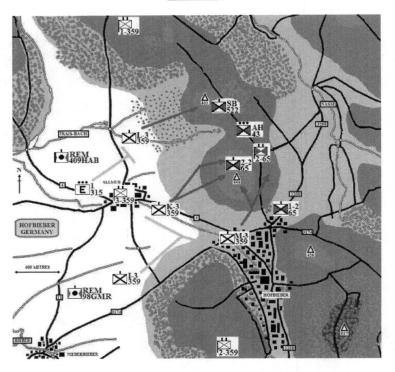

The wounded man had been struck in the abdomen by something capable of opening him up like a butcher's knife.

The bloody entrails were wrapped around his legs where he had thrashed around in extreme pain, at first caused by the wound, and subsequently from the additional damage his own actions inflicted.

Pain and blood loss had reduced the man... *boy*... to a whimpering wreck, and Towers knew he was not long for this world.

He knew the boy well.

He knelt besides Private Jacob Means, son of Mr and Mrs Randolph Means of Gillette, Wyoming, and held the dying eighteen year old's hand as Dressman, one of his old hands, administered morphine in battlefield fashion, straight into the thigh of the casualty.

"Fuck."

514

Means' eyes glassed over and he was gone.

Arranging the boy's hands appropriately, Towers stood and picked up the discarded Garand, placing it in the ground barrel first, so as to mark the location of the body.

"Just a boy, Major... they're always just boys."

Towers slapped Corporal August Dressman on the shoulder gently, understanding that the old veteran had seen more violence in his life than most.

"Move on out... let's catch up with the company!"

A gap had opened up between Towers' group and the hindmost of Love's soldiers.

Which gap ensured his immediate survival.

Fig # 217 - Soviet order of battle, Hofbieber, Germany.

SOVIET FORCES, HOFBIEBER, GERMANY 14TH AUGUST 1946

1258 hrs, Wednesday, 14th August 1946, Height 444, Hofbieber, Germany.

"Comrade Mayor, if I fire now, I'll waste much of my salvo. I recommend waiting."

The rifle battalion's Major was living on his nerves, and the combination of enemy artillery, mortars, and the approaching infantry were bringing him to the edge of his endurance.

"Comrade Starshy Leytenant, I order you to fire your fucking weapons now... right now... at the enemy... right there!"

515

The shaking pistol indicated the men moving towards the northern peak of Height 444, where the rifle battalion commander had placed his most junior and inexperienced company.

"Comrade Mayor, there's movement in the other enemy positions. Look..."

"Give the fire order, Tobulov, give the fucking fire order!"

Ignoring the proximity of the Tokarev's muzzle, and the wild eyes of the critically stressed man, the Guards artillery officer spoke calmly into the telephone, changing the fire order to one that brought down the deadly rain upon the troops advancing on Height 403 instead, out of nothing more than self-preservation.

"Drug-one-one, this is Druzhok-five-two, execute plan dva, execute plan dva, over."

"Druzhok-five-two, Drug-one-one, two minutes, repeat, two minutes. Out."

The Major was rapidly coming apart, and failed to notice the change in his fire order.

"Two minutes? Two fucking minutes? Tell the lazy bastards to fire now... the enemy are moving forward!"

"For the Rodina's sake, will you shut up and let me do my job, Mayor!"

The artillery officer produced a flare pistol ready to fire the agreed signal, and he waved it threateningly at the man who had started to cry.

The Major dropped to his knees and came apart mentally, helped by a near miss from an American mortar round.

A single red flare rose into the sky above the Soviet frontline, sparking frantic activity amongst the defenders.

The attacker US infantry, fearing the nature of the signal, advanced quicker.

Dropping back inside the battalion command post, Starshy Leytenant Tobulov ensured that the men tending to the gibbering officer had fitted the man's equipment properly, following the instructions that the engineer colonel had given that very morning.

Satisfied that all was in order, he donned his own kit and turned to watch the arrival of the deadly barrage.

1302 hrs, Wednesday, 14th August 1946, Hofbieber, Germany.

"Cover!"

The cries went up as men recognised the sound of Katyusha rockets about to arrive in their vicinity.

Over six hundred were in the air and the noise was terrific in volume and terrifying in its intensity.

The rockets started to explode, covering an area between Allmus and Height 403.

The light smoke filled the ground over which the Soviets had attacked, and that was now occupied by US troops going in the opposite direction.

The failed attack had been expected to fail, albeit not so bloodily, and had been designed to provoke a response from the US forces that they believed were gathering for an assault.

That response charged straight into a killing ground from another world.

In February 1945, Soviet forces had stumbled across Dyhernfurth in Lower Silesia. GeneralMaior Max Sachsenheimer, led a German counter-attack and spoiling mission, protecting the Anorgama Gmbh facility, part of the huge I G Farben empire, whilst its deadly product was dumped into the Oder River. Eventually Sachsenheimer's force was driven back, and the Soviets claimed the facility.

Despite the best efforts of the German troops, some quantities of the product remained, and were recovered by the Red Army.

In the chaos that was the Soviet logistical system, some special rocket rounds were accidentally delivered to the front, where Lieutenant General Gluzdovskiy, the commander of the Sixth Army decided to use the tools at his disposal, and ordered the 98th Guards Mortar Regiment to deploy in support of the ragged 117th Rifle Corps.

The surviving Katyushas of the 98th put their special shells on target.

Starshy Leytenant Tobulov didn't bother to call in the results, as he knew the Katyusha unit would be rapidly relocating.

In any case, the gas mask and cape made conversation difficult.

The explosions were... well... different.

Micco risked a look up from his prone position and observed the ground behind him, seeing a hazy, almost light brown coloured smoke screen forming all across the rear.

It was no smoke screen, and obscured nothing, just changed the view enough to be noticeable.

Already on the leading slope, Micco and his men were not engulfed in the same way as the rest of Love Company's soldiers were.

He and his men did not smell the light fruity smell.

Which meant that First Sergeant William O. Micco and his men survived the first use of Tabun nerve agent on the modern battlefield.

"Stop! Stop right there!"

Dressman's voice rose above all other sounds.

In any case, the tableau that greeted them did not encourage forward movement.

Towers was rooted to the spot as the most gruesome play was acted out before his eyes.

Men rose up screaming, others dropped to the ground gasping for air.

Hundreds of soldiers became incapacitated in a moment, as the nerve agent found bare flesh or was inhaled.

Death came quicker to those that drew the deadly agent into their lungs.

Some died within seconds, whereas others gasped for air as they evacuated their bladders and bowels.

"Chewing gum?"

"What's that you say Harry?"

"Chewing gum… smells like chewing gum."

"Oh my god! Major! Get back!"

Dressman had been there before, and pieced together the explosions, hazy vision, and unusual smell.

"Gas! The bastards have fired poison gas!"

There was not a single gas mask in the attacking force, in Third Battalion, or even in the 90th Division.

For the soldiers of Love Company, it was already too late.

Otherwise healthy soldiers found themselves unable to draw breath, or lapsing into a sleep from which there was no return.

Towers was startled by the figure that leapt past him.

"Stop Harry! Grab him someone!"

518

It was too late, and the acting commander of Love Company escaped the grabbing hands and charged forward to help his men.

As Remington ran, his lungs worked overtime, drawing the deadly Tabun into them.

His vision started to fail him and his lungs failed to work as hard as he ordered.

His limb control failed and he tumbled head first into the ground, where his body started to convulse.

Around him, others were in a similarly awful death dance, arms and legs jumping and waggling uncontrolled, as the agent interfered with their nervous systems.

Remington vomited and, face down, inhaled the contents of his stomach, bringing a reasonably swift end to his suffering.

Towers, open-mouthed with shock, watched from a distance. Suddenly shaking himself from his inactivity, he made the only decision he could, assisted by Dressman's hands pulling at his straps.

"Move back... quickly!"

The command group needed no second telling, and displaced back to the command post, where Towers immediately grabbed the telephone.

Out on the killing ground he had left behind, the gentle breeze encouraged the Tabun to spread south and southwestwards.

Shocked beyond measure, he tried to compose himself, and failed.

"Colonel Bell, Sir... Colonel... my boys're all gone... all gone..."

Dressman shouted as he pissed on his comforter.

"Piss on it... anything... get it on your fucking faces... quickly!"

"Who is that shouting? What the hell do you mean, Towers? Talk sense, soldier!"

"Colonel, the commies fired something at us... don't know what it was... poison gas or summat... but all my boys are dead... not shot, not by shrapnel, not blown up... but they're all fucking dying or FUCKING DEAD!"

Bell felt the full force of Towers' anger down the phone.

Clearly the man was unhinged, and Bell needed to act quickly.

"Towers, put your next senior man on the phone right now. That's an order."

519

Retaining enough understanding of the situation, Towers, his muscles twitching, handed the phone across to the only other officer left, a veteran Lieutenant who had recently rejoined the 90th.

The officer opened enough gap from his urine soaked handkerchief to be coherent.

"Yes Sir, Colonel, Sir."

The man's voice was strangely high-pitched, but Bell missed it.

"Who are you, soldier?"

"First Lieutenant O'Halloran, Sir."

"What the hell is happening with Towers? He said everyone's dead. What's he on about?"

"Sir, Major Towers is correct. Third Battalion's been wiped out... they're all dead or dying... all of them."

"All of them? Are you goddamned mad, O'Halloran?"

The Lieutenant's nose streamed, and he started to shake with rage... or shock... or...

Towers, sweating profusely, took the phone from O'Halloran as he folded to the ground, alongside the radio operator, who struggled to draw on the cigarette he had just lit, resigned to his end and preferring to go out with lungs full of smoke than nostrils full of his own waste.

O'Halloran wet himself as he coughed and spluttered.

Towers held the man's webbing to try and pull his face out of the dirt.

"Colonel Bell... we're about... to die...," he felt a wave of instability wash over him, and grabbed the hand holding the telephone in an attempt to hold it steady.

O'Halloran, unsupported, simply collapsed to the floor.

Towers' attempt to rally was unsuccessful and the receiver fell from his grasp.

His vision indistinct, Towers made a barely controlled descent into a sitting position, as his limbs gave up being properly controlled.

The man with the scythe strode the valley floor, and none of the attackers, save Micco and his group, were spared.

Dressman, knowing his end was approaching, spent his last few conscious moments waving his fist at the sky, and screaming at whichever decider of men's fate it was that had spared him the horrors of the Great War, albeit shot and gassed, only to bring him to die so horribly in a German field in 1946.

1358 hrs, Wednesday, 14th August 1946, Height 444, Hofbieber, Germany.

The battalion commander had rushed out of the bunker at some time during the destruction of the US force, and found enough of the Tabun to ensure his lingering but inevitable death.

Amongst the defending Soviet riflemen, seventeen had certainly either succumbed or had a fatal exposure.

There had even been fatalities amongst the guardsmen of the 98th Guards Mortar Regiment, where mishandling and poor sealing of rockets had brought about the deaths of eleven personnel, including the artillery colonel who had delivered the shells and protective gear.

On the slopes of Height 403, First Sergeant Micco and his men remained in situ, unable to go forward, and sure as hell not going anywhere backwards.

The enormity of what had happened behind them shocked them so totally that, when Soviet troops surrounded them, they simply surrendered, and were meekly taken into captivity.

1435 hrs, Wednesday, 14th August 1946, US Twelfth Army Group Headquarters, Ehrenbreitstein Fortress, Koblenz, Germany.

Bradley was enjoying a quiet moment, having just seen off De Lattre of French First Army after a working lunch.

A cool breeze blew through the large hemispherical window, bringing with it light relief, from which he was quickly dragged by the strident ringing of his phone.

"Bradley."

The commander of US Twelfth Army Group listened in shock and horror as what was known about the events at Hofbieber were explained to him by the new commander of Third Army, using the exact words of the report sent by the distraught commander of the 90th Division.

"They did what?"

Feeling a calm descend, Bradley responded in a controlled matter-of-fact way.

"I see. No survivors, Lucian? None at all? Do we know what they've done... what they've used?"

He listened to the words that followed, understanding that, if the report was true, the war had just moved into a phase unlike any other in the history of man.

521

Lucian Truscott asked for orders.

Bradley had none that were any use against poison gas attacks.

"I'll get my technical staff on it straight away. Find out practical precautions. I'll get gas masks movingbto frontlien forces within the hour. I'll also get air pounding anything that could remotely deliver these weapons. Now, I have to call the boss. Good luck, Lucian, and I'm truly sorry."

He killed the connection and immediately sought another.

"Get me General Eisenhower."

1452 hrs, Wednesday, 14th August 1946, 2nd Red Banner Front of Soviet Europe's Headquarters, Grandhotel Pupp, Karlsbad, Bohemia.

"Comrade Leytenant General, an urgent call from General Kurochkin."

The two men were old friends so Trubnikov, recently sent from 3rd Red Banner to command 2nd Red Banner, welcomed the interruption to the medical examination the headquarters doctor was undertaking.

"Enough for now, Comrade. I'm fit as a borzoi."

"Not so, Comrade Leytenant General. Your blood pressure is raised, so avoid stressful activities. Plus, there's some noises on your chest, so no smoking."

In open defiance, Trubnikov made a great play of lighting a cigarette, and grinned at the doctor as he picked up the telephone.

"Trubnikov."

His grin widened as he recognised the voice of his friend, although warning sounds coursed through his brain as he also detected something more sinister in the man's voice.

"Pavel Alekseevich, how…"

Had the doctor been measuring Trubnikov's blood pressure as the commander of Second Red Banner listened to the report, he would have had a fit.

"What? We've done fucking WHAT?"

Across Europe, telephones rang and incredulous ears received the news of the Soviet gas attack.

522

As more and more details were confirmed, anger and disbelief grew hand in hand.

The heads of the Alliance were all informed, and there was a general universal call for a reply in kind but not, as some had expected, or even hoped, for the use of atomic weapons.

In Moscow, Stalin's reaction was measured by the number of arrest orders he issued.

NKVD officers went forth and worked their way through the 98th Guards Mortar Regiment, all the way to the commander of Sixth Army, who blew his own brains out before the arrest squad could do it for him.

Interrogations were swift and brutal, and the Sixth Army lost many of its finest officers for no other reason than a lack of knowledge that Tabun weapons were even present within their unit.

The reasons that had ensured no chemical exchanges in the German War were still sound: more so in many ways.

Stalin talked urgently with Molotov in Sweden, passed on the incredible news, and gave his instructions on how to proceed once the full situation was understood by the Allied politicians.

Zhukov dispatched his two colonels, Ferovan and Atalin, armed with a defined brief to investigate the incident in a different way, and he also ensured that every supply depot was swept for any more such weapons.

Just to make sure, Stalin had Beria do the same.

On the Allied side of the line, lights burned well into the night, on both sides of the Atlantic.

The words were ones of horror and incredulity…

… of retribution…

… of revenge…

… and of The Bomb.

Meanwhile, word spread around the globe.

1857 hrs, Wednesday, 14th August 1946, 733 15th St NW, Washington DC, USA.

Careful not to risk her recently applied nail polish, she lifted the phone to her ear.

"Oh-three-oh-six."

"Hi honey."

"Hello Humphrey, I'm nearly ready. Shall I com…"

"Sorry honey, I can't make it. Things have taken off here in the office. There's an emergency meeting of the committee in half an hour."

"Aww Humphrey. I bought that red dress I was talking about too."

In truth, Olivia von Sandow was not disappointed, as her liaison with the Senator from Illinois had not proved as fruitful as her masters had expected, and the sex was simply lousy.

All that changed in one simple statement.

"So sorry, honey, but it's big, really big. The lousy commies've used some sort of chemical and killed hundreds of our boys, and a lot of civilians in Germany. Between you and me, I guess the bomb'll be back on the table, and I doubt anyone'll try hard to stop it being used."

"Oh no, that's horrible, Humphrey."

"We have all sorts of chemical stuff too, stuff we had set aside for use on the nips. You can betcha that'll be on the table. The Brits are hopping mad too, and they're on board with whatever we decide, so there's no checks from that angle. The whole thing just went to hell in a handcart, Olivia."

She heard his final words and made appropriate noises, and returned the phone to the cradle when she realised that Senator Humphrey Randall Forbes, member of the Armed Services Committee, had rung off.

She quickly decided that this was just the sort of emergency that the rapid contact system was established for, and picked up the phone again and obtained a connection.

"Occidental Grill, good evening."

"Good evening, I would like to book a table for two tomorrow evening at eight in the name of von Sandow, and I would like to make sure that you set aside a bottle of the 1935 Latour Pauillac for me please."

"One moment please… yes, we have a table, and that is reserved for you. Would you like to hold whilst I speak to the sommelier, Madame?"

"No, no need. I have an appointment at the Tabard for seven-thirty… just make sure he sets one by please. Thank you."

"Thank you, Madame. We shall look forward to seeing you tomorrow at eight."

The phone connection had already been broken and Olivia von Sandow, happy she had set up a dead drop with her Soviet master, was making a new call.

"Klaus, it's Olivia. My date has cancelled this evening and I wondered if you would like to take his place. There's a reservation for seven-thirty at the Tabard. You know it?"

To make sure her superior understood, she gave him the urgent code.

"I believe they have some fresh lobster just in."

The meeting was set, and within the hour the head of the German Intelligence Service in the USA was aware that the American government, supported by its staunchest ally, was considering responding with the bomb, or their own hitherto unsuspected stocks of chemical weapons.

Which was not wholly accurate, for Senator Humphrey Randall Forbes did not speak for the White House.

Having powdered her nose, Olivia returned to her seat, confident that the message she had secreted in the cistern of the third stall would soon ensure that her Soviet masters also had the details that Forbes had so willingly surrendered.

2303 hrs, Wednesday, 14th August 1946, Vinogradar Young Communists Sailing Club, Black Sea, USSR.

"Well, Comrade Kalinin, your report?"

The Admiral was so keen to know that he overlooked returning Captain Second Rank Mikhail Stepanovich Kalinin's crisp salute.

Admiral Oktyabrskiy grasped Kalinin's shoulder in a show of emotion.

"Spit it out, Mikhail."

"I have signed off on vessel fifty-one, Comrade Admiral. The Chief Engineer assures me that fifty-four will be ready for my inspection as of tomorrow at 1500. I anticipate, if all goes well, that I will sign her off on Monday at the latest."

Oktyabrskiy clapped his hands in joy, for reasons that were not apparent to Kalinin, who had no idea of the nature and tone of the phone call that the Black Sea Fleet commander had just endured.

"Forget fifty-four, Comrade. You are ordered to commence sea trials."

"When, Comrade Admiral?"

"Your crew have done their training. I've seen your efficiency reports…"

"On the mock-up only, Comrade Admiral. I would require…"

"You have the weekend only, Kalinin. You are ordered to undertake whatever sea trials you dictate to bring fifty-one to readiness and make her operational. Is that clear?"

"Sir… Admiral… this is a magnificent submarine… but if I go to sea in it without a properly trained crew… and I mean not one trained on mock ups… but with water under and over them… I cannot…"

"You will do it, Comrade Kapitan. I have received a direct order, and I pass it on to you. You will take fifty-one to sea at 0900, Monday morning and conduct trails to bring her to a state fit for the Motherland's use… for use as soon as is possible."

Kalinin looked hard at the Admiral, and then at the sleek form of fifty-one, and then back, his face set in resolution.

"Comrade Admiral, you know… you have to know… this is madness…"

"It is an order, Comrade Kapitan."

"It's fucking lunacy, that's what it is, Comrade Admiral, fuc…"

Again, Oktyabrskiy grasped the junior man's shoulder, this time in warning, more than friendship.

"Shut up, you fool, shut up."

The furtive glances that the Admiral shot in all directions told Kalinin all he needed to know about where the order had come from.

"You will do your duty, Comrade Kapitan. You will take her to sea and perform whatever sea trials…," Oktyabrskiy lowered his voice but increased the weight of delivery in such a way that Kalinin got the message loud and clear, "…that **you** dictate… before making her operational. Do you understand, Mikhail?"

"Yes, Comrade Admiral."

"Good."

He released his hold on the submarine commander's shoulder, and his posture became more relaxed.

"I have other news… good news… Comrade Kapitan. Your vessel will be J-51 of the Soviet Naval Submarine force, and will have a name, especially chosen for her by our glorious General Secretary."

Kalinin noted the J-51 with approval, as he and his crew had started calling the Type XXI 'Jana', after the young NKVD officer who had been killed when a crane dropped part of the submarine on her.

526

Oktyabrskiy motioned to a group of four waiting sailors, who struggled forward something, clearly heavy, concealed under a canvas.

"Come, Mikhail."

They descended from the gantry onto the dockside.

The Admiral waved his hands and the sailors dragged the cover away, revealing a nameplate.

Kalinin read the two words.

'Sovetskaya Initsiativa.'

"What do you think, eh, Comrade Kapitan? A fine name, eh?"

"Yes, indeed, Comrade Admiral. One worthy of her purpose."

"Have one of your officers oversee its installation before the official launch ceremony, Mikhail

With a hearty slap on the back and a soft-spoken reminder of his orders, Admiral Oktyabrskiy went on his way.

Watching him depart, Kalinin resolved to call her 'Jana', as 'Soviet Initiative' was far too much of a mouthful.

All you have to do is hold your first soldier who is dying in your arms, and have that terribly futile feeling that I can't do anything about it... Then you understand the horror of war.

Norman Schwarzkopf

Chapter 170 - THE RESPONSE

1000 hrs, Thursday 15th August 1946, Camp Vár conference facility, Lungsnäs, Sweden.

The atmosphere in the bespoke meeting room was little short of openly hostile, the encouraging air of détente and cooperation washed away by the events in Hofbieber the previous day.

Undén called the meeting to order and, as he had agreed, despite the pleading from Minister Molotov, gave the floor to the Allied delegation.

"Thank you, Chairman Undén."

Eyes turned away from US Secretary of State James Byrnes towards the man who unexpectedly rose in his stead.

Ernest Bevin, Foreign Secretary in Churchill's coalition government, was to deliver the Allied response.

"Chairmen Undén, fellow delegates, it with a heavy heart, and with incredulity, that I must report a change to the war situation that has now been confirmed since we last convened."

His West Country accent was difficult for the translators to fully understand, so he spoke slowly, and as precisely as he could.

"At roughly one pm yesterday, in and around the German villages of Hofbieber and Allmus, the armed forces of the Soviet Union employed a deadly weapon against soldiers of the Allied Armies, one employed in direct contravention of the 1925 Geneva protocol for the prohibition of the use of Asphyxiating, Poisonous, or Other Gases, and of Bacteriological Methods of Warfare, which came into effect on the 8th February 1928, and to which the government of the gentleman opposite is a signatory."

He took a sip on his water as the translators caught up.

"Chairman Undén, the Allied Alliance has entered into these discussions in good faith, accepting the generous offer of the Swedish Government to come here and meet with our enemies, to find common ground, and to attempt to establish some means of ending the conflict and returning the world to the peace it so richly deserves... and desperately needs."

Molotov was white, not through fury, but through his embarrassment and his shock at the events being described, even though he had been told the previous evening.

The phone call, from no less than the General Secretary, had been very much one-way, and he was left in no doubt as to what he needed to do when the strangely accented Englishman had stopped prattling on.

"Chairman Undén, these proceedings will be terminated with immediate effect whilst we consider our position, a position that includes a response with any and every means available to the Allied Alliance, including the use of our Atomic weapons."

The entire Allied negotiating team rose as one, intent on departing, but Minister Undén responded loudly.

"Gentlemen, please! Remain seated for a few moments longer, please."

He gestured them to sit, and they did, their theatrical attempt to leave wholly staged for dramatic effect, as they were well aware that Molotov had pleaded with the Swede for first statement, and had no intention of leaving before hearing his words.

"At your request, we will stay, Chairman."

Undén bowed his head graciously in acknowledgement.

It was all theatre, all the dance of brinkmanship and diplomacy, although it didn't sit well with Byrnes, who was all for a 'pistols at dawn' approach.

"Minister Molotov has asked to make a statement on behalf of his government."

The rumbles from the allied side of the table were unusually pronounced, and a number of choice words fell upon Molotov's ears as he rose.

"Chairman Undén, fellow delegates, I stand before you at this grave hour, charged to deliver the most sincere and contrite apologies of the people and leadership of the Union of Soviet Socialist Republics, in specific regard to the highly regrettable incident outlined by Secretary Bevan."

Surprise swept through the Allied negotiating team like an out of control brush fire.

"I can confirm the following circumstances exist regarding the unauthorised and criminal use of a German-manufactured chemical agent on the battlefield around Hofbieber yesterday."

Johann Ludwig Graf Schwerin von Krosigk, the German Foreign Minister bristled at the deliberate negative mention of his country.

"One of our rocket artillery regiments was supplied with some experimental ammunition that had been filled with a noxious substance captured from the Nazis during our victorious advance through Czechoslovakian Silesia in February 1945."

Some of the Allied contingent made notes, whilst others looked for signs of insincerity on the face of the Soviet Foreign Minister.

Curiously, there were none.

"It appears, from our initial investigations, that a number of Red Army officers acted without orders, in secret, and in knowing contravention of the Geneva protocols to which we were, and still are, willing signatories."

That was a huge signal, and it wasn't wasted on a single person present.

"Arrests have been made, from the commander of the Army within whose boundaries this appalling incident took place, down to those who perpetrated the attack. I can confirm that the NKVD officer, a colonel, who seems to have been responsible for delivering the shells to the frontline unit, is amongst those who has been executed on the personal order of the General Secretary, Comrade Stalin."

Molotov knew the man was already dead by a different mechanism, but he had specific orders.

He produced a handkerchief and ran it quickly across his brow as the combination of an unusually warm Swedish summer and the number of bodies crammed into the meeting hall, heated the room up beyond a comfortable level.

Undén made a note to have some fans brought as soon as the meeting broke up.

"The International Red Cross have been invited to participate in our investigations and, short of revealing military information, will, with our agreement, furnish the Allied nations with a full copy of their findings. We similarly agree that the Allied nations may select two persons from a non-aligned and neutral nation to join the investigations."

Pens scribbled noisily as Molotov's words were faithfully transferred to paper for later examination.

"By these demonstrations of our good faith, the Soviet Union hopes to demonstrate that there were no orders... no intent... no wish to operate outside the 1925 Geneva Protocols, and that the incident of yesterday was an aberration beyond its control."

Molotov studied his notes to make sure he got the wording absolutely as he had been directed.

"Once again, Comrade General Secretary Stalin wishes me to pass on the full and total apologies of the Soviet Union for the unprovoked use of chemical weapons by rogue elements of the Red Army, and also the wish that further use can be avoided, either by way of retaliation, or escalation... by any means available to either side."

The meaning of that was very clear to all listening.

"We have come to these proceedings at the request of the Government of our friend, Sweden, in good faith, and with open minds, and have no intent of initiating any unusual act of war, and we hope that our sincerity in that will be appreciated by our opponents, and that further action, of a nature that expands the type of weapons employed, can be avoided."

"Whilst we reserve the right to carry out full military activities, as already decided by all parties in this conference, the Soviet Union makes the categorical assurance that there will be no further use of any weapon cited within the 1925 Geneva Protocols."

Molotov sought and made direct eye contact with his American counterpart.

"By these means, we hope and trust that the Allied nations will forgive this unwarranted attack, accept that it was unintended, accept that we will continue to investigate it, will ensure no repeat, and that they will all return to the negotiating table without further escalation of the conflict."

The Soviet Foreign Minister resumed his seat, his throat dryer than he had ever known.

A full glass of water barely touched the sides, and he set the empty tumbler down.

Still, there was no reply from the other side of the table, but there was much whispering, as lowered heads came together in urgent discussion.

Östen Undén, as disbelieving as the men sat to his right, felt compelled to fill the silent void.

"Minister Molotov, thank you for making delivering that clarification of the circumstances surrounding the unfortunate events of yesterday, and also, I thank you on behalf of the Swedish Government for your candour and renewed commitment to finding a peaceful path forward."

He ignored the looks he was getting from some of the Allied contingent.

"However, it is not Sweden that had been sorely wronged here. It is not Sweden that has been the subject of this heinous attack, in clear contravention of Geneva Protocol."

The looks from the right softened perceptibly.

"It must be for the delegation from the Allied nations to decide, in concert with their governments, how matters will proceed from here. As representative of my country, and in the light of the Soviet statement and full and frank admission of guilt, I can only urge restraint and forbearance on the Allied nations' part. Unless there is anything else?"

Neither side rose or made any attempt to speak further.

"Then I will adjourn this meeting until either side calls for it to be reconvened, at any time, day, or night, from this moment forward. Please, speak to your governments, relay the words that have been spoken here, and remember the spirit that brought these two sides together in the first instance. Thank you. This meeting is at an end."

Undén cracked the gavel down with more force than usual, highlighting his own anxiousness at what might be coming.

The delegations filed out of their respective doors, leaving the Swedish contingent alone.

"Adolfsson... please get some fans installed in here for when we come back."

"Yes, Minister."

His aide knew him well enough to venture a further comment.

"I thought I'd melt at one time. It was hot in here, Minister."

Undén laughed loudly, relieving some of the tension that threatened his enjoyment of lunch.

"Not as hot as it could have been, Björn... nowhere near as hot as it could have been."

Secure communications flowed out from and back into Sweden, as the negotiating teams reported back on the morning's exchanges, apprising the leadership of all sides, and seeking guidance on how to respond.

Soviet information was delivered, revealing that the agent used was Tabun, liberated from the Germans in 1945.

Speer received a number of telephone calls seeking very specific information, and the characteristics of Tabun were soon common knowledge amongst the Allied leaders.

The Allied political leadership assembled in Versailles, and the French, Canadian, Spanish, Polish, and German heads listened, with varying degrees of shock, to the news that the Soviets had brought matters to the table, and the full details of the attack visited upon US forces.

The leaders deferred to Truman on the matter of the contravention of the Geneva Protocol, and he ordered a military operation, a retaliation in kind, to be prepared, using stocks of nerve agents captured from the Germans in 1945, although he conceded that converting the battlefield into a chemical one was not in the best interests of anyone, if only because neither sides soldiers, nor the civilian populations, could protect themselves, or be protected.

Secretly, Truman and his staff had wondered whether the attack would change public opinion on use of the bombs on Russia, but it was too soon to tell.

Truman stressed the fact that, however regrettable, the Hofbieber attack gave the Allies an even stronger bargaining position.

Surprisingly, use of the bomb was not mentioned.

There was little debate on military action, as all understood the need to take advantage of the situation, as the bonus of applying more pressure to the clearly weakened enemy would strengthen their own position further.

Ground and air attacks would be ramped up to a high level... an unsustainable level as General Eisenhower advised... but the benefits of exhausting some of the Allied forces would be far outweighed by the pressure placed upon the Soviet Union and the opportunity to bring an early end to hostilities.

It was the terms of a negotiated peace that caused the greater discussion... and the greater disagreement.

As the discussions focussed on the negotiations, and the recommended cease fire lines and future political boundaries, the German and Polish heads of state became more and more agitated, despite the assurances of further negotiations, post cessation of hostilities.

The meeting broke up for lunch, a break called by Truman, who clearly wanted a period of calm to enable Speer, and particularly the Polish President, Władysław Raczkiewicz, to calm down.

After enjoying a hearty spread, the leaders returned to the room, only to discover that the break had done nothing to soften the two leaders' positions, and that new words, such as treachery, abandonment, and betrayal, figured heavily in their protestations.

It all centred on where the lines would be drawn.

The start negotiating position returned Europe politically to 1938 boundaries, but no one present really expected that to be the end position, and subsequent discussions seemed to end up with Germany minus Prussia at the minimum, and a partitioned and fractured Poland.

As the politicians continued to form their response, the soldiers acted.

1200 hrs, Thursday, 15th August 1946, Eberschutz, Germany.

"Panzer marsch!"

Maybach engines revved, creating a wall of noise, dragging even the least curious civilian to their windows to witness a full-scale panzer attack.

Even the experienced grenadiers of the 78th Sturm Division, responsible for liberating Eberschutz the previous day, watched in awe as the Europa Panzer Brigade ground forward, supported by a wave of aircraft in close support.

The scene was further enhanced as nebelwerfer batteries added their deadly rockets to the attack on Trendelburg.

The Germans were determined to continue to press the Red Army as hard as possible.

Fig # 218 - Soviet initial dispositions, Trendelburg, Germany.

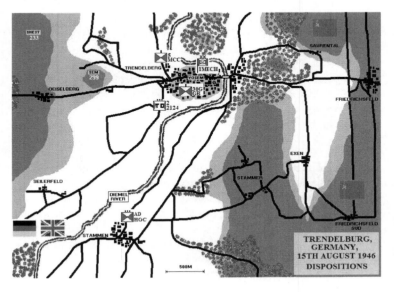

Colonel Von Hardegen observed the plan unfold, his modified Panther G positioned on a small incline that overlooked the first point of contact at Sielen.

Grenadiers from the 14th Sturm-Grenadiere Regiment had smashed into the German village some thirty minutes previously, and quickly overcame the light Soviet resistance. They had also summarily executed the dazed prisoners for the benefit of the villagers, who spoke of the excesses visited upon them by the occupation force.

The lead unit of von Hardegen's force skewed to the right as planned, securing the flank, should there be any enemy forces of note on the other bank of the River Diemel.

If there was, they were wisely staying quiet, as powerful 75mm and 88mm guns maintained in overwatch.

The remainder of Europa continued northwards, and von Hardegen ordered his headquarters unit to push forward to and past Sielen.

Inwardly, he cursed the absence of any means of crossing the Diemel at Sielen with heavy vehicles, the bridging equipment he needed prioritised elsewhere, except for the one bridging tank he had retained for a crucial task.

The original structure at Sielen had long since been deposited in the water by either the Allied air forces, or Soviet engineers, or both.

The only possible crossing point left was the small wooden bridge over the modest Hungerbach on the southeast edge of Sielen, which carried Route 68 over the water, to join with the 67, the road that lead northeast to Trendelburg.

A replacement bridge had been constructed by Soviet engineers and coerced locals, and was constructed in timber cut from the local forests It had easily succumbed to the attention of Allied aircraft. Although still standing, the repairs affected by the Soviets would not stand the weight of anything of any substance, the bridge itself initially constructed for light vehicles, not to allow the passing of heavy armour.

Another reason that the 14th Sturm-Grenadieres had launched a swift attack, without artillery preparation, was so that his own engineers could assess the likelihood of using Sielen as a crossing point for his panzers.

The initial report was enough to make him switch his attentions elsewhere, and instigate his second plan.

Aerial photographs had revealed the possibility of a surviving bridge, damaged but probably bridgeable, which is why he

535

preserved his only bridgelayer for use in Stammen, further up the Hungerbach.

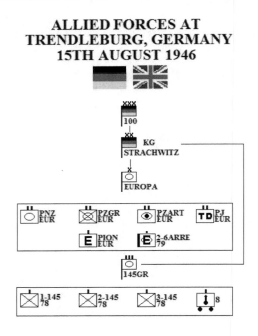

ALLIED FORCES AT TRENDLEBURG, GERMANY 15TH AUGUST 1946

Now leading the advance was his second company, equipped with the new and extremely impressive Jaguar, the very latest vehicle to roll off the production lines from the recovering German industry.

Its 88mm, the same as that which had graced the Tiger II, could dispatch most opponents with relative ease, and in the hands of veterans, such as the men of Europa, it was as lethal a tank weapon as the Allies possessed.

The formation of Jaguars pushed forward, ignoring the light artillery fire that suddenly came their way, manoeuvring almost as if on an exercise.

The 'exercise' turned to harsh reality as one artillery shell found an SDKFZ 251 carrying some of Europa's panzer-grenadiers, spreading the vehicle and men over the German countryside in one bloody moment.

Von Hardegen gripped his binoculars more tightly, knowing he had just seen a dozen men die.

The lead unit increased speed and moved quickly through the choke point caused by the river bend and the two hundred metre high ridgeline to the west.

He waited to see the second phase enacted, and immediately saw the reconnaissance force push out down the riverbank, seeking to secure the positions around the damaged Soviet military bridge at Stammen, something that was key to the success of his plan.

Fig # 220 - Kampfgruppe Strachwitz's initial attack on Trendelburg.

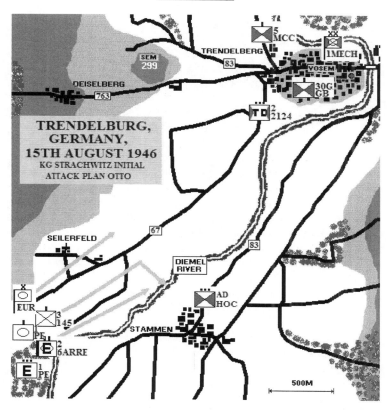

The other key part, a Churchill VII bridge layer, one of a small unit of special tanks seconded from the 79th Armoured

537

Division, announced its presence as it noisily made its way past the headquarters unit, having been called forward by the recon force commander, who was clearly confident enough that he had secured Stammen's west bank to bring up Europa's prize asset.

The Churchill lumbered along slowly, encumbered by the additional weight of the reinforcing metal deemed necessary to make its portable bridge capable of sustaining the passage of the tanks of von Hardegen's command.

Ahead, the lead Jaguars had been taken under fire by something that seemingly didn't trouble them.

The lead vehicles halted and sent shells into three locations, two of which yielded secondary explosions.

Von Hardegen listened to the reports that some 45mm anti-tank guns had been engaged and destroyed in front of Trendelburg.

He checked the position of the bridge layer and silently cursed the slowness of the British-made vehicle, wishing it would move quicker. Further up river, a platoon of engineers had accompanied the recon troops and, equipped with inflatables, had moved over the river into Stammen.

The flashes and sounds of exploding grenades followed by automatic fire indicated that close quarter fighting was in progress.

The radio sang in his ear as the recon commander relayed the contact report to the lead echelon commander, who responded by ordering a platoon of sturm-grenadiers forward, intending that they should cross the river, using the inflatables, and back up the engineers in Stammen.

A pair of Allied aircraft swooped on something out of sight well to the east of the river, and it quickly died, whatever it was, flames and smoke indicating its fate.

A quick look at the map allowed von Hardegen to work out that it had been somewhere around Exen, on the raised ground overlooking Trendleburg.

At various points along the bank of the Diemel, Panthers and Jaguars had taken up position, intent on watching for any sign of movement on the east bank.

One Jaguar had thrown a track, and von Hardegen observed as the venerable Bergepanther recovery vehicle made its way forward to assist.

"Wotan-six, Wotan-six, Walküre-six, over.*"

The message was from the panzer battalion's commander, Oberstleutnant Fürth, who had served with the 21st Panzer Division in North Africa, where he had been taken prisoner.

"Wotan-six, phase two complete. Request permission to execute Otto, repeat, request permission to execute Otto."

Von Hardegen took a moment to see where the Churchill had got to, and made the same assessment as Fürth.

"Walküre -six, Wotan-six, execute Plan Otto. Out."

Although he knew what was about to happen, von Hardegen was still extremely impressed with the discipline of the manoeuvre that turned the First Company of the panzer battalion sharply to the right, suddenly not heading towards Trendelburg, but instead towards Stammen, where the Churchill was just starting the process of bridging between the two stubs of the damaged bridge.

[* - The German Army began introducing a radio regime similar to that of the Allies in early March 1946.]

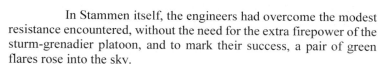

In Stammen itself, the engineers had overcome the modest resistance encountered, without the need for the extra firepower of the sturm-grenadier platoon, and to mark their success, a pair of green flares rose into the sky.

"Driver, advance."

Von Hardegen repositioned himself once more, moving his headquarters quickly through the choke point, but keeping to the left edge of the slope, well away from the focus of the panzer battalion.

Up front, Third Company, with a mix of Jaguars and Panther Gs, had taken up a line abreast advance, still facing Trendelburg, intent on keeping any defenders fixed on them, rather than the flanking manoeuvre being undertaken at Stammen.

A familiar voice announced itself in his ear.

"Wotan-six, this is Siegfried, situation report, over."

The Battlegroup commander, Major General Hyacinth Graf Strachwitz, was a no nonsense type with huge experience and an array of medals to reflect his combat experience.

"Siegfried, Wotan-six, all is proceeding to plan. Executing Otto now. No major resistance encountered, over."

"Received. Out."

Von Hardegen understood that his own report would trigger actions by other units in the battlegroup, and he took a moment to remind his commanders that they should be aware of friendly forces moving forward on their flanks.

As he spoke, the air cover again fell from the sky, clearly working over some enemy unit south of Deisel.

He concluded his warning but remained focussed on the air activity, as more and more aircraft seemed drawn to the area northwest of Trendelburg.

Puzzled, von Hardegen sought out the air liaison officer.

"Mime-two, Mime-two, Wotan-six, over."

The DRL Captain responded immediately.

"Mime-two, Wotan-six, report on air activity northwest of Trendelburg, over."

"Wotan-six, Mime-two, situation unclear. Reports state enemy armoured column under attack. We've no information on any armoured column in that area. The flight leader states they are Soviet tanks and vehicles. I'm trying to find out more, over."

"Mime-two, received. Keep me informed. Out."

Von Hardegen had a sense of something not right, and made a quick decision.

"Walküre-three-six, Walküre-three-six, Wotan-six, over."

The response was swift and he gave the halt order, which was also speedily acknowledged.

"Walküre-three-six, Wotan-six, maintain your present position until further orders. Be aware of enemy armoured force northwest of Trendelburg, in the vicinity of Deisel. Out."

One of the attacking aircraft, bearing the new German state's markings, pancaked onto the ground spewing smoke and flame and bounced three times before flipping on its back.

For the briefest of moments, Stelmakh considered making an attempt to rescue the man frantically pushing at the canopy, but abandoned the idea, understanding that he would not reach the man in time.

There was also a part of him, the part that had lost much of its humanity in the meat grinder that was war, that discarded the notion on the principle that the man had it coming, given what the German pilot and his comrades had done to the column of T34s and infantry.

The mechanised unit had no business being where they were, and had brought unnecessary attention to the area where the small group of survivors from the 6th Guards Independent Breakthrough Tank Regiment were hidden away.

Fire consumed the cockpit within seconds, removing an doubt or guilt before it set in.

6th GIBTR now consisted of nine IS-IIIs in total, organised into two groups, one of five and one of four, plus an headquarters of two T-34s.

The now Captain Stelmakh commanded the larger group of heavy tanks, reflecting his position as the third senior rank within the 'regiment', and his growing reputation as an excellent tank commander and leader.

Two days beforehand, his Order of the Red Star and Order of Kutuzov 3rd Class were supplemented with the presentation of the Order of Suvurov 3rd class.

The young warrior who had once bemoaned his lack of decorations had, in a few months, become the most decorated officer in the regiment, something of which his unit and, in particular his crew, were extremely proud.

Fig # 221 - Soviet order of battle - Trendelburg.

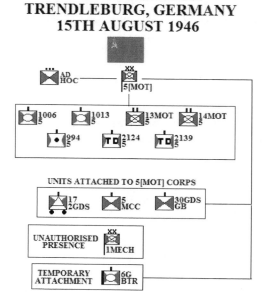

Stelmakh returned to scanning the ground ahead of him, his binoculars picking out the advancing enemy tan...

'They've stopped... the bastards have stopped...'

He tightened his grip as he saw another movement, this time slightly off to the right, and behind the leading force.

'Their leader has sensed something.'

He looked into the sky, seeking answers amongst the whirling Allied aircraft, but found none, so he thought things through.

'They don't know we're here... or they'd be attacking us.'

He picked up the handset to make a report, but checked himself as another of the fighter-bombers took hits from the mechanised units SPAA guns.

It simply exploded in mid-air less than a hundred feet above the ground, showering his concealed infantry with a deadly mixture of fast moving metal pieces and burning fuel.

Watching the horror unfold, he made his report.

"Cherepakha-krasniy-odin, Chorniy-odin, over."

The major commanding 6th GIBTR responded immediately.

"I've seen it. Shit happens. Maintain silence. Out."

The man had been with the 6th for less than a week, and already they knew that his combat experience was considerably more limited than his decorations indicated, and that the main contributions he brought to the unit were bluster and bullying.

"Cherepakha-krasniy-odin, Chorniy-odin, urgent situation report over."

"Spit it out man, Krasniy-odin, over."

"Chorniy-Odin, enemy force heading location Vosem has halted," he gave the code for Trendleburg itself as he took another quick look at the new movement, "And another enemy force is flanking to the west, heading north to pass close to location Sem," he swivelled to check the prominent height and seek out its defenders, but there was nothing to be seen.

And then, suddenly, there was.

"One moment... enemy force is definitely driving at location Sem... tanks and infantry, possibly battalion strength, Chorniy-Odin over."

"Maintain fire discipline. Fire only on my order. Don't panic, man. Krasniy-Odin, out."

If the handset was not a vital piece of his equipment, Stelmakh might well have thrown it in the general direction of his commanding officer.

"Ukol!"

The chuckling gunner, Oleg Ferensky exchanged looks with his loader, before commenting on his commander's language.

"Young ears, Kapitan, the Comrade Loader is blushing."

Stelmakh dropped into the turret and silenced 'Yuri' Ferensky with a single look, sparing a second look for the tank's oldest crewman, who appeared older than any two of them combined.

Lev Kalinov was a quiet and withdrawn man who claimed to be somewhere around thirty years of age, but who looked closer to fifty, as if life's experiences had weighed heavily on his face, a face that sometimes seemed strangely familiar to Stelmakh, and a face that remained straight as he offered an observation to his tank commander.

"I agree, Comrade Kapitan. The man's a total prick."

Ferensky chuckled again, this time from behind his sights as he followed the leading enemy vehicles.

"Comrade Kapitan."

The tone alone was enough, and Stelmakh emerged from the turret with his binoculars already on the way up.

The enemy were charging at Sem, the height west of Trendleburg.

'Ukol.'

He had the thought before he picked up the handset once more and spoke to the 'ukol' in question. Stelmakh's report to his commander was often interrupted and broken, as his words were punctuated by medium artillery dropping on Sem and in the valley beneath.

Taking Height 299, or location Sem as the Soviets called it, had always been part of the plan, which is why two companies of Europa's panzer-grenadier battalion were set aside to storm it and secure it, backed up by anti-tank guns from the brigade's panzer-jager company.

Another part of the plan was the artillery that lashed the height with high-explosives, and that now also dropped smoke along the right flank of the hurrying halftracks, completely obscuring them from Stelmakh's gaze.

The small Soviet-held hill, completely stripped of its trees and bushes by man's combative efforts, was quickly overrun, placing a German force immediately to Stelmakh's right.

Von Hardegen split off two platoons from the main body and brought them up to support his small force, holding back the grenadier attack on Height 233 until they could move up and support.

Soviet mortars were hitting back at Height 299, but there was no sign of any other resistance to the west of the Diemel River.

On the east bank, things were different, as the sharp crack of tank cannon revealed.

Reports indicated that a handful of tanks and anti-tank guns on Stammen heights, overlooking Route 83, had opened fire from concealed positions, causing casualties amongst the leading elements.

Europa's commander dismounted from his tank and left his Panther at the bottom of the slop, von Hardegen moved up a shallow trench and took up a position next to a rusting M-16 halftrack, long since stripped of anything remotely of use or value.

The commander of the grenadier force joined him in surveying the ground ahead of them.

No smoke screen obscured them now, and they examined the route to Trendelburg. Von Hardegen listened intently to the infantryman's report that secondary explosions had been seen when the smoke shells descended.

"Mines?"

"I think so, Herr Oberst. Not large ones, but large enough to take a tyre or a track, I think."

Von Hardegen hummed his response, and switched his attention to the German town that was the object of his attack, wherein, intelligence reported, the commanding officer and staff of the 1st Mechanised Corps were trapped.

Part of Plan Otto was constructed to ensure the enemy headquarters group remained trapped; the part that was now suppressing the Stammen Heights.

He could see one Jaguar burning brightly, and what might be a halftrack in a similar state, but apart from that, there seemed little price paid for the Stammen advance so far.

"We'll stick to the plan as far as you are concerned, Hauptmann. Once the other kompagnie is established on Height 299, with some of my tanks as baby sitters, I might reconsider... but for now, we stick with the plan. Klar?"

"Alles klar, Herr Oberst."

The infantryman scuttled away to make sure his defences were organised, and that the AT guns were properly protected.

A whistle attracted von Hardegen's attention, accompanied by frantic waving from his Panther turret.

He half tumbled, half ran back down the slope, and climbed back aboard his command tank.

"Herr Oberst, Walküre-six, urgent."

He pulled on the throat mike and made contact with Fürth.

"Walküre-six, Wotan-six, come in, over."

"Wotan-six, Walküre-six, phase three complete. Request permission to proceed with next phase, over."

"Walküre-six, Wotan-six. Walküre-two will remain under my command. Proceed as planned. Wotan will support from 299. I will advise if moving. Confirm. Over."

Lieutenant Colonel Furth acknowledged the change and was gone, already initiating the next artillery barrage planned for 'Otto'.

Von Hardegen watched as the elements on the east bank pushed hard up the valley, mirrored by forces to the west, both thrusts surging towards Trendelburg.

His ears heard more firing to the north and he ordered his command tank repositioned so as to observe the attack on Height 233, where some resistance was being encountered.

Even as he watched, he observed a handful of old T34s armed with 76mm guns try and fail to halt the advance, the venerable tanks simply swept aside in a volley of 75mm and 88mm high velocity shells.

1225 hrs, Thursday, 15th August 1946, Astride Route 83, Trendelburg, Germany.

Stelmakh was silently pondering the command and control problems of a tank unit with less than half an issue of fuel in their tanks, less than full ammunition stocks, operating under the umbrella of a powerful enemy air force, and overseen by an officer of dubious worth.

His mind could find no light in the darkness of his thoughts.

The enemy force that had halted before Trendelburg was now moving again, and more of the bastards were knocking away at the heights on his right.

He looked, and looked again.

The enemy forces had exposed flanks, their attempted smoke cover next to useless in the growing breeze.

'We have an opportunity...'

"Cherepakha-krasniy-odin, Chorniy-Odin, urgent situation report over."

545

"What is it about fucking radio silence that you don't understand, Stelmakh?"

'What a fucking idiot.'

"Cherepakha-krasniy-odin, Chorniy-Odin, urgent situation report, enemy flanks exposed to our front, and on location Sem, over."

"Get off the radio… now! Don't reveal our presence or position. Fire discipline. Do not fire, repeat, do not fire. Stay hidden and let them pass. Out."

There was silence in the tank, broken by a contemptuous fart from the driver's position.

"That's my fucking comment on that load of shit. The man's an idiot, Comrade Kapitan. Look at that target… look at it, for fuck's sake! We've got them on fucking toast, and he wants to hide."

"Thank you, General Stepanov."

The growing tension in 'Krasniy Suka' dissuaded the others from any comment or contribution.

Vladimir Stelmakh thought hard, knowing his time for such activity was extremely limited.

He then acted, switching over to his own unit's frequency, and pressed the transmit button.

"All units Cherepakha-Chorniy, Cherepakha-Chorniy. Stand by to engage targets moving to your front."

He unkeyed the mike.

"Yuri… get ready to fire on my order."

"Uh-huh."

The turret moved slightly in response.

"All units Cherepakha-Chorniy, ready…. Ready… fire!"

Five 122mm guns sent their deadly projectiles down range.

"Achtu…"

Someone shouted into the radio, an unknown tank commander who perished within milli-seconds, as three of the massive shells struck home, easily penetrating the side armour of the Panthers and Jaguars leading the drive into the west edge of Trendelburg.

Von Hardegen saw the smoke marks from the enemy positions, but such was the quality of their camouflage that he still could not see where exactly they were, or what they were.

"Gunner, engage… distract them if you can."

"Jawohl."

546

The Panther's turret swung and the gunner found a drifting smudge of smoke. Another immediately declared itself, as the enemy fired once more.

Five of Third Company's tanks now lay smashed on the valley floor, and no enemy had been successfully engaged.

The 75mm spat an AP shell towards the smoke spot, uselessly, as nothing but earth and stone was damaged by its passage.

Europa's commander checked the tanks of his third company and immediately saw that Walküre-three-six was now amongst the casualties.

'Another of the old comrades.'

Third Company had reoriented and were trying to strike back, the powerful 88mm's lashing out at anything that looked remotely like it could be a threat.

An anti-tank gun fired from across the Diemel, striking, but not killing, the nearest Jaguar.

Seemingly with disdain, the turret swung, the driver re-angled the tank, and the anti-tank gun was blotted out in an instant.

The Jaguar commander ordered a purple smoke shell placed on the same location, and the circling attack aircraft swooped down to bathe the area in rockets and napalm.

Walküre-three-six's last act had been to do the same, but the IS-IIIs held fast, knowing that of they moved out of their bunkers, they would be easy meat for the vengeful DRL airmen. However, other Soviet vehicles moving in the open to the north attracted them away from the purple smoke marker, and the remnants of the mechanised unit, plus both of the 6th's T34s, were quickly butchered.

"Chorniy-Odin, Seeniy-odin, over."

Stelmakh directed his gunner to engage a new target before answering.

"Seeniy-odin, Chorniy-Odin, receiving, over."

"Chorniy-Odin, our glorious leader just fireballed. You're in charge. Say the word. Over."

Stelmakh felt the smile start, but resisted celebrating the man's death, even if he was a liability.

"Seeniy-odin, situation report. Engaging company of enemy heavy tanks to my front. Under air attack. Holding. Do you have the other enemy force in sight? Over."

"Chorniy-Odin, yes. Heading north towards objective Shest. Clear shots. We can engage immediately. Over."

"Seeniy-odin. Engage immediately. Do not move out of your bunkers whilst enemy aircraft are here. We relocate only when they are gone. Understood? Over."

The commander of the Seeniy group responded, but Stelmakh heard not a bit of it, his hearing lost to the immense clang of a shell striking his gun mantlet.

"Gunner! Get the bastard quick!"

Ferensky was on the case and sought out the enemy tank.

"Firing!"

The breech hurtled back into the turret as a HEAT shell went from muzzle to target in the blink of an eye.

The front of the Panther went orange and white but, when the bright lights disappeared, the vehicle stood defiant.

But it was silent, a small hole betraying the penetration point where the particle stream overcame the tank's armour.

The men inside had perished instantly.

Third Company had now lost eight tanks, and not one IS-III had been knocked out in return. Now their air cover was leaving, short on fuel, and simply nothing was going right.

Von Hardegen knew his force was in big trouble, particularly as the group attacking Height 233 had been taken under fire by another concealed enemy.

"All units Walküre, All units Walküre, Wotan-six, smoke the target areas, repeat, smoke the target areas, keep it in place until air arrive. Out."

He switched channel immediately.

"Mime-two, Mime-two, Wotan-six, over."

"Wotan-six, Mime-two, go ahead, over."

"Mime-two, limettensaft, limettensaft, Acknowledge. Over."

"Wotan -six, Mime-two. Order is limettensaft. Understood. Over."

Von Hardegen didn't bother to speak to the DRL officer again. Having ordered his own desperate limejuice air strike, he went back on the radio to order a platoon from First Company back to assist Third Company.

A sharp crack on his left hand side summoned him from his thoughts and he risked a quick look.

One of the 88mm Pak 43s had joined the fight, and with good effect.

From its raised position, it had fired at an angle that brought its shell into contact with the open driver's hatch of its target.

The heavy shell passed easily through the flesh and bone and destroyed everything in its path before finally angling upwards and slamming into the underside of the turret roof, when it dislocated the IS-III's heavy metal frying pan shape from its mount.

The growing purple haze prevented the AT crew from putting another shell into the target, just to make sure.

As the smoke started to disperse, another smoke shell was added, maintaining a marker for when the aircraft summoned by the limettensaft order arrived.

Which was reasonably quickly, for it seemed no more than a minute since the message had been sent than a flight of Hs-129s from 13th Sturzkampfstaffel arrived on the scene.

They were eminently unsuited to the work, being better employed against open targets, rather than aircraft hidden in bunkers.

None the less, the DRL pilots tried to make a difference, but the best that they managed was to knock apart the camouflaged bunker surrounding one of the enemy tanks, revealing the nature of their enemy at last.

'Scheisse!'

A common thought amongst the German panzer crew who spotted the low shape of the deadly IS-III.

'Blyad... our bunker's fucked!'

"Driver reverse!"

Stelmakh had no choice, his hidden position savaged by the exploding 30mm shells from the Henschel 129-B-2 aircraft.

The IS-III virtually flew backwards out of the bunker position, and avoided a further attack completely, as the aircraft's shells chewed up the vacant ground and woodwork.

Looking back towards the rear, Stelmakh directed Stepanov to reverse into a nearby stand of trees, near where their secondary position was located.

Two 30mm shells hit the side of the tank, inches apart.

Whilst not a killing hit, the blast wave took hold of Stelmakh's exposed head and dashed it against the cupola. The unconscious officer dropped like a stone to the turret floor, his face a bloody mess, and his mouth smashed; blood and broken teeth created an awful looking injury.

In the driver's position, Stepanov had a similar experience, the back of his head thrown back against the unyielding metal, splitting his skin and knocking him unconscious with his foot on the accelerator.

'Krasniy Suka' started to lose speed as the tree trunks resisted her, eventually stalling as a stout beech proved too much of an obstacle.

Kalinov, ignoring the dislocated finger that had resulted from trying to steady himself, acted swiftly, grabbed a smoke grenade and dropped it onto the engine grille.

"What you doing, Leo?"

Ferensky spoke like a drunk, clearly not totally with it.

"Only chance is if they think we're already fucked. Help me with the Kapitan."

They pulled Stelmakh into an upright position, and Kalinov started to clear away the detritus of his teeth and gums.

As he worked he called to Stepanov.

"Oi! You lazy bastard! Bloody driver!"

He counted eleven smashed teeth in the commander's mouth.

"How's he doing, Leo?"

"Well, it's going to fucking ache a bit, that's for sure, and soup'll be his favourite food for a while."

The darkness of a huge bruise was already spreading around Stelmakh's face.

Ferensky had shaken himself out of the stupor induced by the enemy shells, and stuck his head out of his hatch.

What greeted him was a scene of horror.

Another of the IS-IIIs had been knocked out, this time very dramatically so, and its turret lay some yards away from the spectacularly burning hull.

The remaining two tanks were still resisting but their positions were now exposed, meaning that the enemy tanks were making hits, although the heavy armour of the IS tanks resisted well.

Ferensky's mind registered a sound from another time, a growing screaming wall of sound that he had not heard for many a month.

Automatically he looked to the sky and there it was.

A Stuka.

And another following it.

And another following that.

The screaming intensified as the six dive bombers hurtled down.

The leading aircraft released its bomb, the crutch shepherding it away from the propeller, and the Junkers-87-D started to pull out of its dive.

The 250kg bomb missed its target, but it was close enough to lift the tank up on one side.

Ferensky watched with a fascinated detachment as the offside track of the heavy tank lifted a couple of feet, hung there for the briefest of moments, and then crashed back down to earth again.

He mused what that had done to the boys inside, but the question became immaterial within a few seconds, as the second bomb struck the engine compartment, transforming many thousands of roubles worth of state property into worthless scrap in a millisecond.

The other IS-III crew knew they had no chance, but it didn't stop them from trying.

In actual fact, they evaded the falling bombs successfully, moving skilfully away, whilst keeping their armour towards the Jaguars.

However, two enemy gunners anticipated a turn, and both fired a telling shot.

On Height 299, the Pak 43 gunner sent his shell towards the manoeuvring IS-III, as did von Hardegen's gunner, whose 75mm shell arrived a split second before the heavier AT round.

Both penetrated, and both would have been enough in their own right, but together, they dramatically destroyed the tank and her crew.

The DRH tanks pressed forward, seeing the way open.

Between the two tank forces, men of the Red Army's 5th Motorcycle Regiment, long since parted from their vehicles and employed as infantry, rose from their concealed positions, not to fight, but to surrender.

Europa's tank men had little cause or inclination to take prisoners, and many hull machine guns chattered, knocking the surrendering men back into the holes from which they had emerged.

The motorcycle soldiers dropped back into cover and, without exception, decided to hide rather than fight.

Furth ordered a company of the sturm-grenadiers to move forward and ferret them out.

They were also similarly disinclined to take prisoners and the eventual survivors of the motorcycle unit were few in number.

Von Hardegen ordered Fürth to resume the attack on Trendelburg, leaving a platoon of Third Company to screen the flank, and to take the detached platoon from First Company under his direct command on the west side of the Diemel.

More aircraft were arriving, and some engaged the tanks that were killing his men south of Height 233.

Despite the fact that his command had taken a whipping from the unsuspected enemy heavy tanks, von Hardegen understood that he could still proceed with his attack successfully, although Third Company had taken a severe beating.

With the help of the DRL, the Soviet tanks were overcome, and a sharp assault on height 233 was successful, with few men lost.

At Trendelburg, the double attack enveloped the town, although First Company, now light a platoon, had to move more carefully than was planned.

A short but bitter fight ensued, as the defenders, artillerymen from the 30th Guards Gun Brigade without their guns, fought tooth and nail for every building.

The men of the panzer-grenadier battalion soon learned to bring up one of the Jaguars, using the 88mm gun to more than level the playing field.

Many points of resistance were simply wiped out by high-explosive, until the message got through, and many of the artillerymen started to surrender.

The sturm grenadiers only met brief resistance on the Stammen heights, but it was enough to seriously wound their long time regimental commander, Oberstleutnant Ernst Kaether.

The commander and staff of 1st Mechanised Corps surrendered far too willingly for the tastes of some of the survivors of the artillerymen who had tried to defend Trendelburg.

Time revealed that the commander and his immediate staff had deliberately contrived the circumstances that led to their capture, using the dismounted artillery crews as sacrificial lambs, although, in their haste to escape the dreadful conditions prevalent in the Red Army, they had not realised that the 6th GIBTR was at hand.

Days later, a guard at the temporary prisoner camp, set up just outside nearby Arolsen, casually informed a German-speaking artillery sergeant of the circumstances surrounding the fight and surrender at Trendelburg.

By prior arrangement, the camp guards simply watched on as vengeful motorcycle and artillery troops beat many of their mechanised corps' comrades to death.

None of whom were even remotely responsible for the betrayal.

1607 hrs, Thursday, 15th August 1946, Height 299, Trendelburg, Germany.

Von Hardegen completed his discussion with the infantry commander; a relaxed affair over coffee.

The main topic of discussion was air power, and how having on their side for once made life a lot easier, much easier than it had been in the difficult last months of the previous war.

Kuno von Hardegen was happy to leave the mopping up to Furth whilst his crew worked on getting his command tank moving.

Occasionally, his eyes would be drawn to the sound of an explosion, as something in one of the burning vehicles succumbed to the attentions of internal fire.

A Feldwebel ran up and reported to the Panzerjager Captain, having first deferred to Europa's commander.

"We have a visitor, Herr Oberst."

A brand new command halftrack, led and flanked by four American jeeps, bounded up the slope and pulled up short of the position occupied by the two officers.

The rear doors opened and disgorged an impressive military figure and three aides. The two officers came to attention and saluted the battlegroup commander, Major General Hyacinth Graf Strachwitz von Gross-Zauche und Camminetz.

He returned the salute.

"Oberst von Hardegen...Hauptmann Zander, good to see you both again."

He held out his arm to the Europa's commander.

"Kuno, come walk with me."

The two moved away, heading towards von Hardegen's tank, discussing the successes and failures of the day's battle as they walked.

1611 hrs, Thursday, 15th August 1946, 450 metres south of Deisel, Germany.

The pain was extreme, but Stelmakh still managed to direct his crew.

The tank had refused to start, and Stepanov was nose down in the engine compartment trying to find the problem, aided by Kalinov, who claimed some mechanical knowledge.

The tree that had arrested their reversing manoeuvre now helped greatly in saving their lives, its thick leaves shrouding the two men at work on the back of the heavy tank.

Ferensky had slowly and carefully pulled some more foliage down onto the turret, concealing the hatches, from which he and Stelmakh kept watch.

The main enemy force had long since moved into Trendelburg, but a group of enemy infantry was still to be found within the Soviet infantry positions that had long since been cleared of motorcycle troops.

Stelmakh debated the issue.

Starting the tank would warn the enemy infantry who, in turn, would bring down artillery and call for the enemy tanks' return.

He did not consider surrender.

He did not consider waiting until dark claimed the battlefield.

"So why aren't we waiting until night, Comrade Kapitan?"

In a stuttering and clearly painful way, Stelmakh explained his thinking.

How the regimental fuel reserve was located just north of Deisel, at the express command of their now-deceased leader, rather than filling their hungry fuel tanks.

How he didn't expect it to be there for much longer, especially if the enemy were pushing forward.

How without it they had no chance to get back to their own lines.

Ferensky understood, sort of, and waved his commander to silence.

"I get it, Comrade Kapitan. So we get one bite at this, and one bite only."

Stelmakh nodded painfully and then a distant noise caused his eyes to narrow.

A group of enemy vehicles sped across the high ground, occasionally dropping from view within its undulating folds.

Stelmakh turned to observe the two men head down in the engine compartment, straining his ears to hear the conversation.

"... not an expert, Comrade Driver, but I'd say that this bit should attach to something."

"Ha ha fucking ha. Have you just pulled that off?"

"Nope... it was off all by itself."

"No way, can't be... I'd have seen it straight away."

"Well, you didn't, cos it was."

The squabble was brought to an end by a hand slapping on the tank's turret armour.

Stelmakh said nothing, but they still got the message.

Quickly connecting up the wiring loom, Stepanov and Kalinov gently placed the grilles back in position, before sliding back up to the turret.

Kalinov, grinning from ear to ear, dropped back into the turret, having given Stepanov a look of professional disdain.

"Comrade Kapitan... I missed it. Simple wiring probl..."

Stelmakh held up his hand, cutting the driver short.

His eyes made the enquiry.

"Yes, I'm sure we'll start first time, Comrade Kapitan."

Stelmakh controlled his swollen and bruised mouth well enough to speak clearly.

"Good, very good. Get ready. You remember the route?"

"Yes, Comrade Kapitan."

Stepanov carefully slid across the top of the turret, checked the nearby infantry positions, and slid feet first into his position.

"Crew, standby by."

"Comrade Kapitan."

Ferensky extended an arm, pointing at the object of his concern.

A quick look through the binoculars and Stelmakh's mind was made up.

"Get ready and make it count, Yuri."

"We've only got solid or HE now."

"Make it count then, Yuri."

Stelmakh felt no pain as his mind's resources were drawn to concentrate on timing his move to perfection.

He watched the target move across his front, right to left, spared a look at the infantry positions, and another look for objective Sem, and then back again to the moving vehicle.

"Yuri?"

"I'm on it, Comrade Kapitan."

"Onufriy?"

"Finger on the button, Comrade Kapitan."

"Start when we fire."

"Yes."

"Yuri?"

"On target. Ready."

Stelmakh watched and waited for the perfect moment.

"Fire!"

The armour piercing shell struck the Panther at the join of turret and hull, penetrating with ease.

It failed to explode, but caused severe damage to the workings of the gun and turret, before deflecting down into the front of the tank, moving through the hull gunner, and coming to rest in the transmission.

The smell of blood and tortured metal filled the driver's nostrils and, without orders, he pushed himself up and out of the hatch.

As his ears recovered, he realised the sound that assaulted his ears was that of a man screaming.

A horrified look revealed Kuno von Hardegen stood erect in the turret, but screaming as if mortally wounded.

Another sharp crack marked some large weapon firing, and the driver squealed in fear, expecting another Soviet shell to arrive.

But it was not aimed at him, and he pulled himself back to reality.

The driver hopped up onto the turret roof and took von Hardegen around the shoulders, intent on pulling his commander out of the smoking wreck.

He overbalanced and fell backwards onto the engine grill, unprepared for the lack of weight, as only the top half of his colonel came out of the tank, the lower portion having been severed by the shell.

Von Hardegen let out a single piercing scream… a long scream… a scream revealing the highest level of suffering.

The driver brought up everything his stomach contained, fainted, and toppled off the rear of the Panther.

Von Hardegen started a different cycle of agony, as the hot engine covers added to his extremis, and burnt into the flesh of his shoulders and buttocks, roasting the pieces of tattered flesh and bone that had once been his thighs and groin.

Whilst some of the sturm-grenadiers sought out the Panther's destroyer, a few hardy men ran towards the Panther, intent on offering what help they could.

A Leutnant climbed up on the rear, and also brought up the contents of his stomach. Despite his long years of service, he was unprepared for the horror that lay on the Panther's engine grilles.

The Panzer Oberst had no legs, the shell having struck him precisely on the left hip joint and gone through his body, exiting three inches below his right hip joint, and wiping out everything in between.

Blood, urine, faeces, all were mixed in the liquid that seeped from every part of his ruined body.

The next man up was an old Stabsgefreiter, a senior corporal, a man who did the only thing that could be done.

The bullet blew the back of Kuno von Hardegen's head off, bringing him immediate relief.

The Leutnant, dry retching by now, his stomach emptied, controlled himself long enough to accept back the Luger that the Stabsgefreiter had snatched from his hand.

"Thank you, Poppelmeyer. Thank you... from him."

The old soldier nodded and dropped off the back of the burning tank, picked up the unconscious driver and carried him off to the infantry positions.

As soon as the big gun barked, Stepanov hit the ignition button and the diesel roared into life; 'Krasniy Suka' lurched forward immediately.

Stelmakh had agreed the route with Stepanov so he could concentrate on other matters, such as the 12.7mm machine-gun, with which he discouraged the enemy infantry from becoming bold.

Not for the first time, the IS-III's co-axial weapon had been knocked out, the hit on the mantlet having damaged the barrel.

He remembered the last time it had happened.

Stelmakh dropped into the tank to get another box of ammunition as an enemy shell noisly carried away the 12.7mm. A moment of terror washed over him, and translated itself into a weakening of his bladder and, for the first time for a long time, he wet his trousers.

A few bullets spanged off the armour, as some more resilient members of the sturm-grenadiers took on the huge tank, but Stepanov was already moving as fast as he could towards Deisel, and the turret was turned to the rear.

An enemy weapon fired at them from 'Sem', but the shell missed by some distance, Stepanov's manoeuvring proving successful.

Stelmakh spared a quick look at the targeted Panther and was happy that it was out of the fight.

He ignored the men running towards it, preferring to keep his limited ammunition for any direct threat.

Ferensky shouted into the intercom.

"After his next shot, stop the tank."

"Fuck off."

"I know where the bastard is. I just need a couple of seconds to put one in his lap."

"Fuck off."

"Do it, or the bastard'll fetch us."

"You better not fucking mis…"

The enemy shell streaked past the IS-III and Stepanov hit the brakes.

'Krasniy Suka' slid a little in the rapid manoeuvre, causing Ferensky to adjust more than he planned, but the target was firmly fixed in his sight.

Smokeless ammunition did not save the Pak 43 on Height 299 and the HE shell, even though it missed its target, was close enough to send bits of the crew in all directions.

The tank leapt forward again, some small arms fire earning the sturm soldiers an HE shell by return.

The IS-III dropped into a rut, causing Stelmakh's binoculars to bounce up into his jaw.

He squealed as best he could through his dressing, nearly fainting with the surge of pain that followed.

Kalinov emerged and threw the final smoke grenade, quickly dropping back in as the grenadiers renewed their efforts.

A bullet whipped past his head as he disappeared inside.

He produced a bottle of German apple schnapps from the empty ammunition racks, and offered it up to his commander.

"It'll help with the pain, Comrade Kapitan."

He understood what the man was about to say, and held the bottle closer.

"We've got the last round in the gun, we got the tank and the thing on the hill, the green toads can't hurt us with their pop guns… and you need a fucking drink, Comrade."

Stepanov offered up the clincher.

"Nearly there, and you were fucking right, Comrade Kapitan!"

The IS-III was close to the riverbank, where Stelmakh had hoped to find cover enough for a safer withdrawal.

He took the offered bottle, pressed it to what remained of his lips, and passed out as the alcohol hit his wounds.

Kalinov caught both bottle and man; the former was passed to a very thirsty Ferensky, the latter was lowered to the turret floor with due reverence.

'Krasniy Suka' carried the four men away from Trendelburg, the sole surviving vehicle of the 6th Guards Independent Breakthrough Tank Regiment, and the only Soviet soldiers to escape the defence of Trendelburg.

1352 hrs, Friday, 16th August 1946, Chateau de Versailles, France.

"So, we are agreed, gentlemen."

Churchill posed it as a statement deliberately, knowing that some present would find the terms of their position wholly unacceptable, but were presented with no choice but to accede to the majority position.

"Firstly, as stated by President Truman, we reserve the right to reply in kind to the despicable use of chemical weapons against Allied forces, but will not yet do so, pending the results of the independent investigations into the matter."

He nodded to Truman and continued.

"We will do this as a sign of good faith in the peace negotiations as a whole, and as an expression of our wish to believe that the Soviet Government would not have knowingly undertaken this attack, and in the hope that the veracity of the explanation offered is confirmed independently."

That was the easy part over with.

"We now confirm to the negotiators that our unequivocal position is that Europe will see a full return to the political boundaries in force on 1st January 1938, but that, and I add, only if negotiations seem to be floundering, they have some room to manoeuvre in order to bring about a speedy ceasefire on favourable terms for the entire Allied cause, in as much as we would be prepared to negotiate a temporary alteration to some of those political boundaries, and or lines of military demarcation, in order to bring about an end to hostilities."

Both Speer and Raczkiewicz sneered, knowing the extent that the Allies were prepared to negotiate back to, albeit in the first instance.

Churchill had argued that even a partial return of Polish territory would, in the first instance, be a bonus for the Polish nation, and that further negotiations would undoubtedly see the entire country returned to Polish rule, a point not accepted by Raczkiewicz, and the matter of the restoration of Prussia similarly caused problems for Speer.

None the less, that was the Allied negotiating position, and it was communicated to the team in Sweden.

When the negotiators returned to the table, the Allied response was put by US Secretary of State James Byrnes.

The qualified acceptance of the Soviet explanation regarding the Hofbieber affair was greeted with a gracious nod; less so the reservation of the right to similar retaliation should the stated facts be found to be less than the truth.

Byrnes laid out the 1938 return proposal as the Allies only acceptable position, given the aggressive war that the USSR had inflicted upon a Europe still suffering from the previous conflict.

Molotov listened and immediately rejected the Allies' starting position.

The negotiations started in earnest.

1920 hrs, 16th August 1946, Chateau de Versailles, France.

"Mister President, sir."

Truman wiped his mouth with the delicate silk serviette, removing any hint of the delicious stroganoff sauce.

"Yes, Colonel?"

"Mister President, there is a call for you, from the States."

Truman eyed the delicious beef stroganoff.

"Who is it? Can't it wait?"

"Sir, its Governor Dewey. I tried to put him off but he's very insistent. Says it's an emergency and that you should come to the phone straightaway."

Truman's jaw set in pugnacious fashion, the Missourian immediately roused by the comment.

Churchill raised an enquiring eyebrow, to which Truman could only offer a small shrug.

"Lead the way, Colonel."

"Truman."

He settled himself in the superbly comfortable grand chair, its red upholstery almost embracing him in its soft cushioning.

"Mister President, this is Governor Dewey here."

"Yes, so I was told. So, where's the fire, Thomas?"

"In your office, Mister President."

"Say that again."

"Mister President, I represent a large number of very important and powerful politicians, and I'm here to tell you that we are preparing your impeachment for failing to protect our soldiers to the best of your ability, for failing to fully prosecute the war, and for failing to properly discharge the duties of your office."

"Impeachment... you're way outta line, Governor, way outta line."

"We think not, and we think it's you that's out of line here, and we're going to do something about it."

"For a start, Governor, there is no offence here, not in what you suggest... no treason, no bribery, no crime or misdemeanour of any type, so your move is dead in the wat..."

"You don't define the offence, Mister President. That's defined by Congress, and the part of Congress I represent is minded to impeach you on the counts I have stated."

Truman remained silent, his brain working overtime on his next move.

One suggested itself, and he quickly debated the matter, arriving at an unpalatable conclusion.

"Governor Dewey, I want you to listen to me."

"Won't do any good, Mister President. We're decided. We implement the process as soon as we..."

"Listen to me good now, Governor Dewey. There will be no impeachment, and I'll tell you why."

Truman sucked in a lung full of air and made his play.

"What I tell you now is absolutely top secret and cannot be divulged to anyone. Am I absolutely clear on that point?"

Dewey's silence was deafening, but Truman waited.

"You are clear, Sir."

"I want your word on it, Thomas."

"Sir..."

"Your word or you can do your worst."

Silence.

"I will not divulge any secret matter you inform me of in this conversation, Mister President. You have my word on it."

"Thank you, Thomas. Now, this is for your ears only."

He listened as Dewey asked to have the room to himself and waited until Dewey confirmed he was on his own.

Truman coughed lightly.

"The Allies are presently preparing retaliatory strikes with weapons in kind, which will be available should the circumstances be favourable, and the need arise."

"We've heard rumours, but that's not good enough, Mist…"

"Wait. Our preparations to use the bombs in Europe are ongoing, with training by ourselves and the British Royal Air Force being stepped up."

"Go on, Sir."

Truman took the plunge.

"At this moment, Secretary of State Byrnes is in a secret location, with the representatives of all major Allied nations, and with the Foreign Minister of the Soviet Union, engaged in talks to bring about an end to this war."

"I see."

"Moreover, and I must stress the importance that this knowledge is not shared, Minister Molotov has presented a full and total apology regarding the chemical weapon attack in Germany, one to which we have responded in a conciliatory manner, in order to progress the peace talks."

"But…"

"Thomas… they came to us… they… came… to… us… I have a chance here to turn this whole thing off."

The silence was all-encompassing, and Truman gave the man time to understand the gravity of what he had just said.

"I understand, Mister President."

"You want the boys home. I want the boys home. We both want to win this thing, but maybe we can't. Maybe this is the best way to win, to establish our Alliance after a negotiated peace… a peace settlement that we can drive, given the fact that they came to us because we've hurt them… hurt them bad…"

"How did we hurt them, Mister President?"

"We're not completely sure, but the suspicion is supply, and specifically fuel, Thomas."

Governor Dewey was hooked.

"So you believe we can stop the war right now and…"

"No, not right now. We think that the military pressure should be maintained, lest they forget what brought them to the table in the first place."

"I can see that, Sir. I understand that. But, in the end, we can end this quickly, and restore a great deal of Europe to the way it was?"

"Sure. We intend to negotiate a ceasefire and defined lines, staged withdrawals and adjustments to controlled territories, and we will be able to drive that because…"

"…because they came to us."

"Indeed, Thomas."

"Sir, you know I have a problem with this."

"Yep. You can't tell anyone what I just told you."

"And I have to quieten down a baying pack of governors, senators, and congressmen, just by saying 'trust me'."

"They made you leader, Thomas, so lead them. I need to concentrate on this. If you still want to impeach me when it's done, feel free. I'll stand my own corner. But for now…"

"For now, I will make it go away, but I caution that the process cannot be infinite, Mister President."

"I don't know how long it will be, but you'll be kept informed by my office. I'll leave instructions on the matter. Contact them at any time, Thomas."

"Mister President, good evening, and thank you for your candour and confidence."

"Thank you for your call, Thomas. Good evening."

The phones went silent.

Senators Mead and Wagner had heard Dewey's end of the conversation, and were keen to hear the other side as soon as possible.

"No, I gave the President my word."

"So, what's occurring, Tom?"

"Nothing."

"Nothing?"

Both senators spoke the word incredulously.

"Nothing. We sit on our hands for a while. Things are simply not as they seemed."

"Such as, Tom?"

"I cannot tell you, Bob. I will not tell you, Bob. Everyone is just going to have to trust me on this one, and if they don't, we could foul up a huge chance to bring the boys home."

Wagner nodded, but Mead nodded and laughed.

"You said they came to us, Tom. I can work it out from there."

Dewey went for his poker-face, knowing the snippet he had repeated back to Truman would be enough for Mead.

"They're negotiating then."

It wasn't a question.

563

The cost of freedom is always high, but Americans have always paid it. And one path we shall never choose, and that is the path of surrender, or submission.

John F. Kennedy

Chapter 171 - THE NEGOTIATIONS

1113 hrs, Saturday 17th August 1946, Buckingham Palace, London, UK.

The assembled dignitaries, awardees, and witnesses were hushed as the master of ceremonies announced the very first of those to be honoured.

As was tradition, the award of the Victoria Cross took precedence over all other awards.

"Lieutenant Colonel John Ramsey."

At the mention of his name, Ramsey walked forward.

His face shone with pride, more so at his steady gait, than the moment he was about to experience.

He stopped before the King and saluted, which salute was returned impeccably by the British monarch.

"We meet again, Colonel Ramsey."

"We do indeed, Your Majesty."

"My sympathies at the personal sacrifice you have made for your country. I was so upset to learn of your injuries. How are you getting along, Colonel?"

"Extremely well, thank you, Sir. The medical staff have all been marvellous."

King George VI leant forward.

"I am told your bloody-mindedness has been a fearful factor in your superb recovery, Colonel."

Ramsey smiled.

"One uses the tools at one's disposal, Sir."

"Indeed one does, Colonel Ramsey. Now, we shall proceed."

The King turned and removed the Victoria Cross from the cushion, and attached it deftly to Ramsey's uniform.

"With the thanks of our people, and my own personal admiration, Colonel. You are a true bloody hero. But now, please, take a bloody back seat, man. Give other men a chance to earn some kudos, what?"

Ramsey nodded respectfully.

"I rather fancy that circumstances will dictate that, Sir."

The King leant forward again as the two men shook hands.

"You know, Ramsey, I have heard the circumstances behind this award. Extraordinary, absolutely extraordinary. I have asked my private secretary to bring you to my study when the ceremony is over, if you find that convenient. I simply must hear the story about you and the Russian first hand."

Ramsey smiled at the memory of a man who wore a different uniform.

"It would be my pleasure, Sir."

They exchanged smart salutes and Ramsey returned to the throng, his mind full of pictures of Barnstorf, of McEwan, Green, and Robertson... and of Yarishlov.

The next VC was awarded to Sergeant Carl Jones of the 4th Royal Welch Fusiliers, nine-five to his boys, his selfless act during the last throes of the battle of Hamburg undoubtedly worthy of the highest gallantry award and the thanks of a grateful King and nation.

1258 hrs, Saturday 17th August 1946, Hauptstrasse, Haserich, Germany.

"I have no idea, Frau Hallmann, none at all."

Not totally true, as the markings indicated a military origin, but Postman Pfluggman had a date with a cold beer in nearby Blankenrath.

"What are these marking here, Hans?"

"Military. Maybe some relative's things, Frau Hallmann?"

"Oh, I don't think so. I've no relatives fighting now. Willi was the last one, and he was lost in Austria... so long ago now."

"Perhaps it is his then, Frau Hallman? They find things all the time, you know."

"You think it might be? They never found him. Maybe it **is** his?"

"One way to find out, Frau Hallman. Good day."

The mother of Willi Hallman, now dead, but once an SS-Hauptsturmfuhrer in the Das Reich division, hurried excitedly to the kitchen table, and quickly found a knife to cut open the package.

She ignored the briefcase, and immediately sat down to read the accompanying official document.

Dear Frau Hallmann,

The enclosed briefcase was recovered from the site of a fatal air crash in Austria, a matter which would appear to have been unrelated to you, or any member in your family.

However, a rough handwritten note was discovered in a broken glass phial within it, a note that gave your address.

As we are unable to ascertain to whom the briefcase belonged, and no third party has claimed it, we felt it only proper to forward it to you, without certain contents that were declared the property of the unknown deceased's employers.

We have taken the liberty of copying the message as, in its present form, it is suffering from the effects of handling and its exposure to traumatic forces.

The original is in the marked envelope with the case itself.

The message reads as follows.

Frau Hallmann,
Hauptstrasse,
Haserich,
Mosel,
Germany.
AKNEPSU-65AB141/63RK29-29U532
Für-EAK
Schildkröte.

The Government has satisfied itself that the message is not of a military nature, but would be grateful if, should you discover its meaning, that you communicate with the office indicated below at the earliest possible moment.

With regards,

The dispatching postal official's name was illegible, but was, in any case, unimportant.

The nondescript US Army mail address meant little to her.

What had caught her eye was a set of three letters.

EAK.

Annika Hallmann understood them perfectly, for she had seen them many times before, when the boy had come to play in the fields around her home, and later, when the man had visited her with his wife and two little girls.

The message was '... *Für-EAK.*'

EAK...

Ernst-August Knocke, her godson.

She went to the telephone and sought a connection to a grand house on the outskirts of nearby Riedenhausen.

The housekeeper answered and promised to get the General straight away.

"Kumm."

"Good afternoon, Herr General. Frau Hallman here."

"Ah, Frau Hallmann. Good afternoon to you too. How may I be of assistance?"

"I need to see you straight away, Herr General. Something you will wish to see has come into my possession. Can I cycle over now?"

Kumm paused for a moment, his Saturday afternoon card game in full swing, but his knowledge of Annika Hallmann was enough to know that she would not trouble him if it were not important.

"Yes, of course. Come over immediately. I have friends here, but they are ones who will understand the interruption, and the concept of discretion, should the need arise. I can have the car sent for you?"

"Thank you, but no thank you, Herr General. I will be with you shortly."

"Shortly, Frau Hallmann."

He replaced the receiver and strode back into the orangery, where his friends eyed him quizzically.

"Frau Hallmann is coming over. Something that simply couldn't wait."

They all knew Frau Hallman from her work with their organisation, so the men relaxed as one.

"She'll be a while, so I suggest we play another hand."

The man with the eye patch swept the cards up and shuffled.

"Zu befehl, Brigadefuhrer."

SS-Brigadefuhrer Otto Kumm gathered up the twelve cards that the dealer, SS- Obersturmfuhrer Krause, had dispensed, looked at them with something approaching disgust, and waited for his partner to lead off.

They had two further hands before the game of Doppelkopf was brought to an end by Frau Hallmann's arrival.

The briefcase did the rounds as the woman who had the HIAG's records hidden in her attached barn, explained the note and the significance of 'EAK'.

"I see, Frau Hallmann. And the significance of this other scrawl?"

"Unknown to me, Brigadefuhrer. But clearly my godson is supposed to know. I had hoped you'd know how to get hold of him, as he's one of ours."

Kumm nodded.

"Yes, I know how to get hold of Knocke, Frau Hellmann."

"Can you get this note to him, Brigadefuhrer?"

He looked at his playing partner with a smile.

"I think we can arrange that easily enough, don't you, Willi?"

The ex-SS senior officer simply nodded and savoured his chilled Riesling.

"Yes, Otto. Easily."

Ex-SS Obergruppenfuhrer Willi Bittrich, now Général de Brigade in the French Foreign Legion, finished his wine and accepted the note.

Frau Hallmann cycled home, less speedily, as the road was uphill most of the way.

She wheeled her bicycle into the barn and went in to make herself coffee, unaware that eyes watched her from across the street, and that she had been followed all the way to Riedenhausen, and all the way back.

1333 hrs, Sunday 18th August 1946, Officer's Canteen, US 130th Station Hospital, Chiseldon, UK.

Major Presley had finished her lunch and was relaxing with a cup of the finest Columbian, having reserved the final fifteen minutes before her shift began to read the Sunday Pictorial, and the section relative to yesterday's events at the Palace.

Sipping greedily at the fresh coffee, she examined the picture of Ramsey, complete with his latest Victoria Cross, shortly to become a bar to his original award.

She examined his posture and grunted to herself, proud of the fact that he stood erect and seemingly comfortable, a resolution she found wholly satisfying, given the effort the man had given to getting 'back on his feet'.

Setting the paper against the empty vase, she relaxed into her chair and read the story.

From our Royal Correspondent.

At the investiture ceremony conducted at Buckingham Palace yesterday, Saturday 17th August, His Majesty the King presented Lieutenant Colonel John Eric Arthur Ramsey VC, DSO and three bars, MC and bar, with a second award of the most prestigious gallantry award, the Victoria Cross.

Lieutenant Colonel Ramsey, of 7th Battalion, The Black Watch, was given his second award for extreme gallantry and leadership at the Battle of Barnstorf, which occured during the heavy fighting in Northern Germany that ensued throughout October 1945.

He was severely wounded during that battle, losing both his legs in an explosion, but has since made excellent progress with prosthetics, and was able to walk unassisted to the presentation stool to receive his medal from the hands of the King.

Whilst the second award of a Victoria Cross is unusual, in as much as only three other service personnel have so honoured, this award is totally unique.

The facts of his exemplary conduct initially only came to light because of a hand-written note placed inside his battledress by a senior officer of the Soviet Red Army, a man against whom Ramsey had fought on that fateful day.

The Soviet Colonel, an officer called Jarishlov, commanded the troops who captured Ramsey after the Black Watch officer had successfully, and at great personal cost, destroyed a vital route over the Hunter River, holding up a major enemy attack almost single-handedly.

Badly wounded, Ramsey was given safe conduct back to the Allied lines, from where he was taken to hospital, where US doctors saved his life.

Medical staff found the Soviet officer's note amongst his old battledress some months later, and the process of investigation was started.

Normally, the recommendation for the Victoria Cross should come from an officer at or the equivalent level of regimental command, an, it seemed clear, that the officer recommending in this instance satisfied that requirement.

The cause of disagreement within the hallowed halls of the War Ministry was that the officer in question was an enemy.

The Prime Minister came to hear of the discussions, and directed that additional investigations should be made amongst the survivors of the Battle of Barnstorf, and, if any award was considered due, then it should be made, regardless of the fact that the initiating officer was Russian.

Investigations soon revealed a tale of great heroism and superb leadership in the face of overwhelming odds, over and above that cited by the Russian officer.

The award process reviewed all evidence and decided that the criteria for a second award had been met, and exceeded.

So intriguing was the story that the King invited Lieutenant Colonel Ramsey to his study to discuss the battle and the minutiae of his award in private.

Lieutenant Colonel Ramsey is pictured displaying his new medal, accompanied by his wife, Lucinda, and his senior nurse, Major Jocelyn Presley of the US Army Medical Service, who nursed him through his recovery.

It might surprise the reader that this officer still seeks to be actively involved in the defence of his country, and has recently accepted a position within the Department of Procurement in the Ministry of War.

The Victoria Cross was also awarded to Sergeant Carl Jones, of 4th Royal Welch Fus...

Presley shook her head, part in awe at the man's drive and commitment to the cause, but also partially because he had done his bit, given so much of himself, in literal as well as mental terms, and still could not take a back seat.

She even felt a modicum of anger, something that Jocelyn Presley immediately baulked at, and became angry with herself for having such a thought.

She folded the Sunday paper and left the canteen, determined to throw herself into her work and overcome the negative thought.

"Good afternoon, Lieutenant. Any problems?"

"Good afternoon, Major. Only the usual suspect. Simply won't lie still. Major Levens wrote him up for some more analgesia, but he won't let me administer it."

The syringe and its paraphernalia were set in a kidney dish, ready for use.

Presley checked the documentation and nodded to the nurse going off duty.

"I'll deal with him, don't you worry. Enjoy the rest of your day, Lieutenant."

She strode purposefully towards the man in question.

"Good afternoon, Colonel Crisp. I hear you've been causing trouble again."

1759 hrs, Sunday, 18th August 1946, the Oval Office, Washington DC, USA.

"Three... two... one... and cue."

The microphone went live.

"My fellow Americans, and peoples of the free world, good evening."

Truman's voice resounded from radios and speakers the length and breadth of the United States, and in many corners of the world beyond.

"I am speaking to you from the Oval Office on this most momentous of days, a day when I can bring to you tidings that herald an end to the fighting that has blighted our world for months and years."

"Your government, and those of the Allied Alliance, have been involved in talks with the government of the Soviet Union, talks that were aimed at bringing the hostilities to a swift end, and restoring the political map of Europe to something approaching normal."

"I am here to tell you that a ceasefire has been successfully negotiated and that, as a result, hostilities between the NATO alliance and the Soviet Union will cease at midnight tonight, Greenwich Mean Time, that is to say, in one hour from the commencement of this address."

"This announcement is being repeated across the spectrum of our Allied nations, from Prime Minister Churchill in the United Kingdom, to President Camacho in Mexico."

It was eleven o'clock at night in London, but Churchill had acquiesced to the timetable, knowing that his countrymen would need to know at the exact same time.

571

"We have agreed a ceasefire in order to save more lives, prevent more destruction, and in order to immediately look to commencing the rebuilding of our world."

"There will be a phased withdrawal by all Soviet forces, returning them to the national lines that were in place on 6th October 1939, with some small alterations, from which position negotiations will continue, in order to restore Europe to her 1938 political boundaries."

President Truman moved on to flesh out some of the agreements in place, and some that were expected to be negotiated in future, but not everyone was listening any more.

0008 hrs, Monday, 19th August 1946, the Rathaus, Aachen, Germany.

"Small alterations... bastards."

The nods were universal.

"Bastards. We've lost the initiative."

Speer sat back from his notes, throwing his pen across the table. He already knew what was going to be said in any case.

Guderian wiped his hands across his face, seeking to refresh himself. He had not slept for nearly thirty-six hours.

Von Vietinghoff played with his pen, seeking some solace in its gentle tapping on the table.

Karl Renner, the only Austrian present, remained subdued.

It again fell to Speer to speak.

"So, we have been betrayed once more. Our soldiers have committed to the joint cause to defeat communism, and our weak allies have fallen short of their stated objectives... objectives they swore to me... to us... to uphold, come what may."

He stood and walked around the table, holding his hands behind his back.

"The Communists are weak, they have shown that by coming to the table. They didn't when we were at the gates of Moscow, or laid siege to Leningrad, so they are weaker now than they were then... and yet our glorious allies choose to cease the fight. We have the initiative... we should attack, attack, attack!"

Von Vietinghoff spoke his thoughts, interrupting Speer.

"The initiative is lost, Herr Kanzler. We have surrendered it, but then, they do not have it either. The Communists will use this time wisely. They will rearm and resupply, despite what Truman says. We know they will hide their efforts well enough to get it done, especially if peace provides them with an umbrella.""

They all nodded, knowing that Eisenhower had said as much himself, despite the agreed reconnaissance flights that the Allies could conduct without interception.

"And these demarcation lines... stop in place now... roll back over the winter to October 1939 lines, except for the 'small alteration' of Prussia, which will remain in Soviet hands, to be negotiated at whatever meeting is arranged for Spring 1947, all because the predictions are for another hard winter."

Guderian raised his hand to speak, and did so without acknowledgement.

"If it's like last winter, the armies could not operate, Herr Kanzler."

"So that means that the Communists have until spring next year to sort their forces out. Who knows what weapons they might have to hand by then? They have jets... shitty ones from what Galland reports, but they may get better ones. We've heard about these new tanks, and how they are better than anything else they have."

Speer slammed his hands on the desk.

"All we've done is give the bastards time to prepare!"

He resumed his seat and took on a softer tone.

"Is there anyone around this table that believes this is anything but a ruse by Stalin and his lackeys? To buy time to save his army? Anyone who thinks other than he will use the time to rearm and replenish, whilst our Allies will draw back, weaken themselves, and enjoy the 'hard-won' peace...eh?"

There were no takers.

"I believe that Stalin will start all over again. We've discussed this, and I know you all... all of you..." he nodded to the one man who had remained silent and immovable throughout, "...Agree that we cannot let this peace treaty stand."

The nods were universal.

Guderian interrupted again.

"But, Herr Kanzler, we cannot operate during the winter and..."

"Yes, we know that, Generalfeldmarschal, but we cannot let this peace stand, for it deprives all of us around the table with less than we had before we put these Communist bastards in their place during this last year. So many men have died, so much territory has been lost, and we're just recovering it... and now this?"

The Austrians were the greater winners amongst the group, losing only a small corner of their country, and one that was slated to be recovered during the winter withdrawal.

None the less, Austrian Präsident Karl Renner nodded to show that he was still behind the venture.

Speer acknowledged the commitment with his own simple gesture.

Guderian paused to let the silent exchange run its course.

"Herr Kanzler, we know the reasons behind what you are proposing, but there is a simple matter of logistics and capability that cannot be denied. We cannot do what we have discussed for some time to come... probably two and a half months... which would mean winter, not the Russians, would be our greatest enemy. It must be delayed."

"I agree."

Von Vietinghoff could not do otherwise.

Renner raised his hand and the floor was ceded immediately.

"I'm not a military man, but my Chief of Staff agrees, Herr Kanzler. It cannot be done, so we must bear it."

More than one brain suggested the thought that Austria had little to concern itself with, but all remembered that Renner had aligned himself both before and after the terms of the ceasefire were agreed.

Speer canted his head slightly in acceptance of the Austrian statement.

"So, we seem to be in a position where we have to accept and observe this... temporary settlement... because logistics and winter obstruct us. Do you agree, Herr Präsident?"

The previously silent man spoke in heavily accented German.

"My military advisors tell me this is the only way, Herr Kanzler."

"Thank you, Herr Präsident."

Neither party could yet get used to the fact that they were bedfellows in the enterprise. They both thought that time would possibly forge a stronger bond between their countries, although the enmity and hate of centuries that lay between them now would probably prove the stronger emotions. Just so long as they honoured their agreements, and tackled the mutual enemy.

"So, I seek a voice vote on the matter. A simple yes or no. Given what we have discussed previously, and I will pose the question like this. Do we accept the arrangements negotiated by our Allies without further comment, and appear to be full partners in the venture, whilst making our own plans, roughly as outlined by Generalfeldmarschal Guderian, but accepting that the delay will inevitably mean the enemy will strengthen themselves but..." he acknowledged Guderian, "... That we will also profit from the delay in some ways... or do we not?"

The 'yes' votes were universal.

Speer nodded in acceptance.

"Herr Präsident, Kameraden, on that basis, do we agree to begin our preparations for the spring, with the full intention of implementing our military and political plans at the earliest possible moment post-winter?"

He patted the folder sat in front of him, one of only seven in existence.

It contained their thinking for Operation Undenkbar, in itself a clever name, designed to supposedly mimic one devised by Churchill's henchmen over a year beforehand.

Undenkbar... Unthinkable...

"Do we agree, in principle, to implement Fall Undenkbar in the spring of 1947? I can tell you that the Graf is in favour."

Speer spoke of Johann Ludwig Graf Schwerin von Krosigk

He looked to Guderian who gave him the expected answer.

"Jawohl.

Von Vietinghoff...

"Jawohl."

Karl Renner...

"Jawohl."

The other Austrian member, Adolf Schärf, was absent, apparently suffering from a severe digestive complaint, although the real reason was known only to Renner.

Wilhelm Hoegner, Prime Minister of Bavaria...

"Ja."

All eyes swivelled to the immaculately dressed man at the end of the table.

The moment was too great for a simple word.

It required dignified speech.

"Our countries are traditional enemies, and you have visited unprovoked violence upon my people on at least three occasions within living memory."

He leant forward and clasped his hands together.

"And yet, it seems the only way forward is for my country to ally itself with yours, so that it can be made whole again as, yet again, we find ourselves betrayed by those are supposedly our friends. This also appears to be our best hope for an end to the curse of Communist oppression. So, for the good of my country..."

He opened his hands towards the group, palms first.

"… I say… tak."

'Yes.'

With that one word, Władysław Raczkiewicz, the President of Poland, allied his country and soldiers to those of Germany and Austria, and became a full partner in the plan to rekindle war in Europe.

To be continued......

List of Figures within Initiative.

Glossary.

10th US Mountain Division	_	Only US division trained to fight and operate in extreme cold weather conditions.
3.45" RCL	_	British 88mm calibre recoilless gun. Could fire a HESH shell up to 1000 yards.
88mm Pak 43	_	Potent German heavy anti-tank gun, either carriage mounted or on a cruciform base.
Aardvark	_	Marriage of a Panzer IV hull with an Achilles turret.
Aichi Seiran	_	Japanese submarine-launched floatplane capable of carrying bombs or a torpedo.
AK47	_	Soviet assault rifle, similar to the ST44.
Alkonost	_	Soviet secret agent's codename.
Alligator	_	SP vehicle based on the STUG III chassis, and with an extended fighting compartment to permit installation of the 75mm KwK42 L/70 gun.
Antilope	_	Marriage of an SDKFZ 251 half-track with a Puma turret, containing a 50mm gun.
AP-40	_	German AT round with a tungsten carbide core, which was produced in ever reducing numbers as Germany's WW2 mineral resources became scarcer.
APA	_	The designation used by the USN for an attack transport.
APCBC	_	Armour-piercing capped ballistic capped ammunition.

APCR	_	Armour-piercing, composite rigid ammunition.
APDS	_	Armour Piercing - Discarding Sabot.
ARL-44	_	French heavy tank designed by the CDM during the occupation and produced post-1945. As part of France's desperate attempt to regain a position as a world power. It was an unsatisfactory design.
Armee de L'Air	_	French Air Force.
Asbach	_	German Brandy.
Atlantic Operation	_	The Operation to lure Soviet forces to the southern borders of the USSR by contriving a large fictitious force in the Gulf.
B-26c Marauder	_	US twin-engine medium bomber used by a range of Allied Air Forces.
B-29	_	US four engine heavy bomber, also known as the Super fortress.
B-32 Dominator	_	US four engine heavy bomber.
Bagration	_	Operation Bagration was a Soviet assault in 1944, which virtually destroyed Army Group Centre.
Beaufighter	_	British twin-engine multi-role aircraft used by a range of Allied Air Forces.
Beretta-35	_	.32 calibre automatic pistol with an 8 round clip.
Bergepanther	_	German tank recovery version of the Panther.
Blue Max	_	Nickname for the 'Pour-le-Merite' medal.
Blyad	_	Russian for whore/bitch

BM-8-36	_	Katyusha vehicle with 36 rails for firing M8 missiles.
BTR-152	_	Soviet 6-wheel armoured personnel carrier/
Buzogányvető [Mace]	_	Hungarian twin weapon mount that fired a 100mm anti-tank rocket [HEAT] or anti-fortification round [HE]. It could kill any vehicle on the battlefield in 1945.
C-47	_	US twin engine transport used for paratroopers or supply.
CAP	_	Combat Air Patrol.
CEAM m46	_	French-produced ST-45.
Constellation	_	US Lockheed four-engine transport aircraft.
DC-4	_	US Douglas four-engine transport aircraft.
Dodge WC54	_	US Dodge 4x4 light truck adapted to a number of roles.
DRH	_	Deutsches Republikanischen Heer [Army]
DRK	_	Deutsches Republikanischen Kreigsmarine [Navy]
DRL	_	Deutsches Republikanischen Luftwaffe [Air Force]
DSC	_	Distinguished Service Cross
DSHK	_	Soviet 12.7mm heavy machine gun.
DShKm	_	Soviet 12.7mm heavy machine gun modernised in 1946.
Einhorn	_	Field conversion of the Jagdpanther, with extended rear compartment to allow installation of the 128mm Pak44 L/55.
F4U Corsair	_	US Chance-Vought single seater fighter and fighter-bomber aircraft.

F80 Shooting Star	_ US Lockheed single engine turbojet fighter.
F8F Bearcat	_ US Grumman single seater fighter aircraft.
Feldherrnhalle	_ Feldherrnhalle Panzer Division
FG-1 Corsair	_ US Chance-Vought single seater fighter and fighter-bomber aircraft.
Fischer-Tropsch process	_ A process by which a mixture of carbon monoxide and hydrogen is converted into liquid hydrocarbon
Frundsberg	_ 10th SS Panzer Division 'Frundsberg'.
G43 Gewehr	_ German WW2 7.92mm semi-automatic rifle.
Gamayun	_ Soviet secret agent's codename.
Govno	_ Soviet expression for shit/bullshit/rubbish
GRU	_ Glavnoye razvedyvatel'noye upravleniy - The military intelligence main directorate of the General Staff of the Armed Forces of the Soviet Union.
Handley-Page Halifax	_ RAF four-engine heavy bomber, used by numerous Allied Air Forces during WW2.
Hashem	_ Jewish term used to refer to God.
HEAT	_ High-explosive, Anti-tank. Shaped charge shells that penetrate using the Monroe effect.
Heinkel-162 Salamander	_ Also known as the Volksjager, the 162 was a single-seater jet fighter, made primarily of wood.
HESH	_ High-explosive, Squash head.

HIAG	_	Organisation founded by ex-SS Brigadefuhrer Otto Kumm, which aimed to provide assistance to ex-members of the SS, amongst the issues of which was the fact that their pensions were withdrawn post-war.
HLI	_	Highland Light Infantry.
Ho-105/155 30mm cannon	_	Japanese fighter aircraft cannon, which was basically an upscaled copy of the .50cal Browning.
Ho-5 20mm cannon	_	Japanese fighter aircraft cannon, which was basically an upscaled copy of the 1921 Browning aircraft machine gun.
Horch 1a	_	German 4x4 multi-purpose vehicle.
HS-129/B3	_	German Henschel twin-engine ground attack fighter, known as the Panzerknacker. B3 version was equipped with the 75mm Bordkanone, and was a successful tank killer.
Hudson V	_	US built Lockheed twin-engine light bomber and maritime patrol aircraft.
Hundchen	_	Marriage of an SDKFZ 251 and a Pak43 88mm anti-tank gun. Unsuccessful as it was top heavy.
Hurensohn!	_	German expression meaning roughly 'Son of a bitch.'
HVAP	_	High Velocity, Armour Piercing
HVAR	_	High velocity aircraft rocket.
Hyena	_	Panther hull married to an M4A3 or similar turret, mounting a 76mm gun.

IS-III	_	Soviet heavy tank equipped with a 122mm gun, and designed with improved armour protection.
IS-IV	_	Soviet upgraded version of the IS-III, with increased armour, improved engine, longer chassis, but retaining the 122mm gun.
IS-IVm46/B	_	Soviet heavy tank resembling an extended IS series, with 130mm main gun and many other technical improvements.
ISU-152-45	_	Soviet heavy tank destroyer with improved armour, and an ML-20SM main gun.
Jagdpanther	_	German self-propelled gun on a Panther chassis, armed with the deadly 88mm Pak 43.
Schwarzjagdpanther	_	German production version of the modified Jagdpanther with remodelled superstructure and 128mm Pak 44.
Jaguar	_	Panther modification, similar to the Ausf F.
Job tvoju mat	_	Russian obscenity.
JU-87D	_	German single engine dive-bomber, known as the Stuka.
Kanzler	_	Chancellor.
Katyusha	_	One of a number of rocket-firing mounts, fitted on many different vehicles, from armoured trains, tanks, lorries to riverboats.
Kempai-Tai	_	Japanese Military Police Corps, more known as their secret police.
Kipper	_	A salted or pickled herring, split open in a butterfly fashion, and eaten for breakfast. Honestly!

Lewisite	_	Chemical weapon that causes blistering and lung irritation
Li-2	_	Soviet twin-engine transport aircraft, a copy of the US DC-3.
Little Boy	_	The Uranium-235 bomb dropped on Hiroshima by Enola Gay.
LVT	_	Landing vehicle, tracked. Developed for amphibious supply work, the LVT evolved into a troop transport, and further into gun platforms.
M-16 halftrack	_	US SPAA mount on a halftrack chassis, comprising a Maxson mount equipped with 4 x .50cal M2 heavy machine guns, particularly effective when used against infantry.
M-19 Diamond T	_	US 6x4 heavy tank transporter
M1A3 Garand	_	M1 Garand with modifications to accept a 20 round magazine.
M-29 Cluster bomb	_	US 500lbs cluster bomb containing ninety 4lbs charges.
M39 grenade	_	German egg-grenade.
M43 SP Gun	_	US SP gun mounting a 203mm M115 Howitzer
M5 Stuart Tank	_	US light tank equipped with the 37mm M6 gun.
M8 Greyhound	_	US-manufactured six-wheel armoured car, armed with a 37mm gun.
Martin Marauder B-26	_	US twin-engine medium bomber, known as the widowmaker.
Me-262	_	German single seater twin-engine jet fighter or fighter-

bomber. Known as the
Swallow [Schwalbe].

MI-6 — British Military Intelligence
department, dealing with
foreign affairs.

Mig-9 — Russian single seater turbojet
fighter.

Mikado — Hirohito, Emperor Shōwa, the
Emperor of Japan.

MP-40 — German sub-machine gun.

Nakajima Ki-84 Hayate — Japanese single seater single-
engine fighter, considered the
best available to the Japanese
during WW2.

Nakajima Ki-87 — Japanese single seater single-
engine high altitude
interceptor, designed
specifically for B-29 bomber
interception.

Nebelwerfer — Name was a disinformation,
roughly meaning smoke
thrower, but referred to a
number of different types of
German rocket artillery.

NKVD — Narodnyy Komissariat
Vnutrennikh Del, Soviet
Secret Police.

Offizier-Stellvertreter — The rank was actually more of
an assignment, but is
associated with the higher-
ranking group of NCOs.

Oradour-sur-Glane — On 90th June 1944, members
of the 2nd SS Panzer Division
destroyed the French village
of Oradour and massacred the
majority of its occupants,
apparently in retaliation at a
Maquis attack on their
soldiers.

Panther Felix — French-produced Panthers
with a 17pdr gun, often

		equipped with an M2 MG pintel mount.
Panther II	_	German upgraded Panther, with increased armour and gun mounted.
Panzerschreck	_	German 88mm anti-tank rocket projector.
Pershing M26	_	US built heavy tank armed with a 90mm M3 gun.
Pour-le-Merite.	_	German high honour awarded for military valour or civil honour, discontinued with the fall of the Kaiser.
PPSh-41	_	Soviet submachine-gun, often equipped with a 71 round drum magazine.
Praporshchik	_	Soviet junior officer rank, ranking just under an officer i.e. the highest NCO rank.
Prinz Eugen	_	7th SS Freiwillingen-Gebirgs Division, a volunteer mountain division.
Project Raduga	_	Raduga is Russian for Rainbow.
PTRD	_	Soviet anti-tank rifle firing a 14.5mm round.
Quonset Hut	_	Lightweight curved steel structure based on the British Nissen Hut.
RBFSE	_	Red Banner Forces of Soviet Europe. [Krasnogo Znameni sily sovetskogo Yevrope]
Riegel Type 43 bar mines	_	German designed anti-vehicle mine, notorious for its instability, as wires were very prone to corrosion.
Riken Institute	_	Japanese National Scientific Research Institute, where their atomic bomb project was advanced.

Ritterkreuzträger	_	Knight's Cross holder.
RP-3	_	British air to ground rocket, as carried on aircraft like the Typhoon.
S-2	_	Intelligence officer in a headquarters.
SAAF	_	South African Air Force.
SAAG	_	Second Allied Army Group, a formation created to fool the Soviets about Allied intentions.
SAFFEC	_	South American Field Forces, European Command.
San	_	The San are a tribe of bushmen spread throughout Southern Africa.
SAS	_	Special Air Service.
SDKFZ 251	_	German halftrack in many configurations.
Sen-Toku	_	The I-400 class of fleet submarines, the largest built until the 1960s. Twin hulled vessels carrying a large aircraft hangar, intended to launch air attacks on the west coast of the USA and Panama.
Shinhoto Chi-Ha	_	Upgraded Japanese type 97, carrying the Type-1 47mm gun.
Short Stirling	_	British four-engine heavy bomber.
Shtrafbat	_	Soviet penal unit.
SKS	_	Soviet semi-automatic carbine of 7.62mm calibre, complete with integral bayonet.
Skyraider A1	_	US Douglas single engine ground attack aircraft with high load capacity and excellent loiter time.

SMERSH	_	Acronym for Spetsyalnye Metody Razoblacheniya Shpyonov, a group of three counter-intelligence agencies. Also known as 'Death to spies.'
SPAT	_	Self-propelled anti-tank.
Speiss	_	German NCO, literally 'The Spear', indicted by two white stripes on both sleeves, the duties of an RSM fell to this senior NCO.
Spitfire Mk XI-PR	_	Supermarine Spitfire dedicated to photo-recon missions.
Springfield Rifle	_	US .30-06 bolt-action rifle replaced by the Garand.
ST-44	_	German Sturmgewehr-44, the first assault rifle.
ST-45	_	Further development of the ST-44, but easier and cheaper to produce, these weapons were developed mainly by CEAM.
Staghound	_	US produced T17E1 armoured car, known as the Staghound in British use. Armed with a 37mm M6 gun, plus 2-3 MGs
Stahlhelm	_	A German steel helmet.
STAVKA	_	Soviet term for the High Command of Soviet Forces. Junior to the GKO.
Sten	_	British cheap manufacture submachine gun.
Super Pershing	_	US heavy tank mounting the improved T15E1 90mm gun and extra armour protection.
T20E2 Garand	_	US selective fire version of the Garand, with a 20-round magazine and a recoil checker.

T3 Carbine	_	US M2/3 Carbine fitted with infrared siting and a 30 round magazine.
T34m45/100	_	Standard production T34m44 upgunned to a 100mm with restyled gun mount and extended turret.
T34m46/100	_	Production model similar to the T34m44, but with increased hull armour, front, and side, and a 100mm main gun.
T-44	_	Soviet medium tank carrying either an 85mm or 100mm gun.
T-54	_	Soviet MBT armed with a 100mm gun, superior in performance to the 88mm on the Tiger II. Eventually the 54/55 became the most produced tank in history. RG introduces the 54 ahead of schedule.
Tabun	_	Nerve agent, manufactured in huge quantities by Nazi Germany.
Tam o'shanter	_	Scottish bonnet.
Thompson SMG	_	US designed submachine gun.
Thunderbolt	_	US republic single seater single-engine fighter and fighter-bomber
Trews	_	Scottish tartan trousers.
V2	_	German long-range rocket, also known as the A4.
Vár	_	The Norse Goddess of oaths and agreements.
Vickers Windsor	_	British four-engine heavy bomber.
VNIIEF	_	Soviet Union's Central Research Institute of Experimental Physics.

591

Winchester M-12	_	US pump action shotgun with an external tube 6 shot magazine. [12, 16, 20, and 28 gauge.]
Winchester M-69	_	US bolt-action .22 rifle fitted with a suppressor.
Wolf	_	Marriage of a Panther hull and a Panzer IV turret.
Wound Badge in Gold	_	Awarded for five or more wounds due to hostile action, or total blindness, loss of manhood, or severe brain damage.
X7 Rotkäppchen	_	German wire-guided AT missile used during WW2. Literally 'Red Riding Hood', the missile apparently enjoyed success against the IS series of heavy tanks.
XXI Submarine	_	Also known as the Elektroboote, this was the ultimate in WW2 submarine design.
Zis-151	_	Soviet six-wheeled heavy truck
Zis-6	_	Soviet six-wheeled heavy truck
ZSU-12-4	_	Soviet SPAA mount with 4 x 12.7mm DShKm machine-guns.
ZSU-12-6	_	Soviet SPAA mount with 6 x 12.7mm DShKm machine-guns.

Fig # 222 - Rear cover.

Initiative Paperback rear cover

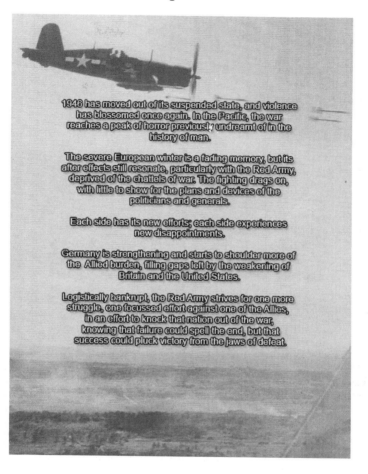

1946 has moved out of its suspended state, and violence has blossomed once again. In the Pacific, the war reaches a peak of horror previously undreamt of in the history of man.

The severe European winter is a fading memory, but its after effects still resonate, particularly with the Red Army, deprived of the chattels of war. The fighting drags on, with little to show for the plans and devices of the politicians and generals.

Each side has its new efforts; each side experiences new disappointments.

Germany is strengthening and starts to shoulder more of the Allied burden, filling gaps left by the weakening of Britain and the United States.

Logistically bankrupt, the Red Army strives for one more struggle, one focussed effort against one of the Allies, in an effort to knock that nation out of the war, knowing that failure could spell the end, but that success could pluck victory from the jaws of defeat.

Bibliography

Rosignoli, Guido
The Allied Forces in Italy 1943-45
ISBN 0-7153-92123

Kleinfeld & Tambs, Gerald R & Lewis A
Hitler's Spanish Legion - The Blue Division in Russia
ISBN 0-9767380-8-2

Delaforce, Patrick
The Black Bull - From Normandy to the Baltic with the 11th
Armoured Division
ISBN 0-75370-350-5

Taprell-Dorling, H
Ribbons and Medals
SBN 0-540-07120-X

Pettibone, Charles D
The Organisation and Order of Battle of Militaries in World
War II
Volume V - Book B, Union of Soviet Socialist Republics
ISBN 978-1-4269-0281-9

Pettibone, Charles D
The Organisation and Order of Battle of Militaries in World
War II
Volume V - Book A, Union of Soviet Socialist Republics
ISBN 978-1-4269-2551-0

Pettibone, Charles D
The Organisation and Order of Battle of Militaries in World
War II
Volume VI - Italy and France, Including the Neutral
Countries of San Marino, Vatican City [Holy See], Andorra
and Monaco
ISBN 978-1-4269-4633-2

Pettibone, Charles D
The Organisation and Order of Battle of Militaries in World War II
Volume II - The British Commonwealth
ISBN 978-1-4120-8567-5

Chamberlain & Doyle, Peter & Hilary L
Encyclopaedia of German Tanks in World War Two
ISBN 0-85368-202-X

Chamberlain & Ellis, Peter & Chris
British and American Tanks of World War Two
ISBN 0-85368-033-7

Dollinger, Hans
The Decline and fall of Nazi Germany and Imperial Japan
ISBN 0-517-013134

Zaloga & Grandsen, Steven J & James
Soviet Tanks and Combat Vehicles of World War Two
ISBN 0-85368-606-8

Hogg, Ian V
The Encyclopaedia of Infantry Weapons of World War II
ISBN 0-85368-281-X

Hogg, Ian V
British & American Artillery of World War 2
ISBN 0-85368-242-9

Hogg, Ian V
German Artillery of World War Two
ISBN 0-88254-311-3

Bellis, Malcolm A
Divisions of the British Army 1939-45
ISBN 0-9512126-0-5

Bellis, Malcolm A
Brigades of the British Army 1939-45
ISBN 0-9512126-1-3

Rottman, Gordon L
FUBAR, Soldier Slang of World War II
ISBN 978-1-84908-137-5

Schneider, Wolfgang
Tigers in Combat 1
ISBN 978-0-81173-171-3

Stanton, Shelby L.
Order of Battle – U.S. Army World War II.
ISBN 0-89141-195-X

Forczyk, Robert
Georgy Zhukov
ISBN 978-1-84908-556-4

Kopenhagen, Wilfried
Armoured Trains of the Soviet Union 1917 - 1945
ISBN 978-0887409172

Korpalski, Edward
Das Fuhrerhauptquartier [FHQu], Wolfschanze im bild.
ISBN 83-902108-0-0

Nebolsin, Igor
Translated by Stuart Britton.
Stalin's Favourite - The Combat History of the 2nd Guards
Tank Army from Kursk to Berlin. Volume 1: January 1943-
June 1944.
ISBN 978-1-909982-15-4

Read the first chapter of Endgame now.

Never was anything great achieved without danger.

Niccolo Machiavelli

Chapter 172 - THE STRAIGHTS

1509 hrs, Monday, 19th August 1946, Chateau de Versailles, France.

Kenneth Strong, Chief of Military Intelligence to SHAEF, stood as his visitor was ushered in.

"General Gehlen. Good afternoon. Tea?"

The head of the Germany's Military Intelligence Section shook his head.

"I'm afraid not, General Strong. I have only a little time. This is an unofficial call, as I told your aide. I must not be missed."

In itself a curious statement, and one that piqued Strong's interest.

"I'm all ears, General."

No words came. Instead, Gehlen extracted a set of pictures from a grey folder and set them out on the desk.

"What am I looking at, General?"

"The Soviet Union's May Day parade this year. I can only apologise, but I did not have sight of these pictures until yesterday, otherwise I would have brought them to you much earlier."

Strong was puzzled.

"But we had a briefing document through, with pictures your agents took on the day… didn't we?"

Gehlen sat back in his seat and shrugged.

"Yes, you did. These were not considered of sufficient quality to have been included in the original submission, neither did they appear to contain anything not covered elsewhere in the original briefing documents."

"But they obviously do, or you wouldn't be here, eh?"

"What do you see, General Strong?"

"Big bloody tanks, big bloody bombs, and some…"

"The bombs, Herr General."

Strong concentrated.

"Big blighters, like I said. I assume the technical people have run up some numbers?"

597

"I regret that there were no pictures of these bombs in the original submission, Herr General. Otherwise, I would have been in your office many weeks ago."

Strong screwed his eyes up, trying to make a deeper appreciation of the grainy photographs.

"Allow me to show you another photograph set, Herr General."

Four more pictures were laid out, photos of excellent quality, precise and defined, showing a large bomb.

"These weren't taken in Moscow in May, I'll warrant."

"No, Herr General. They were taken at Karup air base in Denmark on 12th December."

Gehlen left it all hanging in the air and waited for Strong to put it all together.

"They look the same... admittedly these Moscow ones are a trifle fuzzy, but I think... and clearly you think, they're the same, or at least born of the same bitch."

The German intelligence officer could only nod.

SHAEF's Intelligence Chief had a bell ringing in the back of his brain.

"Karup?"

Strong searched his mind and found the answer in a second.

"Bloody hell! Karup!"

"You understand the problem, Herr General."

"Karup. Where the special unit is based."

"Yes."

"But the special unit has only recently formed there..."

"Yes... but..."

"But the advance units have been there for ages."

"Yes, Herr General. The base was adapted in anticipation last year."

Strong returned to the two sets of photos.

He knew no weapon had been deployed to Europe as yet.

Examining the Red Square photos again, the British officer posed the only question that really mattered.

"So what the merry hell are these?"

"The Karup unit started using weapons called Pumpkin bombs, which have the same size and ballistic characteristics, so I am told."

Which roughly meant, German Intelligence has someone within the unit who supplied that very information.

"A B-29 bomber went missing in December last year... the 13th to be precise. Nothing remarkable, it was on a Pumpkin test-bombing mission in the southern Baltic. I think I now know where it went."

"It came down in Russia?"

"It most certainly would seem so, Herr General, for I suspect these items paraded in Moscow are copies of the exact same Pumpkin bomb shown in the photos from Karup."

The two locked eyes and the possibilities flowed silently back and forth.

Strong gave voice to their fears.

"Or are they?"

Gehlen stood.

"That, General Strong, is something our agencies need to find out very, very quickly."

0101 hrs, Tuesday, 20th August 1946, Two kilometres northwest of Ksar es Seghir, Morocco.

"Hai."

The whispering voice responded in a controlled fashion, such was the tension throughout the submarine.

Adding an extra knot of speed gave Commander Nanbu Nobukiyo more opportunity to control his passage, the strong current having dragged the huge submarine a little closer to the Moroccan shore than intended.

"Up periscope."

The gentle hissing of the extending tube was the loudest sound in the submarine, and drew more than one crewman's attention.

Nobukiyo aimed the periscope at the lights of the Spanish town of Tarifa. He found the flashing light that marked the promontory.

"Mark."

First officer Jinyo made a note of the bearing and checked the ship's clock.

The periscope swivelled towards the Moroccan village of Eddalya, a normally sleepy place that tonight seemed wide-awake, courtesy of two men who were handsomely paid to light a beacon of celebration on the sea shore, ostensibly to hail the formation of the Moroccan Democratic Party for Independence but, in actuality, to provide a navigational point of reference for the passage of some vessels of interest to the Soviet Union.

I-401, Nobukiyo's craft, was second in line, the procession of four vessels led by I-1, with I-14 bring up the tail, sandwiching the two huge Sen-Tokus.

Nobukiyo easily found the beacon.

"Mark."

Jinyo moved to the navigation table and handed the two bearings and times to the navigation officer.

Within seconds, the map showed two intersecting pencil lines, marking I-401's present position.

"As it should be, Commander."

"Depth forty metres. Time to turn?"

Jinyo checked the navigator's work.

"Three minutes, Commander."

"Up periscope."

Nobukiyo repeated the process of getting bearings.

He took a quick sweep round and saw nothing that troubled him.

"Down periscope."

"We've drifted south, commander."

"Increase speed by two knots...recalculate."

The two senior officers exchanged looks as the navigator fretted over his map and slide rule.

"Depth is approximately three hundred and sixty metres here, yes?"

"Yes, Commander."

The navigator interrupted.

"Seventy seconds to turn, Commander."

Nobukiyo grunted by way of reply.

The clock slowly made its way to the appropriate point.

"Lieutenant Dosan. New heading?"

The navigator never looked up from his table.

"Zero-eight-eight, Commander."

"Come to starboard. Steer course zero-eight-eight. Make our depth one hundred and thirty metres."

The orders were repeated, and the huge submarine turned and dropped further into the waters where the Atlantic and Mediterranean mixed.

Nobukiyo thought about the other submarines breaking through the straight at the same time, and of yet others ships, vital to the plan, many miles behind them.

Still out in the Atlantic were the support ships I-353 and the Bogata Maru, the latter now returned to the original German look as the German freighter 'Bogata', although Japanese crew managed her, and the submarine tender modifications were retained.

Bogata had been anchored on the protected east side of the island of Deserta Grande, one of the Madeira Islands.

Beneath her keel, I-353 lay on the bottom by day, surfacing by night, waiting until other arrangements could be brought to fruition.

In the South Atlantic, Nachi Maru and Tsukushi Maru, two submarine tenders under Allied orders, and laden with returning prisoners of war, were ready to do their part when needed.

The Hikawa Maru 2, a hospital ship, also carried Allied servicemen being repatriated, as well as other things more crucial to Operation Niji.

Nobukiyo snatched himself from his musings and put his mind firmly back on the mission in hand.

Commander Nobukiyo took up his seat and closed his eyes, displaying no nerves about the venture they were now engaged in.

After all, many German U-Boats had successfully done the same journey, and in times when the Allies were much more aware.

Now that peace, such as it was, ruled the world, the passage would be that much easier.

Nobukiyo certainly hoped so, for the Black Sea was still a very long way away, even with the Turks turning a convenient blind eye.

Perhaps, by the time it came for them to exit the Mediterranean and seek the freedom of the Atlantic once more, things might be different, but they would climb that mountain when it was there in front of them.

Until then, there was one small fact that constantly niggled away in the back of his mind, a fact he did not care to share with any of his crew.

It announced itself once more, and he felt a chill run down his spine.

As he conned his submarine into the blue waters of the Meditarranean Sea, his mind battled to put the fact back where it belonged.

He failed, and his processes suddenly all locked on to the one inescapable fact.

Once in the Mediterranean, no U-Boat had ever made it out.

[If you have borrowed this work on Kindle, please can you log back into Kindle at your earliest convenience to ensure Amazon receive an update on the pages you have read. Thank you.]

25623703R00335

Made in the USA
Middletown, DE
06 November 2015